W9-BDX-974

THE PROMISE OF JOY

THE PROMISE OF JOY

ALLEN DRURY

Doubleday & Company, Inc., Garden City, New York

All of the characters in this book are fictitious, and any resemblance to actual persons, living or dead, is purely coincidental.

To
Ken McCormick
Editor sapiens et patiens

MAJOR CHARACTERS IN THE NOVEL

In Washington

Orrin Knox of Illinois, President of the United States
William Abbott, ex-President of the United States
Mrs. Ceil Jason, widow of the Governor of California
Robert A. Leffingwell, Secretary of State
Blair Hannah, Secretary of Defense
Fred Van Ackerman, chairman of the Committee on Making Further Offers for a Russian Truce (COMFORT) and chairman of the National Anti-War Activities Congress (NAWAC)
LeGage Shelby, chairman of Defenders of Equality for You (DEFY)
Rufus Kleinfert, chairman of the Konference on Efforts to Encourage Patriotism (KEEP)
Mr. Justice Thomas Buckmaster Davis of the Supreme Court
Robert Durham Munson, Senator from Michigan
Dolly, his wife
Tom August, Senator from Minnesota
Arly Richardson, Senator from Arkansas, Majority Leader of the Senate
Representative J. B. "Jawbone" Swarthman, Speaker of the House
Representative Bronson Bernard of New York
Lafe Smith, Senator from Iowa
Mabel Anderson, widow of Senator Brigham Anderson of Utah
Walter Dobius, a columnist

Frankly Unctuous, a commentator
Other members of the media
Other members of Congress
Members of NAWAC

At the United Nations

Lord Claude Maudulayne, the British Ambassador
Raoul Barre, the French Ambassador
Krishna Khaleel, the Ambassador of India
Nikolai Zworkyan, Ambassador of the Union of Soviet Socialist Republics
Sun Kwon-yu, Ambassador of the People's Republic of China

In Moscow and at the United Nations

Alexei Shulatov, President of the United States of Russia

In Peking and at the United Nations

Lin Kung-chow, President of the United Chinese Republic

NOTE TO THE READER

MOST OF THE CHARACTERS in this concluding novel of the *Advise and Consent* series, and the background of most of its events, will be found in its predecessors, *Advise and Consent, A Shade of Difference, Capable of Honor, Preserve and Protect* and *Come Nineveh, Come Tyre: The Presidency of Edward M. Jason.*

In *Advise and Consent* (written in 1958, published in 1959) will be found the nomination of Robert A. Leffingwell to be Secretary of State; the accession of Vice President Harley M. Hudson to the Presidency; the death of Senator Brigham Anderson of Utah; the appointment of Senator Orrin Knox of Illinois to be Secretary of State following Bob Leffingwell's defeat by the Senate. There also will be found the marriage of Orrin's son, Hal, to Crystal Danta, the marriage of Senate Majority Leader Robert Munson of Michigan to Washington hostess Dolly Harrison and many other episodes leading into later books.

In *A Shade of Difference* (written in 1961, published in 1962) will be found the visit to South Carolina and the United Nations of His Royal Highness the M'Bulu of Mbuele, ruler of Gorotoland, with all its explosive effects upon the racial problem in the United States and the United Nations; the beginnings of the war in Gorotoland; the early stages of Ambassador Felix Labaiya's activities in Panama looking toward seizure of the Canal; the opening moves of California's Governor Edward Montoya Jason in his campaign for the Presidency; the death of Senator Harold Fry of West Virginia and his decision to entrust his son, Jimmy, to Senator Lafe Smith of Iowa; and many other episodes leading into later books.

In *Capable of Honor* (written in 1965, published in 1966) will be found the bitter convention battle between President Hudson and Governor Jason for the Presidential nomination; the selection of Orrin Knox for the Vice Presidential nomination; the escalation of the war in Gorotoland, the outbreak of war in Panama, and their effect upon the Hudson-Jason battle. There also will be found the activities of Walter Dobius, columnist all-knowing and all-powerful; and the ominous formation of the National Anti-War Activities Congress (NAWAC), which turns the convention into a near battleground and puts Edward M. Jason increasingly in pawn to the lawless, the sinister and the violent.

In *Preserve and Protect* (written in 1967, published in 1968) will be found the violent aftermath of the sudden and mysterious death of just-renominated President Hudson; the furious contest in the National Committee between Orrin Knox and Governor Jason in their struggle for the vacant nomination; the open civil rebellion of NAWAC in its drive to nominate—and dominate—Ted Jason; and the climactic episode at the Washington Monument Grounds, where Orrin Knox, nominee for President, and Edward M. Jason, nominee for Vice President, meet the destiny that forms the basis for *Come Nineveh, Come Tyre* and *The Promise of Joy*.

In *Come Nineveh, Come Tyre: The Presidency of Edward M. Jason* (written in 1972, published in 1973) will be found his first unhappy weeks in the White House, with all their attendant perils for the country and himself; how he meets them; and what such methods as his might portend for the United States; and in *The Promise of Joy: The Presidency of Orrin Knox, his* first unhappy weeks in the White House; and how he meets perils dissimilar in nature but perhaps even greater in scope; and what such methods as his might portend for the United States.

Running through all six novels—as it runs through our times—is the continuing argument between those who would use responsible firmness to maintain orderly social progress and oppose Communist imperialism in its drive for world dominion; and those who believe that in a reluctance to be firm, in permissiveness and in the steady erosion of law lie the surest path to world peace and a stable society.

BOOK ONE

1. NOW THE AUGUST DAY has come when he and Governor Edward Montoya Jason of California are to go to the Washington Monument Grounds and there before their countrymen pledge their lives, their fortunes and their sacred honor—and as much cooperation with each other as they can manage.

It is also the day when Secretary of State Orrin Knox, twice unsuccessful candidate for President, now Presidential nominee by fluke of death, circumstance, savagely bitter political battling and a squeak-in vote of 658 for him to 635 for Ted Jason, may find out whether he can trust the attractive, intelligent, equivocal flirter-with-the-violent that fluke and circumstance have thrust upon him as his running mate.

As he finishes shaving and prepares to rejoin his wife, Beth, in the living room of their comfortable, rambling old house in Washington's secluded Spring Valley, he does not know just how much cooperation with Vice Presidential nominee Ted Jason there will be. But he has given Ted his word and he intends to keep it:

There will be as much as he can conscientiously contribute.

He will make a genuine effort.

Ambition and the country have a right to expect no less . . .

Ambition and the country!

How much he has done for both, in these recent hectic weeks that have seen President Harley M. Hudson win renomination in the wildly violent national convention; have seen Orrin become his running mate after a furious struggle with Ted Jason; have seen Harley's death in the mysterious and still unexplained crash of Air Force One, followed by the accession to the Presidency of Speaker of the House William Abbott; and have seen that event in turn followed by the emergency reconvening of the National Committee, whose deliberations, surrounded by a violence even greater than that which shattered the convention, have finally resulted in Orrin's nomination for President and Ted's for Vice President.

Some have said that Ted, Governor of California, descendant of grandees and shrewd Yankee traders, darling of all that aggregation of uneasy citizens whose hopes and fears are symbolized and given voice by radically activist NAWAC—the National Anti-War Activities Congress—has flirted too much with violence.

Some—and they include Orrin and President Abbott—have said Ted has put himself in pawn to violence. Some—and they include Ted's lovely wife, Ceil, who only last night abandoned her self-imposed exile at the great Jason ranch "Vistazo" north of Santa Barbara and flew back to be at Ted's side for today's ceremonies—have said that Ted has betrayed something essential in himself in so doing. And some—and they include all of those and many more besides, both in Washington and throughout the country—have made plain their fear that Ted may never be able to break free from violence and the begetters of violence, no matter how he tries.

And many of these—their uneasy discontent and frequently bitter criticism reaching him through a thousand channels in the past twenty-four hours—have said that Orrin Knox, in accepting Ted as his running mate, has betrayed everything Orrin has stood for in three decades of public life, and has taken a fearful chance with the country's well-being for no other reason than sheer political opportunism and greed for office.

This, he knows, is the chief burden he carries before his countrymen today: the glibly cynical and disillusioned belief, on the part of so many, that Orrin Knox, so long regarded as a man of principle even by those who have disagreed with him most bitterly, is not so principled after all.

This he carries, and with it his worries about Ted, which are fully as lively, did his countrymen only know, as those anyone else may have. But how can he convince anyone of this now? He has apparently made a deal, hasn't he? He has apparently reversed himself 180 degrees to accept Ted as his running mate, hasn't he? He has apparently been just as much of a political trimmer and grasper after power as any he ever criticized in all his long and controversial years as Senator from Illinois . . . and he did not criticize with much charity, sometimes, in those days.

Fittingly enough, perhaps, many of his countrymen are not willing to grant him charity now.

And yet—and yet. Reviewing the immediate past as he casts an appraising glance at the steady eyes, the emphatic face, the brusque and somewhat impatient expression that stare back at him from the mirror, he does not find it in his heart to blame himself too much, even as he concedes that those who question him now do indeed, from their point of view, have more than reasonable grounds. He has had to answer for his decision to his son; and having done that, believes he can in the long run justify it to all but the most deliberately obtuse and intransigent.

In all these furiously tumbling weeks, the moment of greatest truth for Orrin Knox came, as it perhaps did for Ted Jason, on the night when the sinister forces of NAWAC waylaid and beat his daughter-in-law, Crystal Danta Knox, outside the national convention at the Cow Palace in San Francisco. Crystal had lost the son she was carrying, and it seemed for a while that Orrin's son Hal had lost all faith in his country, its political system and the ultimate human decencies that are the only protection men have against the fearful winds of decay and dissolution that howl unceasing around a free but sometimes achingly imperfect nation.

When his father selected for running mate the man Hal regarded as the principal cause of his wife's beating and his son's death, it seemed that Hal no longer had anything at all in which to believe.

But Orrin had brought him back, he tells himself with a sudden grimness that gives sterner lines to the strong, impatient face, and if he could do that, he can bring the rest of them back too. Hal had been utterly devastated by his choice of Ted Jason, yet Orrin had brought him back. It had not been easy. But it had been done.

Their principal conversation on the subject had occurred soon after former Governor Roger P. Croy of Oregon, Ted's campaign manager, had left the Spring Valley house to give the press indirect but unmistakable affirmation that Ted would indeed be the Vice Presidential choice. Shortly thereafter had come a peremptory rap on the study door.

"Who is it?" Orrin had asked.

A voice he hardly recognized had said, "Me."

"Oh," he said, and suddenly felt tense, nervous and sick inside. "Come in."

He glanced up quickly into the haggard, unhappy eyes of his son and glanced quickly away again.

"Sit down."

"I will if you'll look me straight in the eyes," Hal said in a voice so low he could hardly hear it.

"Very well," he said, though it cost him as few things in life had. "Now, do you want to sit down, or had you rather stand?"

"*Why?*" Hal demanded, standing. "In the name of God, *why?*"

"Because there are times when politics offers cruel choices," Orrin said slowly, "and sometimes, even with the best will in the world, one gets caught in them."

"Do you realize that that man, or his people, killed my son and your grandson?" Hal asked in a strangled voice.

Orrin sighed.

"Yes."

"And do you realize that his gangs may do anything—destroy the country—put us under dictatorship—anything?"

"I think there is that potential, yes, if they're not controlled."

"Do you think that millionaire lightweight is controlling them? Was he controlling them this afternoon?"

"Sit down, Hal," he said quietly, "and stop being rhetorical. I know just about everything there is to know about the character and motivations and strengths and weaknesses of Edward M. Jason, I believe. I don't think there's much you can tell me. And I don't think there's much to be gained from our fighting about it."

"But I want to know why," Hal said, sitting slowly down on the sofa. "I want to know *why* my father, whom I have always loved and respected and looked up"—his voice began to break but he forced himself on—"looked up to—why he has decided now that this man is worthy to move up one step from the White House. I don't—I don't even know why you think he's worthy to associate with you *personally*, let alone be Vice President. . . . You've got to tell me something," he said, staring at the rug. "I've got to have something left to believe."

For several minutes Orrin did not reply, though his first impulse was to go to his son and put his arms around him as though he were a little boy. But it died, as such things do, because he wasn't a little boy. Instead he tried to piece together something coherent that would make sense. He wasn't sure it would, in Hal's present mood—or his own, for that matter—but he knew he had to try.

"I think," he said slowly, "that Ted Jason, at heart, is not a bad or an evil man. I think to a large extent he is sincerely convinced that he has a better answer for this country than I do. I think he really believes that if he could be elected President, things would somehow straighten themselves out and he could bring peace to the world at large, and to us domestically. I think he really thinks that."

"Does that give him a license to kill my son?" Hal asked with a withering bitterness. His face suddenly dissolved. "My *son,*" he said in a choking voice. "Like I—like I was for you, when I was born. *My son.*"

Orrin closed his eyes and sat back with his hands over them for a long moment. Then he looked up, though not at his son.

"You make it very difficult."

Again Hal spoke with a devastating bitterness.

"Am I supposed to make it easy?"

"Easier," his father said. "Just a little—easier—that's all. . . . I don't think there's anything you've felt in these past few days that I haven't —well, I'll amend that, because I do remember how it was with you, and I do know you've been feeling things I can only imagine. I don't really *know,* because back in those innocent days this kind of violence didn't stalk America the way it does now. I didn't have to worry about my family then as we all do now. I didn't think I was taking my life and theirs into my hands every time I took a stand on a public issue. But it's getting close to that now. Give us another five years like this, and freedom of opinion will be pretty much gone. Unless"—his expression too for a moment became bitter—"you're on the right side. . . .

"All I'm saying about Ted Jason," he resumed presently, "is that he's in that curious state of mind in which ambition really does dominate all. It dominates so much that everything is related to it. Everything becomes possible to it. Everything seems right to it. Everything can be fitted in . . . and everything that feeds it can be justified."

"And that doesn't make him a dangerous man?"

"Of course it does," Orrin said. "Of course it does. And yet not a *bad* man, in the sense that say"—his eyes grew somber as he thought of Wyoming's demagogic junior Senator, chairman of the National Anti-War Activities Congress—"Fred Van Ackerman is a *bad* man."

"How do you separate them?" Hal asked with a skepticism that at least, Orrin was relieved to note, replaced the bitterness a little. "Behind Ted Jason stands Van Ackerman. And all the rest of them. If you take one, you take them all."

"I think they can be separated," Orrin said, "because I think in Ted's mind they *are* separated. I think if he can be shown what they are, and what they're helping to get the United States into, he will break away from them. Because I think, as I say, that at heart he's a decent and well-meaning man."

"But that isn't why you're taking him," Hal said with a sudden shrewd bitterness. "Not just because you think maybe you can reform him someday."

"Sooner than that," Orrin said. "But, no, you're right. That isn't why."

Hal gave him a long look, so painful for him that he actually squinted as he did so. His father could barely hear him when he spoke.

"You're taking him because of some deal, then."

"No," Orrin said, and thanked God he could say it truthfully. "No deal." A smile lit his face briefly. "Do you really think if I'd made a deal I wouldn't have made it for more than twenty-three votes, boy? What kind of a dealer do you think I am?"

"Well," Hal said, and briefly he too smiled a little, "maybe not. But there must be some reason—some reason. There's got to be something that makes sense"—and again his voice dropped very low—"if you are willing to put the murderer of your grandson on the ticket."

Again Orrin sighed and looked away.

"You do have a way of cutting a man up."

Hal laughed, a dry, humorless sound.

"I'm told it's inherited," he said, and at his father's sudden angry look he did not flinch or drop his eyes. "But that doesn't answer my question."

"I'm trying. Give me a chance, will you? . . . In the first place, Ted isn't a murderer—except as I suppose we are all murderers, who let things slide to a point where—things like that—can happen. Maybe I'm equally guilty, Hal. Did you ever think of that?"

Hal made a protesting movement but his father continued inexorably.

"Maybe I should have stepped aside at the convention. Maybe I should have stepped aside now, when the National Committee had to make its choice of a successor to Harley. Maybe I'm driven by power and ambition, too, beyond the point of decency—many think so, here and abroad. If I'd stepped aside, probably nobody would have hurt your wife and your—son. If I'd stepped aside in San Francisco, Harley would have had to take Ted, and maybe Harley would be alive now: who knows? It's a fair assumption, even though Ted of course had nothing to do in any direct way with what happened to Harley. It was the climate—but maybe I'm as responsible as he is for the climate. Maybe if I'd gotten out of the way, Ted's backers wouldn't have felt they had to get desperate and do the things they have done. Maybe"—and again his eyes darkened at the thought of Helen-Anne Carrew, society columnist for the Washington *Star-News,* ex-wife of America's leading political columnist, Walter Dobius, murdered because she was getting too close to discovering the violent elements behind Ted Jason—"maybe Helen-Anne would still be alive. Maybe all of this is my fault as much as his. Maybe all men who don't deny the ambition for power when they catch a glimpse of where it can lead to are guilty. . . . Did you ever think of that?"

"But you couldn't just walk away and let him have it!" Hal protested in a half whisper.

"No," his father said quietly, "I could not, or I should have betrayed everything I believe in for this country, everything my whole life has stood for. So it isn't so simple. And it isn't for him, either. . . . The country is badly divided right now. We have enemies everywhere, both inside and outside, who would love to see us brought down, even though the fools will go down with us if we aren't here to protect them. We need unity. He does command an enormous support among a great many sincere citizens who really do see in him the hope for peace that they honestly cannot see in me. This extends overseas as well. I've denied him the top spot by a very narrow margin, and many of those people are not going to be satisfied unless they can see him beside me—unless they can feel that he is offering some moderating influence on my policies, which they think are so horrible."

"But you *can't* accept his views on appeasing and giving in," Hal said in the same dismayed half whisper.

"No," Orrin agreed again, "I can't. But one thing he said when he addressed the mob at Kennedy Center this afternoon did make sense, and that is that times change and people change." He smiled a wry little smile, almost wistful. "I'm not anywhere near the positive soul I was in the Senate a year and a half ago, you know. I've been close to the center of the machine for a while as Secretary of State, and I know it isn't so easy. It isn't all black and white and cut and dried; it's a sort of horrible gray, like fighting your way through a dirty fog where everything is hazy and blurred and you're not even sure that the light ahead *is* a light: it may be just a—just a mirage. . . . No, I've changed, and I like to think for the better. And so can he. So *will* he, if I have anything to say about it. And I think I will. . . . He has good qualities—he wants to do what's right for the country, I think—he just needs to be shown. And he does command an enormous popular support—"

"And you want to win the election," Hal interrupted, his tone so bitter again that his father for a few moments was too crushed to reply. "You want the votes he can bring with him. *You want to win.*"

"Yes," Orrin said at last, quietly, "I want to win. Because I think I can save the country and save the general peace, in the long run, and I want to try. . . ."

And there, of course, he had come squarely back to what seemed to him the essential justification of all his acts, as it was Ted's self-justification too: peace, that great will-o'-the-wisp that had provided the basic inspiration for the actions of every American President in the past three decades. Peace, so glittering, so golden, so flickering, so faint. The greatest mirage of them all, for which men everywhere worked and labored and did unto other men horrible things, because to all of them peace did not mean peace unless they could somehow have it on their own terms. . . .

Later on, Hal, who in his bitter youthfulness had probed so many tender things, had given indication that he was forgiving his father, that he was finally convinced that Ted Jason had to share the ticket for the sake of what Orrin had told the National Committee must be an "Era of Reconciliation," both at home and abroad. If Hal had seen it, even the skeptical among Orrin's supporters could be made to see it. Nothing must be allowed to stand in the way of reconciliation among the hostile nations of the earth, and among the violently warring elements in America. . . .

This, in Orrin's mind, transcends all other considerations, and to it he knows he will pledge himself publicly when, before the hour is over, he stands before his country and the world at the Washington Monument to make his acceptance speech and outline the policies he intends to follow if elected in November.

In these policies he hopes he will have the willing support of his running mate, for with that support will come the support of all the many millions who see in Ted Jason the world's best hope for peace. If that support comes, then Orrin will not only win the election. He will also be able to move firmly to increase the chances for peace abroad and to diminish the power of the violent at home.

Without Ted's full support, he knows that in all probability he cannot win the election, for Ted is the darling of the media, whose powerful pens and voices have made him the darling of the people, and Orrin very definitely is not. He has won his fight for the nomination. But his victory is openly and harshly begrudged.

He has not won the support of the media—could not, after all their years of mutually hostile battling over differing views of foreign policy—or of vast numbers of his countrymen who have been conditioned for the better part of three decades to be suspicious and resentful of Orrin Knox. His margin of victory for the nomination was small, his area of really genuine popularity is small. If he wins the

White House, it will be because of votes reluctantly given him as an indirect endorsement of Ted Jason. If he wins, it will not be a recognition of the integrity of Orrin Knox, but a recognition of the popularity of Ted Jason.

This is not as he feels it should be, but being a blunt and pragmatic man, he knows this is how it is. And thus he is bound to his equivocal running mate whether he wants to be or not. All the conflicting elements whom he must somehow weld into a unified force enable Ted to hold him in pawn even more effectively than Ted himself, perhaps, realizes.

Exactly what Ted does realize about his own situation at the moment, Orrin finds it impossible to understand. After all the heated, frustrating and inconclusive conversations he and President Abbott have had with Ted—culminating finally in a flat ultimatum from Orrin that Ted must repudiate NAWAC and all the violent or be barred from the ticket—Orrin still does not know whether Ted has the slightest comprehension of the dangers he has been flirting with in his fight for the nomination—or, indeed, in what Orrin regards as his dangerously flaccid and complaisant attitude toward the never-resting imperialism of the Communist powers.

Ted has been, and remains, an enigma to Orrin, although Orrin thinks he understands the basic motivation, for it has been his own: Ted has wanted to win. So has Orrin, but not at the price of running with the pack that will, he feels, destroy America both at home and abroad if it cannot be checked.

Well, he tells himself abruptly: well. Grim lines come about the firm, emphatic lips. *He* intends to check the pack and, by God, *he will*, both at home and abroad. And if Ted Jason and his friends don't like it, they can lump it. He will have the power and he will use it. They will have met not only their match but their master.

And as abruptly his mood changes, to be succeeded by an instant ironic bitterness as he surveys the world he wants so much to run. What will he have confronting him if he finally achieves his long-held ambition to sit behind the desk at 1600 Pennsylvania Avenue?

Gorotoland, strategic key to the heart of Africa, in flames as its U.S.-supported hereditary ruler, flamboyant "Terrible Terry"—His Royal Highness Terence Wolowo Ajkaje, 137th M'Bulu of Mbuele—battles desperately to hold his throne against the onslaught of his equally flamboyant cousin, Communist-backed Prince Obifumatta.

Panama, in flames as the Communist-backed People's Liberation Movement of Ted's former brother-in-law, Felix Labaiya-Sofra, attempts to overturn the U.S.-backed government of the old oligarchy and seize the Canal.

In both countries, overt support for the revolutionaries, from both the Soviet Union and mainland China.

In both countries, commitments of U.S. forces by Harley Hudson that placed his immediate successor, William Abbott, in a most difficult position both in the eyes of the world and in practical fact—commitments that will put upon Bill Abbott's successor the obligation to end both conflicts and get out as fast as possible, with honor if he can manage it, without honor if he can't.

And domestically, all the anti-war turmoil, recently spilled over into a violence with sinister undertones that lead many to suspect that the excuse of foreign involvement is being used as the fulcrum for domestic revolution.

This lovely picture, full of so many potentially fatal pitfalls for the next American Chief Executive, is what confronts him now. It is, he suspects, the main reason why Bill Abbott has held firm to his decision to serve until January and then return to the House and the Speakership he has held for so many years.

Why in the hell would any sane man want the responsibility?

But, then, of course Orrin Knox knows why, for it is the same reason that motivates Ted, the same that has motivated every aspirant to the Presidency in recent years. Because *he*—in this case Orrin—believes *he* knows best. Because *he* thinks *he* has the answers—or, at least, some of them. Because, though he may not know exactly how he will go about it, he does know that *he* desperately wants to achieve world peace and restore domestic tranquillity, and he honestly believes that *he* is more sincere and more determined about this than all his competitors.

Power is the great desideratum of all who rise above a certain level in American politics. But for the best—and they are many—it is not a completely selfish desire. *Power to do something constructive for the country and the world* is the name of the game, for the most earnest, the most idealistic, the most dedicated and the most sincere. Orrin feels—as all who achieve the highest office have had to feel, to survive all the scars of getting there—that he possesses these qualities in greater measure than anybody. Otherwise, why would he have been permitted to come so far and rise so high?

Just as he reaches this flight of self-righteousness—and just as his innate Knox self-skepticism and sense of balance starts to come to his rescue to keep him from going entirely overboard in self-congratulation—the door to the bedroom opens and the other half of the famous Illinois team of "Orrin and Beth" comes in.

"I know that look," Beth says with a chuckle. "You're telling yourself that nobody, but *nobody,* has more answers to anything than Orrin Knox does."

"Hank," he says blandly, using the nickname he has used ever since she was Elizabeth Henry, fellow student at the University of Illinois, so many years ago, "it is the only possible mood in which to approach an acceptance speech. Particularly," he adds, looking less cheerful, "when you don't know whether your running mate is going to go along with you or not."

"Do you really have doubts?" she asks, coming forward to the mirror and leaning forward to adjust the off-the-face white hat she has chosen to go with the sensible green dress and comfortable white pumps she is wearing for this auspicious occasion. Their eyes meet as he replies thoughtfully.

"I wouldn't say I was entirely confident. Although he did promise me last night that he will absolutely, completely, unequivocally, cross-his-heart-and-hope-to-die repudiate NAWAC, the violent, the Communists and all their sleazy vicious doings."

"The question," she says with an equal thoughtfulness, sitting on the bed and studying the problem, "is whether they will repudiate him. And if they don't, what they will do to you."

"They will go along with me," he says crisply, "as long as Ted is at my side."

"And if he shouldn't be—?" She gives him a quizzical look and he responds with one surprised and skeptical.

"Why won't he?" he asks. "Knowing Ted Jason, I don't believe he's going to give up his position 'one heartbeat away,' etcetera, etcetera, etcetera. After all, if I'm not very successful in the next four years, I might not seek—or win—a second term. And he's still young enough so that either way he'd be set to be the next nominee. He may make a few noises now and then just to show he's still really a stout and independent fellow, but I suspect for the most part he'll stick pretty close to stodgy old reactionary Orrin. Which, after all, is exactly what I want him to do. I need him. By the same token, he needs me. That's why we're together, and, I expect, are going to stay together."

"I think you will intend to," she agrees, still thoughtfully. He takes her up on it sharply.

"Then why won't we?"

"You may not," she says quietly, "be the only people involved, you know. Communists and the violent don't always go away just because people say they should. Sometimes they have purposes more involved than we simple souls can believe."

"But what would be the point in killing him, if that's what you mean?"

"There wouldn't be any point in killing him," she agrees with a certain wry bluntness. "I agree with you, why should anybody kill *him?*"

"Hank," he says calmly, "I am not going to start worrying at this late date about anyone killing *me*. I know some have wanted to, I know some still may; but the great majority are satisfied to have him on the ticket and in a position to become heir apparent—"

"He *is* the heir apparent," she interrupts with a sudden sharpness of her own. "Watch out for yourself."

"I won't believe," he says firmly, "that Ted Jason would be, or could be, party to any attempt on my life."

"Any more than he was party to an attempt on Crystal's," she remarks quietly. "Nonetheless, it happened."

"You and I," he says with equal quietness, "have faced the possibility of assassination ever since I entered public life. It's true, the chances are greater now, the occurrence being a thing that feeds on itself in a world of kooks and crazies—"

"Not always kooks," she says, "and not always crazies. Sometimes very cold-blooded and very calculating people who know exactly what they're doing. It seems to me you're a sitting duck for someone like that."

"So what would you have me do at this late date?" he demands. "Quit? Say, 'I'm sorry, I didn't mean I want to be President, include me out, I'm going home'? Don't be silly, Hank. You're talking like a scared old lady now, not like the next behind-the-scenes President of the United States!"

"Well," she says, smiling a little in response to his deliberately joshing tone, "it may have its humorous aspects, but even so—"

"And why are you so gloomy and apprehensive all of a sudden?" he asks, not knowing now that one day he will look back and wonder if she was the only one of the four about to meet at the Monument Grounds who felt that way. "I've been anointed by the *Times*, the *Post*, the networks, Walter Dobius, the Russians, the Chinese and the whole wide world—not very heartily, but they've done it. Ted Jason is going to keep me on the straight and narrow, the forces of imperialistic reaction have been put in check, God's in his heaven and all's right with the world. We're going to be under the greatest security and protection the country's ever seen, today, so we might as well relax and enjoy it. Anyway, Hank"—and though still joking a bit, he becomes more serious—"you'd better not keep on in this vein or you really will give me the heebie-jeebies. And I can't afford to have them. Too much depends on how we launch this campaign. Plus the fact that it's all out of character, for you. You don't normally go off on this kind of tangent."

"No," she says, rising with a smile and sudden decisive air that brings him a feeling of genuine relief, for he has been more disturbed by her uneasiness than he has wanted her to know. "It isn't, and I apologize for being gloomy. I know we're protected, I know everything is going to be all right. I expect we'd better go down. They must be almost ready for us."

"Of course," he says, suddenly serious, a perverse but inescapable reaction now that she is abandoning the subject, "if you really have a hunch, Hank—"

"Nonsense," she says firmly, linking her arm through his as they hear cars and motorcycles downstairs, a sudden bustle through the lower part of the house which indicates that it is time for them to go and keep their appointment with the country. "It was just a thought, and a foolish one at that. Come along, maximum leader. Your panting multitudes await."

"I hope they'll like what I have to say," he replies, and abruptly he turns and takes her face between his hands.

"Thank you for everything, Hank," he says softly. "For all the kindnesses, down all the years."

She blushes, a rare thing for Beth Knox, looking suddenly very shy and, in some curious way that of course does not exist except in mind and memory, youthful and freshly beautiful again as she had been when they first began courting.

"It's mutual, my dear," she says. She returns his kiss youthfully, too, and then, with a little smile at herself for not resisting the urge to become practical again, "Be good today. They expect a lot from you, and you have a lot to give."

"Hank," he says with a sudden enthusiasm, almost boyish in his turn, "with you beside me, I can't be anything else *but* good. We've got a great four years ahead of us. A *great* four years!"

"Well, we know one thing, anyway," she says with a chuckle as the first sirens begin below. "It won't be dull."

So the hour of acceptance comes bright and hot and clear, and from all the corners of the two cities, all the corners of the nation, the great throng gathers on the Monument Grounds around the stark white obelisk to fatherly George. Krishna Khaleel, the Ambassador of India; Soviet Ambassador Vasily Tashikov and his agricultural/secret police attaché; British Ambassador Lord Maudulayne and Lady Kitty; French Ambassador Raoul Barre and Celestine; and almost all their colleagues of the diplomatic corps, are there. Somewhere in the enormous multitude that laughs and yells and chatters, shoves and pushes and jostles in amiable contest for position, are the brilliant, twisted young black, LeGage Shelby, chairman of Defenders of Equality for You (DEFY); pompous, dough-faced Rufus Kleinfert, Knight Kommander of the Konference on Efforts to Encourage Patriotism (KEEP); and most of their fellow members of NAWAC. (Only Senator Van Ackerman is missing. Whispering now, he is in his fourteenth hour of filibuster against the Administration-backed *Bill to Curb Further Acts Against the Public Order and Welfare.*)

The Chief Justice is there, his wife already upset because she can tell from the way Mr. Associate Justice Thomas Buckmaster Davis is bustling about near the platform that he must have some preferred assignment she doesn't know about. Senate Majority Leader Robert Durham Munson of Michigan and his wife, Dolly, are there, along with Majority Whip Stanley Danta of Connecticut, Crystal Knox's father, and more than half the Senate. From the House, Representative J. B. "Jawbone" Swarthman, chairman of the House Foreign Affairs Committee and possible strong contender for the Speakership next year, and his wife, "Miss Bitty-Bug," are rubbing elbows, not too comfortably, with California's giant young black Congressman Cullee Hamilton and his soon-to-be wife, Sarah Johnson. More than two hundred of their fellow House members are also on hand. All the members of the National Committee have already taken their seats on the platform.

Television crews are everywhere, and through the crowd there are many television sets in place to bring the ceremonies to the farthest reaches. Police with walkie-talkies are also everywhere, moving constantly, efficiently, yet amicably, their presence giving rise to a few catcalls but otherwise no indication of hostility. At regularly spaced intervals groups of four soldiers stand back to back facing their countrymen, guns, bayonets and gas canisters ready. Around the flag-decked platform and the dignitaries' circle at the foot of the Monument, a tight cordon of Marines stands guard. Overhead the ubiquitous helicopters whir and hover.

Yet somehow, despite these precautions, there seems to be something in the air that indicates they will not be needed. Press and police estimate more than four hundred thousand present on this day that belongs to Orrin Knox and Edward Jason, yet with no visible exceptions they seem to be almost on picnic, so happy and relaxed do they look and sound. Even NAWAC's banners are good-natured, and this seems to put the final touches on it:

ORRIN AND TED: THE UNBEATABLES . . . HEY, HEY, GREAT DAY! BAD TIMES, GO AWAY! . . . TED AND ORRIN HAVE GOT US ROARIN' . . . WE'LL HAVE PEACE TOMORROW AND NO MORE SORROW . . .

Presently from far off there comes the sound of sirens, hailed with a great roar of greeting and approval. The sleek black limousine from Spring Valley comes along Constitution Avenue in the center of its police motorcycle escort, turns into the Monument Grounds and proceeds slowly to the foot of the obelisk. Two minutes later, more sirens, another great roar; the sleek black limousine from Dumbarton Oaks in the center of its police motorcycle escort comes along Constitution Avenue, turns into the Monument Grounds, proceeds slowly to the foot of the obelisk.

Out of their cars step the nominee for President and the nominee for Vice President, and their wives, and for a moment, in the midst of a wave of sound that seems to blot out the world, they stare at one another with a questioning, uncertain, hesitant yet friendly look. Then Orrin steps forward and holds out his hand, and as the picture flashes on all the television sets, a silence falls.

"Ted," he says, and his words thunder over the Monument Grounds, the nation, the world, "Beth and I are glad to see you."

"Orrin," the Governor replies, "our pleasure."

Impulsively and with a completely natural friendliness, Ceil steps forward and kisses Beth and then Orrin. Beth gives her a warm hug and then turns to embrace Ted. The television cameras zoom in, the still photographers push and shout and scramble. A shout of happiness and approval goes up from all the vast concourse.

Orrin links his arm informally through Ted's and leads the way to the platform, through the dignitaries' circle where friends and colleagues, opponents and supporters, greet them with an eagerly smiling, unanimous cordiality.

"It seems to be a happy day," Orrin says quietly, words no longer overheard as the police hold back the press. "I'm glad."

"So am I," Ted says. "I think we have a great responsibility."

"We do," Orrin agrees. "I'm going to make a conciliatory speech."

"I too," the Governor says. "I had thought of sending it over for your approval this morning, but—"

"Oh, no," Orrin says quickly. He smiles. "I trust you." The smile fades, he looks for a moment profoundly, almost sadly, serious. "We've got to trust each other, from now on."

"Yes," Ted says gravely. "We must. I think we can."

Orrin gives him a shrewd sidelong glance as they reach the steps of the platform.

"I have no doubts," he says quietly.

"They're going to need our help," Beth says to Ceil as they, too, reach the steps and start up after their husbands.

Ceil smiles, a sunny, happy smile.

"I think," she says with a little laugh, "that you and I can manage."

The wild, ecstatic roar breaks out again as they appear together on the platform, standing side by side, arms raised in greeting, framed by the flags against the backdrop of the gleaming white needle, soaring against the hot, bright sky.

"Mr. Secretary and Mrs. Knox! Governor and Mrs. Jason! Look this way, please! Can you look over here, please? Mr. Secretary—Governor—Mrs. Jason—Mrs. Knox—this way, please! Can you smile and wave again, please?"

Finally Orrin calls:

"Haven't you got enough?"

And from somewhere in the jostling tumult below them, of heads, hands, flailing arms, contorted bodies and cameras held high, there comes a plea of such anguished supplication that they all laugh.

"*Please,* just once more, Mr. President! All together again, *please!*"

"The things we do for our country," Orrin says with a mock despair as they all link arms and step forward once more.

"Yes," Ceil says happily. "It sometimes seems as though—"

But what it sometimes seems to Ceil at that moment will never be known, for they are interrupted.

No one in the crowd hears anything, no one sees anything. For several moments the import of the sudden confusion on the platform does not penetrate.

It is so bright and hot and sunny.

It is such a happy day.

They cannot quite comprehend, in that bright, hot, sunny, awful instant, the dreadful thing that has occurred so swiftly and so silently before their eyes.

It is not clear then, nor perhaps will it ever be, exactly what those who planned it had intended. But whatever they had intended, by some possibly inadvertent and unintentional miscalculation, they have accomplished more.

A husband and wife—but they are not the same husband and wife—

stare at one another for a terrible moment suspended in time and history. Then she begins to scream and he begins to utter a strange animal howl of agony and regret.

Their puny ululations are soon lost in the great rush of sound that engulfs the platform slippery with blood, the Monument Grounds sweltering under the steaming sky, the two cities, the nation, the horrified, watching, avid world.

EDWARD JASON, BETH KNOX SLAIN . . . VICE PRESIDENTIAL NOMINEE, RUNNING MATE'S WIFE ASSASSINATED IN WASHINGTON . . . SECRETARY KNOX, MRS. JASON NARROWLY ESCAPE DEATH IN MELEE AT MONUMENT GROUNDS . . . POLICE HOLD FAKE PHOTOGRAPHER SUSPECT . . . NATION'S LEADERS JOIN IN MOURNING GOVERNOR JASON AND MRS. KNOX . . . PARTY THROWN INTO CONFUSION BY LOSS OF CANDIDATE . . . CONGRESS IN RECESS . . . WORLD APPALLED BY NEW VIOLENCE IN U.S. . . .

And the second day:

JASON, MRS. KNOX LIE IN STATE AT CAPITOL . . . STATE FUNERAL FOR BOTH TO BE HELD TOMORROW . . . SECRETARY KNOX, MRS. JASON "IMPROVING," REMAIN IN SECLUSION . . . PRESIDENTIAL ELECTION SCENE CLOUDED . . . PARTY HEADS CONFER ON NEW RUNNING MATE FOR KNOX . . . ANTI-WAR ELEMENTS RESTIVE AT CHANCE SECRETARY MAY PICK PRO-WAR CANDIDATE . . . PRESIDENT ABBOTT RECONVENES NATIONAL COMMITTEE FOR DAY AFTER TOMORROW . . .

And the third day:

GOVERNOR JASON, MRS. KNOX INTERRED AT ARLINGTON IN SOMBER STATE FUNERAL . . . SECRETARY, MRS. JASON UNABLE TO ATTEND . . . PRESIDENT SAYS NATIONAL COMMITTEE FACES "SUPREME RESPONSIBILITY" IN CHOOSING NEW RUNNING MATE FOR KNOX . . . FURIOUS POLITICAL BATTLE EXPECTED AS PRO-, ANTI-WAR FORCES SEEK TO CLAIM SECOND PLACE ON KNOX TICKET . . . SECRETARY'S SON SAYS HE "MUST AND WILL" CHOOSE HIS RUNNING MATE . . . WORLD STILL STUNNED BY HORROR OF DOUBLE ASSASSINATION AS U.S. POLITICS ROARS INTO HIGH GEAR . . .

And life and history, as they must, go on.

2. "RARELY," wrote Walter Dobius with a grimness that showed in the heavy-handed way he pounded the keys of his electric typewriter at beautiful "Salubria" near Leesburg in the hot Virginia countryside, "has a nation prepared for joy been plunged so rapidly into mourning.

"Rarely have hopes for peace been raised so high, only to be dashed tragically and instantaneously to the ground. . . ."

America's most distinguished political columnist, aware that the readers of his 436 client newspapers were waiting avidly for the definitive word on the tragically sudden change in the nation's political geography, gnawed his thumb knuckle thoughtfully for a moment as he paused to look out the den window at "Salubria's" rolling acres, now somnolent and exhausted in the steaming twilight of the day on which Edward M. Jason and Elizabeth Henry Knox had been laid to rest. Not only his countrymen but the world waited for Walter Dobius. It was an awesome responsibility and, as always, he was prepared to discharge it.

Prepared, and indeed, eager, for now all his work and that of his friends for many patient weeks was abruptly undone, and he knew they faced an enormous task to set it right. Together with his colleagues of the *Times*, the *Post*, *The Greatest Publication That Absolutely Ever Was*, CBS, NBC, ABC, Frankly Unctuous and his other friends of the networks, Walter had labored long and hard to put Ted Jason on the ticket. Not because they loved Ted Jason, but because they hated Orrin Knox. And "hate," though he felt it to be an exaggerated and rhetorical word he never used to himself, was probably not too strong for the combination of contempt, repugnance, disapproval, mistrust and plain, downright dislike with which they had all, over so many long, embittered years, regarded the Secretary of State.

And now, God help the country, there was nothing left to restrain him unless Walter and his friends could do the job. They had entertained great reservations about Ted Jason, who had been equivocal, tricky and devious as he played with the violent in his attempt to wrest the Presidential nomination from Orrin. But at least he had been *Right* on all the essential issues. And in Walter's world, when you were *Right*, you could be forgiven failings that would bring universal condemnation when indulged by lesser men.

Thus Ted's flirting with NAWAC and all its dangerous and even sinister components could be blandly ignored and smoothly brushed over in newsprint and on the tube. The Governor of California believed in Peace with a capital P, he was against the old, outmoded big-stick-brandishing that had so often marred America's past, he opposed the wars in Panama and Gorotoland, he believed in meeting the Communists half- or even more than halfway, he would apparently make enormous concessions to avoid any kind of confrontation with them—he was simply, classically *Right* on the issue that Walter and his colleagues saw as determining whether mankind would live or die.

As such, Ted Jason could be forgiven for being what they had come to perceive in these recent weeks—a weak, vacillating, overly ambitious man. He could not only be forgiven, he could be protected, as they always protected those who agreed with them. Around his essential weakness could be drawn the cloak of an incessant and unvarying drumbeat of press and media adulation. The public could never get through to him because the media kept the public out. Inside the charmed circle of their determined protectiveness, Edward M. Jason flourished and grew great in the eyes of his countrymen, who "only knew what they read in the newspapers or saw on television." What they read in the newspapers and saw on television often was not the truth, but that was beside the point. The point was to defeat that irresponsible, headstrong, desperately dangerous, warmongering fool, Orrin Knox. Anything could be excused and justified in the pursuit of that goal. And anything was.

For some strange reason, however—no doubt caused by the essential frivolity, stupidity and unworthiness of the American people, characteristics often observed and commented upon by their mentors—the massive onslaught of the media had not been enough. Orrin, though politically battered and bloodied, had somehow managed to hang on to a basic constituency in the country whose members persisted in seeing him as a man whose personality was sometimes prickly but whose honesty, courage and integrity were constant. This hard core the media had not been able to erode; and when the showdown had finally come earlier in the week at the National Committee meeting, it had proved to be something more than just a hard core. By some miracle of direct communication that rested more on what people sensed about him than on what they were told by those who tried to persuade them differently, he had been able to get sufficient support to win the nomination. Enough genuinely spontaneous public pressure had descended on the committee to persuade enough—just enough—of its members to vote for Orrin. It had been a very narrow victory but there was no doubt it had been approved by a majority of his countrymen. And even his opponents had been disposed to fall in line when Orrin had decided, with what Walter and his friends could only regard, grudgingly, as genuine statesmanship, to pick Ted for his running mate.

Thereby, as Walter shrewdly knew from his twenty-five years in Washington, Orrin had drawn most of the teeth of his liberal critics—while at the same time producing an erosion of doubt in his basically conservative constituency that he would have a hard time overcoming. A hard time, that is, as long as Ted lived and could exercise an influence on Orrin's policies—as long as he provided a focal point for the liberal point of view that would hold Orrin in check.

But now Ted was gone and the check was no longer there. *Why* was it no longer there?

Suddenly, as he later told his chum the executive director of the *Post,* it was as though Walter heard a great voice from the sky, a genuine revelation. Into his mind like a slither of lightning came the question: *Why was Ted Jason no longer there?* One of the shrewdest political brains in the world came to a dead halt. Across its owner's face passed a strange look of astonishment, speculation and the beginnings of an almost gleeful triumph. Not openly gleeful, for such blatant satisfaction would not have suited Walter's image of himself, but a genuine satisfaction, nonetheless.

He drew a sharp breath and his mind began to race. Out of its headlong plummeting came the column that was to mark the beginning of the last great attempt to get Orrin Knox—the attempt that would carry Walter and his friends into strange and dangerous alliances with deadly enemies of theirs whom they believed, in their naïve sophistication, to be friends.

It was to be an attempt undertaken, by those who launched it, with an absolute self-righteousness and an unshakable, uplifting, thoroughly comforting self-congratulation. Walter and his friends would be convinced, as they had been in the case of so many other savage attacks upon public figures they knew were clearly unworthy to serve the great Republic, that what they were doing was best for America. This justified all, even the type of attack he was beginning now as he turned back to his typewriter with a sudden determination, his pudgy fingers racing over the keys as both his ideas and what his less friendly colleagues (and there were some) called "Walter's hysteria quotient" began to flow:

"In this dreadful hour, when American politics are in disarray and when the peace-loving have lost perhaps their last, best hope who might have restrained a war-obsessed Administration, all Americans who love their country must now reassess their attitudes and approaches to the coming campaign and the election in November.

"As of this moment, it appears an all but total certainty that the nominee chosen to run against Orrin Knox will be the amiable and worthy Minority Leader of the United States Senate, Senator Warren Strickland of Idaho. But when one says 'amiable and worthy' about Senator Strickland one has said it all. He has served for twenty years with notable diligence and unnoticeable accomplishment. Nothing in his record indicates Presidential stature. Nothing in his personality indicates the kind of national charisma that will be needed to defeat Secretary Knox. Secretary Knox," (and Walter gritted his teeth as he wrote it, but one had to give the devil his due, unfortunately) "whatever one may think of his policies, does have a dominant and commanding personality. It may frequently be prickly, sharp-tongued, impatient, intolerant and unattractive" (and that, he thought with satisfaction, put the devil's due in proper perspective) "but there is no denying that it is a powerful one. Like him or dislike him, trust him or mistrust him, Orrin Knox is *there* and he cannot be ignored. That poses, for all those many millions in America who deplore his pro-war policies and his harsh impatience with dissenters at home, a major problem.

"It is a problem, it seems likely, which cannot be solved by voting for Senator Strickland, whose personal friendship and basic sympathies in any event lie with Secretary Knox, even though he is theoretically in opposition. It can only be solved by placing on the ticket as Secretary Knox's running mate a man in the Ted Jason mold, dedicated to the Ted Jason policies—as strongly, immovably and implacably opposed to war, to phony hostility towards our peace-seeking Communist friends, and to the outworn tenets of shotgun diplomacy, as was Ted Jason himself."

(And where, Walter asked himself with a savage inner sarcasm, do you find this paragon? Roger P. Croy, that fatuous fool, the demagogic silver-haired, silver-tongued, former Governor of Oregon who had managed Ted's campaign for the nomination? George Henry Wattersill, that constantly publicized young legal defender of the sick, the misfit and the misbegotten from the underside of America? Some other Senator, shopworn and unappealing even though he might parrot the Jason line? Some other Governor, arriving too late on the Presidential scene for any effective buildup? There was nobody sufficiently big in his own right so that Orrin could be forced to take him, that was the problem. But the thought must be given one more boost for the record, before Walter turned to matters more subtle and long-range.)

"That there are such men in American life," he assured his readers, "there can be no doubt. A dozen, starting with the outstanding former Governor of Oregon, Roger P. Croy, come instantly to mind." (He knew he did not have to name them, because over the years his readers had become so conditioned that if Walter said something "comes instantly to mind" his readers would instantly start racking their brains to *make* something come to mind.) "Therefore, the first task before the vast millions who believed in the idealism, the purposes and the sheer human *goodness* of Edward M. Jason is this: to bring sufficient pressure on Secretary Knox, and on the National Committee, to persuade them to accept such a man.

"To do otherwise—to allow a handpicked Knox Vice Presidential nomination—would be to permit the unthinkable. It would be to endorse the creation of a ticket completely unbalanced, completely lopsided, completely dedicated to the war policies of Secretary Knox and the last two Administrations.

"National tickets must be balanced. It is one of the most honored traditions of American politics. It would be unthinkable to permit a ticket in which the opposing point of view within the party had no voice to speak for it. Balanced tickets have not become a time-hallowed feature of our politics for nothing. *Balance means balance.* It is absolutely imperative if the American democracy is to function fairly for all its citizens.

"Therefore, all those Americans who believed in Edward M. Jason, all Americans of good faith and good heart, must instantly make their wishes known on this issue, in overwhelming force and unanswerable unity. The country can accept no less."

And now with that clarion call to the faithful out of the way, he decided—with a sudden overwhelming dislike for the man who had won the Presidential nomination over his bitter and implacable opposition—that he would give Orrin Knox something to think about. He would not do it frivolously, lightly or vindictively. A genuine thought had occurred to Walter Dobius and he did not consider it at all beyond the realm of possibility that it might be an entirely valid one. Not that Orrin himself could have been personally involved, of course; he would grudgingly but honestly give Orrin that much toleration. But somebody could have been involved . . . somebody could have been. And once he expressed the thought in print, he knew very well that for many millions it would be easy to accept. He and his colleagues lived happily in an age in which they could create "the truth" simply by stating it emphatically in print or on the tube.

If Orrin could not be defeated—and Walter was realist enough to doubt very seriously that he could be—and if he could not be restrained by a running mate handpicked by Walter, his colleagues and the peace-loving elements of the country—then he must be prevented from pursuing his insane war policies by other means.

Righteously, as he always chastised those who deserved it in American public life, Walter began to lay the groundwork—completely and honestly convinced that he was doing so in the best interests of the nation to which he owed, in odd but undeniable fashion, allegiance and a curious kind of jealous and possessive love.

"With this much said," his talented fingers hurried on, "the mind inevitably returns to the terrible events that took place three days ago at the Washington Monument Grounds. And after all due sorrow has been expressed to the Secretary for the loss of Mrs. Knox—after all the universal mourning that has accompanied the end of the amazing career and infinitely valuable life of Governor Jason has been expressed to his widow—the questions begin. Americans have to acknowledge that they are not pleasant questions. But Americans must also acknowledge that they are questions that have to be faced, for they go to the very heart of the basic worth and potential capabilities of a possible Knox Administration.

"If these questions have any foundation at all—and many here in this capital" (another favorite phrase that dutiful readers out in the country could never verify but always accepted) "believe they may have foundation—then they throw the most grave and disturbing light upon Secretary Knox and all around him.

"They raise, indeed, the gravest question of all: *Can he govern?*

"Or will he, ultimately, face defeat at the polls?

"Or, if elected, will he face suspicion, mistrust, incapacity to function—and then perhaps, before too long—impeachment—ouster—disgrace?"

Which was pretty strong stuff, Walter knew. But he was in the grip of a bitter resentment against fate for removing the only hopeful element of the Knox ticket, and anger drove him on to lengths which, even for Walter at his most righteous, were perhaps a little extreme.

"Why was Edward M. Jason, the man who could have restrained the war policies of a Knox Administration, so tragically and abruptly taken from us? Why did there occur a death so convenient to the head of the ticket? What sinister forces, lurking in the background of the Knox campaign, may have been responsible for this terrible event? Did the candidate know—did he even remotely suspect—that some among his conservative supporters might be so radical and so ruthless that they could conceivably go to such terrible lengths to get rid of Edward M. Jason?

"If this should ever prove to be the case—if there should ever appear the slightest suspicion that Orrin Knox—if not directly, then through the fundamental executive sin of not knowing what was going on around him—was in any remotest way culpable for the horrifying murder of his liberal running mate, Edward M. Jason, Governor of California—then he should be driven forever from public life with such a cry of condemnation and revulsion from his countrymen as will ring forever down the corridors of history.

"This correspondent does not say—no responsible observer or leader in this stunned capital says—that Secretary of State Orrin Knox did indeed know, or condone, or participate in, any such dreadful scheme. Yet the somber questions remain:

"*Why was the only man capable of restraining his war policies so ruthlessly and mercilessly gunned down? Who planned it? How did it come about? Why did an event so convenient for Orrin Knox occur?*

"Washington—America—the world—awaits answers to these questions from the only man who can give them—the Presidential candidate. It is the hope here, as it is everywhere, that they will soon be forthcoming."

Which, as Walter told himself again, was indeed strong stuff. Under other circumstances—if, for instance, it had been Orrin Knox who had fallen dead on the platform instead of Ted Jason—Walter might have proceeded in a much different way and turned out to be, in the long run, a much different man. He would then have been dealing with a liberal candidate, but one whose real liberalism and basic human worth he did not trust for one moment. He would then perhaps have been much more the cautionary sage, attempting, as he had so often done with wayward Presidents in the past, to guide Ted Jason into sound and responsible paths worthy of his great office. But Orrin had not died, Ted had; and his dislike for Orrin and Orrin's pro-war conservatism was such that he felt only a cold and self-righteous duty to America in attempting to weaken him as much as he could.

If Ted had lived . . . but Ted hadn't lived, so all that was empty speculation.

Orrin was Walter's problem now, and in his approach to it he felt, and acknowledged, very few, if any, restraints.

His column, appearing next morning in a nation still rocking from three major political deaths in as many weeks, touched off, as he had expected and intended, many consequences in many hearts and places. The media, whose members might have given Ted Jason the benefit of much patience and tolerance had he lived and Orrin died, extended no such kindness, consideration or fairness to the survivor they had opposed so long and so savagely. He was given no quarter, save for a few cursory expressions of sympathy for the loss of his wife. Frankly Unctuous picked up Walter's column that evening on his commentary—dutifully labeled "Opinion" by the network—and his fellow commentators did the same. Agreeing editorials, more cautiously worded than Walter's column but still sounding the same questioning and unsettling theme, appeared in the *Times*, the *Post*, *The Greatest Publication* and all their many editorial imitators across the country. As a result, understandably enough (although there were some slight expressions of alarm and regret in some sections of the media), the black-jacketed forces of the National Anti-War Activities Congress poured into the streets in many cities, their dismay at the death of the man they believed they had forced onto the Knox ticket suddenly given a focus, an idea and a theme. Savage banners demanded a liberal on the ticket, or failing that, the defeat, or death, or both, of Orrin Knox.

Overseas, the views of the mythical and inevitable "man in the street," so avidly sought by American correspondents whenever anything detrimental to America could be used as excuse, revealed the not very startling news that the man in the street—or his interviewers, at any rate—was convinced that there was a very strong likelihood that Orrin Knox had, indeed, had something sinister to do with the death of Ted Jason. Within hours from the time Walter finished his column in "Salubria's" quiet study, his flash of inspiration had traveled the globe with serious effects upon the man who seemed likely to be the next President of the United States.

As the National Committee prepared to meet to select a successor to Edward M. Jason, it was apparent that the Presidential nominee would not have his way without a fight; a fight he was not physically, mentally or emotionally prepared to make, just yet, but one for which history was not being allowed to give him time to prepare.

KNOX FORCES DENOUNCE "ANY INFERENCE, ASSUMPTION, HINT, RUMOR, FABRICATION, SLANDER OR LIE THAT IN ANY WAY LINKS SECRETARY KNOX TO JASON DEATH." PRESIDENT ABBOTT LEADS BITTER ATTACK ON MEDIA FOR "VICIOUS UNDERMINING OF ONE OF THE

MOST DECENT MEN IN PUBLIC LIFE." GALLUP POLL SHOWS 37 PER CENT "FIND IT POSSIBLE TO BELIEVE" KNOX HAD "SOME KNOWLEDGE IF NOT RESPONSIBILITY" FOR GOVERNOR'S ASSASSINATION.

NATIONAL COMMITTEE CONVENES TODAY IN ATMOSPHERE OF CRISIS AS SECRETARY PLANS FIRST PUBLIC APPEARANCE SINCE SHOOTING AT MONUMENT GROUNDS.

3.

HE WAS AWARE that somewhere below there was again the stirring that accompanies official arrivals and departures, and he realized that it must be for him. Although three days had passed he still was not sure he could make the effort. He knew he must, he was the nominee, even through the haze of grief, sedation and swirling confusion he had clung desperately to the knowledge that he had a responsibility that could not be avoided, a responsibility he had desired and must fulfill. It had kept him going—just barely. Then had come the visit from his son and daughter-in-law, accompanied by President Abbott and Senator Munson, shortly after 9 A.M., and with it the realization that it was time to put aside grief, insofar as possible, and return to the world. After that, very slowly and painfully, aided by two doctors, two nurses, Hal and Crystal, he had dressed, taken a cup of broth and some crackers and then asked to be left alone again for a little while until it came time to leave for the National Committee meeting.

With considerable vehemence, Hal and Crystal, as the remaining members of his family (how awful and impossible that fact was to contemplate!), had recommended against his going. With equal emphasis Bill Abbott and Bob Munson, as old and dear friends and colleagues, had argued on the other side. The discussion had been sufficiently tart and sufficiently like old times to drive below the surface for at least a little while the aching knowledge he would live with for the rest of his life: the knowledge that the lively mind that had matched his and kept it company for so many years would never be with him again. How he could get along without it, he did not know: except that he knew he must, and so he knew he would.

But for a few minutes out of the long agony of the past seventy-two hours, there was mercifully little time to think about that. Bill Abbott, with a shrewd understanding of the therapy he needed, opened the conversation with his usual direct, no-nonsense approach.

"You know how Bob and I feel about things, Orrin," he had said, not unkindly but not permitting any sentimentality to creep in, either, "so we won't spend time on that. She was a wonderful, wonderful woman and your loss is the country's more than the country knows, probably. As for *him,*" he added with a bluntness that brushed quickly past the tears that started, in spite of his determination, in Orrin's eyes, "I suppose we must mourn, too, at least for Ceil's sake. I don't hold with the idea that we must mourn for the country, because I think he was a weak and equivocating man whose death was probably for the best. Can't say that in public, of course, or I'd be shot. I made my formal statement and let it go at that. But that's how I feel about him. If he hadn't run with that violent crew and favored appeasing our enemies, I might feel differently. But he did, and I don't. So there it is. . . . Now: who do you put in his place? Got any ideas?"

For several moments Orrin had hesitated, an uncharacteristic uncertainty that revealed to them more than anything else had up to that moment how terribly crippled he was by the tragedy at the Monument Grounds. His voice when he spoke was uncertain, too: not the Orrin they had known, a change alarming because so much depended upon him and he *must* be strong. Otherwise, the world—or America's part of it—could fall apart.

"Who do you—who do you think I should select?" he asked, looking from face to face in a way so supplicating and unlike him that his son, in sheer grief, fright and worry at seeing him so, responded with an almost explosive irritation that made Crystal move quickly to place a restraining hand upon his.

"Well, if you don't know, Dad," Hal said sharply, "then I don't see how we're to know, either. It's your responsibility, isn't it?"

"That," he said carefully, not responding to Hal's tone with a tart rejoinder as he might have in some earlier, more manageable time, "may not be true. That's why I'm asking."

"It will be true," Bob Munson said, his voice deliberately comfortable and reassuring, "providing you make a quick decision and take it to the National Committee this afternoon. They've had three days to stir around but I don't think things are out of your control yet. They'll still follow your wishes, I think, providing you know what you want, and providing you take it to them personally. I don't think this can be done by proxy, even though you know Bill and I and the rest of your friends would do our damnedest for you if you couldn't show up."

"How can he show up?" Hal demanded, as fiercely protective of his father as he had been challenging to him a moment ago, and for the same reasons of grief, worry and alarm. "He isn't in any condition yet to go anywhere, let alone face that crew at Kennedy Center. And maybe"—his eyes widened with a sudden desperate concern and unhappiness—"maybe another mob, as well."

"Orrin Knox has never been afraid," William Abbott said bluntly. Hal rounded on him with a sudden flare of anger.

"Orrin Knox has never had to face anything like this!" he snapped. "Don't you have an ounce of human sympathy, Mr. President?"

"Human sympathy is one thing," William Abbott said with the same uncompromising bluntness, "and politics in this hectic age is another. The longer your father waits to name his Vice Presidential choice, the more chance there is for the Committee to run amuck and select somebody so alien to everything Orrin Knox stands for that he couldn't possibly accept him on the ticket. Only, he may have to, if he doesn't grab the initiative. And then where will we be?"

"In one hell of a mess," Senator Munson said crisply, "with NAWAC running rampant and violence in the streets and the Russians on the prowl and everything as bad as though Ted Jason himself had been elected. To say nothing of the fact that under those conditions Warren Strickland might even win. You don't want that to happen, do you, Orrin?"

But this did not evoke the response Bob Munson obviously hoped it would. Orrin only uttered a tired sigh and inquired in a listless voice:

"Wouldn't that be best for the country, maybe? Just wipe out Ted and me and all the bitter differences we've represented . . . let the country start over again with somebody entirely out of it? Warren would do a good job."

"He would," the President agreed, "but he wouldn't do the job Orrin Knox would. And that's what we want."

"That's what you want," Orrin said in the same listless way, "but it's not what half my countrymen want. More than half, more likely." He sighed again, shifting in his chair in an unsuccessful attempt to relieve a little of the savage pain that still clawed his right shoulder and side. He looked up at the President, standing solid and stolid and uncompromising in front of him. "Why don't I just quit altogether, Bill, and let the Committee start all over? A lot of them would like that."

"You cannot!" the President said with an indignation so sudden and so sharp that it provoked an uneasy stirring from Hal and Crystal. "It would throw away everything. Everything!"

"Everything's gone anyway," he said dully. "Why shouldn't I?"

"Because then," Bob Munson said with a deliberately harsh impatience, "you would simply give further credence to all the rumors and all the vicious things that Walter Dobius and the rest of them are floating around."

"What are they 'floating around'?" he asked with a careful articulation, although he found that he really did not seem to care about something that three days ago would have provoked an aroused rejoinder.

"Awful things," Crystal said quietly, "but nothing to bother you with right now."

"On the contrary," the President said. "On the contrary. I think he needs to know what he's up against."

And with a deliberate, coldly driving emphasis, he told him: Walter's column, the response from Walter's colleagues, the instantaneous reaction from all who had always seized upon the slightest excuse to mistrust him, the worldwide whisper of suspicion and uncertainty that had spread in the past three days. Hal and Crystal watched with open apprehension, but the recital had the effect the President intended and anticipated. Orrin began to grow angry, and with the anger came the first break in the horrified, disbelieving shock and apathy of the past three days. When he looked up at the end of the President's recital it was with a little of the old combativeness in his eyes.

"Then I obviously *have* to go to the meeting this afternoon," he said, and it was not a question but a statement of fact. Both his son and daughter-in-law responded at once.

"You can't go!" Hal said sharply. "You're in no condition to go!"

"You really aren't, you know," Crystal agreed with an undisguised worry. "The doctors told us just before we came in that—"

"He has to go," Bob Munson interrupted harshly. "If he can stand up and walk, he has to go."

"I can stand up," Orrin said, with the first semblance of a smile he had managed since half his world ended with a shot; and he did so, shakily, holding out his hand to Hal, leaning on his arm. "Whether I can walk"—he took a step and stopped with a sudden sharp grimace—"is another matter. But even if I have to be carried—I think I'd better go."

"But, *Dad*—" Hal protested.

"I have to go!" he said sharply, sounding for a moment completely like Orrin again. "Don't argue with me, I have to go!"

But after they had left, Hal and Crystal still greatly distressed and uneasy, the President and Bob Munson uneasy also but convinced they had carried an argument that had to be won, he sat for a long time alone, fighting with himself the battle their remarks had only begun.

How fantastic it was, he thought, his mind gradually beginning to shake off the terrible inertia that had held it since the tragedy, that his friends of the media should leap so soon to the attack. It showed how much they must still concede Orrin Knox to be a major factor to be reckoned with in the destiny of his country. It also showed how much they must still fear and dislike him, for reasons reaching back into all the bitter battles over foreign policy of all his controversial years in the Senate—the battles in which they called him "warmonger" and he called them "appeasers." It was a dislike so intense that it could not rest even long enough to let his wife grow cold. It was not until this moment that he had really understood the full extent of the burdens he was going to have to carry if he managed to win an election which now, thanks to those who had arranged to kill his running mate and his wife, appeared to be very much in doubt.

He marveled, as he heard the sounds of preparation increasing downstairs, and as his nurses looked in from time to time to utter meaningless but cheerful sounds that must be words intended to lift his morale, at how much a tough mind could stand when it had to. He had thought three days ago, in that frightful moment at the Monument when Ceil Jason had started to say something—when there had been an instantaneous blur of sound and motion—when he felt a heavy weight sag suddenly against him and had known instinctively and with an awful certainty exactly what it was—that he would never recover. For the first few hours he had been almost completely sedated, hardly sentient, hardly knowing day from night. After his wound had been treated, sedation had continued for twelve hours and then been slowly withdrawn; but even now, off the drugs completely since last night, the pain reduced to a dull throb that was constant but bearable, his mind was only partially functioning. He prided himself, however, that, even though crippled, it *was* functioning.

He started to promise himself that sometime, when there was time and when he could pay her proper tribute, he would think about Beth —and yet, in that formal a sense, why should he? He would always think about her, to the day he died. She would never leave him. She would always be there, as he knew she was there right now, strong, helpful, companionable, encouraging, just as always, her presence in some ways as real and vivid as though she had never left. At the moment he felt that there should be some formal acknowledgment of grief, since the doctors had absolutely forbade his attendance at the funeral. But perhaps in the long run there need not be. She had always known how he felt. He knew she knew now. It might be all that was necessary.

And having told himself these things so calmly and philosophically —cold-blooded, ruthless Orrin Knox!—he suddenly had a sense of her presence so sharp that his eyes filled uncontrollably with tears and an anguished cry shattered through his mind: *Come back, oh, come back! I miss you so!*

But after a few moments training and discipline began to take hold again, just as he expected them to, just as he knew she would expect them to. The Knoxes had taken a heavy battering during their years of public life and they had learned early to fight back, cut their losses, respond as strongly to events as events responded to them. He would mourn her forever, inside: but now there were things to be done. Aided by the blunt talking of his old and dear friends from the Hill, he began to contemplate at last in unsparing detail what they were.

First he must regain command of the National Committee, which he knew must now be almost out of control as its one hundred members, a national committeeman and a national committeewoman for each of the fifty states, prepared to reconvene once more at riot-torn Kennedy Center to choose Ted Jason's successor as Vice Presidential candidate. The members would be shattered by the twin tragedies at the Monument Grounds, by the abrupt and frightful destruction of the hard-fought compromise finally worked out between the forces of the Secretary of State and the Governor of California. Their mood would be sympathetic to Ceil Jason—much more sympathetic, now, to the anti-war position Ted Jason represented—much more susceptible to the bully-boy tactics of NAWAC, whose increasingly paramilitary activities would be even more militant now.

The Committee, though he had many staunch friends there, would be the first and most difficult hurdle, particularly since he really did not know, at this moment, whom he would recommend as his running mate. If he could have time—a day, even—he could hold conferences, talk it over with the different elements of the party, ascertain the general mood, try to work out another compromise. But he apparently was not to be granted a day. It was clear enough that he must make his fight right now, this afternoon, in public, or the Committee would indeed, as the President had predicted, force upon him someone so far over on Ted's side and so alien to his own philosophies that he would simply be unable to accept him. And then, given the mood in the Committee that such an event would generate, he himself might very well be forced off the ticket and that would be the end of everything Orrin Knox had stood for and fought for in almost three decades of public service.

Many millions, he knew, would regard this as no loss, and there were plenty on the Committee who wouldn't either. So this afternoon was the first and most important stage of the new era he found himself in. He must approach it crippled in heart, mind and body. A wave of bitterness consumed him for a moment. *Haven't You done enough to me?* he demanded of a God he had always considered basically impersonal, impartial and generally uncaring of ordinary mortals, although possibly somewhat more concerned about Orrin Knox. Apparently He wasn't, though: Orrin Knox had another river to cross, and there was no way around it.

And this time, as never before, he was entirely alone.

Again the desperate desolation of the fact savaged his mind, and again, after a titanic struggle with himself, he forced it back and forced himself to go on with the careful calculations an experienced politician in his situation had to make. Grief had to be put aside: for the present, at least, there was simply no time for it.

His alternatives were four, as he saw them.

He could recommend someone exactly in line with his own thinking, someone like Bill Abbott or Bob Munson. Walter Dobius and his colleagues had already made clear that they would do everything in their power to stop that. If Ted Jason had lived and he had died, he knew they would have been 100 per cent in favor of a Vice Presidential candidate whose views exactly paralleled Ted's. The argument of "balance" would be forgotten, all thought of compromise would be hooted down, it would be presented as the greatest possible good for the country that both men on the ticket should reflect the same point of view. But Orrin was the one who had lived, and therefore "balance" was the slogan, compromise was the ideal, and only a ticket that faithfully reflected the sharp divisions in the party could possibly be supported.

So unless he wanted to fight what could well be a losing fight—for he knew there were enough in the sharply divided Committee who felt the same way Walter and his friends did to make it at best a razor's-edge proposition—he had best give up the idea of a completely compatible Vice President.

He could, instead, choose Roger P. Croy or someone equally devoted to the Jason point of view on foreign policy. This would mean that in the event of his own death, all his policies would be reversed, whatever he might have achieved in foreign policy by a sensible and carefully calculated firmness would be wiped out, the world would be—as he saw it—delivered sooner or later to the twentieth century's great new imperialists who operated under the guise of Communist liberation, brotherhood and good will. This he could not countenance, nor could those in the country who looked to him for leadership.

Or he could resign the nomination this afternoon, get out of the fight and let the Committee start afresh. This thought, which he had volunteered so listlessly to the President only a few short minutes ago, now seemed utterly repugnant. Such a move would indeed be to guarantee victory on all fronts to those he regarded, with a considerable contempt, as the appeasers, the trimmers, the equivocators, the foolish and the weak.

He had always believed and acted in a certain way, always represented a certain "tough" attitude in foreign policy. Many millions of his countrymen had depended upon him to do this. They depended upon him still. He would be betraying them and betraying himself if he withdrew.

The skeptical, impatient expression his family, friends and colleagues knew so well momentarily touched his face.

He wouldn't consider it!

He would be a fool if he did.

His reaction revealed that Orrin Knox, having begun to mend, was mending very rapidly.

So only one alternative remained, and that was to find somebody occupying a reasonable middle ground and do his best to persuade the Committee to go along with the choice.

In a sudden flash of inspiration, he knew instantly whom he would nominate.

He did not know how the Committee would take this.

But he knew he would do it.

For the first time since horror struck three days ago, a smile—grim, determined, ironic, not very lasting or much filled with humor, but at least a smile—crossed his face.

Their Presidential nominee, they would find, might be down but he was not out.

When Hal knocked gently on the door a few moments later, his father's response brought a smile, relieved and deeply affectionate, to his face too.

"I'm ready," Orrin announced in a voice still weak but scarcely reluctant. "Lead me to 'em!"

And so the National Committee returned to heavily guarded Kennedy Center, scene just four days ago of the "Great Riot" in which the enormous mob led by the paramilitary forces of the National Anti-War Activities Congress had stormed the doors after the nomination of Orrin Knox for President. Thirty-nine had died on that terrifying, bitter day. Only the subsequent nomination of Ted Jason as Vice President and Ted's dramatically soothing speech to his hysterically violent supporters appeared to have saved the country from revolution.

The memories hung heavy on Esmé Harbellow Stryke and Asa B. Attwood of California, on Anna Hooper Bigelow and Perry Amboy of New Hampshire, on Pierre Boissevain of Vermont and Blair Hannah of Illinois, on Ewan MacDonald MacDonald of Wyoming, on Lathia Talbot Jennings of South Dakota and Mary Buttner Baffleburg of Pennsylvania, and on all their fellow national committeemen and national committeewomen as they prepared to reconvene.

The memories were not eased by the fact that the scene was once again almost exactly as they had left it, and for the same reasons: NAWAC and the violent again were at their stations, and again the Committee was under terrible pressure.

Again the President had ordered out the troops, again the same precautions surrounded the hundred men and women who must select a new running mate for Orrin Knox. Again they were housed at military headquarters in Fort Myer, Virginia, just across the Potomac; again they arrived at the Center in Army cars, protected by motorcycle outriders; again they found themselves under siege. And again the President, as national committeeman from Colorado and chairman of the Committee, had arranged it so that the meeting should be held in the Playhouse, its seating capacity kept to a rigid five hundred: the Committee, three hundred visitors and observers divided as equally as possible between Knox and Jason supporters, and one hundred from the media. This last restriction had produced the same anguished denunciations that had greeted it before, but the President had been adamant. The original meeting had been chaos and circus enough and he did not want this one made more so. Again the *Times,* the *Post, The Greatest Publication That Absolutely Ever Was,* Walter Dobius, Frankly Unctuous and his network colleagues, and all the rest, had cried, "Dictatorship!" and "Suppression of the news!" But William Abbott was a tough old man and he didn't give a damn. Grumbling and unhappy, the media too had its collective memories revivified—creating, as the *Times* remarked acridly, "a sense of *déjà* damned *vu.*"

Around Kennedy Center's land perimeter the President had again arranged for riot-trained soldiers to supplement the District of Columbia police—a thousand this time instead of the five hundred before. An inner ring of riot-trained Marines—also increased from five hundred to a thousand—had been assigned to guard the Playhouse. In the Potomac's Georgetown Channel, Theodore Roosevelt Island and Theodore Roosevelt Bridge, nearest approach to the Center from Virginia, had been closed. Across the river a strip a mile long and six hundred yards deep—again, double last time—had been sealed off to all traffic. In the channel four small armed Coast Guard cutters lay at anchor just off the esplanade, overhead a dozen helicopters were on regular patrol over the entire area, both precautions also escalated. At re-established "Checkpoint Alpha," sole entrance for Committee members, visiting dignitaries and the media, security regulations even tighter than before, if possible, had been reinstated.

And beyond the barricades on the land side, and in hastily re-erected tent towns at the edge of the barred zone across the river, NAWAC and its friends were also back, and also nearly doubled. Just before he left the White House in his heavily guarded limousine to come to the Center, the President had been advised by the Secretary of Defense and the District chief of police that crowd estimates were between a hundred fifty and two hundred thousand, with more thousands still pouring into the capital from every plane, train, bus and freeway.

He too, Bill Abbott felt with a weary sigh as his bristling cavalcade headed west toward the Center, had a sense of repetition so heavy as to be almost unbearable. After all the bitter battling to put together the Knox-Jason ticket, after all the tension, bloodshed and horror, now another horror had been piled on top and everything had been smashed to smithereens. All the careful compromises of democracy, hammered out at such cost, destroyed in a bloody instant by those who felt only contempt for democracy and wished to destroy it . . . or so he analyzed their motives.

He did not know, yet, who had perpetrated the murders at the Monument, but he intended to find out. The commission he had appointed to investigate Harley Hudson's mysterious death had a new mission now. He had conferred with its chairman, the ex-Chief Justice, within two hours after the assassinations. Already the staff was at work interviewing witnesses. He had a strong hunch that there was a link between all these murders and he thought he knew where it came from. He also suspected strongly that those responsible were very well entrenched in NAWAC. If he could find the connection, he would have them—providing he could convince some of his more skeptical countrymen to accept the facts in their columns, news stories and broadcasts. At least he would have the culprits as far as the historical record was concerned.

He was convinced that the trail led straight to the Soviet Ambassador, Vasily Tashikov, and his "agricultural aide," long ago tagged by the FBI, military intelligence and the CIA as being the head of the Russian secret police network, the KGB, for the eastern United States.

If that was true, however, surely a great mistake must have been committed. For surely the man they wanted to kill was Orrin Knox, not Ted Jason, who, on all the evidence Bill Abbott had seen, would have been an easy mark for Soviet pressure had he become President in the event of Orrin's death.

Orrin must have been the target—although, as it was turning out, the President could not really see that the assassins had lost much. The situation that had been created for Orrin was such a tangle that he might end up being unable to govern, too: for different reasons, but as fortuitously for America's enemies. Perhaps, in fact, even more so, since a President under such attack as Orrin was under might be an even easier mark than, in the President's estimation, Edward M. Jason would have been.

Except for one single factor, he told himself with the mildest glimmer of hope as the first outlying fringes of the mob began to appear along his route, screaming obscenities and shaking their fists at the old man who sat stolidly back in the cushions and gave no slightest acknowledgment that they existed.

Except for one single factor.

Long ago, watching the then freshman Senator from Illinois carry some point of debate by sheer logic and strength of character, the late Senator Seabright B. Cooley of South Carolina had been moved to a remark that none of Orrin's friends had ever forgotten.

"There comes a time," Seab had said in his deceptively drowsy, sleepy-eyed way, "when most folks let themselves feel beaten and they give up on an issue. But not Orrin. Orrin keeps at it. You mark my words, now, Orrin will go far. And do you know why? Because Orrin's got somethin' jest a leetle bit extra, that's why. Yes, sir. Jest a *leetle* bit extra."

"Orrin's little extra" had been a byword on the Hill and in American politics ever since; and since it was the quality that had carried him finally, over so many obstacles and so much bitter opposition, to his party's Presidential nomination, it was the thing to which William Abbott was pinning his hopes as his cavalcade, coming now within sight of Kennedy Center, brought to full volume the angry wave of sound that kept him company.

"Orrin's little extra," needed now as it had never been before—first, by Orrin himself, and then, the President was convinced, by the country and the world.

The Secretary of State had looked wan and still in considerable pain a couple of hours ago during their talk at his home in Spring Valley, but on the whole he had appeared to be increasingly strong. Yet William Abbott the lifelong bachelor knew as well as Bob Munson and Orrin's children how terribly much he must be missing Beth, and how terribly heartsick and weakened by her death he must be.

God knew *he* missed her, the President thought, recalling the shrewd, calm, comfortable presence that had contributed so much to the life and career of Orrin Knox. Beth Knox had been a rare woman, and she and Orrin had enjoyed a unique partnership in both marriage and politics. In fact, as in many great political careers of American history, the two had been so intermingled that no one, least of all the participants, could tell where the one ended and the other began. From the very first campaign for the state senate in Illinois it had been "Orrin and Beth" on the billboards and on the hustings; and during all the contentious, controversial, battling years since, in the state senate, the governorship, the United States Senate and finally the State Department, it had been "Orrin and Beth" who had together served, first the people of the state and then the people of the country, with an uncompromising integrity and an uncompromising opposition to all those attitudes and trends which they believed weakening, if not fatal, to the survival of democracy. This had brought them the unrelenting hostility of many in the media, the academic, religious, artistic and professional worlds who did not see the attitudes and trends in the same light they did. But it had not deflected or deterred either of them; nor had it jarred the steady balance or the wry good humor with which Beth, in particular, had responded to the incessant and unrelenting belittlement.

Orrin, of course, had not suffered those he believed to be fools quite so equably. Possessed of great intelligence, a lively temper and a tongue sometimes too willing to be tart and impatient, he had often responded broadside to his enemies instead of trying to go around them. More often than not, this had worked in the Senate, whose members normally favored the more subtle approach but in his case respected his sheer intelligence and the powerful will that went with it. It was not, however, until Harley Hudson appointed him Secretary of State that he became, as he himself acknowledged, a much more moderate and diplomatic soul. Not too diplomatic, for that wouldn't have been Orrin: but at least more reasonable, more willing to compromise, a little less certain that he had all the answers to everything.

Then had come the convention, Harley's decision to run again, Orrin's belief that his dream of the White House was finally put to rest forever; Harley's mysterious death, Orrin's battle with Ted for the nomination, Orrin's squeak-in victory and his realization that he had to give in and compromise with Ted and his supporters if he wanted to win. Out of that had come, suddenly, a man mature in a way Orrin had never really been mature before. And then had come horror at the Monument, and out of that—what kind of Orrin?

The President did not know and his puzzlement must have shown in his face to some degree when he arrived at heavily guarded "Checkpoint Alpha," because the reporters and television cameramen waiting there rushed forward as far as they were allowed, which wasn't much, to shout their frantic appeals for enlightenment. What was the nominee going to do?

"I don't know," the President called out sharply, "and if I did, you know I wouldn't tell you. Why don't you wait and see, as the Committee and I are going to have to do?"

"Old bastard!" the *Post* commented, not too quietly. "He won't tell us anything."

"That's right," the President responded with equal cordiality. "Why should I?"

"The people have a right to know!" the *Post* shouted indignantly; but the President's response was a smile of such openly sarcastic amusement that it almost said aloud, "Look who's talking!" As such it was promptly wiped off the television screens and he was allowed to enter the building without further questioning, followed by mutters quite as savage, if more muted, as any that had been shouted at him in the streets.

So there it was again, he reflected with an annoyance that again showed briefly in his eyes, that eternal hostility that crippled them all, press and politicians alike: for which, he supposed, he was just as much to blame as they were. Certainly Orrin was, for after an early period of trying to appease critics who were implacably against him on the most fundamental of issues, foreign policy, he had come finally to the conclusion that they could never be appeased, that as long as he pursued what they liked to call a "tough" or "pro-war" policy toward the Communists, they were never going to forgive him, never relent, never be even minimally fair. When he finally decided, permanently, that he must take his stand on what he believed regardless of their opposition, he had guaranteed a state of permanent warfare with the media. Sooner or later all those who supported him were drawn into the same vortex and received the same treatment.

How would it be, the President wondered for a moment as he went mechanically through the motions of greeting the troops inside the doors, smiling, confident and apparently fully in command, if the leaders of the media ever found themselves in a situation where their freedoms were really threatened by the policies they had always so vigorously advocated and supported? How would it be if they turned out to be wrong, if suddenly someone they had raised up—even a Ted Jason, perhaps—turned upon them and, using the public support they themselves had created for him, tore them down? How would they enjoy the harvest they had sown for so many long, bitter years? . . . But, of course, he dismissed the thought, it would never happen in America. They would always be free to pursue their harshly unbalanced attacks on all who disagreed with them. They would never have to face the reckoning. They would always be safe, always protected, always free to be unrestrained and irresponsible, for such was what they considered freedom to be. Not even if Ted Jason had become President, he was sure, would any attempt ever have been made to attack or control the media. Not even Ted's most violent supporters would have dared. This was America, and in America such things could not be.

Certainly they would not occur under Orrin Knox, that was sure, even though the President had moments of exasperation and resentment when he almost felt they should. The attack on Orrin now was utterly disgraceful, the wildest and most vicious he had seen in some time, and he had seen a good many in his long service on Capitol Hill. It was not enough that the man must lose his wife to an assassin, he must be accused of helping to plot the whole thing in order to remove someone who disagreed with him from the ticket. What kind of minds they must be, the President thought, Walter who would promulgate such a horrid myth, and his friends who could seize upon and embellish it!

He was frowning when he reached the door of the Playhouse, and it was so they saw him as the guards snapped to attention, and the doorkeeper bellowed, "Ladeez and Gemmun, the Prezdent of the Yewnined States!"—Blair Hannah, Ewan MacDonald MacDonald, Lizzie Hanson McWharter, Mary Buttner Baffleburg and the rest of the National Committee; Robert A. Leffingwell, Patsy Jason Labaiya in heavy mourning for her brother, Lord and Lady Maudulayne, Raoul and Celestine Barre, Vasily Tashikov, Krishna Khaleel and all the other observers domestic and foreign who had been given tickets; the

Times, the *Post*, *The Greatest Publication*, *Time*, *Newsweek*, Walter Dobius, Frankly Unctuous and the other members of the media who were there by virtue of personal stature, prestige of publication, or the luck of the draw. A President upset, and one obviously in no mood to waste time, or to pretend in any way that the business before them was any less serious than it was.

He strode swiftly down the aisle, mounted the small platform, moved to the lectern at its center; turned quickly to note that the official reporter was seated at the small desk to his left, turned back to look directly into the banked lights of the television cameras that flanked the room.

"Please be seated, ladies and gentlemen," he said crisply, and waited for a moment as they did so, their expectant eyes never leaving his face. "By virtue of the authority vested in me as chairman of the National Committee, I declare this new special emergency session of the Committee to be now in session for the purpose of selecting a nominee for Vice President of the United States. If the distinguished national committeeman from the state of Washington will oblige us as he did before"—he paused and a little sigh, tired and sad, escaped his lips—"and how short a time ago that was!—then we shall be very grateful."

"Yes, Mr. President," Luther Redfield said, his voice shaking slightly with the gravity of it; and proceeded in his somewhat florid but desperately sincere fashion to deliver the convocation while they all stood again, heads bowed, and far off the distant sea of NAWAC murmured and rumbled, seeming to lap ominously against the walls of the silent room.

"Mr. President," Roger P. Croy said into the hush that followed, "I wish to offer a suggested resolution of sorrow on behalf of myself and other friends of the late nominee for Vice President—"

"On behalf of all of us, I should think," the President interrupted in a tone he tried to keep impersonal. "I trust the committeeman does not wish the world to think his grief and that of his friends is exclusive."

"Mr. President," Roger Croy said smoothly, "there may be some on this committee less saddened, perhaps, by events, than"—he paused delicately—"some others. For that reason—"

"For that reason, nothing!" the President snapped. "This resolution will be adopted unanimously by this committee. I assume you have also included in it an expression of the Committee's condolences to the nominee for President for the loss of his wife."

"We had thought, Mr. President," Roger P. Croy said earnestly, "that perhaps some proponent of the nominee might wish to offer such a—"

"Shame on you!" the President said angrily. "For shame, Governor! For shame, to try to introduce crude partisanship at such a cruel moment! There will be one resolution expressing the unanimous sense of this committee concerning both Governor Jason and Mrs. Knox, so if you don't have one ready, sit down and let someone else propose it!"

"Mr. President—" Roger P. Croy began indignantly, even as Blair Hannah rose on the other side of the room to seek recognition.

"I have the resolution, Mr. President," he said in a voice filled with contempt for his mellifluous colleague from Oregon; and read it quickly, a dignified, brief and moving valedictory for Edward Montoya Jason and Elizabeth Henry Knox.

"Is there objection?" the President asked, staring about the room with an expression that indicated, as the St. Louis *Post-Dispatch* murmured to the Boston *Globe,* that there damned well better not be. "Then without objection, the resolution of condolence is adopted unanimously by the Committee."

He paused for a moment as the room suddenly became very still. Outside, the mob, following closely on television, also fell silent.

"The business of the Committee," he said slowly, "is to find a new nominee for Vice President. It is not only the tradition, but it is the courtesy we owe him, that the nominee for President should be allowed to make his recommendation to the Committee before we act. Therefore I shall appoint a committee to wait upon the nominee for President and escort him to this chamber at such time as may be mutually convenient—"

"Mr. President," Ewan MacDonald MacDonald inquired in his gentle but not-to-be-trifled-with burr, "can you advise the Committee as to when—or whether—the nominee for President will be able to attend? There are reports and rumors that his health may not permit it. In that case, perhaps we should proceed at once to—"

"Mr. President!" Mary Buttner Baffleburg said, her roly-poly little body seeming to quiver all over with indignation. "Don't you try anything like that, now, Ewan! Just don't you try it! We're not here to allow any railroading today, I can tell you that! Not one bit of it!"

"Mr. President," Ewan MacDonald said patiently, "I admire the zeal with which Mrs. Baffleburg protects her candidate's interests, I always have, but—"

"I don't have a candidate!" Mary Baffleburg said sharply. "I'm waiting for Orrin Knox to tell us who he wants, just as I should!"

"As I say," Ewan MacDonald repeated with a little smile, "I admire your independence, Mary. But some of us feel even more independent. We think we ought to go ahead and name a candidate for Vice President and we ought to do it today, not next week sometime."

"Nobody is proposing 'next week sometime'!" Mary Baffleburg snapped.

"Well, when the candidate can get here," Ewan MacDonald said. "When will that be?"

"I don't know," Mary Baffleburg replied. "But I can tell you this, Ewan MacDonald, if there's any attempt to railroad this or prevent him from speaking, or any attempt to put over somebody he doesn't like on him, then you're in for a fight, I can tell you that!"

And she sat down, pugnacious little face red and puffing, while the cameras lingered upon it with an amused attention.

"Mr. President," Roger P. Croy said quietly, "perhaps *you* can advise us when we may expect the nominee for President to appear. The distinguished committeeman from Wyoming does have a point, it seems to me, despite the rather violent response of the distinguished committeewoman from Pennsylvania. We can't wait around forever, you know. We have to have a candidate for Vice President. Possibly, if the candidate for President does not show signs of sufficiently speedy recovery, we may even have to have—"

"Now, Mr. President, just a minute!" Blair Hannah cried, jumping to his feet, while outside a sudden excited roar welled up from the thousands in the parks. "Just a minute, now! Just what does the committeeman from Oregon think he's trying to do here, anyway?"

"It's obvious what he's trying to do," Asa B. Attwood of California shot out. "He's trying to dump Orrin Knox, that's what he's trying to do, and I tell you, Mr. President, if there is any move to do that more than half this committee is going to walk out and you won't *have* any committee to nominate a Vice President. So I'd suggest the great former Governor of Oregon had better not get too smart here!"

"DUMP ORRIN KNOX!" a sudden chant came on the wind. "DUMP ORRIN KNOX!"

"Yes, 'dump Orrin Knox!'" Asa Attwood echoed angrily. "You just try it, you people. You just try it!"

"Well, now, Mr. President," Roger P. Croy said calmly, "I think the committeeman from California is making a great leap somewhere, I don't know exactly where—certainly not in any sensible direction discernible to me. No one said anything about trying to 'dump' the nominee for President. I just said that unless his health recovers sufficiently and soon, we will be forced by the sheer logic of events to ask him to withdraw so we can nominate someone else. That's simple fact. I don't see how it warrants such hysteria."

"It isn't hysteria," Asa Attwood said, "it's just a statement of fact: you try to dump him and more than half this committee will leave and you'll be high and dry without a quorum."

"It depends on which states leave," Ewan MacDonald MacDonald suggested calmly. "You can take bodies with you, Asa, but you can't take delegate votes. And since we vote according to the number of votes allotted each state in the convention, I think you might find us able to nominate a candidate for Vice President *and* for President, without you and your friends. Maybe you'd better stick around."

"There will be no attempt to dump Orrin Knox!" Asa Attwood said flatly, and far in the distance echo came: "DUMP ORRIN KNOX! DUMP ORRIN KNOX!"

"Mr. President," Helen Rupert of Alabama said with a sudden impatient emphasis that brought quick attention, "can we stop this silly squabble and get on with it? I voted for Edward M. Jason for President in this committee four days ago, but I have no desire or intention to get rid of the man who is our nominee. We have a very distinguished nominee and I intend to support him wholeheartedly now the decision has been made—even more so, in view of recent tragic events. But we do need a candidate for Vice President, and we do need to hear from Secretary Knox. Do you, or does anyone, have any idea when he will come here, or whether he can come here?"

"I was about to appoint a committee to escort him here," the President remarked with some asperity, "but distinguished committeemen seemed to prefer arguing about it."

"But you said 'at such time as may be mutually convenient,'" Roger P. Croy pointed out, unabashed, "and that immediately created speculation."

"Only by those who wished to create it," the President said. "As a matter of fact, I understand the Secretary is ready to come here this afternoon. In fact, I have good reason to believe he may be on his way right now. In any event, I am going to appoint a committee to escort him here, and I would suggest that the committee meet him at Checkpoint Alpha rather than try to venture further from the Center. This will avoid," he remarked, as distant amused hooting greeted the words, "possible uneasy moments for all concerned."

"Will the nominee be sufficiently protected?" Blair Hannah inquired.

The President nodded, his face suddenly grim. "He will be, by troops who have orders to shoot to kill."

"Mr. President," Roger P. Croy said in a sad, unhappy tone, not facing him but staring somberly straight into the cameras, "can't we have an end to all this talk of shooting and killing? Is there to be no end to it, even now, after all these horrors?"

"Talk to your friends," the President said coldly. "It is up to them."

"Mr. President!" Roger Croy said sharply, as along the press tables at the side of the room there ran a little current of whispered annoyance, and from the mob beyond there rose an abrupt shout of angry protest. "That is no way to talk to a member of this committee! Whoever has done these dreadful things in recent days, they are not friends of mine, nor friends of anyone on this committee, nor do any of us have any kind of allegiance or obligation to them. You owe me and all of us an apology, Mr. President. I demand it."

"Apologies will come when apologies are due," the President said with a deliberate indifference. Outside the room the angry protest rose again; inside, many looked annoyed. But he remained indifferent, having decided upon a course of action and not intending to be deflected from it. "To escort the nominee I appoint the distinguished committeeman from Illinois, Mr. Hannah; the distinguished committeewoman from Pennsylvania, Mrs. Baffleburg; the distinguished committeeman from Vermont, Mr. Boissevain; the distinguished committeewoman from Alabama, Mrs. Rupert; the distinguished committeewoman from South Dakota, Mrs. Jennings; and"—he exchanged looks with Roger P. Croy that brought some flicker of amusement to the audience—"the committeeman from Oregon, Governor Croy. I believe if you will now proceed to Checkpoint Alpha, you will find that the nominee is on his way."

And such indeed appeared to be the case, for distant on the angry wind came a rising wave of shouts and screams and animal sounds that portended the arrival of someone mightily displeasing to the mob. In this fashion the nominee for President of the United States arrived at Kennedy Center, on a wave of imprecations, vilifications and obscenities from his fellow Americans; not exactly, as he remarked to his son and daughter-in-law, riding in the heavily guarded limousine with him, a triumphal progress, but the only kind that could be expected, given the situation in which they found themselves.

Nonetheless, for all that he managed to treat it with an outward lightness that got him and his children safely through it despite the jeering hate-filled faces and the occasional egg or rock or brick that bounced off the car, such a response from his countrymen could not help but make him even more heartsick and depressed than he was already. Thus when they finally reached Checkpoint Alpha and were safely inside the military cordon, it was apparent to the searching eyes of the cameras and the press that Orrin Knox was a somber and unhappy man. It was also apparent, from the way in which he leaned heavily on Hal and Crystal, and the awkward way in which he walked, very slowly, very hesitantly, very painfully, that he was still a very sick man. But he was here; and after all the detrimental things had been duly noted by the media, and by the members of the welcoming committee who watched his halting approach with worried and in most cases genuinely upset expressions, a grudging note of admiration began to sound in the comments that went forth on the air, and to appear on the faces of those who watched.

The scene also had its effect in the Playhouse, where two television screens, one on each side of the podium, kept members of the Committee in touch with the outside world. By the time the slow little cavalcade had paused, so that the Knoxes could greet the welcoming committee—even Roger P. Croy, looking somewhat embarrassed, managing a reasonably friendly handshake—a mood of quite genuine warmth had begun to develop; and as they proceeded slowly to the elevators and ascended to the Playhouse, it continued to grow. By the time those in the room heard a stir in the hall, the crack of rifle stocks as the guards came to attention and muffled voices in deferential greetings, the mood was far more welcoming and receptive than anyone would have believed possible a scant fifteen minutes before. Outside, the ominous rumble of the mob continued to surge, a hostile and unrepentant sea. But inside the room where history was to be made Orrin Knox was in far better shape politically than he or his supporters had dared to hope.

When William Abbott said gravely, "Ladies and gentlemen, the next President of the United States!" and the doors swung open to reveal him standing, pale but erect, between his son and daughter-in-law, they found themselves instinctively on their feet, applauding, smiling, shouting their welcome.

Only a few remained aloof—some of the media, either personally unfriendly or professionally unimpressed; Patsy Labaiya, looking grim and unforgiving; Vasily Tashikov, on his feet but ostentatiously unapplauding. But these were hardly noticed in the wave of sentimental warmth that accompanied the family as they proceeded slowly down the aisle, slowly up the steps, to shake hands gravely with the President, giving him the quick, quiet smiles of old friendship, and then take their seats in the three chairs prepared for them at his left.

For a moment, while the cameras dutifully sought out the Munsons, the Maudulaynes, the Barres, Krishna Khaleel, Robert A. Leffingwell, Mr. Justice Davis and many another prominent face, the nominee stared out over the room as though he hardly sensed their presence at all. Gradually they grew silent as the more sensitive among them realized who he must be thinking about; but before the moment could become painful Hal touched his arm, he started, recognition returned, he smiled, more easily now, and acknowledged their greeting. The applause welled up again and drowned out the distant roar, still unabated in its hostility. Finally the applause died down and with it the discontented noises of NAWAC, as everyone began to concentrate, with an almost frightening intensity, on the man who sat, propping himself slightly forward to accommodate his obvious pain, at the left hand of the President.

"Members of the Committee," William Abbott repeated gravely, "it is my privilege and pleasure to introduce to you the Honorable Orrin Knox of Illinois, next President of the United States."

This time the applause, on the part of many, was more dutiful: but it came. Outside there was an automatic booing in response. Again it all died away and a profound, expectant silence settled gradually on the room, the city, the nation, wherever men and women listened—and there were many, many millions who did—to the nominee for President.

As always with Orrin, there was that first long, appraising moment during which he looked quietly at his audience, judged his approach, formulated it, prepared to deliver it; except that, this time, it took him a little longer because, this time, it was far more important. Emotionally, also, it was perhaps the hardest moment of all his long public career. The moment lengthened, tension rose. Finally he began, in a voice still somewhat shaky and weak but growing stronger as he went along.

"Mr. President," he said, while beside him Hal and Crystal watched with an almost fiercely protective attention, "members of the Committee"—he paused, and with his next words, by the strange sentimental yet tough-minded alchemy of politics, they knew it was true beyond challenge, they knew there could really be no question whatsoever of removing him from the ticket—"*my partners in this campaign:* on behalf of my family and myself"—his voice almost broke, then grew steadier—"and on behalf, I know, of Mrs. Jason—we wish to thank you all from our hearts for your expression of sympathy in this most trying hour for us. It means a great deal to have your sympathy and support. We are very grateful. . . ."

He stopped; obviously mastered powerful emotions; went on.

"And so now we meet again, to come to grips with the problem created, by party or parties unknown, for reasons not yet clear but certainly inimical to all that is good and hopeful in this democracy, for you and me.

"History will have its say about Edward M. Jason. I will say only that we had reached an accommodation—sincerely, I believe—that would have permitted us to campaign together and, had we won together, to govern this country effectively together.

"Now the central figure of that hard-fought, bitterly won compromise has been violently taken from us. And together you and I must find his successor. Without too much bitterness, I hope, and without too much political strife. Because we face a very hard battle to win, and to make our ideas prevail."

There was a noticeable stirring in the room, and at the press tables the Los Angeles *Times* whispered to the Cleveland *Plain Dealer*, "*Whose ideas* prevail?" "That's the gist of it," the *Plain Dealer* agreed moodily. "Whose ideas?"

The same thought had obviously occurred to the Committee, for it was clear, from Mary Baffleburg's pugnacious face to Roger P. Croy's openly moody visage, that the candidate had come more quickly and more directly than they had expected to the nub of it. He came even closer, startling them all, in his next words.

"I did not," he said, and something of the tartness of the old Orrin crept back into his voice, "in my zeal to make my own ideas prevail, plot, plan, organize, or connive in, the murder of Edward M. Jason."

There was an audible gasp from somewhere in the room, and from the mob outside a startled, annoyed and restless sound.

"And that," he added quietly, and for just a moment his eyes came to rest on those of Walter Dobius, staring coldly at him from the press tables, "is the first, last and only comment I shall ever make upon *that* vile suggestion. . . .

"Members of the Committee," he said, his tone suddenly conversational and candid, yet filled momentarily with an abrupt and unexpected tiredness, so that Hal rose quickly and stepped to his side, "you will forgive me if I favor my health a little, for the time being. I am on the mend and expect to be campaigning vigorously soon, but right now"—he smiled and shook his head, throwing himself upon their indulgence and understanding—"I must give in, a little. I think if you don't mind, I shall sit down to deliver the rest of this."

And as Hal quickly brought forward his chair and adjusted the microphone, he did so, obviously in some pain but managing to handle the situation with dignity. This did not prevent, however, a distinct shiver of dismay from running through his audience, and indeed through all friendly listeners everywhere. A certain triumphant note came into the noise from the park. At the press table Walter Dobius turned to Frankly Unctuous and murmured, "Absolutely impossible. Abso–lutely impossible!" "But they won't get rid of him," Frankly observed morosely. "No way."

The knowledge that this was indeed true presently brought a quietness to the room again. Beyond its confines the concerned might question, the violent might agitate, the critical might complain. Inside, they knew that for better or worse their hopes were pinned now on the Secretary of State, who simply must get better, as he promised, because there was no one else. Much as some of them might have misgivings, much as Roger Croy might have enjoyed making mischief an hour ago, they all knew that they were drained and exhausted, both emotionally and politically, to the point where they simply could not go through again the sort of battle for the Presidential nomination that they had gone through with Orrin Knox and Ted Jason. It was impossible.

This did not mean, however, that the Vice Presidential nomination would go by default, or that there could not still be a vicious battle over it. To that eventuality the candidate now addressed himself.

"Mr. President and members of the Committee," he said gravely, shifting a little in his chair with a fleeting grimace of pain, "it is customary for one in my position to recommend his running mate. Usually the recommendation has been accepted. Much less often, it has not. I hope today it will be.

"I have not consulted in any way with my choice for this position. Indeed," he said simply, while the buzz of speculation raced over the room, "I have not been able. Yet I am convinced that the one I should like to have–if you agree with me–will serve, and willingly. I can think of no other who could more fittingly fill this position, more fairly and honorably perform the duties of Vice President and yes, if need be, the duties of President. I shall not waste time upon qualifications, for they will be obvious. I shall not waste time upon appeals for your support, for I hope it will be gladly forthcoming. I shall not embellish or expand. I shall simply give you a name, commend it to your most earnest consideration and hope you will agree."

He paused to reach for a glass of water, deliberately building tension, and as Hal quickly handed it to him, his purpose was amply achieved. "God *damn* it," NBC muttered to CBS, pretty well summing up the mood in the room and wherever Orrin's words were heard, "will you get *on* with it!" "Orrin," CBS said, not entirely without a grudging admiration, "still knows how to create an effect."

After taking a quick sip of water, however, it appeared that he would not prolong it unduly. He took out a handkerchief, carefully wiped his lips, carefully put it away. Only a slightly heightened emphasis in his voice when he resumed revealed that he, too, was under tension; though why he should be, he told himself, he did not really know, since his next words would be the simplest and most obvious available—so simple and obvious, he hoped, that he would carry the Committee with him by acclamation.

This he did, though after all the excited speeches of endorsement and agreement by the supporters of Edward M. Jason, after all the mixed but basically friendly comments by his own supporters, after the unanimous vote, the excitement of the media and the naming of a special committee to escort the new nominee for Vice President to Kennedy Center, he found that despite his most earnest efforts, he must start all over again.

It was what he deserved, he told himself wryly later, for thinking he could make everything too easy.

MRS. JASON NEW VICE PRESIDENTIAL NOMINEE. SECRETARY KNOX NAMES HER TO SUCCEED SLAIN HUSBAND. NATIONAL COMMITTEE APPROVES CHOICE BY ACCLAMATION IN WILDLY ENTHUSIASTIC SCENE AT KENNEDY CENTER. FIRST TIME WOMAN HAS EVER RECEIVED THE HONOR FROM A MAJOR PARTY. CHOICE BRINGS ENTHUSIASTIC ENDORSEMENT FROM ALL ELEMENTS. SHE IS EXPECTED TO ADDRESS COMMITTEE THIS AFTERNOON. ACCEPTANCE SPEECH TO BE CARRIED WORLDWIDE. STOCK MARKET RALLIES SHARPLY ON NEWS. PRESIDENT ABBOTT SAYS, "VICTORY OF THE TICKET IS NOW ASSURED."

"DARLING!" Patsy cried, bursting into the guest suite of her house in Dumbarton Oaks with such excitement that she didn't even bother to knock. "DARLING, DARLING! That fantastic, crazy old Orrin Knox! Whoever would have thought he'd have the SENSE? . . . What's the matter?" she demanded, giving her silent sister-in-law a sudden sharp glance in which impatience, annoyance and genuine alarm were about equally mixed. "*What's the matter?* You're not thinking of—you're NOT THINKING OF—"

"Patsy," Ceil Jason said, very quietly but in a tone that for once reduced her voluble and exclamatory sister-in-law almost—almost—to silence. "Will you please go away and leave me alone?"

"But—" Patsy said. "But *they're on their way right now* to take you to the Center! You can't—Ceil, you just CAN'T—"

"I'm going to the Center," Ceil said, her voice filled with an infinite weariness and pain. "Go away."

"Are you going to accept?" Patsy demanded. "You've got to accept! Ceil, you've GOT to—"

"Patsy," Ceil said, "I have lost my husband, I am still in considerable pain myself, I am only just beginning to think coherently again, and there you stand screaming at me. You are beyond belief. Please go."

"Well!" Patsy said. "Well, all *I* can say is—"

"Don't," Ceil said. "Just go."

"Washington cannot remember," Frankly Unctuous said from one of the special broadcasting booths set up downstairs, while all around him press telephones and typewriters rocked and clattered with the joyous news, "an occasion of such spontaneous celebration as is now greeting Secretary of State Orrin Knox's stunning announcement that he has chosen the lovely Mrs. Ceil Jason to be his Vice Presidential running mate.

"As you all know, his choice was immediately and unanimously endorsed by the National Committee, whose members at this moment are upstairs awaiting the arrival of the widow of Governor Edward M. Jason. Her acceptance will indeed, as President Abbott truly says, guarantee the victory of what is still, one may be allowed to happily note, the Knox-Jason ticket.

"That this victory will in turn guarantee a much less rigid, much less doctrinaire Administration on the part of Orrin Knox, is as certain now as it was when Governor Jason was still alive. Indeed, it removes the fears of many, many millions both here and abroad that the Secretary might turn back to the reactionary, big-stick, arrogant, inexcusable American foreign policy he espoused during his years in the Senate, and more recently in Foggy Bottom. It guarantees the same peace-loving, moderate approach that would have been the case had Ted Jason lived to become Vice President: because the same forces which backed him and forced Secretary Knox to adopt a more reasonable policy that would make it possible for Governor Jason to accept a place on the ticket, are also behind his widow. Their influence, through her, will continue undiminished.

"For that, fellow Americans"—and he stared straight into the camera, solemn, earnest and effective as always—"the people of this nation, and the peoples of the world, may be profoundly grateful. We are too close to disaster everywhere to be able to afford a national government which does not make every possible effort to maintain peace.

"Because she does have this massive support which had gathered behind her husband, Mrs. Jason will be far from the ordinary innocuous Vice President. And because she is possessed of unusual intelligence as well as unusual beauty, she would also be, should events ever require it, a most capable and effective occupant of the Presidential office.

"Therefore, Washington rejoices, the nation rejoices, the world rejoices. In a surprising show of statesmanship, Orrin Knox has astounded and delighted everyone. The act augurs well for an Administration which may not be as reactionary as many feared, after all."

"Yes, you snide bastard," Hal Knox said, snapping off the television in the small, heavily guarded room where they had been escorted to wait until Ceil arrived, "maybe it won't be, after all. . . . Well," he said, turning to his father, "you surprised them, all right. That I will have to concede."

"What's the matter?" he inquired mildly, carefully shifting position to favor his wounded arm. "Don't you like Ceil Jason?"

"I think Ceil Jason is such a fine lady and so infinitely above what she was married to," Hal said, "that there's just no comparison. But she brings with her the same crew he did, and I don't know whether, as a woman, she'll be any better able to handle them than he could."

"She has character," Crystal noted quietly. "A great deal of character. She was about to leave him because he wouldn't break away from the violent, wasn't she? She can handle them."

"She won't have to," Orrin remarked.

"Oh, yes, she will," Hal said. "They think they have a claim on her and they aren't going to let her escape it. You may try to protect her and keep them out of the campaign, but they'll be there. They're too determined and too vicious to let go."

"Are you saying *I* can't handle them?" his father demanded sharply.

"You'll try," Hal agreed, "but it won't be enough. After all, you know, you've made yourself even more of a sitting duck than you were before. They missed you the first time. Now they've got another Jason on the ticket. What makes you think they'll miss next time?"

"I must say," Crystal remarked, half amused, half annoyed, "you're a cheerful soul. Why don't you try to be positive, for a change?"

"Well, it's true," Hal said, his face as stubborn as his father's often was. "It's absolutely true and you know it. There still remains one sure way to get a Jason into the White House. So watch out. One sudden death in the Knox family"—abruptly his flippant tone dissolved, his face twisted and turned young and naked with pain—"is enough, thank you."

"All right," Orrin said quietly. "All right. I'll be careful. And so must she. I think one great advantage, however, lies in the fact that she *did* almost leave him because of the way he let the violent move in on his campaign. She didn't approve of that, and I have the feeling she didn't approve of his general approach to foreign policy, either. I'm pinning my hopes to that."

"And to the name of Jason," Hal couldn't resist. His wife made a movement of protest, his father gave him a steady look.

"Yes," he said. "To the name of Jason, also. Do you really think it is not important for me to win this election, Hal?"

Their eyes held unwavering; then Hal's looked away.

"Yes," he said, very low. "It is important. And she is infinitely better than he was. And you have pulled a great coup. And I accept it."

"Then let's stop fighting about it, shall we?" his father suggested quietly. "We're going to need all our energies to win. And there's one other thing to keep in mind, in fairness to me: she wouldn't be on the ticket, in spite of her name, if I didn't really, honestly believe that she is fully capable of being President if"—he paused and gave an odd, fatalistic, almost humorous shrug—"if she had to. She isn't just a political choice, after all. I hope I think a little more of my country than that."

"Of course you do," Crystal said, leaning down to give him a comforting hug and kiss as, far in the distance, they began to hear a deep, rising, profoundly ecstatic sound.

Hal reached forward and turned on the television. There appeared, to the accompaniment of an excited commentary by two of the network's brightest young men, a sleek black limousine accompanied by a police motorcycle escort, nearing Kennedy Center through wildly cheering thousands who packed solid every foot of the way.

"Is she there?" Hal asked after a moment. "I don't see her waving, or anything."

"She isn't the ostentatious public type," Crystal observed. "That's one of the reasons I like her."

"She's campaigned with Ted for years," Orrin said. "You would think she'd be waving a little, at least. Must be some reason for it. Grief, probably."

But, sitting back in the heavily guarded car she shared with Patsy, the Jason aunts, Valuela Jason Randall and Selena Jason Castleberry, and Herbert, the Jason uncle, she refused, for the moment at least, to play the public game. She had always done her duty when Ted was alive, almost never turning down a campaign invitation, traveling with him the length and breadth of their great, fantastic nation-state from the Oregon line to the Mexican border. Ceil Jason, so blonde, so beautiful, so obviously possessed of intelligence, wit and charm, had been, in her more glamorous way, fully as vital a help to her husband's ambitions as Beth Knox, in more old-shoe fashion, had been to Orrin's. Yet now all that seemed very far away: it seemed too much of a burden to wave and pretend to smile. She was still, as she had told Patsy, in considerable pain from the assassin's wildly erratic fusillade. And she had also spent the past two hours in considerable confusion of mind as to how she should meet this most unexpected and fantastic turn in her life created by Orrin Knox.

Now as her triumphal procession began its final approach to Checkpoint Alpha past mobs even denser, noisier and more hysterically happy than those that had gone before, she felt that she *had* decided —on her own, this time, without reference to Ted, or to what he would have wanted, or to what his career required, or to anything but what she, Ceil Jason, knew was best for the country, and for her.

She really felt, thinking back over the hectic time since the news had begun to bombard the house in Dumbarton Oaks via television, radio, telegram and telephone, that these were her priorities: first the country, and then herself. She had always tried to put them in that order, and that was why, only one short week ago, she had come within a hairbreadth of leaving her husband and ending forever the relationship that was then, and always would be, the most fundamental of her existence.

Her feelings toward Ted now were strangely ambivalent, for a just-bereaved wife; being an honest woman, she could not help acknowledging to herself that this was the fact. To the family—Patsy, with her loud opinions and garish dresses, Selena and Herbert with their endless well-publicized espousing of Authentically Liberal Causes, Valuela with her painting, her villa at Positano and her string of never very permanent young men—she had appeared properly grief-stricken and indeed, at heart, she was.

Yet there was something else . . . something else.

Even though she had returned to his side from her self-imposed exile at the great Jason ranch, "Vistazo," north of Santa Barbara, when Orrin gave him the Vice Presidential nomination, still she had rendered a judgment on Ted that she could not evade now. She had rendered a judgment by leaving, and she had rendered a judgment by returning; and essentially, although one brought her close to divorce and the other to reconciliation, they were the same.

Edward Montoya Jason was to her, as to so many, an enigma, even though her life had run beside his for the better part of twenty years. When he had married her—handsome multimillionaire scion of Spanish dons, Indian stock and shrewd Yankee traders taking to wife the beautiful daughter of a modestly well-to-do family in Redding—it had been the great occasion of the San Francisco season, an event noted in *Time, Newsweek*, the New York *Times, Town and Country, Palm Springs Life, Palm Beach Life* and other such knowledgeable recorders of the social scene. When he had gradually moved into full control of the family corporations, Ceil had been his encourager and confidante. When he had entered public life and won the governorship, Californians had taken pride in the most beautiful first lady in the fifty states, who was still their Governor's encourager and confidante. But when the prize of the Presidency began to affect his decisions, his public actions and his private thoughts, his encourager and confidante began to draw away. Her flight to "Vistazo" had been only the culmination and symbol of a long, steady process that had, by then, been under way for five or six years.

So subtly yet so swiftly that it sometimes took her breath away, the Ted Jason who had been so straightforward, honest and filled with integrity when she married him began to trim, shade and equivocate in the governor's office in Sacramento. At first gently, then more openly as she became more alarmed by this, she began to chide him for it, not to the point of open issue but in a way that she hoped would bring him back to her own original concept of him, which she knew had been his concept, too. She was finally forced to the unhappy conclusion that he was not going to come back, that he was set upon a course dictated by ambition from which he would not deflect, even for her. And this despite the fact that they had known, and still knew, a deep and abiding love for one another that seemed to go along in some separate channel quite apart from the steady erosion of integrity and firmness that she was unhappily witnessing, every day.

Until the national convention so recently concluded, and then she knew that there could be separation no longer, that it was all coming together, that the Edward M. Jason who was rising to dominate his nation's politics was simply no longer, nor would ever be again, the Edward M. Jason to whom she still owed, in heart and body, an allegiance she thought she could never abandon.

But the day came—or the night, rather. When Crystal Knox was beaten by the thugs of NAWAC in the ghostly fog outside the Cow Palace—when she lost her baby and almost lost her life—it was a turning point for Ceil Jason as it was for all those most closely involved in the drama of the Presidential nomination.

The National Anti-War Activities Congress had become increasingly threatening, increasingly harsh, but not until that night had it burst into open violence. When it did, everyone of influence and authority had denounced it and demanded its elimination from American life—except the man who had profited most from its political support. Once again, and this time with the lines drawn so tragically that no one could escape their implications, unless it be willfully, he equivocated. And finally, at last, lost—almost—his wife.

Why he had not, she could not exactly define for herself, except that it seemed to come down to one thing—the fundamental decency of the man who was now asking her to succeed her fallen husband.

In her darkest moments at "Vistazo," where she had fled to spend several days alone except for faithful Manuela and Tomás, riding patient old Trumpet down the long meadows to the crashing sea and back again, thinking, thinking, thinking, the thought she had kept coming back to was: *Orrin Knox is willing to trust him.* The corollary to that, of course, was: *Then why shouldn't I?* And finally, after all the arguments were exhausted, after she had fought out all her battles with the handsome stranger who smiled at her from familiar photos in accustomed places, she had come back to that question for the last time, and answered it—as she had not, for a while, been at all sure she would—in Ted's favor. The deciding factor, as she had never had a chance to tell her husband, had been Orrin. If a man with that much integrity and that much experience of politics and the world could place his faith in Edward M. Jason's ultimate decency and ability to break free from the violent, then her last reservations were canceled. She knew politics too, and she knew that much of Orrin's decision had been forced upon him by Ted's supporters and by his own necessity to win. But she also knew Orrin well enough to know that no matter what his own self-interest or political advantage might be, if he really did not consider Ted trustworthy he would not have taken him.

And now Orrin had decided that she should run for Vice President: again, for his own political advantage, but also, she believed, because he really considered her worthy of his trust and confidence. Unlike so many of his critics, she did not underestimate the integrity of the Secretary of State. She felt flattered, humbled and grateful for his endorsement. She had no intention of using it, as many of her husband's supporters were already urging that she do, as a weapon for political trading.

Because, indeed, what would she trade for? Basically she agreed with Orrin (though the fact was unknown to those who greeted her proposed elevation so ecstatically) on most of his major positions. She was against the violent, she was worried about the Russians, she had been privately appalled at Ted's tendency to drift further and further toward an attitude of appeasement, if not downright surrender, in his quest for peace. She was no more certain than Orrin, in fact, exactly how sincere that quest had been. She agreed with Ted that the wars in Gorotoland and Panama must somehow be ended as speedily as possible, but she knew Orrin agreed too. Orrin's proposed methods—or at least his frequently stated intention to get out in a way that would not leave the United States and its allies hopelessly exposed to Communist domination—had always seemed better to her than Ted's. Basic loyalty to her husband had prompted the suppression of her own ideas, even when she had questioned his most. Now there were other loyalties remaining: to the country, to the nominee for President and to herself.

This was what her decision narrowed down to as the limousine drew up to Checkpoint Alpha, the guards snapped to attention, the welcoming committee stepped forward with friendly smiles and a sudden intense and intently watching silence descended on the world. What did she owe the country and Orrin Knox—and what did she owe Ceil Jason? And would it be possible to accommodate them and in so doing make victory in November inevitable?

She was not sure, but she knew she had to try.

Like Orrin, when she arrived she too leaned on her family and obviously favored her wounds. But her charming speaking voice rang out steady and clear as she stepped forward and held out her hand to Roger P. Croy, who somehow managed to be in the forefront of the welcoming committee.

"Governor—" she said, "ladies and gentlemen of the Committee—thank you so much for coming out to meet me. I appreciate your kindness."

"Madam Vice President," Roger Croy said gravely, "you confer the kindness and honor upon us."

"I don't know about that title," she said, smiling a little, with the sudden shift to informality that was one of her principal appeals on the platform, "but anyway, I am glad to be here."

"As we are glad to have you," Blair Hannah said with a fatherly warmth that did much to wipe out the memory of his initial reservations when Orrin had first proposed her name. "Your presence confers great grace upon us all."

At this there was a burst of applause inside the Playhouse, a great shout of happiness and approval from the throngs outside. There followed a few moments of bustle while Ceil shook hands with the rest of the committee and introduced the members of her family. Then the party moved up the steps, the doors were opened, they disappeared inside, the doors were closed again. The tensely watching silence settled once more over all.

"Ladies and gentlemen—" William Abbott said solemnly a minute later as there came again the sound of soldiers coming to attention, rifles being slapped into position, the familiar rituals of pomp and circumstance—"the next Vice President of the United States!"

And again they were on their feet in wild ovation, Committee, guests and media alike, while outside a long crowing roar of triumph rose along both sides of the placid steel-lined Potomac.

She was dressed, reporters noted and the cameras showed, very simply, in a plain black dress with a small black off-the-face hat, black gloves, black shoes. Her flowing blonde hair was severely restrained in an unobtrusive black net. She wore a single white rose over her heart. Her face was pale but composed, her expression reserved, unsmiling but not unfriendly; and no more tense and nervous than might naturally be expected.

She and her family came forward slowly down the aisle while the ovation gradually subsided. Valuela, Selena and Herbert took the seats set out for them at the President's right. He and Orrin stepped forward and greeted her with kisses, which she returned with an obvious fondness, brushing aside tears that for a moment threatened to overwhelm her. The ovation roared up again in wild approval, gradually subsiding as she took her seat. Silence settled again. The President once more formally introduced her. She stood up and came forward to the podium. Applause roared up, terminated. The profound expectant silence resumed. Clearly and steadily, referring only to a few scribbled notes which she arranged on the lectern before her, she began to speak; and many things in American politics were immediately rearranged.

"Mr. President," she said gravely, "Mr. Secretary, ladies and gentlemen of the Committee: like the Secretary, I too wish to begin by expressing my thanks for your expressions of sympathy. They are very"—her voice began to tremble but she steadied it and proceeded —"very welcome and helpful to all of us, in both families. Things sometimes seem to happen that have no reason at all, but we have to assume that there is a pattern somewhere, otherwise we could not go on living. In that faith we are all going forward. Your help and support make it, if not easy, at least less difficult. We feel we are not alone."

She paused, took a sip of water, looked up with a sudden complete candor into their eyes and the eyes of the world.

"Mr. President, I hope you will all believe me when I say that the occasion for my being here came as a complete surprise to me. It is due directly and entirely to the generosity of the nominee for President." ("And his desire to be elected," the *Guardian* whispered to the *Post,* who nodded and smiled an unamused, unforgiving little smile.) "I do not believe he consulted anyone before announcing his choice. Certainly"—and the briefest trace of humor touched her lips—"he did not consult me.

"Nonetheless, Mr. President," she said, while the murmur that greeted this began as she knew it would, "I deeply and most sincerely appreciate the honor."

Again she paused. The tension in the room and wherever people watched or listened suddenly shot up for some instinctive, undefined reason.

"I only regret," she said clearly and distinctly, again giving them her straightforward, candid look, "that it is impossible for me to accept."

"My *God!*" the *Times* exclaimed, as the world exploded into excited sound and at the press tables AP, UPI, CBS, NBC and ABC scrambled their way out of their chairs and raced for the special telephone booths set up in the hall. "My God, *now* what?"

It was apparent from his astounded and dismayed expression, which the cameras faithfully seized upon, that the same question was occurring to the Secretary of State; and it was also clear, from Patsy Jason Labaiya's outraged squawk of "*WHAT?*" to the Indian Ambassador's startled "Oh, my *gracious!*" that Ceil had created a universal astonishment and, for most people, an honest and completely genuine dismay. It was some measure of how much their hopes had become concentrated upon her in the past two hours, of how eagerly and with what relief the enormous burden of expectancy had been transferred to her shoulders from those of her dead husband. It was some measure of how important Ceil Jason in her own right had become since the fateful words of Orrin Knox so short a time ago.

Because of this, her own words now were more fateful still; and after giving them a few moments to sink in, and to allow the general hullabaloo to subside, she went on in her pleasant, cultured voice to explain herself more fully and to do what she could to repay the debt of gratitude she knew she owed the nominee.

"Mr. President, Mr. Secretary, ladies and gentlemen: I do not state this decision lightly, nor have I reached it on any spur-of-the-moment impulse. Believe me, I have given it a great deal of thought in the past two hours. Yet I know if I were to consider it for a much longer time, I should still arrive at the same conclusion. I cannot, and I will not, accept—sensible though I am of the very great honor and responsibility the Secretary wished to place upon me. I do not think it would be fair to him, or to you, or to the thing we must all keep firmly in mind, now more than ever: to the country, which is the charge and responsibility of all of us, most particularly those of us directly or indirectly associated with public office and the public trust.

"I think it is impossible accurately, just yet," she said, and her voice became more quiet, her eyes more somber and haunted, "to assess the life and career of—of my husband. I like to think he brought many good things to the people of our state, and I like to think he represented many good things to people everywhere. We will never know whether he would have achieved them. But I would like to think he would have tried."

("Not exactly a widow's fervent tribute," the *Saturday Review* whispered to the San Francisco *Chronicle*. "I heard there was something funny there a few days ago," the *Chronicle* whispered back, "but I was never able to trace it down.")

"One thing," she said, and at the sudden note of strain and challenge in her voice an alert watchfulness seized the press and all her audience in the room, "disturbed me. That"—and her voice steadied and became quite firm—"was the nature of some of his support."

In the distance, puzzled, uncertain, prepared if necessary to be hostile, an uneasy rumble came from the gangs of NAWAC. It was obvious she heard it, but aside from a heightened color and an even greater firmness in her voice, she gave no sign.

"At the end, I believe he intended to repudiate once and for all the ugly gangs that had gathered behind him under the general banner of the National Anti-War Activities Congress." The uneasy sound howled up instantly into an angry roar. "For his memory, and for my own self," she said clearly above it, "I repudiate them too, in everything they do and everything they truly stand for, under the pious pretense of peace-loving with which they seek to fool the country."

Now the angry roar knew no limits, beating in upon the Committee without challenge for several moments. Then suddenly, started by Ewan MacDonald MacDonald and Blair Hannah, joined in enthusiastically by the President, Orrin and many others, joined in dutifully because they did not dare refrain by Roger P. Croy, Esmé Harbellow Stryke, Patsy, her aunts and uncle, and some others, applause for her courage began and rose until it drowned out, at least in that small room, the ugly sound.

Out in the world the ugly sound continued and would be a long time dying, with fateful consequences for them all.

"I know very well," she said finally, "that in taking this position I am inviting great hostility from these elements, and that is one of the reasons I am withdrawing from the ticket." She smiled slightly. "Secretary Knox has enough burdens without carrying me." The smile faded. "If I accepted the support of the violent, I should be a heavy weight upon him. Now that I have repudiated their support, as I must or betray everything I believe in, I should be a heavy weight upon him. I think I can help him better acting independently from outside. This," she said, and the firmness grew in her voice, "I intend to do."

The angry roar rose again in the distance, again it was drowned out in the crowded room by the applause of her audience, this time wholehearted and, except for some obvious dismay along the press tables, unanimous.

"I intend to do so," she said, "because I believe that in Orrin Knox we have a candidate for President who honestly and forthrightly stands for what he believes, who has nothing but America's well-being at heart and who will not hesitate to do what he thinks is right to achieve that well-being."

("And Ted wouldn't have?" the *Saturday Review* whispered quizzically. "I told you," the *Chronicle* reiterated. "There was something there.")

"I intend to do so," she went on, "because I firmly and completely believe that in his election lies the best hope for our country at this time. He will not appease, he will not trim, he will not equivocate. The whole world knows where he stands, and while some don't like it, I do. And so, I hope and believe, do a majority of our countrymen.

"Orrin Knox repudiates the violent, he repudiates the appeasers, he repudiates the weak of heart and the flimsy of purpose. He will extricate us honorably and effectively from the wars in Panama and Gorotoland, he will preserve our independence and that of the free world in the face of the ongoing threats and subversions of the Soviet Union in its voracious and implacable imperialism. Domestically, also, I believe he will find the way to national unity—"

The noise outside rose in a sudden hoot, disbelieving, exaggerated, elaborately skeptical and sardonic. She flushed but lifted her head with a sharp motion that recalled her husband, and went on.

"—the way to national unity," she repeated firmly, "which can only lie in the repudiation of the violent and the re-establishment of decent compromise and cooperation among all the elements of our society that genuinely want to preserve it."

The careful and deliberate distinction again brought angry noises from outside, a counter of heartily approving applause from within the room.

"For myself," she said quietly when it all died away, "I pledge my full and active cooperation to the election of Orrin Knox in November. I thank him again for his confidence and trust, I thank you for your support, I urge you to help him find a running mate who will do justice to the job that lies ahead for all of us. I will be with you all the way. Goodbye for now, and God bless you."

And with a little bow to the President and Orrin, who led the standing ovation that immediately ensued, she left the platform and moved up the aisle, followed by her family, whose faces were studies of complex emotion. So swiftly yet so gracefully did she go that she seemed to pass among them like some elusive golden presence that they attempted, with a hungry yearning, to touch and hold, yet could not; and was gone, out the door, past the guards, down the steps, into the waiting limousine and away through the now jeering and hostile crowds, almost before they knew it.

There occurred then in the crowded little room an odd phenomenon that no one present ever forgot: a great silence and then a sudden, instinctive, unanimous sigh, a release of pent-up breath and emotion, deep and profound, as they all realized with a shattering impact the loss of certainty that they had suffered in her refusal.

It was followed almost immediately by a sudden restless stirring.

The President, an old veteran who knew all the signs, moved instantly to head off the uproar that was about to occur.

"Without objection," he said smoothly, banging the gavel with a loud *crack!* that startled them into silence and carried the point over many tentative, half-formed protests, "the Committee will stand in recess until noon tomorrow."

"But, Mr. President—!" Roger P. Croy, Blair Hannah, Mary Baffleburg and Esmé Stryke all cried at once. "But, Mr. President—!"

But the President was out and gone, too, as fast as he could move; and after a moment Orrin and Hal and Crystal followed, and then, by ones and twos and threes, the rest, upset, baffled, uneasy, uncertain, beginning as they went the angry and disputative chatter which would now, until such time as they had selected a successor to Edward M. Jason, become the burden of their days.

MRS. JASON REJECTS VICE PRESIDENTIAL NOMINATION. REPUDIATES VIOLENT, PLEDGES ALL-OUT CAMPAIGN FOR SECRETARY KNOX. DECISION LEAVES PARTY STUNNED AND WITHOUT CANDIDATE. BATTLE LINES DRAWN BETWEEN WAR AND PEACE FACTIONS AS PRESSURES MOUNT FOR QUICK DECISION. OVERNIGHT RECESS MAY GIVE SECRETARY CHANCE TO WORK OUT NEW COMPROMISE.

4. BUT IT WASN'T very certain, and as afternoon wore on into evening and then into night, it was again obvious that there were many in influential places who wanted, not compromise, but victory, for their views.

"It is amazing," Walter Dobius wrote rapidly in the den at "Salubria," hushed and quiet in the gently steaming twilight of the lovely Virginia countryside, "how rapidly politics can be rearranged in this fantastic land. One moment Mrs. Ceil Jason, supremely attractive, supremely qualified, supremely able, is the nominee for Vice President. Two hours later, by her own wish and deliberate decision, she is no longer the nominee for Vice President.

"Instead, she is the highly partisan supporter of the man who trounced her husband for the Presidential nomination—and has aligned herself with him in opposition to all those sincere lovers of world peace who formed the principal basis of her husband's overwhelming political support.

"The true motivations for this must always remain a puzzle and a bafflement to all who worked for the cause of Edward M. Jason. His wife gave no real reasons for her decision not to run, other than her repudiation of what she chose to term 'the violent'—thereby ignoring all the millions of perfectly decent, genuine, nonviolent citizens who simply cannot stomach the ill-fated military adventures in Panama and Gorotoland. Nor did she really pay any genuine tribute to her late husband. Her comments were strangely lukewarm, strangely qualified. Almost, her listeners might have believed, she had never really supported him, and was not too sorry he was gone."

Walter paused and reconsidered. *That* phraseology *was* a little harsh. Perhaps he was letting himself get carried away. He struck out the words "and was not too sorry he was gone," and proceeded, with his customary emphatic touch on the keys, to the next paragraph.

"Certainly she does not now support any of the things in which he believed. Since this unhappily seems to be the case, most observers believe it is just as well that she has voluntarily removed herself from the ticket. Her continued presence would have been an unfortunate distraction that would only have strengthened the pro-war policies of the Secretary of State should he become the President. Her presence as an independent campaigner for the Secretary, which is what she apparently intends to be, will be distraction enough. It is better for all concerned, most of political Washington feels, that she be relegated to the status of private citizen—where, it is to be presumed, she will simply be a pale and repetitious echo of the official Knox line."

You hope, he told himself with a certain savage impatience. You *hope* Ceil Jason, the lovely, the intelligent, the powerfully appealing both in her own right and as glamorous widow, will be a pale echo. Otherwise, Orrin still has a plus even if she isn't on the ticket. He stared out gloomily for a moment into the velvet dusk. Believers in Right Causes such as he always had their difficulties. The Lord never made it easy.

"Her withdrawal," he wrote on presently, "of course reopens the great issue of the national convention, and of the National Committee meeting which finally, after intensely bitter controversy, gave the Presidential nomination to Orrin Knox and the Vice Presidential to Edward M. Jason. That question is: Will war or peace be the fate of America in the next four years?

"And will a bellicose Presidential candidate shadowed by the mysterious death of his peace-loving running mate be able to impose his will and place beside himself another who thinks as rigidly as he along the old warmongering, imperialistic lines that have so disfigured the last two Administrations?

"It is time, in the opinion of most observers here, for all who love peace to appeal to the National Committee as they have never appealed to it before.

"By a tragic turn of fate—and by Mrs. Jason's arbitrary refusal to lend herself to the peace-keeping cause—they have been given one more chance to control and, hopefully, nullify, the warlike tendencies of the man who may well be the next President.

"It is to be hoped they will not allow the opportunity to pass."

Nor were they, he reflected with considerable satisfaction as he reviewed the events of the hours since Ceil had made her dramatic renunciation.

The mobs of NAWAC were still in place, encamped in the parks and behind the barbed wire guarding both banks of the Potomac. Their banners were defiant, their mood unrelenting. From their principal spokesman, Senator Fred Van Ackerman of Wyoming, had come a statement opposing any compromise in what he termed "this great battle to save American democracy, and the world."

"It is unbelievable to all dedicated members of the National Anti-War Activities Congress," he went on, "that Mrs. Ceil Jason should have removed herself in such an almost frivolous manner from the cause for which her husband labored and died. It is with a bitter regret that we hear her announced intention to join the pro-war forces represented by the candidacy of Orrin Knox.

"The executive board of NAWAC, acting on behalf of the membership, endorsed that candidacy because its members firmly believed that Edward M. Jason as Vice President would be able to restrain the imperialist adventures of his running mate. It now must reassess that decision.

"It is incumbent upon all members of NAWAC and all who believe in the right of democratic protest against the big-stick imperialist diplomacy of the present American government to examine most carefully any new name proposed to fill the vacancy on the Knox ticket. It is also incumbent upon them to make their opinions emphatically known, and, if necessary, to express most vigorously their opposition to any candidate who does not fully endorse and actively support the peace-loving policies of Edward M. Jason."

In similar vein, and at times in language almost as strong, Supermedia weighed in. The *Times,* the *Post, The Greatest Publication That Absolutely Ever Was, Time, Newsweek* and all their think-alikes across the country joined in sharp unanimous criticism of Ceil for her decision and her support of Orrin, unanimous insistence that only one cast in the mold of her husband could possibly be chosen to fill the Vice Presidential vacancy. Without quite inciting to riot, Frankly Unctuous and his colleagues of tube and airwave did the same. From "activist" professors, clergymen, lawyers and movie stars of a certain headline-avid type came equally fervent pronouncements. Giving them assurance that they were doing the Right Thing for the Right Cause around the world, many leading journals, politicians and ex-pounders-on-American-shortcomings joined the chorus.

So efficiently and effectively did the one point of view blanket the nation and the globe that it seemed impossible that Orrin Knox could, or would, dare to do anything but exactly what his critics wanted.

All this, of course, as his critics well knew, did not take into account Orrin Knox. Even as they attempted to bring pressure upon him, those who knew and had studied him most closely were aware that he would do exactly what seemed best to him. They were taking a calculated gamble that they could stampede him. But none of the knowledgeable believed it would do much good.

Even so, he was not living, of course, in a vacuum; and though his first instinct after Ceil's withdrawal was to cut his ties to the Jason wing of the party and begin working for someone aligned entirely with his own point of view, he knew it could not be done. His constituency, like that of any American President or Presidential candidate in the twentieth century, was far broader than that, encompassing as it did not only the diverse elements of his own party and his own country but those of the entire world as well.

Somehow he must find a path between all the conflicting forces that had suddenly, with Ceil's decision, returned to harass him again. He respected her decision and was delighted with her frank declaration of support, but he wished unhappily that she could have seen her way clear to accepting his offer. It would have simplified many things. Now they were all awry again.

Thinking about this as his heavily guarded caravan moved out from Kennedy Center through the hooting throngs to return him, his family and his immediate advisers to Spring Valley—"WAR GROUP SEEN DOMINANT AS KNOX CALLS IN PRESIDENT, MUNSON, LEFFINGWELL TO ADVISE ON VICE PRESIDENTIAL NOMINATION"—he had concluded finally that he must win by political finesse what he could not win by direct assault. Accordingly he went through the motions as soon as they reached the house and were safely inside. Here, too, there were generally hostile mobs; here, too, a large cordon of troops and police held them back. He was jeered into his own house, and from time to time, as at the Center, distant murmurs of anger or resentment or scorn erupted in the distance. But at least here he was away from the insistent eyes of television and the press, and could deal with his problem in the private consultations which he now felt provided the only medium through which it could be solved.

"Bill," he said without preliminary when they were seated in the comfortable study where he had formulated so many ideas, written so many speeches, read so many books, prepared so much legislation, "how wedded are you to the idea of returning to the House?"

The President blinked and gave him promptly the answer he had counted on.

"Too wedded to accept the Vice Presidency, if that's what you mean, Orrin. You need me as Speaker again. God help you if you get Jawbone Swarthman."

The mention of the voluble chairman of the House Foreign Affairs Committee, hiding his Phi Beta Kappa intelligence behind his deliberately exaggerated corn-pone accent, brought a brief moment of amusement. Orrin nodded.

"I suppose you're right on that. However, I think I could deal with him and it might be that your presence on the ticket would give me just the extra strength I need to win the election *and* carry the House. Which at the moment," he confessed with a sudden glumness, "I am not at all sure I can do."

"I'm not sure either," William Abbott agreed, "but I think you'd damned well better try. I can be more help to you with that, I think, if I stay free of the ticket. Not that I mean any disrespect to you," he added quickly, "or any disloyalty. I think for the sake of the country you've *got* to win. It's just a question of where I can be of most assistance. Plus the fact," he said with a wry little smile, "that I've had it with the White House. I haven't minded being a 'caretaker President,' as the *Times* called me, but I'm one of the few men in American history who is genuinely and entirely ready to step down. The Hill's been my whole life, after all. I don't really enjoy it much at the other end of the Avenue, though I've tried to do my best."

"And have," Orrin said, "and we are all grateful and indebted to you for it."

"All indebted, anyway," Bill Abbott said. "Not all grateful, by any means. . . . No, I appreciate it very much, Orrin, and like Ceil, I'm deeply sensible of the honor. But I don't think you'd better try to name me. It would throw the Committee into the screaming meemies, and we've had enough of that."

"Whoever I name will throw it into the screaming meemies," the Secretary of State said with some of his old tartness. "I've got to expect that. I just want the effort to be worth the uproar." He turned to the Senate Majority Leader, sitting back comfortably relaxed in his chair, but even before he spoke, Bob Munson interrupted with a lifted hand to give the second answer Orrin had counted upon.

"Orrin," he said, "thanks, but no, thanks. Like Bill, I belong on the Hill. You need me there, I can do you more good there, and anyway, the Jason faction would never accept me. There'd be a hell of a fight to no purpose, and the upshot would be that you'd just have to start all over again. Even if we did get my nomination through, Ted's supporters would never give the ticket their wholehearted backing. It would cripple you all the way and might very well lose you Congress."

"They'll never give the ticket their wholehearted support as long as I head it, anyway," the Secretary said in the same tart way. "And I may lose Congress whatever I do. Why not be consistent, as I always have?"

"Until you accepted Ted on the ticket," Senator Munson pointed out with a smile. "You ain't old All-the-Way Orrin any more." He leaned forward, abruptly serious. "No, Orrin, I can't do it for you, much as I'd like to. It would cause too much resentment, too many problems. Let me stay where I am and run the Senate for you. It's what I do best."

"Very well, then," he said, turning to Bob Leffingwell, sitting quietly across from him near the fireplace. The man whose nomination for Secretary of State he had defeated a year and a half ago in the Senate, the man he had told at the convention he would name as his own Secretary of State, tensed and stared at him with a startled disbelief. "The biscuits are getting cold, Bob, but if you can understand the reasons why you're last, and forgive me, I would like to offer it to you. In fact," he added with the sudden amiable air that was one of his appealing characteristics, "I'd like to have all three of you. That can't be done, so I've had to take you in order of rank. So how about it?"

For a moment Robert A. Leffingwell did not reply. Then he said in a skeptical voice, "Surely you must be joking, Mr. Secretary. Surely you cannot be serious. I cannot imagine a choice less suited to the position, or one more likely to provoke a storm in the Committee, in the country and indeed just about everywhere. I just can't believe you're serious."

"I'm not being frivolous, if that's what you mean," Orrin said with some sharpness. "Of course I'm being serious. I have faith in your abilities, otherwise I wouldn't be planning to make you Secretary of State."

"Your faith has changed," Bob Leffingwell said quietly, one last reference to their bitter confrontation at the time of his original appearance before the Senate, "and I am still not sure it has changed for the better."

"*You* have changed," Orrin said, "and that shows much to me."

"It shows weakness and wishy-washiness to many people, including the Jason camp," Bob Leffingwell said. "First I oppose our foreign policy, then I support it, first I oppose you, then I support you—what does it add up to?"

"The same as it adds up to with me, I like to think," the Secretary said shortly. "Some ability to change and grow and accept the facts of a shifting world. Adaptability and character are what it shows to me. I always knew you had the brains, now I know you have the character. I don't appeal to you frivolously."

"And I don't reject you frivolously," Robert A. Leffingwell said slowly, giving the third answer Orrin had counted upon, "but I feel I must reject you." He turned to the others, men with whom he had once differed bitterly but whose views he had come finally to support. "What do you think, Mr. President?" he asked. "What do you think, Senator? Don't I make more sense"—a touch of wry amusement robbed the question of its sting—"than he does?"

"You do to me," the President said bluntly. "It won't wash, Orrin. Too many problems. And this, Bob, with no disrespect to you. Just the practicalities of it, as you say."

"With which I concur," Senator Munson said. "Too many enemies, too much controversy, too many allegations of weakness and equivocation—some of them," he reminded Orrin dryly, "by you—no, it's going to be tough enough getting him through the Senate for Secretary of State. Vice President I can't see at all, I'm sorry to say. I can see his personal merits but I can't see his political viability."

"And political viability, Mr. Secretary," Bob Leffingwell said calmly, "is what you must be concerned with now. So: thank you, but, like the Majority Leader—no, thanks."

"Well," he said with enough asperity to make them think he was really being forced to consider alternatives other than the one he had been considering all along, "then you force me to fall back on my last line of defense. See what you think of it."

He was pleased that they thought it an idea both viable and exciting. A quick phone call produced the astounded but delighted agreement of the potential nominee. A pledge of secrecy sent them out of the house in Spring Valley to face, without response other than patient smiles, the barrage of questions from the waiting press; and he was alone in the study to contemplate what he would do tomorrow when the Committee met again.

As he considered it, and as his three guests considered it after they left him, the logic of it seemed—as logic always does to those who think of it—impeccable.

But this, of course, was planning without really considering the Committee, the media or the friends of Edward M. Jason, all of whom retained their considerable and continuing ability to make trouble.

Again the Committee came, through mobs again unruly and armed forces again at ready, to Kennedy Center in August's suffocating sun. Again he was introduced as "the next President of the United States," again he surveyed them for his long, characteristic moment. Again he spoke, and again controversy rose and raged and swirled about his words.

"Mr. President," he said quietly, looking, sounding and acting much stronger, "yesterday I nominated a great lady for the office of Vice President, and yesterday she declined. I was as astounded as any of you and as fully dismayed. But life affords us no luxury of prolonged regret in these hurrying days. We must move on.

"I am deeply grateful for Mrs. Jason's declaration of support and I know it will help me immeasurably, in the campaign and after. I expect to take full advantage of her generous offer of assistance, for America knows no more intelligent, lovely and capable woman. I am very lucky indeed to have her on my team."

Far came the distant booing, while in the room there was a mixed and uncertain sound as some applauded vociferously, some hesitated, some grumbled among themselves but grudgingly concurred. Ceil Jason as ardent partisan of Orrin Knox was still a difficult concept for many to assimilate: except that, as with so many things in politics, what happens happens, and the astute are well advised to be nimble and make the most of it.

"I could not agree with her more," Orrin said, "concerning the dangers of the violent in this country." There was a sharply rising sound from the world outside: his only acknowledgment was to speak more firmly. "I shall do everything I can to stop them, and I shall do everything I can to drive what they represent out of American life.

"This does not mean," he said sharply over the angry roar that answered, "that honest dissent cannot have a place. Nor does it mean that I shall be arbitrary in my policies or harsh in the treatment of opposing views. It simply means that I shall do my utmost to see that political debate in America is no longer disfigured and besmirched by intolerance, hatred and what has already come very close to civil rebellion." Again the roar rose, again he challenged it sharply. "In my campaign, and in my Administration if such there be, I will have none of it. On that I give you my absolute and unshakable pledge."

Sullen, protesting, angry and unappeasable, the animal sound retorted. Inside, united on this one thing as on perhaps no other, the Committee applauded with heartfelt concurrence, while some among the audience looked skeptical and some among the media made appropriately ironic remarks.

"We meet again today," he said quietly, "with our problem still unsolved. I have considered very carefully several courses of action.

"I could throw the nomination open and let it be decided on this floor. This is what will eventually happen anyway, of course; but to do it without any suggestion from me would be to create even more controversy than might normally be expected. I think there is a responsibility resting on me to again offer advice, and I think many of you feel that I should have the opportunity." There was a restless stirring in some parts of the room, and with a sudden smile he added calmly, "In any event, I intend to take it. . . .

"I could also be arbitrary, of course, and demand that it be my suggestion or no one. This would automatically increase the controversy by a very substantial degree. Nothing would be gained by such an arbitrary policy save greatly increased bitterness, and, perhaps, the complete breakdown of our proceedings.

"By the same token, of course, any similar arbitrariness on the part of those who don't quite see eye to eye with me would produce the same result. Therefore, it seems to me, we had best find another compromise. I have one to suggest. No doubt there may be others. But at least we should begin in a reasonable spirit of discussion. With luck this will lead us on to agreement—hopefully, a reasonably early and cordial agreement. We can then get on with what is, after all, our major business: winning the election."

He paused, took a sip of water, appeared to study his notes for a moment while he let the thought sink in. Again he had issued the tribal call to battle, and again they were realizing, as he knew they would, that their paramount interest as politicians was just what he said it was: winning the election. He hoped, although he wasn't as sanguine as he appeared, that it would help to keep all but the most maverick in line.

"Today," he resumed with a return of the quick, appealing humor, "I am going to offer you a man. I didn't have too much success with a lady yesterday. Maybe I'll do better today. . . ." The humor faded, seriousness returned.

"This is a man well known to all of you, a young but already much-distinguished member of the Congress who has served his country superbly in several fields. Not only has he distinguished himself in Washington, but as a diplomatic representative of his country he has performed with great integrity, under great provocation, in another arena."

In the audience, seated side by side, Congressman Cullee Hamilton of California and Senator Lafe Smith of Iowa, members of the American delegation to the United Nations, suddenly began to breathe very softly and listen very intently, not daring to look at one another, though very many were suddenly looking at them.

"There are others," Orrin said quietly, "to whom I might have turned; others with more years, longer records in national position. But after considering those who to me seemed most deserving, I decided upon this man for four fundamental reasons: he is young, he is experienced, he is supremely able and he is as devoted to peace as anyone in this room or anyone within sound of my voice. Those, I think, are the desiderata which must govern us today.

"He has one other qualification that he was born with"—he smiled, and Lafe, without turning his head, gave Cullee a nudge with his elbow and whispered, "Right on, man!" Cullee, with a great effort, suppressed the start of an excited grin and kept his face impassive. But he returned the nudge. "A qualification which in a sense both is, and isn't, important. To those who attach great importance to it, it may outweigh all his other qualifications. To those who regard him first and foremost, as I know he regards himself, as an American, it will be nice but not overwhelmingly relevant. It may give him a slight edge in working with the many diverse interests among his countrymen" ("And a slight edge in stopping opposition here," the *Times* remarked sardonically to *Newsweek*. *Newsweek* nodded) "but other than that, it is, in the last analysis, immaterial when it comes to judging him. Certainly it has been immaterial in my mind" ("Oh, sure," *Newsweek* whispered. The *Times* responded with a knowing glance) "as I hope it will be in yours.

"Ladies and gentlemen of the Committee," he said with a concluding fall in his tone that brought them all to a tense silence, "you need no lengthy or flowery introduction. You know him well and favorably. I have faith and confidence in him and believe he would make a great Vice President, and also a great President should the need ever arise. His name is Cullee Hamilton and he is presently Congressman from California. I commend him to your most serious consideration."

And he left the lectern and sat down, exchanging a glance with Cullee, who beamed back with such innocently happy excitement that all friendly observers were pleased. Not all, however, were friendly.

From outside there came a long, astounded, uncertain sound. In the room applause rose, pleased and enthusiastic from Orrin's supporters, dutiful—and ready to have second thoughts—from the Jason camp. It was apparent that the second thoughts were swift in coming. Roger P. Croy was on his feet requesting recognition. The President granted it, a certain tiredness in his voice. Roger Croy picked it up at once.

"Now, Mr. President," he said, showing a carefully calculated testiness of his own, "if I bore the Chair, I am sorry, but it does seem to me that we had better stop, look and listen now, rather than later. This nomination by the candidate for President faces us squarely once again with the fundamental issue we have been contending over ever since the convening of the national convention.

"Let me state it with some of his own famed candor.

"It is salvation or disaster.

"It is war or peace.

"It is life or death."

There was an approving roar beyond, a vigorous burst of applause within. Blair Hannah was on his feet, flushed with annoyance. A mask had come down over Cullee's handsome face. He looked somber and ominous. The innocent happiness was gone already. Such was the withering effect of the present suspicious world.

"Mr. President," Blair Hannah said, "I think we can do without the flamboyant rhetoric of the national committeeman from Oregon. The distinguished nominee for President has offered us the name of a candidate for Vice President worthy in every respect of our trust and support. He is a fine young man, able in public service, dedicated to the cause of world peace, thoroughly responsible in every way. He is also—"

"He is also," Roger P. Croy interrupted, "one of the chief architects of a consistently disastrous foreign policy, and the fact that he is black is not going to be sufficient to bamboozle those who abhor that policy into forgetting it. If the candidate for President thinks this, he is unhappily mistaken. He is, as usual, being too clever."

"Mr. President," Mary Buttner Baffleburg cried angrily, roly-poly little body shaking with indignation, "look who is dragging in the race issue here to confuse everything. That—great—liberal, Mr. Roger P. Croy! It has no place in these discussions, Mr. President! It is so much hogwash!"

"Hogwash or no," Roger Croy retorted, flushing but holding his ground, "it is patently clear to many of us that the candidate for President is making deliberate use of it to confuse the issue and secure approval of a Vice Presidential candidate who agrees one hundred per cent with his own point of view."

"Is that bad?" Asa B. Attwood inquired innocently, and at once Roger P. Croy rounded on him with a fine show of righteousness.

"Yes, it is bad!" he said sharply. "And I will tell the committeeman from California why. It is bad because it would reverse the hard-fought decision of this committee when it chose Edward M. Jason. It is bad because it would wipe out all the elements of balance that we struggled so hard to achieve. It is bad because it would make the ticket simply Tweedledum and Tweedledee, betray all the supporters of Edward Jason and give the man who may be our next President virtual carte blanche to continue headlong down the road to endless overseas involvement and endless war. That is why it is bad, Mr. President, and I for one intend to oppose it as vigorously as I know how."

"I think the issue *is* race," Asa B. Attwood said with a calculated indifference, turning his back deliberately upon Roger Croy. "If the committeeman wants to be tagged with that, it's his responsibility."

"The issue *is not* race!" Roger Croy cried, his anger entirely genuine this time. "That is a vicious, unprincipled, unworthy falsehood, I will say to the committeeman from California! It is entirely typical of the tactics with which Orrin Knox and his supporters have acted here, throughout. It is just one more of those vicious, unprincipled—"

"Well, *now!*" William Abbott interrupted with a sudden thunder that startled into silence all except CBS, who murmured dryly to NBC, "I thought *that* would bring a little work with the gavel." And the President did indeed use it, so hard that it seemed it must break the lectern.

"I do not propose," he said, as the room became abruptly silent, keeping his tone level but breathing hard, "that this committee degenerate once more into the name-calling aggregation of political asps that it turned into a week ago. We have some responsibility to proceed in an orderly fashion to make the grave decision that devolves upon us, and I for one don't intend to let us get into personalities if I can help it. The committeeman from California and the committeeman from Oregon will both be in order, because we shan't proceed until they are."

And he stopped and stared angrily at Asa Attwood and Roger Croy until both began to avoid his gaze and subside, looking annoyed and resentful but not quite daring to challenge him. Seated at the President's side, Orrin stared out impassively at the room, face devoid of expression. From outside there came a scornful, mocking sound.

"Now," the President said after a sufficient period of silence had elapsed, "we will proceed. You have heard the nomination, you know the man, you are all aware of all the issues—God knows we have discussed them enough in recent weeks. Your candidate for President has given you his second nomination for Vice President. How many more must he offer before you condescend to act? Who will move that we approve this nomination and give the country what it seeks from us, a worthy and responsible choice for Vice President?"

"Mr. President!" Esmé Harbellow Stryke cried, as across the room a dozen other Jason supporters also sprang angrily to their feet. "Oh, no, you don't, Mr. President! We won't have that kind of railroading here! We just won't have it! There will be a fair and open debate on the qualifications of the proposed nominee, or I for one will walk out, Mr. President, and then where will your precious committee be? And I don't think I will be alone, either!"

And she sat down, her sharp-featured, intelligent face peering angrily about like that of some shrewd little fox. From many of her colleagues came supportive shouts of "Hear, hear!" and from beyond the walls a massive, approving roar.

Abruptly the nominee for President made a sudden decisive gesture, rose and came forward to the lectern.

The President, taken by surprise, said, "Are you sure you want to—?" Orrin nodded with something of his old brusqueness. The President shrugged and turned to the Committee.

"Ladies and gentlemen," he said, "Secretary Knox."

He stood for a moment, supporting himself with a firm grip on the lectern, while his audience first stirred, then settled down. An intent, absolute concentration came upon them. Into it he spoke with a biting impatience and an annoyance he did not bother to conceal.

"Members of the Committee—my co-workers in this campaign: either we choose a nominee for Vice President here today or we open the door to squabbles and divisions that could occupy us for weeks, ending in a party so badly split that we could never win. That is not how I conceive your function. It is to achieve unity, and to win."

"Whose fault are the divisions?" Ewan MacDonald MacDonald inquired in a gentle undertone just loud enough to be heard. There was some amusement in the room, a raucous hoot from the grounds outside. Orrin raised his head with a sharp, uncompromising anger and stared straight at Ewan MacDonald.

"If you think it is mine," he said with a harsh directness that left them breathless, "I am prepared to get out of the way. If you want me to withdraw Congressman Hamilton's nomination, I will do so. If you want me to withdraw my own, I will do so. Is that what you want? Make the motion!"

("*Make* it, God damn it!" the *Times* whispered savagely to the *Post;* but the moment for a decisiveness to match the nominee's was gone almost before it existed. "They haven't got the guts," the *Post* whispered savagely back; and as Orrin had accurately foreseen, they didn't. His gamble was won the instant he took it.)

For perhaps thirty seconds there was absolute silence while his gaze remained locked with that of the committeeman from Wyoming. No one whispered further, no one spoke, no one moved. The world hung suspended until Orrin exercised his option to set it back in motion. When he did, it was his world again. "Orrin's little extra" had once more carried the day.

"Very well," he said quietly, and in the room and outside there seemed to be a universal expulsion of tightly held breath. "So we go forward together. And if we go forward together, *we go forward together*. I have offered you my choice of Vice President. Vote him up or vote him down, but *vote*. The whole world is waiting on you."

And he turned and went back to his chair while the tension held just too long for the supporters of Ted Jason to take advantage of it.

"Mr. President," Blair Hannah said quickly, "I move the Committee approve the nomination of Representative Cullee Hamilton of California to be our nominee for Vice President of the United States!"

"Second the motion!" Mary Buttner Baffleburg cried.

"Vote!" cried the friends of Orrin Knox.

"BOO!" cried NAWAC.

"Mrs. Jennings," the President said quickly, "will you be so good as to act as clerk for us again?"

"Alabama!" Lathia Talbot Jennings cried, so eager to comply that she uttered the name even as she got up and scurried to the stage, trailing a startled amusement in her wake to lighten, if only briefly, the angry moment.

And the vote was on.

When it concluded the President stood for a moment looking over the wildly excited room. Then he faced full into the cameras, the watching nation, NAWAC and the world.

"On this vote," he said, his voice showing just an edge of the universal tension, "the Yeas are 651, the Nays are 642, and the Honorable Cullee Hamilton of California is the Vice Presidential nominee of this party."

After that, for a few minutes, there was pandemonium as the media scurried to broadcast, note and record the reactions of the Committee, the audience and the crowds outside. When all the counterclaims of "Marvelous choice!" and "Railroad!" had been faithfully reported and immortalized, the room settled down again into a restive, buzzing semblance of order. Into it the President said quietly, "Ladies and gentlemen, the next Vice President of the United States."

Cullee came forward to the podium, helping Sarah Johnson up the steps, seating her in the chair hastily provided by one of the sergeants at arms, shaking hands with the President and with Orrin. Then he turned to face the room. His expression was somber. The burst of excited applause that had greeted him from Orrin's supporters quickly died away. In the tumbling minutes since Orrin had offered his name his mind had raced through several alternative things to say. He had finally decided to tell them exactly how he felt. With the honest bluntness that had distinguished his utterances in the United Nations and in the House, he proceeded to do so.

"Mr. President," he said, "Secretary Knox, members of the Committee, ladies and gentlemen:

"I accept your nomination and I shall do everything I can to help this ticket win in November, and to help create a responsible and forward-looking Administration starting next January.

"I don't think," he said, raising a hand to silence the automatic response that came from his friends and Orrin's, "that this will be easy. I don't think any of us should be under any illusions about that. It is going to be very difficult for all of us, and mostly so for President Knox. Let's talk about that for a minute." His expression turned stubborn, curiously youthful.

"To begin with, I don't think either Orrin Knox or I should have to apologize for the fact that I am black. There's not much either of us can do about it at this late date. There it is. If it makes it impossible for some of our colleagues to support the ticket, so be it. I daresay we can get along without them if we have to."

From the press tables there came a hardly muffled snort of derision, from outside a long, rolling roar of boos. Roger P. Croy flushed with indignation and Esmé Stryke's tense little body seemed to quiver with it. But he gave them look for look and went on, unimpressed.

"It looks as though maybe we'll have to get along without some other people, too, and to them I say: we couldn't care less. Neither the Secretary nor I have been beholden to the kooks, the crazies, the vicious or the violent. We haven't had them and we don't need them now. But we do need everybody else—all responsible Americans who believe, as we do, that we must return to a reasonable ground of decency in our public life, while at the same time maintaining a strong foreign policy abroad—above all, a patient but firm attitude toward the Soviets."

("Those damned right-wing clichés again," the *Christian Science Monitor* whispered to the New York *Post*. "We thought we had all that licked with Jason," the *Post* agreed morosely. "And now look where we are. Right back where we started.")

"If this makes the ticket," Cullee went on, and again the sarcasm came into his voice, "just a matter of Tweedledum and Tweedledee, then so be it. I don't think myself that it does, because I have had some differences with the Secretary in the past, and I expect I'll have some in the future."

("But not on foreign policy or defense," Justice Davis murmured to Patsy Labaiya, holding herself ostentatiously rigid with disapproval of the speaker. "Not on anything that *really counts*." "I know," she responded. "It's frightful. *Simply* FRIGHTFUL.")

"So there will be divergences," Cullee said, "and I expect I'll not hesitate to tell the President about them. And I expect he'll hear my advice"—he paused and turned deliberately to Orrin, who nodded (after all, what else could he do? CBS inquired of ABC)—"because that's the kind of frank understanding we have always had, and that's the kind of man he is."

He paused, lifted his head, stared straight out; a thoughtful, almost wondering expression crossed his face.

"This is quite a day," he said with a sudden childlike candor that was most disarming to all but his harshest critics, "for a little black boy from Greenville, South Carolina. There are two people I wish could see me now. One is my mother, bless her heart. And the other is that old curmudgeon Senator from my native state who isn't with us any more, Seabright B. Cooley. I think maybe they'd both be proud. I think so.

"Anyway"—and suddenly he grinned, for a moment unashamedly and openly delighted, before the realities of the world closed down and his expression turned somber again—"*I* am, and that's for sure. . . .

"So," he concluded solemnly, "I accept your nomination. I pledge you everything I have in me. I say with our candidate for President—*let us move forward together*. We have a big job to do. *Let's get started!*"

And he turned, as the applause, now disposed to be generous, rolled up from the room, and from NAWAC's distant hordes the booing answered back, to shake hands with the President, with Orrin, Hal and Crystal, with Lathia Talbot Jennings, who gave him a sudden impulsive kiss and then turned bright pink. Then he and Orrin were standing together at the lectern, hands linked and raised high, posing for the cameras; a reminiscent moment suddenly tense for everyone, but passing this time, of course, without incident in the tightly guarded room.

"This special emergency meeting of the National Committee," the President said, stepping forward to bring down the gavel with a final decisive *crack!*, "stands adjourned sine die. Goodbye, and God bless you all."

And Orrin had the running mate he wanted, and the savage campaign, as of that moment, was begun.

5.

THERE FOLLOWED the seemingly endless, always exhausting succession of conferences, speeches, journeys, statements, appearances, charges, countercharges, challenges and responses which every four years provide the American electorate with some final, fundamental judgment on the man they wish to have as their President.

For the better part of three months, feeling steadily stronger and more like himself, he conducted a grueling campaign—not so much against Warren Strickland, who accepted, with an amiable irony he made known only to a few old friends, including Orrin, his party's Presidential nomination—but against all the enemies, foreign and domestic, who were bitterly opposed to the idea of Orrin Knox in the White House.

These were many, and most were highly vocal. They had begun their outcries immediately upon Cullee's nomination, and their attacks had ranged the spectrum from patronizing comments on the Congressman's youth and general inexperience to bitter attacks upon his record as an advocate of the Hudson-Knox foreign policy.

"It is not only in the specific instances of Gorotoland and Panama that this policy is disastrous"—the *Post* had summed it up at the end of a three-part editorial series entitled "Compounding the Knox Mistake: The Hamilton Nomination"—"but in its general tone and thrust as well. In fact, tone and thrust are its major, and, we feel, most dangerous aspects.

"Tone and thrust are abysmally clear. There is one basic purpose: to oppose, and if possible thwart, the policies of the Soviet Union. And this with a sort of automatic knee-jerk hostility that is based on hysteria, fear, unthinking opposition, inability to accept the facts of our world as they exist—inability to perceive that only by working out a peaceable agreement with the Russians can we possibly hope to save the world—inability, in essence, to live and let live."

Walter Dobius, the *Times,* the networks, Frankly Unctuous and all the busy gaggle of commentators, editorial writers and columnists who customarily tell Americans how to think, agreed.

"Orrin Knox ran his railroad through the National Committee and came out with the yes man he wanted—Cullee Hamilton," Walter wrote. "The country will have a heavy reckoning to make if this prize pair is elected and given a mandate to pursue their unconscionable war policies."

Overseas, too, there were grave doubts expressed, harsh criticisms voiced, deep misgivings murmured at diplomatic receptions and off-the-record talks with foreign leaders, which speedily found their way back to America.

At first the Secretary had been worried that this incessant barrage, which had characterized so much of his own public career, might seriously affect the poise and stability of his youthful running mate. He need not have feared. Their first private talk, a week after the Committee adjourned, found Cullee unimpressed, undeterred and undaunted.

"I gather," he said with a wry smile when they were safely alone in the study of the house in Spring Valley, "that you and I are no damned good."

"*You* are no damned good," Orrin said cheerfully. "I am no damned goodest. How does it feel to be on the ticket with such a scoundrel—and to be such a scoundrel yourself?"

"Mr. Secretary," Cullee said, his smile broadening to a grin, "I couldn't be more pleased." Then his expression abruptly changed, his tone became unaffectedly serious and humble. "I really don't know," he said quietly, "how I can ever express to you my gratitude for your having given me this opportunity. It is more than I ever dreamed—more than I ever had any right to dream. I didn't mean to get so corny in my acceptance speech, I got carried away, I guess, but it *is* true: it's more than a little black boy from Greenville, South Carolina, could ever have expected. Even though some of my so-called friends"—he scowled, his handsome face suddenly uneasy and unhappy—"seem to think it's a shame and disgrace to my race for me to have accepted such an awful, demeaning, patronizing gesture on your part."

"How *is* LeGage?" Orrin asked, and Cullee's expression, always perturbed when he thought of LeGage Shelby, his brilliant former roommate at Howard University, now head of the Defenders of Equality for You (DEFY), became if anything more somber.

"That no-good lightweight is going to do everything he can to ruin us, that's for sure—him and his other buddies in NAWAC. What a crew! They aren't going to forgive you for Ted Jason's not being here—not," he added hastily, "that you had anything to do with *that*. But you know it's a factor."

"Yes," Orrin agreed somberly, "it's a factor. Walter Dobius and his friends keep reviving the suspicion every other day. I'd like to think nobody believed them, but I'm afraid some do."

"Walter and his friends on one side, and NAWAC and that bunch on the other," Cullee said with a grimly humorous smile. "We've got us quite a cross-ruff going, haven't we, Mr. Secretary? If the ghosts don't get you, the goblins will."

"Well," Orrin said, a characteristic tartness entering his tone, "I trust you and I, by running a good, honest, hard-hitting campaign, can take care of them both."

Cullee nodded.

"I think so. I really do. I still think the majority in this country is fair-minded, and I think if we rely on that and state things honestly as we see them, we'll come through all right. . . . So," he added matter-of-factly, "do you want me to attack NAWAC and the media while you take the high road?"

Orrin gave a startled little laugh and shook his head.

"No, you don't need to do that."

"Isn't that the function of Vice Presidents?" Cullee inquired, quite seriously. "I want to do whatever you want me to do, to help."

Orrin smiled and realized anew how fond he was of this direct and uncomplicated heart he had raised to share his problems, and, if November brought its hoped-for reward, his power.

"We'll handle it together. If we have to reply, we'll coordinate and we'll both do our part. But I'm hopeful we can keep it on a plane where we won't have to. Certainly Warren isn't going to lower it. I know that."

"There are those who will," Cullee said. "This isn't going to be an easy campaign, Mr. Secretary."

"I've never expected it to be," Orrin said gravely. "But I think you and I can stand the gaff."

"You can count on me," Cullee said, his face for a second as stubborn as Orrin's could be. "If they think they're going to push little Cullee around, they have another think coming."

And although the campaign almost immediately became marred by violence and by increasing media attacks upon their general probity, character and competence, Orrin had been pleased to find that he had remained true to that pledge. And this in spite of provocations that grew increasingly difficult to take as the weeks hurried on.

NAWAC, at first seemingly stunned by Cullee's nomination, had for several days issued no official comment. Then Fred Van Ackerman, speaking, as he said, for his own Committee on Making Further Offers for a Russian Truce (COMFORT), LeGage Shelby of DEFY, and Rufus Kleinfert, Knight Kommander of the Konference on Efforts to Encourage Patriotism (KEEP), gave the media a position paper which would, he said, form the basis for NAWAC's approach to the campaign.

"The nomination of Congressman Hamilton to run for Vice President with Secretary of State Knox," it read in part, "indicates not only the Secretary's desperate paucity of new ideas to offer the country, but it throws into glaring light the helplessness with which the American voter must face his choices in November.

"Senator Warren Strickland and his running mate are as pro-war as Secretary Knox and Congressman Hamilton. There is no solace in either camp for all those Americans who genuinely desire a world in which Soviet Russia and the United States can live in harmony with one another.

"Senator Strickland and his running mate have no desire to provide such a world. Secretary Knox and Congressman Hamilton have no desire to provide it.

"The American people must therefore return, as in all times of past danger, to a patriotic reliance upon their own efforts to make their feelings known.

"In this effort, the National Anti-War Activities Congress expects to be, throughout the campaign, constantly vigilant and on the alert for any activities or statements by any candidate, or any spokesman for any candidate, which seek to subvert peace. It intends to make its opposition to such anti-peace attempts vigorous and effective.

"All Americans who agree are invited to join us and help conduct this great battle for a sane and peaceful world."

And daily, as the press faithfully reported, new thousands answered the appeal and received their memberships in NAWAC. And daily NAWAC's black-leather-jacketed representatives, increasingly and openly paramilitary, appeared in ever more ominous numbers at campaign rallies, parades, speeches by the candidates, political gatherings of every kind.

For all of them, this was hard to take—for Warren Strickland and his running mate, the amiable Governor of Pennsylvania—for Orrin—for Cullee—for Lafe Smith in Iowa—for Hal, who was running for the House in Illinois—for Ceil Jason, who had suggested that she introduce Orrin at each of his major campaign appearances. Starting with his opening speech in Chicago on Labor Day, she had done so with gracious efficiency and a genuine enthusiasm that added greatly to his campaign. And starting with that day and running right on through, on each occasion the demonstrators and the rioters and the black-suited cadres were there, like a spigot turned on and off by—whom? Perhaps by Fred Van Ackerman, perhaps by some hand more sophisticated than his.

No one knew, and the media treatment of the disturbances was in general so tolerant, good-natured and determinedly unalarmed that it was, at first, difficult to get much attention for warnings about them.

"We note," the *Post* editorialized almost jovially after five or six outbreaks of violence, fortunately not fatal but deeply disturbing in their bitterness, had marred the appearances of the Secretary of State, Senator Strickland and their running mates, "that the peace-loving elements in America seem to be arousing some concern in the camps of the various pro-war candidates who are running for election in November. We cannot find ourselves moved by their expressions of alarm. We think they deserve whatever they get in the way of protest which, while perhaps a little vigorous at times, nonetheless represents the opinion of the overwhelming majority of Americans.

"It may be, as spokesmen for both Secretary Knox and Senator Strickland contend, that there have been threats, possibly even minor examples of actual violence, in opposition to their views. Surely such episodes have been entirely accidental. In any event, we suggest that the candidates have only themselves to blame. Harsh and oppressive policies bring harsh and oppressive responses.

"Basically, the message of NAWAC and other anti-war groups is clear: America wants peace and friendship with the Soviet Union. Is that such a crime?"

Similar opinions appeared in all the usual places. No one of any prominence in the media was in the least concerned. It appeared that violence was about to become a joke. Some counterattack appeared to be necessary, and in a speech in St. Louis in the third week of September, Orrin launched it.

"We have just witnessed," he said, as his upset and excited audience quieted down after the first few hectic minutes of his appearance, "a scene disgraceful to America and ominous for all who believe in the preservation of our free society. Armed demonstrators carrying the banners of a paramilitary, un-American organization have attempted to stop this meeting. They have attempted to stop free American citizens from attending. They have threatened the lives of Mrs. Jason, myself and Congressman Hamilton. They have threatened your lives.

"How much longer will America tolerate such tactics?

"I do not know the limits of America's patience, but I do know mine. I have asked the President of the United States for increased Secret Service protection for Mrs. Jason, myself and Congressman Hamilton. He has agreed. He has also offered to assign Federal troops to any major campaign rallies where Senator Strickland or myself feel their presence to be necessary.

"I do not know whether I will avail myself of this offer or whether Senator Strickland will. But I thank the President for it, because things have passed dangerously far beyond the point of normal political debate in this country when armed elements can threaten, disrupt and disorganize the political gatherings of a free people."

The response had been prompt and outraged.

KNOX, PRESIDENT SEEK TO IMPOSE MILITARY CONTROL OF POLITICAL MEETINGS. USE PRETEXT OF MINOR ANTI-WAR DISTURBANCES TO THREATEN FEDERAL INTERVENTION IN ELECTION PROCESS. MAJOR FIGURES OF CHURCH, THEATER, LEGAL PROFESSIONS JOIN NAWAC IN DENUNCIATION OF "OUTRAGEOUS, UNCONSTITUTIONAL ATTEMPT TO SUBSTITUTE DICTATORSHIP FOR DEMOCRACY." PRESIDENT UNMOVED. WHITE HOUSE SPOKESMAN SAYS OFFER STANDS.

And although neither Orrin nor Warren Strickland availed themselves of it, things quieted down for a brief period and there was a noticeable restraint apparent in the protests staged by NAWAC and others.

The lull lasted roughly two weeks.

Then both candidates received an urgent call from the White House, events suddenly raced into high gear and the campaign became, abruptly, much more hectic than before.

"Let's sit over there by the window," William Abbott suggested in the Oval Office. "I want to get away from that damned desk."

"That's odd," Warren Strickland said with his pleasant smile. "Here Orrin and I are breaking our necks to try to get to it. Is there something wrong with it?"

"He won't tell us," Orrin said. "He doesn't want to discourage us."

"Oh, yes," the President said, "I'll tell you. If it's discouraging, so be it. All I know is, one of you is going to have to take it next January. *I* won't be here, thank God."

"As bad as that," Senator Strickland said.

"As bad as that," Bill Abbott agreed somberly. "Look at this."

And he handed each of them a long manila folder marked "Ajax Only."

"Ajax?" Orrin inquired quizzically. The President nodded.

"That's me. You'll find that all intelligence types around here love to play games with names. Anyway, Ajax is breaking the rules by letting you see this. But I thought you'd better know, because I may have to take action that will arouse some public comment, and I want you both supporting me. That is, if you see fit."

"I'm sure we shall," Warren Strickland said, putting on his glasses, opening the folder and beginning to read. "What is this?"

" 'Hammerlock and Time Bomb: Plans for New Offensives in Panama and Gorotoland,' " Orrin read. "I suppose 'Hammerlock' and 'Time Bomb' are—"

"You guessed it," the President said. "Moscow and Peking. Hammerlock is what the Pentagon thinks the Russians have on us, and Time Bomb is what they think the Chinese are. They hope it's a time bomb against Russia, but nobody's sure at the moment." He gestured to the folders. "Right now, it doesn't look that way."

"No," Warren Strickland said as his eyes sped down the first page. "It certainly does not. . . ."

"So," Orrin said five minutes later as they closed the folders and turned to the President, staring moodily out at the Rose Garden as it lay listless in the last heat of Indian summer. "What now?"

"A signal," William Abbott said.

"How big a signal?" Senator Strickland inquired. "A little modest signal or a great big noisy one?"

"Quite big," Bill Abbott said. "Quite noisy. A worldwide alert of all the armed forces, I think."

"That *is* noisy," Orrin agreed thoughtfully.

"But justified, don't you think?" the President inquired. He gave them both a sharp glance. "Or don't you?"

"Yes, I think so," Orrin said, still thoughtfully. "If what our people say here is true."

"And you have to assume it is," Warren commented.

"Yes, I do," the President said with a certain grimness. "You'll find that. . . . So: if it happens, will you both support me?"

"How?" Orrin asked.

"A joint statement," the President said crisply. "Endorsing my decision, giving it your full support, pledging yourselves to follow through on these policies for as long as necessary to insure restoration of peace and friendly control in those two areas."

The candidates exchanged a thoughtful glance.

"Aren't you trying to tie us down pretty far in advance, Bill?" Orrin asked finally. "I agree with your purposes, and I see the threat, and all things being equal I would expect to continue the same policies myself, but still—"

"We might want to maintain a little more flexibility," Warren said. "It's nothing personal," he added hastily, as the President gave him a sudden searching look. "You know that, Bill."

"Well," William Abbott said, drawing himself up suddenly with all the combined dignity of Mr. President, which he was, and Mr. Speaker, which he had been and planned to be again, "if I had thought I was going to have to beg—"

"Not at all," Warren Strickland said hastily. "Not at all, Mr. President. You know that."

"Of course you do, Mr. President," Orrin said shortly, "so don't be ridiculous. We do have a point, I think. Who knows what the situation will be four months from now, on January 20?"

"It sure as hell won't be any better," the President said bluntly, "if I can't get you two to stand behind me on a firm policy now. Our only chance of salvaging anything in this world, it seems to me, is to *be* firm. Not namby-pamby and mollycoddling around."

"That's hardly fair," Orrin said sharply. "Neither of us has been namby-pamby or advocated 'mollycoddling around.' That's why people such as Walter Dobius are in such a dither. We don't offer them much choice, I'm afraid. Poor things," he added with considerable scorn. "It touches me."

"Yes," the President said with the first note of amusement that had entered their conversation, "I can see that." His tone became challenging again. "What are you going to do, then, leave me out on a limb?"

"Stop putting it on such a personal basis," Orrin said bluntly. "You sound almost whiny, and that isn't like you, Bill. No, we're not going to abandon you, are we, Warren? But we have to think about it."

"What's to think?" the President inquired.

Warren shrugged.

"Our own advantage, I suppose." He sighed. "That's too candid, but it's what it comes down to."

"I hope your own advantage lies in supporting what's best for the country," the President said sharply.

"It is," Warren agreed. "Indeed it is. And is it best for the country to tie our hands completely now, or to maintain, as I said a minute ago, flexibility? That's the issue, Mr. President. It isn't whether we like you personally or not. Lord knows, I hope you don't have any question about that!"

"No, of course not," Bill Abbott said impatiently. "I'm sorry if you think I put it on a personal basis. Maybe I did. I'm worried, that's all. Because of course they may not pay any attention. We may be past the time for signals. That's what I don't know and that's why I feel I need your support. I thought it was only fair to give you advance notice, in any case, since it will be up to one of you before long." He stared out moodily once again at the Rose Garden. "So I guess I'm on my own, then. I'm sorry I interrupted your campaign schedules to have you come here. Nobody knows it, of course, so we'll get you out the South Portico, away from the press, and nobody ever will. Thank you for coming."

And he prepared to stand up, until Orrin raised a restraining hand.

"Now, just a minute," he said. "Just—a—minute, Mr. President, if you don't mind. Stop jumping the gun on us. You know us better than that. Just let us think for a minute, all right?"

"All right," the President said, sitting slowly down again. "Be my guests."

And for another few minutes, silence prevailed in the Oval Office while they, too, stared out at the garden and the gleaming white arcade leading to the Mansion. Then Orrin turned back.

"Very well," he said crisply. "You're the leader of my party. I have to support you—and I do agree. I think we have to take some action and I think the statement can be framed in such a way as to maintain our personal independence later. Warren, what do you think?"

"One can do a lot with words," Senator Strickland said with a smile. "Let's try."

PRESIDENT ORDERS WORLDWIDE ARMED FORCES ALERT TO MEET WHAT WHITE HOUSE STATEMENT CALLS "GRAVE NEW THREATS TO PEACE IN PANAMA AND GOROTOLAND." KNOX, STRICKLAND ENDORSE MOVE AFTER SECRET CONFERENCE WITH ABBOTT. NEW MILITARY GESTURE BY U.S. STUNS WORLD. PEACE GROUPS DENOUNCE "BIPARTISAN BLUFF" AND "CONTRIVED CRISIS" AS MOSCOW DENIES ANY PLANS TO RENEW INTERVENTION IN TROUBLE AREAS.

"If there is any single most deplorable practice which has grown up in this age of deplorable foreign policy," the *Times* exclaimed next morning, "it is the damnable practice of Presidents calling 'worldwide military alerts' every time they want to bluff the Soviet Union into something.

"We do not know what has prompted this latest sensational démarche by the Abbott Administration, but we do know one basic purpose it has: to scare the living daylights out of the country, strengthen the war party and guarantee that both Secretary Knox and Senator Strickland will be tied permanently to an anti-Soviet, anti-peace policy.

"It is not surprising that Secretary Knox has lent himself with indecent haste to this charming project, since he has been one of the chief architects of the policy all along. It is more startling to find a man of Senator Strickland's general probity falling for it. Despite their carefully worded claims of independence, it is obvious that both candidates are now firmly committed to a continuation of hatred, suspicion and fear in the world.

"We would not blame Moscow in the slightest if it calls this bluff. In fact, we hope it does. The Soviet leaders have made it entirely clear, in their angry protest issued in Moscow last night, that they have no intention whatsoever of undertaking any new intervention in Gorotoland or Panama. Perhaps they should, just as a means of restoring some rational perspective to American policy. We strongly suspect there would be no real reaction from Washington, despite stout talk of 'worldwide military alerts.'"

But this, as it turned out, was something that never had to be proved, for nothing happened to change the situation in either of the war-torn countries; and after three days the President announced termination of the alert, receiving additional scathing comments therefor.

In his dusty capital of Molobangwe on the plains of Gorotoland, Terence Wolowo Ajkaje, 137th M'Bulu of Mbuele, breathed a little easier, knowing that the forces of his ambitious cousin Prince Obifumatta were not going to make the all-out drive they had fully planned to make, with Russian and Chinese help, three days before. And at his ancestral home, "La Suerte"—standing for *La suerte está echada*, "The die is cast"—Felix Labaiya-Sofra, Patsy Jason's ex-husband, leader of the Panamanian People's Movement, realized that he must wait a little longer for the help his friends in Moscow and Peking had been within two hours of giving him when the President ordered the alert.

Felix in the lush green highlands of Panama, and Terrible Terry in his ramshackle palace in dusty Molobangwe, knew very well the truth behind the headlines; but at home in America, where uncomfortable and challenging truths about the Communist powers were never permitted credence or sometimes even space by the custodians of American communications, the episode served only to exacerbate a campaign already bitter enough.

POLLS SHOW KNOX SLIPPING STEADILY AS ANTI-WAR PROTESTS MOUNT IN WAKE OF RECENT "CRISIS" ALERT. NAWAC REPORTED CONSIDERING ENDORSEMENT OF STRICKLAND AS "LESSER OF TWO EVILS." SENATOR SEEKS TO FORESTALL MOVE BY DENOUNCING "VICIOUSLY VIOLENT ELEMENTS SEEKING TO CAPTURE MY CAMPAIGN." SECRET SERVICE MAN, TWO PEACE DEMONSTRATORS SLAIN IN CLASH AT KNOX RALLY IN MADISON. PRESIDENT AGAIN OFFERS TROOPS BUT CANDIDATES DECLINE. BITTERNESS GROWS AS CAMPAIGN ENTERS FINAL WEEKS.

So a hot September moved on into an October serene and lovely everywhere across the tense, uneasy land. The polls did indeed show him slipping, though his crowds everywhere were large and enthusiastic and his major speeches well attended and well received. From three decades' experience in politics he knew that if the election were to be held so much as one week later than scheduled, he might very well lose. But he felt he had a margin still, however dwindling;

and since Warren seemed to be having some difficulty, both in separating himself from his would-be endorsers and in establishing a foreign-policy position really separate and distinct from Orrin's own, he considered himself free to state with increasing emphasis exactly where he stood.

His major exposition of it came in the last week of October in Laramie, Wyoming, where he had gone deliberately for two reasons: to endorse the young Congressman who was hoping to oust Fred Van Ackerman from the Senate, and to carry the battle directly to Fred, NAWAC and the violent dissident, on Fred's own home ground. The polls showed Fred slipping badly too. His speeches were becoming daily more strident and inflammatory as a result. With ten days left to election, Orrin decided it was time to administer the *coup de grâce* to both Fred and the elements he represented, if he could. His decision greatly alarmed Hal, Crystal and the President. Warren also telephoned him privately and urged him for safety's sake not to go.

But he stuck to his own counsel, as they had known he would; a decision which, looking back later at the events of that hectic day, he thought he might possibly have modified—or again might not have, since what happened had, in all probability, been the final factor in guaranteeing November's outcome.

They had arrived in Laramie by motorcade from Cheyenne, where they had spent the night; himself accompanied by the Secret Service contingent, his press secretary and a doctor, Ceil accompanied by her aunt by marriage, Valuela Jason Randall, over from her villa in Positano for the final days of the campaign. Orrin had never met Valuela before, but since her arrival the previous weekend he had become rapidly and genuinely fond of her. She was a racy old girl with her startling red wig, her outspoken opinions and her indomitable character, and he found in her, as he had in Ceil, a surprisingly staunch supporter. He knew that she painted, remembered vaguely having seen some of her work—as bright and garish, yet as fundamentally strong and powerful, as she seemed to be herself. He realized at once that she was a very intelligent woman, with a great store of common sense.

"I'm glad to have you with us," he said as they waited in the hotel at Laramie prior to the speech. "I've seen Selena and Herbert occasionally at some of my meetings, but they haven't exactly been friendly."

"Sel and Herbert!" Valuela said, a snort dismissing her sister, Selena Jason Castleberry, perpetually drenched in diamonds and Causes, and their brother Herbert, Nobel prize-winning scientist whose frizzly white hair and excited pop eyes had loomed up quite regularly of late in television shots of demonstrators waving anti-Knox banners. "I consider it greatly to your credit that they're against you. I should worry for the country if they were not."

"I believe I have the cream of the Jason crop," he said with a smile. She chuckled.

"You have in Ceil. I'm just an old baggage who's come along for the fun. Are we going to have any today?"

"I hope not too much," he said. Ceil nodded.

"We've had quite enough already, I think. I'd be just as happy if we could get along without any more."

"Look here," he said, suddenly serious. "If you'd rather not come along to the rally, you don't have to. Why don't you and Valuela stay here and watch it on television? That might be the best idea. Really."

"I'll come," Valuela said. "Nobody knows *me*. You and Ceil are in a different category."

"I'm not going to run away or back out," Ceil said quietly. "I'm not afraid." She smiled wryly. "Any more than I have been."

"This could be the worst," he said gravely. "We're right here on the home ground of the protesters' hero. Somebody may want to finish the uncompleted job."

Her eyes widened as she considered it. But there was no flinching in her tone.

"We've faced that at each major speech."

"Why have you done it?" he asked, thinking back over the weeks since Labor Day, the days that suddenly seemed to stretch so far away into the past that they were almost beyond memory, so crowded were they with a blur of places, people, charge and counter-charge, endless challenge, endless response.

"Because," she replied with a gravity to match his own, "I do genuinely believe that Orrin Knox is best for this country. Believing that, I have felt I must help him." She paused and thought, face earnest and concentrated like a little girl's, and for a moment he could see the sunny, golden little child she must have been. "I have done it for my husband, because I felt that this was what he should have done. I don't know whether he would have—but he should have. I thought I would do it, to—to give him back something in memory that I feel he had lost in life."

"I told you she was the cream of the crop," Valuela said into the silence that followed. He nodded, touched for a moment to the point where he could not trust himself to speak.

"You are so right," he said finally, managing a smile. Outside there came the inevitable stir and bustle, the all too familiar approach of the world's demands. "I think that means us," he said, standing up. "Are we ready?"

"For whatever," Ceil said with a sudden smile, linking her arm through one of his.

"For another grand appearance by two great people," Valuela said firmly, linking her arm through the other.

"So armored," he said with a chuckle, "how could I possibly fail?"

Yet there were several moments that bitter day when he thought he might. The first occurred as soon as they emerged from the doorway of the Hotel Laramie. Several hundred people, divided about equally between his supporters and the dissident, were waiting for them across the street, held back by police and sheriff's deputies. Their appearance brought an instant tumult of sound—clashing, chaotic, mostly indecipherable save for one member of NAWAC who carried a bull horn. Through it he began shouting obscenities at Ceil and Orrin. Instantly fighting broke out, in a moment the area across the street was a confusion of shoving bodies, flying stones, bricks, sticks, flailing arms and tangled legs. The fighting spilled over, broke the police line, surged toward them. Several of NAWAC's black-jacketed bullies, taking advantage of the confusion, formed a flying wedge and started for them. Instinctively Ceil and Valuela flinched and drew back, he turned protectively toward them, their Secret Service cordon closed ranks and hurried them back into the lobby so swiftly that they were inside again before they knew it.

Outside the fighting abruptly stopped, hoots of angry derisive laughter rose from the demonstrators. Television, faithfully recording every moment, carried the spectacle to the world: Orrin Knox, Presidential candidate, driven off the street by a crowd of demonstrators, apparently fleeing in terror for his life. Five minutes later, the street finally cleared, they were hurried into their limousine. A motorcycle escort roared into action. What had been planned as a leisurely triumphal parade through the streets of Laramie turned into a high-speed, furtive scurrying to the rally.

There they were hurried through massed police to the platform. Ten thousand of the faithful were on their feet, chanting and applauding with defiant enthusiasm. But the day had turned sour, the edge had been taken off.

Score one for NAWAC, he thought grimly.

Ceil, visibly upset, introduced him with half her usual effectiveness; the determined shouts of his supporters mingled with the continuing hoots of the dissident, off on the edges of the crowd. He stepped forward, took a deep breath, launched into a powerful attack on violence, called for the defeat of Fred Van Ackerman, began a measured exposition of his views on foreign policy. An object came hurtling through the air, landed at his feet, exploded with a loud *bang!* Instinctively, again, they all shrank back. It turned out to be a plastic bag filled with water; the bang had been contributed by someone else, apparently firing a blank. Again a roar of derisive ridicule broke through the valiant attempts of his supporters to counteract it with their applause: the mood of the day was further shattered. Mocking, evil child's tricks appeared to be succeeding where more serious onslaughts had not.

Yet in the long run, as he concluded later, it probably helped to stem the sapping tide reported in the polls. He finished his speech on a note of rising anger that culminated in a cold denunciation of the violent and all who sought to profit from their support.

At the end of it he let his voice drop to an almost conversational tone. "Mrs. Jason and I," he said, "have been subjected here today to the most recent of a series of deliberate humiliations, some designed to be seriously dangerous, others, like today's, meant simply to cast ridicule and scorn upon the things for which we stand.

"I say to you, my friends, whether they be dangerous or mocking, they have but one purpose and one hoped-for result. The purpose is to intimidate and discredit all who attempt to advocate a firm and even-handed policy toward the Communist powers, and particularly the Soviet Union. The hoped-for result is to turn that policy around and transform it into one of weakness, appeasement, retreat and defeat.

"We are nearing the end of a long and bitter campaign. A week from now we will vote. The events of this day, as of many unhappy days since the campaign began, state the issue very clearly: do Americans wish to cast their lot with those who want to destroy freedom and democracy—those who want, essentially, to destroy America herself by destroying her strength in the face of her enemies—or do Americans want to preserve the freedom and democracy they have, and by using their power constructively, work for a world stable and free from the fear of war?

"It is a very simple issue, though the future of freedom everywhere may be wrapped up in how you decide it."

After that, in the last hurrying days, he had some sense that the trend had been halted, that his chances were again improving; that somehow what had happened in Laramie had brought home, in a way that more awful events had not, the fragile nature of the fundamental decencies and safeguards he believed himself to be defending. Apparently a majority of his countrymen had made up their minds in his favor on that day. A week later they gave him permission to direct their destinies—the first step on a long road whose desperate conclusion not he, nor anyone, could then foresee.

KNOX ELECTED PRESIDENT BY SLIM MARGIN. ELECTORAL VOTE IS 273 TO 262, POPULAR TALLY 85,114,000 TO 81,783,000 FOR SENATOR STRICKLAND. KNOX GETS NOMINAL CONTROL OF BOTH HOUSES OF CONGRESS BUT MANY PEACE CANDIDATES ELECTED, SHARP BATTLES FORESEEN OVER FOREIGN POLICY. ABBOTT, HAL KNOX WIN HOUSE SEATS. VAN ACKERMAN, DEFEATED FOR SENATE IN WYOMING, PLEDGES CONTINUED NAWAC FIGHT.

And pushed to the bottom of the front page in the tide of election news, but augury of many things to come:

VASILY TASHIKOV NAMED HEAD OF SOVIET GOVERNMENT IN SURPRISE KREMLIN SHAKE-UP. AMBASSADOR TO U.S. BELIEVED TAPPED BECAUSE KNOWLEDGE OF AMERICA MAKES HIM BEST EQUIPPED TO DEAL WITH NEW ADMINISTRATION IN WASHINGTON.

HARDENING OF SOVIET LINE SEEN LIKELY FOLLOWING KNOX VICTORY.

6.

AND ALTHOUGH the assumption was only a headlined guess and its confirmation came to him far from the public view, it was rapidly made clear that a hardening Soviet line was indeed what he faced.

Three days after election, sitting in the temporary office the President had kindly offered him in the Executive Office Building across the street from the White House, he received a call from Dolly Munson.

The wife of the Senate Majority Leader looked beautiful as always when she appeared on the Picturephone. She also looked excited and as though she were the possessor of a big secret. She positively sparkled with it, in fact—so much so that he could not resist a little gentle kidding of the sort Dolly often invited from her friends.

"Orrin!" she said. "Guess what!"

"You and Bob are going to have a baby," he said gravely. "Dearest Dolly, how marvelous."

"My goodness," she said, dissolving into a gurgle of laughter, "wouldn't that be a score for the geriatric set! No, it's nothing as dramatic as that. Although," she added with a mischievous expression, "it is *rather* dramatic, I must admit. Yes, I'd say it's *quite* dramatic. Orrin, I want you to come to lunch tomorrow at 'Vagaries.'"

"I always love to come to anything at 'Vagaries,'" he said, thinking with reminiscent affection of the Munsons' beautiful old house, stately and secret among its trees at the edge of Rock Creek Park, "but I'm not sure I can make it at the moment. You see, I hate to inject a practical note into the social schedule of Washington's most famous hostess, but I have just been elected President of the United States, you know, and—"

"You love to say that, don't you?" she interrupted with the cheerful impudence of a dear friend.

"Sure," he agreed with amiable promptness. "Wouldn't you?"

"Considering all the headaches you're going to be taking on, I'm not so sure, Orrin. I'm not so sure." She gave him a shrewd, quizzical look. "Are you?"

"I have to be," he said. "I'm it. Too late to worry about it, now. Isn't that right?"

"Lucky man," she remarked, "if you can tackle it *without* worrying. Knowing you, I don't believe it. But, anyway—I'm glad it's you doing the worrying, and not somebody else. What are you going to appoint Ceil to?"

"Oh," he said with mock surprise. "Must I?"

"You certainly must," she said firmly. "You owe her a great deal. Besides which, she is a lovely lady and a very intelligent one. You'd be foolish not to. Despite what they say, *I* know Orrin Knox isn't foolish. So what's it going to be?"

"What would you suggest?"

"Ambassador to the U.N. She's a natural. Am I right?"

He chuckled.

"Dolly," he said, "you are uncanny. Also infallible. And you are hereby sworn to absolute secrecy."

She gave him a pleased smile.

"I can't even tell Bob?"

"Not even Bob."

"Oh, *good.* That makes it a real secret. Now, about lunch tomorrow—"

"Dolly dearest," he said patiently, "I really can't. It's impossible. I've got to put together a Cabinet and a White House staff, I've got endless planning to do—"

"Bob doesn't know this secret, either," she said. "So how about *that?*"

"Well, I'll admit that's intriguing, but—"

"It's very important, really," she assured him, suddenly solemn. "It's rather like a certain time—when certain people met at 'Vagaries'—to discuss a certain appointment. Do you remember that?"

He stared at her thoughtfully, mind leaping back almost two years: the annual "Spring Party" at "Vagaries"—Bob, himself, several other members of the Senate, several ambassadors, disappearing quietly upstairs to discuss the first nomination of Robert A. Leffingwell to be Secretary of State—one ambassador in particular— . . . light broke.

"That's very clever of him," he said. "To ask you to set it up at 'Vagaries.' No one would ever know, or guess."

"Washington's most famous hostess," she said with some satisfaction, "has her uses. I gather you are now persuaded."

"I may be," he agreed. "What are the conditions?"

"I'm to send a car to pick you both up—I suggested the station wagon instead of the Rolls, figuring that would be less conspicuous—"

He smiled.

"Possibly."

"It has to be tomorrow because he has to leave for home tomorrow night. No time limit, no holds barred. Approximate time of pickup twelve-thirty. Lunch upstairs in the study. No servants around the house—you'll have to eat my cooking. Both of you to come alone. No one else to know."

He gave her a thoughtful look.

"I'll buy everything but the last two. I have got to have my Secretary of State with me, and I think the President should be fully informed. After all, *his* colleagues are going to know. And Bill is still going to be President until January."

"Well," she said doubtfully, "I don't know. He seemed awfully positive."

"So am I awfully positive. Everybody knows that. Tell him and call me back."

"I have to wait until I hear from him," she said. "He's supposed to check back with me within the hour."

"I'll be right here," he said, turning to the papers on his desk with a matter-of-fact air. "Let me know."

"Well—all right."

Half an hour later his secretary announced she was calling again.

"Well?"

"You can tell the President," she said, "but he insists you both be alone."

He thought for a moment, then nodded.

"Maybe it's better that way. After all, in the last analysis that's what it's going to come down to if anything happens—his will against mine. Maybe it's a good idea to take each other's measure, right now."

"He seems to think so," she said. "And I agree. After all, I'm not worried about Orrin Knox's will."

"Neither is Orrin Knox," he said crisply. "See you tomorrow, Dolly. You and 'Vagaries' may go down in the history books yet."

"If we can help straighten out this world," she said, suddenly serious, "I don't care whether we're in the history books or not."

"A worthy sentiment," he said. He chuckled. "Tell me: *are* you a good cook?"

"You may not believe it of Washington's leading hostess," she said, cheerful again, "but I am."

"Good," he said. "I'd hate to get indigestion on top of everything else."

But if indigestion were going to come, he told himself as the station wagon, undistinguished and unnoticed in the rush of noontime traffic as they wanted it to be, approached the Soviet Embassy, it would come from his luncheon partner, not from Dolly's cooking.

Vasily Tashikov looked somber and forbidding as he came quickly out of the iron gates. He glanced neither left nor right, hopped quickly in alongside Orrin, drew himself stiffly back into the corner. Why are they so ostentatiously grim, Orrin thought with an annoyance echoing that of a thousand Western statesmen on a thousand occasions. Why can't they ever act genuinely like human beings? Or did it really matter whether they frowned or smiled? It was all play-acting anyway. The basic attitude and purpose never changed, however many momentary "détentes" came and went in the course of their ruthless imperialism's unrelenting onward drive.

He debated for a moment whether to speak, decided at first against it, his attitude, spurred by annoyance, summed up in the tart reaction: let the bastard make the first move or to hell with him.

Then he thought better of it, for while this might be the way for the new Chairman of the Council of Ministers to act, it was no way for the next President of the United States to act—were he to conduct himself with any kind of responsibility toward his own country and humanity.

He touched the button that raised the window between the chauffeur and the back seat—Dolly's station wagon, like "Vagaries," the Rolls and everything else arising from her very substantial wealth, had all the amenities—and turned in a relaxed and conversational way toward his companion.

"Well, Vasily," he said, "congratulations on your new appointment. It could mean great things for our two countries."

For a moment Tashikov did not reply. Then he shot Orrin a sudden sharp glance from his darkly hooded little eyes and shrugged.

"I would say that depends on you, Mr. President."

"Oh?" Orrin said, annoyance instantly re-established by Vasily's tone. "You don't bear any responsibility, I take it?"

"We are not responsible for the tense condition of the world," Tashikov said, almost indifferently. "We must assume responsibility for trying to straighten it out, however."

"And you can do that best by immediately offending me, is that it?" Orrin asked. He, too, shrugged, and decided suddenly on the only course he felt would impress this small, bullying man who had been Soviet Ambassador in Washington long enough to know better than to try to browbeat Orrin Knox: so why was he trying?

He reached for the button again, rolled down the window.

"Driver," he said calmly, "take me back to the White House, please."

"Yes, sir," the driver said, and automatically began signaling for a turn which would bring him back onto Connecticut Avenue headed downtown.

This, Orrin noted with a satisfaction suddenly grim, brought results. Tashikov leaned forward hastily, an expression of genuine consternation momentarily flaring, as hastily banished, in his eyes.

"This is not necessary!" he said sharply. "Let us proceed, if you please."

"You heard me," Orrin said to the driver.

"No!" said Vasily Tashikov.

"Mr. Secretary," the driver said, beseeching help. "Mr. President—"

"Very well," Orrin said, sitting back, looking with disinterest out the window. "You may proceed."

"Thank you, sir," the driver said in a relieved voice. "I was getting a little confused."

"I think Mr. Tashikov was, too," Orrin remarked. "Carry on."

And again he raised the window, though he continued to stare out with no further attempt to communicate with his companion.

Five silent minutes passed while the station wagon, trailed discreetly by two carefully ordinary sedans, one containing the Secret Service men the President had insisted upon, the other containing four equally sedate, business-suited security guards from the Soviet Embassy, moved on up Connecticut toward Woodley Road.

"Mr. President," Tashikov said stiffly at last, "I do not believe I have congratulated you."

"No," Orrin agreed, not turning his head.

"Then permit me," Tashikov said with a bland little smile which Orrin saw when he became aware of a pressure against his arm and turned to find a hand extended.

"Thank you," he said, returning the pressure with a cordiality exactly matching Tashikov's own, which was not much. "I understand you go home this evening."

"I fly from Dulles at seven," Tashikov said. "There are many things to be decided in Moscow."

"I am surprised you lingered so long."

"Our simultaneous elevations," Tashikov said with a dry little smile, "have provided a fortuitous opportunity. I decided I must not leave without talking to you. It did not seem that I should intrude the very hour after your triumph, for you have obviously been very busy. Nor could I afford to wait very long, either, for matters press upon me, too. This was the latest I could delay. I am glad you have been able to see me."

"I thought it would be of value," Orrin said. He paused and then went on in a deliberate tone. "Providing we can talk sense and not nonsense. Otherwise it will be a useless exercise."

"I would not want our charming hostess to waste her time on a useless exercise," Tashikov said as they turned up Woodley Road and headed for the park. "I shall do everything in my power to make our discussion pertinent."

"I hope so," Orrin said, his tone not yielding much. "Because I shall not have time for anything else."

And to this, though he could not refrain from a scowl, quickly come and quickly banished, his small dark companion attempted no rejoinder until they came within sight of the gleaming white columns of "Vagaries," secret in the trees.

"Well," he said, rather vaguely. "We must see how the time goes. . . ."

For the next half hour or so, it went noncommittally and with a reasonable matter-of-factness on both sides.

Dolly greeted them, her usual charming ease not altogether masking the real excitement generated by her role in this historic occasion; the Secret Service and the Soviet security guards were posted about the grounds with the not altogether humorous suggestion from Tashikov that they be careful and not shoot one another; their hostess took them upstairs to the study, where a small table had been set up; they invited her to join them during the repast; she refused, brought them soup, a casserole from which they could serve themselves, a bottle of wine; bade them farewell, closed the door firmly behind her; and they were alone.

With a certain dogged determination, interrupted only when they asked one another to pass things or offered one another seconds, they plowed through the light but delicious meal, carefully drinking exactly one glass of wine apiece. Then they pushed back their plates, Orrin poured them both another glassful and they sat back and stared at one another for several moments, during which neither spoke, averted his gaze or revealed any particular reaction at all. Then they both spoke at once.

"Mr. Chairman—"

"Mr. President—"

They both laughed without much humor.

"You requested the meeting," Orrin said. "Which," he added quickly, "implies nothing invidious, on your part or mine, it's just the fact. Why don't you begin? You obviously have something on your mind."

"Many things," Tashikov said thoughtfully. "Many things. . . ." He leaned forward suddenly, hunched low over the table. "Mr. President, are you going to continue the foolish United States policy of trying to stem the tide of history which is running inevitably toward the people's revolution everywhere?"

For a split second Orrin almost let his temper take over in response to this tiresome and familiar ploy. Fortunately better judgment prevailed.

"I regard myself," he said calmly, "as about to become the custodian of the oldest genuine people's revolution in history. I would like to think that the tide of history is running our way, yes."

"That is not what I said!" Tashikov snapped, suddenly—although perhaps not genuinely; who ever knew, with them?—angry himself. "I said the *people's* revolution, not the selfish and sinister revolution of capitalism which oppresses the masses and grinds down everything decent in humanity!"

"Suppose we not worry about the masses for the moment," Orrin suggested, "or about capitalism, either. Suppose we talk about naked force and imperial ambition and the points at which your unceasing drive to dominate the world touches upon our vital interests. Those are the things that really matter, between our two countries and between you and me. Isn't that right?"

"Your 'vital interests'!" Tashikov said scornfully. "What are they? A warrant to meddle in Europe, a warrant to meddle in Asia, a warrant to meddle in the Middle East, in Africa, in Latin America, in all the oceans, in all the skies—where does your self-assumed warrant to meddle *not* create 'vital interests' for you, Mr. President? And haven't you had lessons enough in recent years that *you are not wanted* in any of these places? That your 'vital interests' are not vital at all, to anybody but your own greedy capitalist-imperialist society? You have had your lesson with oil, with energy, with the Arabs, the Jews, the Japanese, the Europeans, the Africans, the Latin Americans—where will it end, your eternal meddling? How much longer can you maintain it?"

"We will maintain our determination to resist your imperialism," Orrin said levelly, "whenever and wherever it tries to encroach further upon the right of men and women to decide their own destiny free from dictatorship, military bullying, mind control and secret police. Is that a clear enough answer?"

"Clichés!" Tashikov said in the same scornful tone. "Clichés! What will you do all this noble 'resisting' *with?* You had better study your military defenses, Mr. President, I think. They are not what you apparently imagine."

"I know what they are," Orrin said sharply.

"Not much," Tashikov remarked softly. "Not very much, are they, Mr. President?"

"Do you want to try us, Mr. Chairman?" Orrin inquired with equal softness. "Be my guest."

"Pah!" Tashikov said—and he actually did say "Pah!"—a short disgusted sound that would have been melodramatic had he not been so obviously quivering with anger. "You make idle threats, Mr.

President, idle, foolish and empty threats! You know as well as I do that United States armed forces have been allowed to slide to nothing —*nothing!*—while we have been steadily expanding all over the world. Your Congress and your recent Administrations have deliberately crippled you. We have not understood such insanity but you know we have taken advantage of it, Mr. President. You know we have not been idle. Oh, no! We are everywhere—*everywhere*. You would not dare defy us now."

"We just have," Orrin pointed out coldly. "We had an alert and *you* didn't dare defy *us,* did you?"

"Well—" Tashikov said, openly taken aback for a second but recovering quickly. "Well—that was an error on our part, I will freely admit that. It was an error. We knew you were bluffing and we should have called you. We knew we should. You would have done nothing—*nothing*—because you can do nothing. We knew it. We will not make that mistake again."

"I repeat," Orrin said, trying hard to control his temper and succeeding with a major effort, "try us, Mr. Chairman. Just try us. We have a few things left, you know: enough bombs to destroy you, enough missiles to get them there, enough subs and planes and ships to take you down with us. You would not survive any more than we, were you so stupid as to try it. I hope for your sake, and for ours, and for the world's, that you would not dare to be so monumentally insane and irresponsible."

For a moment it appeared that his antagonist must burst with emotion, so apoplectic did he look; but he mastered it with an obvious effort and spoke in a voice that shook yet held a measured and apparently quite genuine menace.

"I give you fair warning, Mr. President: do not interfere with us. Do not challenge us. Do not attempt to impose your capitalist-imperialist views upon us or upon any of our friends. The result would be dreadful for you. We will not hesitate to punish you ruthlessly. We will not hesitate to use every weapon we have against you. We may give you warning or we may move by surprise before you know it. Either way we will win because we have the power, Mr. President, and your country, by the recent decisions of its own leaders, does not. We have something else, Mr. President, superior to any weapons: *we have the will.* And America does not."

"*I* have the will," Orrin said sharply. His small opponent gave him an angrily sarcastic glance.

"Yes, we concede that. We know in Moscow that *you* have the will. But we also know that almost no one else does. Witness your own campaign, Mr. President. Witness your own victory. America is more divided than ever between the warmongers like yourself and the weaklings who are so in love with the idea of 'peace' that they will give us anything if we but demand it forcefully enough. You have the will, yes, *but how many of your countrymen can you carry with you when the showdown comes,* Mr. President? How many?"

"'*Can*' carry with me? '*When*' the showdown comes?"

Tashikov shrugged.

"We are alone, we are talking facts. That is why I wanted to be alone, to talk facts. You and I know it is 'when,' not 'if.' So be on guard, Mr. President. You will need all your will—because a majority of your countrymen no longer have any to back you up."

He sat back with a sudden triumphant little movement of the body, positive, self-satisfied and smug, staring with bright little eyes as cold as death—whose harbinger they might well be, for Orrin, for both their countries and for the world.

Orrin regarded him for a long moment before he spoke, his face impassive because it had to be: quite literally the most important thing in the world at this moment was that he not show weakness of any kind to Vasily Tashikov. When he spoke it was in a quiet, almost conversational tone.

"You talk insanity, Mr. Chairman. You talk of the murder of the world. You talk of inhumanity beyond inhumanity. You have left the human race and I pity you for it. I pity you for it.

"Nor," he said, and his tone sharpened a little, "am I impressed by it. Never as long as I am in the White House will you force the United States of America to abandon its principles, its policies or its beliefs. If I have to blow up the world I shall do so, to stop you from it. And don't place too much reliance on the fact that others may not agree. *I* shall be President of the United States, and *I* shall do the deciding. Your people tried to kill me once"—Tashikov gave him the sudden black, automatic scowl, but Orrin really was unimpressed and looked it—"they may try again. But if I live and occupy the office to which I have been elected, I will never yield to your blackmail. Never.

"So keep that in mind, Mr. Chairman.

"It is a factor."

And once again across the remains of Dolly's lunch they gave one another grim stare for grim stare, neither flinching, neither averting his eyes, neither, apparently, yielding in the slightest.

The silence was finally broken by Tashikov in a voice so impersonal and devoid of intonation that it seemed almost disembodied.

"We are finished. We had better go."

"I agree," Orrin said. He rose, went to the door, opened it, called Dolly. She appeared at the foot of the stairs, took note of their faces; an expression of alarm, quickly banished, crossed hers.

"It might be best and least conspicuous if you each took your own cars back," she said. "I'll call them."

"Thank you for the lunch," Orrin said.

"It was very good," Tashikov said.

They left.

Behind them she stood in the beautiful doorway of beautiful "Vagaries," hand crushed to mouth, eyes wide with a terrible fear for the world.

"I hope you didn't yield an inch," the President said.

"I did not," Orrin said. "I'm putting my account of the conversation on tape for you. He is very intransigent—very."

"I hope you won't yield an inch in your Inaugural, either."

"I certainly will not."

"Good. But brace yourself. I think they'll stay quiet for the next couple of months, but the minute you're in—watch out. They'll try something."

"I think I'll be ready for them," Orrin said grimly.

"Good," Bill Abbott said again. "Let me know what I can do to help in the meantime."

"Just stand there and keep your finger in the dike," Orrin said with a returning humor.

The President chuckled.

"Trust your Uncle Bill. I ain't about to yield nuthin', neither."

And for the next two months, while Orrin carried on his concluding duties as Secretary of State—met with many visitors—sought and received advice from many people—put together his immediate working staff for the White House, and department by department built up what he considered a very good Cabinet headed by Robert A. Leffingwell as Secretary of State—the President remained true to his word. There were minor skirmishes in both Gorotoland and Panama, but the alert seemed to have temporarily stopped Moscow's tendency to global adventurism. Although he told Orrin he had been seriously considering carrying through with his announced threat to blockade Panama if there was any major attempt by the Soviets to supply Felix Labaiya's forces with additional matériel, the attempt did not materialize and the blockade did not become necessary. An uneasy status quo prevailed over both battlefields. In a public-relations sense this was an awkward and embarrassing situation for the Administration, making it appear over-anxious and bringing many bitter attacks both foreign and domestic. In the practical areas where it counted, it was much preferable to open hostilities.

The only thing more preferable, the President confided with a sigh when they met shortly after the new year to confer on final plans for Inauguration on January 20, would have been peace itself. But despite intensive behind-the-scenes diplomacy in a dozen capitals including their own, no offer that could be trusted to last came from the other side.

"They want to prolong it until you get in and then let you have it," the President warned again.

Again Orrin said, with a calm certainty he did not altogether feel but nonetheless had to show, even to William Abbott: "I'm ready for them."

So the hurrying days moved on to his date with destiny. On the home front the anti-war movement seemed to be in a lull reflecting the lull in the war zones. The economy remained relatively stable, Christmas buying reflected a reasonable market and the customary euphoria of the season. The most noteworthy news item on January 19 was the possibility of snow on Inauguration Day. A major new storm was blowing in out of the West. It appeared likely that Washington would be inches under, and shivering, by the time the official party reached the Capitol at noon the next day.

At 10 P.M. he went to thanksgiving services at St. John's Episcopal Church, across Lafayette Square from the White House. He was accompanied by William Abbott, the old Cabinet, his own Cabinet, Hal, Crystal, Ceil and Valuela; Cullee Hamilton and Sarah Johnson (who would be married at 11 A.M. tomorrow morning in a special ceremony in the Rotunda presided over by the chaplain of the Senate); members of his campaign and White House staffs; Warren Strickland, the Munsons, Lafe Smith and other old friends from the Senate; and such friends from the diplomatic corps as Lord and Lady Maudulayne of Great Britain, Raoul and Celestine Barre of France, Krishna Khaleel of India.

During the services the memory of his wife, kept off in some relatively unhurtful area for weeks by the incessant overwhelming rush of public business, came back like a knife, and for several moments, head bowed, hands desperately clasped together as if sheer physical pressure would help, body shuddering with recurring waves of suppressed sobs, he wept for her. Then the moment passed, a relative peace returned; he was able to stand, looking tired but smiling, at the door to wish them all a calm Godspeed into the night as the services ended.

On the way home he asked to be driven past the Lincoln Memorial, where more than one of his predecessors had repaired in moments of national or personal anguish. Even at that hour, in the wind now growing steadily harder and more cutting off the frozen Potomac, a few tourists were still there. Respectfully they stood back for him and the little group that accompanied him, the inevitable Secret Service, his son, his daughter-in-law, Ceil and Valuela.

Brooding, mysterious, inscrutable, unfathomable, his expression meaning many things to many men, the Emancipator stared down upon him. *Help me,* he thought: *I shall need it.* Impassive, keeping his own secrets, confiding in none, the Emancipator looked over his head into far, unknowable distances.

Hesitantly but warmly the tourists gave him a smattering of friendly applause as he led his party back down the steps.

Even in the short time of their visit the wind had increased, the temperature had dropped.

It was very cold.

Soon there would be snow.

7.

IN THE MORNING, in one of those concerted lemming-like movements toward a common objective which frequently characterize all Right-Thinking members of the media, he was told in editorial, column and telecast, what he should say in his Inaugural Address.

A wondrous blueprint for a marvelous world emerged.

"Now is the moment," the *Times* informed him and the readers it so often led by the hand down the righteous paths they should go, "when Orrin Knox, after falling short of greatness for so many years, may at last achieve it. His Inaugural affords him an opportunity unparalleled in American history.

"Now is the moment for him to lay aside the old, bitter, outworn foreign policies of the past and come forward with a new charter for this nation and for all mankind—a Charter of Peace which will light humanity to happiness and stability for generations to come.

"Now is the moment for him to turn to the nation he and his followers have for so long considered the enemy of America—the Soviet Union—and, trusting in the human decency and fairness of its leaders, as he wishes them to trust in his, say to them:

"'America wants peace. America wants peace with such determination and responsibility that America will do whatever is necessary to achieve it.

"'As a first step, America will withdraw at once from all the hostile, imperialistic, antagonistic military positions which she occupies all around the globe.

"'America will call home her navies, withdraw her armies and air armadas, abandon her incessant spying upon the Soviet Union, give up the fear-ridden, hag-ridden attitude of suspicion which has dominated her foreign policy for so long.

"'America will trust in the sincerity of the Soviet Union's desire for peace, will accept the Soviet Union's good faith, and will build upon it eagerly and willingly as the surest guarantee of peace.

"'America will trust the Soviet Union, for America knows that only in trust between our two countries can real world peace be achieved.'

"Something along these lines, we submit to Orrin Knox, is what he should say to the Soviet Union, to America and to the world today.

"We do not believe, with the small of vision, that this would mean an increase in Soviet intransigence.

"We do not accept, with the myopically fearful, that it would mean any sort of 'surrender' to the Communist ideology.

"We do not agree, with the fainthearted, that it would mean national disaster.

"On the contrary, we believe it would open the door at last to that universal peace for which all nations and all peoples hunger so desperately.

"We hope to hear something like this, today, from our new President."

The *Post,* while less disingenuous in its approach to him, and less sanguine that its hopes would be answered, was equally clear as to what it thought Orrin should do.

"We are doubtful," it said, "that the incoming President of the United States possesses the vision and the statesmanship to do what really needs to be done to cut the Gordian knot entangling U.S.-Soviet relations. But if he did, we think this is what he would do:

"He would declare an end immediately to all the antiquated, outmoded, no longer operative assumptions of fear of the Soviet Union upon which American foreign policy has been built for so many long, sad, futile years.

"He would put his trust in the good faith of the Soviet Union and offer it a gesture of simple decency and good will so monumental and precedent-shattering that the Soviet Union, we believe, would have no decent alternative but to accept.

"Specifically, he would:

"Withdraw American arms from all those places around the protesting earth where American power and imperial arrogance achieve no genuine security for anything, but only create division and hatred.

"Abandon foreign naval bases which keep the Navy where it has no business being, and bring the fleets home where they belong, to serve the only purpose which is rightfully theirs: to defend the United States of America.

"Close the Army and Marine bases which serve only to maintain the fat frauds of the Pentagon in the luxury to which they have persuaded the taxpayers to let them become accustomed. Bring home the troops, reduce their numbers to bedrock, assign them the only task which is rightfully theirs: to protect the United States.

"Shut down the Air Force bases which threaten the world. Ground the high-flying money-gobblers, clip their wings, bring them back to roost at home where they belong, doing the only job that is rightfully theirs: protecting the United States.

"We do not, as we say, expect Orrin Knox to do all, or even a part of, these things. Yet what a glorious day it would be for the world if he did!

"It would not mean, as the doom-sayers would have us believe, an unprincipled and cataclysmic seizing of advantage by the Soviet Union. It would not mean a 'surrender' of the United States to Soviet ambitions and Soviet power.

"It would not mean any of the phony disasters that phony prophets have been forecasting for too many dismal years.

"It would be an act of faith begetting faith, of trust begetting trust.

"It would mean peace.

"We do not think Orrin Knox has the guts or the vision.

"But we would certainly like to see him try."

Frankly Unctuous, looking out from the circle of familiar faces whose owners comprised his network's customary panel of experts on all things domestic, foreign, earth- or universe-shaking, laid it on the line with equal fervor in his customary plum-pudding tones:

"America waits this morning to hear from its new President—waits and hopes.

"Hopes with a desperate hope that Orrin Knox will find in himself the vision and the strength to make of his Inaugural Address a beacon light for all mankind.

"Hopes that the moment will bring him, as it has so many of his predecessors, to a new stage of his life, encompassing a new vision, a new dream:

"The dream of peace.

"How wonderful it would be, America thinks this morning as it awaits his message to us, if he would abandon all those imperial trappings and desperate fears which have for so long made American foreign policy the shame of a trembling world.

"If he would lay down American arms.

"If he would bring home a Navy too far-flung to do anybody any good, let alone America which it is supposed to protect.

"If he would bring home an Army and a Marine Corps too scattered overseas, in places where they have no business, to be of any real value in protecting America if a genuine crunch should come.

"If he would bring home an Air Force whose bases serve only to threaten others, not to protect America.

"If he would trust the Soviet Union, as it is willing to trust us.

"It says it wants peace.

"What a glorious thing if he became the first American President to really believe it, and to act fearlessly in that belief!

"Today America waits and hopes. Will Orrin Knox respond to that waiting, and answer those hopes?"

And finally Walter Dobius, having sat up late at "Salubria" to frame the stern advice which he felt the new President must have if he were to begin his governance aright, his conclusions appearing in his 436 client newspapers across America that fateful morning:

"Orrin Knox faces his greatest test at the Capitol shortly after noon today.

"He will have been sworn in as President.

"He will step forward to deliver his Inaugural Address.

"It is possible for him to go down in history at that moment as one of America's greatest Presidents—perhaps its greatest—or to continue down the same dreary road he has been on so long, of conservatism, reaction, fear, lack of vision, lack of responsibility, lack of the statesmanship that the times, and the cause of peace, demand.

"Two possibilities lie open to him in the speech which will open his Administration and his particular segment of history.

"He can pursue the same old tired, shopworn, exhausted, cliché-ridden, cataclysmically dangerous policies of hatred and suspicion of the Soviet Union that have crippled America and the world so dreadfully in recent years.

"Or he can turn to the Soviet Union, and through it to the Communist world, and with open arms and a confident heart offer the trust and good faith which are the only means of securing trust and good faith in return.

"He can do this, in the judgment of one observer at least, if he will, in this opening statement which will set the theme and mood of his entire Administration, do several fundamental things which have long—too long—cried out to high heaven for doing:

"Abandon the overseas bases of Army, Navy, Air Force and Marines which serve only as a constant irritation in the world—which do not really protect anybody—which are simply the futile gestures of an outmoded dream of 'balance of power' which in the end can only come crashing down in disaster for all humanity.

"Bring the forces home, where they belong, to protect us, not threaten somebody else.

"Make America's defenses truly that—America's defenses. Not the arrogant symbols of an imperial ambition.

"Not the mailed fist of a potential conqueror feared by all the world.

"Not a flaunting of 'American power' or 'American strength' which no longer has any validity in a world moving ever more inexorably toward a true peace among mutually trusting and responsible nations.

"Orrin Knox has it in his power, at this moment in his country's brief and sometimes not entirely noble history, to make a gesture of friendship and faith to the Soviet Union so dramatic and overpowering in its impact that the Soviet Union can only respond in kind.

"If given the opportunity, it *will* respond.

"Let no one be mistaken about that.

"All Americans who truly love their country must hope that God will give Orrin Knox the vision to see his opportunity, and the strength to seize it.

"The benefit to America and to the whole world would be incalculable, and marvelous beyond belief."

So echoed many an editorial writer, commentator, broadcaster, doctor, lawyer, Indian chief, across the land, on this fateful morning of the start of the Presidency of Orrin Knox.

So urged many an editorial writer, commentator, broadcaster, statesman, governmental leader, ordinary citizen, around the globe.

So sang all the hopeful, the idealistic, the yearning, and—in some high and secret places—the calculating and the crafty, at home and overseas.

Alas, as most well knew, their wistfully dreamed and loudly urged vision of a world in which the lion would lie down with the tiger and the angels sing in peace was not to be.

Most of them knew, with a desperate anguish for their fallen hero, that had Edward M. Jason stood on the steps of the Capitol at that moment, he might well have given them what they wanted.

Most of them also knew that to expect such concessions from Orrin Knox was hopeless.

Deliberately informal, almost conversational, calm and flat, his level voice punctured the dream and returned the world to the cold reality of "old, outmoded, cliché-ridden" things.

"My fellow Americans—" he said, and a rustling hush descended upon the sparse crowd that had braved the new-fallen snow and the bright freezing day to come to the Capitol (A scant twenty-five thousand, most observers guessed. "Because nobody really likes Orrin Knox," his enemies said. "Because of the weather," his friends angrily responded), "we meet in a solemn hour for America—as indeed all hours, for America, seem to be solemn now.

"Yet I think we need not despair, for with faith, with diligence, with persistence and with courage, I believe we shall come through as we have always come through before.

"The first thing we must do is clear our minds of naïve dreams, futile wishes and mistaken concepts of where we stand.

"We must take off the blinders and be tough enough to accept, analyze and study the realities that face us.

"Only then can we begin to work our way out.

"We are confronted with two wars in being, and a continuous threat to the peace of the world and our own national existence from the imperial ambitions and imperial conquests of the present rulers of the Russian people."

("There he *goes!*" they wailed in the newsrooms of CBS and NBC, the editorial sanctums of the *Times* and the *Post*. "By *God,* will that reactionary bastard *never* learn!")

"We face a constant drumfire of crippling criticism abroad and would-be crippling subversion at home."

("You *see?*" they cried to one another. "*Jesus!*")

"We have fallen to a dangerously weak and dangerously low level of national defense.

"Too many of us have permitted ourselves to be persuaded by our critics that our history is rotten, our ideals are fraudulent, our purposes are corrupt, our future is hopeless."

("Is there a cliché he's missing?" they demanded of one another. And answered themselves, "Give him time, give him time!")

"Too many of us take counsel of our fears, and not of the basic decencies and basic strengths of this often stumbling but still good-hearted nation.

"How do we handle this rot which eats at us?"

("There he goes!" "It's too perfect—he's unbelievable.")

"How do you expect *me* to handle it?

"This is the time above all times when you have a right to ask a new President that question. It is the time above all times when a new President should answer, as fully, as completely and as candidly as he can.

"First, the wars.

"We are involved in Gorotoland and in Panama for simple reasons which involve the security and the honor—"

("Oh, *no!* Not 'the *honor*'!")

"—of this country and of the non-Communist world.

"In Gorotoland we became caught in the conflicting ambitions of two men, the hereditary ruler, the M'Bulu of Mbuele, and his cousin, Prince Obifumatta, who is attempting to take the country from him. Despite repeated warnings from my predecessors that we would protect our interests—"

("Our interest in oil!" "What else?")

"—American commercial enterprises were attacked, and a group of American missionaries was slaughtered, by the forces of Prince Obifumatta. We decided to give assistance to the M'Bulu, and with our aid, he is presently maintaining his control of the country.

"Prince Obifumatta is receiving heavy assistance from the Soviet Union, and from the People's Republic of China.

"In Panama, similarly aided by the Soviet Union and the People's Republic of China, a revolutionary movement led by the former Ambassador to the United States, Señor Felix Labaiya, is attempting to seize the country and the Canal. We are assisting the legitimate Panamanian government in repulsing this attempt.

"So we have the United States on the one hand, and the Soviet Union and the People's Republic of China on the other, arrayed against one another in two small client states in two widely separated areas of the world. But though the countries are small, the stakes are very high. We know this, and Moscow and Peking know this. And that is why we are where we are.

"Now: how do we terminate these two situations and get out of each with our honor—"

("There he goes again!" "He's got a good cliché going, man. You don't expect him to drop it now?")

"—and with the security of this country and the non-Communist world intact? Because, believe me, my friends, both must be preserved. Gorotoland is the strategic heart of Africa, the crossroads of the continent, which is why the Communist powers are there. Panama's strategic importance to us, and to world commerce, is obvious, I think, to everyone. Neither can be permitted to fall to Communist control.

"At the same time, we do not want, and we do not seek, any permanent controlling involvement ourselves. If we can guarantee Gorotoland's genuine independence, the genuine independence of Panama and the freedom of the Canal to all traffic on an equal basis, then that is all we want.

"How to arrive at these objectives is not so simple. Yet we must try.

"Therefore I am issuing an invitation at this moment to the new Chairman of the Council of Ministers of the Soviet Union, and to the Chairman of the Chinese People's Republic, and such aides and assistants as they may wish to bring with them, to meet me and my advisers in the Palace of the League of Nations in Geneva, Switzerland, at noon one week from today.

"The purpose of our meeting will be to negotiate and settle the twin situations in Gorotoland and Panama.

"As far as I and my advisers are concerned, we are ready to stay in Geneva for as long as necessary to bring these two conflicts to an end which will establish peace and satisfy the legitimate interests of all parties, including the countries directly involved, and the major powers.

"I would hope to have a reply from the Chairman of the Council of Ministers of the Soviet Union, and the Chairman of the People's Republic of China, at the very earliest possible moment—I would hope not later than noon tomorrow.

"I take this action on my own initiative, without prior consultation with anyone, because I believe the search for peace to be my first and overriding duty as your President."

("Well, how about *that?*" they asked one another knowingly at the *Times* and the *Post*—or the *Pimes* and the *Tost,* so mirror-image were they in their attitudes toward him, toward the world and toward anyone who did not agree with their own rigidly intolerant and illiberal views. "Old Orrin is certainly desperate for a gimmick, isn't he?")

"So we come, inevitably, to the matter of this nation's defenses—

because what we do in Geneva, and what we do thereafter, will depend to a great degree on how much strength we can put behind our words. Strength, as history shows, is all the Communists respect. Smiles, blandishments, 'détentes,' agreements, conferences, cozy talks, kindly gestures, 'treaties,' solemn pieces of paper—they all mean nothing.

"Strength is all that matters.

"When we have it, we get reasonable arrangements the world can live with.

"When we don't, we get the back of the hand.

"I do not intend"—and for the first time his voice abandoned its measured cadence, his head came up in a sharply challenging way, he stared straight into the massed cameras—"for the United States in my Administration to take the back of the hand from anybody."

("Twenty minutes after he began speaking," Frankly Unctuous reported with a certain smug satisfaction he could not quite keep out of his voice, "the President has received his first noticeable round of applause.")

"Therefore, I am sending to the Congress this afternoon an emergency supplemental appropriations bill for the Department of Defense in the amount of ten billion dollars. This measure will provide for an immediate expansion of the Army, the Navy, the Air Force, the Marines and the missile and satellite forces of the United States. I shall ask the Congress to give it immediate priority. I hope it can be passed and reach my desk not later than one month from today."

("There he goes, right back to the same old big-stick militaristic policy," they said at the *Pimes* and the *Tost*. "You see, you can trust him: he always blows it." "Damned war-lover!")

"These, my fellow Americans, represent the two basic aspects of the foreign policy of my Administration:

"Frank and candid negotiation, tough but fair-minded bargaining looking toward lasting agreements to reduce tension and bring peace to the world—and the military strength without which that kind of negotiation and agreement is impossible in the modern world.

"Domestically, I hope that my Administration can be equally practical, equally tough-minded, equally firm—and equally fair.

"We have done much in recent years to strengthen ourselves internally. We need to do much more.

"Racial tensions still exist, their causes still abound. We will tackle them firmly and fairly.

"We will do the same in those areas of the economy where labor tensions exist.

"Full medical insurance for all citizens is not yet a reality despite many attempts to achieve it in recent years. We will continue to strive for that goal.

"Energy is still a major problem. We will continue to expand our exploration and development of new energy sources, particularly in the areas outside petrochemicals. We will continue to increase our network of atomic reactors.

"Unemployment remains at a relatively low level, but it is still too much. We will attempt to encourage new businesses and industries to provide more jobs. The gross national product is sagging. We will do our best to bring it up.

"Agriculture will continue to receive the same close attention from my Administration that it has received from others. The price gap between producer and consumer is still too low for the producer, too high for the customer, too close to profiteering for the middleman. We will seek ways to close that gap.

"Inflation continues to plague us—declining somewhat, but still too great for a healthy economy. We will use all the weapons available to government to control it, and bring it down.

"All of these things I pledge to you as our goals in this Administration. I expect personally to give all of them my diligent and continuing personal attention.

"But first we must, if we can, solve the foreign crisis and help the world achieve a viable and lasting peace. And to do that, we need not only an America strong in military defenses but strong in spirit, in hope and in idealism. The climate for that kind of America, my friends, can be set by me—but the achievement of it has to be done by all of us.

"We have here a land which still, for all its troubles of recent years, possesses as much of decency, good will and human goodness as any nation anywhere—more than most, I like to believe, though that may be too prejudiced. But I think not.

"I think that America, with all her faults—and they are many—and with all her strengths—and they too are many—still guards and preserves what remains of human liberty in the world. She does so because it is her historic role, as it was her historic reason for being, in the first place. And she does so because you, a majority of the American people, I believe, still have faith in her and the things for which she stands.

"We Americans are human, and so we are a very complex conglomeration of good, evil, weakness, strength, certainty, uncertainty, carefully considered policy and sudden, unpredictable impulse. We swing like the pendulum sometimes, but always, so far in our history at least, we have come back to middle ground. So I pray it may ever be, for that is our greatest strength: that the storms rise and blow over, and the Republic still stands.

"With your help and your support, we will survive and continue to discharge our duty to ourselves and to all mankind--the duty to preserve, protect, defend and increase freedom in the world. We shall do it with humility but with a conviction that our hearts are good and our purposes sound: with firmness in the right as God gives us to see the right, but always—with firmness.

"Thank you, and God bless you all."

("How's that for waving the flag and drowning in clichés?" they asked one another at the *Tost*. "Of all the crap," they said scornfully at the *Pimes*. "Does he really think he's going to get away with *that?*")

"At the conclusion of his brief speech," Frankly Unctuous reported to his listeners, who were aware of it already, "the President received his second scattering of applause in a routine performance which curiously seemed to stir little interest, and even less enthusiasm, in one of the smallest and least responsive crowds ever to attend an inauguration."

KNOX OFFERS TO MEET IN GENEVA WITH SOVIETS, CHINESE TO NEGOTIATE SETTLEMENT OF GOROTOLAND, PANAMA. INAUGURAL STRESSES MILITARY STRENGTH, RELIANCE ON ARMS TO GAIN "REASONABLE ARRANGEMENTS WORLD CAN LIVE WITH." CONGRESS COOL TO DEMAND FOR NEW BILLIONS FOR ARMED FORCES. ANTI-WAR GROUPS CONDEMN "RETURN TO BIG-STICK DIPLOMACY." SPARSE INAUGURAL CROWD SEEMS UNSTIRRED BY NEW PRESIDENT'S APPEAL TO FAITH IN AMERICA.

Which, he realized as he went through the customary motions of the brief lunch with Congressional leaders, an awkward meal in which everyone carefully avoided the issues he had raised in his speech, was a fairly accurate summation. Neither the audience nor his former colleagues on the Hill had seemed particularly stirred. It would be even more of an uphill battle than he had anticipated.

Yet, he told himself stubbornly while his tightly guarded limousine and its accompanying Secret Service cars fell into line to lead the parade down Capitol Hill, along Pennsylvania Avenue, past scattered but not unfriendly crowds, to the White House and the reviewing stand, this was the way he saw it, and this was how he would proceed. He would not have been faithful to his own beliefs or to his own concept of the country's role in the world if he had attempted to trim, appease or compromise with the many enemies, foreign and domestic, who longed to see America brought down. He would not have been Orrin Knox had he not stated his own view of America, which, balanced between good and bad, came down in the last analysis on the side of the good he still felt to be America's greatest strength.

So if they didn't like it, they could lump it: not exactly, he thought with a wry inward smile, the most effective state of mind for a President of the United States to be in, but one he couldn't avoid sometimes. He knew the practical requirements of getting along with Congress would speedily modify it, if he wished to get anything through that difficult body. And he did want to get his new defense bill through. In fact, it was imperative.

It was also imperative that he get some word as soon as possible from Moscow and Peking. The moment he arrived at the reviewing stand he beckoned to his new Secretary of State, just taking his seat with the Cabinet two rows back. Robert A. Leffingwell worked his way promptly forward to his side.

"Bob," he said in a low voice for his ears alone, as the first band playing "Hail to the Chief" went by, "I want you to go into the Oval Office and open the hot lines to Moscow and Peking. Call me the minute there's a response."

"Yes, Mr. President," Bob Leffingwell said. "Will you pass the word to the Secret Service and Signal Corps so I can get in?"

"It's done," he said, and calling over the chief of the Secret Service, conveyed the instructions.

Then he turned back to the parade, smiled and waved, and began the vigil which was to last, as it turned out, until almost midnight.

"Not only was it a flat, lifeless, disappointing speech," they wrote sternly at the *Tost* for the editorial that would appear in tomorrow morning's edition, "but it carried one extremely ominous note. Our bellicose new President is not only going to 'preserve, protect and defend' freedom everywhere—*everywhere,* mind you—but he is going to 'increase' it. And how does he intend to do that, pray tell, unless he means to launch us on a new imperial conquest of all those many areas of the world where independent-minded peoples beg to differ from his particular narrow concept of what 'freedom' is?"

"There are many things we deplore about the Inaugural Address," they wrote with equal severity at the *Pimes,* "but one thing above all others stands out: the apparent determination of President Knox to return to a concept of armed diplomacy which the failures of two decades have proved to be a ghastly mistake. How can he possibly reach agreement with the Soviet Union and China in this fashion? How can he possibly answer those great nations' sincere desire for peace, and the sincere desire for peace of all the Communist world, by such a belligerent stance? He calls on the one hand for a meeting in Geneva, and on the other for an enormous new shotgun to take along with him in his hip pocket. And the Communists are to believe he comes in peace? We would not consider it likely that they will fall for any such transparent two-faced ploy. Indeed, for the sake of the world's peace, we sincerely hope they will not."

"President Knox's call for a return to ancient American virtues," Frankly Unctuous said in his plummy tones, staring earnestly into the camera, mustache twitching, chipmunk cheeks pursed in disapproval, "might be moving if it were not so outdated—and if it did not contrast so glaringly with his appeal to arms as a guarantee of peace. He apparently sees himself as some sort of world savior, bent upon forcing his concept of freedom upon the entire world. It is the sort of paranoia that in other lands has led to dictatorship, destruction, the death of millions and the death of peace. We sincerely hope Congress will reject his appeal for more military funding—as we hope the Soviets and Chinese will reject his arrogant insistence that they come to Geneva. That is not the way to achieve the peace that we, and all mankind, so desperately desire."

"And so what is one to make of Orrin Knox?" Walter Dobius wrote rapidly in the study at "Salubria," quiet in the hush of the soft Virginia countryside. "Peace in the one hand, arms in the other: was there ever a new Administration that began with more dangerous incongruity for the world? Couple it with an appeal to American 'virtue,' tell the rest of the world how pure, how noble, how ineffably 'good' Americans are, and you have the basis for a completely disastrous course in foreign affairs. Washington hopes desperately tonight that the Congress will have the sense to reject out of hand this bare-faced appeal to an antiquated militarism whose bankruptcy has been demonstrated over and over again in recent years. Washington also hopes that the Soviets and the Chinese will treat his high-handed demand that they meet him in Geneva with exactly the contempt it deserves. Only then, one suspects—after the dash of cold water which he obviously needs—can his fearful countrymen dare to hope that President Knox will settle down and give them the kind of leadership they so earnestly seek and so desperately deserve."

It was not until approximately 11:45 P.M., however, that Walter and his friends of Supermedia were to have their prayers answered. Up to that time, events had moved in the old, traditional pattern: the parade had ended (without a murmur from the hot lines), the First Family and the Cabinet had retired, with Ceil Jason and Valuela Randall, who had been invited by the President to spend the night at the White House, for a private dinner.

Dinner completed, they had emerged to re-enter their closely guarded limousines and depart for the four inaugural balls that were being held that night at the Kennedy Center, the Museum of History and Technology at 14th Street and Constitution Avenue, the Washington Hilton and the Sheraton Park Hotel.

At each of these the new Chief Executive had been greeted by the bedrock faithful, sufficient of whom had turned out to make of the gatherings a scene of reasonable encouragement, excitement and gaiety.

Many who attended had found the President's speech disturbing—not so much because of the basic thesis, with which many of them agreed, but because of the general somber and challenging tone. Although he had carefully avoided putting it on that basis, it had been a little too close to "blood, sweat and tears." Americans as a people did not like to be called to sacrifice, or even to consider the possibility of being called to sacrifice. They had had it so good for so long that they did not want to face the possibility that it might not be so good from now on.

Much as many of them admired Orrin Knox, he had made them uneasy with his stern call for strength as the imperative foundation for peace. They would much rather have had it the easy way, for such had been their conditioning under several Presidents in the recent past. His partisans at the inaugural balls greeted him with a flattering excitement and a genuine warmth because they had always liked and respected him. Their cordiality did not necessarily mean that they would follow him with equal enthusiasm into the future, any more than would Walter and his friends—if it was to be so harsh and demanding a future as he apparently foresaw.

Nonetheless, he was greeted with an encouraging friendliness which he needed; and when he came back to the Museum shortly after eleven-thirty to make the customary brief farewell remarks before returning to the White House and a well-earned rest, a last cordial burst of shouts and cheering accompanied him to the stage.

There he stood for a moment looking out upon them in his characteristic moment of silent appraisal; and then in a relaxed and conversational tone he began to speak.

"My friends," he said, "thank you for a long and most enjoyable evening. You have made me, my family and our friends, feel most welcome. We will always remember the cordial atmosphere of this night.

"Now we must all go home and rest up for tomorrow. I don't know about you"—he smiled and friendly laughter responded—"but for me, it promises to be a busy day.

"I end this inaugural day as I began it: with faith in America—if America is strong; with confidence in the future—if we meet it bravely, firmly and unafraid; with an appeal to the Congress to give us the means to be both strong and brave; and with an appeal to the Soviet Union and the People's Republic of China to meet with me in Geneva to negotiate the basis for a genuine and lasting peace, in the two war zones, and everywhere.

"So far, I must confess"—his tone turned grave, they stirred uneasily, they did not really want to hear it, they wanted to go home drunk and happy, with the difficult world far away—"I have not received any response from them to my appeal. So far they have not given any indication—" He paused abruptly, looked sharply across the mass of jammed-in humanity to the farther door, noted a disturbance there, perceived his Secretary of State pushing forward toward him through the crowd with a determination both obvious and grim. "Or have they?"

Instantly jovial murmurings died, happy smiles faded, drunkenness turned rapidly sober, tension rose. Fear, as palpable as though he could reach out and touch it, was suddenly everywhere.

"Make way for the Secretary of State!" he directed sharply. "Let him through, please."

Probably in seconds, though to everyone in the room, everyone who was watching anywhere, it seemed many endless minutes, Robert A. Leffingwell was at his side, a Signal Corps message was spread before him on the lectern.

He skimmed it rapidly. His face turned stern, he made no attempt to disguise his feelings. That they were angry and not dismayed was probably all that prevented the outbreak of a racing panic in the room and in the country.

His head came up sharply, he spoke in a perfectly level and unemotional voice.

"Please be calm. I must tell you that the Soviet Union and the People's Republic of China have rejected my appeal. They have, in fact, launched massive new offensives in Gorotoland and Panama. American forces have already suffered heavy casualties and are being pushed back. I must return at once to the White House.

"Be of good faith and good courage. Your President is determined to handle this, and will do so.

"God bless you, and good night."

So ended the inaugural day of Orrin Knox, in a wild confusion of frightened people, hurrying autos, a city of celebration celebrating no longer, a nation stunned and desperately anxious to find, somehow, safe haven from history's savage winds.

His anger and determination grew steadily as they rushed him back through suddenly deserted streets to what now was home: the beautiful building, white and ghostly in the snow-laden mists of the icy night, mysterious, shimmering, ominous, remote.

When he got out of the limousine and hurried up the steps of the South Portico, his path flanked by solemn, frightened young Marines at rigid attention, he realized that the temperature was dropping again.

Cold blew the wind off the Potomac, and cold blew the wind in the corridors of the world.

If he had ever had any illusions that his Presidency would be an easy one, this took care of them.

Neither for him nor for his country would the Presidency of Orrin Knox be easy.

BOOK TWO

1. "BILL," HE SAID CRISPLY, "can you get Bob Munson and Warren and get down here as fast as possible?"

"We'll be there in half an hour," William Abbott said from the bachelor apartment at the Sheraton Park to which he had just returned after vacating the White House. It was not, in historical perspective, a humorous moment, but he could not resist a smile. "You mean you want *us* to tell *you* what to do? That doesn't sound like Our Orrin."

"Your Orrin knows what to do," the President said, "and he's already starting to get it done. I want your support, however, and a public statement thereof. And the sooner, the better."

"Yes, sir," Bill Abbott said gravely. "We are at your service."

And within half an hour they were all there, the people upon whom he would rely, now and in the hectic weeks to come: the ex-President; Senator Munson, Senator Strickland; the Vice President, the Secretary of State; Blair Hannah, former national committeeman from Illinois, whom he was appointing Secretary of Defense; Ceil Jason; Lafe Smith; his son.

He was not in the Oval Office when they were ushered in shortly before 1 A.M., but within five minutes he entered swiftly through a side door. They stood and turned toward him with that hushed, expectant, demanding yet beseeching look with which Presidents are greeted on desperate occasions.

"Please be seated," he said quietly. "Thank you for coming." A quick humor, quickly dying, touched his face. "You might know my time in this house would begin with a bang. Nothing dull and routine for good old Orrin." His expression sobered, he spoke gravely and without embellishment.

"I have just been down in the Situation Room. As Bob Leffingwell and Blair Hannah already know, I have taken the actions which seemed to me to be called for in this instance. I could have waited for advice, but of course I have been aware for some weeks of the possibility that something like this might occur the minute I got in here. So I have been mentally ready for it—although actually, I suppose, one never is really ready for anything of the enormity of this.

"I too have ordered a worldwide alert. More to the point, I have ordered an immediate counteroffensive in both Gorotoland and Panama. Additional planes, troops, antiaircraft missiles, ammunition, supporting matériel are already on their way. I have ordered a blockade of Panama. I have again opened the hot lines to Moscow and Peking and I have made clear that I desire to hear from them immediately. I expect that when I do"—he smiled with a certain grimness—"their comments will not be jovial. But at least now they understand that I do want to communicate." He paused and looked slowly around the room at their tense and worried faces.

"I trust what I have done meets with your approval."

His predecessor hesitated for a second, then nodded.

"It meets with mine," William Abbott said. "I couldn't agree more."

"Nor I," said Warren Strickland. "It is risky. But it has to be done."

"I believe so," the President said. "I am also opening a diplomatic counteroffensive, whose chances are rather less, I imagine, than the chances of the action in the field, but it is a necessary concomitant.

"I am instructing our delegation to the United Nations to introduce a resolution in the Security Council tomorrow morning—this morning—condemning the Soviet and Chinese aggressions and demanding their immediate withdrawal.

"This will of course get nowhere at the hands of our enlightened friends from Africa, Asia, Europe, South America, the Middle East and all other points of the fair-minded unhypocritical globe, but it must be done for the record. It will be a difficult and harsh debate, a tense and exhausting initiation for our new Ambassador to the U.N. If you are willing, Lafe, I would like you to continue on the delegation, at least for the time being, to give her such assistance as she may require."

There was a stirring, a sudden comprehension, pleased and congratulatory glances.

"She?" Cullee inquired with a smile. The President nodded and smiled at Ceil.

"She."

"Mr. President—" she protested. He raised an admonitory hand.

"Now, none of that. No false modesty, no telling us how unequipped you are, no begging off from your public duty. I need you, the country needs you, the members of the media need you, the photographers of the world need you—it's absolutely inevitable. I think it will be rather nice for the United States to have the most glamorous ambassador in the world. We need all the image we can get. Right?"

"Mr. President—" she said again, and shook her head. Then she capitulated with a charming smile, suddenly pleased and excited. "Right."

"Good," he said. "You will be a member of the Cabinet, also. . . . Well, then: what I would like right now is a public statement of support, if I may have it, particularly from you, Bill, from Bob and from Warren. I would hope this would help to swing Congress behind me, as much as possible."

"It won't be easy," William Abbott murmured. The President gave him a challenging look.

"Whoever said it would be? But I need, and I want, just as much backing up there as I can get. And who is in a better position to get it for me?"

Bob Munson hesitated for a moment, then decided to speak candidly, for this was no time for anything else.

"You know the situation up there—or maybe you don't, having been so busy getting ready in the last few days. But it isn't all that good, Orrin. It's tight—very tight. The election left us very little room in which to maneuver. You have nominal control, but that's about all. I'm going to have a hell of a fight holding people on my side of the aisle, let alone the whole Senate. Isn't that right, Warren?"

The Minority Leader nodded, his face grave.

"It is, as Bob says, Mr. President, very tight. We've got a breed of new mavericks in there, many of them young, many of them stampeded to lesser or greater degree by the peace crowd—some of them *very* stampeded. Bob's riding herd on an unruly bunch now, and so am I. Whether we can hold them in line is chancy at best." He paused and then added quietly, "Whether we can even retain our leaderships is chancy at best."

"I didn't know it was that bad," the President remarked in a startled tone. His predecessor sighed.

"Not so good on my side, either, Orrin—Mr. President," he said. "The House is in a restless, ugly mood right now. We haven't organized yet, as you know, because I couldn't make a run for Speaker again until I left this place. So we've been poking along for the last few days with Jawbone Swarthman holding the reins, temporarily." He smiled rather grimly. "May not be so temporary, from what I've been hearing in the last twenty-four hours."

"No!" the President said. He stared out the window, a thousand calculations tracing their disturbing patterns on his face. Almost as if to himself he remarked finally, "I can't have Jawbone in there."

"You may have him," Bill Abbott said, "though I'm going to do my best to stop him. But we're on thin ice in this new Congress, Orrin—thin ice."

"And *your* competition?" the President asked Bob Munson. The Majority Leader gave him an oblique glance.

"Who knows?" he inquired with some bitterness as he thought about the cantankerous senior Senator from Arkansas. "Arly Richardson, maybe. The old bastard has always wanted it; he'd give the young fellows a familiar name to rally behind—and he's solid on the war issue, as they see it. Not," he said, quoting the *Post*, "'an Administration lackey,' like me."

"Arly's a damned troublemaker," the President said with heartfelt distaste. He sighed. "And an effective one, unfortunately. Warren, don't tell me *you're* going to be replaced, too."

"No, probably not," Senator Strickland said with a smile. "After all, I'm an almost-President, you know, I led the boys to battle and almost licked you, Orrin. I'd be hard to dump, so soon after election. But," he said, more seriously, "I've got problems, too. This war thing cuts all ways from Sunday, in both parties. I think Bob and Bill will survive, but it's going to be very close."

"Well, then," the President said, instantly practical and impersonal, "maybe I shouldn't embarrass you all by asking your endorsement on what I'm doing in this new crisis. Maybe it should be every man for himself and devil take me if I can't make it on my own." He gave them a shrewd glance. "How about that?"

"Oh, no," Bob Munson said, and "Oh, no," said William Abbott—not quite quickly enough, in the President's estimation.

"Now, see here," he said with the sternness of long-time political and personal friendship. "I don't want any nobility here. I want you two leading that Congress. If it will help you to get re-elected if you disassociate yourself from me on this, I want you to do it. We can worry about regrouping later, after you've won. Don't let it get in the way now, O.K.? I can take the flak alone if I have to. I have before."

For a long moment the ex-President and the Majority Leader exchanged glances, their expressions quizzical, skeptical, informed, sophisticated: balancing all factors, appraising all possibilities, matching Presidential needs, national needs, their own needs. Finally William Abbott broke it with a smile and a shrug.

"Might as well hang together, or we'll all hang separately. Probably will, anyway. No, Orrin—very kind of you, very generous, very thoughtful—but, no. The country really does need a united front right now, so as long as we can hang on, I expect you will have Bob and me. Isn't that right, Bob?"

"Indubitably," Senator Munson said cheerfully. "Let the zombies howl."

"The only thing, Orrin," William Abbott added gently, and something in his tone made them all glance at him with a sudden attention, "is—have you really thought this through? Is this *really* what you want to do?"

"My father doesn't do things unless he wants to do them," Hal said with a sharp defensiveness that brought a momentary smile to the President's lips.

"True enough," Bill Abbott agreed. "I'm just asking if he really does want to do this." He stared thoughtfully at his successor, sitting straight and unyielding behind the enormous desk.

"It's what you did a month ago," the President pointed out with a characteristic tartness. "Greater in degree, but essentially the same thing: confronting them—holding the line—saying: stop *now*, this is it, you asked for it, here it is. . . . Isn't that right?"

"Yes, that's right," William Abbott said, "but I didn't have to go so far. I went part way and stopped."

"A month ago that was sufficient," the President said. "Now we are actually under attack, they've started moving, I had no choice. . . . At least," he added, and an honestly puzzled frown crossed his face, "I *feel* I had no choice. Don't you agree, gentlemen?"

And he turned to the Secretary of State and the Secretary of Defense, heretofore sitting silent and attentive in the semicircle facing the desk.

"The only other option would have been to admit defeat and surrender under fire," Robert A. Leffingwell said. He glanced respectfully but firmly at the ex-President sitting at his left. "Or so it seems to me, Mr. President."

"All right," William Abbott said. "And you, Mr. Secretary of Defense?"

Blair Hannah studied the question throughtfully for a moment, his thin, rather florid face solemn under its crown of silver hair. But his response was equally firm when it came.

"I think so. After all, Mr. President, we *have* been attacked, you know."

"All right," William Abbott said again. "Now," he said, leaning forward, looking intently at his successor, "I assume you know what you have on hand to do it with, Mr. President. I assume the Secretaries know."

"Not very much," the President agreed bleakly. "But that didn't stop you, and I can't let it stop me. We both had to respond."

"In the hope," Bill Abbott said softly, "that a firm and prompt response would bring them to a halt before they realized how weak we really are."

"Yes," Orrin Knox said quietly. "That is the hope. Tashikov told me that they knew, that they would never be bluffed again. Now we shall find out."

"But, Orrin—Mr. President," Lafe Smith protested, "surely we are not as badly off as *that*? . . ." His voice trailed away uncertainly into a silence broken by a harsh snort from the Secretary of Defense.

"Are we not?" Blair Hannah inquired. "Oh, are we not? What do you think you boys on the Hill have been doing in these recent years, cutting our budgets to ribbons, knocking back defense everywhere, reducing our forces and our arms in every sector? You've had a fine time with it, playing the turn-tail-and-make-the-critics-happy game. A fine time!"

"I haven't!" Lafe said sharply, and at his side the Vice President leaned forward, too.

"And *I* haven't," Cullee Hamilton echoed with an equal sharpness. "And Orrin—the President—hasn't. Or President Abbott. Or Senator Strickland. God knows we all have fought and fought and fought to retain an adequate defense. You're a little too generous in passing out the blame, Mr. Secretary."

"Well," Blair Hannah said, more moderately, "of course I didn't mean to be quite so general in my condemnation. I know there has been a constant group constantly fighting, and I know you all belong to it. I apologize for getting too dramatic about it. But, my God!" He paused and took a deep breath. "Do you have any conception of how weak we have really become over the past few years? It's been an absolutely shattering revelation to me since I've begun to find out about this new job, I can tell you. Apparently we've been sleepwalking straight into disaster. And now," he concluded in a voice remote and nearly bereft of hope, "this may be it."

"But you don't really think so," Ceil Jason said quietly, "or you would not have concurred with the President. Nor would any of us concur with him. Isn't that correct?"

Blair Hannah gave her a long look and finally shrugged.

"We have a *fait accompli*, Madam Ambassador," he said. "Of course we support our President."

"If you don't *really* support him," Hal Knox said angrily, "maybe you'd better get out of the Cabinet, Mr. Secretary!"

But at this his father, who had been silently studying them all, intervened with a calm parental firmness.

"Hal, you will be quiet, please. I understand the Secretary's feelings. I understand everybody's feelings. We're in a very tough situation. I'm taking a very great gamble—the gamble that before they really realize how weak we are, the tide will have turned and we'll be on top again. The gamble that this moment will come before we begin to run out of arms, supplies, matériel, ships, planes, guns, tanks, missiles . . . men."

"And how long do we have to prove out the gamble, Mr. President?" Cullee Hamilton asked quietly. The President gave him a long and troubled stare.

"Not long enough," he said at last. "But it seems to me it must be done."

"Very well," William Abbott said quietly. "As long as you have really thought it through, Mr. President; as long as this is *really* what you want to do. Not an impulse, not a flare of temper, not—if you will forgive me—what is known in some influential circles as a 'typical Orrin Knox off-the-cuff reaction.' But a cold sober judgment."

The President gave him too a long, troubled look, and then spoke with a finality that closed the subject.

"We're in a corner, Bill. They've finally made that mistake, the one that we've all tried to avoid for so long. And now there's no way to go but straight out."

"Right," Bill Abbott said crisply, and turned to the rest.

"Well, gentlemen—Madam Ambassador and gentlemen—I'd say that about does it. Let's get started on that statement. Mr. Secretary"—he turned to Bob Leffingwell, tense and worried but determined, as they all were now—"why don't you transcribe for us? Mr. President, what do you want us to say?"

"I think," he said, feeling as though he were very high on some mountaintop, breathing very thin air, not at all sure he would make it safely down but committed beyond recall, "that you might say—"

TOP CONGRESSIONAL LEADERS BACK KNOX WAR MOVES. ABBOTT, MUNSON, STRICKLAND PLEDGE ALL-OUT SUPPORT IN "CRISIS FORCED UPON US BY COMMUNIST AGGRESSION." MANY ON HILL EXPRESS MISGIVINGS ABOUT ACTION. BATTLE OVER LEADERSHIPS LOOMS IN BOTH HOUSES. . . . PRESIDENT NAMES MRS. JASON TO U.N. POST, ORDERS U.S. RESOLUTION CONDEMNING RED DRIVE INTRODUCED IN SECURITY COUNCIL. . . . U.S. COUNTER-OFFENSIVES IN AFRICA AND PANAMA MAKE LITTLE HEADWAY IN FIRST DAY'S FIGHTING. ALLIES HARSH ON PANAMA BLOCKADE. . . . ANTI-WAR GROUPS MUSTER FOR MAMMOTH DEMONSTRATION AT CAPITOL. FIRST POLLS SHOW MANY "APPALLED" BY BELLIGERENT RESPONSE OF NEW PRESIDENT.

"We are appalled," the *Times* said sternly, "by the belligerent response of our new President to the Sino-Soviet drive to restore some semblance of stability and democratic government in both Gorotoland and Panama.

"We would suggest that he is reacting hysterically, and perhaps fatally, to a dangerous but perfectly understandable reaction on their part to inexcusable United States meddling in the internal affairs of these two troubled lands.

"Orrin Knox has been in office twenty-four hours and already he is deepening our commitment to overseas war. He is also flirting, as such moves nowadays always flirt, with the dreadful possibility of atomic retaliation. And for what? A little country far away, in the heart of Africa, whose affairs are no concern of ours, whose people, desperately anxious for democracy, have a right to our support, not our obstruction. And a country, admittedly nearer at hand, whose people also yearn for democracy and for control of the Canal which, in justice and in right, belongs to them to do with as they see fit. . . ."

"Perhaps the most comforting thing about Orrin Knox," the *Post* remarked with a savage jocularity, "is his utter predictability. Twenty-four hours—twenty-four hours? Scarcely twenty-four minutes!—and up he comes with a typical Orrin Knox off-the-cuff reaction. And in this instance, a typical off-the-cuff reaction that could very well blow the world to hell in a hand basket before another twenty-four hours.

"We do not condone the violence of the Sino-Soviet response to endless American meddling in the internal affairs of Panama and Gorotoland, but we can see why they felt they must act. The response of Orrin Knox to their response indicates why they felt they must move quickly and decisively before he could thoroughly muster U.S. power for further meddling. Had they waited any longer he might have been able to mount a real counteroffensive instead of the apparently doomed gesture now under way. And then the fat would really have been in the fire.

"He has appointed Mrs. Ceil Jason to the U.N., and today a U.S. resolution condemning Russia and China will be introduced by her in the Security Council. This will of course bring a counterresolution from the other side condemning American action. This in turn will be followed, we predict, by a speedy denunciation of U.S. interventionism. And then, if our brave new President has the ounce of sense we still like to hope he has, he will take the face-saving opportunity offered and speedily withdraw from his belligerence and let the peoples of the world decide their own destinies without his imperial supervision."

Walter Dobius, more concerned with long-range implications, as he always prided himself he was, laid it on the line to his readers from "Salubria."

"Orrin Knox has thrown down the gauntlet, much more rapidly and dangerously than anyone would have believed, to all who believe in peace and the sane resolution of the conflicts of men. Now if world peace is to be preserved the severest correctives must be applied—by the Soviets and the Chinese on the field of battle and in the United Nations, and by his own people in the Congress of the United States.

"Most observers here in the capital, stunned by this new display of the famed Knox belligerence, have no doubt but that the decision of battle will go against it. Most hope the decision will be rendered with merciful speed before too many more American boys are sacrificed on the bloody ancient altar of balance-of-power diplomacy. Any more, of course, is 'too many more.' Unfortunately some are already lost. We must pray that events will place an immediate limit on further tragically useless deaths.

"There is, however, an aspect more long-range and more fundamental for the future, and that must be decided this week in the Congress. No doubt motivated by reasons of long-time political loyalty rather than good judgment, the ex-President of the United States, who was before, and who aspires to be again, the Speaker of the House; the Majority Leader of the United States Senate; and the Minority Leader of the United States Senate have joined the President in his dangerous gamble. They have pledged him the full support of Congress.

"It is a support, the facts suggest, which they no longer control and can no longer deliver. And a prediction may be ventured that this will be made speedily apparent when all three of these gentlemen seek re-election today to their leadership posts.

"They will be judged by their peers on the issue they have chosen to stand on—all-out support for the President.

"It seems highly likely at this writing that they will be roundly defeated for it."

And Frankly Unctuous, speaking from the Senate Radio-TV Gallery in a pre-session telecast, tied it all together in one of those smoothly rolling packages for which he received one hundred thousand smackers a year.

"Belligerence on the battlefield—and probable defeat there, in the United Nations and in the Congress. These are the prospects that await the brand-new Presidency of Orrin Knox.

"So, tragically, begins his opportunity to change his old warlike image, seize the torch passed on to him by the fallen Edward M. Jason and emerge as the world's hope for peace.

"It is a sad and discouraging commentary on the arrogance of one man.

"No one in Washington, or anywhere else as far as we can discover, condones the perhaps overly harsh Sino-Soviet decision to punish American intervention in Panama and Gorotoland with a swift and decisive move to aid the freedom-loving elements in those two disturbed countries. But by the same token, no one—save a little handful of political faithfuls who may be facing consignment to history's dustbin—approves of the violently overreactive response of our new President.

"Orrin Knox could have gone to the United Nations and asked for its support in this new crisis. Given past American intransigence in the face of U.N. demands for withdrawal from Gorotoland and Panama, this might not have been forthcoming. But at least it would have been the peaceable, the constructive, the responsible method of approach. And it is possible that he might have won a signal victory there and emerged, greatly strengthened, to commence really genuine peace negotiations with Moscow and Peking.

"Now this, in all probability, will never be.

"In Congress, had he not forced ex-President Abbott and Senator Munson to go along with his war policy, he might well have secured their re-election to the leadership posts in House and Senate. Thus he would have assured himself a firm legislative foundation for a reasonable program.

"Now, tied to his falling banner and his failing cause, they will very likely be defeated for the leaderships. Thus he will face heavy problems in dealing with new and less obliging lieutenants on the Hill.

"Washington is talking already of what is being called 'the tragedy of Orrin Knox.' Its theme is false pride. Its fatal flaw is arrogance. Its impact upon all our lives may well make it the tragedy of America."

And in similar language spoke once more all those vocal, vitriolic and well-publicized citizens for whom Supermedia provided the forum and set the pace: so yapped the pack from all its many burrows across the land.

"My God," Lafe Smith said to a silent Ceil as, closely guarded by the Secret Service, they entered the doors of the Secretariat of the United Nations in New York through solid walls of jeering demonstrators shortly before noon, "is there no perspective left anywhere in this crazy land?"

And "My God," Bob Munson remarked to Warren Strickland as they prepared to go in and meet the press on the floor of the Senate just prior to the opening bell, "doesn't *anyone* try to be fair to anyone any more?"

Knowing the answers as they did, all were somewhat prepared for, though unable to reconcile themselves to, the events of that tense, unhappy day.

2. AT THE ENTRANCE of the Delegates' Lounge they met as they had so often met before: the ambassadors of Great Britain, France and India and the leaders of the delegation of the United States. This time, as always, voices hesitated in the crowded chamber, eyes swiveled, thoughts were distracted as attention focused feverishly on the little group that stood, its members somewhat awkward, embarrassed and hesitant with one another, just inside the door of the enormous many-windowed room.

For a moment they eyed one another somewhat warily. Then Lord Claude Maudulayne stepped forward cordially and held out his hand to Ceil.

"Madam Ambassador, may I congratulate you most sincerely upon your appointment. You add a note of grace and beauty desperately needed in these drab and difficult corridors."

"Oh, my, yes!" Krishna Khaleel exclaimed fervently. "You are much the most beautiful thing that has ever happened to the United Nations, Mrs. Jason. *Much* the most beautiful!"

"And possibly," Raoul Barre said dryly, "the most intelligent. Lafe, we are delighted to have you with us again."

"Yes, *indeed,*" Krishna Khaleel agreed. "Even on so"—he paused delicately—"so difficult an occasion."

"Which you will no doubt make even more difficult, K.K.," Lafe said. "How about finding a chair for the most beautiful ambassador in the world?"

"We usually have good luck by the window," Claude Maudulayne suggested, offering Ceil his arm, which she accepted with a smile. And now chatting and joking in their old, relaxed way despite the uneasy tensions that underlay their persiflage, they moved across the room through many smiling faces and warmly extended hands which Ceil took with a series of dazzling smiles that obviously overwhelmed their intently observing audience.

When they were seated with their coffee at a table looking north upon the bleak frozen river and the bleak winter city, she tossed her long blonde hair back from her face and looked at Lord Maudulayne with an ironic expression.

"I would like to be able to accept the congratulations, except that for the moment I'm here under somewhat shaky pretenses. I haven't been confirmed yet, you know."

"But surely," the British Ambassador said, turning to Lafe, "there's no doubt—?"

"No," Lafe said, looking annoyed. "Just a nasty debate from a few hotheads, probably, leaving a bad taste in everybody's mouth and casting a sour shadow on her first day here. It's too bad."

"Of course," K.K. suggested in a wistful tone, "if things were not so—so *unhappy* right now, there would be no need for a nasty debate, would there? And of course if dear Orrin had not been so—so *precipitate* . . ." His voice trailed away, still wistful. Lafe took him up on it sharply.

"Now, see here, K.K.: spare me more of this pious stuff from India. The issue is massive new aggression by the Soviet Union and China which Orrin felt he had to stop. I agree with him and so does Mrs. Jason."

"But not, I think," Raoul Barre observed gently, "a majority of the United Nations. Have you seen the Soviet resolution?"

"We just got in," Lafe said. "Have you seen ours?"

"No," the French Ambassador admitted, "but I doubt if it has much of a chance."

"There is, of course," Claude Maudulayne said, "the matter of the blockade. If it were not for that, possibly—"

"No 'possibly,'" Lafe said, "no way. We're licked on this already, Claude, we always have been, as long as the world is upside down as it is. But we have to keep trying to reassert a little perspective into the historical record, even if it means another lengthy review of exactly why we are in Gorotoland and Panama, and exactly why the Russians and the Chinese are attempting to drive us out."

"There's no time for that," Raoul Barre remarked. "The mood is too ugly and the impatience with the United States too great. It *is* regrettable, Mrs. Jason, that you must face such hostility as you are going to face on your first day here. But as Ambassador Khaleel says, the misfortune arises from your own President."

"How can you say that?" she asked quietly, studying him carefully with her beautiful dark eyes. "He acted in response to aggression, he didn't start it."

"But initially—" Raoul Barre began. She leaned forward.

"No, not 'initially,' Mr. Ambassador. You know what happened initially. Why try to pretend it was not so?"

"Madam Ambassador—" he began.

"*Mr.* Ambassador," she said. "You tell me why you pretend it was not so."

"Oh," he said with a sudden impatience, "we know about the attacks on your missionaries in Gorotoland, the interference with your attempts to find oil and gain a monopoly on it. We know you are afraid of another possible Communist take-over on your doorstep in Panama, of possible Communist control of the Canal. We know all about those things. They do not matter here."

"The truth has to matter somewhere," she said.

"Not here," Lafe agreed dourly. "Not here. And the issue wasn't oil, as you very well know, Raoul. It was murder of defenseless people. And it isn't because we want to benefit ourselves alone that we want to internationalize the Canal and keep it out of Communist hands. Sure, we have an interest in our own security—I should hope—but many more things enter into it." He shook his head and shrugged in sudden disgust. "But you know all that. You *know* all that. And you're right: it doesn't matter here."

"Then where does it?" Ceil asked quietly. "Where will it, ever?"

"If the Communists succeed in taking the world," Lafe said glumly, "it never will anywhere. All opposing historical records will be destroyed, all opposing books will be burned, a new history will be written. I can see it now—*The New History*, subtitled *The Death of the Mind*."

"If, then, as you imply," Raoul Barre said with some asperity, "it is so vital for the views of the United States to prevail if freedom is to be saved, why does the United States so constantly put itself in a position to be so effectively attacked by our Communist friends? Why do you do things such as Orrin has just done?"

"Such as *Orrin* has just done, my God!" Lafe exclaimed angrily. "This is new history, and instant history, with a vengeance. *Who* launched the new offensive in Gorotoland and Panama, just yesterday? *Who* reignited the wars? *Who* took the actions to which the President is only responding? My God, how can you people here do such instantaneous forgetting? . . . But of course," he said more quietly, "you don't. You know. It's just that to face up to the Communists is too difficult, too dangerous, too likely to create obligations for counteraction that you just don't want to contemplate and undertake. You *don't want* to remember history, even the history of literally yesterday, because to remember would require action against those responsible. And you are afraid."

"And what does the United States offer," Raoul demanded, while around the room, observing their now tense and solemn faces, many paused to whisper and to watch, "to help us not be afraid? Withdrawals everywhere in the past few years, arms cutbacks, reduced military strength, inability to enforce your policies, increasing weakness in the face of Communist advances, simple lack of preserving the armed strength required to keep yourselves effective in the world. Why should we join you in strong actions opposing the Communists when you have so little left to oppose them with yourselves? You can't help yourselves, let alone help us. Why should we endanger ourselves for you? You are no longer able to protect us from the consequences."

"We are still able to react decisively," Lafe said, controlling his temper with an obvious effort, "and we are doing so. Any nation which bases its policies upon the assumption that we will fail will be making a grievous mistake, I assure you. We continue to have a strong President with the will to act, and from now on, I believe, things are going to get better."

"Better for what?" Lord Maudulayne inquired moodily, and at his side the Indian Ambassador echoed, "Yes, yes! Better for what?"

"Better for all of you," Lafe said bluntly, "because without us, still, what would become of you?"

"It is very kind of America, dear Lafe," Krishna Khaleel said lightly, "to save us all so regularly, and with such modesty. I suppose it can only happen because America never stops to ask us if we *want* to be saved—at least, from whatever it is America seems to think she is saving us. *My* government is not worried about the Communists, because we are not aligned with anyone. India will survive to watch you all go down, if that should be the case, though of course we do not wish it for anyone. Still, history you know"—his tone trailed off—"it *does* carry certain built-in dangers for those too proud and too arrogant. . . ."

"You see what you are up against," Lafe said to Ceil. "It will be an education."

"It is already," she said with a humorless little smile. "I feel I'm getting a cram course, right here."

"I hope it is preparing you for the next few hours," Lafe said grimly, "because they aren't going to be easy."

"How is Jimmy Fry, old boy?" Claude Maudulayne inquired, deliberately changing the subject to the one he knew would distract his angry colleague from America. At the mention of the handsome, retarded son whom the late Senator Harold Fry of West Virginia, then chief U.S. delegate, had in effect bequeathed to Lafe, the expression of the Senator from Iowa softened and became less tense.

"He's still up the Hudson at Oak Lawn sanitarium, but I'm going to bring him down to Washington tomorrow. I've got a new house on Foxhall Road, you know, and the doctors say it would probably be better for him to be there with me."

"A house?" Krishna Khaleel inquired archly. "For bachelor Lafe, that dashing Romeo of Washington and the U.N.? Is there something in the wind that we don't know about?"

"Dashing Romeo," Lafe said, "is running down. I'm getting too old, K.K. Anyway, I've seen quite a bit of Mabel Anderson during the campaign, and I think she may be coming back to Washington pretty soon."

"You know it!" K.K. said in a delighted tone, genuinely pleased by the thought of Mabel Anderson, widow of the late Senator Brigham Anderson of Utah, dead by his own hand during the bitter Senate battle over the first nomination of Robert A. Leffingwell to be Secretary of State, eighteen months ago. "Lafe, how wonderful for you! We will all be so pleased. When is the wedding?"

"Keep it to yourself, K.K.," Lafe cautioned hastily, "and the rest of you, too, please. Strictly confidentially, she's coming in next week and we expect to be married in a private ceremony as soon thereafter as it can be arranged."

"Congratulations," Raoul Barre said. "She is a very sweet girl."

"A very fine one," Lord Maudulayne agreed. "And a very fine thing you will be doing, for her, for yourself, for her daughter and for Jimmy. I know Kitty will join me in wishing all of you every possible happiness."

"Thank you, Claude," Lafe said. He shook his head, his expression abruptly somber again. "In such an era," he said as if to himself. "*In such an era!*"

"Shall we go in?" Raoul suggested pleasantly, ignoring his sudden change of mood. "It is almost time. Madam Ambassador"—he stood up with a gallant little bow and a charming smile—"will you deign to go in with France?"

"Perhaps I should ask the State Department what it will commit me to, first," she said with an answering smile, rising and taking his proffered arm.

"Nothing too permanent," Raoul said cheerfully, "because the debate is likely soon to separate us again."

"Ha!" she said, giving him a quizzical look. "At least you're honest."

"All of us here try to be," Krishna Khaleel said, burbling along behind as they made their way slowly out through the crowded room to join the colorful throng of the nations moving toward the Security Council. "We all try to be!"

"I'm afraid I am not so generous, K.K.," Lord Maudulayne remarked with a wry little chuckle. "I would not agree that all of us try."

Two hundred miles to the south, standing at his front center desk on the aisle to face the poised pencils and skeptical faces of the reporters who gathered there each noon for the regular pre-session press conference, the Majority Leader of the United States Senate found himself as gloomy and filled with foreboding as his young colleague from Iowa up at the United Nations.

He was uneasy, Bob Munson confessed to himself, uneasy and even apprehensive, for he did not know what this new Senate would do. Orrin's margin of victory had been so narrow that he had barely managed to retain control of the Senate—and the control was only nominal, based on party label, not on any infusion of new Senatorial blood that would look kindly on his policies. It would be slippery going, the Majority Leader told himself: mighty slippery going. And the first step on the uncertain road would come right now in his opening remarks to the media, whose members were obviously ready to go for him with all the knives at their command.

"Senator," UPI said, leading off the questioning, "we hear there's going to be a real battle over the leadership. Are you confident you'll win?"

"I'm always confident," he said comfortably. "That's my job. You boys and girls know that."

"You don't think your stand on the wars will have an adverse effect on your candidacy, then," the *Times* suggested.

"It may," he agreed calmly, "but that will have to be determined when we vote."

"We hear a lot of the members are very upset by the latest turn of events," the *Post* said.

"I'm very upset by Communist aggression myself," he said promptly. There was a stirring in the group clustered around his desk and he thought he heard Warren Strickland, seated just across the aisle, suppress a snort.

"I think U.S. aggression is more to the point," the *Post* said severely. Bob Munson studied him for a moment with deliberate skepticism.

"Oh, do you. Well, I don't. I like to keep my priorities where they belong, not get them all mixed up for ideological purposes. The Communists moved first."

"Wasn't that because they felt world peace would be better served if they moved swiftly to terminate our meddling in Gorotoland and Panama, before it did any more damage, Senator?" the Los Angeles *Times* inquired.

"So they say," Bob Munson agreed. "So they say." He looked at the clock over the Vice President's desk with a sudden interest. "What else do you people have on your minds today?"

"Is there anything more important, Senator?" Walter Dobius snapped. The Majority Leader gave him a slow and thoughtful look.

"Why, Walter, whatever *you* say is important no doubt *is* important. But right now, if you'll excuse me, I have to do a little politicking."

And he gave them a cheerful smile and stepped across the aisle, shouldering them aside until they stepped back with annoyed looks and let him through. As he bent down to murmur in Warren's ear he was aware that they were off up the center aisle to Arly Richardson's seat. The stringy, acerbic old senior Senator from Arkansas had just come in. Around him the dutiful and the anticipatory were flocking.

"Am I going to make it?" he asked Warren quietly. The Minority Leader frowned and shook his head.

"I don't know, Bobby. It's going to be very close. I wish I could help you, but it's the majority's problem. And you know what your caucus did this morning. For the first time in a couple of decades—"

"Yes," Bob Munson nodded glumly. "No endorsement of me *or* Arly—everybody for himself—'an open vote on the floor according to each Senator's conscience,' as that new kid from Oregon put it. Which means not a vote on the leadership, but a vote on the war issue. And the same thing in the House caucus, so Bill tells me. It's wide open. We aren't the issue, the wars are the issue."

"Senator," the *Times* broke in with a certain relish, coming back down the aisle, "Senator Richardson says he has enough votes to beat you for the leadership."

"Claiming isn't winning," Bob Munson said, returning to his desk as the rest swarmed back upon him too. "Why don't you all go and talk to the Vice President? He looks new and lonely up there."

But just at that moment, as he had known from the clock that it would, the buzzer sounded for the opening of the session and they hurried off the floor and back to the Press Gallery above the Vice President's head, there to watch with shrewd, sophisticated (if not altogether unprejudiced) eyes the drama to be played out upon the floor below. Many had liked him over the years, their relations had been quite cordial most of the time, but they were after him now. Some few still remained friendly, but the most influential had chosen their side in the conflict with the Communists.

It wasn't his.

Cullee rapped the gavel with a sudden force that disclosed his nervousness on his first day of presiding over the Senate, and said, "The Senate will be in order! The Clerk will call the roll for a quorum!" in a voice that he hoped was calmer than he felt.

Quorum completed, ninety-nine Senators, exclusive of Lafe, in their seats, an air of tense expectancy began to settle over the chamber. He called on the chaplain to deliver the prayer. Full of fervent appeals to duty in a troubled time, it ended on a note of ringing exhortation to save and preserve the Republic. Those who had a goodly share of the responsibility for doing so looked about them expectantly. Tension grew.

"Mr. President," Bob Munson said, rising slowly to his feet.

"The distinguished Majority Leader," Cullee said, and somewhere among the newcomers somebody murmured audibly, "But not for long."

"Mr. President," Bob Munson said, ignoring the little titter that swept the chamber, "before we get into the business which will occupy us principally today"—he turned and looked, slowly and with apparent complete composure, at his colleagues all around—"namely, the selection of a Majority Leader, and consideration of the President's request for an additional ten billion dollars for the defense establishment, I would like to ask the indulgence of the Senate to take up one nomination, which I hope we can speedily pass upon.

"I would suggest," he said calmly, as Arly Richardson rose to his feet with the obvious intention of challenging him, "that the nominations for the Cabinet be referred to the appropriate committees, for consideration and reporting back at the earliest possible opportunity, as the President needs his official family confirmed and fully operative just as soon as possible. Mr. President, I so move."

"I second that motion," Senator Richardson said with satisfaction.

"Without objection," Cullee said, "it is so ordered."

"The nomination I wish to call up," Senator Munson said, "is that of a most distinguished American who is already at work on the difficult task assigned her by the President—Mrs. Edward M. Jason, Ambassador to the United Nations. I move the Senate approve this nomination, Mr. President."

"Mr. President," Arly Richardson said sharply. "Now, Mr. President, just—a—minute, if you please. The distinguished Senator from Michigan is very adept at sliding over things, but he cannot slide over the fact that all three—not two, but three—of the subjects requiring action today are inextricably tied together. The first is Mrs. Jason's nomination. The second is the choice of a Majority Leader. The third is the request for a supplemental defense appropriation. All three go to the fundamental issue that faces this Senate and this country today: are we for war or are we for peace? They cannot be separated from that issue, Mr. President, and I for one am not going to let the Senator from Michigan separate them. What we vote on one we should vote on the others. Up or down, we should decide, insofar as our responsibility lies in this Senate, the war issue. It is the thread that ties them together.

"Basing my judgment on that proposition, Mr. President, I want my colleagues to know that I shall vote against the nomination of Mrs. Jason, as I shall vote against a war candidate for Majority Leader, and as I shall vote against a supplemental appropriation for defense which can only be used to encourage the President in further military adventurism.

"I say this should be stopped.

"I shall cast my votes to stop it.

"I urge my colleagues, particularly my new colleagues, to do likewise."

"Mr. President," Bob Munson said, allowing a little calculated asperity to creep into his tone, "the Senator from Arkansas in his usual kindly fashion has laid about him with a truncheon, or possibly a trowel, and managed to damage a fine lady and a great American in the process. The appointment of Mrs. Jason has nothing to do with any so-called 'war issue.' It is simply a recognition by the President of her own great abilities—and of the fact, I will remind the Senator, that she is the widow of one whose policies the Senator and many others in this Senate professed to think very highly of, not so long ago."

"She has not espoused those policies for months," Arly Richardson reminded him sharply, "if she ever did. After her husband's death she devoted herself wholeheartedly to the pro-war campaign of the President. At this moment she is in New York advocating the pro-war policies of the President. She has permitted herself to become the handmaiden of Orrin Knox's ill-advised ventures. She is now a strictly partisan person. He means war, she means war. I will vote accordingly."

"Mr. President," Tom August of Minnesota said in his hesitant, almost timorous way, "will the distinguished Majority Leader yield to me?"

"I am always glad to yield to the distinguished chairman of the Foreign Relations Committee," Bob Munson said amiably, "if he will be brief."

"Oh, I shall," Senator August said hastily. "I simply want to assure the Majority Leader that I fully support his endorsement of Mrs. Jason, and while this procedure of calling up her nomination without referral to committee is unusual, still I think the circumstances and her own fine character warrant it. I shall vote for her because I think it important for the President to have the person he wants as Ambassador to the United Nations. I do not say this as any endorsement of his policies in the present crisis, which perturb me very much, I will say frankly to the Majority Leader, but because he naturally wants someone in that post who will support him. If not Mrs. Jason, then it would be someone else equally devoted to his program. So I really think this nomination stands quite apart from any war or anti-war issue. I believe we are lucky to have someone as fine as Mrs. Jason to represent the United States in the U.N. I urge my colleagues to approve her speedily and without further debate."

"Oh, no, Mr. President!" Arly Richardson cried, and from many places around the floor and in the packed galleries (where a sizable scattering of NAWAC's black-jacketed hearties could be seen) there came murmurs of dismay and discontent. "Not so fast, now! I am amazed, I will say to my dear old colleague from Minnesota, absolutely amazed that he would capitulate so fast and so completely to the further step toward foreign entanglement which this nomination represents. We must stop it, Senators! We must stop it at once! The peace of the world hangs in the balance this day, and we must not let Orrin Knox move further down the road toward its destruction. He means war: Mrs. Jason means war. It is as simple as that.

"Mr. President, I move we vote on this nomination without further ado, overwhelmingly defeat it, and place the Senate on record irrevocably on the side of peace!"

A dozen Senators were on their feet demanding recognition, the galleries burst into an excited gabble, the chamber filled with sound chaotic, argumentative, angry, hostile. For a split second the Vice President hesitated. Then he said to himself, *Come on now, old Cullee, you're it!* and banged down the gavel as hard as he could.

"The Senate and the galleries," he said in a voice so loud and emphatic that it startled the room momentarily into silence, "will be in order! This is not a mob scene here!"

("Well, get *him*," the St. Louis *Post-Dispatch* murmured with a startled irony to the Boston *Globe*. "Little Cullee's in the big league now," the *Globe* agreed: "Massah, lif' dat bale!")

"The Majority Leader still has the floor," the Vice President said, more calmly. "What is his pleasure?"

"Mr. President—" Bob Munson began thoughtfully. Then he stopped, cast a quick glance across his restless colleagues and changed tactics without losing a beat. "Why," he said reasonably, "I think the Senator from Arkansas is entirely right. In ten minutes here we have had presented the basic arguments for and against this nomination. You either think the President and Mrs. Jason are working for peace or you don't. You either think the President has a right to choose his official family or you don't. I'm sure most minds are made up. Sure: why don't we vote?"

"Mr. President," Arly Richardson demanded, clearly upset by what appeared to be an abrupt capitulation. "Is this some sort of trick?"

"The Senator is ridiculous," Bob Munson said, turning his back upon him and facing the chair. "One minute ago he was demanding a vote. Now I agree and he gets suspicious. *This* is leadership material? Mr. President, I suggest the absence of a quorum, and I shall then renew my request for a vote."

And presently, after ninety-nine Senators had again been found to be present, and after the chamber had quieted down to a tense silence, he renewed the motion and the vote came: an extremely clear indication, he knew with an inward sigh when it was over, of exactly what Orrin faced on the Hill this day.

"I have been informed by the Secretary-General," said Australia, this month's president of the Security Council, as the session finally, after usual delays, came to order at 12:45 P.M., "that our charming new colleague from the United States has just been confirmed by the Senate. Congratulations, Madam Ambassador."

And he applauded vigorously, beaming across the circular table in a kindly way, while at his side the Secretary-General, that stately, tired old man from Nigeria, and a few others of their colleagues, did the same. Nikolai Zworkyan of Russia, Sun Kwon-yu of the People's Republic of China and the ambassadors of Cuba, Egypt, Ghana and Zambia ostentatiously refrained.

"Thank you, Mr. President," she said pleasantly, "I hope I may be worthy of the honor."

"If there is honor to be found," the Soviet Ambassador remarked, not looking up from the papers he appeared to be reading on the desk before him, his level words like a deliberate physical slap in the face, "in representing a dishonorable cause."

"Mr. President!" Lord Maudulayne and Krishna Khaleel said together in shocked tones, and from his chair, slightly behind and to the right of Ceil's, Lafe said, with no attempt at muffling it, "Son of a *bitch!*" An excited thrill ran through the crowded press seats and the overflowing public galleries. Everyone expected blood on this afternoon when the arrogant United States would surely be humbled, but no one had expected it quite so soon. It promised to be, as the *Guardian* murmured cheerfully to *Paris-Soir*, a real fun time at the good old *Nations-Unis*.

"The Ambassador of the Soviet Union," Australia said severely, "if he cannot behave like a gentleman, might at least behave like a diplomat."

"Mr. President," Nikolai Zworkyan said in a blandly impervious tone that would have done credit to all the shrewd mechanical men who had spouted their rigid ideology from that chair before him, "the Ambassador of the Soviet Union sits here as the enthusiastic choice of his government. He does not sit here as the 51-to-48 choice of the United States Senate, an Ambassador by only three votes. Possibly," he said with an unctuous little bow in Ceil's general direction, "that gives him a somewhat greater reason for being listened to in this chamber."

For a moment Ceil gave him a thoughtful glance. Her color was high but her voice when she spoke was fully under control.

"Mr. President," she said in a clear, steady tone, "I was told when I took this job that there might be tigers in the path. I was not told that there would be vermin."

There was a gasp from all around the room, sudden boos from Zambia, Rumania and Ghana, a wave of hisses from the galleries. She only raised her head a little higher and went on.

"On behalf of my government I send to the Chair a resolution and ask for its immediate consideration by the Security Council."

"Mr. President," the Soviet Ambassador cried, "that is completely irregular, Mr. President! The delegate of the United States should introduce her resolution and give us time to study it, Mr. President. She should not try to spring it upon us when we are unsuspecting and unprepared! It should lie over for twenty-four hours, Mr. President! I so move, Mr. President, and ask for an immediate vote on the motion!"

"Mr. President!" Egypt, Cuba and Rumania cried together, and "Mr. President!" Lord Maudulayne, Krishna Khaleel and Raoul Barre cried with equal vigor.

"The distinguished delegate of France," Australia said promptly. Raoul leaned forward with a sort of bored weariness that brought him immediate attention, as he intended it should.

"Mr. President," he said, "does it occur to no one, including the Soviet Ambassador, that we should at least find out what we are being called to vote upon? I would like to know, at least, what the United States proposes. Is that small boon permissible, I will ask the Soviet Ambassador?"

"It is irregular, Mr. President!" Nikolai Zworkyan said angrily. "It is completely irregular, what is being proposed here by the delegate of the United States and supported by the delegate of France! I oppose it, Mr. President, I oppose it!"

"Must I," Raoul inquired in the same bored tone, "go so far as to make a formal motion that the resolution of the United States be read to the Council—and we will then have to vote on *that?* I would assume such pettifogging to be beyond the reach even of the delegate of the Soviet Union, Mr. President. But I will so move if he forces me."

"Well," Zworkyan said, glowering about with a carefully calculated air of indignation, "the Soviet Union does not choose to engage in that scurrilous type of debate, Mr. President. The Soviet Union believes the issues here are too grave for that type of thing. The delegate of France may indulge himself in name-calling and hostile words, Mr. President, but we will not!"

"Christ," Lafe said, again making no attempt to keep his voice down. "What a hypocrite!"

"The Chair," Australia said hastily, "will ask the Secretary-General to read the resolution of the United States for the information of the Council."

And after waiting a moment to make sure that the Soviet Ambassador would indeed conclude the bluster and subside, as everyone expected, the Secretary-General read in his clipped British-American accent:

"Whereas, the armed forces of the Union of Soviet Socialist Republics and the People's Republic of China have today launched unprovoked aggressions in the nations of Panama and Gorotoland, and whereas such unprovoked aggressions interfere with attempts to negotiate a peaceful settlement of those two conflicts, and are a major and obvious threat to world peace; and,

"Whereas, the government of the United States, acting in accordance with the Charter of the United Nations, has accordingly taken steps to strengthen the chances for world peace and enhance the opportunities for meaningful negotiations in those two countries by opposing the unprovoked aggressions of the Union of Soviet Socialist Republics and the People's Republic of China; and,

"Whereas, the President of the United States in his Inaugural Address called upon the Heads of Government of the People's Republic of China and the Union of Soviet Socialist Republics to meet with him in Geneva to negotiate peaceful settlements of outstanding world problems; and,

"Whereas, the Heads of Government of the Union of Soviet Socialist Republics and the People's Republic of China have not yet signified their intention to attend such a meeting in the interests of world peace:

"Now, therefore, be it resolved:

"That the Security Council endorses the actions of the United States in seeking to strengthen world peace and enhance the opportunities for meaningful negotiations in Gorotoland and Panama, and calls upon the Heads of Government of the Union of Soviet Socialist Republics and the People's Republic of China to meet forthwith in Geneva with the President of the United States and begin at once meaningful and constructive negotiations looking toward peaceful solutions of the outstanding issues which threaten world peace and the future of mankind."

("Incredible arrogance!" the *New Statesman and Nation* told the *Times of India.* "Unbelievable effrontery!" the *Times of India* told the *New Statesman and Nation.*)

"Mr. President," Ceil said quietly, "I move the Council now vote on the resolution of the United States."

"Mr. President!" Nikolai Zworkyan exclaimed angrily. "Mr. President, such incredible arrogance, such unbelievable effrontery! I do not see how the Security Council can tolerate it for one minute, Mr. President! Accordingly"—and for a brief second, like a tiny gleam of light in his theatrically thunderous face, a self-satisfied little smile broke through and disappeared again—"the Soviet Union has no choice but to offer its own resolution. Mr. President, I call up the resolution of the U.S.S.R. introduced this morning, ask the Secretary-General to read it, offer it as an amendment to the resolution of the United States and request an immediate vote."

And with an air of triumph he made no attempt to conceal, he rose briskly, walked around the table, placed a copy of his resolution smartly on the desk in front of Australia and returned to his seat. Sun Kwon-yu of China watched with a bland, impassive face.

"The bastard's in order," Lafe leaned forward to whisper angrily in Ceil's ear, "but protest it."

"Mr. President!" she said quickly. "Mr. President, the United States objects to this obvious attempt to deny the Security Council a chance to vote on the merits of our resolution. We protest this unprincipled attempt to . . ."

"Madam Ambassador," Australia interrupted regretfully but firmly as a little rustle of scornful laughter swept the room, "I am afraid the delegate of the Soviet Union is entirely in order. I am afraid I must ask the Secretary-General to read the text of the Soviet resolution."

And after a moment, as Ceil sat slowly back in her chair and turned upon Nikolai Zworkyan a thoughtful, sardonic gaze, the dignified old man obliged again:

"Whereas, the government of the United States has been guilty of consistent violations of world peace in the countries of Gorotoland and Panama; and,

"Whereas, these unprovoked aggressions and acts of war by the government of the United States have continued for many months in direct defiance of the United Nations and its coordinate bodies, the Security Council and the General Assembly; and,

"Whereas, the United Nations and its coordinate bodies have several times attempted to restrain and terminate these aggressions and acts of war by the government of the United States, only to be thwarted by vetoes of the government of the United States in the Security Council and open defiance of obvious overwhelming sentiment in the General Assembly; and,

"Whereas, the governments of the Union of Soviet Socialist Republics and the People's Republic of China, determining that as peace-loving democratic states they must come to the aid of this body in the face of United States war aggressions, have proceeded to take such necessary steps as they deem advisable to repel such aggressions and restore world peace in Gorotoland and Panama:

"Now, therefore, be it resolved:

"That the United Nations, acting through the Security Council, does approve, endorse and support the necessary steps taken by the People's Republic of China and the Union of Soviet Socialist Republics to halt United States aggression against world peace, and pledges its support in all ways required to assist the Union of Soviet Socialist Republics and the People's Republic of China in maintaining world peace and order in Gorotoland, Panama and all other areas of the world where peace is threatened by aggressive designs of the government of the United States;

"And further be it resolved:

"That the United Nations demands that the United States cease and desist immediately and forthwith from all military actions of whatever nature in Gorotoland and Panama, and that all United States personnel, military and otherwise, be withdrawn immediately from those two countries; and further:

"That the United Nations demands that the President of the United States meet immediately following such cease-fires and withdrawals with representatives of the People's Republic of China and the Union of Soviet Socialist Republics to negotiate settlements in Gorotoland and Panama that will restore world peace, establish democratic regimes in those two countries and terminate the possibility of any further aggressive war adventures by the government of the United States anywhere in the world."

"Mr. President," Nikolai Zworkyan said calmly into the expectant silence that followed, "the U.S.S.R. demands a vote."

"Mr. President," Ceil said with equal calmness, "if the delegate presses his resolution the United States will veto."

"And if the delegate presses *her* resolution," Zworkyan snapped, "the Soviet Union will veto. So I would say to you, Madam Ambassador: let us vote and be damned. And when we have done so, let us take it to the General Assembly and see who wins there!"

"Mr. President, Mr. Speaker, sir!" Jawbone Swarthman cried to William Abbott over the noisy tumult of the House, and in the excited galleries and across the buzzing floor it could be seen that he was waving a piece of wire-service copy taken from the tickers in the Members' Reading Room just off the floor.

"See here what happens, Mr. Speaker, Mr. President, sir, when this Administration carries its ill-advised war policies to that great forum of the nations up there in New York, that great United Nations up there! Why, sir, this Administration gets *licked*, it gets *defeated*, it gets *humiliated!* Hear this, now, Mr. President, Mr. Speaker, sir! Just hear this!"

And whipping a pair of pince-nez from his vest pocket he popped them on his rosy button of a nose, held the wire copy at arm's length and read in a loud accusatory voice:

"'UNITED NATIONS, NEW YORK—The Security Council today handed the new Knox Administration a stinging defeat by voting 9–4 for a Soviet-Chinese resolution condemning United States aggressions in Panama and Gorotoland, demanding immediate U.S. withdrawal from those two countries and calling on President Knox to attend an immediate peace conference with representatives of the Soviet and Chinese governments.

"'The resolution was vetoed by Mrs. Edward M. Jason, newly appointed U. S. Ambassador to the United Nations. But while the veto killed the resolution, it did not erase the overwhelming condemnation of the President's war moves of the past twenty-four hours contained in the votes of other Security Council members.

"'Only Australia, Norway and Lesotho, nonpermanent members of the Council, joined the United States in voting against the Soviet-Chinese resolution. Two other permanent members, Britain and France, abstained. Neutralist India joined Chile, China, Cuba, Egypt, Ghana, Rumania, Zambia and the Soviet Union in voting for the resolution.

"'The Council then turned to an opposing United States resolution seeking condemnation of the Soviets and Chinese for their response to American moves in the two war-torn countries in Africa and Central America. It was expected that the vote on that resolution (Note to editors: Expected within the hour) would represent a similar overwhelming rebuke to the Knox Administration's policies.'

"So, Mr. President, Mr. Speaker, sir!" Jawbone cried triumphantly, the corn-pone accent that concealed the shrewd Phi Beta Kappa, *magna cum laude* graduate of Duke University Law School at its most fulsome and florid.

"*So!* What does *that* say for the policies of this new President we have, I ask you? What does that say about his aggressin', his movin' in on li'l ole Gorotoland and Panama, his *gettin' tough* with them, when all they's tryin' to do, Mr. President, Mr. Speaker, sir, is just to have theyseffs a li'l ole democracy, a li'l ole bit of freedom, a li'l ole *self-determination* without the big ole imperialist Yewnited *States* gettin' in there and tryin' to mess things up! That's what it's come to, Mr. Speaker, Mr. President, sir, jes' messin' things up! Now, isn't that right, I ask you? Isn't that right?"

"Is the gentleman," William Abbott asked ominously from the chair he was reoccupying until the House made up its mind on a new Speaker, "asking me?"

"Yes, sir!" Jawbone said stoutly. "Yes, sir, I *am* askin' our beloved ex-President, our beloved ex-Speaker, here, seein' as how we're now in the midst of a debate in which he's tryin' to persuade this House he ought to be Speaker *agin.* Yes, sir, I do ask you, Mr. Speaker, Mr. President, sir, since you been makin' yourself the o—fficial spokesman for this dangerous new Administration we got down there in the White House now. I *am* askin' you, I say to the gentleman from Colorado, and I tell you *this House wants to know what you goin' say in reply!* Yes, sir, *we want to know!*"

"Well, sir," the ex-President said in an acid tone, gesturing to the Minority Whip, an amiable gentleman from Missouri, to take over the Chair, "I'll tell the gentleman and this House, since they want to know. I'll tell them!"

And he rose and came slowly down to the microphones in the well of the House and stood there for several moments staring out impassively upon his restless colleagues and the standing-room-only crowds in the galleries. He looked as he had always looked when he held the reins of the House—stolid and unimpressed, solid and powerful—a natural force, great in the land, and muchly to be reckoned with.

Except that this time he was fighting for his political life, and here in the body he had dominated for so long, everyone knew it.

"Members of the House," he said quietly, while a hush, attentive, respectful—and avid for his downfall—settled over floor and galleries.

"The chairman of the House Foreign Affairs Committee, my dear old friend the gentleman from South Carolina who aspires to unseat me this day"—there was a ripple of laughter, not quite as plentiful or encouraging as he had hoped—"stands up here waving a piece of paper and then proceeds to read us the slanted interpretation of the media as a valid and factual contribution to this debate. I don't think it is, I will say to the House, and I'll tell you why.

"When I became"—and he used the title simply, for he intended it to impress and knew it would many of them, though possibly not enough—"President of the United States, I found a situation facing me that required drastic action on my part if the peace of the world and the security of the United States were to be preserved.

"My predecessor, the late Harley M. Hudson, had determined to take strong steps, including armed intervention, in the countries of Gorotoland and Panama, because American missionaries and American interests had been attacked in Gorotoland, and because a rebel movement in Panama was threatening overthrow of the government there, and capture of the Canal.

"I continued those policies because I agreed entirely with his analysis of the two situations and with his methods of handling them. I didn't apologize then and I don't apologize now. And I don't think"—his tone became flat and emphatic—"that President Knox has to apologize either."

At this there was a sudden stirring, a clearly hostile rumble of protest across floor and galleries. His voice became, if anything, more emphatic.

"The Soviet Union and the Communist Chinese, planners, suppliers and day-by-day managers of these two attacks upon the United States and the peace of the world, have tried unsuccessfully in the United Nations to stop American moves to produce a reasonable status quo and a reasonable basis for negotiations in both afflicted countries. We have exercised our veto to stop them. Today we are exercising it again. I hope we will continue to do so whenever necessary."

Again the rumble of protest, louder, more excited.

"Mr. Speaker," he said, turning to the Minority Whip in the Chair, "may we have order in the House, please?"

"The House will be in order," the Minority Whip said promptly, banging the gavel. "And the galleries, too. Otherwise the Sergeant at Arms will be asked to clear the galleries." The rumble died, still protesting. "The gentleman will proceed."

"Thank you," William Abbott said. He looked somberly around the restless room. "Recently the Communist powers have become bolder. Two months ago they were on the verge of an all-out offensive to renew the fighting, which had sunk to a point of near stalemate, during which we have been working diligently through every available channel all over the world to begin genuine peace negotiations. In response to very full and complete intelligence information on this contemplated move, I ordered a worldwide alert of all American armed forces. I intended the alert as a signal to the Communist powers that they would be met by complete American opposition if they continued with their plans for an offensive.

"The signal sufficed. They abandoned the offensive—until the day when they thought the United States would be off balance, namely the inauguration day of a new President. Immediately after he offered them the olive branch and asked them to meet him in Geneva for a full-scale review, and hopefully a full-scale settlement, of the outstanding issues that divide the world, they struck. Now they are putting forward the phony topsy-turvy theory that their aggression was in answer to a nonexistent American aggression. So far they have had their usual success in persuading those many members of the United Nations who hate the United States anyway.

"I hope they will not have a similar success in this Congress."

Again there was angry protest.

Into it the supporters of a strong American policy found themselves speaking with an ever-harsher, ever-blunter emphasis, regardless of what their own best political strategy might be.

"Yes!" Bob Munson said angrily, his tone so sharp that the sounds of protest momentarily died away. "Yes, I say to this Senate, I hope the Communists will not have a success in this Congress similar to the success they seem to be having in the United Nations this afternoon. They can always persuade enough haters of America to go along with them, up there. God help us if there are that many haters of their own country here!"

"Mr. President," Arly Richardson said with equal sharpness, "will the Senator yield? What does the Senator think he gains by attacking those who disagree with him as 'haters of their own country'? There are very many perfectly sincere and genuine doubts about the actions taken in the past twenty-four hours by the new President of the United States, and I for one do not intend to have my patriotism or my integrity impugned when I oppose those actions. I won't have it, Mr. President!"

"Very well," Bob Munson said promptly, "I withdraw any unintentional or inadvertent impugning of the patriotism and integrity of the Senator from Arkansas, or anyone else who agrees with him. But I do not withdraw my criticism of his general approach to these matters, because I think it to be absolutely vital to the future security of this country and the group of independent nations that we not flinch or falter in this new confrontation with the Communist powers. I think it is absolutely imperative that we support the President a hundred per cent without any breaking of ranks that would encourage the Communists to believe that we are weak, or wavering, or ready to surrender in the face of their new aggression."

"'Their new aggression'!" Arly Richardson echoed scornfully. "What about ours? That is what we are responsible for, I suggest to the Senator, not somebody else's. What do we do about *ours?* How do we extricate ourselves from this predicament into which the new President, in his characteristic fashion, known only all too well to this Senate where he served so many years, has plunged us with his usual impulsiveness and lack of forethought? That is what I think this Senate must decide. And, Mr. President," he added, in an emphatic and pointed tone, "I do not think it can do it under an inflammatory, demagogic, subservient leadership which has already committed itself lock, stock and barrel to the President's ill-advised, irresponsible course."

"Now, Mr. President!" Bob Munson said, and it was obvious he was keeping his tone level with some difficulty. "How the Senator can so quickly and easily absolve the Soviet Union and the People's Republic of China from any guilt or culpability—how he can talk blithely about 'our' aggression and totally ignore theirs, which began this latest confrontation—is literally beyond me. It sounds illogical to the point almost of unbalance, Mr. President. I just don't get it, and I wish the Senator would explain."

"Mr. President," Tom August said in his hesitant, apologetic way, "I should like to try to answer the Majority Leader on that point, if I may, because here, of course, we part company.

"The news from the United Nations, Mr. President, indicates clearly what the situation in the world is at this hour. Other powers, observing the actions of the new Administration here in Washington, have reached the conclusion that there would have been no Communist moves in Gorotoland and Panama had the United States not already been in those two countries, and had we not, under the two previous Administrations, consistently defied U.N. attempts to get us out. Therefore, Mr. President, what appears to be an overwhelming majority of the United Nations—at least in the Security Council and, I suspect, when it goes to the General Assembly later today—has decided that it is the United States that is basically culpable for being there in the first place, not the Soviet Union and the People's Republic of China for following the U.N.'s wishes and seeking to get us out.

"That is the fact of how they feel, Mr. President, and"—he looked with an apologetic stubbornness at Senator Munson, who was regarding him with an open disbelief—"I am afraid that is how many Americans feel, too.

"Therefore, it becomes difficult for many of us in the Senate, and I believe in the House as well, to support President Knox in this instance. And also, I believe"—and while the apologetic air deepened, so did the stubbornness—"to support a candidate for leadership who has chosen to identify himself intimately and beyond extrication with the policies of the President."

"I have identified myself with the policies of the President 'beyond extrication,' as the Senator puts it," Bob Munson snapped, "because I do not see how any sane man concerned for his country's future can do otherwise. The Senator knows why we were in Gorotoland and Panama 'in the first place.' Every informed man and woman in sound of my voice, every informed man and woman in the country and in the world, knows why we were there 'in the first place.' We were there because we, and indirectly but quite effectively, the chances for world peace, were attacked. No amount of quibble or double-talk can change that fact of history. Furthermore, we are presently engaged in direct military action solely and entirely in reply to a new and completely unprovoked Soviet and Chinese aggression. No vote of the U.N. can change that fact.

"Why should I not support President Knox's response to it 'beyond extrication'? To do any other, it seems to me, would be to abandon both what I have believed in all my life, and the survival of this country. I am not afraid to seek re-election to the leadership on that basis."

"If the Senator persists in that position," Tom August said with a sort of wistful regret, while a few seats away Arly Richardson looked both grim and triumphant, "then I am afraid I, and many others, are going to have to vote against him."

"If the gentleman from Colorado, our great ex-President, ex-Speaker here, persists in that position," Jawbone Swarthman cried with an almost exuberant indignation, "of supportin' this new President in all his wild-eyed adventures *no matter what,* then I say to this House I'm goin' to have to vote against him, and I think a lot of others are too! Not only vote against him, but vote for somebody who's a little better in tune with what's goin' on in this world. That's all I can say!"

"Well," William Abbott said bluntly, "you might as well nominate yourself, Jawbone. Or have you primed somebody else to do it?"

"I suspect there will be some who will," Jawbone said with a serene dignity. "Yes, sir, I will say to the gentleman I suspect there will be some who will. But that doesn't change the mistaken nature of the gentleman's position, I will say to him. I know what he did as President, I know what he did here as Speaker before, we all know he's a great public servant, we all know he's one of the greatest that ever served this Republic. But lots of us here feel he's all wrong, and we feel this new President down there is all wrong *this time*. I'll remind the gentleman from Colorado, the ex-President, ex-Speaker here, it's a *whole new Congress*. And it just doesn't like all this foreign adventurin', I'll say to the gentleman, all this interferin' and meddlin' and usin' American boys to fight other people's wars all over this whole *globe*. No, sir, *it does not!*"

"And so what do *you* offer as alternative?" Bill Abbott demanded, and in the galleries and over the floor there was an uneasy shifting and even a few muted boos and hisses at his tone. "Appeasement? Surrender? Turn-tail-and-run? Just suppose you were President of the United States, confronted with the sort of sudden offensive that confronted Orrin Knox twenty-four hours ago, what would you have done, I'll ask the gentleman from South Carolina? Given in? Pretended it wasn't happening? Retreated without a protest? Surrendered without a fight? Which of those policies would you approve and support if you were Speaker? Just exactly what do you offer, I ask the gentleman? You aspire to leadership: what kind of leadership? I think the House has a right to know, since the gentleman is so hostile to the policies of the President, and my own."

"Well, sir!" Jawbone cried, and it was obvious that now he thought his once-powerful opponent had delivered himself up to him. "Well, sir! Let me tell you what I'd support, Mr. ex-President, Mr. ex-Speaker, sir! Let me tell the gentleman, and tell this House as well, since he challenges me! *This* is what I'd follow. Yes, sir!

"First of all, I'll say to our dear friend from Colorado, our distinguished ex-President, ex-Speaker—"

"For God's sake, Jawbone!" William Abbott snapped, abandoning parliamentary courtesy but provoked beyond endurance. "Knock it off!"

"—Mr. ex-Speaker, sir," Jawbone repeated blandly, ignoring him, "*first* of all, I never would have put us into those two itty-bitty good-for-nothing spots in the first place. Not that I don't have every respect for the great people of Gorotoland," he added hastily, "and the great people of Panama, and not that I don't respect their li'l ole right to determine their own destinies, but *for that very reason* I'd never have got us into those messes in the first place. And secondly, *if* I did,

I'd sure not have handled it like Harley Hudson, God rest his soul, and you, Bill, and now ole Orrin there. I'd sure not have gone in there breathin' fire and throwin' bombs and sendin' troops and generally messin' up the whole peace of the world. No, sir, I would not!

"I'd have gone to the U.N. right off, that's what I'd have done. I'd have said, 'Now, looka-here, you-all, we got us a li'l ole problem here, and we want you fine gentlemen of the earth to *help us out*. We want you to help us handle it in a peace-lovin', peace-respectin', *decent* way like you-all gentlemen want us to do!'

"I'd say, 'Now, pass us a li'l ole resolution here declarin' as how we want a *real* peace in Gorotoland, a *real* peace in Panama, and you help us get it. You order a cease-fire, you set up a peace-keepin' force, you call a peace conference and we'll attend and we'll abide by it. We'll abide by it, win, lose or draw,' I'd say, 'we'll abide by it! Yes, sir! And if you-all say, *"Git!"* then we'll *git*,' I'd say. 'You won't find us cheatin' around tryin' to hang in there and impose our armed will on those two itty-bitty ole countries! You won't find the good ole U.S. of A. empirin' and conquestin' and generally raisin' unmitigated hell tryin' to get *our own way*. No, sir! We'll take you-all's way because we believe that's the way of peace! We surely do, now! We believe that's the way of peace!' "

"And what if—" William Abbott attempted, but as he knew from experience, Jawbone in full flood was not one to be interrupted short of terminal catastrophe.

"Yes, sir!" Jawbone cried sternly. "*That's* what I'd have done, and we'd never even *been* in the spot where we are now! Never even *been*, I'll say to our dear ex-President, ex-Speaker here! Never even *been!* But if we *had* been"—and his voice became abruptly quieter and more confidential—"if we *had* been, and I'd found what Orrin Knox found waitin' for him when he hit that big room down there at 1600 Pennsylvania, why I'd have said *this* to our friends in Moscow and Peking. I'd have said, 'Sure, you-all, I see where you got a right to be a little bit annoyed with the good old U.S. of A.,' I'd say. 'I see where you got a feelin' you needed to do *somethin'!*' I'd say. 'And while I mebbe think you been jes' a li'l bit *extreme*, mebbe, jes' a li'l bit *harsh*, I can understand it, now, I surely can! So why don't we all go to that good old United Nations up there in New York and give 'em our problem, now, and see if mebbe we can't all sit down together—*not* offerin' harsh resolutions against each other, *not* tryin' to gain advantages over each other, *not* tryin' to make points—jes' talkin' together quiet and friendly-like to try to work this out. Meanwhile,' I'd say, 'we won't fire back at you-all. We'll jes' sit tight. We won't run but we won't go forward—we won't run but we won't go forward. We'll jes' sit tight and let that good ole U.N. bring us together, and we'll do it with *love!* We'll do it with *peace in our hearts!* We'll do it with *care for mankind* and *love for ev'body,* because that's how we feel the good old U.S. of A. ought to act in this world of ours! Yes, sir, that's how we feel the U.S. of A. *ought* to act!'"

And he paused triumphantly as a great wave of cheers and applause burst from floor and galleries and continued for a full minute as the Minority Whip in the Chair banged the gavel and tried without success to restore order.

"Yes, sir!" Jawbone said in a tone of finality and satisfaction, and appeared about to sit down. But even as he started to, one of the new young members—William Abbott thought it was a Representative Bronson Bernard of New York, but he wasn't sure, there were so many rigidly determined young faces in this new House—hurried forward and thrust another piece of wire copy into Jawbone's willing hand. Jawbone promptly waved it high above his head.

"Look now!" he cried. "Hear this, Mr. ex-President, Mr. ex-Speaker, sir! Hear this, my dear colleagues of the House!

"'UNITED NATIONS, NEW YORK—The war policies of the Knox Administration suffered their second devastating rebuke in less than an hour today as the Security Council voted 9–4 against a United States resolution condemning moves by the Soviet Union and the People's Republic of China in Panama and the African nation of Gorotoland.

"'The resolution was vetoed by both the Soviet Union and China. The United States was joined only by Australia, Norway and Lesotho in voting for it. Two other permanent members of the Council, Britain and France, again abstained. Neutralist India joined Chile, Cuba, Egypt, Ghana, Rumania, Zambia, Russia and China in voting against the American resolution.

"'Both Soviet Ambassador Nikolai Zworkyan and the new United States Ambassador to the U.N., Mrs. Edward M. Jason, announced plans to take the issue immediately to an emergency session of the General Assembly scheduled for 6 P.M. tonight.

"'Observers were unanimous in predicting that the United States position would again go down to crushing defeat in this evening's session.'

"You see?" Jawbone cried. "You-all *see!*"

"Mr. Speaker," someone shouted into the excited babble of the House, and William Abbott could see that it was indeed Bronson Bernard, flushed and quivering with the excitement of his dramatic debut on the national scene, "I nominate the great chairman of the House Foreign Affairs Committee, our distinguished colleague Representative J. B. Swarthman of South Carolina, to be Speaker of this honorable House!"

"Mr. President," Tom August said with a wistful regret into the excited babble of the Senate, "I nominate the distinguished senior Senator from Arkansas, our good friend and colleague Arly Richardson, to be Majority Leader of the United States Senate."

"VOTE! VOTE! VOTE!" the friends of Jawbone cried in the House.

"VOTE! VOTE! VOTE!" the friends of Arly cried in the Senate.

And although both William Abbott and Robert D. Munson were dutifully nominated to their old jobs by loyal friends in their respective chambers, the results were what they had both expected.

And so, as they watched in grim defeat from their respective chairs, was what happened immediately thereafter.

"On this vote," the Clerk of the House intoned solemnly as he finished a tally that cut, with the war issue, across both parties, "the vote for the distinguished gentleman from Colorado is 110, the vote for the distinguished gentleman from South Carolina is 332, and the distinguished gentleman from South Carolina, Representative J. B. Swarthman, is elected Speaker of this honorable House."

"On this vote," the Clerk of the Senate intoned solemnly, "the vote for the distinguished senior Senator from Michigan is 26, the vote for the distinguished Senator from Arkansas is 71, and the Senator from Arkansas, Mr. Richardson, is elected Majority Leader of the United States Senate."

"Mr. Speaker!" Bronson Bernard shouted, a happy, righteous triumph in his voice. "I move that the President's request for an emergency ten-billion-dollar supplemental appropriation for the Department of Defense be sent to the Armed Services and Appropriations committees for careful consideration in the regular order."

"Without objection," Jawbone cried, ignoring the few unhappy voices that shouted indignant protests from the floor, "it is so ordered!"

"Mr. President," cried the Senator whom Bob Munson had referred to a scant hour before as "the new kid from Oregon," with a happy, righteous triumph in his voice, "I move that the President's request for an emergency ten-billion-dollar supplemental appropriation for the Defense Department be sent to the Armed Services and Appropriations committees for careful consideration in the regular order."

"Is there objection?" Cullee Hamilton asked hesitantly, looking down at Bob Munson in his new seat off to the side in the front row of the majority.

“Mr. President,” Bob Munson began, rising to his feet and rallying strength from some reserve he was surprised to find still untapped, “I object—”

“Then we will have a vote!” Arly Richardson snapped. “Does the Senator from Michigan doubt it will carry?”

Bob Munson looked about him for a moment and then shook his head as though trying to clear it of heavily encumbering cobwebs.

“No,” he said quietly, and in spite of himself a sudden sad little sigh, quite audible and leading to some snickers in the galleries, escaped his lips as he sat slowly down again. “I do not doubt that.”

“Very well,” Senator Richardson said coldly. “Mr. President, I join in the request of the distinguished junior Senator from Oregon.”

“Without objection,” Cullee said glumly, conceding a defeat his curious new office permitted him to do nothing about, “it is so ordered.”

KNOX WAR POLICIES IN CHAOS AS CONGRESS REVOLTS AGAINST NEW PRESIDENT. U.N. GENERAL ASSEMBLY JOINS SECURITY COUNCIL IN OVERWHELMING CONDEMNATION OF U.S. MOVES IN GOROTOLAND AND PANAMA. NEW HILL LEADERSHIP, WORLD ANIMOSITY MAY FORCE AMERICAN WITHDRAWAL FROM WAR ZONES. KNOX COURSE MAY END IN WORST U.S. DIPLOMATIC AND MILITARY DEFEAT IN MANY YEARS.

PRESIDENT CALLS EMERGENCY SESSION OF OLD AND NEW LEADERS TO WHITE HOUSE TONIGHT. ANNOUNCES HE WILL ADDRESS AMERICAN PEOPLE TOMORROW MORNING ON “GRAVEST CRISIS TO FACE REPUBLIC IN MY LIFETIME.”

PEACE FORCES JUBILANT AS “GET TOUGH” ATTEMPT HEADS FOR COLLAPSE.

3. “WELL, SIR, MR. PRESIDENT,” Jawbone said brightly when they were all assembled in the Oval Office at 10 P.M., “here we are.”

are.”

“Yes,” he said, his flat tone conceding nothing. “Please be seated, Mrs. Jason, gentlemen. They’ll be bringing coffee and sandwiches in a minute.” His tone became dry. “Also liquor. We may be in for a long session.”

"Long as you like, Mr. President," Jawbone said cheerfully. "I daresay we're all game."

"I am," William Abbott said, helping Ceil to a chair, taking one beside her in the semicircle that faced the desk, now covered with documents and reports. "There's a lot to talk about."

"Yes," Arly Richardson agreed with some acidity. "Indeed there is."

"So I have invited you," the President agreed, his tone still flat and impersonal. "I am glad you all could come."

And he looked slowly around the semicircle from face to face: Jawbone, Arly, Ceil and the ex-President; the Vice President; Senator Munson, Senator Strickland, Senator August, Lafe Smith; the Secretary of State, the Secretary of Defense; his son. Stacked rather in his favor, he had to admit, only Tom August, Jawbone and Arly really in opposition—but now, of course, their opposition was a vital matter. He decided to address himself to it immediately the refreshments were served.

Ten minutes passed in stilted chitchat about the weather, which was still dreadful, a massive new snowstorm whipping out of the West and across the frozen Potomac with paralyzing cold and gale-force winds, pounding in on the beautiful old house, piling the deserted streets high with drifts—the only reason, they all knew, that there were not at this very moment huge hostile anti-Knox crowds filling Pennsylvania Avenue and Lafayette Park across the way. During the interval waiters came in, placed coffee, sandwiches, cakes on a small table set up in the corner, liquor, ice and mixes on another next to it.

When they were gone he looked straight at the new Speaker and the new Majority Leader and demanded,

"How much trouble are you two going to make for me?"

"Well, now, Orrin—Mr. President, sir," Jawbone began hastily, "you mustn't take that hostile attitude, now, you really—"

Arly Richardson cut across his bluster, his voice as cold as the wind off the river.

"As much as the Congress decides you deserve," he said, and even considering his long-time jealousy of Orrin, his harsh comment brought a surprised intake of breath around the room.

"I see," the President said thoughtfully. "That seems frank enough. In effect, then, I really have no leader in either house, do I?"

"Oh, now," Jawbone began, "let's don't get off on this kind of foot now, Mr. President, sir, let's don't get all hostile and unhappy right away, now—"

But again Senator Richardson spoke with a bluntness to match Orrin's own.

"That depends entirely on what you do," he said, somewhat more reasonable in tone but as adamant as before. "On some routine matters, I would think you would have the full cooperation of the Speaker and myself for whatever you want to do. On some other matters—" His voice trailed deliberately away.

"And those, of course," Orrin said, "are exactly the matters most vital to this country, and the world."

Arly shrugged.

"As you like, Mr. President. It is not the Speaker and I who have devised the collision course America is on now."

"Right," Orrin agreed promptly. "That has been devised in Moscow and Peking."

"With some help," Senator Richardson said dryly.

"*From the beginning,*" the President said, returning him stare for stare.

"Well, now," Jawbone began nervously. "Well, now, Mr. President—"

"*From the beginning,*" the President repeated calmly. "When are you going to bring up my defense bill, Mr. Speaker?"

"Why, as soon as it's gone through the committees," Jawbone said. "As soon as it's gone through the committees and everything's in order. Can't be any sooner than that, Mr. President. You know how the House works."

"Slowly," Orrin agreed. "And you, Mr. Majority Leader?"

"In the regular course."

"That will be weeks."

"So?"

The President gave him a steady look.

"So I need it now."

Senator Richardson shrugged.

"Congress won't give it to you now."

"Bill—" the President said, turning to his predecessor and the former Majority Leader, "Bob—what can you do for me?"

"Mr. President," William Abbott said regretfully, "you know: not very damned much. We've both been royally repudiated, and through us, you have been too." He smiled ruefully. "It doesn't exactly give any of us leverage."

"I hope to provide the leverage with my speech tomorrow morning," the President said. Bob Munson frowned.

"It's a very uphill battle," he observed. The President responded with a sudden blaze of the old Orrin.

"But *why is it?*" he demanded sharply. "Why *is* it an uphill battle? The facts of history are on my side, the truth of history is on my side—"

"But not," the ex-President said glumly, "the frightened pretenses of history or the desperate willful blindnesses of history, or the terrible refusal of history to look harsh and demanding facts in the face. All of those things are rampant in America today. You know what the media will say tomorrow morning, have been saying for twenty-four hours—one long threnody of Pretend It Isn't So, just as they've always done. Even more hysterical, now that you've cut through the pretense and acted on the reality." He paused and fished in his breast pocket for a piece of paper. "I've been brushing up on my Solzhenitsyn these last few days," he remarked when he found it, "because he's an inside expert who knew what it's all about and had the guts to say so." He put on his glasses and read slowly:

"'The timid civilized world'—and, he might have added, *the leadership of its journalistic, educational and intellectual communities*—'has found nothing with which to oppose the onslaught of the sudden revival of barbarity, other than concessions and smiles. The spirit of Munich is a sickness of the will of successful'—and, he might have added, *intellectually arrogant*—'people; it is the daily condition of those who have given themselves up to the thirst after prosperity'—and, he might have added, *the favor of the intellectually fashionable*—'at any price.

"'Such people . . . elect passivity and retreat . . . just so as not to step over the threshold of hardship today. . . .'

"They think 'tomorrow . . . it will be all right. But it will never be all right. The price of cowardice will always be evil.'

"He knew," William Abbott concluded gravely. "And the delicate way our great liberals tiptoed around him, first applauding, then becoming fearful of his terrible Russian honesty, then fading quietly away from their tentative and timorous defense of his views because his words threw too cold and glaring a light on their own frightened and responsibility-evading approach to the horrors of Communist reality, bore him out. He was the great touchstone of the liberal conscience. And the liberal conscience failed him, in America as everywhere, because it lacked the guts to face up to the truth of what he said about his own country, whose false myths of peace and freedom they wanted so desperately to preserve, for the sake of their own cowardice." He sighed and concluded quietly, "You, Mr. President, occupy the same unhappy ground."

"But from a different base," Orrin said quietly, "because I am President of the United States."

"It may not be enough," Senator Richardson remarked with a sort of superior certainty, and Cullee Hamilton turned on him with a sudden burst of anger.

"Why isn't it enough?" he demanded. "Why are you so smug about it, Senator? What makes you think, just because you got elected this afternoon, that you have all the answers?"

"Because I did get elected this afternoon," Arly said with some asperity, "and the issue was clearly drawn between the war policies of this President and the peace policies that a majority of his countrymen, and obviously of the whole world, want him to follow."

"Not the whole world," Ceil said quietly. "Peace has nothing to do with it, up there in the U.N. It's Get-America Day every day, and peace is only the excuse."

"You seem to know a lot about it for one who has only been there one day," Senator Richardson snapped. She gave him a cold little smile.

"One day at the U.N. goes a long way," she observed. "Take my word for it, Senator." The smile turned colder. "Thank you, incidentally, for your gallant support of my nomination."

"The issue is clear-cut," Arly said, flushing but standing his ground. "It goes right down the line."

"So it does," she agreed, her look dismissing him, "which is why I hope the President is going to make it very clear to the country tomorrow."

"It won't matter," Arly said stubbornly. "You can't conceal the facts with words."

"Oh, yes, you can," Robert A. Leffingwell said quietly. "You manage, Senator."

"A fine comment," Arly Richardson said angrily, "for one who must depend upon the Senate's indulgence to win confirmation to the Cabinet."

"I had your indulgence two years ago when I could excuse and justify the Communist rationale," Bob Leffingwell replied with an equal anger. "Now I don't accept it any more and so I haven't got your indulgence. I've changed and you've changed, Senator. Again, as you say, the issue cuts all down the line."

"And are Mr. Leffingwell and I," Blair Hannah spoke for the first time, with a dangerous quiet, "to infer from your remark that we cannot expect the indulgence of the Senate for our confirmations?"

The Majority Leader studied him thoughtfully for a moment.

"There may be some—protracted argument," he said finally. "How long may depend upon how long the President persists in policies with which the Congress does not agree."

The President leaned forward and did some thoughtful studying himself, staring straight at the sharp-featured old colleague who had given him so much trouble during all the years of their joint Senate careers.

"So you're going to try to blackmail me, are you, Arly?" he inquired softly. "Won't give me my Cabinet unless I come to heel. They'll be delighted with that in Moscow and Peking."

"They'll be delighted in Washington, too," Arly snapped, and got up abruptly. "I'm going to get a drink."

"Bring me one, too," Orrin suggested acidly to his departing back. "Scotch. Strong. I've got to wash a lot of bad taste out of my mouth."

"Well, now!" the Speaker said hastily. "Well, now, you-all, you-all, now! That's no way to talk, now, that's no way at all. We got us a problem, here, and what we got to do is *solve* it, not go off bein' *hostile* to one another. We *got* to work together, now, we just *got* to!"

"Sure," the President said. "On your terms."

"Isn't that what anybody wants, Mr. President, sir?" Jawbone demanded. "Isn't that what anybody wants?"

"I need the support of Congress," Orrin said levelly, "or the United States of America is going to have to surrender."

"Oh, now!" Jawbone cried. "Oh, fudge, now! Those are very dramatic words, Mr. President, sir, but I don't believe 'em. I just don't believe 'em, now! It isn't all that bad!"

"Of course it isn't," Senator Richardson agreed, returning with his drink and—creating a brief moment of amusement in the midst of tension—one for the President, which he placed on the desk in front of him before returning to his seat. "Of course it isn't. We may take some humiliation in the world if we withdraw under pressure, we may look a little foolish, I'll grant you. But"—his expression turned adamant—"we have invited the humiliation, and we deserve to look foolish."

"And what happens to us," Warren Strickland inquired quietly, "if we are humiliated, and if we do look foolish? What happens to the world's respect, what happens to its willingness to believe in our credibility or rely upon our actions, what happens to our allies who see us turn tail and run in the face of the most blatant and open confrontation? Who will ever rely upon us again?"

"Old arguments," Tom August said in his hesitant, regretful way. "Old, tired arguments that went out with Vietnam and other ill-fated adventures, and whose discrediting *should* have pointed the way toward a different course in Panama and Gorotoland. Except, of course" —and the regretfulness deepened—"that they did not."

"But, Tom," Bob Munson said, "for God's *sake*, man! How you people can so blithely ignore the fact that *their aggression came first*—"

"That does not excuse my country," Senator August said with a certain prim and unshakable disapproval, "when it does the wrong thing."

"Tom," Senator Strickland said, his tone showing the strain of many years of arguing with the chairman of the Senate Foreign Relations Committee on this same general subject, "how can you possibly, as a rational man, accept the Soviet-Chinese claims as to how this thing began?"

"He doesn't accept them as a rational man," Lafe said shortly. "He accepts them as a frightened man."

"And why shouldn't I be frightened," Senator August demanded with an almost quivering impatience, "when I see my President plunging us into new wars and bringing on a direct confrontation with the Communists? Why shouldn't any sane man be frightened?"

"Any sane man should be frightened," Lafe agreed shortly, "but only cowardly sane men should run away."

"'Cowardly, cowardly'!" Tom August mimicked in a bitter voice. "What does your bravery add up to? I suppose it's brave to want to blow up the world!"

"Tom," the President said with a sudden sharp annoyance, "will you stop sniveling? Nobody wants to blow up the world. All I want to do is—"

"Whatever you *want* to do," Senator August interrupted, looking, as always, mouselike but doggedly determined, "the end result is going to be just what I said unless we can deflect you from this crazy course."

At this a silence fell, while the President studied him thoughtfully for several moments. Then he leaned forward and observed softly:

"And I suppose 'deflecting' me, as you put it, involves holding up my Cabinet and refusing to give me the military strength I need to see this thing through."

"You will have your Cabinet in due course," Arly Richardson said, "but I doubt if either house will approve your budget for military expansion."

"Then apparently," the President said, bleakly but with no signs whatsoever of any intention to yield, "I am on my own."

But since he was still, after all, the President, and since some instinct for national survival restrained even the most adamant of his responsible older opponents from going the ultimate distance in trying to break him, his remote and unreachable tone brought a hurried response from the Speaker.

"Oh, now, Mr. President, sir," he said hastily, "now, come, now! We got us a way out of this tangle, now, you know we have! It's right there waitin' for you. All you got to do is jes' follow that *Yew*nited Nations resolution! It's as simple as that, Mr. President. All you got to do is agree to a cease-fire and mebbe withdraw jes' a few li'l ole troops, now, jes' a token I'm sure would do it, and then ev'thang would be quieted down and you could go and meet with our friends in Moscow and Peking, there, and say to 'em, 'Looka-here, now, you-all, *we want peace!* We want to get *together* with you-all! We want to settle this here whole *mess* that's tyin' up the world, and get on with the business of peace! That's what we want, now, so let's you and me *get at it!*' That's what you could do, Mr. President, sir. That's what we're all *prayin'*, us good friends of yours in charge of Congress now, that's what we're all *prayin'* you'll do."

For another long moment Orrin Knox studied him thoughtfully. Then he spoke in a tone perfectly calm, completely unmoved.

"Let me make it clear to you that this is one President who will never negotiate with the Communist powers under duress. I invited them to talk: they preferred war. So be it. When they prefer peace, we will talk—not before. They have chosen the path we go down. I will follow as long as they wish. When they are ready to talk peace and mean it—when their actions on the battlefield prove it—when they show honesty and good faith and really end hostilities and aggression—then I will talk. Not before."

"The day may come," Senator Richardson said into the silence that followed, his voice filled with a bleakness to match Orrin's own, "when you will have no choice."

"Not if you give me the support and the weapons I need," the President replied.

"And that," Arly said, "many of us in good conscience cannot do."

"Then," the President repeated, "I am on my own."

And this time there fell a silence that no one bridged, as he stared at them and they stared at him, and in the room tension and uncertainty and dismay and fears of the unknowable future filled their hearts. Presently, with hurried, awkward goodbyes from his opponents, heartfelt handshakes and worried, hesitant encouragements from his friends, the meeting broke up and they went out into the driving storm and the bitter night.

As their limousine chugged heavily away, the ex-President and the former Majority Leader looked back for a moment at the great house, now shadowy, mysterious, remote and somehow terribly lonely, in the heavy gusts of snow.

"I wonder," Bob Munson said gloomily, "if we're doing the right thing to encourage him, Bill? I wonder if maybe he's terribly wrong, and we're just encouraging him to take us down a dreadful path that can only end in— . . ."

"I don't know," William Abbott said. "All I know is that you can't have doubts, in that house. You have to be sure. You can't afford to look back, once a decision has been made."

"I'd like to have just two more opinions put before him tonight," Senator Munson said. "If you agree, let's call them from the car right now."

But after they had called, and after the British and French ambassadors had agreed out of old friendship and deep concern to make their own calls to the President, nothing had changed, in the desolate night. Lord Maudulayne and Raoul Barre assured him of their understanding, respectfully but firmly deplored his course, respectfully but firmly urged that he bow to world opinion, hinted sadly, reluctantly but pointedly that their governments might have to attempt to run the blockade of Panama if he persisted, concluded with further assurances of friendship and sympathy, and hung up knowing they had not persuaded or deflected him in the slightest. For them, too, the night turned colder and the winds of the world howled louder down the corridors of history.

After checking the reports from the battlefields—finding the initial American setbacks at least temporarily halted, the fighting momentarily stabilized—he saw only two more people before he went to bed. He was in the Lincoln Bedroom getting ready when there came a quiet but emphatic knock on the door.

"Yes?" he said, taking his bathrobe from the closet, tying it quickly around him as he went forward. "Who is it?"

"It's us," Hal said. "May we come in for a minute?"

"Sure. Want something to eat?"

"I don't," Hal said as they took the two armchairs facing the bed, "but Crystal's ravenous."

"Oh," he said with a sudden pleased expression. "I trust this has the usual conventional significance."

"It does," she said, blushing a little, with a charming smile. "There just hasn't been time to tell you."

"I'm very pleased," he said soberly, giving her a kiss which she returned with genuine affection. "Take care of yourself."

"Will you take care of her?" Hal asked quietly. "Of them?" And suddenly the world's cold winds were inside blowing about them all.

"Children," he said soberly, "I will if God gives me strength. And if He wants me to."

"You must be sure He does," Hal observed, "because you certainly didn't yield any ground over there in the office tonight."

"Did you want me to? You didn't say."

"No," Hal said slowly, "I didn't want you to . . . I think."

"Aren't you sure?" the President demanded. "Because if my own family isn't sure, don't tell me. I don't want to know." His voice grew somber. "I can't afford to know."

"I believe in what you're doing," Crystal said earnestly. "I don't see any other way."

"I don't either," Hal said, still slowly. "I guess what I want—" He paused, his eyes widened in thought just as they had ever since he had been a little boy. "I guess what I want is to be sure that you're sure."

"Didn't I sound it, in the office?" his father asked.

"Oh, sure," Hal said. "You had to sound that way, in front of them. I mean inside."

"I thought the inside showed through. I intended for it to."

"Well, yes," Hal agreed thoughtfully. "I guess you could say it did."

"So?"

"I guess," his son said in a troubled voice, "that I wanted to get it again, straight, from you. I guess I'm scared as hell, frankly. I guess I want you to reassure me." He stared at his wife for a moment, her eyes intently fixed on the President, then back at his father. "Can you?"

For a moment Orrin paused, staring down at the worn rug that covered the floor. Then he looked up directly at these two who now, in Beth's absence, held his heart.

"Children," he said, beginning to walk slowly up and down as he talked, "children and friends, because I like to feel that's what you are. A long time ago, Hal's mother and I decided that whatever I had to face in public life, I would do my best to meet with honesty, with courage and with integrity. We agreed that I would do this even if it meant my political career, even if it meant the end of all our dreams and hopes. I like to think that I have remained generally true to that, over all these years. I am proud and satisfied that this has been the case.

"But until thirty-six hours ago in front of the Capitol, that philosophy and that way of doing things basically only concerned the four of us,

Hal—your mother, yourself, Crystal and me. If I blew it, the people of Illinois might conceivably suffer on some issue I was fighting for, but not too much—not in any way that some other Senator couldn't recover for them, if they threw me out. Basically I was gambling only with the fortunes of Orrin Knox, and the Knox family.

"Now," he said, and his tone became even more thoughtful and somber, while outside the snow slapped savagely against the panes and the cold wind snarled, "much, much more is involved. Now I literally hold the fate of the country in my hands. Now I gamble not with my own ambitions and the Knox family, but—in a sense that sounds maudlin because it is so terribly true—I gamble with the fate of all mankind, and with the whole wide world. . . .

"Still and all"—and he stopped his pacing and his voice grew stronger as they listened with absolute attention—"I think the basic principle still holds. I think I must still try to do what I believe right, as honestly, courageously and with as much integrity, as I can. I hope that when all is said and done, this will be seen to have been the right and only course to follow. . . .

"I can't promise you, I can't promise anyone, that my course will succeed. About all I can give you, and about all I can give the country when I speak tomorrow, is the modest hope that maybe if we do right and are unafraid, right will prevail and humanity will prevail. That is all I can offer. Whether it will be enough to persuade the Congress, convince the Communists and swing the country behind me, I have no way of knowing. But I will try. . . .

"Does that answer your question?"

"It answers mine," Crystal said softly, but it took a moment more for his son to answer.

"As near as it can be, I guess," Hal said finally, his eyes, too, far away in contemplation of terrible alternatives.

"'As near as it can be,'" his father echoed. "Which, I guess, is about as near as I can come."

A few minutes later they left him, Crystal having deliberately lightened the mood by suggesting to Hal, "Come on, let's go down and raid the kitchens. I'm famished!"

By midnight all the lights in the family quarters of the White House were out. Of the three Knoxes remaining, only the President, after a brief colloquy with Beth, who seemed to approve of what he was doing, went immediately and deeply to sleep.

Whatever the coming day might bring, he was at peace in his own mind that he was doing the best he knew, as honestly as he knew. He hoped this would be sufficient—had no way of knowing—but absolved himself from worry, feeling his cause to be just, his purposes to be honorable and his determination unflinching.

At 11 A.M. Eastern time, 10 A.M. Central, 9 Mountain, 8 Pacific, he appeared on television, radio and worldwide satellite network in an attempt to impart this conviction to his countrymen and the world. He did not know how he would be received. But no uncertainty appeared in his calm manner, his steady look or his slow, emphatic words.

He knew his critics would be frothing at the end but he hoped his enemies would be confounded and his supporters of good heart. Only time could tell. Words could do a great deal, and he certainly intended that his should. But only the unfolding of events could provide the final key.

"My countrymen," he said gravely, "I had not thought to address you so soon again. Only vicious, unprovoked and completely unjustified sneak attack by the enemies of this country and of independent nations everywhere has made it necessary that I ask your attention now."

("You see?" Walter Dobius demanded of Frankly Unctuous as they sat together in front of a television set in the Senate Press Gallery, surrounded by respectful colleagues. "Right away, the blind, chauvinist appeal." "Imperialism dies hard," Frankly agreed in his customary profound and portentous manner.)

"You all know the reasons why we are engaged militarily in Gorotoland and Panama.

"In Gorotoland, American missionaries were wantonly murdered and American interests were wantonly attacked by Communist-backed rebel forces.

"In Panama, Communist-backed rebel forces are attempting to overthrow the legitimate government and capture the Canal.

"In both places, my predecessors, President Harley M. Hudson and President William Abbott, felt that the imperative interests of the United States and the independent world were at stake, and that we must intervene. Even aside from the direct attack upon the nationals and the interests of this country, Gorotoland is the strategic heart of the African continent. We cannot let it fall to Communist control: therefore we are there. The Panama Canal is one of the jugulars of the world's commerce. We cannot let it fall to Communist control: therefore we are there."

("How's that for gunboat diplomacy?" they demanded at the *Pimes*.

"At least the bastard is being honest about it," they said with savage irony at the *Tost*. "Thank the Lord for small favors.")

"You will remember"—the President said with a certain savage irony of his own—"at least, some of you will remember, even though many members of the media seem to have forgotten—"

("That's right!" they snapped at CBS, NBC and ABC. "Blame the God-damned media!")

"—that when I came into office, scarcely forty-eight hours ago, the battlefields had been quiet for several months. During this period of stalemate, President Abbott, and I as Secretary of State, made a number of secret approaches, through many channels, to Moscow and Peking, offering substantial concessions to bring about the start of genuine negotiations. All of these attempts were rebuffed. The Communists for the time being did not want war—the worldwide alert ordered by President Abbott discouraged them from that desire—and they did not want peace. Stalemate seemed to suit their purposes, and stalemate was what they deliberately maintained.

"It seemed to me that my inauguration, providing as all inaugurations do something of a clean slate, a new beginning, a fresh approach to problems which never change but which can sometimes be helped by a fresh approach, offered the opportunity for some dramatic new move." His expression for a moment became wry, then hardened again. "It evidently appeared this way to the Communist powers also. There was, however, one difference. I thought it provided the opportunity for peace. They saw it as providing the opportunity for new war.

"My own course, in any event, seemed clear-cut to me. In the concluding moments of my Inaugural Address, I issued a public invitation to the leaders of the Soviet Union and the People's Republic of China to meet with me in Geneva to settle these and other outstanding issues jeopardizing the general peace. I issued this invitation in entire sincerity and good faith, in the hope that it would break the logjam that continues to cripple humanity, as it has for more than four weary decades, interrupted only by a few so-called 'détentes' abandoned as soon as it suited the Communists.

"I suspect that not even those certain members of the media—"

("Boy, is he *hostile!*" they exclaimed at the *Tost*. "I really don't know why," they told one another, quite genuinely puzzled, at the *Pimes*.)

"—have forgotten what happened next.

"Instead of an honest, honorable, cooperative reply to my invitation, the Soviet Union and the People's Republic of China launched an immediate sneak attack on American forces in the two countries. I must tell you, in all candor"—his expression became somber—"that so far, these sneak attacks are meeting with considerable success. American forces have been pushed back, American positions have been seriously threatened. There have been some casualties—not many—except that one is too many.

"I have had two courses open to me in response. I could withdraw American forces and sue for peace—in other words, surrender. Or I could attempt to maintain our positions, in the hope that a vigorous and undismayed response would persuade the Communist powers that we mean business and do not intend to be driven out.

"This latter course seemed to me the only one consistent with our desire for peace."

("'Peace'!" Walter Dobius echoed with a bitter sarcasm. "What a mockery," Frankly Unctuous agreed.)

"The only way, I believe," the President said, "to persuade the Communist powers that we have no intention of running, but do desire to negotiate seriously, is to remain in place, if we can, until they have decided that this latest aggression on their part is not going to produce the American collapse they desire. Once they are convinced of that, I believe we can talk. But not," he said firmly, "until then."

He paused, took a drink of water, resumed gravely, looking straight into the cameras.

"I say 'if we can' remain in place, because I do not believe that this is any time for your President to be less than candid with you. It is not easy at this moment, and it is not going to be easy in the days and weeks ahead.

"The sneak attack caught us at a disadvantage, even though we have substantial forces and matériel on site in both Gorotoland and Panama. More must be supplied. The counterpressure must be maintained if meaningful negotiations are to come about. Past history, in Vietnam and elsewhere, shows that such negotiations only happen when the Communists face matching strength. They never happen when the Communists face weakness—then negotiations mean nothing but camouflaged surrender to the Communist position.

"There is also one other reason for maintaining pressure, even though it seems remote, and that is that there might conceivably be some rift in the apparent unity with which the Soviet Union and the People's Republic of China are cooperating. They have never cooperated before, certainly never on a military venture. There is a remote possibility that something may conceivably happen between them if we remain firm."

("How's that for being a junior-grade Machiavelli?" they asked one another at the *Pimes*. "There isn't a single low-down trick he won't use when he gets desperate, is there?" they asked one another at the *Tost*.)

"We cannot, however, depend on that remote possibility. We must depend on ourselves and on the historical truism that one can only negotiate with the Communists from strength, never from weakness. We must stay strong, and we must endure. Then in due course we may hope that we will be able to achieve meaningful negotiations that will look toward peace not only in Panama and Gorotoland, but in other areas of the world as well.

"To stay strong, however"—and his tone became thoughtful almost conversational—"we need the foundations of strength. And the foundations of strength only you, the American people, working your will through your Congress—"

("Here it comes, now!" the Speaker exclaimed as they sat watching in the Majority Leader's private office just down the hall from the main Senate door. "It won't do him any good," the Majority Leader said with a flat certainty.)

"—can provide. I hope you will do so.

"In my Inaugural Address, aware of the state of American forces, which in some areas leaves much to be desired after the legislative depredations of recent years, I announced that I would send to the Congress a request for an emergency ten-billion-dollar supplement to the funds for the Department of Defense. The events of night before last, events which still continue in Gorotoland and Panama, make this even more imperative. Accordingly, I submitted the request to both houses yesterday morning.

"It is apparent already that there is substantial, and, I believe, ill-informed, opposition to this request. Some of it, particularly from new members, is genuinely ignorant of the exact state of our armed forces. Some of it is dominated by long-standing animosity toward me personally. Some of it is designed to curry favor with certain influential elements in America who are desperately afraid to face up to the obligation to act which would be imposed upon them if they actually admitted the true nature of the Communist threat.

"All of these forces have combined to slow down, already, the momentum which a request of such urgency, in such a time of crisis, should receive at the hands of the Congress.

"Therefore," he said, and he looked with a particular intensity into the cameras as though he could hold the eyes of each individual listener among his country's diverse millions, "I am appealing to you this morning to assist me in persuading the Congress to act favorably on this issue which is, I believe, of absolute desperate necessity to the well-being and actual survival of the United States.

"I appeal to you to make your wishes known. Telephone, send wires, send letters—and do so at once. We face a desperate crisis in the world and we must see it through to a conclusion which will save ourselves, and save mankind, from a catastrophic disaster that would make peace forever impossible."

An even greater earnestness entered his voice.

"We must remain strong. We must discharge our obligations in the two war areas overseas. We must continue to press for negotiations from strength. It is the only way we can ever achieve them, and through them, achieve a lasting world peace."

He appeared for a second to conclude. Then he laid aside his papers and leaned forward, and now he was talking to them person to person, informally, in their own living rooms or wherever they might be.

"Last night, shortly before midnight, my son Hal and daughter-in-law Crystal came to me in the Lincoln Bedroom of the White House, where I was getting ready for bed."

("*Oh,* oh!" they chortled at the *Tost.* "Hit the Maudlin Button, everybody!" they gurgled at the *Pimes.*)

"My son Hal, as you know, is a newly elected member of the House of Representatives. My daughter-in-law Crystal lost her first child as a result of a beating by members of the National Anti-War Activities Congress at the national convention last August.

"Now my daughter-in-law tells me that she is pregnant again, and she and my son, deeply worried like all of us by the events of the past forty-eight hours, asked me what I intended to do, and what I could offer them in the way of assurance to help them through these difficult days.

"What I said, essentially, was this:

"Long ago, when I first entered public life as a member of the lower house of the Illinois legislature, I agreed with"—there was an almost imperceptible hesitation—"my late wife that whatever I had to face as a public servant I would do my best to face with honesty, with courage and with integrity. We agreed that I would do this even if it meant my political career, even if it meant the end of all the dreams and hopes of myself and my family.

"I think I have remained generally true to that, over all these years, and I hope my friends among you will be satisfied, as I am, that I have been generally able to keep that pledge made so long ago.

"Up to the moment when I took my oath as President, however"—and his tone became somber as it had with his children the night before—"I was staking only my own fortunes and those of my family on this personal standard. Now, much, much more is involved. Now—and I do not say this to shock or frighten you, but because it is true—I literally hold the fate of the country in my hands—and even more. Now—in a sense that sounds maudlin because it is so terribly true—I hold in my hands the fate of all mankind, and that of the whole wide world. And so, of course, do the leaders of Russia, and the leaders of China.

"I believe, however," he said quietly, "that the basic principle still holds. I think I still must try to do what I believe right, as honestly, courageously and with as much integrity, as I can.

"I hope that when all is said and done, this will be seen to have been the right and only course to follow. . . .

"This does not mean," he said gravely, and even his bitterest opponents were quiet among themselves in the face of the naked honesty with which he was taking them into his confidence, "that there will be any easy answers, or any easy path to go down. It does not mean that there will be comfortable solutions or a smooth way out. It doesn't even mean that I will succeed in the course I believe to be right.

"I may"—his eyes looked far away, but his expression did not waver—"I may destroy the whole globe. I can do it—any President can, in this age of horrible weapons and instant war, just as any leader of Russia, or any leader of China, or any leader of any smaller power who wants to precipitate world disaster, can do it.

"I would hope that the collective common sense of mankind will prevent that outcome, but it may not.

"Certainly it will not if that collective common sense is not applied as severely to Russia and China as it is being applied to us, in the United Nations and elsewhere. . . .

"So, then"—and again his gaze became intent and concentrated, so that many felt he was speaking directly, and only, to them—"I can't promise you, I can't promise anyone, that the course I have chosen, the course of strength and firmness, will succeed. About all I can give you is the modest hope that maybe if we do right and are unafraid, right will prevail, and humanity will prevail.

"That is all I can offer: no certainty, but a modest hope. I need your help, I need your support, if that hope is to be achieved. Give it to me, and I say to you: be of good faith, and be not afraid. Together we will win through."

And he sat back, and for a long moment, while the national anthem began and his firm, emphatic face, flanked by the American flag and the flag of the President, faded slowly from the screen, there was silence among all his friends and all his enemies, all who had heard him in his own land, and all around the globe.

But not, of course, for long.

KNOX SAYS HE CAN DESTROY WORLD. DEFIES U.S. AND WORLD PEACE SENTIMENT, PLEDGES ALL-OUT FIGHT IN GOROTOLAND, PANAMA. ASKS COUNTRY TO PRESSURE CONGRESS TO ASSURE PASSAGE OF TEN-BILLION ARMS BILL. ADMITS COURSE MAY NOT SUCCEED BUT OFFERS "MODEST HOPE." SEEKS TO DRIVE WEDGE BETWEEN RUSS AND CHINESE.

MOSCOW, PEKING DENOUNCE SPEECH AS "MOUTHINGS OF MADMAN . . . FUTILE IMPERIALIST MANEUVER TO DESTROY UNITY OF WORLD REVOLUTIONARY MOVEMENT." PLEDGE CONTINUED ALL-OUT DRIVE TO "STOP U.S. INSANITY EVERYWHERE." WORLD CAPITALS DISMAYED BY PRESIDENT'S BELLIGERENCE. MANY SEE END TO ALL HOPES FOR PEACE.

CONGRESS REFUSES TO DEBATE ARMS BUILDUP DESPITE ATTEMPTS BY ABBOTT, MUNSON TO FORCE ISSUE TO FLOOR IN BOTH HOUSES. SENATE LEADER ANNOUNCES CABINET APPOINTMENTS WILL BE DELAYED "UNTIL THIS WAR MADNESS IN THE WHITE HOUSE COMES TO AN END." WHITE HOUSE CLAIMS TELEGRAMS RUNNING "TWO TO ONE" FOR PRESIDENT, BUT HILL LEADERS GIVE OPPOSITE PICTURE.

NEW EMERGENCY MEETING OF SECURITY COUNCIL RENEWS DEMAND U.S. WITHDRAW, DIRECTS KNOX TO MEET "FORTHWITH" WITH SOVIETS AND CHINESE. PRESIDENT IMMEDIATELY REJECTS "INSOLENT AND ONE-SIDED ATTEMPT TO FORCE THE HAND OF THE AMERICAN GOVERNMENT." GENERAL ASSEMBLY RESOLUTION URGES U.N. MEMBERS TO USE "EVERY MILITARY AND ECONOMIC WEAPON AT THEIR COMMAND" AGAINST U.S. . . . PEOPLE'S REPUBLIC OF SAUDI ARABIA LEADS SIX COMMUNIST MIDEAST OIL STATES IN IMMEDIATE EMBARGO ON ALL SHIPMENTS TO U.S.

REDS MAKE NEW GAINS ON BATTLEFIELDS. U.S. CORRESPONDENTS SAY AMERICAN SUPPLIES DANGEROUSLY LOW. NAWAC LEADS MASSIVE PEACE DEMONSTRATIONS IN WASHINGTON, OTHER MAJOR CITIES.

And now here the slimy bastards were on his own front stoop, the Vice President thought with a bitter annoyance as his chauffeured limousine turned in the drive of the modest home he and Sarah were still occupying, up Sixteenth Street. They would be moving in a week to the quarters at the old Naval Observatory on Massachusetts Avenue which Congress had finally provided for the Vice President after a couple of centuries of careful consideration, but for now it was still the old homestead, where he and Sue-Dan had gone through the final agonies of their mismatched marriage, and where he had undergone more than one bitter clash with at least one of the individuals who waited for him now.

He had come home early because the Senate, having slapped down the President's request for speed on the Defense Department emergency appropriation, and having compounded the defiance by deliberately holding up speedy confirmation of the Cabinet, had then gone into a three-day recess, presumably to give the President time to think about it. Lord knew *he* was thinking about it, and his thoughts were not very friendly to the body whose presiding officer he had become. It was also apparent, after several sharp arguments over parliamentary procedure between himself and Arly Richardson, and himself and several of the new young members who were egging Arly on, that many in the Senate were not thinking very friendly thoughts about him, either. He was the principal symbol of the Knox Administration on the Senate side, and as such was obviously bearing the brunt of a lot of the antagonism over Orrin's policies. He did not really mind this, since he believed in them; but being by nature one who usually liked people and liked to get along with them, he was finding it a strain. And, he knew, there would be a lot more to come.

But that it had to enter his own house was something he resented intensely. In fact, when Sarah had come home from her first meeting of the Senate Ladies' Club to hear from faithful old Maudie about the ominous phone call she had received, and had then called him, much upset, he had exploded with a wrath far from his easygoing manner.

"God damn it!" he had exclaimed, making his secretary jump. "Why the hell can't that trash come and see me here, in the open, instead of sneaking around behind people's backs? I guess," he had added dourly, answering his own question, "it's because that's the only way they know how to operate, behind people's backs. . . . I want you to be witness, Darletta"—his voice took on a sarcastic singsong as he listed the titles—"Mr. Le*Gage* Shelby, chairman of Defenders of Equality for You—*DEE*FY—and Mr. Rufus Kleinfert, Knight Kommander of the Konference on Efforts to *En*courage Patriotism—KEEP—and Senator —*ex*-Senator Van Ackerman, thank the Lord, chairman of the Committee on Making Further Offers for a Russian Truce—*COM*FORT—and also and incidentally, chairman of great old *NAWAC*—are coming to my house in half an hour. I don't know what they want, but knowing that trash, I imagine it isn't anything nice."

"Do you want me to come along and take notes?" Darletta asked matter-of-factly, brisk and efficient as ever, which was why he had brought her from his modest offices in the House down to these much more stately and elaborate quarters he now occupied in the Executive Office Building, across the street from the White House.

"No, thanks. Sarah will be there, and so will Maudie, my good old maid. I just want you to note that the Vice President left his office at 4 P.M. to meet these characters. If I'm never heard from again, the world will know who saw me last."

"I always thought," she said with a sudden little twinkle, "that just being Vice President was enough to guarantee that nobody would ever hear of you again."

He stood up with a chuckle and put on his coat.

"Girl," he said, "movin' downtown has made you right sassy, now—right sassy. Watch it, or I'll stand on my dignity. I'm very dignified, you know."

"Yes, sir," she said cheerfully, scooping up the correspondence they had been working on together. "I'll remember that."

"You do it," he said, as his chauffeur appeared at the door.

"Mr. Vice President," he said, removing his cap and bowing low, "your car is ready, sir."

"You see?" he demanded.

"I see," Darletta said with a smile. Then her expression turned serious. "Be careful with those people," she said, and he could see she was seriously worried. "They're bad business."

"Do I know," he agreed somberly. "*Do* I know."

And so here he was at the front door, guarded by Secret Service but otherwise as modest as any on the block. Inside there waited for him—what? He hoped to goodness Sarah and Maudie were away in their own parts of the house and not making any attempt to entertain his unwelcome visitors. Sarah, however, opened the door, her eyes and a certain hurried note in her voice revealing tension.

He kissed her quickly, whispered, "Where are they, in the living room? Have they been giving you a bad time?"—received her quickly nodded "Yes" to the first and "No" to the second—and feeling somewhat relieved, said in a normal, cheerful voice, "Why don't you go back and help Maudie, and I'll be along in a few minutes."

"We'll expect you in about fifteen minutes," she answered with equal clarity. "We have to go over those plans for the party, you know."

He mouthed, "Party?" with an exaggerated surprise, gave her a grin as she disappeared swiftly down the hall; straightened his shoulders, stepped forward quickly and opened the door to the living room. His visitors stared at him with varying degrees of expectation and insolence. 'Gage Shelby and Fred Van Ackerman, he noted, were doing pretty well on the insolence. Rufus Kleinfert was his usual stolid, dumpy self, his expression not indicating much of anything.

They also, quite deliberately, did not rise for him, which annoyed him further.

"Yes?" he said, unable to keep all the hostility out of his tone. His old Howard University roommate and buddy reacted with the split-second timing with which he had always reacted to Cullee's moods.

"*Yes*," LeGage Shelby snapped. "*Yes*, Cullee, we're here."

"'Mr. Vice President,'" he corrected coldly, his own temper, also, as fragile as ever, doubly so as there surged into his mind the loss of Sue-Dan and all the other scores he had to settle with 'Gage.

"We won't get out, Mr. Vice *Pres*ident," Fred Van Ackerman said, giving the title a deliberate insolence, "until we've said our piece. So settle down."

"Yess," Rufus Kleinfert agreed, in the thick Pennsylvania-Dutch accent that thirty years in Texas oil had never quite eradicated. "We have verry important matters to discuss."

"O.K.," he said, dropping his massive frame into his favorite armchair, which they had somehow managed to overlook—if they had realized it was his favorite, he knew, damned 'Gage or smart-ass Van Ackerman would have had it already. "What can I do for you?"

"As if you will," 'Gage said. "But maybe," he added darkly, "you'd better."

"What's this?" he demanded, his tone deliberately bored, deliberately going into the lazy cadence of his native South Carolina, which he knew would infuriate 'Gage. "You-all threatenin' me again, boy? You know that don't cut no stuff with me, boy."

"'*Boy*'*!*" LeGage exploded furiously; and then, with an obvious and mighty effort, forced himself back under control. "We didn't come here to play games with you, Cullee—Mr. Vice President," he corrected angrily as Cullee raised a casual but definitely warning hand. "We're here to talk serious business."

"Good," Cullee observed in a pleased tone. "Being Vice President *is* serious business."

"Why stop there?" Fred Van Ackerman inquired with the cheerful brashness he sometimes used to camouflage his more outrageous proposals.

For several moments, while he stared at them blankly, his eyes traveling slowly from face to face and back again, an absolute silence held the room. Finally he broke it, very softly.

"Just what are you driving at, Senator? Just what slimy thing are you thinking about now?"

For a split second a blind anger flared in the shrewd face across the room. Then, in one of the lightning changes of mood so characteristic of the ex-Senator from Wyoming, it was succeeded by an impudent smile.

"Not slimy at all," Fred Van Ackerman said blandly. "Just a perfectly reasonable way for a deserving young black boy from South Carolina and California to ascend the ladder of political success to its very utmost, topmost, God damned most-most rung. That's all, Mr. Vice President. Just a chance for a little job advancement, if you handle it right."

"There won't be an election for four years," Cullee said in a puzzled tone, playing it straight even as he wished desperately that there were some way to signal Sarah, to get a tape recorder going, to preserve somehow this fantastic conversation which was swiftly moving into areas far beyond anything most of their countrymen could ever dream.

"Won't be an election," LeGage agreed. "May be something else."

"Yess," breathed Rufus Kleinfert with a heavy expiration.

"Tell me about it," Cullee suggested, his tone still puzzled, almost dazed. "I'm not sure I understand—"

"Oh, you understand, Mr. Vice President," Fred Van Ackerman said calmly. "You understand very well."

"No, I don't," he said. "I really don't. Tell me."

"All right," Fred said coldly, deciding suddenly to go along with it. "Pay attention, now. Half-Ass Orrin is destroying the country—"

"And world peace," Rufus Kleinfert interjected.

"—and world peace. If he stays in office we're going to be in such a hell of a mess that nobody is ever going to get us out—*if* he stays in office."

"So?" Cullee asked blankly.

"So we've got to get rid of him," LeGage snapped.

"I suppose somebody could try to impeach him," Cullee said with an innocent thoughtfulness, "but really—"

"Impeachment!" Fred Van Ackerman said scornfully, neither tone nor words extending charity to his former colleagues on the Hill. "Those lily-livered pantywaists! Even if they had the guts, which they don't, impeachment would take months. Half-Ass is ruining the country in days."

"Well, I don't know, then . . ." Cullee said doubtfully. "I don't think he would resign. I mean, even if I tried to persuade him—" He broke off with a deprecating laugh. "But of course *I* couldn't, I'd have too much interest in it."

"We all have an interest in it," LeGage said sharply, "and we can't afford to wait 'months,' either."

"Of course, maybe," Cullee said slowly, "if you-all in NAWAC keep up these mass demonstrations like you put on yesterday all over the country, then maybe—maybe he might just decide that he really should quit, you know?"

"Orrin Knox?" Fred Van Ackerman snorted. "He won't quit until he's carried out on a stretcher."

"Which is exactly what you bastards want for him, isn't it?" Cullee demanded with a sudden furious anger, abandoning pretense, speaking with all the revulsion he had always felt for this sleazy crew. "I ought to go to the FBI and have you all put away forever!"

"How could you?" Fred Van Ackerman demanded with an evil innocence of his own. "You haven't got any witnesses that *we've* said anything. In fact, we haven't. *You* said it, not us. Maybe they ought to put *you* away."

"Now, you listen to me," Cullee said, hunching forward in his chair, breathing heavily, stabbing the air with an emphatic hand as he spoke. "I don't know what kind of an evil bargain you have in mind here—or rather, I know damned well—but it couldn't ever work even if the world were as insane as you insane bastards seem to think it is. Because even if you got rid of Orrin, as I suspect you've gotten rid of some others, you'd still have me. And I wouldn't change his policies one little bit, because I believe in them. *I believe in them.* I admire his principles, I admire his integrity, I admire his guts. I think he's got the only way out of this mess, and I'm supporting him one hundred per cent. So what good would it do anybody to have me in there?

Even if I—" He suddenly paused and his tone became absolutely calm and absolutely disgusted—"even if anybody on God's green earth would enter knowingly into such a scheme as you three sickies have in mind. I repeat, you *are* insane—criminally insane.

"And when I think of all the innocent fools all over this country who tag along behind you thinking you're really interested in peace and in the welfare of the United States of America—well"—he sat back with a disgust, a weariness and a frustration so deep that he could hardly articulate them—"I pity them. I pity us, the whole country, that we've gotten so far off the beam about this."

"And who's put us off the beam?" LeGage demanded with a sudden furious anger of his own. "Who's extending the war, ruining the peace, making it impossible for us to talk to the Russians and the Chinese, making it impossible to get negotiations going, leading us back, back, *back* to old discarded things that have never worked and never will work? Who, I ask you, Mr. Big-Shot Vice President? *Who?* The damned President, that's who! Damned Orrin Knox with his arrogance and his impatience and his know-it-all mighty superior ways and his damned stubbornness that's going to send us all straight to hell in another week or two if we don't stop him *now,* that's who!"

"You sound like my ex-wife, boy," Cullee said with a renewal of the lazy tone, knowing instinctively that the moment was over, he was back in command. "You seein' much of that sexy little gal these days?"

"You leave Sue-Dan out of this!" LeGage snapped. "You leave Sue-Dan the hell out of this!"

"She's my ex-wife," Cullee pointed out in the same lazily infuriating way. "What's the matter, is she your *ex*-girl friend? I thought you were a better swinger than that, boy. Used to be when I knew you. . . . Though you do have to be pretty busy to keep up with that little Sue-Dan, I'll admit," he added admiringly, never showing the knifelike pain that still shot through him at the thought of her. "Yes, sir, pre—tty busy."

"Ah!" LeGage cried, a frustrated, infuriated, inarticulate sound, jumping to his feet and whirling away to a window in sheer exasperation. His movement gave Cullee the chance he wanted and he too rose slowly to his full six feet six and looked down at them as from a great height of disgusted judgment.

"Now, you scum," he said softly, "get out of my house and don't you ever—*ever*—come near me again. Any of you! Now, *git!*"

And he walked across the room, opened the door to the hallway, turned back and gave them a somber glare.

For several seconds they returned it, 'Gage still quivering with fury, Fred smiling with the air of unimpressed insolence he usually managed to maintain, Rufus Kleinfert, as always, deceptively stolid and stumpy for one who must be shrewd, considering how many millions he had amassed in the slippery sludge of Texas oil.

"NAWAC," Fred Van Ackerman promised pleasantly as he picked up his coat and slipped it on, "will get you for this, Mr. Vice President. You and your precious Orrin, too."

"I said *git*," Cullee said, "and I mean *git*. That way! Out!"

"You're all wrong!" 'Gage cried bitterly, turning back for a moment in the door, his voice as urgent and woebegone as it used to be in climactic moments of their bitter pitched arguments over race and policy at Howard University, so long ago. "All wrong, Cullee!"

"I'll chance it," the Vice President said, just before he slammed the door upon them. "I'll take that chance."

"What did they want?" Sarah asked, coming swiftly to him along the hall, eyes wide with fear and worry.

"Crazy things," he said, feeling suddenly heavy and burdened and old far beyond his forty years. "Crazy, crazy things. And they aren't alone, either. That's the awful thing. They aren't alone."

Nor were they, though the five shrewd and highly intelligent individuals who faced one another via Picturephone linkup along the Eastern seaboard would have denied with the utmost vehemence the charge that their basic motivations and ultimate intentions were very close to those of the ruthless trio who dreamed their dreams of violence behind the façade of NAWAC's innocent millions. The principal proprietors of American public opinion were about their business of eliminating the opposing point of view again, and now, as always, their consciences were clear because their purposes, as they always managed to convince themselves, were patriotic and pure.

"I believe," Walter Dobius said—and his colleagues could see that he was in what some of them referred to as "Walter's super-doomsday mood"—"that America faces at this moment the gravest crisis in her entire history. I believe that we must stop Orrin Knox or we are literally fated to die, as a nation and as a people. I hope you all feel the same urgency."

"Is that why you wanted to talk, Walter?" the kindly old man who presided over *The Greatest Publication That Absolutely Ever Was* inquired with his customary gentle irony. "I had thought we on this journal had already made our concern quite clear."

"We, too," the *Times* observed, and "We, too," the *Post* agreed. Frankly Unctuous cleared his throat and looked grave.

"I can see Walter's point, however," he observed judiciously. "I think now we must *really* fight this arrogant man in the White House. Otherwise, I would estimate that the Republic has perhaps another two weeks to live."

"I'm not so sure I give it that long," the *Post* remarked gloomily. "But certainly *we* are doing everything we can to make *our* feelings known."

"I think it is time to call for impeachment, or resignation, or both," Walter said firmly, "to pursue him relentlessly on every front, every aspect of his life, his career, his philosophies, his program. It is time to turn Orrin Knox inside out and expose him to his countrymen for what he is, the most irresponsible, warmongering, unpatriotic, unworthy, dangerous and disastrous individual who ever sat in the White House. It is time to be as absolutely ruthless and uncompromising toward him as he is toward everyone who disagrees with his insane death-making policies.

"We can oppose him, Walter," the *Times* remarked, "and God knows *we* are, but we also have to maintain at least an aspect of objectivity, you know. We can't be too rabid. Otherwise we would lose public confidence in the fairness of the press. Then we would really lose all hold on them."

"'Objectivity'!" Walter snapped. "'Rabid'! Is *he* objective, I ask you? And who is being 'rabid' in Gorotoland and Panama? Stop giving me empty words and hit him, hit him, *hit him!*"

"My goodness," the proprietor of *The Greatest Publication* said gently. "You *are* concerned, Walter, aren't you?"

"And why shouldn't I be?" Walter inquired bitterly, his stubborn face flushed with anger. "When a President has consistently ignored every piece of sound advice that we in the media have been giving him all his public life, what else does he deserve from us? And now the situation is absolutely desperate—*absolutely desperate.* Surely we are not going to hesitate now!"

"I am not," Frankly said flatly. "And I think I can speak for my colleagues of the networks. Anything you can find to use against him, we will report. And I shan't hesitate for a minute to comment on it, either. Nor, I think, will the others. It is literally a matter of saving the United States of America. It seems to me that anything is justified in that cause."

"Well, of course we have the means," the *Post* acknowledged.

"God knows we've used them before. We can attack, as you say, Walter, his morals, his family, his life style, his character, his income tax, his financial dealings, his sex life—if Orrin Knox ever had any! I mean, all this is very simple and easy to do. And damned effective, too, I will admit, if you keep hammering at it loud enough and long enough."

"And we can find plenty of people in Congress to help us out," the *Times* noted. "Hints, rumors, innuendos—speeches, attacks, charges, investigations—you name it, we've got it. But," he added thoughtfully, "if you don't mind too much, Walter, we would like to confine it to the issue, because we think the issue is much more important. The issue is war or peace, quick or dead, disaster or joy. What more do we need than that?"

"I am inclined to agree," the head of *The Greatest Publication* said. "I agree with your basic thesis, Walter, that this is a desperately anxious time, but I think there is plenty to be said about it without resorting to gutter tactics."

"Oh, I don't know," the *Post* said dreamily. "*We've* found them very effective."

"Anyway," Walter said impatiently, "they aren't 'gutter tactics.' They're perfectly legitimate dissections of a man's basic character and career, vital to an appraisal of his present policies. They supplement the arguments on the issue, which I grant you are very important—overwhelmingly important. Certainly no one can honestly say that I haven't been making the arguments on the issue! My God, I've been arguing the issues with Orrin Knox for twenty years!"

"And very well, too," the head of *The Greatest Publication* said soothingly. "You wouldn't be America's leading columnist otherwise."

"You can do as you like," Walter said, his face getting the balky set they knew so well, "but I am going to attack him in every way possible. I think we must hit him and *hit him hard.*"

"I'm with you, Walter," the *Post* agreed, abandoning discussion with a sudden decisiveness. "He is on an insane collision course and he must be stopped. We'll use everything we can."

"I, too," Frankly Unctuous said firmly.

"Even if it may tend to obscure the real issue?" the *Times* inquired thoughtfully.

"Even if it may inflame even further the leaders of NAWAC and the violent and incite them to more God-knows-what?" *The Greatest Publication* inquired gently.

"Even so," Walter Dobius said coldly, his tone abandoning once and for all any remotest shred of tolerance that might still be lingering in his heart for Orrin Knox. "Even so."

"I wouldn't have asked for this interview," he said with a sudden nervousness that surprised him, "except that you ought to know what I've been through this afternoon."

"Sit down, Cullee," the President said with a relaxed courtesy that might have been light-years away from the hectic moment in which they met, and from the house that was the fulcrum of the world's animosities, hopes, disparagements, concerns. "I'm going through a bit, myself."

"Yes, I know," the Vice President said hurriedly. "I didn't mean to imply—"

"Oh, I know," the President said with a smile. "Ignore me. I'm just letting off steam. What happened to *you* on this happy day?"

His expression hardened as Cullee told him. When the recital ended he hit the desk with the flat of his hand.

"Those sons of bitches," he said quietly. "I've always regretted society doesn't have an automatic trapdoor for that type, preferably over a pool of piranhas. It would simplify matters. But we don't, so here we are. Are you ready to take over if they get me?"

"Mr. President!" Cullee said in an alarmed voice, forgetting for a moment Orrin's propensity to make rather grim jokes at times of tension. "They aren't going to get you!"

"They may," the President said, his voice becoming somber. "They may. I'm very well protected, but sooner or later somebody may get through, just as they did at the Monument Grounds." His expression darkened. "They're after my family again, you know."

"No."

"Yes. And you'd better look out for yours. Do you have enough protection at your house?"

The Vice President hesitated for a moment, then gave him an honest and troubled look.

"I could use more."

"Right," Orrin said promptly. "Excuse me." He buzzed his secretary, asked for the chief of the Secret Service, reached him immediately, gave a quick order, turned back. "Five more men will be on the job in fifteen minutes, so you can rest a little easier. They added three more on the Spring Valley house last night, even though it's empty now, with Hal and Crystal living here. Crystal had planned to go back this afternoon to get some clothes but we had the detail do it for her, after the threats."

"What threats?"

"Death, doom and destruction to the two of them if I don't change my policies. The same line you got, from the same sources, I suspect—although of course they've gathered so many kooks around them that it could be somebody down the line. But I rather think not."

"Evil days," Cullee said moodily. The President nodded, with a certain grim irony.

"And all my fault, too, as you can hear all over. Are you still glad you joined this Administration, Cullee?"

"I believe you're doing what's right," Cullee said simply.

"Thank you," the President said gravely. "So do I. However—" He picked up a sheaf of papers and handed them across the desk. "Look at these for a minute."

There was silence while the Vice President read. Presently he looked up.

"It doesn't look good," he admitted uncomfortably.

"It does not," Orrin agreed. "Their initial momentum is still running, we're still falling back. Losses are mounting, matériel is being wiped out. Britain and France and the rest are beginning to talk seriously about running the blockade in Panama. Everything appears to be going wrong." He gave his Vice President the sharp, direct, undodgeable look his friends and colleagues knew so well. "Shall I give up?"

Cullee answered without hesitation.

"How can you?"

"Yes," the President said. "That is the question, which I resolve in favor of my policies because I do not see any other way out of the situation our enemies have created. I am afraid, however, that in the classical pattern of difficult democracy it is going to get worse before it gets better."

"I'm not dismayed," the Vice President said.

"Nor I. Troubled, of course—far more troubled than my critics will ever grant me—but not dismayed. This dismays *them*, no doubt, but I won't yield to them, Cullee." He paused and repeated softly as if to himself, "I won't yield to them. . . ." He looked at the snow, still hitting the house in occasional spits and flurries, the great storm reluctant to yield its hold on the desolate gray world. "I wonder what Ted would have done," he said in a musing tone, "if I had died at the Monument and he had come to this chair. Appeased, maybe? Been tough, maybe? Fought it out, or gulped and gone under? Nobody knows, but I do know one thing"—his tone became wry—"whatever it was, he would have had the media behind him with a whoop and a holler, that's for sure. At least until it got too late, even for the media. . . . Well—" He stood up, held out his hand, prepared to say goodbye. As he did so the buzzer sounded urgently several times. "Yes?" he said, switching on the intercom, sitting slowly down again.

"Mrs. Jason on the line," his secretary said.

"Yes, Ceil," he said, turning on the Picturephone, gesturing Cullee to come stand beside him. "What is it? *What is it?*" he repeated sharply as her face, strained and obviously agitated as he had never seen Ceil Jason's face agitated, came on the screen.

"Mr. President—" she began, seeming to have difficulty with her breathing. "Mr. President—"

"Take your time," he ordered calmly. "The Vice President is here, as you can see. We'll wait."

"Yes," she said; and after a moment, pushing her golden hair back, clearly fighting for control and presently achieving it, she was able to speak more quietly and coherently. "We have had some trouble up here."

"You haven't been hurt?" he demanded sharply.

"No," she said. "No. But"—her face threatened to crumple again, then steadied—"but someone was. My—my chauffeur. We were about to leave for the Secretary-General's cocktail party and he went—went out to the car a moment ahead of me and started it up. I was about to get in when I decided that I wanted to change my purse. So I went back up to the suite and did so, and just as I stepped out the door again, it—it went off."

"A bomb," he said, not a question but a flat, weary statement. She nodded.

"Yes," she said, her voice threatening to break again. "It was apparently set to go off about—about five minutes after the engine was started. If I hadn't gone back to get my purse—" She shivered and stopped.

"Was he killed?"

"Y—yes."

"I am so sorry," he said gravely. Suddenly his voice exploded in an angry, frustrated burst. "God *damn* it to hell! I could murder those bastards with my own bare hands." Then he, too, with an obvious effort, regained control. "Who did it?"

"We don't know yet," she said. "The Secret Service and the New York police are already here and I think the FBI is on the way."

"Who do you think did it? Some of our charming countrymen, or some of our charming friends in the U.N.?"

"It could be any one of fifty up here. But I have the feeling it was —our own people."

"So do I," he said. "How ironic that Ted's most devoted followers should now be trying to kill Ted's wife." He paused and thought for a moment. "Of course, I don't have to tell you to take all necessary precautions—"

"There are ten additional Secret Service men here already," she said with the start of a shaky little laugh, "and a couple of policewomen. I can't even—even powder my nose alone, right now."

"That's good," he said. "And don't try to, either, at any time in the foreseeable future. Maybe someday things will calm down, but not before the wars are over. And when that will be, I can't predict. . . . Well"—a sudden cold decisiveness came into his tone—"there have been other things in the last several hours and I think it's about time I did something about them. You and Cullee listen, now. I'm going to dictate a statement and I want you to make whatever suggestions you think necessary." He flicked the intercom, buzzed his secretary. "Come in here a minute, Dottie. I've got something for you."

MRS. JASON NARROWLY ESCAPES DEATH IN BOMB BLAST. HER CHAUFFEUR DIES IN CAR BOOBY TRAP. ATTACK BELIEVED CAUSED BY CONCERN OVER KNOX WAR POLICIES.

PRESIDENT ISSUES ANGRY STATEMENT, DISCLOSES THREATS TO SON AND DAUGHTER-IN-LAW. ANNOUNCES STEPPED-UP SECURITY FOR "ALL MEMBERS OF MY PERSONAL AND OFFICIAL FAMILY." VICE PRESIDENT GIVEN EXTRA GUARDS. NAWAC LEADERS DENY RESPONSIBILITY BUT WARN THAT "HE WHO RESORTS TO SWORD MUST EXPECT TO FIND SWORD USED AGAINST HIM."

REPORTS FROM WAR ZONES INDICATE U.S. FORCES STILL IN RETREAT AS POWERFUL RED OFFENSIVES ROLL ON.

"And so Orrin Knox has reaped the first—or is it the second, or third, or how many? Whatever it is, the number will assuredly grow—bitter fruit of his obdurate, intractable and foredoomed policies," *The Greatest Publication* commented. "An innocent man is dead and the President's Ambassador to the United Nations has narrowly escaped death. Mrs. Ceil Jason, who only five months ago lost her husband to assailants unknown, has now herself come within seconds of suffering the same fate. It should be enough to give a prudent man pause—since it is his actions which have apparently led straight to this unhappy event. . . ."

"An innocent chauffeur dead," the *Times* said with equal severity, "Ambassador Ceil Jason almost dead, the President's children and his Vice President subjected to threats of terrible violence unless he changes his policies—only an Orrin Knox, we suspect, could continue his stubborn course under circumstances such as these. How much longer must all around him—how much longer must his helpless country and the world—suffer from the intemperate and ill-advised war program of this most erratic and unfortunate of Chief Executives? He takes upon himself a fearful burden, to play so lightly with the lives of all of us entrusted to his care. How much longer, we wonder, will the Congress and the country suffer him to continue without imposing checkreins he cannot imperially ignore? . . ."

"So the insanity goes on," the *Post* exploded. "So the insane stubbornness of Orrin Knox goes on. It staggers the mind, where it does not desolate the heart. How many must die, on the battlefields and in his own immediate group, before he gets it through his head that America and the world simply do not approve of his ruthless, arrogant, foredoomed war policies? Only one truly paranoiac, truly schizophrenic, we suspect, could play so lightly with the fate of men and nations. Starting on Page 1 today we present an analysis of the President by one of New York City's most brilliant young psychiatrists. Entitled *Orrin Knox: Achieving the Unbalance of Power,* it promises to give Americans a profound insight into their most unfit President ever. We commend it to all citizens who wish to understand this strange man who is riding the juggernaut straight down the road to national and world disaster. . . ."

"Washington waits and wonders tonight," Frankly Unctuous said gravely—"another of Frankly's wait-and-wonder nights," his less respectful colleagues assured one another at the Press Club bar—"about the strange course of the strange man who has just assumed the awesome powers of the American Presidency. Confronted by the death of an innocent black chauffeur, the near death of Mrs. Ceil Jason, dire and terrible threats to the safety of his own son and daughter-in-law, his Vice President, his official family, he staggers blindly on, deeper and ever deeper into the morass of endless war. At such a time, subject to the whims of such a man, Americans can only pray—and try to understand. Today a major contribution to that understanding began, first of fifteen lengthy segments, in the *Post*. Written by one of New York City's most brilliant young psychiatrists, it is entitled *Orrin Knox: Achieving the Unbalance of Power*. It will be published next week in paperback by the *Post*. We urge all citizens anxious to understand their unhappy driven President to write the

Post immediately for a free copy, enclosing twenty-five cents for postage and handling. Simply address it: *Unbalance,* Washington, D.C. . . ."

"Only a true megalomaniac," Walter Dobius advised his 436 client newspapers, "would continue to pursue the course of Orrin Knox against all the odds—personal, national, international—psychological, diplomatic, military—which confront him. Such a megalomaniac, one suspects, is Orrin Knox, now falling further and further into the bottomless pit of a war he can neither win nor, apparently, end.

"Or, perhaps, one should say 'neither win *nor bring himself to end.*' Because there is growing concern here in Washington that the new President may be a man so hounded by psychological fears and darkly driving obsessions that he may be spinning out of control and close to crack-up. If so, terrible times lie immediately ahead for this hapless country and the helpless world so endangered by his haunted compulsion to exercise supreme power, whatever the cost.

"Illuminating this tragic side of the President's nature, suspected by so many who have known him during his Senate years, is a new book, soon to be available to all Americans, that began running today in the *Post.* Written by one of New York City's most brilliant young psychiatrists, it is entitled *Orrin Knox: Achieving the Unbalance of Power.*

"The unbalance of power it is, achieved by a man who really is, many fear, unbalanced. The thought can only bring to men everywhere the icy dread of what such a President can do to the world.

Well, he thought that night with a tartness they all would have recognized, there was an icy dread, all right: in him, for what they would do to the country and the world if he knuckled under and let them get away with it. Having found so far that they couldn't shake him on the issues, they now were turning to all the tricks of sneak-and-peek journalism that had become so fashionable in such august places in recent years. The psychiatric study, that favorite ploy, was now under way: it was inevitable that it should have appeared first where it did. Next would come the hints about income tax, the attempts to becloud his financial record, the attacks on his personal life, the sly rumors and innuendos of some vague private failing, the smirk, the snigger, the leer, the lie. It was a well-honed and by now quite respectable technique, elevated to one of the basic principles of modern reporting by journals that had once prided themselves that their integrity would never allow it. Integrity was a long time gone, now, and every public man sooner or later had to defend himself against the hit-and-run tactics of those who wrapped themselves with a smug self-protective righteousness in the flag and the First Amendment to do their devious work.

Well: he had survived this sort of thing before, and he would survive it now. Whether he would survive the attacks of more responsible institutions such as the *Times,* which still possessed sufficient integrity to confront him on the merits, was another question. Because, being an honest man, he knew there was much to be said on the other side.

All of his public life, and ever more sharply in recent years, they had been challenging him on his basic attitudes toward the Communist world and his policies for working out a livable accommodation with it. They did not agree with him that firmness, diligence, prudence, forethought, a strong defense, a strong skepticism and a strong will were the prerequisites of living with the men of Moscow, Peking and their satellites. They felt that faith, hope, charity, concession, withdrawal, one-sided trust, the endless building of paper houses of treaties, agreements, "détentes," would ultimately persuade a ravenous aggression to abandon its perfectly candid and never-changing aim of destroying democracy and the freedom of the human mind.

They had fought very hard, as they always did, to try to win the Presidency for the man who seemed best to symbolize their grimly held belief that comfortable, amiable retreat was more productive than uncomfortable, stubborn strength. This last time their hero had been Ted Jason, and because the violent had clustered around him, Orrin's more worthwhile critics had found themselves in strange beds with strange bedfellows. They still were, as witness the riots and threats of NAWAC side by side with the solemn lashings of the *Times,* the nasty gut-fighting of the *Post.* Starting at those extremes, the troubled reaction to his policies spread on down through the populace, on over the world. Orrin Knox the candidate had meant a tough foreign policy to those who had fought him and those who had supported him. Orrin Knox the President meant the same thing, enlarged a thousandfold.

And many, many millions, he knew, were perfectly sincere, perfectly genuine, perfectly patriotic and disinterested in their opposition to him. He would never be given credit for understanding their point of view, because it suited his critics better to portray him as being as rigid, illiberal and intolerant of the opposing view as they were. But he knew, and he felt that many of his countrymen knew, that he did understand their point of view, and that only because he honestly could not accept it did he hold tenaciously to policies that could, in the present instance, truthfully be called warlike.

Yet he did not see how he could do other. He wanted a livable accommodation with the ever-surging, ever-probing, ever-imperializing Communist tide—and to him "livable" was the key word.

What could you live with? That was the heart of it. Long ago in World War II, he remembered, the columnist Dorothy Thompson had done a piece on "Who Would Go Nazi?"—a cleverly bitter speculation on which among the many public figures of whom she disapproved would embrace fascism if it should, as then seemed very possible, conquer the world.

The same thing might be done now, on the other side. "Who Would Go Communist?" Who—as she had then portrayed them and as many still were, weak of will, avid of ambition, consumed by fears for personal safety, the desire to be on the winning side and the arrogant intellectual conviction that they could handle anybody and survive—would go Communist?

He suspected there were quite a few, leaving well aside the never-resting minority in all countries around the world who were already actively committed. The media were always the first who had to bow to Communism when it took a country, because in the electronic age they were the keys to the control of public opinion. Therefore they were placed immediately under dictatorship. Inevitably many among them would point proudly to past sympathies and claim that this gave them a right to survive: because they had always "understood." They would eagerly and naïvely "go Communist." But this would do them no good. Having been free, inevitably in short order they would try to act as though they still were free. And immediately they would be eliminated, because the mindless state can brook no opposition from the mind.

For this reason he believed, although they would never concede it to him, that in a fundamental way he was protecting Supermedia and its friends as much as he was protecting anything else when he advocated a firm policy vis-à-vis history's latest imperialism. It lent an extra impatience to the mood with which he thought of them. They thought they could embrace those who wished them death, and survive, did they? They would find out damned fast, if it ever came to that.

The same thing applied to the many millions who, conditioned by the constant drummings of Supermedia through newsprint, screen and tube, felt a perfectly innocent aversion to his policies—regarded him as warmonger and warmaker—desperately feared what they were told was his "belligerence," his "arrogance," his "intransigence" and his "refusal to negotiate for peace." He was protecting them, too, though they were daily conditioned to give him no credit for it.

Having said all this, however, there remained a cold reality of which he was entirely aware:

What he was doing *was* dangerous. The policies he was pushing *did* carry the potential of final disaster. He *was* gambling. The outcome *could* be terminal.

Orrin Knox indeed was dealing in the fate of mankind. He did not blink the awful thought. The only difference between him and his critics was that he believed that some things were more important than disaster—that some things were still worth fighting for, whatever the risks—that there were still principles valid enough to warrant saying, "*No!*" and taking one's stand in the path of Juggernaut.

He believed this because, being a close student of history, a discipline now highly unpopular with entire generations, he had observed that time and again when men finally reached this conclusion, when they finally took leave of their fears, when they finally dedicated themselves selflessly to the principles of freedom, justice, truth and the other frayed but still valid achievements of the independent mind, the Lord sometimes moved in and rescued them. Events turned their way. They held firm against all potentials of disaster, all prophets of doom—and somehow, somewhere, frequently at the very last millisecond before midnight, things shifted in ways unpredictable, and they survived and made it through and saved what they were fighting for.

It was to this, he thought now as he prepared to leave the Oval Office and return to the Mansion and a sleep that might be broken at any moment with news of further disasters on the field of battle, that he clung, against reason, against logic, against the facts as they appeared to be aligning themselves all along the perimeters of the beleaguered democracy he led.

He knew his forces were in retreat—he knew the country's sadly reduced military strength permitted him very little margin and very little time—he knew he was engaged on a gigantic gamble that could end everything—but he knew he had to stay with it, at least a while longer. The end result might be defeat, disaster, surrender . . . but it might not be.

He could not, being true to what Orrin Knox had always believed and been, remaining true to his oath to preserve, protect and defend the Constitution and the nation it governed, open the door and invite disaster in. It might come through his policies, and if it did he would have to face it as best he could and take the consequences. But he could not, and he would not, give in to it without a fight. "Cooperating with the inevitable" had never been his style, because he had learned in life that the inevitable was frequently only as inevitable as men, in their fear, caution, lack of courage or cupidity, made it.

He walked slowly back to the Mansion along the arcade overlooking the snow-buried Rose Garden.

It was almost midnight.

Orrin Knox was receiving the full impact of the world's terror, hatred and dismay.

But Orrin Knox was not yielding.

So the fifth day of his Presidency passed into night, with no prospect of salvation to relieve its gloom and no ray of light as yet visible at the far end of the dark passage through which he and his country were struggling.

4. NOR DID SALVATION come any closer in the week that followed, nor did any faintest glimmer reveal itself ahead. Day marched after day and on each the forces that threatened his country grew stronger on the fields of battle, the gloom that gripped his countrymen became deeper, the frantic howls of his critics domestic and foreign wailed ever louder around an increasingly isolated White House. American troops, planes, tanks, their retreats stabilized—but only just—continued to fight savage holding actions, a growing number captured, a growing number dead. Television and the press dwelt long and lovingly on every American reverse, every American mistake, their treatment of the enemy so sparse and gentle that one might almost have thought the United States was the sole country involved. Inevitably this had what he thought of as "the Vietnam effect" on his countrymen. Daily he sank lower in the public-opinion polls, daily his supporters grew more discouraged and more timid, daily more and more in Congress charged, denounced, demanded, daily the number who dared speak out in his behalf declined. The U.N. met, raged, passed new resolutions, raged some more when he had Ceil veto them. Rumors increased that Britain and France might be joining the Communist powers to form a naval task force to challenge the blockade of Panama. Hysteria soared. Still the basic deadlock remained. He kept himself aloof, made no further statements, held to his own counsel. He would not yield, the Communists would

not yield, his critics foreign and domestic would not yield. The world screamed toward a climax of hatred and terror at whose center he appeared to be as serene and unshakable as though nothing at all untoward were going on.

But it took its toll, and all who were close to him knew it.

On the tenth day of his Presidency it took a toll he did not know that he could stand.

But he saw it through and stood even that, though looking back he marveled that he had.

"Bill—" he said, coming forward late in the winter-dark afternoon to shake hands with his troubled predecessor. "Bob—Warren—please be seated. And don't look so solemn," he added with a smile. "It isn't as bad as all that."

"It isn't?" William Abbott inquired with a sigh. "You must know something we don't know."

"I know we're holding them," he said crisply.

"But at what a cost!" Warren Strickland said quietly. "At what a cost!"

"And would you be doing it any differently if you sat here?" he demanded sharply; and after a moment the Senate Minority Leader also sighed.

"No . . . I guess not. But it is imperative that we have some hope, Mr. President. We must have *some* hope." The room became silent as he asked a quiet question: "Is there any?"

He studied their worried faces for a moment, elbows on chair arms, chin on fingertips in his characteristic pose. All were deeply troubled, all were looking to him for reassurance. For the first time it crossed his mind that even these might leave him, if the agony went on long enough.

"Hope?" he echoed, the thought giving his tone an extra edge. "Hope? Yes, I can give you hope: the hope that a just cause will ultimately win, that courage and decency will ultimately prevail, that freedom and democracy will not go down if brave men remain unflinching in the defense of them."

"We're brave men," Bob Munson said, as quietly as Warren. "But we need encouragement."

"I have been in office ten days," he said, his tone still edgy. "The new fighting has been under way ten days. *Ten days* is sufficient to judge the way a war is going? *Ten days* is enough to give up hope?"

"Nations have fallen in far less in this century," Bob Munson pointed out. "And today time telescopes even more. . . . No," he said gravely, "we aren't judging the war—finally—Mr. President. We aren't giving up hope—finally. But we are telling you that things are getting increasingly tight, on the Hill, in the country, everywhere."

"And you think I don't know it?" he demanded, unable to keep some bitterness out of his voice. "I'm told it in every broadcast, every newpaper, every phone call, every piece of mail that reaches this house. I feel it in my bones as much as you do—you can't be in politics as long as I've been and not have a gut instinct for what the country is thinking. At least I can't."

"And still you remain unshaken," William Abbott said thoughtfully; and then with a wry smile added, "But of course you do, just as I did, and just as any other character worth his salt in this office, does. . . . Except that this time"—and again he sighed, heavily and unhappily—"this time, I just don't know. . . . I just don't know."

"Well, I do," he said with an outward calmness he did not entirely feel. "I do, Bill. And so did you, up to now. What's happened?"

"The wars," the ex-President said. "World opinion. Domestic opinion. The U.N., nattering away. Congress, still holding up your Cabinet. The defense bill you have *got* to have to keep going, still pigeonholed. The whole head-on, intransigent atmosphere. No slightest sign of charity or compassion or understanding for you anywhere, at least in any influential spot in this country. Or the world, for that matter. The whole thing, Orrin. It's just beginning to wear me down. As it must," he concluded gravely, "be wearing you down too, though you seem remarkably resilient . . . at least on the surface."

"And surface," he remarked dryly, "is what the world goes on." His expression changed, sobered. "No. I *am* worn down, Bill. Desperately so. But I will not—I cannot—give in and change course now. I simply cannot do it, because the minute I did, everything would be lost." He looked from somber face to somber face. "Is that why you asked to see me? To urge me to give in?"

"Not to give in," William Abbott said quietly. "You know none of your real friends wants you to do that. Just to—bend a little, perhaps. Give a bit. Don't be quite so—arbitrary."

"This *is* a change," he said, finding it hard to keep the anger from his voice. "You three telling me this? I can't believe it!" He mastered his annoyance with an obvious effort, forced his tone to become more reasonable. "All right then: how do I 'bend a little'? How do I 'give a bit'? How do I become less 'arbitrary,' when I face an absolutely unbending, ungiving, completely arbitrary adversary? We've all known each other all our political lives, nobody on the Hill has been any closer over the years: advise me. I'll listen." A fleeting smile crossed his face, but the moment was too serious for it to linger long. "I may not do anything about it, but I'll listen."

"Have you considered," Bob Munson asked, "reopening the possibility of a conference? As you say, we *are* holding them—"

"Barely."

"Yes, barely—but we are. Mightn't this be an opportunity to start talking?"

His expression became set.

"It's got to be more solid than this."

"But will it be?" Warren Strickland inquired.

"Can it be?" asked William Abbott.

"I don't know," he said, "but I've got to hold on and hope."

"*Can* you hold on?" Bill Abbott asked. "Can we even hold what we've got, without a bloodbath even worse than we're having right now? My part of the war was relatively easy, things were pretty calm over the past six months. Now we're into Operation Meatgrinder—"

"Who came up with that one?" he snapped.

"It's on the Hill. You'll see it in your friendly media tomorrow morning. I'm not saying I agree with the spirit in which it's used, but in essence—"

"Yes?" the President inquired with an ominous quiet.

"In essence," the ex-President said calmly, "that is exactly what it is, Orrin, and you know it."

"I cannot give in," the President repeated, his voice curiously remote but unyielding. "And I cannot talk—yet."

"You may never have a better chance," Senator Munson remarked.

"At least some gesture—?" Warren Strickland suggested. "Some sign of willingness to meet, if only to take the propaganda initiative away from them? It would make it so much easier for you—and for the sizable number who still, I think, support your course, although with growing difficulty."

He gave them a long, moody, searching look.

"How long can you fellows continue to support it?"

"How long can you?" his predecessor inquired with equal moodiness.

"As long as I have to!" he said sharply.

"Not quite, I'm afraid, Orrin," William Abbott said somberly. "Not quite."

"I *have* to, Bill!" he exclaimed in an almost desperate way. "I simply *have* to! Until *they* agree, until *they* make a sign, until *they* come halfway. There's no other alternative at this moment." His tone became suddenly almost beseeching, almost wistful, an Orrin they had very rarely seen in all their years of close association. "Now you *know* that . . . don't you?"

"We'll stay with you just as long as we can," Bob Munson assured him quickly, deeply troubled by this insight into depths of Presidential anguish. And Warren Strickland, leaning forward with equal haste, agreed, "Of course we will—and beyond that if need be. Although"—he shook his head with a worried frown—"we probably won't have much company."

"I can't help that," he said, voice low, eyes far away, mind somewhere in the bitter night. "I have got to do what I think is right for this country and the world even if they both hate me forever in the process. There is no other way . . . *is* there?" he demanded of his predecessor with a sudden reviving challenge, a sudden return to the Orrin Knox they knew so well. "*Is* there?"

William Abbott studied him for a long time.

"We'll be with you a while yet," he said finally. "But, Orrin," he added quietly, "for your sake—for the country's sake—for everybody's sake—I hope it doesn't have to be too long." He too looked far away. "I don't know whether we could all stand it."

"If I can, you can," the President said, sounding fully himself again, but softening the near-flippant tartness with a smile.

"Yes," the ex-President agreed, "*if* you can."

"Try me," he said with a suddenly reviving cheerfulness, for he was confident now, with a sudden upsurging relief, that these old friends would not desert him, no matter who else might. With them, his family and a few others, he felt his strength was as the strength of millions.

And so he continued to feel after they left, despite the continuing burden of discouraging reports that continued to flow to his desk from the Situation Room. The mood continued until shortly after 11 P.M., when he decided to go to bed; then it changed.

He had just reached the Mansion and stepped off the elevator onto the second floor when one of the young Secret Service men on duty throughout the heavily guarded house hurried forward down the long central hall. Something about the agent's haste, his manner, the way he was carefully suppressing emotion though so obviously in the grip of it, sent a cold shiver through his body.

"Yes?" he called sharply. "What is it?"

"Mr. President," the agent said. "I'm afraid there's bad n—"

"My children," he interrupted flatly, a great abyss seeming to open up at his feet, the house, the world, everything, almost literally spinning away from him, beyond grasp, beyond redemption.

"Yes, sir," the agent said, his voice shaking a little now. "I am so sorry. We just this minute received word—"

"What?" he asked, a monstrous impatience seeming to seize his whole being. "*What is it, man?*"

"They've been kidnapped, sir," the agent said hurriedly, his earnest young face white with strain. "They went to the benefit at Ford's Theater, and just after the performance ended, while they were waiting to get into the car, a group of six people—"

"Why weren't they guarded?" he demanded, his voice grating harshly in the hushed corridor.

"Three of our men died, sir," the agent said simply; and for several seconds neither of them said anything more.

Then he sighed from some great depth, passed across his eyes a hand that shook, and in a voice that was lower and by some miracle almost normal, said quietly:

"I'm sorry, I apologize. I should have known. Who did it?"

"We aren't sure, sir," the agent said, voice calmer now, officially matter-of-fact. "They were masked, four men and two women, armed with submachine guns and grenades. I should add that four spectators were also shot, two of them seriously. It could be NAWAC or one of its violent subgroups. The FBI is working on that angle, I believe."

"Have we heard anything from them yet?"

"No, sir, not a word. They headed up Sixteenth Street and apparently went into Maryland. The hunt is being concentrated around Silver Spring and Chevy Chase. I think"—he paused, swallowed painfully, and went on—"I think I should tell you that it is our people's impression that these are fanatics who may not stop at—at anything, sir."

"Oh, they'll stop," he said with a bitter weariness, "if I pay the price. I'm sure they'll let me know, soon enough."

"Yes, sir," the agent said, young face sadly troubled; and the President felt it was comforting that he should still be hesitating there, not quite sure whether to leave or offer to stay, when another agent appeared down the hall carrying an extension telephone.

"A call for you, sir," he said; plugged the instrument into an outlet along the wall, handed it to him and added quietly, "It's being monitored, of course." Solemn and wide-eyed, the two of them watched as he said sharply:

"Yes?"

"We have them," the voice said calmly, "and we will kill them unless you withdraw from Gorotoland and Panama and meet with the peace-loving powers to negotiate an end to this war madness once and for all."

"There are other kinds of madness," he said.

"Maybe," the voice agreed, still calmly. "But we have them, and those are our conditions."

"You have a deadline in mind," he suggested, playing for time, mind racing, desperately seeking some ground for rational appeal. The response showed him there was none.

"You just begin getting busy. We'll let you know when we decide on a deadline."

"What kind of a deal is that?" he demanded.

"A deal in which we hold the trumps," the voice said, "so don't delay, Mr. President. We would hate to have to kill your son and daughter-in-law just because you were too stubborn and bullheaded to listen to reason."

"No reason," he said. "Insanity."

"Insanity or no," the voice repeated, this time allowing itself a slight edge of anger, "we have them and we will do as we say unless you do as we say. So think it over, Mr. President. There is very little time."

"How much?"

"See how fast you can move, Mr. President," the voice suggested. "Give it a try. You may surprise yourself."

"But—" he began, anger and desperation in his tone. The other hung up with a decisive click, the line went dead.

"I must go back to the Oval Office," he said, mind whirling, certainty and conviction now far away. "I must decide what to do. Will you—?"

"We will take you over, sir," the agents said as one, and he responded, "Thank you," with a gratitude so humble and lost-sounding that they gave each other frightened glances behind his back.

But at his desk, after talking to Bill Abbott, to Bob and Dolly Munson, to Warren Strickland, to Cullee and Lafe and, finally, the call he dreaded, to Stanley Danta, Crystal's father, he managed to regain a measure of control.

Aided most by Stanley's reaction, which was of course greatly disturbed but quietly and courageously sympathetic and understanding, he thought it all out, entirely alone, for half an hour. Then he got his press secretary out of his bed across the river in Alexandria and dictated a brief statement for immediate release.

Then he went back once more along the arcade beside the Rose Garden, passed through the hushed corridors of the Mansion past the suddenly increased guards who now seemed to be everywhere, made his lonely ablutions and climbed into his lonely bed in the Lincoln Bedroom.

Throughout the house they marveled at his iron calm, but alone in the room he cried repeatedly, and did not sleep.

KIDNAPPERS SEIZE PRESIDENT'S SON AND DAUGHTER-IN-LAW AT FORD'S THEATER. THREATEN DEATH UNLESS WARS END AND IMMEDIATE PEACE CONFERENCE IS HELD.

KNOX ISSUES STATEMENT DEFYING "INHUMAN BLACKMAILERS," SAYS HE WILL ACCEDE TO DEMANDS "ONLY WHEN THERE IS GENUINE SIGN OF TRUE, PEACEFUL COOPERATION FROM THE COMMUNIST POWERS."

FBI REPORTS "NO VALID CLUES AS YET" TO FATE OF YOUNG CONGRESSMAN AND WIFE.

WORLD APPALLED BY DANGER TO CHIEF EXECUTIVE'S CHILDREN.

"The world," Walter Dobius wrote rapidly at "Salubria" in the ice-still afternoon, "is appalled today not only by the dreadful dangers that must be presumed to be faced by Rep. Harold Knox and his lovely young wife, but by his father's apparently obdurate intention to risk the sacrifice of their lives so that he may continue to pursue his intransigent war policies in the face of almost universal condemnation—condemnation which has now, all too tragically, been brought home to his own doorstep. Only an Orrin Knox, it seems likely, would be so callous in the disregard of human life—in this case the human life which, presumably, is nearest and dearest to him. . . ."

"It does not surprise us," the *Post* snapped, "when Orrin Knox callously sacrifices the lives of other people's sons in the pursuit of his mad war policies. But it does both surprise and appall us when he appears ready to sacrifice the life of his own son, and that of his daughter-in-law as well. Not since Adolf Hitler, we suspect, has there been a world leader so ruthlessly determined to have his own way and so completely devoid of human feeling in the pursuit of it. . . ."

"Up to this point," the *Times* remarked gravely, "there may have been some few left in the world who could still see the rationale for the policies of the new President. Now there must be very, very few—if any. His only son and that son's charming wife are held hostage by individuals apparently driven to absolute frustration by the President's stubborn and unyielding stand. Using a method which must be deplored but which nonetheless can be understood in the context of these unhappy times, they are seeking to make their point to the President in a way he cannot avoid. Apparently so far the attempt has failed and he intends to continue, at what dreadful danger to his own family only time can tell, the actions that have now brought retribution, with classical fury, upon his own house. . . ."

"At dreadful cost," Frankly Unctuous solemnly told his millions of devoted listeners, "President Knox has clung to the wreck of his policies overseas. Now that cost, measured already in terms of the deaths of other men's sons, appears likely to be measured in terms of the death of his own son and his son's wife. That is the frightful option that has been presented him by those whose methods the decent must condemn, but whose motives must certainly arouse a sympathetic response in the hearts of many. Very few, it seems, want these foreign wars. Everyone wants peace. Orrin Knox has adamantly refused to accept these realities. Now he faces them on his own doorstep. Horrible tragedy may lie ahead for a family already shattered by the death last year of Mrs. Beth Knox. Are policies so universally challenged really worth these two innocent young lives? So far the President apparently believes they are. Yet not even Orrin Knox, the world must hope, can be quite that heartless and inhuman. . . ."

"I don't think he cares for you very much," the voice observed from the other side of the heavy oak door.

"He cares for us enough, you filthy bastard," Hal retorted.

"My, my," the voice said with some amusement. "The young tiger roars like the elder. But both, alas, are in the same cage."

Hal uttered a scornful snort.

"Christ, you sound pompous. What guru book did you get that out of?"

"Listen, you fucking smart-ass," the voice snapped, suddenly as young and bitter as he, "you'd damned well better watch your language. We've got you and your precious Crystal and we can do whatever we want with both of you. So keep that in mind, sonny boy. You'll both be healthier if you do."

"You don't intend for us to be healthy," Hal said, and at his side Crystal made the small stirring that he knew meant: take it easy. But he was too carried away by anger and disgust to respond to a gesture so clearly inspired by apprehension. He was consumed by rage and disgust, caught in the grip of a terrible contempt for all the scum of the recent earth, some of whom had apparently become their captors. He could not be conciliatory, though he knew perfectly well their lives might depend upon it. "You've made your demands and he isn't listening, is he? He isn't going to bow down to you dirt, is he? You insane psychotics have met your match, haven't you?"

"Don't you want him to bow down?" the voice inquired presently, obviously mastering itself to speak more calmly. "Maybe he would if you asked him."

"Why should I ask him?" Hal demanded. "I agree with what he's doing."

"Oh, you do now," the voice conceded. "But suppose we send one of Crystal's ears to him, for instance? It's been done. Or," it added on a sudden note of inspiration, "some other portion of the anatomy? Would you ask him then, maybe?"

"You wouldn't dare," he said, in a savage voice, though his heart felt that a cruel hand had twisted it in two, and beside him his wife shot him a glance in which terror, for the first time in the twelve hours since their kidnapping, clearly showed.

"No?" the voice inquired, its owner obviously feeling that he held the whip hand again. "What's to stop?"

"He will never give in to you," Hal said, forcing his voice to stay steady, "no matter what you do. And the world will never forgive you if you hurt us."

"Most of the world thinks what we're doing is great, man," the voice assured him with considerable satisfaction. "Most of the world thinks it's about time somebody put some sense into your old man. And what about you, honey child, Crystal baby? What if we send old Dad sonny boy's ear? Or maybe"—it chuckled happily—"some part of him that you like better? Then what?"

"You can't frighten me," she said, though her voice trembled.

"Oh," the voice said, "I think we can. Because it isn't talk, you know. They absolutely don't know where you are, and they absolutely aren't going to find you. And if proud Mr. President doesn't give in, that's absolutely going to mean one big hell of a lot of trouble for you kids. Just be sure of that, O.K.? . . . Well," it added with a sudden note of finality, "that's enough talk about it for now. We'll be serving you some food pretty soon, and you can watch the TV in there and find out how little is being done for you, and after a while we'll talk again. And maybe if old Pops hasn't done anything for us by that time, we'll have to see what we can do for him. And for you kids, too, of course."

"Run along, monster," Hal said, trying, and managing, to sound unimpressed.

"Don't think we won't enjoy cutting you up, smart-ass," the voice snarled, young and full of hatred again. "It will be a pleasure."

"Shove off, Dracula," Hal said coldly. "Go and scare old ladies."

But after the voice's owner, absorbing this in silence with an obviously great effort, had gone away, he and Crystal held each other very close while he stroked her hair gently and said, "Hush . . . hush . . . hush . . ." over and over again, in response to the terrified incoherent sounds that escaped, despite her most gallant efforts, from her shaking lips.

NO WORD FROM KIDNAPPERS AS SECOND DAY PASSES. PRESIDENT APPARENTLY HOLDING FIRM TO REFUSAL TO DEAL WITH COMMUNISTS DESPITE PERIL OF CHILDREN. NEW AMERICAN REVERSES REPORTED IN PANAMA, GOROTOLAND. JOINT NAVAL TASK FORCE BELIEVED READY TO CHALLENGE PANAMA BLOCKADE. NAWAC, OTHER PEACE GROUPS RIOT IN MAJOR CITIES. CONGRESSIONAL LEADERS HINT "DRAMATIC ACTION" IN TODAY'S SESSION.

In the White House, gray-faced, stern but outwardly calm, he went about his duties and made no further public comment.

"Mr. Speaker!" Bronson Bernard cried in the House, his voice trembling with excitement but armored in righteousness, and, "Mr. President!" shouted the mint-new young Senator from Oregon, in tones equally insistent and portentous in the Senate, "I have a resolution to submit for immediate action!"

"The Clerk will read," Jawbone Swarthman responded with an eager encouragement in the House, and, "The Clerk will read," Cullee Hamilton responded with a cautious correctness in the Senate.

Both Clerks, grown gray in the service of their respective houses, proceeded to do so in voices that reflected the excitement and tension that quickly grew across the crowded floors and in the crowded galleries.

Four hours later after savagely bitter debate in both houses, the word went out that Orrin Knox had been pushed still further to the wall.

IMPEACHMENT RESOLUTION FILED IN HOUSE. MEMBERS VOTE 310–111 AFTER WILD DEBATE TO DIRECT JUDICIARY COMMITTEE TO START IMMEDIATE PRELIMINARY INVESTIGATION. SENATE PASSES PARALLEL RESOLUTION URGING HOUSE TO ACT, BEATS BACK ATTEMPT BY SMALL

PRO-KNOX GROUP TO DECLARE MOVE UNCONSTITUTIONAL. VOTE OF 68–31 APPARENTLY ASSURES CONVICTION IF HOUSE ACTS FAVORABLY ON FIRST STEP.

And still he continued, increasingly strained, increasingly stern, but still with a businesslike and apparently unbreakable calm, to discharge the duties of the Presidency in his increasingly isolated house, issuing no further public comment.

"Mr. President," Blair Hannah said, and his voice, like so many in these cataclysmic, on-rushing days, trembled with his effort to keep it calm. "My colleagues and I"—he gestured to the Joint Chiefs of Staff, aglitter with medals, standing almost as if at attention to his right—"feel that you must be told that we have very little extra reserves left to fight on with in Gorotoland and Panama unless you can persuade Congress to authorize an immediate appropriation for the Department of Defense."

He looked up quietly, spoke with what appeared to be an unmoved matter-of-factness.

"How much equipment do we have mothballed and in storage?"

"A substantial amount, Mr. President," the Chairman of the Joint Chiefs said. "But it will take many weeks to bring most of it back into shape. And we may not have," he added bleakly, "many weeks."

"How long *do* we have?" he inquired bluntly. The Secretary of Defense and his colleagues exchanged a quick glance.

"Perhaps two weeks at present levels of demand," Blair Hannah said.

"I should like you," he said quietly, "to launch a massive counteroffensive on both battle fronts not later than four days from today."

"But, Mr. President—!" the Joint Chiefs exclaimed as one man in stricken voices; and Blair Hannah gave him a look in which dismay, disbelief, compassion and something close to pity competed.

He did not flinch, nor did his level gaze drop from theirs.

"Can you do it?"

"At the cost of thousands of lives," the Army Chief of Staff protested in a desperately unhappy voice.

"And hundreds of planes," the Chief of the Air Force agreed in the same anguished way.

"And possibly hundreds of ships," the Chief of Naval Operations concurred quietly. "Mr. President—" He hesitated and then went on with a dogged determination, "Is it really going to be worth it? Do you really think it will accomplish anything? Have you information that leads you to believe such an effort will have a productive effect upon the enemy?"

"I have approximately the same information you do," he said quietly. "And a belief that they are weaker internally, and vis-à-vis each other, than we can know from the outside. I believe that if we keep up the pressure just a little longer, the Soviet Union and China will either suffer internal revolutions or begin fighting each other. That is what I believe."

"But it is only a belief," Blair Hannah said quietly. "You really have no proof."

"Maybe 'belief' is too strong a word," he agreed, but there was no indication whatsoever that he regarded the admission as weakening his position in any way. "Maybe 'hope' is the operative word. Therefore"—his tone hardened—"you will launch a massive counteroffensive on both battlefields not later than four days from today."

He stood up, never having asked them to be seated, and moved toward the door to show them out. As he did so he turned back for a moment to his Secretary of Defense, his tone more relaxed and informal.

"Blair, I'm sorry we haven't been able to wangle confirmation for you yet, but we're working on it. I don't think it will be too long."

For a moment Blair Hannah gave him a sharply contemplative look.

"You sound as though life were still going along quite normally," he observed in a puzzled tone. "How do you figure that?"

"It will," he said calmly, "if you will all cooperate and if the Lord, as I believe, still takes some interest in America."

"Maybe He does," Blair Hannah said bleakly, "but I'm damned if I see much sign of it at the moment."

And by six o'clock that night the word that always leaks through the sieve that is Washington had leaked, as usual, from someone in the Pentagon who belonged to a generation well-trained in the uses of publicity to thwart a President.

"According to well-informed military sources," Frankly Unctuous said with a despair and disgust in his voice so great that it might have led to some questioning of his journalistic integrity if that had been a subject that still concerned anyone, "President Knox is apparently planning a major new offensive in the two tragic wars in which America is hopelessly entangled. All one can say is, God help this poor nation and all the peoples of the world whose hopes for peace are so inextricably bound up in what we do! . . ."

"A move of uttermost desperation appears to be shaping in the White House," the *Times* wrote. "President Knox, the kidnapping of his son and daughter-in-law still unresolved, beset now by the drive for impeachment in both houses of Congress, is reportedly about to resort to the last weapon of the frantic: a wild military gamble, a renewed offensive in Gorotoland and Panama, a foredoomed, blood-drenched exercise in futility. . . ."

"Orrin Knox, teetering on the brink of what can only be described as mental unbalance for some days now," the *Post* said, "is apparently slipping over. New U.S. military offensives are rumored in Gorotoland and Panama, new sacrifices of men and matériel—and with it, almost assuredly, the sacrifice of his own son and daughter-in-law, for certainly their captors will not accept this new defiance of the wishes of the peace-loving without reacting strongly. Poor Orrin Knox—poor America! And poor world, that must suffer such a man. . . ."

"Orrin Knox is apparently passing across that border that divides the rational from the irrational, the quick from the dead," Walter Dobius wrote for his 436 client newspapers. "Washington buzzes today with the latest rumor about this strange, stubborn man who is defying the lessons of history and the wishes of the world in his adamant opposition to the peace-seeking efforts of the Communist powers. The rumor is that he has ordered a new offensive on the battlefields—a new, empty, foredoomed, grandiose, blood-drenched military venture. When all the Communists want is peace. When all the world wants is peace. All humankind—all nature—all everything, everywhere—wants peace. And still Orrin Knox resorts to war. The threat of impeachment, the probable murders of his children—nothing seems to deter this strange, lost man. The Angel of Death wings low over America tonight. How much longer can Orrin Knox go on?"

Yet in the White House, his face growing gaunter with strain and worry but his mood outwardly as firm and unshakable as ever, he went about his duties calmly and issued no further public word.

"Mr. President," the general director of the *Post* said, and on the Picturephone his face too showed strain and worry and, also, a fear and shock that immediately commanded his listener's attention. "Mr. President, I thought you should know that—that we have—"

"What?" he interrupted, and something of the old sarcasm he was accustomed to show this individual whose publication had hounded him so many years, broke through. "Written another editorial calling me a madman?"

"No, sir," the director of the *Post* said quickly. "Please, Mr. President. This is too serious for that. This is too—"

"And that isn't serious?" he demanded sharply. "When you bastards denounce and demean me every day of my life, doing everything you can to make it impossible for me to function, as you have tried to do to so many of my predecessors? That isn't important, man? My God, you tell me what is!"

"I will, Mr. President," the director of the *Post* said, neither his face nor his voice displaying the anger that Orrin might have expected from him under other circumstances; so that for the first time a frightening chill began to run along his spine.

"What is it?" he demanded sharply. "What's on your mind? I haven't got all day."

"This," the general director of the *Post* said: and reaching somewhere off-camera, he produced and held up for the President to see an object that for a moment made his head swim, his eyes blur and his body actually start to slump against the desk.

"It isn't real!" the director of the *Post* cried hastily. "Mr. President, it isn't real! But the hair—we think the hair—is."

Forcing himself to open his eyes and study the grimacing blood-daubed head that the general director held balanced on one trembling palm, he could see that it was made of Styrofoam, that its features were crayoned in, that to its scalp were pasted several large swatches of blonde hair which he recognized instinctively as Crystal's. Across the bottom of its jagged severed neck was a large card on which were scrawled, also in blood, the words: "Hello, Daddy. This is Crystal, Daddy. Crystal wants peace, Daddy. Or do you want a piece of Crystal, Daddy?"

"How did you get it?" he asked at last, a sick horror in his voice. The director of the *Post* replied in the same tone as he set the awful grotesquerie down on the desk beside him.

"It was sent to me via United Parcel Service delivery van about fifteen minutes ago, apparently as a means of assuring the widest possible publicity—which," he added as the President stirred and started to say something, "we will not give it unless you want us to, Mr. President. Do you want us to?"

"Oh, yes," he said, his tone suddenly cold with anger as the true monstrosity of it hit him. "I want to see if you have guts enough to show the world the kind of people you're running with these days."

"Very well," the director of the *Post* said sharply, his tone too reverting instantly to its long-time hostility. "I only wanted to help—"

"On the front page," the President suggested harshly, knowing he shouldn't but too tired and embittered to hold himself back. "With a banner. Rub their noses in it. Write an editorial. Tell us how proud you are of your fellow workers in the cause of getting Orrin Knox. Show them what monsters you have created with your damned destructive attitude toward your own country all these years."

"*We* have created?" the director of the *Post* demanded, stung into the open anger and contempt he had always felt for this obdurate public figure who had always failed to respect the *Post*'s ineffable worth and unassailable virtue. "*We* have created? Whose are the war policies that have brought about this terrible climate in the country? Who is about to lead us into further insanities to throw after those already committed? Who is about to take us straight into a defeat from which we may never recover?"

"And who wants a 'peace' from which we may never recover?" the President demanded with equal anger. "A 'peace' which is nothing but surrender, God save the mark!"

For a long moment their eyes held in furious dislike. Then the President broke the moment with a contemptuous gesture.

"Publish if you have the guts," he said. "And be proud of your co-conspirators against the peace of the world and the perpetuation of the United States of America."

And reaching over before the director of the *Post* had time for more than the start of some incoherent, blurted, bitterly protesting reply, he snapped off the machine and sat back, breathing hard.

Then presently the utter horror of it hit him, and for a time he sat in the silent office, arms clasped tightly in front of him, body shaken by a silent shuddering so strong he began to think he could never control it. But presently he managed. Presently some steadiness returned. Presently, white-faced and drawn but again outwardly calm, he rang for his secretary and resumed his routine duties.

Outside, the dark winter afternoon died into night. On the streets the extra editions of the *Post* and the *Times* appeared with the horrible picture and the horrible news and the hysterical denunciatory editorials. And everywhere across the country, in print, on the air and in pompous public comment, the chant resumed.

Some few there were who understood the terrible ordeal he must be going through, and who were compassionate and courageous enough to oppose the tide and express admiration and sympathy for his determination to do the right thing as he saw it for his country and the world, even against such terrible odds.

But mostly the chant was the usual chant, for that was the popular and fashionable thing, and indeed for many the honest one: the awfulness of obdurate, unyielding, blood-thirsting, war-loving, mass-murdering, peace-destroying, humanity-betraying Orrin Knox.

WHITE HOUSE SAYS PRESIDENT WILL HAVE NO COMMENT ON DEATH EFFIGY OF DAUGHTER-IN-LAW. FBI SAYS NO DIRECT WORD RECEIVED FROM KIDNAPPERS, STILL DRAWS BLANK ON WHEREABOUTS OF MISSING CONGRESSMAN AND WIFE. PENTAGON REFUSES TO CONFIRM OR DENY PLANS FOR U.S. COUNTEROFFENSIVE. PRESIDENT ANNOUNCES HE WILL PAY CABINET OUT OF OWN EMERGENCY FUNDS, BUSINESS OF GOVERNMENT WILL PROCEED "REGARDLESS OF WHETHER SENATE CONFIRMS THEM OR NOT." TEMPORARY LULL GRIPS WAR ZONES AS RUMORS OF "LAST CHANCE" U.S. BLOW CONTINUE TO COME FROM MANY CAPITALS. MOSCOW, PEKING IGNORE REPORTS, SHOW NO SIGNS OF MAKING ANY NEW OVERTURES TO BELEAGUERED PRESIDENT.

But that, of course, as so often happened with the media's flat reports to the world of what was or was not going on, was not the way the President heard it. He had felt with some instinct beyond instinct, some inner belief that had really been all the support he had known in the past forty-eight hours, that a break was coming somewhere. To that conviction he had sacrificed most of what remained of his good standing with his countrymen, nearly all of his remaining influence with the world, very possibly (although he did not believe it, otherwise he really could not have gone on) the lives of the two beings who now were all the family he had left. And still the break had not come.

But now, at precisely 11:23 P.M. by the gently humming, softly flicking digital clock on the night stand beside his bed, it did.

"You would not come to me," a voice he instantly recognized said softly from the blacked-out screen of the Picturephone, "so I have decided to come to you."

"Where are you?" he demanded sharply. "And how did you get to this country without being recognized?"

"Simply. An 'elderly clerk' flew over, complete with white hair, beard, mustache, scarf, overcoat, important papers. There was no trouble. I am at the embassy. I shall expect you within the hour. I trust there will be no more nonsense about standing on dignity. Bring friends, if you like"—he chuckled slightly, without much humor—"I have brought some with me. If I might suggest: The Vice

President. President Abbott. Senator Munson. Senator Strickland. Secretary Leffingwell. Secretary Hannah. Within the hour."

For a moment he did not reply. Then with equal firmness he said:

"It may take a few minutes to rouse the others, but as nearly as possible we shall be there—within the hour."

"Good. Now we may do business."

"Perhaps."

"Within the hour."

"I said so," he reminded with a sudden annoyance he made no attempt to conceal. "Within the hour."

"Good."

Despite the best efforts of everyone concerned, however, it was closer to an hour and fifteen minutes when their small convoy of two limousines and two Secret Service cars crunched over the icy snow to the door of the embassy. The streets had been almost entirely deserted, it seemed likely that no more than a dozen startled citizens had seen them pass. None of them could have known what the unmarked cars portended.

They got out. The iron gates clanged open. The small figure of the Chairman stood outlined in the flood of light.

"You are late," he said in an accusatory voice, offering no other greeting. "Come!" And he turned on his heel and disappeared, leaving them to follow unescorted through two lines of black-suited guards obviously trying hard to look as grim and unfriendly as possible.

"What is this?" William Abbott demanded in a deliberately loud and disgusted voice.

"I am a bad boy," the President said grimly, "and I think we are in for a very unpleasant session."

But none of them was prepared for the type of unpleasantness it turned out to be. They had expected bullying, denunciation, ranting, threats—a reprise of every major Soviet diplomatic démarche of the past three decades. Instead it began as a quiet, almost conversational discussion by their host, who, once he had them seated on one side of a long rectangular table, placed himself and six advisers, four in the uniforms of the military forces, on the other. During this he spoke no word, greeted none of them by name or title, maintained an aspect as ostentatiously cold and rigid as any of his guards along the corridor. After a couple of abortive attempts to speak to him, they accepted this, became rapidly as grim and matter-of-fact as he.

By the time he had the meeting arranged to suit him it had already, without a word spoken on either side, moved beyond the conventions of preliminary cordiality to the point of open hostility. This was apparently how he wanted it, and this, they promised themselves, was how he was going to get it.

"Mr. President!" he said finally, when all apparently satisfied him. "Gentlemen: I have called you here to receive the terms on which the Soviet Union will make peace with you, not only in the nations of Gorotoland and Panama but everywhere throughout the world. I have called you here secretly, and have come here myself secretly, because I thought we could better conclude our business free from the pressures of an open meeting held before the eyes of the world. I hope this meets with your approval. Apparently it does, for you are here.

"You are here, I think"—and his tone became quite pleasant for a moment—"because you are beaten and you know it. Ah, yes, I know!" he added quickly, as an angry stirring came from across the table. "You don't wish to have it stated so bluntly, you don't wish to admit it, you say *I* am the one who sought this meeting, not you. Nonetheless, you are here, and the reason *I* sought it, gentlemen, is because it seemed to me there was no point in further bloodshed when your cause is already lost. It seemed to me that sheer stubbornness on the part of the President might prevent the only outcome —genuine peace—that the world can or will accept. Therefore I came to you, for we should not permit the world's wounds to bleed any longer. If you do not feel this responsibility, Mr. President, *I* do. So *I* moved. It is all very clear."

"Where are the Chinese?" the President inquired. For a second the question appeared to have the effect he sought. But Vasily Tashikov was not a clever man for nothing, and quickly he laughed and dismissed it with a deprecatory wave of the hand.

"The Chinese!" he repeated cheerfully. "The Chinese!"

"Yes," Orrin said, "the Chinese. Where are they?"

"Why, in Peking, Mr. President! In Peking, where I am scheduled to arrive tomorrow, carrying word that you have accepted our terms. They are expecting me. I shall report to them. I am their agent here. That is where the Chinese are," he said, and for just a second an emphatic hardness came into his voice. "In Peking, where they belong. And, of course," he went on smoothly, "beside us on the battlefields, fighting successfully in the people's cause to conquer the imperialist capitalist aggressions of the United States."

"And you're going there tomorrow," the President said slowly, ". . . with our agreement to your terms."

"There is no doubt we will have it," Tashikov said calmly. "There is no doubt at all. Because, let us survey the fields of battle and see where we stand.

"Let us take Gorotoland first. The forces of the usurper Terence Ajkaje—"

"The hereditary ruler," Cullee Hamilton interrupted, "much as I dislike him."

"The usurper Ajkaje," the Chairman repeated firmly. "The forces of the usurper, and the forces of the United States, which, in defiance of the United Nations, world opinion and a majority of your own people, still persist in trying to save the usurper, have been driven steadily back to the point where they are now virtually surrounded and doomed to surrender at any moment. Furthermore, their supplies are reaching a dangerously low point, and let us be honest about it, Mr. President, Mr. ex-President, Mr. Vice President, all of you gentlemen: *there is nothing more which can be sent them.*

"We know that," he added firmly as Blair Hannah shifted in his chair, "because we have sources in the Pentagon quite as good as yours, Mr. Secretary. History has shown on many occasions in recent years that there are people in the Pentagon who love world peace more than they love their own peace-betraying country. They tell us things; they give us documents. So do not try to bluff us. The matériel is not there. The manpower is not there. The support of Congress is not there. Nothing is there but the stubborn unwillingness of the President to face facts. *And this we know.*" A sudden anger crossed his face for a moment. "So please do not try to treat us like children. *We know.*

"So, then: we come to Panama. The situation there is the same. You are beaten back, you are defeated, you are on the verge of surrender. The corrupt regime you seek to preserve can give you no assistance, there is nothing in your own larder: your war machine is about to starve to death for lack of supplies, just as it is in Gorotoland. Nothing can reverse this trend—*nothing.* And this, too, *we know.*

"Therefore, Mr. President and gentlemen, we think it is time to talk."

"Why?" the President asked, looking tired but determined.

"If for no other reason," Tashikov said in a tone almost pitying, "because you are likely to lose your son and daughter-in-law if you do not. Now, do not misunderstand me!" he said sharply as his listeners on the other side of the table shifted angrily in their seats.

"My government has absolutely nothing—*absolutely nothing*—to do with the insane psychotics who have your children—"

"Except to create a climate in the world in which psychotics feel free to roam," William Abbott said bitterly.

"Absolutely nothing!" Tashikov snapped, ignoring him. "We deplore it, it is not our doing, and besides, we do not need it. You are defeated anyway. Why should we indulge in unnecessary violence, when you are finished? It would be pointless. We do not do pointless things. Therefore, for myself and my government, Mr. President, I say: we regret this, and we do not condone it. We hope they return to you safely. *But:* it is your decision whether they do. No one else can decide it for you. You and you alone hold the fate of your young Congressman and his wife. As of course," he added softly, "you hold the fate of many other fine young Americans and their wives. . . .

"So, then. Beaten in Gorotoland. Beaten in Panama. Beaten in Congress. Beaten in world opinion. Beaten in the minds of a majority of your countrymen. And still you fight on. In fact, you even talk of a new offensive—"

"That worries you, doesn't it?" the President said. "You don't like that, do you?"

"No, we do not!" Tashikov snapped. "Because we think it is insanity. Because we think it can only mean further useless bloodshed. *Because we know you cannot win.*"

"But you don't really know that," the President said softly. "That, you really don't know. And you wonder. And it worries you. And so you are here, not because *we* are weak but because you are afraid that we may still be stronger than you when it comes to the test . . . and because, I think, you are afraid that you may not be able to hold things together on your side much longer, if the wars go on. You must win soon or not win at all. Isn't that the truth of it, Mr. Chairman?"

"No, it is not the truth of it!" Vasily Tashikov cried. "That is bluff! Empty bluff! I will show you the truth of it, Mr. President and gentlemen, since you are so pigheaded and so blind. Comrades!" And he rounded so suddenly on the generals and admirals seated beside him that a couple of them actually jumped. "Bring out your charts! Bring out your photographs! Bring out your maps! Show these arrogant madmen what their true military situation is!"

And for the next half hour he and his colleagues proceeded to do so: the bomb-carrying satellites hovering everywhere over the earth; the submarines on station off both coasts of the United States; the secret missile bases in Cuba and elsewhere in Latin America; the secret installations in the untracked Arctic wastes of touchy, unsuspecting Canada; the worldwide network of air bases; the fleets of conventional naval craft afloat in every sea; the millions of men and women under arms; the worldwide network of spies, saboteurs and informants working ceaselessly inside the United States and everywhere else to assist the imperial ambitions of the nation whose smugly satisfied leader sat across the table uttering occasional little grunts of satisfaction as his officers displayed their deadly wares.

It was an amazingly candid and amazingly complete accounting, provided for one purpose only: to scare the Americans into surrender without further defiance.

When the recital ended there were no visible signs that this had been accomplished; although the President, looking thoughtfully from face to face, wondered what the reaction would be when they got away from this carefully orchestrated pressure chamber and were back on their own home ground.

And so, obviously, wondered the Chairman and his colleagues as, stolid and impassive save for Vasily, who could not resist little chuckles and chortles and happy sounds from time to time, they surveyed the outwardly impassive but inwardly shaken Americans across the table. At least they thought the Americans must be shaken, so admittedly impressive and overwhelming was the array of horrors spread before them. Yet here, as always, men failed to comprehend innate American optimism; nor did they give sufficient weight to "Orrin's little extra."

Presently, as the Chairman looked at him expectantly and challenged, "*Well,* Mr. President?"—it came out.

"Once before," the President said, and the room was very still and they listened very closely for intimations of fear which did not come, "I was privileged—or unfortunate enough—to attend a meeting in Geneva somewhat similar to this. You will recall, Mr. Chairman, for you were there too, that the principals were the two gentlemen then occupying the Presidency and the Chairmanship. You will recall as vividly as I, Senator Munson and Senator Strickland, who also were there, what happened from your side on that occasion: virtually the same thing, and for the same reason—to frighten the United States into giving in without further ado to every insane ambition of the Soviet hierarchy.

"And you will further recall the response of the President of the United States, that good man, Harley Hudson: he told you you were crazy, and he got up and walked out. And that"—he pushed back his chair and stood up—"is, I think, a fine practice for American Presidents to follow in situations such as this. And so I shall make it my own. Gentlemen—"

And he gave Tashikov a cursory nod that barely maintained civility, turned and walked out, followed, after a moment's startled hesitation, by his countrymen.

Behind them as the gates slammed shut they could hear Tashikov shouting into the frozen night, "You will be sorry for this, Mr. President! *Knox, you will be sorry!*"

But he did not turn back, reply or in any way acknowledge this kindly farewell, any more than Harley had under similar circumstances two years ago—though now the stakes were even higher, the risks of defiance even greater and the consequences, in every sector, even more dreadfully in doubt.

When they reached the White House, passing once again through the silent and now completely deserted streets, it was almost 2 A.M. and bitterly cold. But although they all looked tired, none more desperately so than himself, he turned to them with a businesslike manner when they got out of the cars under the South Portico.

"I hate to hold you here at this hour and under such circumstances, but we've obviously got to talk. The staff will make you comfortable in the solarium and I'll join you there in twenty minutes with the latest war reports and anything else of significance."

When they were reassembled, furnished with coffee and doughnuts, coats off and relaxing, as much as possible under the circumstances, in the solarium's comfortable family chairs and sofas, he said, "Now, tell me: Have I destroyed the world?"

"Not yet," Bill Abbott said with a grim little smile. "But it may come in ten minutes."

"Did you believe all that?" Cullee asked, and Blair Hannah looked a little blank.

"How can you not?" he inquired. "It conforms generally to what we know from our own intelligence reports. Yes, I believe it."

"And I," Robert A. Leffingwell said.

"And I," said several others.

"Then," the Vice President said quietly, and now they all turned to the President where he sat, a little apart, in a deep rattan chair with bright, chintzy, summer-cheerful pillows that seemed almost frighteningly incongruous with the conversation, "where do we go from here?"

"We proceed with the new offensives I have ordered in Gorotoland

and Panama," Orrin said with equal quietness, "and we wait and see."

"When will they occur?" Bob Munson asked.

"Within hours," Blair Hannah said.

"And for all practical purposes," William Abbott said heavily, "they will take everything we've got."

"For all practical purposes," the President agreed, still quietly, "they will take everything we've got."

"And if they fail?" Warren Strickland asked.

The President looked him straight in the eye and did not flinch.

"Then I suppose the United States for the first time in its history will have to sue for peace on the battlefield. And I shall undoubtedly be impeached."

"And what will happen to the United States then, Mr. President?" Bob Leffingwell inquired.

"I do not know," the President said, and a certain iron entered his tone, "because I do not contemplate that the United States will fail."

"But if it does, Mr. President," his predecessor inquired with a grave persistence.

"I do not contemplate that," Orrin repeated quietly, and William Abbott said in a tone both disturbed and compassionate, "But you must. . . ." He sighed heavily and leaned forward. "Orrin, you are asking us to take an awful lot on faith—your faith. You're taking a terrible responsibility and asking us to share—"

"No more terrible than you took with the alert," the President said sharply, "no more than many of our predecessors have had to take, in their time. . . . And you don't have to share it with me, any of you, if you don't want to." His tone hardened. "You can go now, nothing's to stop you. Blair and Bob Leffingwell, you can resign if you don't want to be responsible." A grim little humor touched his mouth for a second. "You haven't been confirmed anyway, so what's there to resign from? None of you has to stay with me, none of you has to help me—"

"As long as the armed forces will obey you," Bob Munson suggested. The President paused in mid-sentence.

"I am the Commander in Chief!" he snapped. "Furthermore, while they're concerned and upset, as we all are, as Blair and I both know they are, from the talk we had with them yesterday, still they will do their best for me because that is their training and their loyalty. And, I might add, this conforms to their instinct as military men—

their instinct that there comes a moment when, if everything is tossed on the dice, if the moment is seized with courage and vigor, all will come right. They are going with me at this very moment, making the preparations I have asked them to, because in their hearts this is the way they would like to have it decided, cleanly and quickly and on our terms . . . which I do believe," he concluded gravely, "can be achieved in a swift, decisive act."

"If it is swift," William Abbott said moodily. "If it is decisive. If it is clean, if it is final . . . none of which is certain on the dusty plains of Gorotoland or in the jungles of Panama."

There was a silence and into it Cullee Hamilton spoke finally in a hesitant yet determined tone.

"There is one other way, Mr. President. It goes against your grain, it goes against mine and, I suspect, against that of all of us here. And I hate to give any credit to that jackass Jawbone for suggesting it: nonetheless, he did. And that's to stay in place. Simply to send in enough to stabilize the battlelines, regain as much as possible where we've been pushed back, which can probably be done with a third of the effort you're contemplating—and then sit tight. Go back to the U.N. Continue the diplomacy. Fight the propaganda war. Hold where we are—and wait for some break to come. It could perhaps be done that way. It's a possibility. . . ."

"But not, I think," the President said, "a very good one. We had stalemate when Bill was in the White House, and what happened? We tried diplomacy, we tried deals, we tried secret negotiations, we held where we were—and the minute they thought we were off balance, they struck. And they'll strike again, whenever they think they have the chance. They don't give up. . . . No," he said, and his tone again became firm, so that they felt a near hopelessness as they listened, though basically they sympathized. "I don't want stalemate, because I think that only means a delayed victory for them later. Rightly or wrongly—history will have to decide—I lived that day at the Monument Grounds and Ted Jason died. If it had been the other way around, he would be sitting here now, and no doubt you'd have stalemate, delay, maybe even appeasement and surrender—we'll never know. But *I* lived and *I* was elected, and even though many had misgivings about me, the majority elected me knowing that I have always advocated a firm policy, a direct policy—a 'tough' policy, if you like. So for better or worse, that's what we've got. That's my nature and my philosophic belief and my personal conviction—and so that is how I am acting, not as Ted

Jason would, because I am not Ted Jason, but as Orrin Knox, because I am Orrin Knox."

He looked at their tense and worried faces. Old friendship, understanding, sympathy, affection, softened his face and his voice as he concluded.

"I know this is not easy for any of you. I know you are afraid—as, let's face it, I am afraid. If any of you wants to walk out of here and repudiate me, I shall certainly understand and I shall certainly not hold it against you—you know me well enough to believe that, I hope. But being what I am, I cannot do other than I am. I should like to have you with me, and I appreciate, more than words can adequately express, your affection and concern, which I reciprocate. But I must do it my way, for that is the way in which I believe.

"The consequences to my country, the consequences to"—for a second his voice trembled, then grew strong again—"to my family, the consequences to me, may be incalculable. But *I believe* there is a place for right and justice in the world and *I believe* it has come to me, in my turn, to try to save them. I know history is full of men who believed they were doing this, only to find that history did not agree with them, and it turned out eventually that all-unknowing they were doing something entirely different. But I can only remain firm, and try. Because that is my being—that is what I am."

When he concluded there was another silence, very long and very solemn this time; and only after several minutes had passed did William Abbott, looking tired and old but still indomitable, stand up, put on his coat, his topcoat and his hat.

"Orrin," he said, holding out his hand. "I don't know where we will all be in three or four days. But I suspect I'll be standing with you, wherever it is."

"And I," Cullee said, shaking hands, too. "And I," said Bob Munson and Warren Strickland, and Robert A. Leffingwell and Blair Hannah.

And so with great emotion the moment ended and they went forth from the White House into the ghostly night, to be driven home through ghostly streets to their respective abodes.

As often happened, because the Sheraton Park was on the way to "Vagaries," the ex-President rode with the ex-Majority Leader.

As he dropped Bill Abbott off at the hotel shortly before 3 A.M., Bob Munson broke their hitherto silent ride to say with a heavy sigh:

"Well, many of us have always believed his way was the right way. We just never quite thought anybody would ever have the chance to really prove it out. Now he's got it, and he's doing it, and he isn't letting anything deflect him."

"And," Bill Abbott said, "I think we had better all pray like hell, for him, and for the country, and for everybody, everywhere."

If the President had entertained any naïve hopes that the events of the night would remain private, or that they would be fairly stated if they did not remain private, those hopes were exploded at noon in the world's headlines:

TASHIKOV IN PEKING, REVEALS SECRET WASHINGTON MEETING WITH PRESIDENT. SOVIET LEADER SAYS KNOX ADAMANT IN PUSHING NEW OFFENSIVES IN WAR ZONES. HE AND CHINESE WARN PRESIDENT "MUST BEAR FULL RESPONSIBILITY FOR ALL CONSEQUENCES WHICH WILL AUTOMATICALLY FLOW FROM ANY NEW U.S. AGGRESSIONS." PROMISE "SEVEREST POSSIBLE RETALIATION UPON U.S. IF WAR-MAD POLICIES CONTINUE."

WHITE HOUSE REFUSES COMMENT.

CIVIL DEFENSE UNITS TAKE STATIONS THROUGHOUT COUNTRY.

ATOMIC GIANTS APPEAR HEADED FOR DIRECT CLASH.

And three hours later, in a corollary perhaps inevitable, given the nature of the world in the declining years of a sick and sorry century:

SON'S FINGER WITH WEDDING RING SENT TO PRESIDENT IN SPECIAL-DELIVERY PACKAGE. CAPTORS ISSUE STATEMENT TO ALL MEDIA: "REP. KNOX AND HIS WIFE WILL DIE AT 8 A.M. TOMORROW UNLESS U.S. WAR PLANS ARE HALTED IMMEDIATELY. THE PRESIDENT MUST APPEAR ON TELEVISION AND CONFIRM THIS TO THE WORLD, OTHERWISE HE WILL SEE HIS CHILDREN AGAIN, BUT NOT ALIVE."

WHITE HOUSE REFUSES COMMENT.

Somehow he got through the afternoon, checked plans with the Pentagon, managed to maintain an iron control in the sight of the staff, managed to be the President, apparently undaunted and undismayed. At one point he did retire for a brief "nap," during which he broke down completely—let the tears and agony come for the better part of fifteen minutes—then told himself that he had chosen his course, he must follow it to the end and must be brave—brave . . . and so presently reappeared and went back to work, eyes red-rimmed, face drawn and white but adamantine again as he went about the final details of preparation. You could not deal with such people. Recent years had proved that you simply *could not,* or not only two lives, but all, could be lost.

At various points his predecessor, Cullee, Stanley, the Munsons, Warren Strickland, the Maudulaynes, the Barres and Krishna Khaleel all called to express awkward but desperately earnest sympathy; tinged, inevitably, with an overtone of fear as to what was going to happen. He thanked them all gravely, reiterated his confidence that all would be well, gave no sign of yielding. Saddened and as desperately unhappy as he at the abysses, personal, national and international, which seemed to be opening beneath their feet, they too went back to their accustomed routines, achingly precious now that all routines appeared on the verge of dissolution. Somehow the day, the world, life, the universe, inched forward, slowly, slowly, under the dreadful burden of what appeared to be about to happen.

At 9 P.M., one hour from the time when he was to call the Pentagon with the final code word to launch the attack, the appointments secretary announced that an unexpected visitor wanted to see him. Any other time he might have refused, but now there was nothing left to do but await the hour and try not to think any more about anything, if he could help it. His visitor, of whom he had always been very fond during their days together in the Senate and at the U.N., might provide welcome diversion.

"Show him in," he said, and after a moment the appointments secretary did so, saying, "Senator Smith," in a quick, almost embarrassed way and then withdrawing hastily as Lafe came forward hesitantly toward the desk.

"Lafe," he said, holding out his hand.

"Orrin—" Lafe said, "Mr. President—" He shook hands, hard. "I am so sorry."

"Sit down," the President said. "Don't be sorry. There's so much to be sorry for that it's beyond—don't be sorry. I am grateful to you for coming. I need company, right now. None better for me, I suspect. What's on your mind?"

"The continuity of life," Lafe said, quite unexpectedly for a practical mind not often given to philosophizing. "Two things have happened to me today and I thought you might like to hear about them. Not that they are very important in view of—of what you're facing—"

"Of what we're all facing," he said gravely, and Lafe nodded unhappily.

"Right . . . But, anyway, they mean something to me, and I thought maybe they might mean something to you, and that maybe

—maybe you'd be a little heartened by them. So," he added somewhat lamely, "I thought I'd just come by and tell you. No other reason. I just thought I'd come by and tell you because I thought —maybe—right now—you'd like to hear something good—unimportant, I suppose—but good. . . ."

"I would be delighted," he said with a momentary return of the old ruefully humorous Orrin, "to hear something good, however unimportant." Quite abruptly, quite beyond his control, his eyes filled with tears. Lafe's responded, and for several moments they both stared hard out the window at the frozen night and said no more.

"Well," Lafe said finally, his voice trembling a little but managing to stay reasonably steady, "the first is that I asked Mabel to marry me this morning and she said yes."

"How wonderful!" he exclaimed. "Lafe, I am so pleased for you both. That *is* good news, indeed."

"I thought it was nice," Lafe said carefully, "particularly since she's been so bitter about politics since Brig died, and so determined to stay in Utah and not venture out."

"Why should she now?" he asked, mood abruptly changing, with a detached and almost ironic curiosity that, even in this moment, was also typical Orrin. "Are things any better?"

"No," Lafe said with no attempt at dissembling. "But I think she finally decided that it was best to be together with someone you love if—if things are really going to come to the final showdown."

"I would like to be able to do that too," he said with a sudden terrible bleakness, "because I think perhaps they are. But at the moment, those I love are not—not here."

"I know," Lafe said in a tone as desolate as his. "Is there any way you can—any way—"

"No," he said in the same far-off, abandoned-by-the-fates voice. "There can be no weakening by the United States in this situation or, I am convinced, the United States will go under. This means there can be no weakening by the President of the United States. So I am caught." And suddenly, pounding his fists on the arms of his chair with a furious futility that shattered his companion completely for a moment, he cried, *"Caught, caught, caught!"*—and covered his face with his hands, eyes closed, rubbing his forehead slowly, pressing hard as if to drive out the demons that resided there.

For several minutes, while Lafe watched with a fearful absorption, he said no more. Then finally he looked up and in a voice that by some miracle managed to be relatively steady again, asked:

"And what is the other good thing?"

"Well, you know Jimmy Fry," Lafe began with care, because this was perhaps his most emotional subject, perhaps even more than Mabel, particularly since they were sharing it together.

"Yes," the President said. "I know Jimmy. Have you—?"

"Orrin, we've broken through!" Lafe cried exultantly. "We've broken through! He spoke to us! He *said* something! We're getting through at last, Orrin! We're getting through!"

And this time it was his eyes that unexpectedly filled with tears, the President's that responded.

"I'm delighted," Orrin said gravely. "I am so glad for you and Mabel, Lafe. Tell me about it."

"Well," Lafe said, blowing his nose vigorously and plunging gratefully into his narrative, "it happened this morning after Mabel agreed to marry me. I have that new setup for us all on Foxhall Road, you know, and I brought Jimmy down to it from the sanitarium on the Hudson several days ago. He seemed to stand the trip very well, and to accept the new surroundings very well—not that we really knew, because, as you know, it has never been possible to communicate. But this morning, after Mabel said yes, we decided we'd take Pidge and go and tell him."

"How is Pidge?" the President asked, with a brief but affectionate smile for Mabel and Brig's lively six-year-old.

"Oh, she's fine," Lafe said, proud and fondly parental. "Bright as a button and getting brighter every day. And fascinated by her new big brother, which I expect is why it happened."

"He spoke to her, then," Orrin said.

"Nope," Lafe said firmly, "he spoke to *all* of us."

"All right," the President said, again with a fleeting smile. "Go on."

"We went into his room and he was sitting by the window staring out at the trees—that heartbreaking blank look that his father and Cullee and I have seen so many times up at Oak Lawn. So Mabel and I went over toward him and suddenly Pidge went into a little dance and began to sing, 'Mommie's marrying Uncle Lafe! Mommie's marrying Uncle Lafe!' And then when he didn't respond, she went up to him and pulled at his arm and said, 'Hey, Jimmy! I said Mommie's marrying Uncle Lafe! Aren't you happy?' And, Orrin"—his tone became hushed—"do you know what he did then? First of all, he actually turned his head toward us, which he's hardly ever done before. And then he said—*he said,* Orrin—in a sort of croak, like a robot, almost, but quite distinctly—'That's nice. Are we happy?' And Pidge crowed,

'Yes, we *are* happy!' And he said, again in that mechanical sort of way, but making sense, 'Yes, we are happy.'

"Then"—Lafe smiled a little—"Mabel cried and Pidge cried and I cried—and Jimmy just sat there and never said another word, and hasn't since. But he did it, Orrin—Mr. President—*he did it*. And if he's finally done it, then he can do it again. I've been on the phone to doctors all day, it seems like, and they seem to think that now we've finally broken through, we can go on from there if he has love and care and patience. And God knows he's going to have them. So," he concluded, and again for a moment before the realities of the hour closed in on them again he sounded excited and happy, "that's my second piece of good news. A pretty good budget for one day, don't you think?"

"A wonderful budget," the President said, and for a moment he, too, seemed taken out of himself to participate in a happier world. "I am so glad for you on both counts, Lafe. You have a kind heart, one of the kindest I know, and you've earned the happiness. . . . And it is reassuring, what you call 'the continuity of life,' even"—and the lighter mood ended for them both as swiftly as it had begun, the awful burden of the moment came rushing back—"even in such a world."

And abruptly lightness was gone, brightness was gone, the night was filled once more with fear and horror and awful things. And again the President's expression changed, he put his face again in his hands, began again the slow, steady rubbing of his forehead to drive out the demons there.

"When does it begin?" Lafe asked softly.

The President lifted his head, glanced at the clock.

"Twenty-six and one-half minutes, may God have mercy on us all."

Lafe's answer was a quotation, uttered so low that the President could hardly hear him:

"'Let us wear on our sleeves the crepe of mourning for a civilization that held the promise of joy.'"

"Oh, no," the President responded in an agonized whisper. "Oh, no. Don't say that, Lafe. It isn't true. Not yet. . . . Not yet."

But in all the night that lay over Washington, the night that lay over the world, no man at that moment could discern the hope that might disprove it.

"Would you like me to wait with you?" Lafe asked finally. The President nodded.

"Please." A last glimmer of Orrin shone through before he returned head to hands and began the strong, persistent, driven rubbing of his gray but unshakable face. "I can't think of better company to pray in."

So the minutes passed and approached the hour, and so in their hearts and in the hearts of men everywhere hope died further—and further—and further— . . . until approximately eleven minutes before the President was to open the direct line to the Pentagon and give the order.

He was mentally readying himself to do so, trying not to think of his son and daughter-in-law about to die, trying not to think of many other brave people about to die, trying not to think of the world's agony he was about to increase, trying to draw from some ultimate reserve some ultimate strength, when suddenly there came a hurry and a bustle and the loud cries of excited voices in the hall, and even as they looked up astounded the door burst open and Blair Hannah rushed in shouting:

"Mr. President! Mr. President! Good news! Good news!"

And so, of a dreadful sort, it was; and so he found himself, as the phrase shot ironically through his mind, saved by the bell.

Saved by the bell.

But who could say for how long?

Or why?

No one would ever know what happened—what general, colonel, major, captain, lieutenant, sergeant, corporal, private, fired the first shot—what terrible, years-long, deliberately government-created tension finally exploded in what brain or heart.

It did not matter.

It happened, and the world went mad.

The first headlines shouted:

SOVIET, CHINESE TROOPS CLASH IN FIELD IN GOROTOLAND! BLOODY BATTLE FLARES BETWEEN ALLIES!

Two hours later they screamed:

ASIA IN FLAMES! SINO-SOVIET CLASH SPREADS INSTANTLY TO HOMELANDS! COMMUNIST GIANTS CLASH ALL ALONG FOUR-THOUSAND-MILE BORDER! SAVAGE FIGHTING BETWEEN RUSS AND CHINESE! HONG KONG REPORTS CHINESE MAKE INITIAL GAINS, SOVIETS PUSHED BACK!

Three hours after that, sounding, most believed, the death knell of the planet:

ATOMIC WAR!!!

SOVIETS HIT CHINESE WITH MISSILES, CHINESE RETALIATE! REPORT SEVEN MAJOR CITIES WIPED OUT, HUNDREDS OF THOUSANDS DEAD! RADIOACTIVE CLOUD DRIFTS TOWARD SOUTH PACIFIC! WORLD ON BRINK OF ARMAGEDDON!

But this was not quite true yet, for, terrified and sobered by what they had done, the giants paused:

BOTH SIDES HALT ATTACK! MOSCOW DEMANDS IMMEDIATE CHINESE SURRENDER OR "COMPLETE DESTRUCTION OF ENTIRE COUNTRY!" CHINESE DEMAND IMMEDIATE SOVIET SURRENDER OR "TOTAL ANNIHILATION OF SOVIET IMPERIALISM, NATION AND PEOPLE!" ULTIMATUMS EXPIRE AT MIDNIGHT! FATE OF EARTH AT STAKE!

But midnight came and went, and Earth, though just barely, was still here. And then came finally the face-saving power-preserving that had to come if the terminal insanity of mankind was not, at last, to occur:

RUSS, CHINESE TURN TO U.S. AS RUMORS OF UPRISINGS AGAINST BOTH GOVERNMENTS REACH OUTSIDE WORLD!

BOTH SIDES APPEAL TO KNOX TO MEDIATE!

PRESIDENT HOLDS KEY TO SAVING GLOBE FROM FINAL DESTRUCTION!

Saved by the bell.

And now the bell was tolling for him.

BOOK THREE

1. "HI," SAID THE VOICE he had never thought to hear again. "You're a hell of a hard man to get through to, I must say."

"It's a little busy around here," he responded, half laughing, half crying, with relief. "Where are you? Are you both all right?"

"We're at the East Gate," his son said. "We're both all right." He hesitated and his excited tone turned grave. "It hasn't been easy, but we're both all right."

"Thank God for that," he said simply. "Get in here as fast as you can."

"On our way," Hal said.

While he waited for them to walk down the drive, into the West Wing and along the chaotic, crisis-humming corridors to the Oval Office—one of the longest three-minute spans he had ever experienced—the gamble he had taken with their lives suddenly assumed such an enormity in his mind that he felt he could hardly breathe. It had been a desperate gamble, a terrifyingly honest gamble, a gamble he had sincerely believed to be his only recourse. At the time, under the remorseless pressures that then existed, it had seemed the only thing he could do. Now, as always with desperate solutions when pressures are suddenly removed, it appeared utterly unreal, unnecessary and monstrous.

So it appeared to him who had done it. How must it appear to those who had been its potential, its almost certain, victims? How would his children regard him now, who had just yesterday forced himself to sentence them, in effect, to death?

The agonized uncertainty must have been in his face when the door opened, for they paused on the threshold, as he paused behind the desk, and for a tense, unreal moment they looked at one another like strangers. Then Crystal gave a little cry and rushed forward into his arms, Hal followed, and they all found themselves laughing, crying and hugging one another at the same time.

He needn't have worried: they understood. A dreadful weight lifted suddenly from his heart.

"Well," he said shakily, "sit down and let me look at you."

"Shouldn't we—?" Crystal began. "I mean, can you—aren't you too busy to waste time on us right now?"

"Good God," he said. "*Waste* time on you?" A sudden twinkle came into his eyes. "What else is there to waste time on?"

"Now *that,*" Hal said with mock severity, "is being downright disingenuous."

"Yes," he agreed; a little silence fell; and they studied one another again, not this time with tension or strangeness, but as three who had passed through the fire together.

"How did they treat you?" he asked finally. "Aside from—aside from—"

"It wasn't pleasant," Hal said gravely, and for the first time he brought his bandaged left hand, which he had been half concealing at his side, into full view and rested it carefully on his knee. "And Crystal lost a little hair. But on the whole"—his eyes looked far away, remembering—"it wasn't bad. And," he added in the words his father still needed to hear, "we knew you had no choice. And we believed in what you were doing. So that made it a little easier to face what—what we thought we might have to face. Other than that, though," his tone became more conversational, and less tense, "it wasn't too bad. They fed us reasonably well and kept us isolated or blindfolded all the time. We never saw them, but I would say there were about five, wouldn't you, Crys?"

"Yes," she said. "A white man and a white woman, two black men and a black woman. About our age, we thought, most of them well educated and cultured and very hep on the world—as they see it. Which isn't"—she smiled wryly—"quite the way we see it."

"How did they let you go?" he asked. "Did you see them? The FBI will want to get all this right away, of course."

"They turned us out in Rock Creek Park about half an hour ago," Hal said. "Fortunately we found a cab right away. We promised them we wouldn't talk to the FBI." His expression turned as wry as his wife's. "You've no idea what good friends we parted when it suddenly became clear that we were all on the same side after all, trying to settle this hellish mess in Asia. But for once," he said, and his face became grim, "a Knox is deliberately going to break his word. We'll tell the FBI everything we can possibly remember about the scum and I hope they find them and shoot them down 'while trying to escape.'"

"They won't do that," Crystal said, "because now everything's changed and we *are* all on the same side. Our little episode will be lost, forgiven and forgotten in the rush of things. It will be a long time before anybody will start thinking about it again. And then it won't matter."

The President nodded.

"Very true and very shrewd. A great wave of let-bygones-be-bygones is sweeping over the world today. But tell the FBI anyway. There may come a time when the balance returns. When it does"—his expression for a moment turned as grim as his son's—"I too will be in favor of rather severe exactions. . . . I want you to know," he added quietly, "that I'm so grateful to have you back that I—that I"—his eyes filled again with tears, but he went on—"that I can't really express it."

"You ain't the only one, Pop," Hal said with a deliberately cheerful flipness that set them all laughing together, albeit a little shakily.

"No," his father agreed, blowing his nose. "Why do you suppose they really let you go?"

"No point in holding us any more, is there?" his son inquired with a touch of Knox tartness. "Who wants to do anything to bother *you?* You're the world's great hero now, aren't you?"

And so he seemed to be, he reflected after they left to go back to the Mansion to talk to the FBI and then get some much-needed sleep . . . so he seemed to be. Orrin Knox the world's villain was suddenly Orrin Knox the world's savior. Of all the great ironies of history, he thought, surely this must be one of the most exquisite.

He looked at the reports, maps, papers strewn everywhere across the enormous desk and gave way for a moment to a helpless laughter—so overwhelming were the things that confronted him. But, like his children's when they left him, it was a relieved and almost happy laughter, for at least now he had options once more. Now he was in charge of things again. Through him the world had one last chance to save itself. Once again Orrin Knox was the master of events, not their plaything.

And the greatest irony of all was something that had occurred to him instantly, though in the terrible crisis that confronted mankind it might not occur to most others until very much later on, if then.

He was saved by the bell—not by any effort of the American President, not by any recognition by the world of America's decent purposes, not by any triumph of American principles or American courage or American strength, or his own principles or his own courage or his own strength—but simply because two ravenous beasts of history's jungle had, for reasons known only to them and already, he suspected, forgotten in their joint terror at the awful results of their mutual hatreds, turned on one another.

He could not claim that America had brought sanity back to the world: the endless patient efforts of succeeding Administrations had not accomplished what a single rifle shot in Gorotoland had done. He could not claim that Orrin Knox's genius or patience or integrity or human worth or diplomacy had contributed anything to bringing the world back to its senses: some unknown soldier's blind instinctive reaction to an enemy he had been taught for years to hate had done more than Orrin Knox, for all his piety and wit, could ever do.

Nor was there any endorsement of Orrin Knox's policies, any vindication of the beliefs and principles for which he had stood all his life. He had always argued for firmness and unwavering strength in the face of Communist imperialism. So, he had held out for firmness and unwavering strength, and what had it got him? It had been on the very verge of getting him complete disaster, when a sheer fluke of fate had saved him from it.

If anything, he could thank, not himself, but the insane antagonisms, suspicions and mutual jealousies of the leaders of the two Communist giants who for years had trained their citizens to hate one another. Now history with its terrible impartial justice had permitted those leaders to achieve their purpose; and like all who were permitted to achieve a purpose so obscene, history had handed them with it the bones of ruin and the skull of death.

And so they were turning to him—not because firmness and strength and courage and integrity had been rewarded—but simply because slavery and deceit and terror and imperial ambition had been rewarded, with an impartial and devastating irony, even as they were being shown to be futile, empty, pointless and bad.

Irony piled upon irony. His way, perhaps, had not been right, for often enough in history it had led straight to disaster. Appeasement had not been right either, for often enough in history it too had led straight to disaster.

So where was the middle ground, and what was the answer?

There was no time left for mankind to find out now. And that, perhaps, was the most savagely delicious irony of them all.

At any rate, he had people to see and things to do; and now, in these first hectic moments after he had received the formal appeals from Peking and Moscow, he decided he had no time for philosophy, only for action. He made his first decision, called his press secretary. Within twenty minutes a distraught and nervous press corps, as terrified and fearful of what might happen as the rest of humanity, was crowding into the East Room.

He entered, they rose with an instant and unquestioning respect they had never before, he noted with a grim inward humor, shown to Orrin Knox.

The press secretary said: "Ladies and gentlemen, the President of the United States."

He said: "Please be seated."

And subjected them to a slow, searching examination: these hostile faces and bitter tongues that had tried so often to trip and trap him in the past.

There was none of that now. Just fear and supplication, the arrogant and the vindictive humbled at last.

"Ladies and gentlemen," he said—adding, directly into the cameras—"my fellow countrymen: Less than twenty-four hours ago, as you know, the armed forces of the Soviet Union and the People's Republic of China clashed in Gorotoland. Immediately thereafter the two countries were at war all along their Asian border. Within a matter of hours they had exchanged atomic attacks with great and as yet unknown loss of life, and had inflicted upon one another devastating destruction of a number of cities. They had also loosed a radioactive cloud which is even now as I speak drifting into the Pacific Basin toward Australia, New Zealand and the islands of the South Pacific.

"The atomic exchange and the general fighting then ceased. Each country served an ultimatum upon the other. The ultimatums expired at midnight last night, and nothing happened, because by that time, I suspect, both sides were finally aghast at the dreadful things they had done. Some last shred of sanity apparently revived in both Moscow and Peking. This morning, as you all know, they have turned to the President of the United States to mediate their dispute.

"I must now decide whether or not to do so."

"My God, Mr. President," the *Post* blurted in a tone both astounded and fearful, "surely you don't have any doubt?"

"Well," he said reasonably, "why shouldn't I? Two days ago you people regarded me as the world's most hateful and irresponsible man. The same opinion was firmly held and loudly voiced in many places throughout the world, most notably in Moscow and Peking. Perhaps I am not worthy of so great a responsibility. Many of you have frequently told me so, at any rate." His gaze, which had been wandering thoughtfully over a good many faces that flushed and eyes that dropped as he spoke, came back to concentrate on the *Post,* pale and standing as if mesmerized at his chair. "Isn't that true?"

"Sir—" the *Post* began. "Mr. President—"

"Isn't it true that I am the world's most worthless and reckless man?" he demanded sharply, giving no quarter now to those who had never given any to him. "Isn't it true that such a worthless individual has no right to intervene in the affairs of the world which are so much better managed by the great minds of Moscow and Peking? Nine-tenths of you in this room have told this to your country and the world—and have believed it as much, I daresay, as you believe anything—as far back as I can remember. You have been particularly harsh in the two weeks since I entered this office. I repeat, where do you find in me the characteristics that make me worthy of this great responsibility now?"

And he resumed his bland, patient, implacable searching from face to face.

For several long moments no one said anything. The *Post* sat slowly down again. The *Times* started to rise, thought better of it. Frankly Unctuous and the networks were similarly dumb. At last in the front row a familiar figure stood up, short, rather dumpy, determined, grim—for once not sure of himself, for once not pompous and all-knowing—but at least, thank God, the President noted with an inward satisfaction and a considerable respect, having the guts and the simple character to do it.

His tone, however, did not yield an inch as he inquired coldly:

"Yes?"

"Mr. President," Walter Dobius said carefully and with obvious strain. "It may be that when the history of our times is written—*if* it is written—it will be found that you were right and we were wrong in our differing positions on foreign policy. Apparently—for the time being, anyway"—and it was obvious that the words came hard and that he wasn't yielding entirely, though honest enough to yield a good deal—"it appears that you were right.

"Therefore," he said firmly, looking around him at his colleagues with a defiant but determined air, "I for one am ready to apologize for some of the harsher and perhaps more—unrestrained—things that I have said about you in my column. I would suggest to my colleagues, and respectfully to you, Mr. President, that this is no time on either side to harbor grudges. We are all in this together. And frankly"—and the pompous delivery relaxed abruptly into perhaps the most human tone the President had ever heard him use—"it certainly is one hell of a mess, isn't it?"

"It is," he agreed; but did not, for the moment, say more, only continuing to look at Walter with an impassive and politely inquisitive air.

"So," Walter went on finally, just before the moment became too long and awkward, "I wanted to apologize, as I say, and express the hope that perhaps our contacts on both sides can be more—more amicable—from now on." He paused and then went doggedly on, in a tone as close to humble as years of mutual dislike could ever permit him to become toward Orrin Knox. "Is that agreeable to you?"

For another moment or two the President did not answer. Then he nodded and said in a voice that still retained, as Walter's did, a basic reserve, but was otherwise as accommodating as bitter memories would allow:

"Yes, it is, and I thank you, Walter, for having the decency to say these things. I hope they reflect the attitude of most of you, and I shall do my best to cooperate; because it is, as you say, one hell of a situation."

At this there was a little relaxation, the start of a relieved amusement: he was going to be agreeable, after all. "Good old Orrin," the *Times* murmured, quite spontaneously, to the Boston *Globe,* and the *Globe* agreed quickly, "Yes!" with a fervent relief, both quite innocently unaware of the irony of their heartfelt approval after all the harsh things they had said and written over such a long and contentious time.

"I said a few moments ago," the President went on, and his tone now was quite calm, "that I had to decide whether or not to mediate the war between China and the Soviet Union. Perhaps I should have said that *they* must decide whether or not I am to mediate it, because if they want me to"—his tone turned stern—"there are certain conditions they are going to have to meet. And I am not going to hesitate at all in stating them, for to me they seem to be essential for re-establishing peace—everywhere. And what seems best to me," he added dryly, "now seems to be somewhat more important and effective than it was twenty-four hours ago.

"I should tell you that these conditions are being transmitted formally at this moment to the governments in Moscow and Peking. But I use the terms 'Moscow' and 'Peking' for convenience only, because both governments are in hiding underground. We think we know where they are and we are trying to reach them, but in case we don't, possibly you ladies and gentlemen can help with your news stories, broadcasts and transmissions."

He paused and looked straight into the television cameras which were carrying his words around the globe and, most specifically, to the frightened individuals in Peking and Moscow whose ruthless and crafty ways had failed them at last. He then began to enunciate, quietly and firmly and still in an almost conversational tone, the list of conditions that were to leap into the headlines and go down in history, for such time as it might still be recorded, as "the Ten Demands."

"The first condition I had intended to make has been met. It will probably not weigh as substantially in other hearts as it does in mine, yet without it, so far as I was concerned, nothing else could have been done. My son and daughter-in-law have been freed, unharmed save for"—and his even tone wavered just a little before he went firmly on—"the ring finger of my son's left hand. They are in good health and in good spirits and are now in the White House. I am glad to have them back."

There was a spontaneous, completely genuine, completely warm burst of applause and congratulations from his audience. For a moment they were united in human feeling. Then he withdrew to the remoter and more imperial plane that events had now given him the obligation to occupy. His voice became colder and more impersonal.

"The second requirement before I will consent to participate in a possible settlement of the Sino-Soviet War is the immediate and complete withdrawal of all their armed forces from the nations of Gorotoland and Panama.

"This has been accomplished *de facto* in large part in the past twenty-four hours since fighting broke out between them, because both countries are rushing their troops home as fast as possible, and their forces in both places have already been cut to half, or below. This pell-mell process is continuing at this moment and should be pretty well completed, our intelligence reports, by nightfall. Our forces are already reoccupying the positions we had lost. By tomorrow morning we shall be in complete control of both Gorotoland and Panama.

"Nonetheless, I want an official statement from both governments confirming their withdrawal when it has been completed.

"The third requirement is the formal recognition by Moscow and Peking"—far away in dusty Gorotoland a giant, gorgeously robed figure leaped up with a shout of triumph, and somewhere in the steaming jungles of Panama a small, neat, dark-visaged man cried out, at his rebel command post, in protest and despair—"of the government of His Royal Highness Prince Terry in Gorotoland, and of the legitimate, constitutionally elected government of Panama."

("He's going to get his way at last, isn't he?" *Time* murmured to the St. Louis *Post-Dispatch*. "Well," the *Post-Dispatch* said with a wry shrug, "I guess he deserves to, now.")

"I might add," the President said—and in Gorotoland the gorgeous figure paused in mid-crow to frown uncertainly, and in Panama the small, neat, dark-visaged man looked up with some glimmer of reviving hope—"that after both countries are pacified, we will ask—*and we will expect*—the United Nations to call and supervise elections for the creation of genuine, popularly elected governments.

"The fourth condition is the immediate internationalization of the Panama Canal, the Suez Canal and the Dardanelles—each of those international waterways to be under the control of commissions established by the United Nations, each commission to be composed of six members appointed equally by the United Nations and by the power presently holding, or in Panama's case sharing, control of those waterways.

"I realize," he said, "that this is a condition beyond the power of the governments of the Soviet Union and the People's Republic of China to enforce. It *is* within the power of the governments now exercising or sharing control of those waterways. World opinion, which at this moment, I think, is in such a state of justified terror that it cannot be denied its demand for global stabilization, will expect these countries to comply. It will be," he said with a mixture of gravity and irony, "their contribution to the cause of world peace.

"The fifth condition is that the Soviet Union and the People's Republic of China will agree to an immediate reduction, by at least one-half, of their conventional armed forces, and the immediate and permanent elimination, under United Nations supervision, of all their atomic weapons, all their atomic missiles, all their atomic submarines and all their weapons of germ warfare.

"The United States," he added calmly as a murmur spread over the room and even in shaken Moscow and Peking frightened men began to look stubborn, "will participate in, agree to, and be bound by, exactly the same limitations, once our forces have been repaired to the parity destroyed by the fighting in Gorotoland and Panama."

("There's the catch," William Abbott murmured to Bob Munson as they watched with most other members of Congress in the packed, standing-room-only chamber of the House, where a giant television screen had been installed for the occasion. "And thank God for it," Bob Munson said. "We've got to be equal, we can't ever again be less—or they more." The ex-President grunted. "They'll never be more again. They're on the ropes." "I devoutly hope so," Senator Munson said.)

"The sixth requirement if I am to participate actively in seeking a settlement of the Sino-Soviet War," the President continued, "is that there will be established under United Nations supervision an International Relief Commission to extend aid impartially to victims of the atomic bombings in both warring countries, and, if the atomic cloud does not dissipate, in the South Pacific.

"I want the agreement of the governments in Moscow and Peking that they will each contribute equally—*and substantially*—to this relief work. The United States will match them dollar for dollar, and if other nations of the world should wish to contribute, as I am sure many will, they will be welcome.

"The seventh requirement is the establishment of a United Nations force, entirely independent of Moscow and Peking and without consultation or reference to them, to patrol the border between them. Because of the length of the border, this will require many men and much matériel and money. The United States stands ready to make a major contribution of all three to this effort. It expects all other nations of the world that can possibly do so, to do the same.

"The eighth condition is the abolition of the veto in the Security Council of the United Nations."

There was a startled sound in the room, in Congress, in the crowded Delegates' Lounge of the United Nations, in Moscow, in Peking—everywhere.

"The United States," he said calmly, "will work actively, and vote, for abolition of the veto and the substitution of a simple majority. We would expect all sane men who now see what has grown out of the veto to do the same."

("Easily said," Raoul Barre murmured to Lord Maudulayne. "It must happen, it must," Lord Maudulayne said, and Krishna Khaleel echoed earnestly, "Oh, yes!" "So?" said Raoul Barre, surveying the hushed, tensely listening throng of the nations with a tired, appraising air. "So?")

"The ninth requirement is the permanent end of all imperialistic ventures by the Soviet Union and the People's Republic of China—an end to international troublemaking and an end to international meddling. A formal commitment by both countries to devote themselves hereafter to the peaceful development of their own societies, within their own borders. A formal commitment," he repeated emphatically. "A real one, and a lasting one.

"Tenth, and finally, the convening of a conference of the United States, Great Britain, France, Japan, and other interested major powers, in Geneva, to consider other pending world issues, make recommendations for their settlement, and agree upon the terms for enforcing those recommendations. . . .

"Those are the conditions under which I will stand ready, if they are accepted, to fly immediately to Moscow and Peking to assist in restoring peace between the Soviet Union and China, and peace in the world.

"I would hope that sanity, which now seems to be returning in those two capitals, will prevail.

"I would hope that the Soviet Union and China will swiftly agree to the conditions which specifically concern them. I would hope other countries would do the same in such areas as the internationalization of the waterways and the establishment of the peace-keeping force.

"I want to point out to the Soviet Union and to China that they are already partially devastated by this war.

"I want to point out that they have unleashed atomic warfare, and that if it is resumed, the chances are that not only will they be completely devastated, but that the rest of us probably will be too.

"This is a prospect," he said dryly, "which should induce serious thought and swift compliance in Moscow and Peking.

"I think I speak for the entire rest of the world when I say that we sincerely hope that it will do so—and at once.

"Ladies and gentlemen, that is all I have to say at the moment. I will keep you advised of further developments as they come. But I think perhaps you should look for your next news break to Moscow and Peking. Thank you very much."

"But, Mr. President—" a dozen voices cried in varying degrees of protest, anguish, desperation and curiosity.

But he was off the podium and out the door with a smile and a wave, and that was all they heard from him that day.

Back in the Oval Office fifteen minutes later he faced the four men he had asked to come down to see him. This time there was no doubt as to who was in command. The Speaker, the Senate Majority Leader, the ex-President and the ex-Majority Leader were as shattered by events as anyone else and as anxious to know what he intended to do.

This did not prevent a few examples of the candor customary between old political friends and enemies, but at least it relieved him of the necessity of begging for what he needed. He began by asking for it point-blank.

"Arly," he said, as soon as greetings had been exchanged and seats taken, "I want that Cabinet out of that Senate by tomorrow afternoon, and no more nonsense about it. I also want the supplemental Defense Department appropriations."

"At the same time?" the Majority Leader asked with the start of his customary contrary skepticism. The President cut him short.

"How much time do you think we have?"

"Well—" Arly began, still in a contentious tone. Then he shrugged and dropped it. "The Cabinet's no problem. But you aren't going to get any ten billion by tomorrow afternoon."

"I don't want ten now," he said. "I'm only asking that we come back to parity with what's left of the Soviet and Chinese strength and that's still considerable, in spite of everything. I think three will do it, and I do want that. Pronto."

"You can't get those committees to move that fast," Senator Richardson began, and again the President cut him short.

"The hell I can't. They rolled through hoops every hour on the hour for Franklin Roosevelt, and that was a domestic crisis. Now we've got the whole world threatening to topple in on our heads. They'll move. You tell them I said to cut the crap and *move*. I want that bill on the floor, together with the Cabinet, by noon tomorrow, and I want it passed by tomorrow night. Otherwise I'll be drastically weakened when I go abroad to try to settle this thing, and if anybody on the Hill wants to take responsibility for that, then he's a bigger fool than I think anybody up there is. So let's *move*. O.K., Arly? All right, Jawbone?"

Arly Richardson gave him a look in which the jealousy and disapproval of years received, for a second, its last concentrated expression. Then he shrugged and looked away.

"You're the boss," he said, the words not coming easy, but there was no alternative. "Whatever you say."

"And you, Jawbone?" he inquired sharply. The Speaker, who had been staring out at the snowy world, jumped as though he had been shot.

"Well, now, Mr. President, sir," he began, "well, now—"

"Have you been listening to what I've been saying?" he demanded with a sudden sharp impatience.

"Yes, sir, Mr. President," Jawbone said. "I surely have, now, I surely—"

"Then your committees will start work at once, even if they have to sit all night, and that appropriation will be on the floor tomorrow noon," he said in an even voice.

"Yes, sir," the Speaker said with an abruptly reviving cheerfulness. "Yes, *sir*, Mr. President, we'll do it. We'll *do it!*"

"Good," he said dryly. "I knew I could count on you, Jawbone."

He turned to the ex-President.

"Bill, I want you and Bob to do everything you can to help them, of course. I think that for the duration of the crisis I'm going to form what I think I'll call 'the Council of National Unity'—you four, the Vice President, the Secretary of State and the Secretary of Defense, Ceil Jason, the Minority Leaders of House and Senate, probably the Chief Justice, and maybe"—he paused and smiled a little—"just because he would be so pleased to be in on it, and so chagrined if he weren't—maybe that distinguished jurist, Mr. Associate Justice Thomas Buckmaster Davis."

"Tommy?" Bill Abbott inquired with a smile. "You'll never get him to stop talking long enough to get anything done."

"Oh, yes, I will," the President said comfortably. "I know Tommy."

"So do we all," Bob Munson said, though not critically, for everybody was fond of Tommy, for all his fussbudgety ways. "What are we supposed to be, a sort of regency while you go abroad? You *are* going abroad, you say: you aren't going to ask them to come here?"

"No, I think not," he said thoughtfully. "That might make them almost too much the supplicants."

"Which of course they are," Senator Munson remarked, "so why be gentle with them? They got themselves and the world into this hellfire mess, so why shouldn't they come to you? They'd damned well make you come to them if the situation were reversed."

"Well, it isn't," he said shortly, "and I just happen to feel it's best, Bob, that's all. We've got to maintain some of their dignity, on both sides, or they may start fighting again. And then the world would really be lost. I tell you," he added, and his voice became somber, "we're right up against it in a way you fellows may not realize, yet. There's no room for any slippage. They're terrified and exhausted right now, but give them a week or two to recover and who knows that they won't go insane again?"

"Surely they won't resume fighting *now,*" Arly Richardson said, "after atomic war—after all the destruction—after bringing the world right to the edge of nowhere. That *would* be insane!"

"Arly," the President said patiently, "it is my observation after a long period in public life that men in general *are* insane. They do something and get scared as hell, and for a brief time they act sensibly. Then the pressure eases and they begin to feel their oats again, and pretty soon they're insane again. Now, sanity dictates that neither Russia nor China nor us nor anybody will ever again use atomic weapons or do what has just been done. But just wait a few days: they'll be back snarling at each other, and then next they'll be finding pretexts, and before we know it there'll be some more big booms, and next time we'll probably be dragged in, and that will truly be the end of Earth. So I have a very limited time in which to move: ten days *at the most,* I would say. I'm planning to leave for Moscow tomorrow night as soon as you've finished work on the Hill. *If*—" He paused and again his expression became somber. "If, that is, they accept my conditions."

"Which are tough," William Abbott observed. "But—"

"It's a damned tough world right now, Bill," he said gravely. "I've got to be tough. It's probably the first and last chance anybody is ever going to have in this world to be that tough about the things that really matter to world peace. I've got to, because the opportunity, I think we can safely say, is never going to come again."

"Which doesn't mean that they will have sense enough to see that," Senator Munson remarked.

"No," he agreed quietly. "But we should be getting some indication pretty soon."

"I guess we'll just have to pray, as you said, Mr. President, sir," Jawbone remarked brightly. "I guess we'll just have to pray, now, and hope for the best."

"I guess we will, Jawbone," he agreed. "Meanwhile, you all go back to the Hill and do your damnedest for me, will you?"

Senator Richardson gave him a quick, sardonic look as they stood up to go. But his glance was not as hostile as it used to be.

"I don't think we have any choice, do you?" he inquired; and, surprisingly, held out his hand in a manner that was almost cordial.

"I don't think you do, Arly," the President agreed, shaking it gratefully, "but I really appreciate your cooperation."

"You have it," the Majority Leader said. And added somberly, "To what end, God alone can tell."

"He'd better help us!" the Speaker exclaimed in a tone that admonished the Almighty. "He better had, now!"

"You tell Him, Jawbone," Bill Abbott said. "He'll listen to you."

But whether He really would, the President had no way of knowing as the day wore on with no word from Moscow or Peking. Hysterical news reports, headlines and broadcasts continued to come out of both countries, filtered through censorship and cataclysm but providing overall a graphic picture of atomic devastation, vast and growing popular unrest, desperate governments trying to maintain control in the midst of the chaos their deliberate policies had created. Under any other circumstances he would have rejoiced to see them destroy one another like two scorpions in a bottle; but the sheer size of the conflict, and its atomic corollary, made it impossible to take so objective and detached a view. The argument had to be settled before any more millions died, any more cities were destroyed, any more atomic poisons were loosed in the atmosphere to imperil the world. He had made his conditions tough, but it was time to be tough. Heads had to be knocked together on a global scale for the sake of humanity, and this, as he had truly said, was very likely the first and last chance history would ever provide for anyone, President or whatever, to do it.

At noon he received his first encouragement: Turkey and Egypt announced, in simultaneous messages to him and to the Secretary-General, their unconditional acceptance of his plan to internationalize the Dardanelles and the Suez Canal under commissions to be composed of six members each, three to be named by the United Nations and three by the controlling power.

Simultaneously the Secretary-General announced the formation of an International Relief Commission to provide relief for the victims of the atomic exchange in Russia and China, and in the South Pacific if necessary. He added that he was pleased to announce that fifty-three nations had already signified their intention to contribute "very substantial sums, extensive medical supplies and a large number of trained medical and relief personnel" to the effort.

In addition, a proviso the President regarded as much more important than the internationalization of the waterways, the S.-G. announced the formation of a United Nations peace-keeping force to patrol the Sino-Soviet border and again was able to report, with great pleasure and obvious encouragement, that already forty-six countries had signified their intention to contribute "troops, matériel and necessary supporting funds" to the force. Fear, shock and horror, for the moment at least, were doing wonderful things to the world.

Through the press secretary the President issued a statement that he was "highly gratified and greatly encouraged by the overwhelming response of the nations to the desperate need for cooperation and stability."

And it genuinely did please him, and it was apparent from media response, from the hundreds of thousands of wires, cables and phone calls that were coming in, and from the reaction of everyone he saw in the course of the day, that a genuine wave of good feeling, unity and even self-congratulation was sweeping the world. Men *could* cooperate, they *could* work together, they *could* bury their differences and strive in harmony for stability and peace—for a moment or two—and if they were scared enough.

The moment *was* here and they *were* scared enough. Out of these two facts he had to fashion, in desperate haste and with all the leverage events had placed so unexpectedly in his hands, something that would prove of lasting value when the moment had gone, when fear had eased and when all the petty jealousies, suspicions, self-interests and cupidities were free to roam the globe again.

The imperative need to do this was brought home to him poignantly once again—he did not really require the reminder, but perhaps it was good to have it—when he received a frantic call in mid-afternoon from the President of Indonesia and the Prime Ministers of Australia and New Zealand, linked to him via satellite and Picturephone. All were close to tears as they reported that rioting and looting had broken out in their countries and that in consequence they had imposed martial law. But they confessed that they were not too hopeful that they could maintain order in the face of the wave of terror that was sweeping the Antipodes and the South Pacific as the atomic cloud moved slowly south.

All besought his help, but there was not really too much that he could do. He had ordered weather planes aloft from Hawaii and American Samoa and their reports were going simultaneously and without censorship to Jakarta, Canberra and Wellington, and to Pago Pago for broadcast to all the islands of the South Pacific. There was some indication that the cloud was rising slowly into the stratosphere and beginning to dissipate in the face of strong winds, but its ultimate fate was as yet unknown. He promised as much aid as the United States and the U.N. could possibly deliver if the necessity should arise, and urged them to be of good cheer and good faith. He commiserated with them as sympathetically as he knew how. Beyond that he was helpless and they knew it.

The monstrous fruit of the Soviet-Sino exchange would either reach another deadly flowering or it would not, depending entirely upon the whim of nature and the sorely tried compassion of the Lord.

Meanwhile, the day moved on. On the Hill, Arly and Jawbone opened the sessions with grave speeches to hushed chambers, urging support of the President. A long string of fervently agreeing speeches followed in both houses. The Appropriations and Armed Services committees went to work at once, issuing firm pledges to have the Defense Department bill ready by noon tomorrow. In the Senate the committees that had jurisdiction reported at once on the Cabinet nominees they had been stalling for almost two weeks: by 3 P.M. that same day all were approved.

There was a little questioning as to why the President had chosen the forum of a press conference instead of a speech to Congress in which to assess the situation and announce his "Ten Demands," but this was successfully, if ominously, satisfied by William Abbott.

"I believe his reasoning was," he said slowly to the intently listening House, "that at this stage of it, it was best to keep it on a direct but relatively informal basis. I would expect that within the next few days, or possibly even hours, he will come here and talk to us, if one of two things happens: if the situation greatly improves . . . or"—and his voice took on a somber note that sent chills through all who heard him—"if it gets worse. . . ."

At nightfall there was still no indication from either Moscow or Peking as to which it might be. He could imagine the frantic arguing and debating and pulling and hauling that must be going on in both capitals, and thought grimly: you asked for it, you bastards, now *suffer*. But presently, as the hour neared 6 P.M., he decided it was time to put in a prod.

Once again he called in the press corps, now grown to nearly a thousand from all over the country and all over the world. The East Room was so full of reporters, cameras, lights and confusion that the ushers abandoned any attempt to maintain seating space, folded up the collapsible chairs and cleared the room of them. He took notice of this when he reached the podium, grave-faced and unsmiling, to face an equally grave and unsmiling press corps.

"I'm sorry we can't seat you, ladies and gentlemen," he began, "but there are so many of you now that I'm afraid it's going to be S.R.O. from now on. . . .

"I told you," he continued, and his tone became grave, "that I would keep you advised of developments as soon as they come.

"I must report to you that so far there have been none—aside, of course, from the magnificent responses of Turkey, Egypt and many, many other nations of good will and good heart, in the areas outside the control of Moscow and Peking.

"From those two capitals, however, I have received no message and no response.

"I cannot conceive that the men in control there—if, indeed," he added quietly, "they are still in control there, which we don't know at the moment—are so insane that they are contemplating further hostilities. Possibly they are contemplating direct negotiations, in which case, more power to them. I have no pride of authorship, and if they can achieve a settlement without me, then by all means let them go to it.

"But if they are not contemplating direct negotiations, and if they still want me to arbitrate, then they had better speedily reach a decision to that effect and let me get started. Because the situation is still dreadfully desperate, and the longer they wait, the more chance there is that it will once more tip over into war. And that, I think, would be too awful to even think about.

"So if they want me, I'm here. But"—his tone became as hard and unyielding as he thought the situation demanded—"I am not going to wait forever. I'm going to give them just so much time to make up their minds—and don't anybody make any mistake that it's going to be very long, because it isn't—and then if they don't want me, I'm going to get out of it.

"This, with you ladies and gentlemen as witnesses, constitutes fair notice. I would suggest to Moscow and Peking that they respond pretty soon, or the United States will turn to the rest of the world and together we will all do our best to quarantine their madness as much as possible, and to try to organize some sort of stability and safety for ourselves without them, if it can be done.

"That's all, ladies and gentlemen. Thank you very much."

And again, before their desperate shouts for more could reach crescendo, he was off the podium and out.

PRESIDENT URGES RUSS AND CHINESE REACH SPEEDY DECISION ON TEN DEMANDS, LET HIM KNOW WISHES FOR ARBITRATION. WARNS HE MAY WITHDRAW AND HELP ORGANIZE PEACE FOR WORLD WITHOUT RED GIANTS. NO WORD YET FROM WARRING CAPITALS. GROW-

ING CIVILIAN UNREST REPORTED AS ATOMIC CASUALTIES CONTINUE TO MOUNT. HONG KONG AND RUMANIAN LISTENING POSTS SAY CIVIL WAR "IMMINENT" IN BOTH COUNTRIES UNLESS PEACE SOLUTION FOUND.

WORLD WAITS.

And he waited, remaining in the Oval Office, eating a hasty bowl of soup and a sandwich with Bob Leffingwell, Blair Hannah and the Joint Chiefs while they received the latest intelligence reports, which, worldwide, showed—nothing. No word from Moscow and Peking, no feelers sent out through anybody else—silence: indicating, he knew, great agony of spirit, great contention, perhaps actual killings, in some desperate, last-minute bunker-type struggle for control, inside the inner circles.

They finished dinner, the others stayed awhile, returned to Foggy Bottom and the Pentagon . . . time passed.

The press secretary reported that the members of the media were clamoring for another conference, he sent back word that he had nothing to report, would see them when he did . . . time passed.

He looked over the latest reports, noted final consolidation of U.S. control in Gorotoland and Panama, called the Presidents of Turkey and Egypt and the Secretary-General to congratulate them on their prompt cooperation, began to get ready to leave the West Wing . . . time passed.

He returned to the Mansion, looked in on Hal and Crystal to find them both dead asleep and snoring gently like tired little children, smiled to himself, went to the Lincoln Bedroom, got ready for bed, went to bed . . . time passed.

Fitfully around midnight, his exhausted mind finally abandoning its almost incessant whirligig of thoughts, worries, plans and alternatives, he fell at last into an uneasy slumber . . . and time passed.

At 2:30 A.M. exactly the Signal Corps awoke him to announce that the first faint, broken, erratic, almost indecipherable signals were coming from the underground fortresses where the men of Moscow and Peking were hiding.

At 3:15 A.M., looking tired but no tireder than his audience, he faced a gray-faced press corps, many of whose members had kept the vigil without even trying to go to bed.

In his hand he held two sheets of paper. The lights, cameras and eyes of most of his own country and much of the world were upon him as he began to speak in a grave and measured voice.

"We have received," he said, and instantly the already great tension in the East Room leaped upward, "the first official word from the governments presently in power in Moscow and Peking." He paused for a moment and then went on. "I say 'presently,' because I do not think, in view of their statements, that those apparently still in charge there will be allowed by their peoples to endure much longer.

"These two statements, which the press office is presently mimeographing for you and will have ready in just a few minutes, accept nothing, acknowledge nothing and concede nothing."

There was a groan of disappointment. He nodded.

"I share your sentiments. I feel as though I am dealing with literal madmen. The same old gobbledygook about each other and about us—the same old rehash of ideological clichés—the same intransigence, not modified one whit by what has happened between them—a complete rejection of all my suggestions with not even the slightest hint of willingness to negotiate, with me or with each other—the same dead end—literally, *dead* end.

"These are the old, tired, propaganda words of old, tired party leaders who seem unable, even now, to break out of the empty and foredoomed patterns of belief that have brought them to this final, awful confrontation.

"They would be pathetic were they not so dangerous to the actual life of mankind upon this planet.

"I reject both these statements as worthless, meaningless, subversive of the world's desperate hopes for peace and deliberately traitorous to the universal cause of mankind.

"The only thing these statements do *not* do is threaten the immediate resumption of atomic war, though, as you will see, they both leave the possibility open. This tiny bit of forbearance may conceivably be a slight—a very slight—cause for hope.

"I call once again upon the so-called leaders of Soviet Russia and the People's Republic of China to accept my arbitration of their dispute. I remind them that they came to me, not I to them: and they came, the world thought—not only thought, but knows—*in extremis*. In that situation, I agreed to arbitrate.

"I still stand ready, but they must modify their views. They must show themselves truly humbled by the awful, the terrible, the monstrous thing they have done to one another and to the world's chances of survival.

"They must come to the table prepared to lay down their arms once and for all. I have taken it upon myself to state conditions but I believe they are the conditions that most of the world now favors. Certainly the response of recent hours shows that there is just one desperate yearning in most human hearts—outside the two nations and, reports of growing civil disturbance tell us, within them as well.

"That desire is peace.

"I am here to arbitrate if the present leaders of the Soviet Union and the People's Republic of China want peace."

He paused once again. Then he concluded, a somber finality in his voice.

"If they do not want peace, then my message to them is as clear and specific as I can make it:

"Let them bomb each other and be damned."

And this time, though there was a shocked gasp from his audience, there was no clamor for him to remain, no gossip or light talk as his audience trailed slowly out. Nobody ran for the telephones, nobody pushed and shoved, nobody looked anything other than grim, gray and sad. No one, either in the room or wherever men heard his words, was any less somber than he as he turned and walked swiftly out.

MOSCOW, PEKING REJECT TEN DEMANDS, DENOUNCE U.S., EACH OTHER. RUSS SAY PRESIDENT'S CONDITIONS ARE "SINISTER CAPITALIST PLOT TO JOIN CHINESE IN OVERTHROW OF THE SOVIET UNION." CHINESE CHARGE CONDITIONS ARE "ONLY THE SURFACE ASPECT OF SECRET U.S. ALLIANCE WITH RUSSIA TO DESTROY CHINA." NO RENEWED WAR BUT NO PEACE, EITHER.

PRESIDENT SENDS ULTIMATUM AS RED LEADERS REFUSE TO CHANGE POLICIES. KNOX MAKES FINAL OFFER TO ARBITRATE, HINTS POSSIBLE OVERTHROW OF GOVERNMENTS, TELLS PRESENT LEADERS: MAKE PEACE OR "BOMB EACH OTHER AND BE DAMNED."

MANY WORLD LEADERS PLEDGE CONTINUED SUPPORT FOR PRESIDENT'S TOUGH STAND.

But how long he could hold them, or how long he could hold his own country and its media, he did not know.

In the event, he was happily surprised.

He had given himself ten days.

For a while, it appeared that he just might do it.

"We cannot support too strongly," the *Times* said with a fervent enthusiasm that brought a wry smile to the lips of the man it had damned so long, "the courageous stand of President Orrin Knox as he leads the struggle to restore peace and sanity to a horrified world. Never have the many fine qualities of the American Chief Executive been more dramatically displayed than in his present unwavering determination to end the awful conflict between Russia and China. Never has his leadership been more admirable or more deserving of his countrymen's endorsement.

"That endorsement, we believe, he has a thousandfold. When the two Communist giants launched themselves upon the ultimate insanity—the atomic insanity—last week, it appeared for a few horrible hours that the planet Earth was indeed about to go down to that fiery death so often predicted by its more pessimistic inhabitants. Then, it appeared, sanity returned. The fighting stopped. An appeal was made to President Knox by both sides.

"Seizing the opportunity, the President agreed to arbitrate under certain conditions. These conditions, we submit, while severe in some respects, were no more than world peace requires. The only condition on which he might be faulted—his insistence on American control of disputed Gorotoland and Panama—was eased by his immediate promise of free and fair elections in those two countries to permit establishment of independent governments agreeable to their peoples. All other conditions seem to us, as they must seem to fair-minded men everywhere, both judicious and imperative.

"Now those conditions have been rejected out of hand by what we can only describe as the madmen of Moscow and Peking. The fighting has stopped but all the ancient paranoia against America, and against each other, remains. Even from the bunkers, the hatred and blind stupidity snarl out. Against such a background, Orrin Knox emerges ever more clearly as the potential savior of mankind.

"We applaud his decision to stand firm. We endorse his devotion to peace. We agree that if the madmen of Moscow and Peking will not listen, they should indeed be left to 'bomb each other and be damned,' even though this will impose fearful and perhaps insurmountable burdens on the rest of humanity.

"There comes a time when one must stop appeasing and compromising and stand firm. President Knox, with his customary admirable candor and great strength of character—the two pillars upon which the fate of mankind rests at this moment—knows that this is the time."

"Orrin Knox," the *Post* agreed in an equally glowing deathbed conversion, "has emerged within the past thirty-six hours as one of the most decisive and farsighted Presidents this country has ever had. Beyond question he has emerged as the one most suited to this time of terrible crisis. His courage, his decisiveness, his grasp of world realities and his great vision of world peace maintained by firmness and unswerving strength, make him the man for the moment.

"And what a moment! The Soviet Union and the People's Republic of China, locked at last in the terrible struggle their viciously irresponsible leaders have been getting ready for, over many years—the struggle they have managed to persuade their helpless peoples was inevitable. And so it became inevitable, in a way they never planned and never dreamed in all their evil calculations.

"Into this situation stepped President Knox with a calm assurance which must be applauded by sane men everywhere. His willingness to arbitrate was based on ten conditions; all, with very few modifications, were exactly what was demanded by the awful occasion.

"Now he has been answered with spite and contempt by what he rightly calls 'old, tired party leaders who seem unable, even now, to break out of the empty and foredoomed patterns of belief that have brought them to this final, awful confrontation.' Even in this most desperate hour for them, and for the world, they cling to the old paranoia about America and about each other. Faced with possible civil war that could topple them all, they are yet so rigid and so locked into ideology that they apparently cannot bend. They were terrified when they called upon the President; it has taken their insane arrogance and stupidity less than twenty-four hours to return.

"We applaud the decision of President Knox to stand firm—because, as history has repeatedly shown, standing firm is the only way to establish, and maintain, world peace.

"America and the still-sane portions of the world know that in Orrin Knox they have a leader of honor, of integrity, of courage and of strength—a man who cannot be swayed by fear or favor. We applaud his efforts and we pledge him our unstinting and unwavering support. In common with all humanity, we look to him to save us, for, indeed, there is no one else."

"This is the finest hour of Orrin Knox," Walter Dobius solemnly informed his devoted following, "and never has he risen more nobly to the demands of history than he is rising now. Cool, courageous, determined—unflappable, unshakable, indomitable—once again, Illinois has sent the nation, and this time the world as well, a great man to meet great challenges.

"Certainly those challenges at this very hour are greater than any ever faced by any American President or, indeed, any world leader at any time. Actual atomic war has been unleashed. At this moment its full effects upon Australia, New Zealand and the entire South Pacific Basin, let alone upon the devastated peoples of Russia and China themselves, cannot be accurately predicted. The world knows they are awful, and the world knows that unless a recurrence is prevented, we may all shortly find that universal peace will finally be achieved by universal death.

"Therefore the efforts of President Knox to arbitrate the dispute, and simultaneously to readjust conditions in the world to prevent the possibility of future war, must command the respect and the fervent and unstinting support of every sane man, woman and child on this planet. Events have given him the master hand, and to date he is playing it in masterful fashion. His 'Ten Demands' are strong but basically all of them are sound and imperative for world peace. Their summary rejection by the present leaders of Moscow and Peking has brought the only response from him that it could bring: a rejection in turn, and a demand that they either come to their senses or, as he puts it not a shade too strongly, 'bomb each other and be damned.'

"That they will be damned if they do so is certain, though not of much solace to a world which could in all likelihood go down with them. But there is another possibility, raised by the President and supported by growing reports out of both countries: these monstrous men who are playing fast and loose with humankind may very well be toppled from their positions of power by their own people. This possibility alone is enough to justify the ruthless pressure the President is applying upon them. Either way, the pressure seems the best chance to bring peace. If any sanity remains at all in the bunkers of Moscow and Peking, peace will come, and on the President's terms.

"America is fortunate to have so strong a leader at such a time. Nothing has better become the courage and integrity of Orrin Knox than the calm and imperturbable fashion in which he is handling this greatest crisis ever to confront the inhabitants of the globe."

And on "Opinion" that night Frankly Unctuous sang the same fond tune, and on the other networks, and from all of America's other influential journals and public voices, came the same sweet grateful caroling.

Fear was doing great things to the media, too. Orrin Knox was a great man at last. With an ironic set to his mouth and an ironic gleam in his eye, he saw, read and heard them all in the Oval Office, which was now the hub of the world; made no comment, issued no further statement, appeared no more in public that day. The next morning, as he had directed, the United States asked for a special emergency session of the United Nations Security Council, to convene at noon.

"Delegates to the United Nations," Australia said, and his deep-set eyes blinked away tears and his fine, white-haired head shook visibly from the tensions he was under, "you will forgive the President of the Council if he is somewhat distraught this morning. My country is still under threat from the atomic cloud, as are our colleagues from the Philippines, Indochina, Malaysia, Indonesia, New Zealand and all our sister island states and races of the South Pacific Basin. I am advised by the President of the United States, who has just telephoned me"—there was a stir in the full-to-spilling-over room—"that there are some signs the cloud may be starting to dissipate. But we don't know yet for sure, and until we do—until we do," he said almost humbly, "we must all be very concerned. So you will please forgive all of us from that area if we labor under handicap today. . . ."

He paused and looked around the table at the strained and somber faces of the nations, his eyes coming to rest finally on Nikolai Zworkyan of the U.S.S.R. and Sun Kwon-yu of the People's Republic of China. Both looked gray-faced, ridden by many devils, haunted by many ghosts; but in one last show of professional bravado both were striving desperately not to show it, to look stern, arrogant, contemptuous of the rest of the world and of each other, as they had on so many other occasions when they were deliberately subverting world peace and withering the hopes of mankind.

Their expressions brought a sudden anger into the voice of Australia as he resumed.

"This emergency session of the Security Council has been convened at the request of the United States of America. It is undoubtedly the gravest and most important meeting that has ever been held by this body or by any other international organization in the history of the world. I would suggest delegates address themselves to it with the solemnity and responsibility demanded by the awful crisis that confronts humanity.

"The disinguished delegate of the United States."

"Mr. President," Ceil said, her lovely face showing strain and worry but her lovely voice steady and clear, "the United States has requested this session for the purpose of introducing two resolutions which my government hopes will be speedily passed by the Council. I send the first to the desk for the Secretary-General to read."

In his grave and measured tones, very deep, very impressive, the dignified old man from Nigeria complied.

"Whereas, the President of the United States has been requested by the governments presently in power in the Soviet Union and the People's Republic of China—"

"Mr. President!" Nikolai Zworkyan and Sun Kwon-yu cried angrily together, but Australia brought down the gavel with a harsh and uncharacteristic violence that revealed the terrible tensions he was under.

"The delegates will be in order!" he cried. "There will be time for debate later! The Secretary-General will proceed with the reading!"

"—governments presently in power in the Soviet Union and the People's Republic of China," the Secretary-General repeated calmly, "to arbitrate the dispute which has brought war between their two countries, unloosed atomic devastation and jeopardized the peace, health and safety of the entire world; and,

"Whereas, the President of the United States, agreeing to arbitrate, has imposed certain conditions designed to restore and strengthen world peace; and,

"Whereas, these conditions have been endorsed and supported by the overwhelming majority of the nations but have been summarily rejected by the governments presently in power in Moscow and Peking:

"Now, therefore, be it resolved:

"That the members of the United Nations, acting through the Security Council, demand that the governments presently in power in the Soviet Union and the People's Republic of China immediately accept the conditions of the President of the United States and permit him to begin immediately arbitration of their dispute, so that peace may be restored to their two countries and the threat of atomic destruction of the earth may be swiftly and permanently removed."

"Mr. President," Ceil said quickly as the Secretary-General concluded, "I move that the Security Council—"

"Mr. President!" Zworkyan and Sun shouted again, together.

"The delegate of the Soviet Union," Australia said in a tone that begrudged every word; and added with a bitter resentment he could not quite keep out of his voice, "The delegate of the present government of the Soviet Union."

"Yes!" Nikolai Zworkyan cried, and this time his anger, which had so often been phony before, was obviously so genuine that he could hardly speak clearly through his rage. "Yes, that is exactly what is going on here, an attempt to undermine and ruin us! That is what is happening in this great United Nations which is supposed to be so vital to peace! An attempt to subvert and ruin us, Mr. President! An attempt to destroy and subvert us! There is your great United Nations, this wonderful thing!

"That is not," he said, breathing heavily but managing to calm his voice a bit, "what the United Nations is supposed to be, Mr. President. It is supposed to save nations, not destroy them. It is also," he added, casting a sudden savage glance across the table at Sun, "supposed to stop aggression. It is supposed to stop threats to world peace. It is supposed to punish aggressors. *Punish them,* Mr. President! *Punish them!*"

"Running dog of a capitalist whore," Sun said quietly. "Your worthless country has betrayed the revolution and you will be destroyed for it."

"Mr. President!" Zworkyan exclaimed, again so angry he could hardly articulate. "Mr. President, I demand that the United Nations expel the so-called People's Republic of China because of its great crimes against humanity!"

"That is out of order, Mr. President," Raoul Barre said shortly from across the table. "It is also insane to be indulging in these frivolous exchanges when your two countries are bleeding to death."

"His anti-revolutionary fascist clique began it!" Zworkyan shouted.

"His neo-imperialist capitalist cult launched a sneak attack upon us!" Sun shouted back.

A roar of boos and hisses swept the room, coming from delegates at the table and from the clerks, secretaries, guards, newsmen and members of the general public who filled every seat, stood in every aisle and crowded thick along the walls.

"The Security Council will be in order," Australia said sharply, "and so will everyone else. Visitors are reminded that they are here as guests of the Council. Any further disturbance and the room will be cleared. This is terribly serious business."

"Mr. President," Nikolai Zworkyan said, his breath again coming audibly in angry gulps, "the Soviet Union will veto this stupid resolution of the imperialist American President and his Chinese co-conspirators who have started unprovoked atomic war against my country."

"Mr. President," Sun Kwon-yu responded, equally agitated, "the People's Republic of China will also veto this resolution of the fascist American President and his Russian running dogs who have launched unprovoked atomic war against my country."

"Mr. President," Ceil said, and for once her voice, too, showed open anger, "I agree with the delegate of France, this is insane. It is also absurd and ridiculous and, were it not occurring in a context so dreadful and terrifying, with the world literally facing destruction if atomic warfare is resumed, almost laughable.

"But, Mr. President," she said, her voice becoming quieter and the room becoming completely hushed as she spoke, "it can never be laughable, for it is too horrible. At this moment an atomic cloud, as the distinguished President of the Council says, is drifting toward his country and toward many other countries in the South Pacific. At this very moment cities in Russia and China lie devastated under the sky, utterly destroyed. At this very moment thousands upon thousands are dead, and more thousands, many of them suffering horrible wounds, are crawling somehow from the ruins of what used to be houses and are wandering dazed through what used to be streets. . . . And the delegate of the Soviet Union and the delegate of the People's Republic of China sit here attacking the man who holds the key to peace, attacking my country, attacking each other, like a couple of hateful schoolboys: a couple of infantile, spiteful, hateful schoolboys. It is monstrous. It is beyond belief. It inspires in me the thought that they deserve exactly what they get, and that very possibly the wisest course of this United Nations would be to do just what my President said: let them bomb each other and be damned.

"But, Mr. President," she went on with a sigh, "of course mankind, for its own salvation if not theirs, cannot be so irresponsible. We have to make some attempt to restore sanity and save the world—we have to make the try. President Knox needs your help and your support—he needs a united world behind him. Please give it to him, I beg all of you who are not directly involved in this matter, for that will be a great affirmation to all the billions who depend upon us here that the world wants peace, must *have* peace, *will* have peace. . . .

"I know, Mr. President," she concluded quietly, "that the two culpable governments will, as their representatives here have told us, veto this resolution. The United States will take it immediately to the General Assembly, where we all know its success is assured. We will then introduce our second resolution. Mr. President, I ask for a vote on the pending resolution."

"Yes," Australia said gravely. "The order of voting will begin today with Lesotho. The Secretary-General will call the roll."

And so in thirty minutes the headlines said:

SOVIETS, CHINESE VETO U.N. SECURITY COUNCIL RESOLUTION BACKING KNOX, DEMANDING END TO ASIAN CONFLICT. ALL OTHER MEMBERS OF COUNCIL UNANIMOUSLY SUPPORT PRESIDENT.

And one hour later they said:

GENERAL ASSEMBLY PASSES U.N. RESOLUTION BACKING KNOX BY NEAR-UNANIMOUS MAJORITY. RUSS AND CHINESE ONLY HOLDOUTS AS WORLD BODY SUPPORTS PRESIDENT, DEMANDS ACCEPTANCE OF CONDITIONS, END TO WAR.

And two hours after that they said:

GENERAL ASSEMBLY PASSES U.S. RESOLUTION DEMANDING CHARTER AMENDMENT TO END VETO IN SECURITY COUNCIL, OVER VIOLENT SOVIET-CHINESE OPPOSITION. MEASURE GOES TO COUNCIL, WHERE VETO STILL HOLDS UNTIL AMENDMENT IS APPROVED.

SAVAGE DEBATE BEGINS IN COUNCIL AS MOSCOW AND PEKING EXCHANGE NEW THREATS, AGAIN CONDEMN U.S. PEACE ATTEMPTS.

"Members of the Security Council," Australia said with a noticeable tiredness—as they all were tired, after the hour of bitter Council debate earlier, followed by four hours of bitter General Assembly debate, followed by only a brief dinner break before they carried their battle again to the Council—"we are now seized of the resolution of the United States, supported by the almost unanimous recommendation of the General Assembly, to amend the Charter of the United Nations to eliminate the veto of the permanent members and permit action on all matters by simple majority vote. Does the delegate of the United States wish to speak to her amendment?"

"Briefly, Mr. President," Ceil said, her face showing the strain of her many sharp exchanges with Nikolai Zworkyan and Sun Kwon-yu, but her general air composed and confident. "The hour moves on, both here and in the ravaged areas of the earth, and we should not take more time than necessary to state our positions.

"That of the United States is expressed in the resolution. We believe the veto, over the years, to have been perhaps the single most crippling feature of the United Nations. The fact that we have used it in the last two sessions to ward off what we have believed to be serious threats to world peace—"

"Ha!" the Soviet Ambassador said with an elaborate snort.

"—serious threats to world peace," she repeated gravely, "does not change our fundamental belief that it has always been unwise, unnecessary and a fatal flaw standing in the way of a truly functioning world body.

"Now the veto, like so many other things, is thrown into glaring perspective by the terrible events of recent hours in Asia. If it stands, the present governments of Russia and the People's Republic of China can, if they so desire, block all effective activity by the peace-keeping force which has been created to maintain peace along their joint border; block effective activity of the International Relief Commission just established by the Secretary-General to aid the Russian and

Chinese peoples and those other peoples who may be hurt by atomic fallout; disrupt and prevent any effective further operation of this body as it tries to re-establish world stability; and generally thwart and make a mockery of anything and everything we may try to do in this greatest of all crises.

"Based on the last five hours, there is no doubt that the veto would be used by these two governments to do all these things.

"I find it impossible to understand," she went on, "the Soviet Union and the People's Republic of China in their actions and attitudes here today. It is also evident, from the almost unanimous votes so far in both bodies, that the rest of us are equally baffled. It appeared a few hours ago that their governments were aware of the dreadful situation they had created; it appeared they understood that not only their own fate but that of all mankind was involved in what they were doing—and so they stopped. And they appealed to President Knox for mediation.

"But this no longer seems to be the case. Even though intelligence reports reaching mine and many other governments confirm that the leaders of both Moscow and Peking are in hiding, underground and far from those two supreme target cities, still they go on maintaining this dreadful charade of hostility toward one another and contempt for the rest of the world. We thought they had learned something. Obviously they have not. They still could resume at any moment the conflict that could destroy us all. It is truly terrifying.

"Already the sane world has moved far in the direction of stabilizing itself in the face of this crisis. Removal of the veto is a further imperative step. As the Charter now stands, this can only be done with the cooperation of the Soviet Union and the People's Republic of China. My government begs them to weigh this matter with the most solemn consideration, to put aside their differences and their foredoomed attitudes and to join all of us in taking this absolutely fundamental and imperative step.

"I would hope, Mr. President"—and she paused and looked slowly around the circle from face to somber face—"that other members would join their voices with mine in urging this course of action upon the two contending powers."

"We will," Lord Maudulayne said promptly. "To Her Majesty's government it is common sense—the last common sense, perhaps, that the globe will be vouchsafed. We too appeal to the People's Republic of China and the Soviet Union to ponder, to reflect and to comply."

"France most earnestly does the same," Raoul Barre agreed gravely.

"Oh, and my government, also!" Krishna Khaleel echoed fervently.

"We do appeal to the governments of the Soviet Union and the People's Republic of China. India feels that she has been a staunch and steadfast friend to them for many years—a friend when others, perhaps, were not. Therefore we feel that we have a right, possibly a greater right than some others, to join now in urging our friends in Moscow and Peking to yield to the collective conscience of mankind in this matter. We do hope"—he turned with a sudden urgent movement toward the Soviet Ambassador, dour and silent, the Chinese Ambassador, grim-faced and tight-lipped—"we *do* hope—that you will permit this to be done. Please, we beg of you. *Please!*"

"It is not easy for my government," Cuba said, nervously fingering his luxuriant mustache, "to part company with our great friends of the Soviet Union and the People's Republic of China, whom we have always admired and respected and with whom we have had the closest relationship in opposing the imperialist ambitions of the monopoly-capitalist oligarchy of the United States. However"—and for the first time in anyone's memory, he actually broke down and talked like a human being instead of a Communist automaton—"all those things now seem very far away, I must say to our friends of the Soviet Union and the People's Republic. We are terrified of what may happen to humanity if you do not speedily desist and join us all in building a new and safer world. You are trying to kill each other," he said, his voice breaking in a sudden harsh rush of emotion, "but you risk killing all of us! You must not, I say to you! *You must not!* Join us in repealing the veto—join us in all our efforts to save the world! We beg of you—we beg of you!"

"My government also," Rumania said in his harshly guttural English, "has always been a friend and supporter of the Soviet Union and the People's Republic of China. But we can go with them no longer. The games are over, the puppet show has stopped. We are concerned here today with no less than the death of the world. You must yield to the needs of humanity, my friends of Moscow and Peking, or be damned with all of us, forever. The veto must go, the peace-keeping force must be permitted to function, the relief commission must go forward with its work, you must use the sincere good offices of the President of the United States to settle your dispute, you must permit sanity to return and be maintained. There is no other way. My government, too, begs you to permit this fundamental step of repealing the veto. It begs you to participate fully in all the other proposals put forward by the President and endorsed by all the nations save your own, for the very salvation of mankind. You must, my friends, *you must.* There is no other way. *And there is no time.*"

Presently, as Zworkyan and Sun continued to sit silent and glowering, the roll of the Council was concluded. Chile, Egypt, Ghana, Lesotho, Norway, Zambia and Australia had all joined their colleagues in appealing to the two contending powers. Neither ambassador responded, and so at last Australia turned to them directly and asked in a stern and challenging voice:

"Do the two powers concerned wish to address the Council, or shall we vote?"

Nikolai Zworkyan raised his hand at last and leaned forward to his microphone.

"Mr. President," he said in Russian, his words translated swiftly, with all the proper indignant inflections, by the U.N.'s skilled translators, "my government has listened here today to the mouthings of children. Yes!" he repeated sharply as a gasp of dismay swept the room. "The mouthings of children! You wish us to yield to the imperialist warmongers of the United States, the military-capitalist oligarchy whose puppet is Orrin Knox! You wish us to destroy all the safeguards that protect my country and the cause of world revolution! You wish us to permit the capitalist-military puppet Knox to join the vicious betrayers of the revolution who pretend to have a 'people's republic' in Peking! 'People's republic'! It is a fraud, Mr. President, a fraud and a mockery! They are murderers of the revolution, Mr. President, they wish to join the capitalist-military puppet Knox to destroy the Soviet Union! We will never permit it! *Never, never, never!*"

And he sat back, glowering angrily about as a despairing murmur swept the room and around the circle his colleagues stared at him with absolute dismay. All except one, who leaned forward to grasp his microphone with both hands and spit into it a venom equally harsh and equally far away from all the mortal concerns that now confronted humankind.

"Mr. President!" Sun Kwon-yu snapped in a fluent and hurrying English. "Mr. President, my government has listened patiently to all the empty frightened words of petty powers who wish to destroy this United Nations and the people's revolution. We reject them. We reject the attempt to destroy the United Nations and bend it to the will of the arch-conspirators, the arch-devils who are trying to destroy the People's Republic and the people's revolution, namely the U.S.S.R. and the United States! We reject the running dogs of capitalism who sit in Washington, the whoremasters of anti-revolution who cower in Moscow. We reject their conspiracy, we will destroy their evil. We will never yield to them, Mr. President! *Never, never, never!*"

"Mr. President," Ceil said into the hush that followed, "may I ask the two delegates, are they able to be in touch with their governments?"

"I do not need to be in touch!" Zworkyan said angrily. "I know what they want!"

"The people's revolution does not need consultations!" Sun spat out. "Its representatives know from birth what is right!"

"Then we are hearing simply the old clichés," Ceil said quietly, "the mechanical mouthings of machines that are broken at the center. Mr. President, I think we should vote on the resolution of my government."

"I agree," Australia said, his voice shaking with emotion but firm. "The vote will begin with Norway. . . . On this vote," he reported formally five minutes later, "the Yeas are 13. Two of the permanent members having voted No, the resolution is defeated."

"Mr. President," Ceil said into the hubbub that instantly filled the room and was as instantly silenced when she spoke, "I wish to inform the Council that the President of the United States will speak to the peoples of the Soviet Union and the People's Republic of China one half hour from now. I suggest the Council stand in temporary recess to hear his address."

"Mr. President!" Zworkyan and Sun cried together.

"Without objection," Australia said loudly, banging down the gavel, "it is so ordered."

"He isn't wasting any time, is he?" the New York *Times* remarked as he and his colleagues watched the milling crowd empty quickly out toward the General Assembly, where several huge television screens were being hastily set up. The London *Observer* nodded. "There isn't any time left to waste," he said. "But, Orrin, my friend," he added as they too left the press section and headed for the Assembly, "you'd better be good."

And good he was, for he had known for some hours that he was going to have to do exactly what he did.

Far off in some other world almost forgotten, it had been considered, by all those critics who now fawned desperately upon him, abominably bad taste for the democracies to attempt to do to the Communists what the Communists were always attempting to do to them. Even when the Communists succeeded, as they had on a good many occasions, any suggestion that the democracies do likewise had always been greeted with frantic denunciations from the most influential journals and opinion-makers of the West. So it had been very rarely that democracy had used against Communism the principal weapons

Communism always used against democracy: internal subversion and the deliberate overthrow of opposing governments.

Now, however, he knew that it must be done, and because of the circumstances he had no doubt that he would succeed. Nor did he have any doubt that the method he intended to use was the only one. He was dealing with a billion captive, terrified, frantic people and there was no time or place for diplomatic niceties or sweet civilized exhortations. The hour compelled him to be as rude, crude, bluntly shattering and effective as he could possibly be. He must address them like a sledgehammer. The certainty lent an extra incisiveness to his voice as he faced the cameras of the world and began with a slow and somber emphasis:

"People of Russia, people of China!

"I speak to you from the outside world which looks to you to save yourselves and humanity from final destruction.

"You, the people of Russia and the people of China, have in your own hands the power to do this.

"You are the only ones who have this power.

"It does not belong to the cowardly leaders of Moscow who at this moment are hiding safely in underground caves near Kiev while you suffer the awful consequences of atomic attack.

"It does not belong to the cowardly leaders of Peking who at this moment are hiding safely underground in the mountains near Chungking while you suffer the awful consequences of atomic attack.

"It belongs to you, the people.

"You, people of Russia, people of China! It is to you I talk, not to your cowardly leaders who are safe and sound while you suffer.

"I have tried to talk to those cowardly men and they have refused me. The outside world has joined me in appeals to them, and they have refused us all.

"They would rather have you suffer, while they stay safe from harm, than end your suffering and make peace.

"They would rather have your wives, husbands, sons, daughters, mothers, fathers, families, friends, die in the ashes of your shattered cities than give up their own lust for power and their own insane ambitions.

"They would rather have all of you suffer torn flesh, terrible wounds, awful atomic sicknesses, horrible deaths, than give up their insane lust for power and their insane hatred for one another.

"People of Russia, people of China! You do not hate one another, for all men are brothers. You do not want to war upon one another, for war only means the destruction of everyone. You do not want to suffer horrible things because cowardly men in secret caves decree that you must die while they remain hidden and safe.

"You want peace, as we, all the other peoples of the world, want peace. You who are still living want to bury your dead, bind up your wounds, rebuild your lives and your families, return to your quiet ways and live together in peace.

"Evil and cowardly men who control your two governments do not want this.

"They want you to suffer.

"They want you to know terror.

"They want you to die.

"Destroy them, people of Russia, people of China! Rise against these monsters who have already devastated so much of your two countries!

"Already they are making new threats against one another. Already they are calling for new war. *This means that you will die.*

"Destroy them before they can cause the final destruction of the Celestial Empire and Mother Russia! Save your countries from them! Kill them before they can kill you!

"You have the power and you can do it.

"The cowardly leaders of Moscow are hiding in underground caves near Kiev. The cowardly leaders of Peking are hiding in underground caves near Chungking.

"Find them! Search them out! *Destroy them! Kill them before they can kill you!*

"People of China, people of Russia, take back your countries into your own hands. Take back the power these monsters have used to kill your wives, husbands, sons and daughters, mothers, fathers, relatives, friends. Look at your wounds. Look at your dead. Look at yourselves, poor hunted animals whom these men would utterly destroy.

"Find them, kill them, destroy them! We, the world, will help you. You will be free. You will be safe. You and your families and friends will not die any more. You will have peace, with each other and with all the world. We will greet you with open arms when you have done this, and there will be peace and no more war.

"They are hiding near Kiev.

"They are hiding near Chungking.

"Find them, kill them, destroy them!

"Kill them before they can kill you!

"People of Russia, people of China, do it *now!*

"Now!"

Which was not, he reflected again wryly as his somber face faded away and the flags of the United Nations, minus the Soviet Union and the People's Republic, floated past in silent review before the screens went blank, exactly the sophisticated, prim and proper language one might use in a parliamentary debate. But when one was dealing with more than a billion captive, terrified, frantically desperate people there was no time for subtlety, smooth words or gentleness. It was a time to be rough, tough, blunt and crude, as stripped down to naked essentials as the situation itself.

Although he knew there had been feverish attempts directed from Kiev and Chungking to jam his words, he was confident that the massive transmission mounted by his own government and assisted by all the rest had reached its target. He did not have to wait long for confirmation.

"Mr. President!" they cried again, together, their voices sailing up hysterically as they demanded recognition from a stern and righteous Australia in no mood to be tolerant or forgiving.

"Yes?" he said icily. "What do the delegates from the Soviet Union and the People's Republic of China wish to say to us now? What further wrecking of mankind's hopes do they have in mind this time?"

"Mr. President!" Nikolai Zworkyan wailed in English like the trapped and wounded animal he was. "Mr. President, my government protests the monstrous attack of the President of the United States! My government calls upon the conscience of this Council, yes, the conscience of the United Nations, the conscience of the whole world, Mr. President, to oppose the dastardly attempt of the President to destroy the government of the Soviet Union! We appeal to the world to help us, Mr. President! This is against all the decencies of mankind, Mr. President, all the civilized methods of dealing between nations! We beg of you, members of the Council, help us against this monstrous man! Help us! . . ."

But around the silent table and across the silent room, there was no indication of help for Nikolai Zworkyan and his terrible government, facing at last the judgment they had invited so many times, over so many cruel, destructive, ruthless years. Only an impassive pitiless quiet, in which sane men watched with a dispassionate interest, as they might observe the writhings of a dying snake.

"Does the delegate of the People's Republic of China have anything to add?" Australia inquired in the same icy, unforgiving tone.

"Mr. President!" Sun Kwon-yu exclaimed, his voice, also, trembling between anguish and hysteria. "Mr. President, my government too protests the evil attack of the President of the United States! It is terrible, Mr. President! It is monstrous! It is uncivilized! It is bar-

baric! It is the act of a savage! The world must help us against this evil, evil man, Mr. President! The collective conscience of mankind must rise against this murderer, this destroyer! Where is the United Nations, Mr. President? Where is the United Nations? It must help us! It must help us—*help us!*"

But again there was only the impassive pitiless quiet; and into it Australia remarked finally, in an impassive pitiless voice:

"The Council has heard the two delegates. Does any member of the Council wish to comment or respond?"

He looked slowly from face to unyielding face around the circle. No one moved, no one spoke. They simply watched, with a stillness awful and implacable. Finally Australia leaned forward again.

"Is there any further business to come before the Council?"

"Mr. President," Ceil said, her voice showing strain but coming clear and steady over it, "I move the Council reconsider the vote on the resolution of the United States amending the Charter to abolish the veto."

"Mr. President!" Sun and Zworkyan cried together again; but this was the last time, for even as they hunched forward in frantic desperation over their microphones there appeared at separate doors of the chamber a white-faced, frightened Russian and a white-faced, frightened Chinese. And after they had rushed forward to their respective delegations at the big circular table there followed several minutes of wild, excited talk, exclamations, shouts, groans, angry and frightened arguments. And after that, the delegate of the Union of Soviet Socialist Republics and the delegate of the People's Republic of China leaped from their chairs, stared wildly about for a moment like men demented, as indeed they were, and rushed from the room, followed in pell-mell, tumbling, terrified haste by their disheveled countrymen.

A wild excitement filled the room, rose to a crescendo, stopped abruptly as Australia crashed down the gavel and shouted, in a voice unsteady but triumphant:

"The Council will be in order! The Council will vote to reconsider the vote on the resolution of the United States! The vote will start with Australia! The Secretary-General will call the roll! . . .

"On this question," he announced five minutes later, voice still unsteady but now even more triumphant, "the vote is 13 for, none opposed. The resolution is again before the Council."

And five minutes later, triumphant again:

"On this question the vote is 13 for, none against. The resolution repealing the veto is adopted.

"This emergency session of the Council now stands adjourned—to await," he added with a sudden inspiration that obviously delighted him, "the pleasure of the President of the United States."

"My God," Walter Dobius said to the general director of the *Post* three hours later in an East Room of the White House so full of bodies that it seemed they must begin piling up to the roof if one more was allowed to enter, "how he must be feeling! *How he must be feeling!* All the things we've said about him . . . and now he has overturned the world."

"And who's to put it back together?" the *Post* inquired moodily. "Do you think he can? A world in the image of Orrin Knox?"

"I think," Walter replied, "that from now on we are going to have to accept the fact that this is the kind of world it's going to be. . . . And not so bad, either," he added after a moment with an honesty that did not sound at all grudging. "I think he's been very, very good in these last few hours."

"He has been rather amazing, I'll admit," the *Post* conceded. "And now, I suppose, he's going to tell us who he has appointed to run Russia and China."

But he did not go quite that far, nor could he. Instead he began by announcing formally the unbelievable facts that they had all guessed must be so, when the press secretary had announced this sudden new conference so soon after the abrupt departure of the warring delegations from New York.

"Ladies and gentlemen," he said gravely as the room quieted down to an attentive hush and the cameras concentrated once again upon the face that for the time being dominated the world, "I have asked you to come here tonight so that I might confirm what your own sources are beginning to report to you from overseas:

"The government of the Soviet Union headed by Chairman Tashikov and the Politburo of the Communist Party has been overthrown." There was a deep gasp, for it *was* unbelievable. He continued calmly. "The government of the People's Republic of China has been overthrown. Revolutionary juntas are in control in both countries.

"Although sporadic skirmishes are continuing in both countries, there has apparently been very little successful resistance from the old regimes. It appears that most local party leaders in the towns and villages have been slaughtered by the people and the major national leaders are either already executed or soon will be.

"Apparently when the structures began to crack they cracked all the way, very fast. Apparently, as we have long had reason to suspect, there has been no real loyalty to any of the individuals in positions of leadership, *as individuals*—no personality who could hold either country together. Just politburos and committees, which, unfortunately for them, aren't very lovable. Both countries have been laboring along under terribly repressive artificial superstructures created by their respective Communist parties. Both have apparently been ready for revolt for quite some time. The awful nature of the war was the catalyst—my speech perhaps provided the extra push—and suddenly it's happened.

"The new government of Russia, which is returning to Moscow, has informed me that it wishes to be known as 'the United States of Russia.' The new government of China, which is returning to Peking, has designated itself 'the United Chinese Republic.' The United States has already recognized both these governments and urges all countries to do likewise."

He paused, reached for a glass of water, took a sip, looked out thoughtfully, resumed.

"I think I should tell you that both governments have invited me to come over and help them settle the war. I have accepted these invitations. I shall leave tomorrow for Moscow and will go from there directly to Peking. Possibly in the interests of reaching agreement I may then return to Moscow. In any event, I intend to stay there until things are buttoned up—if they can be buttoned up." He looked suddenly somber. "They had damned well better be. . . .

"Those of you who wish to accompany me should make arrangements immediately through the press office. Estimated time of departure for Moscow is 9 A.M. tomorrow. We will take as many press planes as necessary to accommodate all of you who wish to go."

He smiled, and for the first time since the crisis had begun, looked fully relaxed and at ease.

"Tonight I shall reward you for your long and faithful vigil through these two fantastic days by answering questions. I am sure you have some. Walter?"

"Mr. President," Walter said, and his colleagues listened respectfully as they always did to this long-famed, distinguished figure—and so did Orrin, though he could not keep a little twinkle out of his eyes which was not lost on Walter—"evidently, if this change has come about so rapidly in both countries, it must pretty much have come from within, mustn't it? They must have been palace revolutions, backed by the military, right?"

"You're a shrewd man, Walter," the President said, neither sarcastically nor effusively, just stating a fact he had always recognized, no matter what their bitter differences. "I would say your assumption is correct—at least so we believe on the basis of the information we have now. We haven't very much, yet, you know—just the bare bones. It will become clearer when we get there."

"And when it does, Mr. President," Walter pursued thoughtfully, "what is it that leads you to believe that the new governments, being palace-revolutionary, military-backed governments, will be basically any different in their views, or any less intransigent, than the old ones?"

The President studied him for a moment, as thoughtful as he.

"To tell the truth, Walter," he said slowly, "I don't know the answer to that yet. I don't think anybody does, except maybe the new men in charge over there—and I suspect maybe even they don't know. I hope to get there in time to persuade them, if they have any funny ideas.

"But"—and his voice became flat and emphatic, the old Orrin—"I can tell you this: by God they had *better* be willing to be less intransigent, by God they had *better* be willing to cooperate with what the world wants them to do. This is the last chance they have, probably the last chance any of us has. It has *got* to work, and they have got to help make it work.

"I am confident that they will realize this, and that we will find when we get there an attitude of cooperation and willingness that will restore peace and save the world."

"You hope," Walter observed moodily.

"Yes—" he said, and though there were quite a few more questions before they pushed one another out the doors to file their bulletins and hurry to the press office to make their arrangements for the trip, the exchange with Walter was obviously the gist of it:

"—I hope."

With a fervent unanimity that in a grim sort of way amused him, all the most powerful among his countrymen hoped with him.

"The opportunity which now opens before the President of the United States, and the background of events against which it will unfold," declared the *Times*, "are absolutely breathtaking. All who hope for the salvation of the world—and that must include every rational being on this planet—can only pray that all will go well with Orrin Knox as he embarks upon his great, historic journey.

"Two powerful governments which only yesterday seemed solid and unshakable, pillars of the earth's society as we have known it for so many years, are utterly gone, vanished in the irresistible popular rebellions of half a day. 'The Union of Soviet Socialist Republics'—

'The People's Republic of China'—they are as dead as Nineveh and Tyre. Today there stride forth upon the world's stage new alignments of power, new men in charge of these two giant countries whose actions have such a profound bearing upon the future of all mankind. They call themselves 'the United States of Russia' and 'the United Chinese Republic.' To the U.S.R. and the U.C.R. we say: 'Welcome to the councils of the nations. May your success be great and your lives be long.'

"Like President Knox, all Americans must hope that the new governments in Moscow and Peking will seize the opportunity to settle their differences, join in organizing the peace and cooperate in the great new era of international relationships already well launched by the President's proposals, the support of nearly all other governments and the unanimous actions of the United Nations.

"Indeed, there is no alternative. The new governments of Moscow and Peking must cooperate with the rest of humanity. Otherwise, humanity is lost. . . ."

"It is significant," the *Post* pointed out, "that Orrin Knox did not reiterate his famous 'Ten Demands' before agreeing to mediate the war between Russia and China. Several of those demands have already been met, in any event; but we suspect there was much more to his restraint than that. We suspect that there has occurred an act of supreme statesmanship on his part, typical of the shrewd skill with which he has manipulated the cataclysmic events of these fantastic days.

"It could be argued that by imposing conditions they believed they could not accept, he goaded the former leaders of Russia and China to continue their intransigence to the point where it brought about their inevitable downfall. And by treating their successors gently, with great consideration and respect and without 'demands' or arbitrary conditions, it can be argued that he is going as far as he possibly can to encourage them to be accommodating, responsible and truly cooperative with the rest of the world as it seeks to re-establish lasting peace.

"It is a great gamble by a man who has become, under the stress of great events, a great statesman. He bestrides the world like Colossus, not only because there is at the moment no one else, but also because he has found within himself the resources to rise to the moment and meet its awful challenges. Wishing him well with all our hearts, we pray for him knowing that in so doing we pray for ourselves. . . ."

"President Knox," Walter wrote rapidly in his study at "Salubria," snug and comfortable while a new snowstorm out of the West slapped with a softly soggy persistence at the old leaded windows, "takes with him on this great new adventure in peace the hopes and prayers of all mankind. Events—events almost beyond comprehension, so shattering and awesome have they been—have conspired to place in his hands the fate, quite literally, of the world. It is a moment that has no parallel in the past and quite likely will have no parallel in the future. Never again, in all probability, will any single man have such influence and power as now rests in the hands of Orrin Knox. The situation is unique. We must thank whatever fates preside over the destinies of America that she has produced a man who is able to handle it.

"Very shrewdly, the President is not attempting to pressure the new governments in Moscow and Peking—that 'United States of Russia' and 'United Chinese Republic' whose names sound so strangely upon the world's unaccustomed ear. Very shrewdly, he is walking softly, though he carries the biggest stick any man has ever held. Very shrewdly, he is approaching, equal to equal, with dignity, courtesy and respect, the new governments which now control the two vast countries whose relations hold the key to the fate of all mankind.

"Washington is confident that Orrin Knox can meet the challenge. Events have given him the opportunity to become the world's supreme statesman. His own indomitable character offers unshakable assurance that he will do so, and that through him we all will be saved from atomic destruction and returned to the paths of peace. . . ."

"America watches with hope, awe and confidence," Frankly Unctuous assured his innumerable listeners in a special broadcast just before midnight, "the remarkable statesmanship of Orrin Knox as it nears its apogee. Man and moment are met as never before, perhaps, in history.

"Overnight the whole framework of world civilization as we have known it has been rendered obsolete. New governments sit in Moscow and Peking, new names join the roster of nations: 'the United States of Russia' and 'the United Chinese Republic' stand where only yesterday the monstrous monoliths of Communism affronted and dismayed the world.

"New governments—new opportunities—new hopes. This is the finest hour of Orrin Knox. All of us join in prayers for his success, knowing that if he succeeds the world will succeed, and that peace and progress will rescue us from the terrible shadow of clashing rivalries and atomic war.

"History has given to Orrin Knox an opportunity never accorded another man. He approaches it with courage, with faith and with all the resources of the tenacious character Washington has come to know so well over his long years of public service. Now America gives this man and this character to the world—with unanimous prayers for his success and unanimous confidence in his leadership. . . ."

"My, my," he said dryly to his predecessor as Frankly's plump, self-satisfied face faded with a fervid solemnity from the screen, "how times have changed. I seem to be quite a guy, don't I?"

"You *are* quite a guy," William Abbott said quietly, and in his eyes and the eyes of the others gathered around the desk the President could see that, yes, he was. Yet to himself, and it was probably his saving grace, he was still just Orrin Knox, President, with a fearful job to do: not a miracle man, not a new Messiah, not the greatest this or the most marvelous that, not history's infallible statesman who could rearrange the nations forever and ever, but just—Orrin Knox, President, with a fearful job to do.

"Well," he said with a smile almost rueful, "that may or may not be. But I do know this: there's a hell of a tough few days just ahead and I'm going to need all of you to advise me every minute of the way. I'm glad most of you can go with me."

Bob Munson chuckled and replied with the candor of old friendship.

"Let's don't overdue the humility bit. You didn't really think there was a soul in the world who could refuse if you asked, did you?"

"Well, no," he admitted with a sudden cheerful grin, "but anyway, I'm grateful. It's going to be very comforting to have you along. I'm sorry"—he turned to the Vice President, sitting somewhat disconsolately to one side—"that I can't take you, Cullee, but somebody has to mind the store. There's still a country to administer here and I don't know how long I'll be gone."

"How long do you think?" the Vice President inquired. The President's eyes narrowed.

"A week—two. Probably not more, because it should be quite clear by that time whether we're really entering a new era or heading right back into the old one."

"Surely after all that's happened, Mr. President," Justice Davis said earnestly, "*surely* you're going to achieve exactly what you're setting out to do, a settlement of these difficulties between China and Russia and a genuine, lasting peace in the world. The thought that you might not is truly too dreadful to contemplate."

"Yes," he agreed gravely, "and I try not to contemplate it. On the other hand, we're dealing with some tremendous volatiles here and nobody knows yet whether they're going to shake down peaceably together, or not."

"They've *got* to," Justice Davis said fervently. "They have *got* to."

"That's why I'm taking you along, Tommy," he said with an affectionate smile. "Because somebody has to hold high the banner of What *Must* Be Done. And you, my idealistic if occasionally somewhat annoying old friend, are it. You will keep our feet on the paths of righteousness."

"You should be glad to have someone do it," Tommy Davis said, a little huffily but with his usual basic good nature. "It isn't going to be easy."

"That's right," the President agreed, somber again. "That is absolutely right. That's why I've asked this group to go with me." He looked along the semicircle of intent faces that stared solemnly at him as the storm raged outside and the clock within neared midnight: the ex-President, the Speaker, the ex-Majority Leader of the Senate, the new Majority Leader of the Senate, the Secretary of State, the Secretary of Defense, Justice Davis and his son. Himself and eight companions, starting out to save the world. *May God give us strength,* he thought with a sudden profound melancholy, startling because until that moment he had not really realized how apprehensive and uncertain he was of this chaotic future he was supposed to dominate so completely, according to his new-found friends of the media.

May God give us strength.

He lapsed for a moment into an obvious brown study, which alarmed them. To break it, Hal asked finally:

"What *is* the situation over there, anyway? Do we know?"

"Pretty much what I told the press conference," he said, rousing out of it, relieving their worry with his practical, same-as-ever tone. "A general massacre of local party officials in both countries, capture and execution of all the national leaders except a few they apparently intend to put on trial. I understand that our dear old friend Vasily is one of these."

"I don't like the sound of that," Bob Leffingwell said slowly. "That sounds too much like the old pattern. I'd much rather have an honest-to-God, emotional, across-the-board slaughter than an artificial, staged, propaganda trial with all the standard gimmicks. That could be a straw in the wind, couldn't it?"

"I hope not," Blair Hannah remarked, "because if it is, it isn't a good one."

"No," he agreed soberly, "it is not. However, that appears to be what is shaping up—in Russia, anyway. It may be just the ingrained habit of six decades of watching the Communists operate, or it may be a reversion to type. We'll hope it isn't the latter. Reports from China are more obscure. In any event, gentlemen"—and again his eyes swept the semicircle—"I think we are going to have our work cut out for us—even if," he added, "I do come riding on a white charger, armored to save the world."

"What do you intend to do?" Arly Richardson asked, and the Speaker echoed, "Yes, sir, now, Mr. President, what do you intend to do, now, Mr. President, sir?" in his inimitable, predictable way.

"I intend to be somewhat tougher than the *Post* seems to contemplate," he said, "but basically, they've pretty much got the pitch. I'm not going to push anybody unless I have to. I hope to God the Russians and Chinese have acquired enough sense so I won't have to. If I do, however, I shall not hesitate."

"They would be absolutely insane to head back in the same direction the old regimes were going," Bill Abbott said. He smiled a wry smile. "That doesn't say they won't, of course."

"No," he said, "but I intend to make it very clear at the outset that I'm not having any of that. And actually—I mean, there they sit, both countries half destroyed, populations in absolute panic, the world in the same condition, the South Pacific still threatened by the cloud, the globe still entirely capable of being blown up at any moment if the war resumes and spreads—how can they possibly be other than humbled and responsible men?"

"We must think so," Tommy Davis said solemnly. "Orrin—Mr. President—*we must think so*. We must not let doubt come in. We must believe—we must have faith—we must go forward. We dare not admit to ourselves the possibility of failure, for if we do, then the world is really lost."

The President gave the little Justice once again an affectionate, almost paternal smile.

"Tommy," he said, "you're good for me, just as I knew you would be. We will have faith, as you say. We will go forward."

Next morning when they departed for Moscow, that was the spirit in which they went. They flew from Andrews Air Force Base, and as far as eyes could see, their countrymen filled every available field, open space, building top, road, runway, just as they had along the entire length of the fifteen-mile drive from Washington.

He had decided, overriding the Secret Service, that they would go by motorcade instead of helicopter because, as he said, he wanted as many as possible to see them off. The mass outpouring of support he expected would be enormously strengthening for them, he believed; and when the mass outpouring proved to be there despite the new-fallen drifts of snow—streets and freeways solid with humanity every inch of the way from the White House, through the city, out into Maryland and so to Andrews—he had found it exactly as uplifting and encouraging as he had anticipated.

He had even received the final accolade, he noted with a wry little smile as they rode along, he and Cullee in the first limousine, William Abbott, Bob Munson, the Speaker and the Majority Leader in the second, Hal, Bob Leffingwell and Blair Hannah in the third. At regular intervals along the way stood the solemn-faced, black-jacketed stalwarts of NAWAC. Each held a banner: GOD BLESS PRESIDENT KNOX, OUR GREAT LEADER, AND SPEED HIM ON HIS WAY TO PEACE FOR ALL HUMANITY.

"Apparently," he remarked to Cullee, "I've made the grade." The Vice President snorted and murmured something not complimentary to Fred Van Ackerman and his merry men. Fear was still doing wonderful things to the world.

"Mr. Vice President," he said, speaking from the red-carpeted platform set up alongside the plane, the chill wind ruffling his sparse, uncovered hair, "my fellow countrymen:

"We go in faith and in hope to do what we can to help our friends in Russia and China make peace, and to restore the future of the world.

"I think we can achieve this. The obstacles are many, the hurdles difficult. But we go in good faith, believing we will find good faith greeting us. If this be so, we cannot fail.

"There is a good omen for our journey and I want to share it with you. I am advised by the Weather Bureau and by our armed forces that the atomic cloud which has been threatening Southeast Asia, Indonesia and the nations of the South Pacific Basin now appears definitely to be disintegrating at a high altitude that will not harm human life."

There was a great welling up of heartfelt, thankful sound, from his immediate audience and from everywhere over the earth where men heard his voice and watched his calm, wind-buffeted face.

"I agree with you," he said. "It is a marvelous thing, and one for which we can all be greatly thankful. Yet the event gives us all pause, because it reminds us what did happen, and what can happen again unless my colleagues and I are successful in our mission.

"I repeat: we can be successful if we are met with good faith and cooperation in Moscow and Peking. I believe we will be. I believe the massed heart of mankind is insisting upon a genuine world peace at last. I believe that this is a force too strong to be denied. My colleagues and I go as its servants, with nothing to be gained for ourselves or our country but the satisfaction of knowing that we have been able to help.

"That satisfaction I believe we shall have, because I believe peace will be achieved and with it the dawning of a new day for all mankind.

"Goodbye and God bless you. Pray for us, and we shall do our best. I am confident we will return with peace, for you and for everyone."

Again there was a great upwelling of sound, a sort of universal cry of yearning and hope. Then the platform was removed, they boarded Air Force One, the doors were closed, the engines roared, they were up and away, followed by the two packed press planes.

For a long, long time after the planes vanished into the sullen overcast, those they had left behind stood staring up, hushed and solemn, not moving, not speaking, hardly even breathing, so great was their agony of hope . . . until at last they began to break up and move away and drift off, to return to their homes and the vigil that now took over the world.

BOOK FOUR

1. THEY STOPPED OVERNIGHT in London; he conferred briefly with the Prime Minister and the Prime Ministers of France, West Germany and Italy, who had flown in for the meeting. There were pledges of support, fervent expressions of hope, stout assurances of future cooperation in all the things necessary to stabilize the world. He accepted them gravely and with profound thanks, though in the back of his mind a little clock kept ticking away: *one week—ten days—two weeks—one week—ten days—two weeks*. It was not only the Russians and the Chinese he had to hold to the timetable of fear, it was everyone else. Let things drag on too long and the whole thing would begin to disintegrate, the moment would be lost, cooperation on all sides would fritter out in a revival of traditional rivalries, hesitations, self-interests, unwillingness to work together, loss of heart, loss of determination, loss of courage. Time was his ally and his enemy: he did not know which side of its Janus head would be turned to him at the end of his journey. It behooved him to move fast.

Spurred by this, he did not tarry long but flew on very early in the morning to Moscow. Bonfires had been lighted the night before all along the route, in Newfoundland, Iceland, the British Isles: tiny beacons of hope and encouragement to wish him and his colleagues Godspeed on their difficult journey. Now as dawn came slowly to Europe through the pall of winter an occasional rift in the clouds disclosed that in every village, on every hilltop, little groups of people were standing in the snow to wave as the plane that carried the hopes of mankind passed over.

"They wish us well," William Abbott remarked.

He nodded.

"It is nice to know."

"Very," Bill Abbott said. "We need their prayers."

"Yes," he said, and a sigh, sudden and unexpected, escaped his lips. "More than they know."

Presently Arly Richardson, staring moodily out at the drifting clouds, leaned forward abruptly.

"What's this?" he asked. "An escort?"

And so it seemed to be, for Air Force One was suddenly surrounded by what appeared to be at least two dozen jets, taking positions alongside with friendly dips of their wings and a certain almost festive rakishness in the way they flew. In a moment the captain came on the intercom.

"We are being officially greeted, Mr. President. Their commander says he can speak English. I'll have him on in a moment."

A second later, guttural and at times uncertain but obviously full of a boundless excitement and good will, they heard their first words from the new Russia.

"Hello, great American President and his friends!" a youthful voice cried cheerfully. "On behalf of the President and Cabinet of the United States of Russia, we welcome you! On behalf of the free people of the United States of Russia, we welcome you! We are happy you are here to help us. We make you welcome. Welcome, welcome! We want to join you in making peace. We make you welcome. Welcome, welcome! *Welcome!*"

And in a burst of exuberant spirits, the lead plane peeled away for a series of rolls and spins, followed instantly by its fellows, so that for several minutes the sky was filled with cavorting jets, some of them coming dangerously close, but all plainly in the hands of jubilant, friendly and excited men.

During the display, he went forward to the cabin. When things had calmed down again and all their escort seemed to be in place, he spoke in response.

"Gentlemen of the United States of Russia, this is the President. My friends and I are very happy to visit your country. We too hope we can all work together for peace. We will do our best to make peace come. We need the help of the President and Cabinet of the United States of Russia. We need the help of you, the great free peoples of the United States of Russia. Let us go forward together, my friends. Let us have peace!"

"Yes!" the youthful voice came back triumphantly. "We will have peace, comrade!" There was a pause and a burst of laughter. "We are not supposed to say that any more, Mr. President, please forgive me! We say 'citizen' now. We will have peace, great citizen of the world! Welcome to Russia! Welcome, *welcome!*"

And once again he whirled away, followed dutifully by his colleagues, and for several minutes more the sky was filled with exuberant acrobatics.

"Well, now, that sounds right friendly, now!" Jawbone exclaimed, a happy smile on his face as he watched the agitated heavens gradually calm down again. "It really does sound right friendly."

"Yes, it does," Bob Munson agreed from across the aisle. "And one of the most interesting things about it, to me, is that at this very moment, with the country partially devastated, torn by civil war and presumably in near chaos, they are still able to put in the air twenty-four completely air-worthy jets in the hands of twenty-four supremely competent pilots. It is a thought," he added dryly, "for today."

"Indeed it is," Bill Abbott said soberly. "Indeed it is."

As they flew on, the clouds became sparser and eventually thinned out altogether. The snowbound land appeared. They flew over many villages and small settlements; from quite a few, pillars of smoke climbed high in the frigid air.

"Revolution," Hal observed. "They must still be fighting in many places."

"Yes," Bob Leffingwell agreed. "It is a sight the world had never thought to see."

"But inevitable," Justice Davis remarked. "Always inevitable, as long as they had the oppressive government they did."

"Why, Tommy," the President couldn't resist, "I never knew you realized that. I thought it was always hail-to-them and hell-to-us, with you and your friends."

"I can't speak for all my friends," Tommy Davis responded somewhat tartly, "but *I* always realized it."

"You did?" the President pressed.

"I did," the little Justice said firmly, turning away to look out the window.

"Well, good for you," Orrin said, winking at Bob Munson down the aisle. "I never would have suspected, but it's good to have you on our side."

"Thank you," Justice Davis said with dignity.

Before long the gray outlying tentacles of a great city began to appear. Soon their captain was advising seat belts, they were on their way down. With a last exuberant farewell flip of wings their escort peeled away. Air Force One and the two press planes came in alone.

They traversed the runway, turned, came back, stopped precisely in front of a platform similar to the one they had left twenty-four hours ago at Andrews. The door opened, he stepped forward, bundled in a heavy black cashmere overcoat but hatless in the icy wind. Below he saw a jumble of cameras and photographers, many of them his own countrymen racing from the planes behind. A cluster of eager official faces looked up. He stood for a moment smiling and waving, then proceeded down the steps followed by his colleagues. Off to the right a band struck up a tune he did not recognize but guessed, from a certain heavy Slavic pomp, to be the new national anthem. It was followed, as he stepped down onto the red carpet and proceeded to shake hands with the first of his welcomers, by "The Star-Spangled Banner."

He and his companions were surrounded immediately by eager, excited men speaking fervent words of greeting, shaking hands repeatedly with great emphasis, almost, it seemed, dancing jigs of joy. Then there came a little stir, the rest fell back. Out of the tumultuous crowd a stocky, gray-haired man stepped forward.

"You must be—?" Orrin said, holding out his hand with a questioning smile.

"This is General Shulatov, our new President," someone said proudly, and for just a second the dismay he felt must have been apparent in his eyes, for someone else said hastily with a nervous little laugh, "*Citizen* Shulatov, Mr. President, *Citizen* Shulatov!" and he laughed with an exaggerated heartiness and said, "Of course!" as he shook Citizen Shulatov's hand with a very vigorous handshake.

Then he was on the platform, and at his side Citizen Shulatov was speaking in a heavily accented but quite fluent English that echoed from the loudspeakers across the snowy tarmac, and via satellite across the world.

"Mr. President: the President, Cabinet and free peoples of the United States of Russia greet you! We welcome you to the new Russia. We are pleased and honored that you have come. We are grateful for your journey in the name of peace, and we pledge our full cooperation in achieving peace.

"Peace is the highest aim of any government. It is the aim of my government. To assure that we will have peace, the free peoples of Russia have awakened from their many decades of tyranny to demand that we have peace. Because of peace, vast changes have occurred in our country in the past forty-eight hours. We have destroyed the tyrants, just as you asked us to do. A great many of the war criminals are dead; some few are captive and will stand trial. We have a new government whose major purpose is to have peace.

"The President, Cabinet and free peoples of the new Russia welcome you, Mr. President. Tell us what you want us to do in the name of peace, and we will do it. We pledge you that. Welcome to you and your friends, in the name of Mother Russia!"

And with a sudden emotionalism whose sincerity the President was unable to judge accurately at that moment, he turned and enveloped him in a bear hug, kissing him vigorously on both cheeks.

When he had extricated himself with a somewhat embarrassed but good-natured smile, he stepped forward to the microphones and his voice too boomed forth to watching humankind.

"Peoples of free Russia—" He was conscious of the slightest stirring at his side, knew his point had scored, and did not regret it. "Mr. President, members of the Cabinet:

"My colleagues and I are here to aid you in every way we can to achieve peace not only for yourselves, but for the world.

"As you have said, Mr. President, vast and earth-shaking changes have taken place here in the past forty-eight hours. The world has watched in awe and amazement as long decades of tyranny have been swept away, to let in freedom and prepare the way for peace. A great revolution has occurred in your great country—a true revolution at last, a revolution for liberty, a revolution for peace.

"Now the hard tasks of government begin. Now the difficult building of true liberty and true peace must start. Now you must move out into the world to rejoin mankind, after many long years of imprisonment by false leaders and merciless tyrants. Now you must earn peace, and with it the respect, admiration and support of all the world's peoples.

"This will demand of you great statesmanship, great integrity, great vision. It will demand of you the sacrifice of some of the ambitions that brought about war." Again he was conscious of the smallest, slightest stirring at his side. "It will demand of you a new spirit of brotherhood toward your neighbors to the east." The stirring for a second was quite obvious. "It will require a willingness to work together with the new United Chinese Republic. It will require that you find a middle ground with the now free peoples of that vast country—those peoples who, like you, have at last thrown off the chains of tyranny and begun the search for genuine freedom and genuine peace.

"In that search, my friends and I are here to help in every way we can.

"We are not here to demand, except as the massed heart of mankind gives us the right to demand, any conditions for peace.

"We are not here to dictate, except as the massed heart of mankind wants us to dictate, how peace should be achieved.

"We are simply here to help find peace, because peace *must* be found."

His voice and expression turned somber.

"You have suffered terribly in the past few days, peoples of the new Russia. Neither you, nor the Chinese, nor anyone anywhere else in the world, must ever suffer such terrible things again. . . .

"Mr. President, members of the Cabinet, my friends and I thank you for your greeting. We look forward to working with you for the best interests of your free peoples, and of all peoples everywhere. We hope peace may swiftly come because time is very short."

There was a burst of clapping, rather more dutiful, he felt, than not.

He turned to Shulatov, shook hands firmly and, this time, managed to get through another bear hug and bussing with a dignity that much amused his son, as he was aware when he caught his eye over his host's burly shoulder.

Then they were in the official limousines, the sirens were screaming, they were whisked away to the Kremlin over the icy roads and through the cavernous, icy streets. Many, many thousands were out to see them, whether ordered or spontaneously, they had at that time no way of knowing. At regular intervals along the way tanks, soldiers, heavy guns, were at attention as they passed. Overhead more exuberant jets were flying. They arrived at their Kremlin quarters in a curious state of mind, determinedly optimistic, desperately desirous that all would be well—but wary.

An hour later they faced their hosts in closed session in a huge oak-paneled room in what had been the private quarters of Vasily Tashikov. They knew this because Shulatov told them so with an air of considerable pride when they were ushered in.

"That traitor," he added with a grim satisfaction, "who now awaits in Lubyanka the judgment of the people. We despise him, Mr. President! We despise him! He will receive the punishment he deserves for his rash, ill-considered, foolish acts. Of that the world may be sure."

"He was certainly no friend to world peace," Orrin observed noncommittally. Shulatov snorted.

"He betrayed Russia! He *betrayed* her! He will never be forgiven for it by this country. Never!"

"He betrayed her by failing to win the war, I take it," the President suggested matter-of-factly, and for a split second his host almost agreed. Then he smiled with a sudden bland candor and shook his head vigorously.

"No, no! Certainly not! He betrayed her, as he betrayed all the peoples of the world, by launching an atomic attack upon our great neighbor China and thus bringing destruction upon Russia and panic to the world. It was a double betrayal. Is that not right, Mr. President?"

"That is how we see it, Mr. President," Orrin agreed with an equal blandness. "We shall watch the proceedings of his trial, and those of his colleagues, with great interest."

"They will begin very soon," Shulatov promised, again with a grim satisfaction. "But enough of those unhappy people. We want you to meet our new government." He gestured to the group of a dozen men who stood together at the other end of the room, watching them with bright smiles and very close attention. "Come, bring your friends and we will all get acquainted."

And for the next fifteen minutes they did so, a rapid drumfire of names, Cabinet titles, faces. No one again introduced anyone as "General" or "Admiral"—"Citizen" was the term carefully used in all instances—but he got a very distinct impression of an automatic deference, an automatic ranking that seemed to run through their relations with one another. He could tell that his friends were receiving the same impression and were made as uneasy as he. But of course none of them indicated concern by so much as the lift of an eyelid, reserving that for some later private place, if in this honeycomb still redolent of tyranny there should prove to be any such.

Presently Shulatov gestured to a huge oaken table at one side of the room. His colleagues dutifully took their seats, the Americans followed. The two Presidents seated themselves last, opposite one another. A silence fell.

Shulatov leaned forward.

"My colleagues and I," he said, "are at your service. Tell us what you want us to do."

"Tell us what you are willing to do," he suggested.

Shulatov looked a little taken aback.

"Mr. President," he protested earnestly, "it is you who must tell, not we. It is you who come here with the full authority of the world to assist you. It is not for us, the inheritors of a desperately stricken country, to make conditions. It is you."

"No, you tell us," the President said. "That way we will know how difficult our task is to be."

"You do not deny you come with conditions," Shulatov said, and all down his side of the table bright, attentive, intently smiling faces leaned forward to hear the answer. The President decided to meet the issue head on.

"No, I don't deny that. They have been published, you have read them. Some may be easier to achieve, with your new government; some may not even be necessary any longer. Those are the first things we must find out. We cannot do so unless we can understand your feelings and your mood. Please describe them to us. What are you willing to do, to accomplish peace?"

Shulatov made a little conceding gesture with his head and shoulders. His expression darkened.

"Our feelings and our mood, and what are we willing to do. . . . Our feelings are very deeply shaken, Mr. President, I will tell you that, and our mood is very somber. We have lost a dozen cities—more than the outside world yet knows—we have suffered massive losses of our armed forces on the Chinese frontier, we have suffered perhaps ten million civilian deaths and as many more casualties. Yes!" he repeated sharply as a sudden intake of breath came from several on the American side of the table. "Ten million deaths, and as many more casualties. Chaos exists in much of Russia, spurred by the civil rebellion which has brought my colleagues and myself to this table. It is worse than the world knows. It is dreadful. We are reeling from it. What can our feelings and our mood be, other than horror, sadness, fear of the future, chagrin? We would not be human otherwise—and now this has become a very human country again, Mr. President. We are raw and quivering from border to border, from end to end. So you see why we wonder when you ask us what we are willing to do. *We* are in no position to make conditions. Only those who have been spared what we have suffered can make conditions. Is that not so?"

For a long moment the President studied him thoughtfully again. Then he responded quietly:

"Nonetheless, we would still like to know: what are you willing to do?"

A look of impatience crossed the face of the President of the United States of Russia; down the table his colleagues shifted uneasily. But the President of the United States of America did not relax his steady gaze, and after a moment Shulatov leaned forward and spoke with an intense but controlled force.

"We are willing to do whatever will bring peace to Russia and peace to the world! Anything! Anything! We cannot stand a resumption of war with China. We cannot afford to have more armed forces destroyed, more cities destroyed, more lives destroyed. We cannot afford it. We cannot stand it. We *must* have peace. We must have security. We must be safe in our homes and our country again. We will cooperate in any way we can to achieve this."

"Will you go to China with me," the President asked, "or let them come here, or meet with them in some neutral place, to settle your differences? Will you do that for your country, and for peace?"

But even as he spoke he knew the answer, for this time there was a noticeable stiffening in the bodies across the table, a visible frowning in the faces. The question was a test—it had come to him in a flash—he had tossed it out the moment it occurred to him, knowing its answer would reveal many things. The nature of the answer did not surprise him.

"Is *that* a condition, Mr. President?" Shulatov asked with a quietness suddenly inimical, and dangerous. He shrugged.

"Not necessarily," he said calmly. "Let's say a reaching for clarification. You will not tell me what you are willing to do—or at least you are very general about it. I thought I would give you a specific that would help me find out." He looked thoughtfully away, along the table at his own silent colleagues, the now tense and jittery Russians. "It has."

"Mr. President," Shulatov said with an earnestness that, he knew, hid anger, "do not play games with us. Do not use your superior power and superior position to patronize the new Russia. We do not like it. It will accomplish nothing. It will simply antagonize us and stiffen our resistance. It will revive all of our suspicions of the West, it will make us—"

"Listen to me!" he interrupted sharply, hitting the table with the flat of his hand. "Stop propagandizing and listen to me! I have suggested nothing unfair, unusual, extraordinary, inimical, hostile to you or to peace, dangerous to Russia or in any way whatsoever threatening to your independence, security or well-being. I have suggested a perfectly common-sense, down-to-earth practical thing without which there can be no negotiation, no understanding, no peace. *What do you mean* by reacting this way to it? Have you learned nothing at all from this past week in your country? If that is the case"—he sat back and looked away to some distant point, face grim and set—"my colleagues and I are flying home today and the damnation of the world will be upon you for destroying the last hope for peace."

But this time, as he had known, he did not have to carry out the threat to leave: stating it was enough. A visible change came over the face across from him, and across all its companion faces along the table. At first with difficulty, then suddenly very smoothly, the transition was made from anger to agreement. President Shulatov was smiling in a placating, self-deprecating, almost humble way.

"Mr. President," he said, "I must apologize to you, to your friends, to *my* friends, to everybody! The tensions of these past few days have been very great. It is my task to bear them without breaking, but I am afraid I came very close to it just now. Of course you are reasonable, of course you are practical. We do indeed wish to talk to our friends in Peking, to the new government there, to the free peoples of China, relieved of their bondage as we have been. Of course we must meet them face to face. Do not let my reaction, hasty and ill-advised, antagonize you. We will work it out. There are difficulties and details, but"—he waved a calm, dismissing hand—"we will work them out—with your assistance, Mr. President. Always with your assistance, true friend of peace, great citizen of the world to whom the world looks!"

"Thank you," he said, not trying very hard to keep a certain dryness out of his voice. "Then we agree on that fundamental point."

"We do!" President Shulatov said triumphantly. "We do! And now, perhaps that is enough for the first session? You must all be very tired. Perhaps a rest—then cocktails—then dinner? We will show you that the new Russia still knows how to feed her friends well, Mr. President! You will enjoy it."

"I know we will," he said. "I agree, this is probably enough for a preliminary session. Your social program sounds fine to us. First, though, I expect we will have to meet the world press."

"They are waiting in the Great Hall of the Kremlin," Shulatov said, rising; and all down the table, his Cabinet followed suit. "We knew we must accustom ourselves from now on to their kind attentions."

Orrin and his party rose, too.

"I'm afraid so," he said with a smile he permitted to appear fully relaxed again. "You may have the first word."

"After you!" Shulatov said with a sudden boisterous laugh. "After you!"

But in the Great Hall, when Orrin insisted, his host did speak first.

"Ladies and gentlemen of the press," he said to the eager audience in which could be seen Walter Dobius, Frankly Unctuous, the *Times*, the *Post* and nearly six hundred others, many familiar, many not, "we have opened our discussions on a friendly and constructive note. We do not yet have specifics to announce to you but the mood is good, my friends. The mood is good!"

"Do you agree, Mr. President?" a British voice called out, and he faced them with an easy smile and nodded.

"Oh, yes. We are well under way. My colleagues and I are convinced we can make speedy progress in the next few days."

"No swifter timetable than that, Mr. President?" Walter Dobius asked.

"It will be as swift as both sides can make it, Walter," he replied. "I think the world can be sure of that."

"Come drink with us at eight P.M.," Shulatov called out with a cheery wave, taking Orrin's arm as they turned away. "We will have a real Russian banquet for you!"

And so they did: an hour of preliminary drinking, seven courses of food, vodka, mixed drinks, wines, liqueurs, cigars, much standing about with the media afterward, many questions, all blandly fielded by both Americans and Russians: an air of friendship, understanding, joviality. For all that it seemed to have affected the comfort and well-being of the new government of Russia, the war might have been on another planet. So also, thought the President with misgivings he knew were shared by his colleagues, might have been any real progress toward understanding and agreement. But so skillful were both sides in maintaining the façade of cordiality that the first wave of headlines served only to increase the world's hopes and allay to considerable degree its fears:

KNOX, NEW RUSS GOVERNMENT IN CORDIAL FIRST MEETING. BOTH SIDES REPORT "FRIENDLY AND CONSTRUCTIVE PROGRESS" TOWARD AGREEMENT. AMERICANS SAY RUSSIAN LEADERS ARE "DETERMINED TO HAVE PEACE." RUSSIANS SAY AMERICANS "COME IN GENUINELY HELPFUL SPIRIT, AS TRUE TRUSTEES FOR THE WORLD." OPTIMISM REFLECTED BY BOTH SIDES.

At 10 A.M. the next morning they met again.

"Mr. President," Orrin said when they were seated, "before we turn to other subjects I have a matter which has been presented to me by a committee from the press. I think it is important enough to discuss right now."

Shulatov looked surprised for a moment. Then he laughed with an easy amusement.

"I was told there was some disagreement over something, but my people said it had all been settled."

"Apparently not," the President said. "At least, not to the satisfaction of the media."

"Are they ever satisfied?" Shulatov inquired with a comfortable chuckle.

"Nonetheless," he said firmly, "this time they have a point. I understand your government is refusing them permission to visit the countryside. Not only that, but they have been refused permission to visit even the city. They tell me they are confined to the Kremlin."

"They will be taken on a tour of nearby villages this afternoon," Shulatov said with some impatience. "What are they complaining about?"

"They don't want a formal tour," the President said. "They are a free press. They want to see for themselves. It was our understanding that this is now a free country and a free people. Are we mistaken in that?"

"Of course you are not mistaken!"

"Then why must the press of the world be restricted in what it does here?" the President inquired.

"You must understand, Mr. President," Shulatov said slowly, patience abruptly replacing impatience, "that conditions are still very chaotic, in the city, in the countryside and indeed throughout the whole country. It is only forty-eight hours since the last atomic bomb from China fell on us, you know. Many areas are still literally unsafe for anyone, let alone reporters, to venture into. Other areas are still in a state of flux. Still others require firm controls to stop looting and restore civil order. It is all very chaotic still. We cannot be responsible for reporters wandering about."

"I think they can understand and accept the reasons why they cannot yet be allowed to go east to the actual war zones," the President said, "but I don't think they can understand why they cannot go into Moscow itself or into a reasonable radius around the capital to see what actual conditions are in the countryside. They aren't going very far, they want to stick close to what we're doing. But they can't understand why they can't be free to see for themselves what is happening in nearby areas. Nor," he added firmly, "can I."

"We do not want to be responsible—" Shulatov began in the same patient way. But the President interrupted.

"These are grown men and women, Mr. President. They can be responsible for themselves—with, of course, adequate protection, which I am sure your government will furnish them. I think you had better let them go; otherwise, I know them, and I can assure you that there is going to develop very rapidly the suspicion that your government has something to hide."

"Mr. President—" Shulatov said with a flare of anger, controlled but emphatic.

"*Do* you have something to hide?"

"Mr. President—"

"Then," he said calmly, "I think you had better let them go."

Once again their eyes locked across the table. But the President of the United States of America did not yield, and presently the President of the United States of Russia flushed and glanced away.

"Vorosky!" he snapped. "Go and do as the President requests."

"Hal," the President said quietly, "I think you had better go along and report back to me that it has been done."

"Yes, sir," his son said; and in a moment he and an obviously disgruntled, but perforce compliant, Russian walked together out the door.

The room was silent for several moments. Finally Shulatov leaned forward.

"Mr. President," he said carefully, "I told you yesterday that you must not patronize or order my government to do things. We are a free country now, a free government and a free people, and it will only disturb our negotiations very seriously if you persist."

"I shall certainly persist in standing up for what is right," the President said calmly. "And 'being free' is more than words, Mr. President. It is actions and it is good faith and honesty. My colleagues and I—and I think the world—intend to hold you to it. So if it annoys you, I am sorry. But I suggest to you that the situation is frightful enough, here and in China and potentially in the whole world, so that you must not only talk freedom, but *be* free. Isn't that right?"

And again he stared impassively at his host, whose eyes this time did not drop. Instead they crinkled suddenly into amicable laughter, and all along the table his tense and uncertain colleagues took their cue and began to chortle too.

"Of course you are right, Mr. President," Shulatov said, "of *course* you are right. It was a momentary annoyance on my part because the press is so—so *insistent*. We do not like them to tell us what we have to do!"

"I don't like it either," Orrin said, laughing with a deliberate amicability also, "but they do it to me all the time. So, then"—he leaned forward briskly, his tone becoming businesslike and matter-of-fact—"there are certain necessities for peace which we hope your government will willingly and speedily agree to. Are we ready to discuss them?"

"As you like, Mr. President," Shulatov said, and sat back in his chair in a relaxed and expansive way. All down the table his Cabinet did the same.

"Very well," he said. "When the state of war between the former Communist government of Russia and the former Communist government of China reached an impasse after the atomic exchange, and the leaders turned to me to arbitrate, I announced certain conditions. Some of you may have heard of them in the past several days, some of you may not, depending upon where you were and what you were doing prior to taking power."

"Most of us were quite busy, Mr. President," Shulatov interjected in an amused tone. "Quite busy."

A little ripple of laughter went up and down both sides of the table.

"Yes," the President said, "I imagine. Let me review them for you, then.

"The first was that the government of Russia and the government of China would immediately withdraw their forces from Gorotoland and Panama and give to me a formal statement that it has been done. I assume—?"

Shulatov nodded.

"It is moot. We are out of both places. We have no intention of returning. It is no longer a concern to the new government and the peoples of Russia. The Foreign Secretary"—he looked down the table to a bushy-haired, middle-aged figure who nodded vigorously—"will furnish you your statement by the end of the day."

"Good," he said. "And you will recognize the legitimate governments of Gorotoland and Panama, and will pledge your support and assistance in an international commission to supervise free elections in both countries."

"Assuredly," Shulatov said with a dismissing wave of the hand. "And, Mr. President"—he smiled—"it will be real cooperation, from *this* government. We have enough problems right here. Russia's days of fishing in troubled waters are over, we hope forever."

"We hope so too," Orrin said with a humorous exaggerated relief that brought answering chuckles from many along the table. "There were several conditions outside the competence of your two countries, such as internationalization of the Dardanelles, Suez and the Panama Canal. Thanks to the prompt cooperation of the governments of Turkey, Egypt and just yesterday the restored legitimate government of Panama, this has been agreed to.

"There was the establishment of an International Relief Commission under United Nations supervision to assist your stricken peoples and the stricken peoples of China, and also peoples of the South Pacific Basin who might be injured by the atomic cloud thrown up by the war. The cloud has fortunately dissipated but the need in your two countries remains. All the other nations in the world have pledged monetary and medical assistance. I assume your government will do whatever it can to aid its own people in cooperation with the international commission."

Again his host gave the little dismissing wave.

"We will certainly do everything we can for our own people, and we welcome with the utmost gratitude the assistance of the nations of the earth. We will cooperate."

"Good," Orrin said. "The next proviso, which has already been met by the Secretary-General and the willing contributions of more than sixty nations as of this morning, with more scheduled to announce their contributions very soon, is the establishment of an international peace-keeping force to patrol the frontier between Russia and China." He paused and looked at the faces across the table. He could see that a curtain, subtle but unmistakable, had come down. "This will require," he went on calmly, "the full cooperation and support of both governments. I trust yours can see the necessity of such a *cordon sanitaire,* and I trust it will assist fully."

"Where," Shulatov inquired cautiously after a moment, "would this force operate, Mr. President?"

"Why," he said, "along the border."

"It is a very long border. Where?"

"At posts spaced out at regular intervals, I would assume. Perhaps a hundred miles apart, so that they could patrol fifty miles on each side."

His host studied him thoughtfully, while along the table his Cabinet stayed very still.

"Who would establish the locations?"

"The United Nations general command," the President said, looking deliberately blank. "Who else?"

"I had thought the governments of Russia and China, in consultation and agreement with one another," Shulatov said slowly.

"Could you reach agreement?"

"I believe so."

"I am afraid the world may not be so confident. I think it may insist upon an impartial body doing the job."

"Would that not be a very substantial infringement of our sovereignty?" Shulatov inquired.

The President looked surprised.

"You are belligerents. I don't believe the world would trust you to reach agreement, or, if you did, to establish patrol posts in any pattern that would really do any good."

"Has the United Nations discussed this?"

"Establishment of the peace-keeping force, yes. Precise details, no."

"Then this is really just America's idea, just your idea?" Shulatov asked slowly.

"I believe it represents the consensus of the nations," the President said, permitting a certain asperity to enter his voice.

"But you do not know," his host observed calmly. "Perhaps it should be discussed in the Security Council."

"It will be," the President promised. "But," he added as a certain aura of satisfaction flickered along the table opposite, "you know the veto no longer exists."

"No!" his host exclaimed, and many others on his side echoed, "*No!*" and fell into agitated whisperings and murmurings among themselves.

"Yes," he said. "The Charter was amended the night the former governments fell. There is no more veto."

There was a pause while Shulatov stared very thoughtfully into the depths of the table's gleaming surface. Then he raised his eyes, his face a bland mask that revealed nothing.

"We will have to consider this," he said in an almost offhand way. "What else do you have for us?"

"Two final things," the President said. "A pledge from your government, and from the government of China, that you are abandoning permanently, once and for all, imperialistic, expansionist policies everywhere in the world; that you formally renounce all desire and ambition to intervene in the affairs of other nations; that you will devote your funds, your energies, your purposes, to the peaceful development of your own societies."

Again there was a silence while his host thought. Again he looked up with bland eyes in a bland face.

"I have already told you that the new Russia has no more interest in overseas adventures. Obviously, however, we do have an interest in the existence of friendly governments on our borders. We would like to be assured of this—if not through our own efforts, then through international guarantees from all the nations."

"No nation at this hour wishes to be hostile or covetous toward any other," the President said. "You do not realize the state of mind of the world right now. You do not understand the impact the outbreak of atomic war has had upon the world. Nobody wants conquest any more. Nobody would threaten you."

" 'At this hour,' " Shulatov echoed. " 'Right now.' Perhaps you speak truly, Mr. President. You wish guarantees against a renewal of imperialist conquest by us. Perhaps we have an equal right to ask guarantees against imperialist conquest by anyone else—even including the great United States of America."

It was the President's turn to look thoughtful; and after a moment he smiled, not without humor.

"Perhaps you do," he agreed. "Certainly you will have this guarantee from the United States the moment you give a similar guarantee. I cannot command the other nations, but I think I can safely say that they will unanimously do the same."

"But first we must give our guarantee," Shulatov remarked slowly.

"Yes," the President said crisply. "You are the belligerents, you have been the aggressors. You owe the world something, Mr. President."

"My government and I have not been the belligerents," Shulatov remarked, "nor the aggressors. We have been in power scarcely forty-eight hours. It is the old government you must blame, not us."

"You are responsible now," the President said. "Do not be disingenuous, Mr. President."

Shulatov smiled, also not without humor.

"We *are* responsible," he agreed. "For a great country and a great people. Forgive us if it makes us appear overly cautious, but it *is* a great responsibility. . . . This, too, we must consider. . . . Is there anything else?"

"Yes," the President said, and along his own side of the table he could feel a tensing, a quieting, a suddenly wary watching; for this was the nub of it and no one could say what would happen next, though they all had their ideas.

"The final condition," Orrin said, and his voice was level, firm and as calm as though he were discussing the time of day, "is that the United States of Russia and the United Chinese Republic will immediately reduce, by at least one-half, with further reductions to follow, their conventional armed forces, and will immediately and permanently eliminate, under United Nations supervision, all of their atomic weapons, atomic missiles and atomic submarines, and any and all stockpiles and weapons of germ warfare.

"The United States," he went on, his voice rising a little in response to the sudden agitation across the table, but still firm and calm, "will participate in, agree to, and be bound by, exactly the same limitations, once our forces have been repaired to the parity destroyed by the fighting in Gorotoland and Panama. Congress has already approved the funds to do this, and we are therefore ready to commence these negotiations at once."

And he sat back quietly while on his own side of the table his friends kept their faces as impassive as his, and on the other side the agitated movements and sounds and conferrings continued for several moments in a fiercely agitated undertone.

Presently it died away; and the President of the United States of Russia, whose face had been a study in racing emotions, became calm and uncommunicative once again.

"This, too, Mr. President," he said quietly, "we must consider. . . . And now!" He stood up abruptly, his colleagues followed suit, he beamed upon the Americans. "Again we have a party for you! This time it is lunch. You will find that our lunches are as good as our dinners. Come, let us—"

"Mr. President," Orrin said, remaining seated, voice still firm, and unimpressed. "We must ask that you stay here and discuss these most serious matters. It isn't noon yet."

"You will wish to rest and relax a little before lunch," Shulatov said cheerfully. "We can meet again at six P.M., if you like, after everyone has had a chance to recover from lunch. You will need it, believe me, Mr. President, you will need it!"

"At six P.M.," Orrin said in a level voice, "we will discuss and reach agreement upon the three matters in dispute. And we will stay here until we *have* reached agreement."

"As you like," Shulatov said, almost airily. "As you like, Mr. President. But: one thing. They are not 'in dispute.' The government of the new Russia would never want to dispute with our good friends from America. Say they are 'matters of concern and discussion.' We simply want to consider them for a brief time, in private, by ourselves. Surely you and your friends cannot object to that—you no doubt wish to do the same. So come, now, Mr. President! Let us meet our friends of the press again, then let us rest, then let us have a beautiful lunch, then let us rest again, then let us discuss again. O.—K.?"

"O.—K.," the President said with a grim little smile. He stood up. "But we want no more evasions," he added flatly. "There isn't time."

"We know," Shulatov agreed. "We *know*. Let us go and meet our disgruntled friends of the press, Mr. President. Maybe by now they have had their little tours!"

But they had not, and they were disgruntled; and this time there was sharper questioning, harder to evade; and into the second wave of headlines there crept a note of uneasiness and worry that disturbed the waiting world.

RUSS REPORTED BALKING AT CONDITIONS FOR PEACE. SECOND MEETING WITH AMERICANS GOES LESS SMOOTHLY. HIGH U.S. SOURCE INDICATES "SUBSTANTIAL DIFFERENCES ON POINTS VITAL TO WORLD STABILITY." NEW RUSS GOVERNMENT SHARPLY RESTRICTS PRESS VISITS TO COUNTRYSIDE DESPITE U.S. PROTESTS. GROWING CONCERN FELT IN WORLD CAPITALS AS HINTS GROW OF RUSS INTRANSIGENCE. NEW CHINESE GOVERNMENT SAYS "THIS IS WHAT WE EXPECTED."

And this time the jolly cocktail party and the jolly lunch were not quite so jolly; and when they met again at 6 P.M. the atmosphere was tense and edgy as both sides proceeded along the paths they had decided upon in their respective private conferences held in the late afternoon.

"Now, Mr. President," he said, "let us return to the three items in dispute." Shulatov raised a hasty hand, there were little murmurings and protestations down his side of the table.

"Not 'dispute,' Mr. President," he said earnestly. "Surely, not 'dispute' after all our constructive progress and all our friendly exchanges. Surely 'dispute' is too harsh a word!"

"Constructive progress on minor points, friendly exchanges over food and liquor," he remarked dryly. "No progress on major points, no real friendship away from food and liquor. Isn't that right, Mr. President?"

"We feel the greatest friendship for you and America, our true friends who are here to help us!" Shulatov said indignantly, and indignant echoes raced one another down the table.

The President smiled, somewhat grimly.

"And we feel the greatest friendship toward the free peoples of Russia, Mr. President. We would like to feel friendship toward their government. It cannot come if their government turns back to the old, discredited ways. It cannot come if their government defies the will of mankind and refuses to make peace. It cannot come if their government is crafty and devious and seeks to cling to the ways of war. That way lies disaster."

Shulatov studied him for a moment, face blank, eyes bland. Then he leaned forward.

"Mr. President," he inquired softly, "what would you do if my government refused to cooperate with these conditions of yours—with this 'will of mankind' you talk about? Would you threaten us, Mr. President? Would you go to war with us? How would you make us behave?"

Inwardly he thought with a sigh: *exactly so.* Outwardly his expression was as implacably bland as Shulatov's.

"I think it would be necessary then," he said pleasantly, praying that his companions would remain as bland as he, gratified to find the prayer answered, "to organize a world expeditionary force, enter your country, overthrow you and install men with more responsibility."

"You would not dare!" Shulatov cried with a sudden naked anger, too startled and upset to dissemble. *"You would not dare!"*

"What could stop us, Mr. President?" he inquired in the same pleasant tone. "Your country is still in terrible turmoil, as you have told us yourself, you have no really effective control of it as yet, your people are tolerating your military government"—there was a movement, instantly stifled—"only until they can determine whether or not it is genuinely seeking peace. How could you stop us? Revolution and rebellion are still in the air here, the tinder is still dry. All we need do is cross your borders and you will be gone in half a day like your predecessors. Isn't that true?"

Their eyes met, held, locked. This time Shulatov did not look away. Instead his angry expression dwindled, dissolved, was replaced by a serene conviction.

"Mr. President," he said softly, "first, last and always the people of Russia are *Russians. They* might overthrow us, Mr. President, but they would not let *you* do it. Never would they cooperate with you in any way. Never would they do that. Such a step would simply unify them totally against you. . . . But!" His amicable expression broadened into a smile, he made a little dismissing gesture with his hands, he shrugged. "It is foolish, this hostility, these threats. We are not being crafty, we are not being clever, we are not 'clinging to war.' We want peace, Mr. President, *peace!* We do not want further troubles with anyone. We have too much to do right here."

"Then let us return," Orrin suggested quietly, "to the three items in dispute. The first, I believe, is the peace-keeping force to be established along the border with China. Will you permit this force to enter the country peaceably and take up its stations along the border, or will you not?"

Again there was a silence. Everyone tensed again. He looked at Shulatov, Shulatov looked at him. Finally the Russian made an almost hopeless gesture toward his colleagues.

"Mr. President," he said, "I think you expect too much of me. You say will *I* permit the force to enter, will *I* do things. But we are a democracy now, Mr. President—we are a democracy! It is not *I* who can decide everything, it is my colleagues whom I must consult. It is *they* who must decide. And, Mr. President, they are troubled. They are disturbed. They are anxious, as I said earlier to you, about this international force. They believe it only fair that the force include substantial contingents of forces from the United States of Russia. They tell me I cannot agree to an international force unless it does include such contingents. So you see, Mr. President"—his expression looked genuinely worried—"my hands are tied. I cannot tell you what *I* would do about such a force, because it is not *I* who have the power to decide."

"How long do you think it will be," he inquired, controlling his anger with a major effort, "before your colleagues can decide?"

Shulatov appeared to be genuinely concerned and baffled. He shrugged.

"I cannot say, Mr. President," he replied, almost wistfully. "It could take some time."

"And what restrictions would your government attempt to impose on the force?" he asked. "How many Russian troops would you want to have in it, where would you allow it to be stationed?"

"All that would have to be considered, Mr. President," Shulatov repeated earnestly. "It would have to be considered. It would take *time!*"

"There is no time," he said harshly.

"But there must be," Shulatov protested, "there must be! Our country is in chaos, as you say. We face an enormous task in restoring stability. We have a million things to think about. It will take time—"

"I am going from here to Peking," he said in a level voice, "probably tonight. I expect to be there no longer than two days, when I shall return. That is the time you have, Mr. President. Furthermore, if there is any Russian representation at all on the peace-keeping force it will be token only, probably no more than a hundred observers." Again there was the agitated stirring from across the table. He ignored it. "The same will apply to the Chinese. The force will be under the sole and exclusive control of the United Nations command. It will choose its own bases, it will organize the border patrols as it sees fit, it will do whatever is necessary to keep the peace between you. That is its purpose. You will cooperate with it or no, but that is how it will be done, Mr. President. I suggest to you that it would be more profitable for you to accept in good grace than to interfere and oppose. That could only cause a unified wave of hostility against your government from the entire world. You dismiss the consequences lightly but I assure you they would not be light, Mr. President. If you do not believe me, continue on this course and see what it brings you.

"Two days from now," he said flatly, his tone brushing aside the angry expressions across the table, "I want your agreement to the free entry and free operation of the international peace-keeping force. We turn now to item Number Two in dispute, your guarantee that you will permanently abandon conquests and interference beyond your borders in return for an equal guarantee from all other nations toward you—including, as you rightly insist, my own country. Your point is valid and it will be taken into account in this way: a formal statement to this effect will be drawn up by your government, by the new government of China, by my government, and I am quite sure by all other governments. These guarantees will be issued simultaneously in all capitals on a day and at an hour not later than one week from today. You will not be in the position of being the first one, or the only one, nor will China. We will all give our guarantees together, so that there can be no question.

"Does that seem fair enough to you, or must you take further 'time' to consult with your colleagues? If so, I would urge you all to consider it speedily, as I remind you that I shall be returning in two days."

He paused expectantly while down his side of the table his colleagues sat very still and across the way a jumble of emotions crossed the faces of the President of the United States of Russia and his Cabinet. Finally Shulatov's expression relaxed and he spoke with a deprecating wave of the hand.

"If it is done simultaneously in all capitals by all nations," he said calmly, "I believe we would see no objection."

"Good," Orrin said with equal calm. "I commend you on your spirit of cooperation and your contribution to world peace. We come now to the final item on the agenda, the mutual reduction of armaments by the United States of Russia, the United Chinese Republic and the United States of America. Have you and your colleagues had time to study this question?"

Shulatov stared at him for a moment. Then he observed carefully: "It is something which must be given great thought."

"Not much," the President said. "Either you are willing or you are not. Are you?"

"On the terms stated by you earlier?" Shulatov inquired cautiously. "By at least one-half?"

"By at least one-half, with more to follow."

"Mr. President," Shulatov said earnestly, "we could not possibly pledge our country to that course without the most careful consider—"

"China will do the same," the President interrupted. "We will do the same. Other powers are not obligated, but if we three do, there will be such a lessening of tensions in the world that it is highly probable that many of them will follow. In any event, to put it bluntly since we are talking privately with complete candor, we three are all that matter, in this area. If we disarm and bind ourselves not to intervene elsewhere, the danger of world conflict is automatically reduced to virtually nil."

Shulatov nodded.

"But first it must be Russia and China."

"Yes," the President said with an almost indifferent firmness, "it must."

"How do we know that China will agree? How do we know that you will agree?"

"Because my colleagues and I tell you we will," the President said flatly. "As for China, that is the principal reason why I am going there."

Shulatov shot him a shrewd glance.

"You may not find it easy."

"That's right," the President agreed quickly. "Why don't you come with me?"

The response, as he had known it would be, was an instant withdrawal and closing off, accompanied by an uneasy shifting down the table. The President of the United States of Russia gave him a look very close to scorn.

"Now, Mr. President," he said coldly, "you play games with me."

"Not at all," Orrin said with an equal coldness. "You told me in our first meeting yesterday that you would meet with the Chinese. That was your promise. Is the new government of Russia to prove as treacherous as the old? Is that the message I must take back to the world? Mr. President!" He leaned forward earnestly. "Let us stop sparring. I assure you, you *must not* fall back into the old patterns. You have described very movingly the devastation in your country. It exists at this moment, it will exist for many weeks. If we cannot bring about a lasting peace between your two countries it may resume and grow infinitely worse, not only for you but for all of us. *You must not forget that,* Mr. President. I repeat, will you go to China with me? It may be an extraordinary suggestion in some respects, but this is an extraordinary moment. Come with me and we will all sit down together, with our advisers, and work it out. The world demands it of us, Mr. President. We cannot betray the world."

"I cannot betray Russia," Shulatov said, and spontaneously his Cabinet burst into applause that lasted for several vigorous seconds before it died down amid excited approving glances and warm congratulatory looks.

"Two Presidents of the United States," Orrin said quietly, indicating William Abbott sitting solid and impassive on his right, "are here to tell you that no one is asking you to betray Russia, Mr. President. We are asking you not to betray this great chance for peace which has come out of this terrible war. Surely you can leave aside the propaganda and the inflammatory remarks and acknowledge that."

"Mr. President," Shulatov said, and now there was a certain finality in his tone that dismayed the Americans, though none of them gave the slightest indication, "you proceed to hold out the carrot, having found that the stick will not work. Please be assured that we understand your position. Try to understand ours. We do not trust the Chinese. We do not trust the sudden good will of the world. We do not, to be completely candid, trust you.

"We still possess very substantial arms, Mr. President. Oh, do not think we are as weak and helpless as some would like to believe! Russia is not weak, Mr. President: Russia is strong! I told you earlier not to patronize us or try to dictate to us. *Russia is strong!*"

"Russia," he responded crisply, "is also bluffing. Russia is not as strong as all that, Mr. President. Your hold on the country is flimsy at best, the situation is still chaotic everywhere outside this Kremlin fortress, these arms you talk about are largely directed at this moment toward your own people, to prevent rioting, looting and attempts to overthrow *you* as you overthrew your predecessors—and you know it. I warn you, Mr. President: you say the stick has not worked. *It has not even been tried yet.* I am giving you and your government the chance to cooperate peaceably with the world. I am not going to hold the offer open forever. Will you or will you not?"

Again their eyes met and locked; and eventually, this time, it was Shulatov's that dropped—but only to lift again after a moment to meet his with another bland and disarming smile, accompanied by a characteristic shrug.

"Mr. President," he said patiently, "there is no need for us to become heated. You truly say that things are very difficult here for me and our new government. The people demand of us stability and leadership: much remains to be done. Surely you can see that my colleagues and I cannot possibly leave at this moment to go to China with you. It would be impossible. Later, perhaps . . . later. But not at this moment. . . .

"Mr. President"—his tone and expression became earnest, respectful, politely admonitory—"*you* go to China! Take with you our assurances of friendship, our willingness to cooperate, our desire for peace! Tell our new counterparts in Peking that we understand their problems as I am sure they must understand ours. Make your suggestions to them, Mr. President—urge them to cooperate as you have urged me! Be our emissary as well as the world's. And then—return to us! Bring us back their agreement and their pledges and their plans for compromise! Bring back *their* promise to allow an international police force to invade their country, *their* promise to withdraw behind their borders, *their* program for disarmament. And *then* we will sit down with you and, using their agreement as basis, we will plan for peace and decide how to stabilize the world.

"But do not ask me to agree to anything without knowing what they will agree to, Mr. President. Surely, you must see I am not being unreasonable about that!"

And earnest, respectful, politely friendly if just possibly a touch self-satisfied, he sat back and looked blandly up and down the American side.

And again the President of the United States thought bleakly to himself:

Exactly so.

Outwardly, however, he gave no sign. After a moment he nodded thoughtfully.

"What you say seems reasonable enough, Mr. President. And of course the Chinese will want to know your position also. What am I to tell them? That you completely reject an international peace-keeping force along the border to protect them from another sneak attack? That you refuse to enter into an agreement not to cross your frontier again and invade their territory? That you intend to rebuild your armaments as fast as possible to the point where you will once more be a major threat to them?"

This time, he noted with a grim satisfaction, the consternation was on the other side and it had hit so fast that there was no time to dissemble. Shulatov and his colleagues looked openly dismayed. It was not with any bland smile that his antagonist responded to him now.

"Mr. President!" he cried indignantly. "How dare you misrepresent our position so unfairly? I have never said any of those things! I have never said one of them! Not once have I ever—"

"You haven't said the opposite," Orrin remarked in an unimpressed tone. "You have had your chance to agree to these protections for the Chinese and for yourselves and for all of us, and you have refused. I submit I am not being unfair at all, Mr. President. The logical inference to be drawn from your position is exactly as I state it. I shall so inform the Chinese."

"Mr. President," Shulatov said, and with what was quite clearly a major effort of will he forced his voice down, his breathing into a more normal rhythm, his face into calmer and less agitated lines. "Mr. President, I ask you not to draw inferences and not to prejudice our case with the Chinese by such statements. I have said we do not trust them, true, and I have said we must have certain things for our protection, true, but I have never said we wanted more war with them or had any desire to attack them again. I will never say those things, Mr. President, because they are not true."

"Very well, then," he said, "I must have your promise that I can tell them that you wish to reach a genuine cooperative agreement on these three basic points. And I must have your promise that when I return here, you *will* agree and you *will* cooperate. Otherwise, I shall have no choice but to tell them exactly what I said."

He sat back and folded his hands before him on the table, his expression impassive and unyielding. Many things crossed the shrewd face opposite: obviously a major internal struggle was under way, accompanied by little flutters down the ranks of the new government.

Finally Shulatov leaned forward, extended his hands palm upward, shrugged, smiled.

"Mr. President," he said, tone once more most reasonable, "let us not complicate matters. I have told you right along that we are willing to help stabilize the world—indeed we have no choice, we must, for the sake of Russia. So you state it as you please. We will do what we can to help. My government and I agree to that." He looked sharply along the table. "Is it not so, citizens?"

"Yes, Citizen!" murmured many voices, and many bright, eager smiles and head-noddings besought the friendship and understanding of the American side.

"Then I think," the President of the United States of America said, "that we had better go see the press and tell them what our understanding is."

"By all means," agreed the President of the United States of Russia most heartily. "By all means!"

And presently, after they had stated it in a press conference that was held to a terse fifteen minutes in the crowded Great Hall of the Kremlin, it appeared in headlines that did not erase the growing misgivings throughout the world that Earth's agony might not be over yet.

KNOX, SHULATOV REACH "AGREEMENT IN PRINCIPLE" ON ARMS CUT, END TO IMPERIALISM, INTERNATIONAL PEACE FORCE. DETAILS TO AWAIT PRESIDENT'S RETURN FROM PEKING, WHERE HE FLIES TONIGHT. SPORADIC CIVIL FIGHTING CONTINUES IN MANY AREAS OF BOTH COUNTRIES AS NEW GOVERNMENTS SEEK TO STRENGTHEN HOLD. DEATH TOLL FROM ATOMIC EXCHANGE EXPECTED TO NEAR THIRTY MILLION AS REFUGEES POUR IN.

CHINESE EXPRESS "GRAVE DISAPPOINTMENT" AT LACK OF FIRM AGREEMENT IN MOSCOW. PRESIDENT MAY FACE TOUGH NEGOTIATING IN NEXT PHASE OF PEACE EFFORT.

And that he would, he thought with a sigh as Air Force One and its accompanying press planes rose into the air above Moscow and turned east: that he would. Tougher, in all probability, than what he had faced here, now that the Chinese were receiving an increasingly clear picture of Russian intransigence.

The way was open, now, for a return to the old ways of obstruction, subversion, evasion, deceit.

The way was open for a return to war.

"Tell me," he said abruptly as they reached cruising altitude and leveled off for the long night journey, "was I too harsh, do you think? Should I have been milder? Should I have been tougher? Do I interpret the situation correctly, or am I all wrong?"

Around the little conference table in the forward cabin they stared back at him with somber faces. His predecessor, by tacit agreement, led the response.

"I think you did about as well as possible under the circumstances," William Abbott said slowly. An expression of sudden disgust touched his face. "I don't believe the tricky bastards have learned one damned thing."

"I couldn't agree more," Senator Munson said. Senator Richardson uttered a confirming grunt.

"It seems to me," he said, "that it's as though the war had never been.

The atomic exchange, the devastation, the dead—none of it ever happened. The military just took over from the commissars, and here we go again."

"What do you think, Tommy?" the President inquired. "You're our resident optimist. How did they seem to you?"

"Not good," the little Justice said in a somber tone, his normal ebullience given way to a profound uneasiness. "I kept hoping they would give you a really affirmative response. But"—his face turned bleak at the thought of what this could mean—"they did not."

"No," he said with an equal bleakness, "they did not. So where do we go from here—assuming, as Arly does, I think correctly, that what we are facing is a military take-over under the guise of a civil revolt? Should I go all out in threatening them? Or should I keep trying to reason?"

"Why were any of us ever naïve enough to think," Bob Leffingwell inquired moodily of no one in particular, "that when the Communists finally fell it would be anything *but* a military government that would succeed them? You keep a nation in chains for six decades and the machinery of oppression isn't going to vanish that easily. It's just going to acquire some new managers."

"Yes," he agreed. "So do I get tougher, or do I go along with the pretense that it's a democratic civilian government that I can maybe, just possibly, if I talk long enough and gently enough, persuade to return to sanity and join the rest of us in keeping the peace?"

"It did not appear to me," Blair Hannah remarked, "that any amount of talk and gentle persuasion is going to do the least bit of good. It appeared to me that force is still the only language they understand in Moscow."

"So what do we do then?" the President inquired somewhat tartly. "Lead a world crusade to isolate and conquer Russia? I think I made the threat strong enough to give them something to think about, but they aren't fools. Shulatov knows as well as I do that such a thing would be enormously difficult to organize, if it could be done at all. He knows time is on his side if he wants to keep on being intransigent." His face again turned bleak. "He knows it isn't on mine."

"But he knows his country is half ruined," Hal protested. "He knows its peoples are in such a state of panic that they could turn on his government tomorrow. He knows he can't risk more atomic war—"

"And even under those conditions," his father said in the same bleak way, "men will gamble on the edge of hell that somehow *they* are the ones who are going to manage the trick of continuing to be evil, and still survive. He and his government apparently think they can do it: *they think they can do it*. Somehow *they're* going to be able to cling to all their ambitions, all their deceits, all their selfishness, all their cupidity, all their defiance of the hope of nations, the word of God and the rule of love, and come out on top, free to go right on destroying the peace, destroying mankind, destroying the world."

"They must not be allowed," Justice Davis said, his face white with the strain and worry of it all. "*They must not be allowed.*"

"They will not be," the President said flatly. "Although," he added with the quick, wry honesty that had always characterized Orrin Knox, "at the moment I'm damned if I know how I'm going to stop them. . . ."

"A great deal will depend on what you find in Peking, won't it, Mr. President, sir?" the Speaker inquired into the silence that followed. "Hadn't maybe we'd best wait and see what we find there, instead of worryin' too much about it right now? Isn't there somethin' might happen there that will show us the way? Aren't we mebbe worryin' too much?"

"That's a comforting thought, Jawbone," the President agreed with a certain dryness, "and I'd like to believe it if I could."

"You got anything better to believe, Mr. President, sir?" Jawbone inquired quietly. "You got anything better to believe, now?"

For a long moment Orrin studied him thoughtfully. Then he nodded concession.

"No: you're right, Jawbone. I haven't got anything better to believe."

"Then let's hope, Mr. President!" the Speaker cried triumphantly. "Let's hope! Let's don't be mopin' and moanin' 'cause they's been a li'l ole temporary setback, a li'l ole temporary hostility, mebbe, in Moscow. They'll come around, Mr. President, they'll come around! Wait until they see you cozyin' up to the Chinese, Mr. President. Wait until they see that! They'll come around, mighty fast!"

"Is that what I'm really going to have to do, Jawbone?" he inquired moodily. "Is that what it's really going to take?"

"You said yourself," Bob Munson pointed out with equal moodiness, "that men don't change. They still understand the balance of power, even now."

"Power politics!" Hal exclaimed bitterly. "Power politics! The same old thing! Is that what he's got to do? Who's going down the same old path, then? Who's subverting peace and endangering the world and flirting with war, then? Can't *we* ever do anything better, either—even now?"

"I pray we can," Justice Davis said with a desperate gravity into the silence that abruptly fell again. "*I pray we can.*"

"Don't you think, Tommy," the President asked quietly, "that I am praying too?"

And that, essentially, was all that he or anyone could do, although their inconclusive talk went on for another half hour until he finally pointed out firmly that it was past midnight, they wouldn't get much sleep at best, and they had better try to get at least a little.

After they retired to their seats and he to the President's private cabin, he sat for a long time staring out into the blackness that enclosed the three tiny cylinders of light hurtling his party and the press toward Peking. They were on a far-northerly course to avoid passing over the major war areas, and only once was the blackness broken in the more than two hours that he sat sleepless and brooding.

Far below he saw a minuscule illumination, hazy, obscure, almost hidden: the fires of a village or hamlet, he supposed, somewhere in the vast empty reaches of Asiatic Russia. *Hello down there,* he thought. *Do you know we are passing, and are you praying too?* But no answer came back, and swiftly the pinpoint vanished.

Presently he buzzed for the White House physician, asked for a sleeping pill, received it. Presently he slept, as did, he hoped, most of his companions on this strange fantastic voyage into the future—or the past, as the fates might eventually decree. Very soon would come Peking, and they would need their strength.

2.

THIS TIME they were not met by an escort. Their captain reported contact with Peking when they crossed the border, rousing them from fitful, uneasy sleep. But no exuberant jets sailed up to meet them in the growing light, no cheerful young voices cried out an innocent enthusiasm soon to be subverted by cold and calculating elders. At regular intervals impersonal voices contacted them, at regular intervals the captain reported the contacts. It was all very businesslike, and in a way it was more encouraging and more heartening than the puppy-dog effulgence with which they had been met when they entered Russia. At least they were not being misled, however innocently, about the mood they would find when they landed.

"There's one thing to be said for starting at dead level," Bill Abbott remarked finally. "You know the only place you can go is up."

An hour and a half later, somewhat groggy from lack of sleep but shaved, dressed, decently fed and in a reasonably optimistic mood, they saw beneath them the endless drab roofs and occasional shining temples and palaces of Peking; and presently, to further terse commands from the airport, their convoy came down, the doors opened, from the press planes the reporters and photographers swarmed forward, and at the top of the steps the President of the United States appeared and stood for a moment, silent and unsmiling, looking out into the gray, hazy, ice-cold morning.

Below he saw a red carpet, a group of men as drab and gray as the morning. He stared at them, they stared at him: no false exuberance, no artificial welcome here. The only sounds and the only signs of life came from the photographers shouting and tumbling over one another in their frantic competition. He suddenly found the atmosphere as stagy, in its way, as Moscow's false and phony airport camaraderie. He permitted his face to register annoyance, holding the expression long enough for the cameras to record it. Then he lifted his head with a sharp impatience and started down the steps. As if on signal a rickety band off to one side began playing "The Star-Spangled Banner," and suddenly smiling men were stepping forward to hold out their hands and welcome him in polite and carefully modulated phrases.

A minute later, standing before the inevitable microphones alongside the lean-faced, impassive man to whom the rest deferred and whom they introduced to him as "President Lin Kung-chow," he heard words of greeting that immediately presented him with the problem he faced.

"Mr. President," Lin said in a smooth and thoroughly adequate English, "on behalf of the peoples and the new democratic government of the United Chinese Republic, we greet you and welcome you gratefully to our land.

"We are pleased that you take the time to visit us, and we hope your stay will be fruitful for China, for peace and for the world.

"We are especially pleased," he said, and his voice, still smooth, turned subtly harder and more emphatic, "that you have first visited Moscow and then have come to us, because it has given you the opportunity to find out the attitude there. That attitude, Mr. President, does not promise well for the future of world peace.

"Here in China, where we have suffered great casualties and devastation because of the unprovoked sneak atomic attack of the former Russian government, we had hoped that the new government would be as dedicated to peace and understanding between our two countries as we. Alas, Mr. President, we do not find this so. We have followed the results of your visit to Moscow with great interest. They have not encouraged us, Mr. President. We feel a deep concern for the world because of the way you were treated there. We feel little has been learned by the new leaders of Russia. We regard this as a great tragedy for us and for the world—but most of all, for the great Russian peoples, who will only suffer further if their new leaders do not permit them to make peace with us.

"Mr. President"—he turned and looked directly at Orrin, who with considerable effort was managing to conceal his concern and remain impassively listening—"we pledge you the full cooperation of the United Chinese Republic in your great journey for peace. We will work with you, Mr. President. Together we will lead the world back to sanity. Together we will make peace. You may rely on that."

And with a grave little bow he gestured to the microphone and stepped back. Orrin stepped forward and stood for a moment as calm and impassive as his host. There and wherever men watched his face and heard his voice, a profound hush fell. There raced through his mind several courses of action. He decided, characteristically, upon one as blunt and straightforward as his host's.

"President Lin," he said, his words booming through the misty air while a wan sun struggled unsuccessfully to break through, "my colleagues and I appreciate your cordial and constructive greeting.

"We, too, Mr. President, have been profoundly disappointed by the attitude we found in Moscow." There was a movement of satisfaction at his side, a sudden intake of breath from many in the media. "We, too, had hoped to find a more open and more willing approach to the problems of peace. We, too, had hoped there would be more understanding of the true situation that faces the world, more genuine willingness to give up old attitudes and forge new approaches to it. We came away, like you, disturbed and apprehensive.

"But, Mr. President"—and though he was speaking to the Chinese he knew his message would not be lost upon Shulatov and his colleagues, to whom it was really addressed—"we are not discouraged. We are especially not discouraged now that you have spoken. We are, in fact, much heartened by your willingness to cooperate with us and with all the peoples of the earth in our great universal search for peace. We are glad you are with us. Together, as you truly say, we will achieve our goal.

"It is my intention, Mr. President," he said, and now he was again addressing his host and the message was not lost there, either, "to return to Moscow after I leave here. I shall convey to the leaders of the United States of Russia the results of our talks. I shall relate to them the examples of your willingness to cooperate. I shall tell them of your unselfishness, your vision, your statesmanship. I shall tell them of the sacrifices you will gladly make for the common cause of humanity. I shall tell them how China has rejoined the world of sane and responsible nations. I will tell them of her sane and responsible leaders.

"Then, Mr. President, I think we may find a different attitude in Moscow. Inspired by your example, I believe the United States of Russia will join us in our search for peace. I believe then we will all be together, and together I believe we will achieve our common goal of peace and safety for all men, happiness and prosperity for all nations.

"Mr. President and gentlemen of the United Chinese Republic, we stand ready to assist in any way we can. Let us begin."

He turned and shook hands gravely with his host, turned back and waved for a moment, smiling now, at the applauding crowd of officials, colleagues and newsmen; caught the eye of Walter Dobius, crowded up close beneath the rim of the platform, and exchanged a glance in which Walter said as clearly as if he had spoken aloud, *You hope!* and he replied with a grim yet jaunty determination, *Yes, I hope!*—and presently was in a limousine, followed by his party, the Chinese and the press, being hurried away along ramshackle, winding streets, past undemonstrative but politely attentive crowds, to the American Embassy.

Because of the night flight, they would spend most of the day in bed. Promptly at 8 P.M. they would meet their Chinese counterparts in the embassy for the first of their projected talks. Their attitude was slightly more optimistic, but here, also—wary.

"Mr. President," Lin Kung-chow said gravely after the introduction of his Cabinet, "I first would like you and your friends to see photographs of some of the things China has suffered in these past few days. Then you will better understand us and why we feel as we do on certain things. Later, if you have time, we should like to fly you and the press to various points in the devastated areas so that you may see for yourselves."

"We may not have time," Orrin said, "but if we do, we shall certainly accept. In the meantime, I think it would be very helpful to see your pictures."

"Thank you," Lin said. He pressed a button under the table edge. A group of youthful army officers entered and set up a screen and two projectors, one for slides, one for movies. The room settled down, the lights went off, a machine began to whir. The slides came first.

For approximately fifteen minutes flattened buildings, shattered cities, wasted farmlands, bloated livestock, sagging bridges, leveled hills, crossed the screen to the steady *click-click!* of the projector. At several points, including panoramic shots of absolutely leveled Suchow, Lanchow and Harbin, Lin raised a hand, the projector stopped, the images remained for terrible, lingering moments on the screen. For the rest it was a steady parade of dreadful devastation, Hiroshima and Nagasaki multiplied a hundredfold.

Then came the movies. They too were approximately fifteen minutes in length. Gaunt specters crossed the screen in rapid procession, some in panic, some in shock, some literally torn in half, some mere bloody scraps of flesh hanging on what used to be human frames. Before the showing ended, Tommy Davis, Hal, Blair Hannah and four of the Chinese had to leave the room. It was only by the exercise of the sternest self-control that the rest did not follow. After the final frame—another long pan of Harbin with the still-wriggling stump of what had once been a baby looming large in the foreground—the lights went up to reveal two dozen very shaken men. For several long moments no one stirred. Finally President Lin spoke in a choked voice heavy with emotion.

"This is what happened to China. It can never be forgiven. Never!"

"I don't blame you for feeling that way," the President said, his own voice showing the strain of what he had just seen, "but you must remember the same thing happened to the Russians, too."

"They began it!" Lin said sharply.

"Did they?" Orrin asked. "Will anybody ever really know?"

"They began the use of nuclear weapons!" Lin said in the same sharp tone. "There is no dispute about that."

"That is true," the President conceded. "But don't you think they have paid for it a hundred times over?"

"A thousand would not be too much," Lin said coldly. "And I do not understand that you found any evidence of reformation as a result of it."

"Some," the President said. "Not as much as we would have liked, but some. I can tell you one thing, however"—and his tone grew as cold as Lin's—"if you persist in vengeance and vindictiveness—if you are unable to realize that both your peoples, and in a sense all peoples everywhere, have suffered equally—then there will be no hope for peace and this mission is aborted before it begins. Is that the news you want me to take back to Moscow? Is that the message I am to report to the world? *More* of this insanity? Is that what you want, Mr. President?"

"No," Lin said harshly, "it is not what China wants. But China does want the guilty punished. There can be no lasting peace without that."

"Then there can be no lasting peace," the President said crisply, "because if you have no charity, no compassion and no willingness to let bygones be bygones in the realization that all have suffered equally, then there is no foundation, no bridge, no nothing. You might as well begin fighting again and I might as well go home."

"There can be a peace with justice," Lin said, his tone more reasonable, and along his side of the table impassive men of one skin color but many diverse physical types nodded earnest agreement. "That is the only kind of peace there can be."

"Then perhaps our first objective," the President said, his tone more friendly, "should be to define justice. Perhaps if we can agree on that, we can go from there. What is it, in the view of the new government of China?"

"A Russian apology, before the world, for the nuclear sneak attack upon us," Lin said promptly. "A pledge never to do it again. Russian reparations to rebuild our cities and care for our people. A reduction of arms so that Russia will never again be able to wage war. An abandonment for all time of Russian imperialism. A Russian guarantee of our borders forever."

"And what will China give in return?"

"Why should China give anything, Mr. President? China is the aggrieved party."

"I repeat," he said sharply, "we will never know who began this war, which started in Africa under circumstances that will never be clear. I grant you," he continued firmly as Lin gave him a stubborn look and started to interrupt, "that the Russians—the old government, the Soviet government—launched the first atomic attack, and that it was a sneak attack. But that came within the context of a war already begun, and I suspect that the only reason China did not strike first was because she was not quite prepared to do so."

"China would never launch nuclear war!" Lin snapped indignantly.

"China did not launch it," the President said flatly, "and that is the only fact I know. . . . In any event, it happened. I can tell you on the basis of my visit to Russia, Mr. President, that China did her part once the issue was joined. You inflicted very heavy devastation upon Russia, too, you know. The Russians could show you slides and films just as dreadful. What I am here to find out is: *Where does it stop?* Where do we put the period and say, 'The End'? When do we start forgiving and start building the new peaceful world that mankind now wants? You and the Russians have absolutely terrified us, Mr. President. You have opened the abyss that has been waiting at our feet for nearly four decades. We want to know how to close it over again. We want to bury it forever and go forward in peace. If we can't do that, it will open again and next time we will all be swallowed into it.

"What will you do to help prevent that? That is what I want to know."

"We have defined justice," Lin said, and for the first time there came into his eyes something of the infuriating blandness that had met them in Moscow. "And we have described how it may be achieved. Perhaps that is a good point from which to begin trying to answer your questions."

"Mr. President—" he began earnestly. Then he dropped it and his tone became blunt and pragmatic. "Very well, I will tell you where we will begin. You say you want a reduction of arms so that Russia will never again be able to wage war. Let us start with reduction of arms, Mr. President. It is the main thing I have come abroad to achieve. Let us talk about it."

Lin gave him a polite little bow, looking every inch the self-composed Mandarin, and suggested softly:

"Please."

"Very well," he said again, unable to keep annoyance from his tone. "You want Russia disarmed, the world wants Russia disarmed. Russia wants *you* disarmed, the world wants you disarmed. Let's get down to specifics right now. We'll start with your navy, since that's the smallest element in your military machine. You have one small aircraft carrier, thirty destroyers, seven submarines, a handful of support craft. Suppose we keep it at one aircraft carrier, but reduce you to five destroyers, four submarines—"

"Who will reduce us, Mr. President?" Lin inquired, still softly, while down his side of the table impassive men leaned forward in polite inquisitiveness.

"The world will unless you do it yourselves," Orrin said tartly. "The world is not willing to put up with any more nonsense from the big powers on this score. Of course, Mr. President, I hasten to add that you will not be alone in this. Russia will do the same. We will do the same. There will be a general disarmament, I believe, all around the world. As the largest, we three will yield the most, which is only right."

There was a silence while his hosts looked carefully at one another and then turned their impassive gazes once more upon him. Finally Lin Kung-chow leaned forward slightly and uttered two words:

"Russia first."

"Nobody first," he said firmly. "All of us together."

"Russia first," Lin repeated, suddenly as firm. The President, too, leaned forward.

"Mr. President," he said calmly, "this will not work. You are past this kind of bargaining. There is no more bargaining left, for you or Russia. You and the Russians sit atop your charnel houses and you both try to bargain. It is past that. History has moved on. A new world was born this week: it will never return to the old. That new world demands that you disarm, that Russia disarm, that we disarm. None of us can withstand that demand."

"Russia first," Lin Kung-chow said quietly. "Russia first."

"No!" he said sharply. "Together. *Together!*"

"*Russia first,*" Lin said, and abruptly, with another graceful little bow, pushed back his chair and stood up. All along the table his countrymen gracefully did the same. "Mr. President, you and your party are still tired, one imagines: our discussions can only weary. Tonight I think we have reached an impasse, I trust only temporary. Perhaps tomorrow morning we can reach a better understanding. The wise man does not exhaust himself in such a circumstance: he seeks refreshment, of the body and of the spirit. We have prepared a banquet for you in the Great Hall of the People—which we now know as 'the Great Hall of the Republic'—and there our many friends of the press are waiting for us. Let us go. Tomorrow we will meet again. Perhaps then we can find agreement. Come"—he bowed again with a graceful gesture—"let us go."

"At ten o'clock tomorrow morning," the President said pleasantly, "my colleagues and I will be here prepared to sign an agreement reducing armaments drastically for our three nations."

Lin bowed again with a smile equally pleasant.

"As you like," he said. "Now, come! They are waiting for us."

And in the Great Hall, responding easily to the insistent questions of the anxious media, both of them managed to put what he thought of as "a good first face" on the matter. But his countrymen of the press were more experienced and quicker to jump to disillusionment after their sojourn in Russia: they were not fooled, desperately as they all joined him in hoping for meaningful agreement. Instinct told them there was trouble, and not even a ten-course banquet as lavish as anything they had been tendered in Moscow was enough to forestall the unhappy pessimism of their reports.

PRESIDENT, CHINESE FAIL TO REACH UNDERSTANDING IN FIRST MEETING. BOTH SIDES CLAIM "CORDIAL ATMOSPHERE" BUT U.S. SOURCES SAY REAL AGREEMENT "NOT IMMINENT." DISARMAMENT BELIEVED TO BE MAJOR STUMBLING BLOCK. REPORT CHINESE INSISTING ON RUSS CONCESSIONS BEFORE THEY MOVE.

MOSCOW ASSAILS "DELIBERATE OBSTRUCTION AND HOSTILITY BY NEW PEKING GOVERNMENT." WARNS "RUSSIAN PATIENCE NOT INEXHAUSTIBLE." SHULATOV CLAMPS ON PRESS CENSORSHIP, BANS FREE MOVEMENT BY INTERNATIONAL RELIEF COMMISSION. SAYS IT WILL BE PERMITTED TO DISPENSE AID THROUGH MOSCOW ONLY.

CAUALTIES CONTINUE TO SWAMP ALL FACILITIES IN BOTH COUNTRIES AS OUTBREAK OF TYPHUS REPORTED. DOCTORS FEAR PLAGUE.

"Mr. President," he said next morning, "my colleagues and I have prepared, as I told you, a formal disarmament agreement for the signatures of your government, the Russian government and our own. Prior to discussing that, however, I should like to explore with you a little, if I may, your state of mind concerning what has happened to you. How seriously do you and your government regard it, how much impact has it had upon you, do you have any human emotions about it, any worry, any fear, any unhappiness? Or has it all been just an unfortunate incident that you are already forgetting?"

For a moment Lin Kung-chow looked at him with an unbelieving stare. Then he leaned forward and spoke with an open intensity that made no attempt to hide itself behind bland words and bamboo curtains.

"Mr. President!" he said sharply. "Mr. President! Surely you make jokes with us, surely you make a mockery. We have shown you the pictures, we have told you our attitude toward those who did these horrors to us. *It is our country* which has been devastated, Mr. President. Why must you make jokes about our 'state of mind'?"

"I am not making jokes at all," he said calmly. "My question is prompted solely by the fact that yesterday you seemed not at all concerned with the possibility of starting it all up again. You appeared to be so intent on vengeance against the Russians that you paid no attention to the broader implications of what the two of you have done to mankind and the jeopardy you have us all in if you should resume fighting. It all seemed very irresponsible to my colleagues and myself. We decided we would like to know whether you really care about what has happened, or whether it is all some sort of bloody game that you can resume at will without regard to the safety of the whole world."

"Mr. President," Lin said angrily. "Mr. *President*—" and stopped, genuinely at a loss for words.

"Then perhaps," he suggested calmly, "you should reconsider your attitude of yesterday and give more careful consideration to the realities we all face. . . . Now, for the time being, I'd suggest we put aside the question of disarmament and turn to the other matters that must be decided. I don't know how much you know of what has been going on outside your country in the past few days, but you may have heard that I made several specific proposals for things that might be done to re-establish and maintain world peace.

"Several are outside your competence, involving such things as the Suez and Panama canals. There are other proposals, however, in which your direct involvement is necessary. Perhaps we can discuss them now."

"Yes," Lin agreed, his tone easing a little, his colleagues relaxing a shade of their intent and wary concentration.

"With the proviso," the President added, "that we will come back to the disarmament question after we have completed these other matters."

"We will discuss it," Lin said.

"More than that," the President said pleasantly. "We will sign it. So, then: the other proposals. The first is the International Relief Commission which has been established under United Nations control to aid the victims in the two countries. Money, medical supplies and medical teams are already on their way from the other nations of the world, the commission has been established and is already beginning operations. It is desired that the United Chinese Republic also pledge as much as it possibly can to the efforts of this organization. Is that agreeable?"

"We are doing everything we can to assist our own people," Lin said.

"The commission is an international effort, a common pool. You may find yourselves also assisting the Russians, as they may be assisting you. Is that thought too abhorrent for you?"

There was a pause, an obvious tightening of tension across the table.

"We should of course require that we be consulted on any such action," Lin said finally. "You must understand that our first obligation is to our own people."

"*You* must understand that the nations of the world with great generosity are also making great contributions to help 'your own people.' We expect the same generosity from you and from Russia."

"Have you got it from them?" Lin inquired quickly. "The news from Moscow would not seem to say so."

The President shrugged and managed to make the gesture look entirely convincing.

"The news from Moscow," he said calmly, "is not the final word. Right now we are interested in the news from Peking. We expect your contributions to go in the common fund. You will be represented fully on the commission. It will make the distributions. All right?"

"I think we must wait," Lin said politely, "for the final word you mention. When we know what that is, then we shall know better what we must do. For the time being, I should think we would wish to distribute foreign aid through our own administrative channels here in Peking, just as they are doing in Moscow."

"They are not doing it yet," he snapped, thinking: *Damn the Russians.* "Nor will they do it. That is bluff. I suggest to you that the bluff will be called and I suggest that you are in no position, either one of you, to dictate the terms of this humanitarian effort. Let me ask you, Mr. President: does your country need this help or does it not? It can always be withdrawn, you know."

"It will not be withdrawn," Lin said calmly. "The United States has so conditioned the world to these humanitarian impulses in recent decades that it could not possibly be withdrawn. Your own people would condemn you for a heartless monster if you used aid as a club against us, Mr. President. Is that not the case?"

"My own people and the peoples outside your two countries, Mr. President, are in such a state of fear and worry at this moment that they will condone almost anything that will force an end to this conflict. Make no mistake of that."

"Nonetheless," Lin said softly, "I think aid will not be used in such a fashion." He looked along the table at his solemn colleagues. "But let us not argue. We will consider it." Vigorous nods agreed.

"Please do," he said dryly. "It would be of great assistance."

"Assuredly," Lin said politely, and the President could see that irony was going to get him nowhere, if, indeed, it was even understood. He made his tone deliberately matter-of-fact.

"Also in the international area, the United Nations has created an international peace-keeping force, to which most of the nations are contributing men and matériel, which will take positions along your border with Russia for as long as necessary to guarantee a permanent peace."

There was a silence. The faces across the table remained carefully bland. It was obvious, however, that a great deal of thinking was going on.

"Where along the border?" Lin inquired cautiously.

"Wherever the United Nations command deems advisable," he said crisply. "I believe the plan is, at intervals of no more than a hundred miles, with regular patrols out fifty on each side."

"It is a very long border," Lin observed, echoing his counterpart in Moscow.

"Whatever is necessary will be provided."

"Who would establish the locations?"

"The United Nations command. Who did you think?"

"It would appear to us," Lin said slowly, again almost word for word repeating Shulatov, "that the governments of China and Russia should do it, in agreement with one another."

"What reason do we have to believe you could agree?" the President asked bluntly. "Your disagreements have brought this horror on the world. Are we to believe you could agree now, on something so sensitive?"

"It should be done by us," Lin said stubbornly.

"Both your countries will be represented on the international command," the President said. A shrewd little glint came into his host's eyes.

"By how many?"

"By approximately one hundred observers each," he said flatly, and ignored the audible grunt of dismay that echoed down the opposite side of the table. "Mr. President," he said, leaning forward. "Do you really think that you and your opponents are in any position to bargain with the world on these matters? You are the aggressors. You are the warmakers. You are the destroyers of the earth, unless we can all stop you. You are no longer great arrogant independent powers who can toss around the very life of this planet as though it were a bauble for you to play with. You have been called to account, by your own actions. It is time for you to be responsible to the world. The world must have guarantees that you *will* be responsible. And so it will be done."

For several moments after he sat back, there was silence in the room, the Chinese staring at the Americans and the Americans staring back.

Finally Lin spoke with a cautious articulation.

"I would assume that the details will be discussed in the Security Council."

"No doubt," the President said, "but of course you know the veto no longer exists."

"*No!*" Lin said in open dismay, and all down his side of the table a genuine consternation broke the determined calm.

"Yes," he said, in the same words he had used to Shulatov. "The Charter was amended the night the former governments fell. There is no more veto."

Here, as in Moscow, there was a prolonged silence while the news was absorbed; and here, as in Moscow, there was, finally, the same response.

"It will be considered," Lin said. "Are there other things?"

"A formal statement of withdrawal from Gorotoland and Panama; recognition of the new governments now in power, a pledge to support the democratically formed governments which will presently be elected there under United Nations auspices."

Lin nodded, his expression for the moment friendlier.

"There is no problem. The new China has no more interest in imperialistic adventures. You may tell the world, Mr. President, that from now on we intend to stay home."

"Good!" Orrin exclaimed with the same exaggerated relief he had used in Moscow, and briefly they were all united in a wry amusement. "In that case, then, you will have no difficulty in subscribing to a formal pledge that you are abandoning permanently, once and for all, imperialistic, expansionist policies everywhere in the world—that you formally renounce all desire and ambition to intervene in the affairs of other nations—and that you will devote your funds, your energies, your purposes, to the peaceful development of your own society within your own borders."

Abruptly the amusement ceased. A very careful silence followed. Into it Lin finally spoke in a very careful voice.

"It is one thing, Mr. President, to renounce imperialist adventures far from home in the Third World area. But . . . other matters . . . closer at hand . . . perhaps require . . . more consideration. For instance: I believe even the great United States, which is now indisputably the world's most dominant power—indeed, who else is there? —requires along her borders the presence of friendly people, does she not? So we, too, have an interest—quite aside from our Russian border—in Indochina, in Japan, in India, in the Himalayan states. Can the United Nations guarantee us friendly governments there? If not, we would not wish to pledge ourselves not to be concerned."

Once again, as he had in Moscow, the President tried to put it in perspective. But he realized his difficulties more vividly now than he had then: these were people who literally still did not know what was going on in the outside world.

"Mr. President," he said earnestly, "I understand that your own concerns here in China have very naturally prevented you from keeping up with the state of mind of the rest of the world. I realize it is only my word and that of my colleagues which can tell you of it. But the nations are terrified, Mr. President. Their peoples are frantic with fear. You do not understand what the fact of atomic war has done to the world. None of us has designs on anything but achieving a peace that will at last be really genuine and really lasting. Everyone has renounced conquest. The nations want only to live in peace with one another. No one will threaten you. Your borders are quite, quite safe."

"Now," Lin said, his tone faraway and sad. "*Now* they are safe. *Now* the nations feel this way. When will they change, Mr. President?"

"When they see that China and Russia are *not* changing," he said. "Then they will change, Mr. President. Do you wish to assume that responsibility?"

"Our responsibility is China," Lin said simply, as Shulatov had said about Russia. "We can only consider these things in relation to that. . . . We will consider it," he said finally. "It must be considered. . . ."

"Please do," the President said quietly. "With great care, and with great prayerfulness, because so much depends upon it. . . . And so we return," he went on, and on both sides of the table tension and uncertainty were instantly present again, "to the question of disarmament."

"Mr. President," Lin said quickly, "before we do, if I might venture to suggest: this has been a long and tiring session this morning. Again, we have prepared a meal for you and our friends of the press." He smiled. "A noontime meal, not too strenuous, but ample. Why do we not meet the press and have our meal, and then we can meet again, say, at four P.M.?"

"Before we meet with our colleagues present, Mr. President," Orrin countered quietly, "I should like to meet with you alone. Could we do that at four and meet with our advisers at six?"

For a moment his host looked uncertain, wary and exceedingly cautious. Then he thought better of it, relaxed and smiled.

"I see no harm."

"I hope I see positive good," the President said. "Fine. Then let us go and talk to the press, and then we shall eat."

"Yes," said Lin, still smiling. "Let us do that."

At the press conference something of this final little show of amicability transmitted itself to their questioners. The headlines indicated some improvement: though if truth were known, the President thought grimly, there really was none.

SECOND PEKING MEETING GOES BETTER. KNOX, LIN SAY DISCUSSIONS "MAKING PROGRESS." BOTH SIDES APPEAR MORE CONFIDENT OF AGREEMENT. MOSCOW WARNS AGAINST "ANY ATTEMPT TO FORGE U.S.-CHINA ALLIANCE AGAINST RUSSIA." FIRST PURGE TRIALS START IN KREMLIN WITH FORMER PREMIER TASHIKOV ON STAND.

REPORT RIOTING IN BOTH COUNTRIES AS WOUNDED DEMAND INTERNATIONAL AID SUPPLIES. U.N. OFFICIALS STILL UNABLE TO REACH WAR ZONES.

"Mr. President," he said, "I wanted to talk to you privately because I do not think you yet realize the absolute necessity of reaching a real agreement here, particularly on the subject of disarmament. You simply do not realize the state of the world."

"I realize the state of China," Lin said with a grim little smile. "That is quite vast enough for one man's comprehension."

"Yes, I agree with that. Nonetheless, you must look beyond. You must relate it to all the nations and to the desperate condition of mind of all the peoples. I told you the world is terrified, Mr. President: the word is not too strong. All the distant memories of Hiroshima and Nagasaki that were becoming faint, all the thoughtless learning-to-live-with-it that had become such a habit when people thought about nuclear warfare, all the comfortable belief that it-can't-ever-really-happen-because-mankind-is-too-intelligent-to-destroy-itself were wiped out in a moment when the first bombs fell in Asia."

"The first bombs from Russia," Lin said, smile fading, grimness growing.

"Yes!" the President said sharply. "The first bombs from Russia. But only because China didn't get there first. . . . In any event," he said more calmly, ignoring the sudden angry look his last words had produced, "the bombs fell, hell opened, Doomsday crashed upon the world—or would have, had the two governments not thought better of it and drawn back. But not before they had given us all a graphic example of what Doomsday could be like had things gone just one step further. I think the world is united in believing that if you resume fighting, that one step further will be taken and presently we will all be sucked down into the vortex you will have created. Your former governments were the governments of war. You are supposed to be the governments of peace. That is why I am here, and it is to that I pin my hopes. But, Mr. President, it cannot be done without your cooperation."

"Why ours?" Lin demanded harshly. "Why not the Russians'? Why must you try to bring pressure upon *us?* It is because you have not been successful in applying it to the Russians. That is why."

"Explain to me, Mr. President," he said softly, "why it is necessary for me to bring pressure upon *anyone*. Why must I argue with you? Why must I argue with Shulatov? Why are not the facts of your own two devastated countries enough? What more do you need, complete and total annihilation of the earth before you will believe that peace is necessary?"

"We have told you we believe peace is necessary," Lin said, unmoved, "but it must be peace with justice. We have told you what justice is. Why must *I* argue with *you?*"

"Because that way lies just one result," he said, forcing himself to speak with a patience he did not feel, so many were the hobgoblins of the world that screamed silently around his head in the quiet and secluded room in the American Embassy. "That way lies exactly what I have just said: complete and total annihilation of the earth. What becomes of China and Russia then? What becomes of 'justice,' as you call it, which is really only vengeance and hatred and the same old vindictive path to disaster? What becomes of all your pomp and pretense? Nothing, Mr. President: *nothing!* China will be a desert. Russia will be a desert. America and all the rest may very likely be a desert. The globe itself may burst. Who will ever know of Lin Kung-chow and Orrin Knox and Alexei Shulatov then? We do face Doomsday, Mr. President. Someone must be brave enough to take the first step to lead us back. If you have any conscience at all—if you *really* care for China, and it isn't all just talk—then consider that, Mr. President, I beg of you: consider it!"

And for several minutes, while they stared at one another with a gaze that did not flinch or falter on either side, Lin did.

At last he made a little shrugging gesture with his hands and let them fall before him on the table.

"Mr. President," he said quietly, "*you* are a brave man, to lead the world as you are, to come to Moscow and to Peking as you are. I believe you when you describe the feelings of the nations. I believe your sincerity when you express your own feelings. I also agree"—he sighed, and for the first time in three days the faintest gleam of hope entered the mind of the President of the United States of America—"that others must follow your lead in taking the steps back from Doomsday. But, Mr. President, *we cannot do it alone*. There must be equal response from Moscow. And so far"—he shrugged again, this time with a bleak and desolate air—"you have not been able to secure it?"

"Nor can I," he said evenly, "without some gesture of agreement from you. Can you do nothing at all to help us, Mr. President? Out of all of China's ancient wisdom, can humanity receive no help in its awful hour?"

"But why must *we*—?" Lin began; and the President interrupted gravely:

"Because that is how it is. Because someone must have charity—someone must be the leader—someone must be brave. Can you do it?"

Again there was a long silence, again their gazes held. And again, at last, there was the little shrugging, desolate, unhappy gesture from his host.

"You have a disarmament agreement," Lin said, voice low. "What does it say?"

"Yes," he said, taking it from his coat pocket with a hand that noticeably trembled, pushing a copy across the table. "We may amend the preliminary language as you like, but the essential clause is the agreement of China, Russia and the United States to reduce all armaments at least one-half by six months from now; at least two-thirds a year from now; and to small defense forces only, thereafter. All such reductions to be accomplished under United Nations supervision. All excess armaments, where not destroyed, to be turned over to the United Nations for an international peace-keeping force in which all three signatories pledge themselves to participate fully whenever and wherever needed."

Once more silence held while Lin Kung-chow studied the paper at great length; at one point started to push it back, then thought better of it and drew it back to study again; and finally folded it carefully, placed it precisely in front of him and looked up.

"All I can do at this point," he said slowly, "is agree in principle that China will give these proposals the most serious consideration"

—he raised a cautionary hand as the President shifted uneasily in his chair—"at a conference to be held in Geneva, starting one week from today"—the President started to smile—"*providing*"—the President's expression froze—"the new government of Russia makes the same pledge when you return there tomorrow."

With an air of great relief, the President finally did smile and, rising, extended his hand, which Lin shook with a quick, hard emphasis.

"Mr. President," Orrin said, his voice filled with an emotion he made no attempt to hide, "I thank you indeed. That is not everything—but it is much; and using it as a foundation, I think together we can build a peace. I shall take back the word to Moscow, and I anticipate that there your wonderful example will produce the results for which the world prays."

"I hope so," Lin said with a return to bleakness, "for if it does not, your fears of Doomsday may yet come true."

"They cannot," he said firmly, "for mankind has a destiny better than that."

"I hope so," Lin said again in the same bleak way. "I hope so. Shall we call our colleagues in and tell them?"

And after they had done so, with much hand-shaking, congratulating, hope-expressing and inner doubts and reservations, they again met the press; and this time the public emphasis was all positive, and around the world men's hearts lifted and men's hopes soared.

DISARMAMENT! KNOX, LIN REACH AGREEMENT IN PRINCIPLE ON SPEEDY REDUCTION OF FORCES, PROPOSE GENEVA CONFERENCE TO SETTLE DETAILS. PRESIDENT TO RETURN TO MOSCOW TONIGHT.

RUSSIANS WITHHOLD COMMITMENT, SAY THEY MUST "STUDY ALL PROPOSALS CAREFULLY BEFORE REACHING DECISION."

FIRST PLAGUE VERIFIED IN MANCHURIA.

Again they left an airport, again his tired but indomitable caravansary took flight on yet another lap of its gallant journey: from Cathay to Muscovy, he thought, with an ironic little inward bow to history's romantic echoes—from Cathay to Muscovy, and what would brave Marco Polo find there?

Not too much to encourage him, he feared, studying the intelligence reports that lay before him in his private cabin as the scattered lights of Peking faded away below. The picture was still chaotic in all the vast war zone, and in the capital of the new Russian state there appeared to be no lessening of the hard line that had openly developed since his departure. Shulatov and his colleagues were running true to form, apparently: in some ways it seemed there had been no change, so smoothly and swiftly had the new military government moved into the patterns of the old Communist regime. Censorship, suppression, intransigence, defiance, a harsh suspicion of the outside world and a harsh rejection of its desperate yearnings for peace—like the Bourbons, the Russians seemingly had learned nothing and forgotten nothing. It demonstrated, he supposed, what the Communists had always maintained: that the human mind could indeed be permanently conditioned and that once it was programmed in a certain direction it would continue on that line regardless of circumstance.

Yet surely the lessons of the war could not have been dismissed so cavalierly; surely the hourly evidence of disaster could not be so summarily ignored. The country was still in near chaos, the walking wounded were still moving west in a vast, bloody tide, the ruined cities were hardly beginning to move with life, and the life, such as it was, could only be described as ghastly. Virtually insuperable burdens weighed upon the new government, monumental tasks so great that it could not possibly achieve them without the assistance of the world and a condition of universal peace—and yet, like animals snarling from a cave, Shulatov and his colleagues were busy defying the opinion of the world and the peace of mankind, seeking old, outworn advantages in an old, outworn context that no longer existed except in their own suspicious imaginings.

Nonetheless, of course, they *were* imagining, and they were conducting themselves as though the imaginings were still real. Wrongly but sincerely, they believed. As long as they did, the world had a terrible problem—he had a terrible problem. And he was not at all sure that Lin's concession, meager and tentative as it was, gave him much to maneuver with.

In a sense the Chinese, too, were living in the old context. They did not appear to be quite as paranoid as the Russians, but almost. As nearly as he and his colleagues had been able to ascertain, the new Peking government was civilian, not military, and that perhaps gave its members some small handhold upon humanity that seemed to be lacking in Moscow. But it was fragile at best, and it was only as a great personal tribute to him that Lin had taken even the small step he had. If it were rejected in Moscow—if there was no answering glimmer of humanity—if no sound of recognition came back across the roiling void—then God help us all, he thought grimly: God help us all. For the time was growing very short and the margin for error was eroding very rapidly away, not only in Cathay and Muscovy, but everywhere.

Already, the intelligence reports disclosed, there was a recrudescence of self-interest, a resurgence of suspicion, a return of greed, a revival of moral and ethical cupidity. France the eternal loner was already secretly at work trying to sell arms to the breakaway satellites along the old Soviet European border. Rumania and Hungary were already indicating interest. Poland and Czechoslovakia, learning of this, were turning in desperation to Britain. Britain had as yet given no answer, but the reports indicated that Her Majesty's Government might not be averse to the idea. In the Middle East the collapse of the Soviet regime had been followed by revolts in the six Communist Arab oil satellites: West Germany and Japan were helpfully rushing "technicians" and "advisers" to the Gulf. Pious India was secretly moving troops into position all along the disputed Chinese border areas and had already issued secret ultimatums to Nepal and Bhutan which clearly foreshadowed the rapid demise of those tiny remaining Himalayan kingdoms and a probable drive to seize border areas. A Japanese fleet was secretly steaming toward the Kuriles, another toward revolt-torn Taiwan. The Communist government of Cuba had been overthrown and the United States, the CIA reported to him proudly, was secretly preparing to rush arms and aid to the rebel forces. This at least he could handle, and he sent an immediate and toweringly angry order to stop all such plans at once, for it was desperately important that the hands of his own country be clean if he was to continue as peacemaker. Elsewhere in South America, in a sort of weirdly irrational reflex from the terror of the atomic exchange, Brazil had begun to skirmish with Paraguay, and Chile and Argentina were exchanging ultimatums. In eight African countries, governments which heretofore had been to some extent restrained by world opinion were systematically slaughtering every man, woman and child of their minority tribes.

So the time was exceeding short and getting shorter. It was not only the leaders of Russia who had learned nothing and forgotten nothing: many governments were in the same condition. The peoples of the earth might be sincerely and frantically terrified, sincerely and frantically willing to renounce all the old patterns for the sake of universal peace, but many of their leaders were not. And very soon, if the leaders were permitted the time, they would be able to persuade their peoples to relax, forget, resume their old hatreds, their old fears, their old mistrusts and their old foredoomed ways of dealing with one another.

For a few precious seconds out of mankind's long and twisting history—which he no longer thought of as peaks and valleys, but rather a long, sinuous, sidewise progression that moved from here to there along an almost level plain, never sinking very much, never rising very much, just managing to go from point to point erratically as greed and passion directed—there was a chance for genuine peace. The greatest chance there had ever been, born out of the greatest terror. But it would not last—it would not last. Unless it was seized now, it would vanish forever and the world would turn back again into the dark and dreadful night from which it very likely would never be able to emerge again.

He sighed, a lonely and desolate sound. The three bright cylinders with their hopeful cargo hurtled on through the night, back across devastated Russia to Moscow again. How could he make men *see?*

3.

"WELL?" SHULATOV INQUIRED, and all down the table the members of his government leaned forward with a politeness as attentive and bland as his. "What news do you bring us from Peking, Mr. President?"

"I bring you, as you know," he said quietly, "a disarmament agreement. It has been signed in hope and good will by the President of the United Chinese Republic and the President of the United States of America. We hope it will speedily receive the signature of the President of the United States of Russia."

"What are its details?"

"You do not know," he said pleasantly. Shulatov gave him bland look for bland look, and shrugged.

"Hints—speculation—newspaper reports. Nothing official. We have been waiting for you, Mr. President, to tell us."

"So I shall," he agreed, still pleasantly. "So I shall." He pushed a copy across the table. "The standard preliminaries, as you see, including the sentence, which I believe to be true, that *'The signatories recognize that this may in all likelihood be the last chance the world will ever have to achieve a lasting peace.'* Then into the gist of it, which is essentially: the agreement of China, Russia and the United States to meet in Geneva in one week to begin work on reducing all armaments by at least one-half within six months; at least two-thirds by a year from now; and to small defense forces only, thereafter. All such reductions to be accomplished under full and unrestricted United Nations supervision. All excess armaments, where not destroyed outright, to be turned over to the United Nations for an international peace-keeping force in which all three signatories pledge themselves to participate fully whenever and wherever needed. Final details to be worked out at the conference."

"Is that all?" Shulatov asked with a little smile.

Outwardly perfectly calm and perfectly amicable, the President returned the smile.

"It is quite enough if all of us will abide in good faith by its provisions. Does the United States of Russia intend to?"

"Mr. President!" Shulatov exclaimed, with another smile and that bland shrugging motion the President had come to dislike intensely. "Give us time, give us time! We have not even signed it yet. We have barely even *read* it yet. We need time to study, to consider, to analyze, to prepare ourselves for this great, revolutionary change in the world's way of doing things. We need time, Mr. President, *time!*"

"The President of China and I signed in half an hour," he remarked, and down his side of the table his colleagues stared at the Russians with a bland skepticism of their own. This apparently rankled, for there was an uneasy stirring and Shulatov responded with a sudden sharpness.

"I do not care what the President of China did!" he snapped. "I am the President of Russia and it is Russia I am concerned with!"

"As I am concerned with America," Orrin said in a tone that grated, "and he is concerned with China. Yet with both these great concerns we were still able to master our suspicions and our fears and do what we believed best for our own countries and the world. Why is this difficult for you, Mr. President? Are you afraid of something?"

Shulatov gave him a sudden sharp glance.

"I am afraid of the secret alliance the United States has apparently made against us with the new government of China."

"There is no alliance!" the President exclaimed angrily. "*There is no alliance.*"

"So you say," Shulatov remarked with an insolent politeness.

"So I say," he agreed, mastering his annoyance with a great effort and speaking in a matter-of-fact tone. "So, Mr. President, if you will please affix your signature, we will move on with preparations for the Geneva conference. In the meantime I have been authorized by the Secretary-General, who telephoned me in Peking last night just before I left, to lay before you his insistence that both the International Relief Commission and the international peace-keeping force be permitted *at once* to operate freely and independently in your country in order to do the jobs the world wants them to do."

"Did you convey this to the President of the new imperialist regime in China?" Shulatov inquired, and again it was all the President could do to keep his temper. But somehow he managed to speak calmly, though the Russian's choice of words had sent a shiver down the American side of the table.

"I did indeed," he said.

A shrewd little gleam came into Shulatov's eyes.

"And what was his response?"

"He said he would wait and see what you decided to do."

"And I," Shulatov said with a sudden grim satisfaction, "will wait to see what *he* decides to do. So it appears we must *all* wait awhile on those two issues, does it not, Mr. President?"

And along his side of the table his colleagues nodded brightly and chuckled agreement with one another.

For a long moment Orrin studied them, while through his whole being there rushed a wave of dismay and disgust so great that he thought for a second it might physically paralyze him. The Russians were so mistaken—so utterly, eternally, forever-and-ever Doomsday-mistaken—that he wondered how he could ever get through to their closed and terrifying minds.

Perhaps he could not. But he knew he must make one last try. It had worked, not much but enough to keep hope alive, in Peking. It might—just might—work here. If it did, he might yet be able to build upon it.

"Mr. President," he said slowly, keeping his voice calm, his manner relaxed but earnest, "you and Lin Kung-chow and I, quite literally, I believe, hold the fate of the world in our hands. Up to now when men have said this or been told this it has been a cliché. But at this moment, with atomic war having occurred, with its terrible consequences still ravaging your two countries as they will for many months, with the whole world waiting petrified to see whether it too must be drawn in if hostilities resume, the cliché is no longer cliché but reality.

"Upon me, and upon Lin Kung-chow, this fact imposes a great responsibility which we are trying, however falteringly and imperfectly, to live up to. *He* has great doubts, *I* have great doubts. But we are trying.

"Both of us recognize that it will be many weeks, possibly months, possibly years, before all the obstacles to a permanent peace can be removed. But we must try. We must begin.

"The same responsibility, Mr. President, rests upon you.

"These three issues are the start. All are fundamental. If they are solved, all else will fall into place. The International Relief Commission *must* be allowed to move freely, to distribute its aid independently of either your government or the Chinese government; otherwise it becomes no more than a political arm of those governments. The international peace-keeping force *must* operate independently in a buffer zone between you; otherwise it will lose all effectiveness in preventing further war should either of you be so unwise as to start it. Disarmament *must* be accomplished, and very drastically, if war is not to recur. And it *must* be done with complete and open inspection and control by the United Nations, because that is the only way to guarantee that it will be done honestly and effectively.

"There is no way around these three propositions, Mr. President, unless it is to go around them and straight back to war, devastation, chaos, the final ending of the world. You are an intelligent man, your colleagues are intelligent men. Surely you see that.

"Why, then, will you not join President Lin and me in making the effort? It is true it requires great courage. It is true it requires great faith. It is true it requires patriotism—not just patriotism to our own countries, which is easy, but the most difficult patriotism of all, which is patriotism to the Idea of Man. We must keep alive humanity, Mr. President. Our own countries will get along all right if we do that.

"President Lin and I have made a small beginning. We beg you to join us. The whole world begs you to join us. Can you not find somewhere in the heart of Mother Russia the courage and the faith that will let you do it, and so save us all?"

While he spoke, the faces across the table were a study in impassive politeness, showing nothing, giving nothing, yielding nothing. When he concluded there was a lengthy moment during which the expressions did not change. Then Shulatov leaned forward and spoke with a controlled but implacable fury that was instantly echoed in the frowns and theatric glares of his colleagues.

"Mr. President! Do not come here and appeal to Mother Russia! Do not come here and seek to confuse us with fine words and false appeals! We know the reality of it, Mr. President, we know how the world is. *We* must guard Mother Russia, Mr. President, not you. *We* must protect our people, not you. We will take care of Russia, Mr.

President. You and the Chinese gangster may worry about the rest of the world, if you like: we pity you, for you will lose your own countries in the process. We will never lose Russia! *Never!*"

Again, and for the last time, their eyes held in an angry, unwavering, unyielding grip. Then Orrin broke the furious silence, managing somehow to speak quietly despite the whirling fire-storm of emotions that raked his being.

"Mr. President, you are a fool and your government is a fool. I will not say, 'May God help you,' because you do not deserve it and I believe He knows you do not deserve it. I will simply say that my colleagues and I pity you as we have never pitied men in all our lives, because you are signing your death warrant. And the thing that makes it so utterly horrible is that you are very likely signing the death warrant of the world as well. . . ." He stood up abruptly, pushed back his chair. His friends did the same. "Now," he said, breathing heavily but managing to keep his voice steady, "I shall go and talk to the press."

"Talk to them, then!" Shulatov cried, leaping to his feet in a blind rage which was echoed by the shouts, groans and furious murmurs of his equally athletic colleagues, who jumped up all around him. "Tell them your lies, damned American, and see if we care! *See if we care!* We despise your lies! We *despise* them!"

But the world cared, even if the Russians did not; and very shortly men and women everywhere were in the grip of a fear made even more terrible by the fact that for just a little while they had seen in Orrin Knox's mission the gleaming hope that fear might be conquered at last.

U.S.-RUSSIAN TALKS END IN "COMPLETE DISAGREEMENT." NEW RUSS GOVERNMENT SCORNS KNOX DISARMAMENT PLEA, REMAINS ADAMANT IN REFUSAL TO PERMIT INTERNATIONAL AID, PEACE-KEEPING FORCE. PEACE HOPES FADE AS WORLD FEARS NEW WAR. PRESIDENT TO RETURN TO PEKING FOR FURTHER "URGENT CONSULTATIONS" WITH CHINESE.

PLAGUE SPREADING INTO SIBERIA.

"Orrin," William Abbott said quietly, shaking him out of his quick, exhausted nap at the American Embassy before takeoff for Peking, "the Chinese are calling."

"Yes?" he said, instantly awake. Faint and wavering but distinct enough to be understood, a tiny voice said in broken English, "Mr. President?"

"Yes, yes," he said impatiently. "What is it?"

"This is the Foreign Minister. President Lin wishes me to tell you that he does not wish to see you."

"You tell President Lin," he said with all the authority of a very tired but very determined man, "that I will arrive in Peking tomorrow morning and that I will come to the Presidential palace at ten A.M. to see him. I shall be accompanied by the world press. If he wishes to turn me away at that point, he may do so. But I will be there. Good day to you."

And without waiting for response he replaced the receiver with a decisive emphasis that probably hurt the Foreign Minister's ears even over that distance.

"Is he running out, too?" Bill Abbott asked quietly.

The President sighed.

"We're getting boxed, Bill. I don't know what we're going to do about it."

"Keep trying," the ex-President suggested.

"Oh, yes," the President said.

The face was very still, expressionless, completely frozen, completely closed. They talked alone for the last time, without preliminaries or pretense.

"Why are you here?" Lin asked.

"You know why," he said.

"He would not agree."

"He would not agree."

"Then why are you here?"

"Because our two countries must continue to seek peace, regardless."

"We cannot, as long as Russia remains an active threat on our borders."

"We must."

"We cannot."

"Mr. President," he said, "I come back to what I said before. The fate of the world demands that we do. We have no alternative. It does not matter that the Russians will not join us. We have the world behind us. We need no more."

For a moment the frozen mask broke, a human face looked out. A sudden piercing glance came his way.

"Why do we not join together," Lin suggested softly, "and destroy

Russia, you and I, while she is weak and unable to withstand the two of us?"

"*No!*" he said with a horrified revulsion he made no attempt to conceal. "*No!*"

The mask closed again, the human aspect disappeared.

"Very well. It is '*No!*' for us, also."

"That is your final word?"

"That is our final word." Very suddenly the mask cracked again. "Why would they not—?" Lin cried with a naked anguish. "Why would they not—why can't the world—why—?"

The mask re-formed as abruptly as it had shattered and again he said in a cold and distant whisper:

"That is our final word."

"Very well," Orrin said with a dragging sigh that seemed to come from depths below depths. "Very well."

"What will you do?" Lin whispered.

"I will go home to America," he said with an infinite tiredness. "I will go home."

But of course, being himself, and being the President, he did substantially more than that.

KNOX ASKS URGENT SESSION OF UNITED NATIONS AS PEACE JOURNEY ENDS IN FAILURE. MOSCOW, PEKING ADAMANT IN REJECTING ALL NEGOTIATION ATTEMPTS.

PRESIDENT TO CONFER WITH U.S. MILITARY CHIEFS IN HAWAII ON WAY HOME. ABBOTT, TOP CONGRESS LEADERS JOIN HIM IN CALL FOR IMMEDIATE TEN-BILLON-DOLLAR INCREASE IN DEFENSE FUNDS.

WORLD TENSION GROWS AS RUSS AND CHINESE REPORTED MOVING NEW TROOPS TO EDGE OF ATOMIC WAR ZONE.

No official saw them off at Peking airport, as none had seen them off in Moscow. Cars appeared, baggage was loaded, they were driven by mask-faced men through deserted streets. Behind them came the press buses, their occupants for once subdued and silent. The mission begun in such desperately high hopes was ending in profound depression, uncertainty and fear.

Around the small conference table in Air Force One they faced one another with the air of veterans of a long and tiring siege, though actually they had only been gone eight days.

"I feel," he remarked, "as though we've been gone forever. And yet"—he paused, his eyes widened, looking into troubled distances —"I don't see what else we could have done. We had to go."

"Certainly we did," Arly Richardson said, almost impatiently. "You had to make the attempt."

"As you have to keep on making the attempt," William Abbott said, "at the U.N.—at home—everywhere there's the slightest chance."

"Yes," he said. "Bob"—he turned to the Secretary of State—"I want you to issue at once, as soon as you get back to Washington, the full transcripts of our formal meetings with Shulatov and Lin. I will give you detailed memos on my two private talks with Lin, which are to be included."

"They won't like it," Bob Leffingwell said. The President smiled without much humor.

"I'll manage to stand that. I want the world to know exactly what we all said and exactly what it is up against in these two new governments."

"It should create some sympathy for China, I would think," Bob Munson remarked. The President nodded.

"I would certainly think so. Which may come in useful later."

"You aren't going to take sides, are you?" Hal asked in some alarm.

"I don't know what I'm going to do yet," he said with a sudden impatience of his own. Then he smiled and softened it. "I'm sorry, Hal, I don't mean to take your head off. I can't conceive at this moment of taking sides in a military sense, but there's still an enormous task ahead in the U.N. and in mustering public opinion both at home and abroad. The fact that China at least made a small gesture in the direction of peace is one of the things that may be helpful. God knows," he added wryly, "I'm going to need everything I can muster."

"Mr. President, sir," Jawbone said, "I think ole Arly and I can get you that new defense bill through in about two hours flat when we get back to the Hill, don't you, Arly, now?"

Senator Richardson, who obviously did not altogether enjoy being referred to as "ole Arly," replied with a certain annoyed dignity:

"I don't think there will be the slightest trouble on the Senate side, do you, Bob?"

"Not a smidgin," Senator Munson agreed. "We can get it in and out of committee in an hour and then I think it will almost—almost—pass without debate. Except that I'm sure both you and I will want to give our personal impressions of what went on over there, as I suppose you and Bill will too, Jawbone."

"Oh, yes," the Speaker agreed. "I want to tell 'em, sure enough. That ole Russian, shruggin' and smirkin', and all!"

"Well," the President suggested, "don't make it too lurid. Just stick to the facts, they're ominous enough. I think in Hawaii, Blair, that I'd like you to stay with me for my talk with the Joint Chiefs of Staff. I'd like the rest of you, with the exception of you, Bill, to split off and return to Washington and get to work on it at once. I'd like you to come on to the U.N. with me, Bill, if you will. I'm going to fly direct to New York from Hawaii, I'm not going back through Washington."

"Fine," the ex-President said, and the Secretary of Defense nodded agreement. He gave the President an appraising glance and spoke with the candor of long political association.

"What are you planning with the Joint Chiefs? Just window dressing?"

The President gave him an equally candid smile in return.

"Essentially, yes. There's no great need for them to come, of course, but I want to arrive day after tomorrow in New York with both a top-secret meeting with them, and the new defense bill, under my belt. This will be a signal to our friends in Moscow and Peking, I hope, that if they want to play the old game, the United States is ready. Not that we intend to, of course, because I am determined"—his face became grim as he repeated—"*I am determined* to find peace, somehow, out of all this. But it isn't going to hurt to use a little psychological warfare. I need clout and I intend to have it."

"We'll get it for you, Mr. President, sir!" Jawbone assured him earnestly. "We'll get it for you!"

"I appreciate that," he said, without irony.

"Actually, Dad," Hal said soberly, "what *can* you do?"

He stared down at the table for a moment before replying. Then he sighed.

"Yes, exactly so: what *can* I do? Put the case—make it as strong as possible—hope the nations are still terrified enough so that I can swing them behind me—and get the word back to Moscow and Peking that if they do not cooperate in both creating and keeping the peace, they will suffer real and immediate consequences of a nature they will not be able to withstand."

"In other words," Hal said bleakly, "more war and bigger war and final war."

"Not if I can get the support of the world," his father said stubbornly. "Not if the nations will get behind me."

"It's a gamble," his predecessor observed with a sigh of his own.

"I have to gamble, Bill," he said simply. "It's all that's left."

Understanding this, they fell silent and stared soberly at him, who had to carry the frightful burden of the gamble, with concern, affection and the desperate resolve to help him in every way they could, so much depended upon that one determined mind and that one undaunted heart.

PRESIDENT, JOINT CHIEFS ANNOUNCE HAWAII ACCORD ON "ALL NECESSARY STEPS TO STRENGTHEN U.S. POSITION." ARMED FORCES PUT ON IMMEDIATE WORLDWIDE ALERT. CONGRESS RUSHES NEW TEN-BILLION DEFENSE FUND THROUGH BOTH HOUSES IN THREE HOURS.

NATIONS GATHER IN NEW YORK FOR TOMORROW'S U.N. SESSION.

"MAJOR SKIRMISH" RUMORED ON RUSS-CHINESE BORDER.

4.

"THIS SPECIAL EMERGENCY SESSION of the General Assembly will be in order," said Brazil, this month's president, with a smart rap of the gavel. "It is my privilege and honor to present to you the President of the United States of America."

There was a roar of applause as he appeared on the podium. It was quickly stilled. Desperate and worried, the eyes of the world devoured him. He stood staring out for a moment in his characteristic thoughtful way while the final whispers and rustles died. He began to speak in a level, almost impersonal voice.

"Mr. President, my colleagues of the United Nations: I come to you after spending ten days in another world.

"I wish that I could report to you that from it I have returned with peace for all mankind.

"Honesty prohibits such a claim.

"You all have followed the reports of my mission in the world press. Most of you, I am sure, have read the transcripts, released yesterday by the Secretary of State, of the meetings my colleagues and I had with the President of the United States of Russia and the President of the United Chinese Republic.

"They were not," he said, and his words were received with a long-drawn sigh as though they had not quite believed it, had been clinging to some last, wan hope, until he spelled it out for them, "encouraging.

"They were, in fact, disturbing, dismaying and terribly depressing.

"They placed upon me, and upon you, the burden of deciding where the world proceeds next in the search for peace. Apparently, for the time being at least, the world is not going to receive the willing cooperation of the new governments of Russia and China.

"Therefore, what do we do now?

"It first occurred to me to urge a worldwide quarantine of these two governments until more moderate counsels prevailed within their ranks. On reflection, that seemed a self-defeating idea. Intransigent as they are, dangerous as they are in their present mood to the entire world, still it would seem best to maintain a dialogue of some kind, keep open all the channels we can, keep talking in some fashion, however unsatisfactory, in the hope that before long we shall be able to persuade them to cooperate in the things that must be done.

"Providing you and I stand firmly together, I do not think this will take very long. Both countries, as you know, are still close to chaos. The hold of the new governments is shaky at best. Monumental problems of human rehabilitation and physical reconstruction face them both. They need the world as much as the world needs them. It is my hope that they too are reflecting, and that before long they will join willingly in the great endeavor of universal peace.

"As a first step in achieving the world stability which is absolutely imperative, I move, Mr. President, on behalf of the American delegation, that the General Assembly forthwith and unanimously declare that the vacant seats on the Security Council and in the General Assembly formerly held by the Union of Soviet Socialist Republics and the People's Republic of China be filled immediately by the United States of Russia and the United Chinese Republic."

A great excited burst of cheering and applause welled up from floor and galleries, and all across the great garish room delegates from many countries were on their feet shouting, "Second!" and "Vote!"

"You have heard the motion of the distinguished President of the United States of America," Brazil said when he had finally restored order with vigorous bangs of the gavel. "All in favor—"

"AYE!" roared the Assembly, galleries and all.

"All opposed—"

But of course none were, and into the babble of happy excited voices Brazil shouted, "It is unanimously approved and ordered and the rosters of the Security Council and the General Assembly are again complete with the addition of the United States of Russia and the United Chinese Republic!"

And once more there was prolonged and happily excited applause, finally dying down into a humming and optimistic murmuring into which his next words came, as he intended they should, like a bucket of cold water.

"And now, my friends of the United Nations"—and something in his voice instantly hushed the room—"having taken that generous and worthy action, we must return to the realities.

"I have had, as you know, extensive discussions with the Joint Chiefs of Staff. I have placed the armed forces of the United States of America on worldwide alert. I have requested, and the Congress has approved with a unanimous bipartisan vote, an emergency defense fund of ten billion dollars.

"Why have I done these things, when no enemy exists in the world to challenge the United States?

"Because I feel that such actions may contribute to a better working relationship with the new governments of Russia and China. Because I believe that for the moment, hard though it is to imagine, they still think things can be settled by the same old outmoded, warlike means that have brought them to the sad condition they now suffer. Because I believe that this United Nations must be, if you like, the watchdog—the active watchdog—of the peace.

"You know that the new governments have refused to allow the humanitarian activities of the International Relief Commission, to which we all are contributing, to proceed independent and unhampered. You know that they have refused to permit the entry into their countries of the international peace-keeping force, to which nearly all of us have also contributed. You know that they have refused the offer of the United States for a graduated and speedy reduction of all armaments to simple defense forces, and the creation of a permanent United Nations Peace Force to keep the peace everywhere.

"Therefore measures stronger than words may be necessary to secure their cooperation. We of the United States of America have made certain that we will be able to contribute to those measures if it be the will of the United Nations to invoke them."

He paused, took a sip of water. He could sense an uneasy stirring in his audience, for the first time felt a resistance growing. He had expected it. His concluding words were calm, confident, deliberately impervious.

"Mr. President, my colleagues of the United Nations: it is the thought of my government that substantive action along these lines should originate in the Security Council, and therefore we are now formally asking for such a session, to be held at two P.M. tomorrow afternoon. This will allow time for the delegates of the United Chinese Republic and the United States of Russia to arrive and take their seats. It will also give all members of the United Nations time to consider the course of action we should adopt. My delegation will have a resolution to introduce which we hope will offer a reasonable basis for discussion and decision. In due course we will offer a similar resolution in the General Assembly. We hope they will win the approval of all of you."

He paused and looked out thoughtfully once more before concluding.

"My friends of the United Nations—my friends of the world: this is a grave hour, undoubtedly the gravest ever to confront humanity. The very life of the globe is at stake. I have tried, alone save for my trusted advisers, to resolve its terrifying imperatives on your behalf. Unfortunately my individual efforts—what might be called 'the first round'—have failed. It is my hope that the 'second round'—in which the world will stand united behind, and insist upon, the things that must be done to create universal peace—will be successful.

"With your help and support, peace will prevail.

"It will prevail because it must.

"Otherwise we all are truly lost."

And with a grave bow to Brazil, he stepped quickly from the podium and disappeared into the corridor behind, from which he was rushed away by the Secret Service to his heavily guarded penthouse in the Waldorf-Astoria. Behind him he left a United Nations restless with uncertainty and a world press seething with speculation. Here and there from overseas came the first open intimations of a hesitation, a wavering, a pulling back. As he had foreseen, time was running out on the world stage as it was apparently running out in the war zone. He found to his gratification, however, that his own media were still solidly behind him.

"We find ourselves," the *Times* summed up for them all in the stately tones he had not heard for ten whole days, "in complete agreement with the address of the President to the United Nations—as we also find ourselves in agreement with the measures he has taken to put the United States in readiness to cooperate with whatever action the United Nations may decide upon in the special emergency session of the Security Council.

"There was a time when the President's policy of military preparedness might have been regarded as saber-rattling. Viewed in the light of the tragic failure of his peace mission to Moscow and Peking, it appears no more than necessary prudence. It also opens the door to bold and affirmative United Nations action to save the peace—if the U.N. will *be* affirmative, and if it will be bold.

"With great generosity and statesmanship, the President led the way in welcoming the new Chinese and Russian governments into the world body. Now generosity and statesmanship must be demanded of those governments. If they do not respond, other measures may be necessary. Ticklish though they might be, we applaud the President's courage in facing them unblinking and unafraid. . . ."

"This special emergency session of the Security Council," said Australia in a voice that reflected the enormous tension in the room, "will be in order. Have the delegates from the United States of Russia and the United Chinese Republic presented their credentials?"

"No, Mr. President," the Secretary-General said gravely, "they have not."

"Are they on their way, does anyone know?" Australia inquired.

Norway raised his hand.

"I have been asked by both governments to announce that their delegates have landed at Kennedy Airport and are on their way here at this moment. They are expected to arrive momentarily."

"Very well, then," Australia said, "if there is no objection, we will take a fifteen-minute recess pending their arrival. I would suggest delegates remain near at hand, because we wish to resume as soon as they are here."

During the interval the excited buzzing that had begun when the United States delegation took its seats again filled the room. The President himself was here, walking in at the head of his colleagues, the ex-President, the Secretary of State and Ambassador Jason. The President and William Abbott looked rested and calm, Robert A. Leffingwell a little preoccupied as befitted one who had just flown up from Washington. Ceil was dressed in a gracefully tailored deep-blue suit which set off her blonde beauty to perfection.

She looked, as the London *Times* murmured to his New York counterpart, like a piece of bone china, an exquisite figurine. "But one," the New York *Times* remarked, "which isn't going to break." "None of your group looks that way," the London *Times* observed. "They all look tough this morning." "It's a tough world," the New York *Times* said. "Right," the London *Times* agreed. "What are they going to propose that we do about it?" "I haven't quite got the scoop, yet," the New York *Times* confessed. "Orrin is playing this one very close to his vest. Apparently no copies have been distributed and none are going to be until he speaks." "You mean we have to fall back on good old-fashioned reporting?" the London *Times* inquired wryly. "For shame!" "It may not be easy, either," the New York *Times* said. "Lord knows what he's going to come up with, but I suspect it's going to be serious." "I suspect so," the London *Times* said with a trace of gloom. "Damned difficult situation all around, isn't it? *Damned* difficult." "We still have faith in our Orrin," the New York *Times* said with an attempt at lightness. "Although"—lightness vanished—"we think he may be treading on very dangerous ground." "Who isn't, these days?" the London *Times* asked with a shrug less carefree than it looked. "Who isn't . . . My, everybody's really here today, aren't they? Most of the Assembly must be on hand, too." "They want to see," the Louisville *Courier* said from the row behind, "whether Orrin is going to blow us up, close us down or just give us a lecture." "More than a lecture, I suspect," the London *Times* said. "I say—" he added excitedly, as there was a sudden stirring, an instantaneous rush of excitement, a tumble of photographers surging backwards into the room, dancing frantically ahead of the small gray-clad group that entered slowly but purposefully from a door to the left. "Is that the Chinese?" "I believe it is," the *Courier* confirmed with equal excitement. "But who is it? Do you know what Lin looks like? It couldn't be he, could it?"

In the chair Australia too obviously had some doubt, rapping automatically for order but looking uncertain until one of the gray-clad figures detached himself from the group now settling into the section formerly occupied by the People's Republic of China and came forward to whisper in his ear. There was an instant attentive hush.

"Ladies and gentlemen of the Council," Australia said, voice trembling with emotion, "it gives me great pleasure to welcome the President of the United Chinese Republic and his delegation."

Applause burst, rose, roared. Everyone was standing in instant ovation, faces were smiling, doubts were momentarily submerged in a wave of friendly greeting. It had barely begun to subside when from the door to the right there came another tumble of photographers, an instantaneous focusing of attention, a new wave of excitement and tension. There entered another small group of men, these clad entirely in blue-serge business suits. Solemnly they came forward amid the watching hush to take their seats in the section formerly reserved for the Soviet Union. Once again a messenger went forward, once again Australia made the announcement in a voice strained with excitement.

"Ladies and gentlemen of the Council, it is my great pleasure to welcome the President of the United States of Russia and his delegation."

Again delighted applause burst, rocked, roared. Again there was standing ovation, happy faces, eager smiles.

"Well," Orrin murmured behind his hand to William Abbott as they finally resumed their seats, "I got them this far, anyway. At least they're in the same room."

"That's something," the ex-President agreed with a wry little smile, "although I wouldn't count on its being too much."

"No," the President said. "I'm not."

And with a slow and deliberate stare he looked along the circular table until his eyes found first Lin's and then Shulatov's. Neither gave him the slightest sign of recognition, so after a moment he gave to each an obvious and sardonic little bow, which set off a new ripple through the gradually subsiding room.

("Ah, *ha!*" said the London *Times,* and the New York *Times* agreed somberly, "'Ah, *ha!*' is right.")

But for a few fragile seconds more the illusion was preserved that there might be some chance of harmony here, even though the eyes of the three principals did not meet again, nor, in fact, did the eyes of the warring two ever meet at all. It was with an increasingly nervous air that Australia delivered his formal welcome.

"Mr. President," he began, and corrected himself with a hurried little laugh: "Mr. Presi*dents!* It is my official honor and great personal pleasure to welcome you, your delegations and your two great countries to the Security Council of the United Nations. I think I may take the liberty of speaking for the Assembly as well, and for our various subsidiary and associated units, when I say that we are all delighted to have you here.

"You will find here many nations and many peoples disposed to be friendly and helpful to you in this time of universal crisis. You will also find"—and his voice became more solemn and more emphatic as his nervousness vanished in the desperate earnestness of the moment—"an overwhelming desire to achieve world peace and to join, everyone together, in building a new and better world.

"In that endeavor, Mr. Presidents, we welcome, we hope for, we pray for and we dare to think we may expect the friendly and willing cooperation of the United Chinese Republic and the United States of Russia."

He paused and looked expectantly at Lin and Shulatov. Expressionless, both looked back. Tension in the room suddenly returned a hundredfold. He resumed in a tone that momentarily seemed nervous again but grew increasingly stronger and sharper as a genuine indignation took over.

"Mr. Presidents," he repeated, "we hope for, we pray for *and we expect* the friendly and willing cooperation of your two great countries. It is in that hope and expectation that we welcome you here today. The peoples of the world join your own peoples in hoping that out of our deliberations may come a new dawn for the world.

"Because, I assure you, we are sick unto death of constant night.

"On behalf of my colleagues and myself, and of all the nations, I greet you. We await with interest any comments you may wish to make upon assuming your seats. . . . Mr. President?" And he looked at Shulatov with an expectant gaze that did not permit evasion.

After a long moment the Russian shifted in his chair.

"Thank you, Mr. President," he said in a voice almost inaudible, since he did not lean forward to the microphone. "The government and peoples of the United States of Russia appreciate your words."

There was a silence. It lengthened. Finally Australia asked blankly, "Is that all?"

But Shulatov, face still impassive, made no reply. And presently, his voice showing now an outright annoyance, Australia turned to Lin.

"Mr. President," he said, trying to keep the impatience out of his voice but not succeeding altogether, "do you wish to respond?"

Again there was silence, accompanied by rapidly rising tension. Then Lin leaned forward to his microphone.

"On behalf of my people and government," he said in a soft, rapid voice, "we thank you for your greeting."

And he too sat back and said no more, while again the silence grew.

"Very well," Australia said at last, a noticeable tension in his tone. "Then the Chair recognizes the chief delegate of the United States of America, who has requested permission to speak."

("It doesn't look good," the New York *Times* whispered glumly to the London *Times*. "Maybe better this way," the London *Times* whispered back. "It may make it easier for your man to rally support for what he wants to do." "Don't bet on it," the New York *Times* responded still glumly. "This whole thing could get away from him in a minute.")

Of this, of course, he had long been aware, and so it was with more than his usual deliberation that he looked slowly around the watching circle of delegates, looked thoughtfully around the room, looked for a second squarely into the cameras in the booths above, returned his gaze finally first to Shulatov and then to Lin, neither of whom, as before, responded in any way. Then he leaned forward to his microphone and began to speak in a slow and measured manner.

"I had thought, Mr. President," he said, and his tone was cutting, "that here in these surroundings, at least, we might find a little less intransigence and a little more gratitude for what the nations of the world are doing in welcoming thus tolerantly to our councils the two governments who still have it in their power to make fatal mistakes and destroy us all in the process."

There was a murmur of surprise, agreement, some scattered concern at his bluntness.

"Mr. President," he went on calmly, "I find it impossible to believe that the President of China and the President of Russia, with both of whom I had the most confidential and candid discussions within the week, should come here today and not understand the seriousness of the moment. I know they do, Mr. President. Therefore I think they are being deliberately contumacious in their responses to your welcome and in their apparent attitude toward the vast majority of mankind which this United Nations represents.

"I think they should understand," he said softly, "that this is not wise. . . .

"Mr. President"—so abruptly that the change of mood threw them slightly off balance, as he intended, he took a sheet of paper from his vest pocket and put on his glasses—"I have here a resolution which I shall read to the Security Council, and then request a vote." And calmly he began, while along the circle Shulatov and Lin, abandoning their elaborate pretense of disinterest, leaned forward intently to listen.

"Whereas, it is imperative for the peace and safety of the population of Earth that the present conflict between Russia and China be speedily ended, and that there be no more war; and,

"Whereas, the United Nations has established an International Peace Force to achieve these purposes; and,

"Whereas, the United States of America has voluntarily offered to undertake an immediate disarmament program to reduce its armed forces to a defense-force level and contribute to the International Peace Force all funds, troops and matériel which the United Nations command may require for the successful completion of its purposes in China and Russia and its permanent mission of peace; and,

"Whereas, the United States of America, acting on behalf of the United Nations, has approached the governments of the United States of Russia and the United Chinese Republic seeking their agreement to an equal disarmament; and,

"Whereas, such agreement has been deliberately and contumaciously withheld by those governments; and,

"Whereas, those governments have even gone so far as to ban the International Peace Force from its peace-restoring mission on their territories; and,

"Whereas, the world no longer has the time or patience for such frivolous, irresponsible and inexcusable defiance of the will of mankind—"

He paused, and all over the room there was a gentle and unanimous sigh of tension.

"Now, therefore," he said, and his tone grew stronger and his expression cold as he looked directly at Lin and Shulatov and bit off the words, "*be it resolved:*

"That the United Nations, acting through the Security Council, hereby deplores and condemns the intransigent refusal of the governments of the United States of Russia and the United Chinese Republic to cooperate with the International Peace Force and the plan for disarmament of themselves and the United States of America; and, further,

"That the United Nations, acting through the Security Council, hereby calls upon the governments of the United Chinese Republic and the United States of Russia to begin negotiations with the United States of America tomorrow at ten A.M. in the city of Geneva, Switzerland, on the details of disarmament; and, further,

"That the United Nations, acting through the Security Council, hereby calls upon the governments of the United States of Russia and the United Chinese Republic to admit within their territories, for the purposes of restoring and keeping the peace, the International Peace Force, immediately, forthwith and at once; and, further—"

("Where's the stinger?" the London *Times* whispered. "It's coming," the New York *Times* responded. And so it was.)

"—Be it resolved that if the governments of the United Chinese Republic and the United States of Russia do not immediately, forthwith and at once comply with the terms of this resolution, the International Peace Force, backed by the entire resources of all the members of the United Nations, be directed to enter the territories of those two governments immediately, forthwith and at once and take whatever actions may be necessary to restore and keep the peace for the safety and preservation of all mankind.

"Mr. President, I ask for a vote on the resolution."

And he sat back in the midst of sudden exclamation, babble and uproar, as members of the media dashed out to file bulletins, members of the audience exchanged excited comments, delegates turned to one another and to their staffs in great agitation and concern, and along the circular table both the President of the United States of Russia and the President of the United Chinese Republic began shouting for recognition with an angry and frantic haste.

To their outraged cries Australia took plenty of time to respond; and when he did, it was in a dry and hostile tone.

"Yes?" he inquired. "The distinguished delegate from the United States of Russia has changed his mind and now wishes to speak to us, does he? The distinguished delegate from the United Chinese Republic is similarly moved, is he? What do the distinguished delegates wish to say to us?"

"Mr. President!" they cried simultaneously—paused—glared at one another—tried again simultaneously—paused—glared again.

A little nervous tittering began in the room. Australia intervened.

"Allow me," he said with an elaborate politeness. "Strictly on a basis of seniority, because the immediate past government of Russia entered this body prior to the immediate past government of China, the Chair recognizes the President of the United States of Russia for remarks which we all trust will be brief."

"Mr. President," Shulatov said, and he was visibly shaking with a rage that was unmistakably genuine, "it is impossible for the government and the great peoples of Russia to sit here in my person and accept the insults and crudities of the American President. It is impossible!

"We are not your slaves, Mr. President! We are not the playthings of the United Nations! We are not children, to be pushed about in our own country by imperialistic adventures sent to us in the guise of 'peace-keeping'!

"No, Mr. President! We are a strong people and a proud people, and we do not accept this kind of bullying! We defy the United Nations, Mr. President! We will fight if you cross our borders. We will fight, and we still have much left with which to do it. Do not forget that, Mr. President! Many planes, many men, many guns, many tanks, many bombs—yes, atomic bombs! We still have some left, Mr. President! We do not want to use them upon the world, but we will, Mr. President, we will, if you treat us in this fashion! We promise you! *We promise you!*"

And glaring defiantly around the table he slumped back in his seat and turned his back upon Lin, who now received recognition from the Chair.

"Mr. President," he said in his softest whispery voice, and instantly the room, in tumult after Shulatov's defiant challenges, hushed to a deathly quiet.

"It is not the purpose of the United Chinese Republic to engage in wild accusations or violent threats. However, I should be remiss as head of the new Chinese government were I not to say that any such violent incursion into our territory as is proposed by the President of the United States of America could only be viewed with the greatest misgivings by the Chinese people. In fact, Mr. President, I do not believe my government could restrain them from expressions of resentment which might almost be termed extreme. We, too, still have many men under arms, many guns, many tanks and many atomic bombs. We, too, might find ourselves impelled by circumstances to take retaliatory action which would be regrettable.

"We submit, Mr. President," he concluded gently, "that the possibility is worth consideration before hasty and ill-advised decisions are made here that might be regretted later."

And he too sat back, folding his arms carefully across his chest and, for the first time, glanced blandly in the general direction of his antagonist from America, who now leaned forward with an air he hoped was sufficiently skeptical and impatient to shore up the wavering he expected.

"Mr. President," he said, permitting a certain scorn to enter his voice, "I suggest to the Security Council that we not be intimidated by the threats of two governments which are literally on the ropes. I have been to Russia and China, I remind this body, and it is all these two governments can do at this moment to keep control around Moscow and Peking and a few other of their major cities. Their populations have received terrible blows, many of their cities are in ruins, famine and pestilence stalk their lands, civil rebellion still flares in many areas and they themselves could still be overturned in a day as they overturned others—with my help, I remind them. It is for this reason that the International Peace Force must act, and act at once. It is for this reason that it will receive no really effective opposition in either country at this moment. To threaten that it will is to indulge in empty bluff. And the two Presidents know it.

"To them I would say, 'If you don't want this to happen, the way to prevent it is very simple:

"'Disarm. Cooperate. Be reasonable. Work with us and with each other. Help us keep the peace.

"'All attempts to secure your cooperation by other means will cease instantly the moment you indicate your willingness to help us. . . .'"

He turned directly to Lin and Shulatov.

"Will you do that?"

He paused and waited, and for a long moment, while the tension rose to a level almost unbearable, no one in the room spoke or stirred. Shulatov remained expressionless, turned away from the table, rigid and unyielding. Lin stared straight ahead, blank and impassive. The moment lengthened.

"Very well," he said quietly. "Mr. President, I renew my request for a vote on the resolution."

"Yes," Australia said promptly. "On this roll call the voting will start with Lesotho. The Secretary-General will call the—"

But here attrition set in, and although he knew he would fight it to the end, the President of the United States of America also knew that in all probability he was beaten before he began.

Time had run out and the gallant dream of saving mankind by relying on its sanity was over.

"Mr. President," Raoul Barre said, clearing his throat with a precise and delicate sound, "if the government of France might be permitted a comment?"

"Certainly," Australia said, his expression showing that he and Orrin were thinking the same thing.

"Thank you," Raoul said with a little smile. "I promise I shall be brief.

"Mr. President, we are faced with what appears to be an insoluble impasse, a direct confrontation between the desires of the world for peace and the desires of the governments of China and Russia for the recognition of their sovereign independence and their right to be consulted without coercion or threat. These are the things we all wish to retain, as sovereign governments. We cannot, I submit, be too unsympathetic toward these desires nor too arbitrary in our dismissal of them.

"To do so," he said, while both Lin and Shulatov began subtly but unmistakably to relax, "would be to set a precedent which perhaps might come back someday to haunt any one or all of us. We must be careful about that.

"Mr. President"—he gave Orrin a direct, gracious little bow—"the world can never be grateful enough for the magnificent effort you have made in its behalf over these past ten days. You have traveled many, many thousands of miles, conducted detailed and exhausting conversations, sought with all the resources of a courageous heart and a supremely intelligent mind to bring about an end to the war between Russia and China and a start upon that era of permanent universal peace which men and women everywhere desire with all their beings. We cannot thank you enough for that.

"But, now, my colleagues of the Council, it may be that the time for what might be termed such—such"—he hesitated delicately—"crisis diplomacy—is over. It may be that the time has come to discuss and to reason, to abandon arbitrary demands or commands, to consider the finding of a middle path between the understandable desires of the governments of Russia and China to be treated as what they are, sovereign powers, and the possibly somewhat"—again he made a delicately regretful gesture—"overly emphatic, shall we say, approach of the world's leading citizen, the President of the United States of America.

"In that effort to find a middle path," he concluded blandly, "the government of France, as always, stands ready to offer its good services and friendly counsel."

"Son of a bitch!" Bill Abbott whispered to Orrin. "Wouldn't you know!"

"Every time," Orrin agreed somberly. "Every time."

"Do you want me to reply to him?" the ex-President asked.

"Sure," the President said. "Why don't you?"

"Mr. President!" William Abbott said, raising his hand for recognition.

"The distinguished delegate, the former President of the United States of America," Australia said, and again the intent and listening silence came.

"Mr. President," Bill Abbott said, his tone only a little sardonic, "I think I speak on behalf of the American people, whom we represent here, when I thank the distinguished delegate of France for his kind words regarding President Knox. We are glad he appreciates the very extensive and exhausting hard work the President has done in the past ten days for the people of the world, in attempting to end the war between Russia and China and in attempting to erect the foundations of permanent peace.

"It is nice to know how warmly France supports him in that effort.

"In his zeal to find the 'middle path' he talks about, however, it appears to my delegation that the French Ambassador may be treating just a shade too gently the arbitrary and uncooperative attitudes of the new governments of Russia and China—particularly the government of Russia. You will recall, because you have all read the transcripts, that the new government of Russia from the beginning was opposed to any concessions to world needs in the way of disarmament and universal peace-keeping. Indeed, it has refused to allow even a purely humanitarian effort, the International Relief Commission, to move freely within its borders to do the enormous work of human rehabilitation which is still untouched in the war zone and in the cities devastated by the atomic exchange. And incidentally, let's don't forget that's what we're discussing here—*atomic exchange.* It happened two weeks ago, and we are dealing here with the dreadful potential that at any second it can happen again. Let's don't forget that. . . .

"The new government of China, it must be remembered, took at least a first step toward cooperation. The idea of meeting in Geneva to start work on the details of disarmament came from the distinguished delegate who sits at this very table, the President of the United Chinese Republic. Whatever his position here today, he *did* make the original offer, Mr. President. He withdrew it only when it became clear that the President of the United States of Russia intended to reject out of hand the whole idea. Some tolerance must be accorded President Lin for that. Equally, condemnation must lie where it belongs, with President Shulatov.

"Presently, however, both appear to be defying the will of the United Nations and the earnest, one could say almost frantic, desire of the world's peoples for peace. So they must be on an equal footing as regards the resolution introduced by my delegation—although in its operations later, perhaps, the world might again remember, with gratitude, the initial good will of President Lin. . . ."

("How to separate two dogs who both hate cats," the London *Times* whispered. "A nice trick," the New York *Times* agreed. "If you can do it.")

"So, then," William Abbott said, "we return to the resolution and what should be done by the world in the immediate situation. The United Nations is faced by open defiance of its will. The war is not ended, only suspended.

"Casualty reports are still coming in and it now appears that upward of thirty million are dead or dreadfully wounded. Many cities lie devastated. Typhus, plague and other war-borne diseases are racing across the face of middle Asia. At any moment, as I said, it can all erupt again. Is there time, I ask the Council, for the delicate 'middle path' diplomacy advocated by our friend from France?

"I do not think so, Mr. President. I do not think so. I think the stakes are too high, the gamble too terrible. We must move and move *now* to make very sure that the war will end and not break out again. We must guarantee by the massed weight of all the nations the cooperation and disarmament we cannot seem to secure by persuasion. The United States resolution, like the United States offer of cooperation, is very strong, and necessarily so. It seems to us, Mr. President, that the saving of the world both requires, and is worth, a few strong measures."

He sat back and the President murmured, "Good try, Bill."

"Yes," William Abbott agreed grimly. "But they're both too smart to answer when they have others to do their work for them."

And another hand went up and Lord Maudulayne said politely, "Mr. President?"

"The distinguished delegate of the United Kingdom," Australia said, and again the room was silent while Shulatov and Lin, both now much more openly at ease, looked blandly, for the first time, at the President of the United States of America.

"Mr. President," the British Ambassador said, "Her Majesty's government wish to associate themselves completely with the position taken by the government of France."

There was a sharp intake of breath from around the room.

("The landslide begins," the New York *Times* said grimly. The London *Times* looked vaguely polite but said nothing.)

"We, too," Lord Maudulayne went on, "gladly render to President Knox the great tribute which all nations must accord him for his most gallant and valiant endeavor in the past ten days. It has been a supreme effort on behalf of all mankind, and nothing can ever take away from him the honor and gratitude which will forever be his.

"But, Mr. President"—his tone, too, became politely regretful—"it is with considerable sadness that we say that we cannot follow him now. We, too, believe that the hour has come for gentler and more friendly methods. We believe that the new government of China has indeed, as President Abbott reminds us, given proof of a basic willingness to cooperate; and we feel that if a similar willingness can be elicited from the new government of Russia, we will be well on our way to a constructive—and peaceful—solution of the world's problems.

"It is our belief that the United Nations, far from offering the two governments the mailed fist on an or-else basis, should instead offer its good offices to provide the atmosphere in which such a voluntary agreement can be reached. We believe the two governments clearly understand the anxiety of the world and its earnest desire that they end the war, become friends and so provide a firm foundation for universal peace.

"We believe the world can then begin work on the noble objective of a general and very substantial disarmament, to which Her Majesty's government has always given their most earnest adherence.

"My government, too, Mr. President, like the government of France, wish to offer their good offices in achieving all these results so greatly to be desired; and accordingly Her Majesty's government, in equal partnership, good faith and good will with the government of France, offer this resolution which I send to the desk and ask the Secretary-General to read."

And while a youthful member of his staff walked around the circle to hand the paper to the Secretary-General, he smiled in a kindly way at Orrin and Bill Abbott, as though he might have been seeing them at one of Lady Kitty's teas. The President and ex-President smiled somewhat grimly back.

"Be it resolved," the Secretary-General read in his gravely beautiful voice, "that the resolution of the United States of America be amended as follows:

"Strike all after the first four paragraphs and substitute the language herein subsequent, so that the resolution in final form will read:

" 'Whereas, it is imperative for the peace and safety of the population of Earth that the present conflict between Russia and China be speedily ended, and that there be no more war; and

" 'Whereas, the United Nations has established an International Peace Force to achieve these purposes; and,

" 'Whereas, the United States of America has voluntarily offered to undertake an immediate disarmament program to reduce its armed forces to a defense-force level and contribute to the International Peace Force all funds, troops and matériel which the United Nations command may require for the successful completion of its purposes in China and Russia and its permanent mission of peace; and,

" 'Whereas, the United States of America, acting on behalf of the United Nations, has approached the governments of the United States of Russia and the United Chinese Republic seeking their agreement to an equal disarmament; and,

" 'Whereas'—and here, Mr. President," the Secretary-General interpolated, "begins the new language—'such agreement should be reached in an atmosphere of willing cooperation and amity if it is to be firm and lasting; and,

" 'Whereas, it is the duty of the United Nations to encourage and support such a willing, cooperative and friendly atmosphere with due regard and respect for the independence, sovereignty and legitimate self-interest of all the governments of the world:

"'Now, therefore, be it resolved:

"'That the United Nations hereby urges the convening of a world disarmament conference in Geneva, to begin one week from today, such conference to consist of all interested governments that may wish to send delegations; and further be it resolved:

"'That all governments that wish to participate should attend such disarmament conference in good faith and good will, with sincere determination to achieve an agreement that will both respect the independence, sovereignty and legitimate self-interest of all governments, and provide a firm and lasting foundation for universal peace; and further be it resolved:

"'That the operations of the International Peace Force should be conducted in the spirit of this resolution, with due respect for the independence, sovereignty and legitimate self-interest of the governments of the United States of Russia and the United Chinese Republic, and that the said governments are hereby urged to cooperate in sincerity, good will and good faith with the operations of the International Peace Force.'"

The even, dispassionate voice of the Secretary-General stopped. Into the silence the President of the United States of America inquired with a blank surprise:

"Is that all?"

"That is all, Mr. President," the Secretary-General said gravely.

"The United States of America," Orrin said, and there was an instant uneasy murmuring through the room at his tone, "would like to comment. I ask recognition for the distinguished Ambassador of the United States."

"With pleasure," Australia said. At her microphone Ceil leaned forward, looking a little tense but otherwise perfectly composed.

"Mr. President," she said, "I am afraid that the amendment offered by the governments of the United Kingdom and France does not go to the heart of the matter. No doubt it is offered, as the distinguished Ambassador of the United Kingdom says, in 'good faith and good will, with sincere determination to achieve an agreement,' but after we have accepted that fine declaration of intent we must move on to find out exactly how it is to be achieved. The prospects as he outlines them, I am afraid, are bleak.

"The world is confronted here, I suggest to the Council, not with good will, good faith and a sincere determination to reach agreement, but with stubbornness, hostility and an outright refusal to cooperate with the International Peace Force, a duly constituted arm of the United Nations, and a similar refusal to cooperate with a genuine attempt to secure universal disarmament. Why, then, must we bow to this kind of response? Why must we humble ourselves before it and use soft words? Why can we not have the courage to judge it for what it is, a blatant attempt to bluff the world into backing away from its imperative need for peace, so that these two governments may once more return to the old ways of hatred, mistrust, conquest and war?

"I submit, Mr. President, that the governments of France and the United Kingdom are unwittingly playing the game of a new imperialism. They mean well, their desire that we all love one another is very nice, but let us face it: we don't all love one another, and unless there is a strong, powerful, no-nonsense international force to step between us, then many of us will go on warring. And with a third of Asia already devastated by the atomic exchange, we simply cannot afford that any longer. It will mean the death of us all.

"We must take strong and affirmative action to support the International Peace Force we have established. We must insist upon a genuine and very thorough disarmament of the major powers, and soon thereafter of all powers. We must face head on and unafraid exactly what confronts us at this moment in the world's history.

"President Knox has offered a tough resolution because these are tough times. The only way to survive them is to be tough. We most respectfully urge the Council to meet the challenge, defeat the amendment, support the resolution. Otherwise, in the estimation of my government, we are signing a sure ticket to disaster."

"Mr. President!" Krishna Khaleel cried quickly as she pushed away the microphone and sat back. "Mr. President, India wishes to be heard, if you please!"

"Certainly," Australia said with a certain sarcasm. "No one would deprive India of that privilege."

"Mr. President," Krishna Khaleel said sternly, picking it up at once, "you may jest and be sarcastic, but this is serious business here. Rather serious business, I think!

"My government, Mr. President, appreciates the good faith and serious intent of the governments of the United Kingdom and France. It also appreciates the good faith and serious intent of the government of the United States of America. And it understands and sympathizes with the concern and anxieties of the new governments of Russia and China."

("That pretty well covers the field," the New York *Times* murmured. "But wait," the London *Times* advised. "Out of it all will come a synthesis uniquely Indian.")

"*However,*" K.K. said, and his tone became severe, "my government does *not* agree that the President of the United States of America, my dear old friend Orrin Knox, is approaching this in the right fashion. In fact, we are concerned that the record of the past ten days may indicate that he possibly has *never* approached it in the right fashion.

"Oh, Mr. President!" he cried, as Orrin shot him a skeptical glance and stirred in his chair. "We *appreciate* his sincerity! We *appreciate* his honor! We *appreciate* his idealism! It is simply his *methods* we deplore!"

Despite the gravity of the moment, there was a burst of genuine amusement, momentarily uniting them all. Even Lin and Shulatov condescended to smile.

"What?" K.K. cried indignantly. "What, then, have I said something funny? Is it so jolly here that delegates can laugh and chortle at me amongst themselves? Is it a matter for fun-making of India, then, Mr. President, I demand to know!"

"The delegate is advised," Australia said, making himself suitably solemn, "that fun-making of India is the last thing anyone has in mind. Does he care to proceed, or shall we—"

"Yes!" K.K. exclaimed. "Yes, indeed, I care to proceed! And," he added with a sudden determined dignity, "I shall do so in my own way, if the Council please. . . .

"Mr. President, President Knox and his delegation confine themselves in their resolution to two points only, the International Peace Force and disarmament. But, Mr. President, the initial 'Ten Demands' of President Knox, made almost three weeks ago, and the transcripts of his conversations in Moscow and Peking, indicate that the United States of America has much, much more in mind. It has in mind, if you please, the entire rearrangement of the globe, an entire revolution in the way the world does things, an entire change for humanity. And I submit to you, Mr. President, that all this rearrangement, if it were carried out, could only end in the complete and final dominance of the world by the United States of America.

"No, no, now!" he cried, holding up a warning hand as there came again from the American delegation an indignant stirring. "Do not interrupt me, my good friends from America! I do not say this is your deliberate intention, but let us examine the record and see. Let us look at all the peripheral things that hide beneath the twin shadows of International Peace Force and so-called disarmament. Let us see!

"The basic drive and end result here, Mr. President—it is implicit, oh, yes, it is implicit!—is to deny to *all* nations the right to have friendly powers along their borders, to deny to *all* nations the right to defend themselves against hostile elements from outside, to open *all* nations to incursion by so-called International Peace Forces and other international bodies. It is to demand of *all* of us that we disarm, that we renounce *all* interest, even the most beneficent, in anything that happens beyond our borders—that we simply withdraw from the world, as it were, and leave it to those who know best—who have always known best, about everything—our good friends from America. That is the real thrust here, Mr. President, whether they realize it consciously or not.

"It is true that they talk of disarmament, equal disarmament, but when you start with two great powers dreadfully weakened and a third great power still very strong, then if they all go down at the same pace, who still emerges at the bottom in the strongest position, Mr. President? And if we all join them, weak and secondary as we are—and you will recall that the transcripts disclose President Knox advising President Shulatov that in fact it is only those three who matter at all in this context, not your country or mine, Mr. President, or any of the rest of us—then if we all join them in this so-called disarmament, who still emerges at the bottom the strongest over all of us? None other than our good friends from Washington, innocent and idealistic as they are!

"I do not say, of course, Mr. President," he said, and his voice filled with a heavy irony, "that it would not be best for us all to be so advised and so led by superior intelligence from America. But I wonder, really, if that is what we all want?

"I suggest, Mr. President, that the Council should adopt the amendment offered by my dear old friends the Ambassador of the United Kingdom and the Ambassador of France, and we will then proceed in an orderly fashion, as world society has always proceeded, to discuss—to consider—to reason—to compromise—to reach a fair agreement—to solve our problems in the old, good, traditional way!"

He sat back with a satisfied air while across the chamber there swept a sudden spontaneous wave of applause and approval that brought to his face a smile of gratified triumph and to the face of the President of the United States of America an expression of deep and somber concern.

He made no attempt to conceal it when he raised his hand for recognition, and when Australia gave it to him he made no attempt to keep the concern from his voice.

"Mr. President," he said, and for the last time the Council and all its many guests quieted down intently to hear him speak, "how far we have moved from the simple terror with which these past two weeks began. How quickly we have forgotten why we are here. How rapidly has the impulse for salvation died.

"For make no mistake, my friends of the Council—make no mistake, anyone, anywhere. Salvation is what concerns us here. Salvation is what we will throw away if we do not insist that powers that have it in their hands to destroy the world be brought under control and be relieved of that capacity. And by that I say to my friend from India, I do mean all of us, and I mean *all of us equally.* I will not dignify his unworthy absurdities by commenting on his charges against the United States of America. My offer of full disarmament for us, and my own actions in the past ten days in attempting to bring peace, speak for themselves. If they cannot be honestly understood, then I pity those who deliberately misinterpret them."

("Old boy's annoyed, isn't he?" the London *Times* observed. "Can you blame him?" inquired the New York *Times.* "Oh, *well,*" said the London *Times.*)

"Mr. President," he said, ignoring K.K.'s flushed face and offended stare, "I wish to address myself for the last time to the choice between the quick and the dead. We can indeed go on in 'the old, good, traditional way.' We can indeed 'consider' and 'discuss' and 'reason' and 'compromise.' We can indeed talk, talk, talk while time disappears and God's patience with us runs finally out. Sure! Let's do that. Let's take all the time in the world, with skirmishing already beginning again along the Russo-Chinese border, with pestilence spreading from the dead cities, with twenty million walking wounded wandering the roads of central Asia. Let's wait until they walk right into this Council chamber, Mr. President! Let's wait until we join them, in the final walk to nowhere.

"Yes!" he said, and now the room was absolutely hushed in the face of his obvious terrible anger. "Let's wait—let's wait. Let's don't do anything tough. Let's don't do anything strong. Let's don't step on anybody's toes. Let's take counsel of our fears and give free reign once more to our cupidity. Let's revive all our self-interest, our suspicions of one another, our hostilities, our selfishness, our fear of genuine sacrifice for peace, our eternal cowardice in the face of moral principle. Let's go through the same old story that brought us up to the flash point of two weeks ago, and very shortly we will get flash point again. And then, my timorous friends, God help us. God help us, every one.

"Mr. President," he concluded with a harsh abruptness, "we can only decide this by a vote. I request one."

But of course it did not come then, because on an issue so grave every member of the Council had to make a record, for however long the record might be read. One by one the others said their say, Australia, Chile and Cuba, Egypt and Ghana, Lesotho, Norway, Rumania and Zambia. Almost two hours passed before Australia could put the question.

"The vote comes," he said finally, "on the resolution of the United Kingdom and France to amend the resolution of the United States of America. The voting will begin with Lesotho. The Secretary-General will call the roll."

"Lesotho," said the Secretary-General; and after a long moment, during which tension rose sharply in the room and in the world, the giant black chieftain of the Sotho who represented Lesotho said slowly:

"No."

There was a babble of noise, a scattering of applause, some boos.

"Norway."

"No," said Norway firmly.

The boos increased.

"Rumania."

"Yes."

Applause rose defiantly, boos were almost submerged.

"The United Kingdom."

"Yes," said Lord Maudulayne crisply, and this time the applause far outweighed the boos.

"The United States."

"No," said Orrin Knox, and this time the boos far outweighed the applause.

"The United Chinese Republic."

"Yes," Lin said softly, and applause was vigorous, friendly, encouraging, boos few and far between.

"The United States of Russia."

"Yes!" said Shulatov defiantly, and he too received the same warmly generous response.

"Zambia."

"But, *yes!*" said Zambia, and there was approving laughter, though still, here and there, a few boos.

"Australia."

"No," Australia said quietly, and there were plenty of boos.

"Chile."

"*Sì!*" Chile said with a cheerful grin, and laughter approved him.

"Cuba."

"*Sì, sì!*" said Cuba, and the laughter grew.

"Egypt."

"No," Egypt said stoutly, and the boos resumed.

"France."

"Yes," said Raoul Barre, and applause rewarded him.

"Ghana."

"Yes," said Ghana, and the applause, hardly pausing now, rolled on for him.

"India."

"Yes!" Krishna Khaleel said triumphantly, and applause welled up in final triumph as he beamed and smiled.

"On this vote," Australia announced, dispirited and openly unhappy, "five members have voted No, ten have voted Yes. One permanent member has voted No, but since the veto no longer exists, the amendment of the United Kingdom and France is approved by a vote of 10 to 5."

For a moment the room was silent, as though for a last split second men took thought of what they had done. Then applause and cheers welled up and carreid on their tide all who believed and most of those who doubted. Only a few here and there sat silent and depressed.

"The vote now comes on the resolution of the United States as amended," Australia said finally. "The voting will start with Norway. The Secretary-General will call the roll."

And five minutes later, no minds persuaded, no positions changed, the euphoria of the moment continuing to drive them on, he found himself announcing:

"On this vote the result again is ten Yes, five No, and the resolution of the United States as amended by the United Kingdom and France is approved."

"Mr. President," Orrin said, his voice bringing instant quiet again to the room, "the mood of a majority of the United Nations, as expressed by these two votes and by the very great applause given the results by the many members of the Assembly who are in the chamber, is very obvious.

"Accordingly"—he paused and his voice sounded suddenly very tired—"my delegation will not offer its resolution in the General Assembly."

There was a wild excited surge of applause and cheering. Across it his voice cut cold, flat, devoid of emotion.

"I think, however, that the world should have a chance to find out what kind of progress we have made here this afternoon."

He turned directly to Lin, small, closed off and remote, and to Shulatov, grimly and openly triumphant.

"Will you," he said, "meet in Geneva one week from today with each other and with all interested members of the United Nations to begin good-faith—specific—detailed—negotiations looking toward genuine universal disarmament? And will you give a pledge—implicit in the Council's demand for peace and solemn request for such negotiations—that you will not resume war with one another?"

"Now you attempt to broaden it—" Shulatov began angrily. But the President of the United States of America was having none of it.

"*Answer me!*" he demanded harshly. "*Will you do it?*"

For a very long moment the President of the United States of Russia gave him stare for stare. Then his glance moved to the President of the United Chinese Republic and his eyes widened.

"We must give substantial thought," he said, biting off each word, "to whether or not we will sit down with the assassins of Asia."

There was a gasp of dismay that would have been laughable under some other circumstance, so naïve was it that anyone should actually be surprised. But it was not laughable now.

"As *we* must give careful study," Lin said in his sibilant near whisper that yet carried clearly to the ends of the electronically bound earth, "to whether we will soil ourselves by talking to the evil scum who launched atomic war upon our country."

"Mr. President," Orrin said evenly, "I suggest the Council adjourn."

"Yes," agreed Australia in a bleak and desolate voice. "There doesn't seem to be much else to do."

And so presently, disturbed, unhappy, uneasy, apprehensive, those who had been excessively hopeful, or afraid to face facts, or both, in the United Nations that day, trailed out and away to their respective abodes and destinations; and fear, the child of wavering resolution, which had been so briefly banished, returned a thousandfold to haunt the globe.

RUSS, CHINESE DEFY U.N. CALL FOR DISARMAMENT CONFERENCE AFTER SECURITY COUNCIL TURNS DOWN

KNOX DEMAND FOR STRONG MEASURES TO MAKE THEM COMPLY. FATE OF ARMS PARLEY IN GENEVA UNCERTAIN AS WARRING GOVERNMENTS LEAVE NEW YORK.

REPORT FURTHER SKIRMISHES ALONG BORDER, "SIZABLE" AIR BATTLE OVER SINKIANG PROVINCE.

PRESIDENT TO ADDRESS JOINT SESSION OF CONGRESS AT NOON TOMORROW.

"My colleagues of the Congress," he said somberly in the hushed and overflowing chamber of the House, "my fellow Americans everywhere:

"I wish that I could report to you the full success of my mission to China and Russia and to the United Nations in New York. But through the good offices of the media you have accompanied me every step of the way. You know as well as I do the exact status of things.

"I shall not try to gloss realities with fine words or phony optimism. I have tried to make it a basic principle throughout my public career never to fool the American people. That principle has never been more important than now.

"The world has been, and it remains, in extremely desperate condition. The new governments of Russia and China are in the grip of a mutual suspicion and hatred as deep as any that afflicted the old governments of Russia and China. This is understandable, since the men running the new governments came to maturity and lived all their lives under the old governments and were scientifically and deliberately trained, as few men in history have ever been scientifically and deliberately trained, to hate one another.

"The war grew directly out of that state of mind. It may be resumed at any moment—directly out of that state of mind. I have tried, and failed, to break the psychological barrier. Those who built it built too well. There was, as you know, one brief flicker of compromise from President Lin of China. It was summarily destroyed by President Shulatov of Russia. Somehow we must deal with the consequences.

"When I say 'we' must deal with the consequences, I no longer mean 'we' in the sense of the world community, for as you also know, that too offers little hope. Yesterday in New York the nations of the world were called to judgment and found wanting. They too suffer from old fears, suspicions, greeds, timidities. They had rather trust to a vague and amorphous 'good will' which does not exist in the face of the practical realities of national self-interest.

"The practical realities of national self-interest, in fact, encourage them to continue on the same selfish and foredoomed course that has always ruined the world. The practical realities of self-interest—and the fear of being vigilant in the defense of good, and firm in the opposition to evil.

"So there is little hope there. In New York yesterday I abandoned the niceties of diplomatic language. I put it on as tough and naked a basis of strength versus strength as it actually is, and as it actually has always been. I was met with polite words about 'good will'—and 'good faith'—and 'sincere negotiations'—and 'the United Nations urges.'

"The United Nations 'urging,' wistful people of any kind 'urging,' are completely immaterial to the world's crisis.

"It is urging from strength that matters.

"And there is no strength."

He paused to take a sip of water, and in the Press Gallery above, AP murmured to UPI, "Wow! Tough words from our Orrin." "Tough times," UPI remarked. "Look at the Congress. He's scaring 'em to death."

And indeed they did look as strained and somber as he. But whether it was fear or resolution could not be determined at the moment. He offered a silent prayer that it was resolution, and moved somberly on to the conclusion of his brief remarks.

"Therefore, we must turn for strength to where strength is, and that is right here in America.

"We do not know, at this moment, whether the war will resume in Asia. Sporadic skirmishing, a resumption of aerial warfare, have already occurred. At any second it may all flare up again into all-out atomic war. I would say the chances of this, based upon the attitudes of the new governments, is probably 70 to 30."

There was a gasp from the Congress, the standing-room-only audience, the media.

"Face it," he said grimly. "Face it. The games are all over. It is all real now. . . .

"What do we do, in this land, in such a situation? I shall of course send a delegation, headed by the ex-President of the United States, the Secretary of State and leading members of Congress from both parties, to Geneva a week from today. I expect them to find there many other delegations. But I do not expect them to find the only two delegations whose presence really matters—the Chinese and the Russians.

"We will go, and go, as our friends in the United Nations put it, in good faith. But I am extremely dubious that we will find anything there to justify hope about the future of the world.

"It comes back, then, to where it has, perhaps, always been ultimately heading in these recent hectic decades: back to the United States of America—going it alone.

"There is still enough hopeful humanitarian spirit left in the country so that some critics will accuse me of launching with that statement 'a new isolationism.'

"I wish as devoutly as any that the world would permit us to still *be* hopeful and humanitarian. But I would not call it a new isolationism, because 'isolationism' in its critical sense implies that there is something good and valid and viable to be isolated *from*.

"On the basis of the past two weeks, I do not realistically see that in the world today.

"I would prefer to call it America relying on America because there just simply isn't anyone else to rely upon.

"You of the Congress have just passed at my request a ten-billion-dollar emergency defense budget. I had fully intended, when I made that request, to use it simply as a bargaining point, and to abandon all of it except the very minimum necessary to maintain small defense forces—*if the Russians and the Chinese would do the same.* Now it appears they will not. So I shall use it as I am constitutionally bound to use it, to preserve and protect the United States of America.

"I am very much afraid that it is time for us in America, in an old prairie frontier phrase, to 'turn our backs to the wind and hunker down.'

"Devastation such as the world has never seen has occurred in Asia. It may resume again at any moment. If it does, no one can predict where it can be contained—if it can be contained. No one can predict whether we can survive the hurricane if we do 'hunker down.' But it does not seem to me that there is, now, any other sensible course for us to follow.

"It may be that we will be the very last citadel left to save whatever mankind has achieved of culture and civilization. It may be that we will survive to put the world together again—or we may just as likely go down with it. It is all uncertainty, all conjecture, all dark and desperate, all filled with frightful peril for us all.

"But we must be brave—and we must be strong—and we must look to our own defenses—and we must hold ourselves ready to help where we can—and we must pray.

"The Lord has preserved us through many perils, for some purpose. We must be confident that He will continue to do so. I make no pretense to you whatsoever that it will be easy. But I call on you to join me in meeting whatever the future holds, with courage, with determination, with unity and with faith in ourselves, our traditions and our purposes.

"I shall keep you advised at every opportunity of events as they develop, and of what your government is doing to meet them. Goodbye and God bless you until we meet again."

That it might be soon, the early-afternoon headlines reporting his speech made clear:

KNOX CALLS ON ALL AMERICANS TO BE PREPARED FOR WHATEVER FUTURE MAY BRING. SAYS CHANCE OF RENEWED ATOMIC WAR MAY BE "70–30." WILL SEND DELEGATION TO GENEVA DISARMAMENT TALKS BUT WILL ALSO BUILD DEFENSE TO HIGHEST PEAK. ASKS NATION TO "TURN BACKS TO WIND AND HUNKER DOWN." GETS MIXED BUT GENERALLY FAVORABLE RECEPTION FROM TENSE CONGRESS AS NEW WAR CRISIS GROWS.

By 6 P.M. events had taken a more ominous turn:

MAJOR NEW FIGHTING, GROWING AIR CLASHES REPORTED ON RUSS-CHINESE BORDER. HONG KONG OBSERVERS FEAR NEW ATOMIC EXCHANGE, POSSIBLE GERM WARFARE.

By 10 P.M. the news was more ominous still:

CHINESE REPORT BIG BREAKTHROUGH IN GROUND AND AIR FIGHTING! RUSSIANS HURLED BACK OVER HUNDRED-MILE SECTOR! NO NEW A-BLOWS YET, BUT OBSERVERS BELIEVE ATOMIC FIELD WEAPONS, LEAD-SHIELDED TANKS USED IN FIERCE NEW CHINESE ONSLAUGHT.

And shortly after that, a reaction that was, in its ultimate implications, perhaps most ominous of all for the United States of America:

NATIONAL ANTI-WAR ACTIVITIES HEAD URGES PRESIDENT TO INTERVENE ON SIDE OF RUSSIA. NAWAC'S VAN ACKERMAN SAYS "AMERICA MUST SAVE THE CIVILIZATION OF THE WEST FROM THE GODLESS YELLOW HORDES OF ASIA."

With his sure instinct for the jugular and his sure understanding of the lowest common denominator of his countrymen's fears, Fred had put his finger on what now rapidly became the heart of the matter.

5. "ORRIN," WILLIAM ABBOTT SAID from the Capitol shortly after noon next day, "we've got trouble up here."

"No doubt," he said with an inflection both weary and disgusted. "It hasn't taken them long, has it?"

"Not after what's happened in Asia, and Fred's statement, and the way it was all played up in the media this morning," the ex-President said. "Apparently some people have been hankering for an excuse to take sides ever since we left Peking. Now it's become respectable."

"Not all *that* respectable," he said. "I've read the *Times* and the *Post* too, you know, and watched 'Today' and all the rest of them. They've naturally given it all the news play, but editorially they're being very cautious and still very supportive of me. There haven't been any calls to chaos except Fred's—which is standard procedure for him, of course. He had to find some issue."

"Don't underestimate this one, Orrin," Bill Abbott warned. "This one hits home with far more people than we'd like to think."

"Oh, I know," he agreed, his tone less weary, sharper now with intimations of coming battle. "But how can people be so inconsistent? One minute they're terrified to death of atomic war, literally scared silly—and the next they want us to jump in on the side of one of the belligerents and send ourselves down the chute with them. It's insane."

"As I've heard you remark on various occasions," his predecessor noted, "people frequently are insane. Reason says one thing, fear says another: occasionally they coincide but more often they part company. And when they do, you know which one wins out. . . . Intellectually they know we shouldn't get involved, because their great fear of atomic war agrees with their intellectual conclusion on that point. But they also have a great fear—never honestly acknowledged any more—very old, very atavistic—going back through who knows what eons—of different skins and different faces. All races have that fear, they as much as we, although in this country we've tried sincerely to get rid of it, with good and earnest intentions, in the last few decades.

"But now, suddenly, atomic war has stripped all pretenses away. Everybody has reverted to basic emotions—terrified of atomic war but terrified of the alien races, too. Now the question has been raised, as inevitably it would be raised in the event of war between Russia and China: our race or the alien race?

"I've always thought Fred Van Ackerman was a minor Hitler: he has the same genius for going straight for the most ugly and elemental instincts of the human animal. And mark my words, Orrin: all it takes is for one man like that to open the door. Then a few others begin to follow—then still more join—then, under the pressures of popular hysteria, and being themselves only human, the institutions and elements which represent respectability and responsibility gradually begin to come around. And then suddenly *everything* becomes respectable and responsible. And before you know it, the herd is on its way, running wild and impossible to control.

"We're heading straight into a terrible problem, my friend. Don't underestimate it."

"I don't underestimate it," he said sharply. "All problems are terrible today. What indications do you have up there that have you so upset all of a sudden?"

"Both Jawbone and Arly have just had their regular pre-session press conferences—you'll be getting them on the news tickers in a minute. I dropped in on Jawbone's, which he didn't like, and Bob Munson eavesdropped on Arly's, which *he* didn't like. Both are wavering—not openly yet, but beginning. And now there's some young kid from New York—I think his name is Bronson Bernard—who is taking Fred's lead and starting to make a speech about it here in the House. And Tom August is up in the Senate and God knows what *he's* going to say. So"—his expression was lit for a moment by a grim humor—"maybe *we're* the ones who should turn our backs to the wind and hunker down."

"Not me. I sail straight into it. You know that."

"You may have to do something," William Abbott said, "because instinct tells me it doesn't look good."

"I've known since the beginning that the moment would come when it wouldn't look good," the President said. "I've had a timetable ticking in my mind for two weeks. I've known I could use fear as an ally but I've known that unless I was terribly lucky it would turn against me.

"I only made one mistake: I thought that when world fear lessened to the point where international cooperation began to fall apart again, in this country fear of the consequences would unite my own people behind me in staying aloof and holding the high ground for civilization. I didn't quite imagine that fear would divert into new channels and send them plunging in another direction—in the direction of taking sides. . . .

"And after all," he said, with a sudden impatient movement of the shoulders as though shrugging off unnecessary burdens, "who says it's going to, Bill? Just a few calculating adventurers like Fred Van Ackerman and a few waverers like Arly and Jawbone. That doesn't mean they'll carry the whole country. What are we doing, letting ourselves be hounded by *that* fear?"

"You study those editorials and those press conferences and keep your eye on what happens up here today," William Abbott suggested.

"Naturally," he said, impatience open now. "What else would you expect me to do?"

"I don't quite know," his predecessor said soberly. "What *will* you do?"

"Probably make a couple of speeches, if I have to," he said with an almost flippant irony.

"What will they be?"

"The first will be: 'Come on, gang, hold the line!'"

"And the second?"

"The second—" He paused, his eyes widened in thought, he saw many things, none he wished to communicate at the moment, even to this dear old friend.

"Yes?" the ex-President persisted.

"The second will be what-I-do-then."

"Which will be?"

"Christ, Bill!" he said. "Don't bug me!"

"Just so you know," William Abbott observed with a certain flippant irony of his own. "Just so you have it firmly in mind."

"Don't Presidents always have everything in mind?" Orrin inquired. "That's what Presidents are for."

William Abbott studied him for a long time. Then he grunted.

"I hope that won't be it," he said finally. "Let me know any way I can help."

"Thanks, Bill," the President said with a genuine gratitude. "It won't be if I can help it. The best thing I can ask of you at the moment is: get in there and fight."

"I'm on my way," the ex-President said. "Young Bronson is going to hear from me."

"And Tom August from Bob Munson, I trust."

"All troops are at battle stations," Bill Abbott said.

"I, too," said the President. He paused, his eyes again far away, his expression infinitely sad. "Such hatred," he said. "Such terrible hatred, to mount such an offensive even now in the condition they're in, to make such a desperate onslaught in spite of all their devastation and chaos."

"Lin wanted to be helpful," William Abbott observed.

"Yes," the President agreed. "For a very little minute, he did. I should have held that minute, Bill. I shouldn't have let it get away." He sighed. "I tried. But it just wasn't good enough."

"You did all you humanly could," the ex-President said sharply, "so stop worrying about it. You can't look back, it's futile and impossible. Too much lies ahead."

"Yes," he said slowly. "Too much lies ahead. . . . Thanks for calling." His expression eased a little. "Go on the floor and give 'em hell."

"I'm on my way," Bill Abbott said with a reviving cheerfulness. "I'll be in touch."

And for the next few minutes, as the President turned back to the mammoth desk covered with intelligence reports, newspapers, news digests, news-ticker tape, letters, telegrams, he too felt a little more cheerful, for some reason he could not exactly define—having to do, he supposed, with the fact that there was only so far down you could go, then you had to start going up again. And admittedly the press reaction helped. So far they were holding the line. But how long, if their own long-standing intellectual sympathies with Russia and their fear of China, as human as anyone else's, became imperative?

"This newspaper," the *Times* had said this morning, "cannot and will not join the call of former Senator Fred Van Ackerman for a kind of revived racism that would drag this country willy-nilly into the revived war in Asia.

"We can think of nothing more tragic than to intervene in that terrible conflict—and for such a repugnant and unworthy reason.

"The intervention itself would be dreadful. The reason would betray all that this nation stands for, and all the small hopes left to mankind that the world can somehow work its way out of this awful situation.

"Even if intervention could be possible without drawing America and the entire world into the vortex of renewed atomic war, such a reason would defeat all we might achieve—if we achieved anything. And it is almost beyond belief that we could.

"Earnestly and sincerely for several decades now, America and the world have tried to slough off the burden of racism, the blind and crippling feeling that one particular skin color or facial configuration is somehow, in and of itself, superior or inferior to some other. We had thought that idea had been buried once and for all. Now

Senator Van Ackerman, using the public platform accorded him by the original worthy purposes of the National Anti-War Activities Congress, is apparently trying to revive it, and to use it as a fulcrum to send this nation rushing to the defense of the new government of Russia.

"Perhaps, by some fantastically remote way of reasoning, there might be some argument to be made for intervention in the war. We can just barely conceive of it. But surely an absurd and foolish attempt to revive the myth of 'the Yellow Peril' is not the one.

"We would suggest the ex-Senator turn his talents back to the original purpose of NAWAC—namely, no war at all. He should be supporting the President's determination to stay out, not trying to subvert it by attempting to revive racism. Certainly he should not be raising at this point in history the specter of 'Yellow Peril' to encourage an intervention that could very likely only end in complete disaster for the whole world. . . ."

"Shades of William Randolph Hearst!" the *Post* exclaimed. "The world is on the brink of terminal disaster and here comes Frantic Freddy Van Ackerman trying to revive 'the Yellow Peril'!

"We had never thought we'd live to see the day.

"In fact, none of us may live if we *do* see the day.

"We reject the notion that the United States of America should, or could, intervene in the conflict between Russia and China. Until we see extraordinarily convincing arguments to the contrary, we shall continue to support President Knox's determination to build up this nation's strength as a balance for the world, and to *stay out*. We agree with him that intervention would be insanity, at least under any circumstances foreseeable now.

"We particularly agree that intervention on the basis of such a repugnant, antiquated, mindless racism as ex-Senator Van Ackerman proposes is utterly unworthy of America and all it stands for. It would be unbelievable. We refuse to contemplate it. There might by some fantastic stretch be reasons to intervene, but 'Yellow Peril' is not one of them.

"'Yellow Peril' indeed! Somewhere in these dreadful days we must summon up sufficient laughter to hoot the idea off history's stage. If it did not come from the head of NAWAC—whose purpose, after all, is supposedly *No War*—it would not even deserve a moment's attention. Since the source unfortunately demands that it be noticed, it should receive what it does deserve, namely scorn and derision. . . ."

"Washington," Walter Dobius wrote busily in the Senate Press

Gallery after attending Arly Richardson's press conference, "has been affected more than some of its leaders might like to admit by the startling move of former Senator Fred Van Ackerman in calling upon the President to intervene on the side of Russia in the rapidly reviving Russo-Chinese war.

"This turnabout on the part of the leader of an organization supposedly dedicated to no more war is surprising enough, and can only be put down to the political adventurism which has too often darkened his name. That it should turn upon so reactionary a point as an attempt to revive America's ancient and unworthy fear of the so-called 'Yellow Peril' is profoundly disturbing.

"If there were, by some remote and fantastic stretch of imagination, any reason at all for taking sides in Asia's tragic and cataclysmic conflict (and while it could conceivably happen, none comes to mind at the moment), then certainly this echo of the dead past is not one of them. Yet there are some in the Congress who already appear to be toying with the idea. And with ideas like that, certain ideas that spring from humanity's grossest atavistic instincts, history has shown on far too many tragic occasions that it is not necessary to lower the dam very far before the tide rushes in."

(Which, Walter thought, pausing, was something of a mixed metaphor, but expressed it. He was a shrewd student of his countrymen and he did not for one moment discount either the impact or the potential of Fred's surprising statement. He was also a highly experienced reporter, and it had not taken him more than an hour wandering both sides of the Capitol to catch the atmosphere among far too many members: it was electric. The fact scared him, he was honest enough to admit to himself, to death.)

"President Knox," he went on, "has clearly and unequivocally stated what the great majority here still feel: that America should stay aloof and do what she can to save civilization and provide a stabilizing influence in the chaos that will ensue if Russia and China do indeed battle to the death.

"But whether that majority will hold may now be in doubt. It is amazing that one man's statement can have this effect. The reason is both simple and ominous: it can only have such an effect when it synthesizes what many men are secretly thinking.

"This may be the bleak reality that confronts the President, though all responsible citizens in this fear-haunted city hope not. . . ."

And Frankly Unctuous, just back from Jawbone's press conference, spoke from the House Radio-TV Gallery in the same vein:

"Here on Capitol Hill, where only yesterday President Knox called his country to a vigilant neutrality in the steadily re-escalating conflict between Russia and China, there is already evident today an erosion of the firm and united purpose he sought, prompted by a startling, and at first blush ridiculous, statement from the head of the National Anti-War Activities Congress.

"Former Senator Fred Van Ackerman called upon the President last night to intervene on the side of Russia. He said the President should do so because 'America must save the civilization of the West from the Godless yellow hordes of Asia.' He further said that 'the heathen, pagan society of the Chinese mainland is inimical to all the ancient values of European culture and tradition which have come down to us in this country.' He also said that 'unless China is stopped, she may conquer Russia and then pour across the land mass of Eurasia and eventually into the ultimate reaches of the Pacific Basin, not excluding our own shores.' He also said, 'The time to stop her is now. The nation that is attempting to do so is Russia. The nation that must help Russia save civilization as we know it is the United States.'

"He did not quite dare say, 'The nation that must help Russia save *white* civilization as we know it is the United States,' but that was the clear import of his statement.

"Overnight Senator Van Ackerman has revived 'the Yellow Peril.' And it is typical of this dreadful moment that his words should be running like lightning through the country and here on Capitol Hill.

"Intervention in the terrible conflict in Asia would be almost suicidal for the United States, something to be undertaken only for the most dire and compelling of reasons. 'Yellow Peril' is not such a reason. Yet already many members of Congress have received telegrams and phone calls endorsing Mr. Van Ackerman's position. And already the matter has become a living issue in the pre-session press conferences of the Speaker of the House and the Majority Leader of the United States Senate.

"Sometimes issues come alive not because of what men say, but because of what they refuse to say.

"Representative J. B. Swarthman and Senator Arly Richardson are honorable men, men who accompanied President Knox on his gallant but failed effort to bring peace to the world. Yet today both refused to denounce unequivocally and categorically former Senator Van Ackerman's statement. Both were pressed to do so by the media. In identical language both said that Congress 'must refrain from judgment and await developments.' Both clearly and deliberately passed up the chance to reject Senator Van Ackerman's action and condemn his sentiments.

"Evasion of issues, history shows, does not stop them. More often, it encourages them. Many here are fearful today that in encouraging the revival of 'the Yellow Peril,' some leaders of Congress may be helping to open a Pandora's box."

As he finished reading and listening to these expressions of opinion, as he quickly scanned the news-ticker reports on Jawbone's and Arly's comments, the President still did not feel unduly alarmed. Supermedia and all the little media were still behind him at the moment, and while Arly and Jawbone had indeed been somewhat equivocal, still they were in a position where they had to work with all sides, consider all shades of opinion, be careful not to antagonize any of their colleagues unduly—

Or—he brought himself up short—did they?

Wasn't he falling back into the easy thinking of the Hill when that, too, had been destroyed forever by the awful realities of the atomic exchange? Wasn't he letting himself be persuaded, as the Hill always could be persuaded, that compromising with wrong part way was always better than rejecting it outright—which might really make enemies and upset the whole comfortable pattern of getting along together?

Wasn't it all much grimmer and much more stark than that?

He had told them so just yesterday, and he had believed it. He believed it still. Then why should he consider for even a second forgiving the rationale of those who might be wobbling in their support of him now?

It was all very typical of the evil genius of Fred Van Ackerman, he thought. Fred was indeed a little Hitler, one of those fortunately rare types who know exactly how to appeal to all the lowest instincts of their fellow beings. And of course, as Walter had so accurately observed, the reason Fred was able to achieve such successes of evil was because they were hidden there waiting for him, needing only to be called out with the right words and the right timing. His appeal could succeed, as Walter said, only because it synthesized what many were secretly thinking.

That was the honest fact of it.

Damn mankind, the President thought with a sudden savagery, which could be held to the paths of principle such a tiny, tiny time before it wandered off again down the paths of prejudice, self-interest, cupidity and weakening of will.

Already his secretaries were reporting a tide of telegrams and telephone calls to the White House, running overwhelmingly in favor of Fred's position. Already Bob Leffingwell had called from State to report that he was receiving very delicate but nonetheless pointed intimations from a number of diplomatic contacts that possibly, just possibly, the West might have to consider going to Russia's assistance if the tide should really turn against her—"Nothing definite, you understand," Bob said with a savagery of his own. "Just a hint here and a whisper there. But they're wavering, Mr. President. They're beginning to shift."

In hours now, probably, NAWAC would be back in the streets demonstrating for aid to Russia. And before you knew it, there would be a "National Committee to Save Western Culture," or some such fancy title, its solemn rationale presented in a full-page ad in the New York *Times,* its letterhead brimming over with the names of distinguished liberals and conservatives alike, all united at last in one great common cause of saving the West from Fred's "Godless yellow hordes of Asia."

Overnight, thanks to one shrewd political gambler who still knew how to be as troublesome outside the Senate as he had been in it, the mood and climate had changed. But again, the President admitted with a grim honesty—only because men wanted it to change. Fred could never have done it alone.

So he cursed again, knowing even as he did so that accursed or no, mankind was still his burden, and particularly that segment of it that had grouped itself together more than two centuries ago under the working label "United States of America."

His anger, impatience and frustration would pass, as they were doing already even as he expressed them to himself in language vivid and violent.

The burden would remain.

And how to carry it now, if the drive to force his hand gained momentum, as of course it would if Chinese successes grew?

Suddenly he was not at all as calm as he had been a few moments ago at the end of his talk with Bill Abbott. Suddenly a great urgency filled his mind and heart. His instinct was as good as Bill's and Walter's and Frankly's and it told him the same thing as theirs told them. His half-joking comment to Bill about Speech One came to mind: "Come on, gang, hold the line!"

Already—such was the pell-mell headlong rush of these dread days in which everything was compressed and crowded into little—it was time for Speech One.

He called in the press secretary and told him to schedule it for 9 P.M.

Meanwhile the tempo of debate at home accelerated. So, too, did events abroad.

"Mr. Speaker," cried young Bronson Bernard of New York, fiery and consumed with the significance of the moment and himself, "I well know that it is considered not quite right for a member so young as I to join so actively in debate after being here so short a time. But, Mr. Speaker, I submit that it is exactly my youth which gives me the right to speak. For I am of that generation which stands to lose most if the culture of the West goes down.

"Oh, yes, Mr. Speaker," he cried, as there was some murmuring among his elders on the floor and among the media in their omniscient galleries above, "let us make no mistake about it! We who have always abhorred and forsworn war can feel it in our bones: now war is coming rapidly closer to all that we hold dear. It may take weeks, it may take months or years—it may, so fast is the world spinning, take hours. But sooner or later, if it is allowed to run unchecked, the challenge will be here. The last line of Western defenses will be gone, and we will remain to face the dread onslaught alone.

"So, then, Mr. Speaker, I ask you, is it beyond sensibility to take counsel now—to take *action* now—to prevent the arrival of that fearful hour?

"The President of the United States of America spoke to us just twenty-four hours ago in this very chamber and called upon us to go it alone. He urged a new isolationism, a new withdrawal into Fortress America. Given any other set of circumstances, that might be the right, the honorable and the safe course. But look at the circumstances now—and look at the consequences if we do as he suggests.

"There is a chance that the conflict now resuming and apparently heading toward new heights of fury will burn itself out, leaving both participants too exhausted to ever resume again. The world thought that moment had been reached two weeks ago. It was not. And it is entirely possible that it may not be reached now, particularly if one side or the other speedily wins dominance. Particularly will it not be reached if that side which is alien to all the culture and traditions we of the Western world have so patiently built up over so many centuries is the one that emerges triumphant.

"Then, Mr. Speaker, we would indeed face the situation described so vividly by the chairman of the National Anti-War Activities Congress in his statement last night: a situation in which China would swarm across Russia and into Europe, toppling all our friends like dominoes as she goes, a situation in which she could then be expected to move swiftly into the Pacific Basin and before long even to our own shores.

"This, I submit, Mr. Speaker, we cannot permit. We cannot afford to let a way of life and a political philosophy hostile to our own dominate a third of the earth's surface and eventually encircle us. We must take preventive action and take it while we still have an ally who can assist. We must not wait until Russia surrenders and then find that we *really* have to go it alone.

"To do so would be to betray all the principles of freedom and stability that we have always cherished and defended. We must be courageous now and defend them again, while there is still time and while our decisive assistance can swiftly tip the balance the other way and bring a speedy and relatively harmless end to the conflict. We owe it to ourselves and to that Western cultural tradition that is being defended now at great cost in blood and treasure by the United States of Russia. Let us help her, Mr. Speaker! Let us give her the aid she needs to finish the job, before it is too late!"

And he gave his head a sudden emphatic shake and sat down, to the mingled applause and boos of his colleagues and the galleries.

Shrewd and experienced observers in both places thought the applause was somewhat greater than the boos. The ensuing silence was more than a little challenging as the ex-President of the United States arose slowly, looked thoughtfully about the crowded chamber and began to speak.

"Mr. Speaker," he said, "I have listened with amazement to the address of the new member from New York. He is, as he says, young, and he professes to speak for the young and, I take it, the liberal young.

"How ironic it is then, to hear all the arguments of the conservative position vis-à-vis the Soviet Union in past years coming back to us out of the mouth of the liberal young gentleman from New York! How ironic and how laughable, were it not so tragically mistaken, it is to hear him repeat, in defense of Russia, the same old clichés about the civilization of the West, the defense of freedom, the domino theory, the alien culture that may overwhelm our friends and creep upon our borders!

"One might laugh indeed. Except that it would be very sad laughter.

"The President of the United States of America certainly did urge yesterday a new isolationism in which America would stay out, preserve that Western culture the gentleman is worried about, and hold herself ready to step in and bind up the wounds after it is all over. No other power now possesses the resources and the strength to do this. If the war in Asia escalates further and ends in the complete exhaustion that seems likely, someone will have to do it. If we get directly involved, we will be exhausted too. Also we will very likely suffer some of the same atomic devastation that has already hit Russia and China, and may very soon hit them again.

"It seems to me, Mr. Speaker, that to intervene on one side or the other would be insanity. Our only role, our only salvation perhaps, is not to get drawn in. It is to stay out, stay strong and await events patiently and firmly, without fear or hysteria or taking sides in any way.

"The gentleman from New York, and those who agree with him, who no doubt will also speak here this afternoon, takes a moral stance and talks nobly of Western culture. No such nicety hampered the head of NAWAC when he issued his statement last night. He sought, apparently with some success, to revive the myth of 'the Yellow Peril' —to put it on a racial basis, to arouse old hidden fears of Orientals, to call up the old bitterness of race against race. Oh, I know, Mr. Speaker," he said calmly as Bronson Bernard half rose from his seat in protest, "I know these are not the words of the gentleman from New York. He does not possess the crude arrogance which we who know the former Senator from Wyoming have come to recognize as his trademark. Representative Bernard is not that blatant, nor does he relish quite that cruelly the game of forcing people to face their lowest impulses in the mirror. That is the game, and in its own twisted way quite possibly the genius, of the former Senator from Wyoming.

"It is not a game we can afford in the present crisis, because it will blind us to our own best interests, and the best interests of the rest of the world. To return to racism would be fatal. To let ourselves be stampeded into this horrible war on the ground that one side is 'ours' in the racial sense, while the other is 'alien' and 'hostile' simply because it has a different skin color, would be to abandon all sense of balance and all judgment. We would really lose, then, and nobody would gain.

"It seems to me extremely unlikely at this moment that we will intervene in the war. If by some unforeseeable set of circumstances intervention should ever become necessary, then it would have to be on a cold-blooded, reasoned, entirely dispassionate basis. It could not be on an emotional basis of racism and fear of other skins and other colors. That would be an outcome supremely tragic not only for us, but for the entire world.

"Mr. Speaker, I hope the debate as it proceeds today will discuss this. Let's keep it to the issue raised by the head of NAWAC. Already he has aroused a very substantial feeling in the country. The fact that its thrust is entirely opposed to NAWAC's anti-war tradition—the fact that a great many people who believe in no-war are nonetheless hastening to join his campaign—is evidence of how deeply the racial issue cuts in spite of all the pretenses of our recent years. It must not dictate what we do in this terrible war. The consequences of the wrong guess are too awful to contemplate."

"Mr. President," Senator August said with an air of offended dignity as great as that with which Bronnie Bernard was rising to reply at the same moment in the House, "I do not accept the argument of the distinguished Senator from Michigan, Mr. Munson, that this is a racial issue, or that race in any way enters into the grave decisions that America must make in the next few days or even hours. That is as repugnant to all decent Americans as anything could possibly be. It is an attempt to draw a deliberate red herring across—"

"Mr. President," Bob Munson interrupted, "will the Senator yield to me? What does he think our former great and beloved colleague, the head of NAWAC, has done in his statement? His statement was racism pure and simple. His entire argument for intervention is racism pure and simple. And from around the country, Senator, your telephone calls and mine, your telegrams and mine, your mail and mine, is reflecting already a startling and ominous response to exactly that racist line of the former Senator from Wyoming. How can we pretend the issue is anything else? It is the white race against the colored that Van Ackerman is trying to promote. He uses the term 'yellow hordes' deliberately, as he uses all evil terms that suit his purposes deliberately. So why should the Senator from Minnesota try to pretend that there is some high moral purpose to be found in the intervention argument?"

"Mr. President," Tom August said, flushing but standing his ground doggedly as he had so often in foreign-policy debates, "I agree with the Senator that the general tone and many of the terms used by the former Senator from Wyoming were unfortunate and conducive to unhappy interpretations. But to some degree—and I say this only because I think the Congress should weigh carefully the whole question of intervention—Senator Van Ackerman did make a point which obviously worries many of his countrymen. And that is whether this country should stand idly by and watch the death of a nation which, for all its difficult aspects and uncomfortable past, still possesses certain basic similarities of tradition and culture and history with our own."

("Wow!" UPI murmured to the *Post* in the Press Gallery above. "These are liberals?" The *Post,* somewhat ahead of his editorial board downtown, gave him a cold glance. "Sure," he said. "Why not? You aren't saying the Chinese are like *us,* are you?")

"It is true," Senator August continued, "that the new Russian government was hostile and uncooperative during the recent peace journey of the President of the United States of America. It is true that there was a very slight glimmer of cooperation, for a very brief moment, from the President of the new government of China.

"But that is not enough, Mr. President, to justify our sitting by and permitting Russia to go down, when Russia is the only bulwark we have against the spread of a culture which is not, no matter how it is rationalized, similar to our own.

"If Russia goes down in Asia, Mr. President, what will there be to prevent the onrush of Chinese imperialism across European Russia and into Europe itself? And on the other side, it is but a short distance to India and the Pacific Basin, and then, before very long, possibly our own shores as well.

"Everything we have always stood for, in terms of individual freedom and international cooperation, would go down before this onrushing tide. Our friends and allies in Europe and the Pacific would go under like dominoes, one by one. We would then truly stand alone, not in the idealistic sense President Knox attempted to portray yesterday, of the great preservator of civilization, but as the last forlorn citadel of civilization, doomed to fall. What will it profit us then, to have been noble and refrained from intervention? Not a thing, Mr. President! Not a thing!"

"Mr. President," Bob Munson said with a patience he tried to keep from sounding too exasperated, "the Senator from Minnesota is begging the question. He is also overlooking two fundamental facts.

"The first is that there is no evidence at the moment that Russia is actually facing defeat, so what is all the shouting about? She has apparently suffered some reverses in the past few hours in a sector of one hundred miles, more or less, along a border of some four thousand miles. Does that spell the end of a great power even under such conditions as now prevail over there? Is that why we are letting Fred Van Ackerman and a lot of our timid countrymen stampede us into discussing intervention? One hundred miles out of four thousand? And a reversal that may itself be reversed even as we are speaking?

"Shame on us, Senators, to let ourselves be stampeded like this! This is no way to find our way through the very terrible difficulties we face right now. It is desperately important that we remain absolutely calm and objective. We are getting much too emotional.

"Secondly, let us remember, always remember, that this is *atomic war* we are discussing. A week ago this was still a fact so vivid that it terrified us all. Today, even though it may be resumed on a large scale at any moment, the human mind has somehow adapted itself to the point where we are discussing, quite matter-of-factly, quite as though it had no relation to atomic war, whether or not we should intervene. We are talking as though it were a conventional war, some ordinary dispute in foreign affairs, something customary, common, familiar.

"Already, perhaps, it *is* familiar—such is the dreadful adaptability of the human mind.

"I sometimes think the sheer adaptability of the human mind will be the death of us yet.

"Maybe this is the time.

"So, I suggest to Senators, and indeed to all our countrymen, that we remember that Russia may not be at all in a situation where she needs intervention. Certainly she hasn't asked for it. A hundred miles out of four thousand! A temporary reverse! What are we talking about?

"And secondly, let us remember that it is still *atomic war* that's involved here—dreadful, awful, cataclysmic, horrible *atomic war.*

"We need arguments more noble than racism to warrant even thinking about intervention under conditions such as these."

"I still say we cannot afford to stand idly by and watch a basically similar society go down before a culture that is foreign to our ways and our traditions, and is apparently bent upon all-out imperial conquest," Tom August replied stubbornly in the hushed, uneasy Senate.

"I still say," William Abbott said, "that we need something more than an evil racism and the phony threat of 'alien culture' to warrant our even thinking for a single moment about intervention in atomic war."

"I still say this House would be derelict in its responsibility if it permitted Russia to go down without assistance before the advancing tide of a way of life that is completely foreign and completely inimical to ours," Bronson Bernard replied stubbornly in the hushed, uneasy House.

In the Senators' Lobby, just off the floor of the Senate, and in the Members' Reading Room just off the floor of the House, the news tickers suddenly came to life. Bells rang, keys chattered. Responding swiftly, Representative Henry "Pep" Kowalski of Michigan and Senator Warren Strickland of Idaho ripped off the message, read it hastily and carried it with trembling hands into their respective chambers.

FLASH, it said. CHINESE DRIVE MANY MILES INTO RUSSIA AS FURIOUS DEATH CHARGE CONTINUES. REPORT RUSSIAN RESISTANCE CRUMBLING AT MANY POINTS.

This was followed moments later, while proceedings in both houses stood in temporary suspension as members crowded around to pass the news from hand to hand, by another

FLASH—RUSS LAUNCH NEW ATOMIC ATTACK ON CHINESE CITIES. CHINESE RETALIATE.

And an hour later, both houses in recess but nobody leaving, members milling about talking worriedly to one another, calling back and forth to members of the media and visitors in the galleries above, all pretense of business and order gone, everyone desperately worried and waiting for no one knew what, there came yet another

FLASH—MOSCOW APPEALS FOR IMMEDIATE U.S. INTERVENTION.

And so the bell tolled once more, and perhaps for the last time, for the President of the United States of America.

BOOK FIVE
THE PROMISE OF JOY

1. "MY COUNTRYMEN," he said at 9 P.M., looking tired, strained but unyielding, "you all know the terrible news that has come to us in the past couple of hours from Asia.

"In a desperate mustering of her remaining strength, China has managed to break through the Russian lines over a relatively broad sector—according to reports reaching me just a moment ago, about three hundred miles. Her troops, tanks and atomic field weaponry have penetrated in depth about a hundred miles, and they are still advancing. Russian resistance in many sectors of the front seems to be collapsing.

"In response, finding herself being pushed back on the ground and in the air by the desperate fury of the Chinese assault, Russia has resorted once more to atomic attack on a score of Chinese cities, some hit two weeks ago, some new targets. For the first time Peking has been attacked, and is partially destroyed.

"In response to that, the Chinese have renewed atomic attacks on an equally large number of Russian cities, including for the first time Moscow.

"So the war has been fully resumed, in even more awful form than before.

"And as of this moment, the Russians, whom the world had confidently expected to win if war should come again, are losing.

"As a result, as you all know, I have received a desperate and urgent appeal from Moscow that the United States intervene on the side of Russia.

"This appeal," he said, and he looked somberly straight into the cameras, "has already, as you also know, received considerable support in this country. No doubt that support has increased a hundredfold in the past couple of hours. No doubt it will increase still further if Russian defeats continue.

"You have a right to know—the world has a right to know—what your government intends to do about it."

He paused, took a sip of water with deliberate slowness, raised his eyes again to the cameras. An enormous tension gripped the watching earth. Across the street in Lafayette Square, where NAWAC and its sympathizers had mustered a crowd estimated at more than one hundred thousand in the past two hours, someone shouted, *"Save the West!"* and there was a great answering roar of endorsement and support.

"For the time being," he said slowly, "we shall do nothing other than offer our good offices should both sides wish to make another attempt at peaceful negotiations."

In Lafayette Square the roar turned to a savage groan, and throughout America similar groans competed with relieved applause wherever his countrymen watched. At the moment, he would have been pleased to know, the balance was still about fifty-fifty, not yet as far gone on the other side as he feared. He devoted himself in his closing brief paragraphs to an attempt to shore up the neutrality he considered so desperately imperative.

"This decision will appall some of you and gratify others. I can only hope a majority will presently conclude that it is right.

"In any event," he said quietly, "it is the course your government will pursue until the situation in Asia is better clarified by events.

"We will do so for the same reason I gave the Congress scarcely twenty-four hours ago—because we must stay out, stay strong, and stand by to help restore some semblance of civilization in Asia when the combatants at last either collapse exhausted or decide to talk again.

"We shall do so because we believe that neither antagonist, whatever the temporary Chinese gains at the moment may be, can really conquer the other. The countries are too vast, the populations too huge, the administrative problems in the wake of such a war too humanly impossible. Neither China nor Russia can do it. In the long run they simply cannot win. Therefore, they must eventually stop fighting. Given the already extensive weakening of their forces in the first exchange, and the great fury with which they are fighting now, the end cannot be very long delayed.

"When it comes, we must be in the clear and in a position to help, for the need will be enormous.

"We cannot do this if we allow ourselves to be drawn in now. We must be calm—be patient—be firm—be unafraid—and be uncommitted to either side. Any other course, in my judgment, would be disastrous not only for us, but for people everywhere who look to us to restore some order and balance after this terrible contention ends.

"I urge you not to worry, and to be of good heart. Your government has carefully and prayerfully considered what it should do. It acts always with your best interests and the safety of America in mind. It is also acting, we believe, in the best interests of the warring powers and all other nations that may be affected by their warring—in other words, all of us.

"Our refusal to respond to Moscow's appeal does not mean that we are choosing sides, favoring China, knocking down Russia or anything else. It just means that we are trying to be calm, to be sensible and to act with responsibility, forethought and careful planning in a most dreadful and difficult situation.

"God bless you, and good night."

AID-RUSSIA RESOLUTION INTRODUCED AS CONGRESS MEETS IN EMERGENCY NIGHT SESSION FOLLOWING PRESIDENT'S SPEECH. BITTER DEBATE ROCKS BOTH HOUSES. FOREIGN COMMITTEES TO TAKE UP MEASURE TOMORROW MORNING, TRY TO GET IT TO FLOOR AT NOON.

RUSS FALLBACK CONTINUES AS CHINESE DRIVE AHEAD THROUGH DEVASTATED LAND. VAST NEW CASUALTIES REPORTED FROM LATEST A-BOMBING. NEW CLOUD DRIFTS TOWARD EUROPE.

PRESIDENT CALLS MIDNIGHT TALK WITH CONGRESSIONAL LEADERS, TOP ADVISERS. POSSIBLE VETO SEEN IF RESOLUTION PASSES.

"Thank you all for coming," he said, "particularly after such a hectic session. Why was it felt necessary to hold one, by the way?"

"Well, sir," Jawbone replied promptly, "it was jes' obvious that there was pressure buildin' there, yes, sir. Pressure buildin' up so high we had to do *some*thin', Mr. President, sir. Seemed to me we jes' needed a safety valve in view of Russia's appeal, and the way things are goin', and your speech, and all."

"Some safety valve," he said dryly. "Did either of you know the resolution was coming?"

"Tom August was going to introduce it this afternoon," Arly Richardson said, "but I persuaded him to hold it until you spoke. I couldn't get him to hold it any longer. And apparently Bronson Bernard and his friends were waiting in the House."

"Yes, sir," Jawbone agreed.

"You still didn't have to meet until noon in the regular order of things," the President said. "Why the emergency session? Isn't life dramatic enough, these days?"

"We have our right to drama, too, Mr. President," Arly said with a dryness to match his own. "As Jawbone says, a safety valve. Actually, I didn't think feeling had started to run quite so high as it apparently has. We really had a bitter debate, as you know."

"We, too, Mr. President, sir," Jawbone agreed emphatically. "We, too!"

"In which," he said, "my two leaders in the two houses not only didn't come to my support but actually cooperated in plans to get the resolution through as fast as possible."

"We have to live with one another," Arly Richardson said almost indifferently.

"Why?" he demanded, trying not to sound as frustrated as he felt. "You traveled with me, you saw the situation. Why do you want us to get involved? What earthly good would it do this country, or anyone else?"

"It isn't the good it would do, exactly, Mr. President," Jawbone said carefully. "It's jes' a kind of feelin' that mebbe, if things are gettin' so bad over there, if Russia's really gettin' desperate and on the ropes, then, mebbe it's right what Fred Van Ackerman and them say—mebbe we *should* stand by the people that's basically like us. Mebbe we *should* defend the world against those yellow hordes. Eight hundred million of 'em, Mr. President—almost *one billion*. Look at 'em now, pushing and sweepin' through the Russian lines in a livin' tide because they jes' don't give a damn about human life, they got so allfired much of it. They jes' don't *give* a damn. And where does that leave us if they beat Russia and turn our way, Mr. President? Where does that leave us?"

"He answered that in his speech," Bill Abbott said with an angry impatience. "It isn't going to happen, this sweeping over Russia, this sweeping over the world, this—this 'threat to our own shores,' as your side put it in the debate. Russia's too big, they can't conquer her, any more than she can conquer them."

"Eight hundred million on a death mission against two hundred million?" Arly Richardson asked with an angry impatience of his own. "Use your arithmetic, Bill!"

"I am using it!" the ex-President snapped. "I am also, I hope, using a little common sense. My God, man, you people want us to get involved in atomic war—*atomic war*. What's the matter with you, anyway?"

"Now, just a minute," Senator Richardson said sharply. "Just a minute. Do you mean to tell me that if we come in fresh, select a few targets, get in and out fast, against a nation that has just suffered its second round of atomic devastation, a nation that is engaged completely and absolutely in a titanic struggle with its neighbor, that we would suffer the same way either one of them is? It would be a surgical strike, Bill. In and out. Not a bog-down. A *surgical* strike."

"Yes, I know that's the pet phrase you all came up with tonight," Bill Abbott said, "and no doubt it's the pet phrase we'll begin to hear from the media if you've managed to get them on your side, which I hope to hell you haven't because this is tough enough without them yapping and yammering. 'Surgical strike,' all very neat and clean, against 'yellow hordes' we won't admit are 'yellow hordes,' because that upsets our concept of our noble selves. 'Surgical strike'! It doesn't work that way in this day and age. We'd never get home scot-free."

"It *would* work," Jawbone insisted stubbornly. "Yes, sir, Bill, it *would*. And as for those 'yellow hordes,' now, they *are* hordes and they *are* yellow and they *aren't* like us, and I say we've got to stop 'em! We've got to stop 'em right now while they're busy and can't handle both Russia and us together. *That's* what makes sense, Bill, not maunderin' on about neutrality and savin' the world and such."

"Is that what it is?" the President demanded sharply. "'Maundering'? And who's talking about 'saving the world' if you aren't?"

"Many, many people in Congress and throughout the country," Arly Richardson said, "are coming to think that our way of saving it is better than yours. We honor your motives, Orrin, as I hope you honor ours, but we really think, for all its risks, our way might be better. The situation has simply become that bad."

"And it doesn't seem that bad to me?" he inquired, and pushed himself back with ironic disbelief. He placed his hands before him on the desk for emphasis. "*Look:* against all reason, against all logic, against all their own best interests and the best interests of humankind, these two giants have let themselves be driven by the worst elements in human nature, by hatred and fear, into warring upon each other, at what an awful cost. And now you want me to let us be driven by hatred and fear into jumping in, also against all reason, all logic, our own best interests and the best interests of humankind. I won't do it. *I won't do it.*"

" 'Won't' is a big word, Mr. President," Arly said softly, "when your country and the Congress say, 'Will.' "

"They haven't said it yet," he replied sharply, "nor will they, if I can help it. I will not have my hands bound. I must be free to decide what is best as circumstances dictate. I want that resolution stopped before it gets to the floor. Bob and Blair"—he turned to the Secretary of State and the Secretary of Defense—"I want you to go to the Hill first thing tomorrow morning and lobby everybody you can get hold of on those two committees. I won't ask you to help, Arly, or you either, Jawbone, because it's obvious I've already lost you both. But I'd like you to, Bill, and you, Cullee and Hal, and I'll ask Bob Munson and Lafe and Warren and Stanley and some others, and we'll put up a hell of a battle, anyway. And if worst comes to worst"—he paused and looked slowly from face to face, expression grim and unyielding—"I always have one little string left in my bow."

"If it goes through the way I think it may go through," Arly told him, "we'll have enough votes to override your veto."

"Oh, no, you won't," he said firmly, praying he was right.

"We'll see," Senator Richardson said calmly. "We'll see."

"So we shall," he agreed, rising to his feet, extending his hand in good-night to each in turn. "It's past midnight, the day will come fast and be busy for us all. Thank you for coming. Cullee"—the Vice President, who had remained silent and somber throughout, paused in his turn toward the door—"stay for a minute, will you? There's something I want to talk to you about."

"Sure," Cullee said, his tone surprised. "Good night, Arly," he said half humorously as he sat down again. "Watch out for my rulings this afternoon. I'm going to be awfully tough."

"But fair, I assume," Senator Richardson said.

"It's my curse," the Vice President agreed. "I try and I try, but there you are. Good night, you-all."

And to the chorus of their farewells the door closed, the room fell silent, the President of the United States of America looked long and thoughtfully at his Vice President, who looked thoughtfully and earnestly back. Presently Orrin smiled.

"Never a dull moment, is there?"

"No, sir," Cullee said softly, "there sure isn't. Are we going in?"

"I said we weren't," he reminded sharply. Then his expression changed to one of honest admission of the facts. "I shall do my level best to keep us out. I pray I can succeed. If, however, the lemmings are determined to plunge over the edge, I may find myself forced to yield."

"On the Russian side?"

He sighed.

"Cullee, I am damned if I know, and that's the truth. They don't deserve it, and certainly they don't deserve it on the basis of the sleazy reason put forward by little Mr. Van Ackerman and already echoed by so many upstanding and righteous citizens in Congress and elsewhere. Certainly not on the basis of 'the Yellow Peril.' On the basis of the balance of power, which is evidently the only way even the slightest vestige of peace can ever be maintained by selfish, imperfect and greedy humanity, then perhaps there is an argument. But," he added quickly, "I am not in any way committing myself to that. I'm not committing myself to anything. I'm sitting tight and waiting to see how long the furor lasts and whether it is really going to be sufficient to force my hand."

"It's getting stronger," Cullee said unhappily. "That was a hell of a debate and there'll be another today. The chances of that resolution going through are increasing by the minute."

"That's what I wanted to talk to you about—two things, actually. The first is that the chances of my being assassinated, which have never been exactly minimal, have now gone up a thousandfold with NAWAC back in the field and the anti-neutrality hysteria mounting. The amalgamated kooks of the land have their favorite target back again, now: I was a hero for a little while, but no more. And not only the kooks, but those who view murder as an extension of politics, as well.

"Somewhere here—where is it?" He riffled through the mass of papers on the desk. "Here it is—I have just received the official report of the commission investigating Harley Hudson's death, Ted Jason's death and—and Beth's death. Starting with Harley, it was a thoroughly well-organized plan to change the succession of power in this country in favor of the old Soviet Union. If I hadn't escaped at the Monument by some fluke of fate, it might very well have succeeded. As it was, it cost the deaths of a President, a possible future President and my wife. The old Soviet Union isn't here any more, the matter is relatively moot for the time being and I'm not going to release it until enough time has passed to give a little historical perspective—but there it is. The same elements that were devoted to Communism are still in NAWAC and are still, I have no doubt, devoted to Russia itself. Therefore, they'll be after me. Add to them the hysteric, the paranoiac, the unbalanced, the erratic who flock to any cause and who now have the biggest cause in history to throw them off base, and you have odds that would give any insurance company pause.

"And that, my boy, is where you come in."

For a moment the handsome black face before him looked bleak and stricken. Then the Vice President shrugged and managed a smile.

"It goes with the oath of office. I'm ready. Although I wouldn't be honest"—the smile grew a little—"if I didn't say I hope to hell you live, Mr. President. *I* don't want this mess!"

"It is one, isn't it?" he agreed somberly. "It is the mess to end all messes. . . . Well, good: I was sure you weren't afraid of it, but it's good to hear you say so."

"What's to be afraid of?" Cullee inquired. "I'm here—you're here—we have the job to do. If you go, I take it, that's all. You got me into it—with my willing cooperation—and it can't be helped." The smile grew broader. "I'd sure pray a hell of a lot, though."

"Don't think I'm not."

"We're all praying with you," Cullee said. "And for you." . . . The moment ended, his tone turned matter-of-fact. "What was the second thing you wanted to talk about?"

The President gave him a shrewd, appraising look and spoke with the bluntness characteristic when he faced an awkward subject.

"Race. Color. 'The Yellow Peril,' which for many whites, by implication and extension, is the peril of all skins that aren't white . . . and whether a black Vice President feels strongly enough about the attempt to make race the fulcrum for intervention so that he will come to my assistance and attack it for me."

It was Cullee's turn to give him an appraising look.

"When I first got to know you," he said finally in a slow and thoughtful voice, "I was suspicious, as a lot of people were, of the 'conservative Orrin' stereotype. I thought it applied, much more than it did, to practically everything that came along, domestic or foreign. Being black, I was extra touchy on that subject and extra anxious to find signs that you were racist and hostile. Well, before long I found, as any honest man would find, that conservative old Orrin wasn't all that conservative, either domestically, in foreign affairs or on the subject of race. I realized he was a human being just like everybody else, pretty middle-of-the-road, and on some things, in fact, much more 'liberal,' whatever that means, than his 'liberal' critics gave him credit for." He smiled. "I really quite got to like the guy. In fact, I became a respecter, an admirer and a believer. Then we had that long talk when you were Secretary of State, before Seab Cooley died, and that did it. I enlisted for the duration, and here I am. So what do you want me to do?"

"Say something from the chair tomorrow noon, and make it as strong as you can. It will upset the Senate, because they regard the Vice President as the President's agent, rightly or wrongly, and they don't like him to get too involved. But on the other hand, this is an upsetting time and I guess we can take the flak—I guess we don't have much choice. I don't think the resolution is going through either house by anywhere near the margin Arly thinks. I have too much faith in the basic decency of the American people—perhaps falsely," he interjected ironically, "but there it is. But it *is* going to be very tight, and I feel that you really have almost a duty to speak out—not necessarily a duty to me, though I appreciate very much what you say about me, but to your own race and to the general concept of this country as a basically decent and hopeful place. Will you do it?"

Cullee looked relieved.

"I've been wanting to, but I was waiting until you were ready to ask me."

"I'm asking."

"With pleasure," the Vice President said. A sudden scowl crossed his face. "I suppose that bastard Van Ackerman will come out of this stronger than ever."

"If any of us comes out of it," the President said, "he may. I'm surprised LeGage is sticking with him on this, though."

"Maybe I'll talk to him, too," Cullee said, scowl deepening. "He needs it."

"I'm really surprised he hasn't split from NAWAC over the race issue," the President said. The Vice President smiled.

"I said I'll talk to him," he repeated. The smile faded. "It probably won't be easy, the hard-nosed bastard, but I'll try."

It was, however, much easier than he had thought it would be, when, fifteen minutes later, his chauffeur drove him into the grounds of the Vice President's official residence at the Naval Observatory up Massachusetts Avenue. Lights were on in the house, and in the drive he saw the sleek and highly expensive sports car that the chairman of DEFY managed to maintain with the aid of the dues of his organization's many humble and earnest members.

Cullee's mouth set in a thin line. The good feeling he had carried from the White House after his cordial and affectionate good-night from the President vanished. He entered the house prepared for battle.

Surprisingly, it did not come. 'Gage was cold sober and in a cold rage, but for once it was not directed against Cullee and all the old twisted jealousies that Cullee's successes as a man and as a public servant had so often aroused in 'Gage's seething mind and volatile heart. It was directed against exactly the man Cullee and the President wanted it to be.

LeGage, too, it seemed, had been as startled and angered as Cullee by Fred's arrant appeal to racism. He, too, had seen the implicit transition Bill Abbott had perceived, from fear of "the Yellow Peril" to fear of "the black peril," in the minds of their more frightened and intolerant white countrymen. He, too, had been dismayed, frightened and infuriated. And he, too, had come to ask Cullee to speak out.

"Now, why," the Vice President asked slowly, "should I do that? Why do you want me to help old Orrin out of this mess? After all, you didn't think so much of old Orrin lately, as I recall. Why shouldn't I just play it cool and stand to one side while the whiteys fight it out? Why should *I* get involved?"

"Because Orrin Knox is right!" LeGage exclaimed with an impatient anger.

"Right on staying out?" Cullee inquired in the same slow and quizzical tone.

"Right on race!"

"W-e-e-ll," Cullee said with a deliberately infuriating slowness, "I . . . don't . . . know. . . ."

"Oh, stop it!" LeGage exclaimed, angrily and not entirely consistently. "There's no comparison between Orrin Knox and Fred Van Ackerman! That dirty bastard *never consulted me,* did you know that? I may just leave him, yet—I may just quit NAWAC and take my people with me. I may!"

"If you'll do that," Cullee said quickly, "I'll speak in the Senate this afternoon and be as tough as I know how."

LeGage studied him carefully for a second. A grim little smile touched his lips.

"Let me work on him first," he suggested softly. "Maybe we can scare him out of it."

"And you can stay in NAWAC and have your cake and eat it, too," the Vice President said. "Oh, no."

"You don't understand," LeGage said sharply. "That dirty bastard *never consulted me*. He never did."

"And if he had," Cullee said in the indifferent tone with which he could always upset 'Gage, "you would still have gone right along with him and tried to get us in on Russia's side, anyway. That's what NAWAC's always been about, boy, isn't it?"

"He's using race," LeGage said stubbornly, for once not rising to the bait, "and when he uses race—any kind of race, *boy*—he's attacking you and me. And you know it as well as I do."

"O.K., so *I'm* going to attack him."

"And *I'm* going to talk to him!"

"Make it fast," the Vice President suggested, "because it's two A.M. now and I'm going to be speaking in the Senate in just about ten hours."

"All right, I will!" LeGage cried angrily.

"Let me know how you make out, boy," Cullee urged in a kindly way. "Lots of luck."

And satisfied, when LeGage stormed out of the house five minutes later, that he had programmed him sufficiently for the target, he spent another half hour making notes for his speech to the Senate and then went up to Sarah, and bed.

"The *Post*," said the *Post* when it reached the streets three hours later, "has never knowingly condoned, or approved, or participated in, anything that even remotely smacked of racism.

"Nor will we now.

"Nor will we ever.

"Race as a reason for intervening on the side of Russia against China in the terrible new battles in Asia is a vicious argument that all responsible Americans, all who value their country's traditional decencies, must abhor and reject.

"We cannot state strongly enough our eternal opposition to the attempt to portray the current controversy as a contest between the white and yellow races, and to use that as an argument to intervene on behalf of the white race.

"It seems to us, however, that there are other grounds—still not decisive, still not entirely valid, no doubt subject to change at any moment as the tide of battle flows—upon which it might be possible for the United States of America to exercise a restraining, and probably decisive, influence upon the war.

"The first reason for intervention, of course, is that it would almost certainly end the war at once, which is something all sane men in the entire world desire. If done as its Congressional proponents conceive it—a 'surgical strike,' swiftly and antiseptically administered for the sole purpose of ending the war—it would carry its own justification.

"The second reason for intervention (while we do not for one moment accept the idea of one 'culture' being superior to another) is that it is true that Russia does, generally, represent the European tradition, the European way of looking at things, the whole complex of ideas, ideals, emotions that we have come to lump, historically and sentimentally, under the general label 'Western Civilization.'

"The third reason for intervention is that the Chinese, while in many ways an admirable people who in recent years have accomplished much, still do undeniably spring from a background, a tradition, a history which is uniquely and specially 'Eastern' and essentially much different from ours.

"China is—and it does no good to blink the fact—an alien country.

"Alien to our history, alien to our thinking, alien to our ways.

"Therefore, given Point One—that our intervention would almost certainly be decisive—the question arises, would we wish to make our intervention on the side of the culture that is traditionally and in every other way closest to ours, or do we wish to cast our lot with a nation—if one can call such an amorphous and unwieldy aggregation of disparate peoples 'a nation'—which is entirely alien (and, in essence, actively hostile) to everything in which we have always believed, and for which we have always stood?

"The issue is now before Congress in clear-cut form. We urge all Americans to consider most prayerfully which course they would like their government to take, and to so advise all of their public servants, from White House to Hill, who have anything to do with making the decision. . . ."

"The *Times,*" said the *Times,* "has already rejected, totally, completely and beyond any slightest implication of doubt, the racist argument for intervention in the Asiatic war put forward by ex-Senator Fred Van Ackerman.

"We are pleased to see that the brief resolution of support for Russia now pending in both houses of the Congress nowhere rests its argument upon such an evil and reactionary foundation.

"Rather, it places the issue where we believe it belongs—between two ways of life which have traditionally always been at odds and alien to one another—the 'East,' to use a term of easy reference, and the 'West.'

"That America does, in fact and in truth, belong to the 'West,' and that nine-tenths of all those nations and peoples with whom we have always felt kinship and sympathy also belong to it, cannot be denied.

"That Russia, although to some degree bridging East and West in her Asiatic reaches, also belongs to it cannot be denied.

"That China definitely does not belong to it, with equal emphasis cannot be denied.

"Therefore, Americans have much more than race to support their arguments for possible intervention—if, indeed, intervention in so dreadful a conflict should be desired by the majority.

"There is the fact that it is a contest between a tradition and culture essentially like our own, and a tradition and culture essentially different from and alien to our own.

"There is the fact that American intervention can almost certainly end the conflict completely, efficiently and at once. Particularly would this be so if it were done as the 'surgical strike' its proponents in Congress envisage: quickly in and quickly out, for the decisive and worthy purpose of ending the war.

"There is the fact that intervention, if used at all, would logically seem best justified and best employed on behalf of the side which is traditionally 'ours,' rather than the one traditionally hostile to us.

"The resolution embodying this belief is now before the Congress. We do not yet join those who say America *must* intervene. But for all those Americans—and surely they are nearly all of us—who are at the moment prayerfully and earnestly studying the situation, we commend the resolution as a point from which to approach a decision which, while tremendously painful, may yet prove to be both necessary and inevitable. . . ."

"Here in this city of great issues and great tensions but not always great men," Walter Dobius wrote rapidly at lovely "Salubria" buried in the snow, "the leaders of America are about to come to grips with the most fateful questions in American history: shall this nation intervene in atomic war in Asia, and if so, on whose side and for what purposes?

"Hourly, indeed almost momentarily, the conclusion is being reached in many powerful minds and hearts that yes, we may yet have to intervene if the Russian forces continue to be pushed back by the innumerable millions of Chinese who are now flooding forward in a great death tide, blinded to everything but the grim determination to crush the hated enemy.

"And if we find that we must intervene, then the second question becomes all-important: on whose side shall it be, and for what purposes?

"Intervention in atomic war is something so terrifying and abhorrent that only the most compelling of reasons should prompt our action. Yet it is not, as has already been brought out in Congressional debate, an absolutely fatal and final act. Rather, to use the term first proposed by Senate Majority Leader Richardson, it can be a 'surgical strike,' quickly and efficiently done. Indeed, it would have to be: anything else would be catastrophic. Its principal purpose would be to end the war.

"No more worthy purpose, possibly no more compelling purpose, could be found.

"Yet there is, in the minds of many here, a second purpose, almost as compelling as the first: the fact that the Russians, for all their sometimes difficult and prickly ways, are nonetheless in essence 'people like us'—and that the Chinese, for all their praiseworthy efforts to improve their sorry lot in recent years, are not.

"This is not in any way to embrace the viciously childish 'Yellow Peril' argument put forward by ex-Senator Van Ackerman. It is simply to recognize the fundamental human and ethnic fact that the Chinese have an alien background, an alien history, an alien tradition, an alien ambition in the world—and that if it is really coming down with great rapidity on the battlefield to a question of 'them,' meaning the Eastern tradition, or 'us,' meaning the West as symbolized now by the embattled Russians, then Americans may find they have no choice.

"Such is the mood, and such are the considerations, which underlie the bitter Congressional debate, now entering its second day, on the Richardson-Bernard resolution calling for American intervention on the side of the Russians. It is beginning to appear to many that there can be only one safe and honorable decision if civilization as we know it is to be saved. . . ."

"Washington," Frankly Unctuous said solemnly on "Today," "awaits, as does all America, the results of Congressional debate on the Richardson-Bernard resolution calling for American intervention on the side of the desperately retreating Russians.

"It is believed here that the outcome in Asia may be measured in hours rather than days. A dreadful urgency impels all who have responsibility for the decision.

"So it is not surprising that the resolution is gaining strength with a rapidity which indicates its likely passage sometime in the next forty-eight hours—not because of an argument so unworthy as former Senator Van Ackerman's 'Yellow Peril,' but simply because the war appears to be resolving itself into a contest to the death between an alien way of life, on the one hand, and all those dearly held traditions which we in this country and in Europe lump generally under the phrase 'Western civilization,' on the other.

"Many here are coming swiftly to the conclusion that Western civilization is indeed at stake in the savage death struggle in Asia. The immense tide of Chinese, sweeping forward in almost uncountable millions into Russia and toward the West, carry with them a tradition and history which are different from, and alien to, everything for which America and her allies have always stood. Russia is the bastion that today holds the line against the surging tide. The bastion is terribly shaken and may fall. Shall we let it go, or shall we help it, and so shore up and restore again the safety, stability and future of the West?

"Many fear intervention in atomic war, and with great reason. But, as Congressional proponents of the resolution have made perfectly clear, the intervention contemplated here would not be a bogging down in the endless morass of a land war in Asia. It would in no way entangle America for years, or waste her men and treasure, or commit her to a lengthy and devastating conflict. Rather it would be what Senator Richardson calls 'a surgical strike,' quick, clean, efficient—ended with luck in a day or two, certainly in less than a week.

"And it would be *over*, which is the important thing, and *over* in the cause of saving Western civilization from the essentially alien culture which now threatens to overwhelm that civilization's gallant defenders in Russia. It is this productive prospect which is beginning to appeal to so many here. . . ."

In a White House pulsating with the excitement of the great crisis, he put aside the papers, snapped off the nattering machine, passed a hand that trembled a little with strain and tiredness across his eyes.

So turned the tide, embellished with graceful phrases, adorned with elegant ratiocinations, laced with dainty hesitations and delicate reluctances, but moving, just as fast as they could make it go, steadily and implacably away from neutrality and toward intervention on the Russian side.

And the gut reason was not that they were still involved in their long-standing, fatuous and desperately self-destructive love affair with Communism and the Soviet Union, but that they were simply becoming scared to death of exactly what they pretended not to be scared of.

"The Yellow Peril" was condemned with a fine indignation: then the fear implicit in the slogan was trotted out and made respectable under other language. The "threat of alien culture" was treated to dutiful scorn; then its implications were embraced and made respectable a moment later.

Thus were liberal consciences appeased. Thus was consistency maintained. Thus was hypocrisy transformed into forthright candor.

He sighed again.

They were on their way. The next step would be Fred's word "hordes," together with an animal fear of onrushing China; and then would come the renewed attacks upon the President.

They had carefully refrained today from mentioning him at all, but if he stood firm for neutrality it would be only a very short moment, now, before they would renew, with an even greater zest inspired by fear, their violently virulent anti-Knox diatribes of the pre-war period.

And everybody would be back once more to square one.

He decided he would not let this aspect go by default, any more than he intended to let the rest of it go by default. He picked up the Picturephone and spoke directly to the editorial director of the *Times,* the executive chairman of *The Greatest Publication That Absolutely Ever Was,* the general director of the *Post,* the directors of ABC, CBS and NBC, to Walter and to Frankly. Cullee would speak to the Senate in a couple of hours, he said, and he would like them to join him in his office to listen. Startled and reluctant, but perforce bowing to the weight of his office if no longer to him, they said they would be there.

AID-RUSSIA RESOLUTION GAINING GROUND STEADILY AS CONGRESS PREPARES TO MEET FOR SECOND DAY OF TENSE DEBATE. HINT "MAJOR ADMINISTRATION SPOKESMAN" TO MAKE SURPRISE STATEMENT ON WHITE HOUSE POSITION. SOURCES SAY PRESIDENT STILL FIRM IN DETERMINATION TO VETO.

RUSSIANS CONTINUE TO FALL BACK AS CHINESE HORDES POUR THROUGH DISINTEGRATING LINE. REPORT "YELLOW WAVE" RACING HUNDREDS OF MILES TOWARD MOSCOW. OBSERVERS SAY "PERHAPS FIFTY MILLION CHINESE" OVERWHELMING RUSS IN HUMAN DEATH TIDE. MANY UNARMED BUT SHEER HATRED OF RUSS DRIVING MASS FORWARD TO SWAMP DEFENDERS. ATOMIC LULL GIVES CITIES RESPITE AS HUGE NEW CASUALTIES REPORTED ON BOTH SIDES.

DEATH DRIVE RACES TOWARD EUROPE AS FEARFUL WORLD AWAITS U.S. ACTION. PANIC SPREADS AS ATOMIC CLOUD DRIFTS NEARER.

"Members of the Senate," Cullee said shortly after noon, and in the Oval Office as in many other places his countrymen concentrated on his handsome, troubled face, "I ask your indulgence for a few brief minutes while I state my views on the pending resolution. It is a matter of such enormous importance that I feel the Vice President, like anyone else, has a right to be heard.

"I realize that this is somewhat irregular, although not without precedent. But I feel that my race gives me the right to comment on an issue which is essentially an issue of race: and so I shall."

There was a restless stirring across the floor and in the rapidly filling galleries, where for the first time in several weeks a few of NAWAC's black-jacketed hearties could be seen. In his seat beside Powell Hanson of North Dakota, Johnny DeWilton of Vermont murmured, "That's a good point for Arly to answer. Wonder how he'll do it." "If he has an ounce of sense," Powell murmured back, "he'll keep his damned mouth shut altogether."

"Members of the Senate," Cullee went on earnestly, "it is quite obvious to everyone familiar with the Hill that sentiment has grown very rapidly for the Richardson-Bernard resolution in the past few hours. And the reason for that, however much it may be obscured by other arguments, is race-based fear.

"It is not that a major power is seriously threatened—it is that a major *white* power is seriously threatened by a non-white power. That is what sets the pulses racing here and sends the shivers down so many backs. That is what makes the true hidden argument for intervention such a shabby and truly tragic one. For it goes back to old blind hatreds that we had thought the world was civilized enough to have overcome.

"Perhaps men can never really become that civilized. But I suggest to you, members of the Senate, that now of all times is the time they should try.

"At the moment, it appears that the Chinese attack, literally insane in its fury, is pushing the Russians back with steadily increasing rapidity. At the moment, we don't know when or where this process will stop. Already the media, whose major elements are beginning to swing very noticeably in the direction of intervention as their proprietors grow more fearful"—this time the uneasy stirring occurred in the Oval Room, though no one spoke—"are using headlines and reports to inflame public sentiment and quite possibly exaggerate the success of the Chinese drive.

"I am authorized to say to you, members of the Senate, that no reliable intelligence has yet reached this government that the Chinese onslaught, heavy as it is, has threatened any decisive portion of the Russian land mass. Cities and civilians have been killed but not much territory has been consolidated—at least not on the mammoth scale the headlines would have you believe. Headlines which refer to 'Chinese hordes' and say that they are 'pouring' everywhere through the Russian lines give a false emphasis. There is an unconfirmed report that a 'yellow wave'—and note that terminology, Senators—is 'racing' toward Moscow. Its progress, which is not accompanied by any newsmen but is only filtered through Hong Kong, not always a very reliable listening-post, is measured not in miles but in 'hundreds of miles.' Unidentified 'observers'—a word which all Americans know by now means the reporter who happens to be writing the story, with all his human failings and his human prejudices and his strong personal likes and dislikes—tell us that 'perhaps fifty million Chinese' are 'overwhelming' the Russians. Their progress is referred to consistently now as a 'death wave' or a 'death surge' or a 'death tide.'

"From a position of reasonably sincere neutrality when the contest seemed equal, the media are now plunging headlong toward intervention and toward the war which only yesterday, it seems, they abhorred and violently condemned.

"It appears once again that in the American media, as on this Hill, the basic controlling principle is still that fine old saying, 'It all depends upon whose ox is gored.'

"The ox this time is white, and the reaction in this country is already becoming blind, emotional, unrestrained and terribly dangerous to the best interests of America."

He paused and again there was an uneasy movement in the room and in the galleries. Into it someone suddenly shouted, "Black and yellow, black and yellow, hit 'em hard and hear 'em bellow!" There was an instant disturbance as heads turned, startled comment exploded and elderly Senate guards glared dutifully around in a stern and admonitory manner.

Cullee looked completely taken aback for a second. Then he crashed down the gavel with a heavy hand and spoke with a naked anger.

"Yes!" he said. "That's the next step! Get frantic about the yellow races and then get frantic about the black races! And then, my slimy friend in the gallery, whoever you are, you've got a hell of a lot of people in this world to be frantic about!

"Members of the Senate," he continued more calmly, mastering his anger with an obvious effort, "that is exactly what we are heading into, if we allow our approach to this war to be influenced by racial fears. *We cannot afford to do this.* Nothing can more certainly ruin our good judgment concerning our best interests in this terrible conflict, and nothing can more certainly divide us internally and get us to fighting among ourselves.

"Both of these results, I suspect, are exactly what those who are whipping up racial antagonisms have in mind. I suspect this is particularly true"—his voice became heavy with sarcasm—"of that great statesman, the former Senator from Wyoming, who was the first to inflame this issue and get us all to thinking along these lines. That's exactly what Fred Van Ackerman and his slimy NAWAC would like to achieve."

This time there was a genuinely ugly booing from many places in the galleries. This time he glanced up with an angry scowl but otherwise did not respond.

"Members of the Senate," he said earnestly, "there are many extraordinarily compelling reasons for staying out of this tragic war. Not the least of these is the likelihood that we might not be able to keep it from spreading, that no 'surgical strike,' however well and hopefully planned, could keep us from being dragged in deeper and deeper. Then we, too, in all likelihood, would suffer terrible atomic damage. We are not immune from such things. It would be very possible.

"Rather, we must stay out, as the President has said, holding ourselves ready to mediate, help and restore. We must never let ourselves be motivated by racial fears that can only subvert our judgment and turn us against one another.

"The Chinese are not landing on Long Island or Hawaii. They are not attacking us. They are making one last desperate effort and whether it succeeds, as momentarily seems possible, or loses, they are not going to be able to do anything more for a long, long time.

"The Congress must not tie the hands of the President with this resolution. We must not take sides. And above all we must not give way to ugly racial fears, for they become us not at all and weaken us most fearfully."

"And to that, gentlemen," the President said, reaching over to snap off the machine as Arly Richardson rose in the Senate and prepared to make his reply, "I for one say, 'Amen.'" He looked at them calmly across the big desk. "What say you?"

There was an uncertain silence and then by instinctive agreement they turned to the gentle old man who was executive chairman of *The Greatest Publication That Absolutely Ever Was.* He cleared his throat, studied the President thoughtfully for a moment and spoke with a careful deliberation.

"With his general sentiments, Mr. President," he said, "I think we all, of course, agree in principle. Whether the principle can be applied across the board in the present situation . . ." His voice trailed away, then resumed in what appeared to be a tone of genuine curiosity. "May I inquire, Mr. President, why you have asked us to come here? It seems to me a rather puzzling—"

"No, it doesn't, at all, Arthur," the President interrupted. "It seems to you perfectly obvious, just as it does to me: I need your help."

"In what way, Mr. President?" the editorial director of the *Times* inquired blandly. And the general director of the *Post* added with equal blandness:

"Why?"

It was his turn to study them thoughtfully, these eight stubborn faces already closed off and turned away from him, whose owners exercised so much completely uncontrolled control over what America thought—responsible to nothing at all but their own ruthless prejudices and arbitrary beliefs. He realized with a wry inward humor, not really very amused, that they were all much more comfortable now that they were on their way back to where they belonged—opposing Orrin Knox.

"The way in which you can help me," he said quietly, "is by devoting yourselves to keeping the country calm, and by continuing to oppose, with every means of influence you have, the racial frenzy against the Chinese which is fueling the drive for intervention. If you should join the hue and cry for that reason—or indeed for any reason—it could force my hand and, I believe, help to destroy possibly the last chance to save the world. I am asking you to support me in what I am trying to do. It is as simple as that."

"Mr. President," Walter Dobius said, his tone, while equally quiet, filled with a growing indignation, "I for one resent the implication of your remarks. I think we are doing our best to keep the country calm, to judge the whole situation calmly, and to advocate what we think is best for the country and the world, which is just as much our responsibility as it is yours. We are against racial frenzy as much as you, Mr. President. You aren't unique in that."

"But you aren't quite as firm against intervention as you were a little while ago, are you, Walter?" he asked.

"No, we're not," CBS said sharply, "because the situation has changed so rapidly in the past forty-eight hours that it's no longer as simple a question as you make out."

"Oh?" he inquired. "Have I made it sound simple? Forgive me, gentlemen. That was furthest from my thoughts."

"It seems to me," NBC remarked, "that all of us, be it in editorial, column or broadcast, have made several very valid points in the last few hours. The first is, of course, that you *can* end the conflict by intervening, and nobody else can. The second is that it is indeed a conflict between two cultures, to one of which we belong. The third is that if Russia does go down, if the balance of power is destroyed permanently by the onrushing hordes of China"—he flushed at the President's sudden quizzical expression but managed to amend with reasonable dignity—"if the balance of power is permanently upset in favor of China—then there is a strong possibility that we will sooner or later be attacked ourselves. We all seem to be agreed that those things are valid. I don't know why we should pretend they aren't."

"We regret as much as you do, Mr. President," ABC pointed out earnestly, "that some people are using race to stir up trouble, but there it is."

"Exactly," Frankly Unctuous agreed. "We have all deplored that. But we can't shut our eyes to the realities of world affairs."

"Which I am," he said sharply.

"You are not doing that, Mr. President," the *Post* said with a calm arrogance that took his breath away, "but it may be that you are confusing your own conclusions about these things with what is really best for the country."

For a moment the President stared at him with an open disbelief.

"Well, by God," he said finally. "So *I* am the one who is confusing his own conclusions about these things with what is really best for the country, am I? Well, well."

"There is possibly a legitimate difference of opinion, Mr. President," the chairman of *The Greatest Publication* observed gently. "None of us is impugning your motives."

"Nor am I impugning yours," he said. "I am simply saying that underlying all these rationalizations is an ugly racial fear—an ugly gut terror—of what our friend from NBC and many, many others, I remind you, refer to as 'the onrushing hordes of China.' This to me is more terrifying than the Chinese themselves, because in one phrase it throws us back a hundred years or more into a blind emotionalism that simply cannot produce the kind of steady thinking we must have in this situation. It just can't produce it."

"But, Mr. President," the *Times* said with a noticeable patience, "your general condemnation cannot possibly include us, because we have all specifically said in the past twenty-four hours, and less, that *we too* deplore racism, that *we too* want calm and careful policy. So—you puzzle us. We feel you are talking about one thing and we are talking about another."

"Not really," he said. "Not really. We are both talking about intervention."

"And your only argument for being against it," Walter said, "is that in some people's minds it may have a racial reason!"

"That is not my only argument against it," he said angrily. "My argument is that possibly the only way we can save the world and ourselves is by not intervening, by staying free, keeping our strength together, standing ready to pick up the pieces. Not by letting ourselves be stampeded by fears of 'onrushing hordes'—"

"I am so sorry," NBC said dryly. The President ignored him.

"—'onrushing hordes' and 'alien cultures,' or by dreams of 'the balance of power,' and my presumed ability to end the conflict by the simple act of waving some sort of magic wand and crying, 'Stop!' Good lord, do you know what intervention would mean? It would mean missiles and planes and bombs and, yes, maybe men and a great many men, before we were through. It would mean total commitment. 'Surgical strike,' you are all saying now, making it sound very neat and sanitary. War isn't like that, at least on the scale that's under way now. It handles things strictly on its own terms. It runs wild. That's your intervention for you!"

"Nonetheless, Mr. President," the chairman of *The Greatest Publication* said gently, "we for our part seem agreed that there may be very valid and compelling reasons for going in—particularly if the Russians continue to fall back in such disarray as they are now doing. If this continues, Mr. President—and there is no indication right now that it won't—then I think we are agreed that we must continue to call the shots as we see them."

He gave them a long look, from face to set, unyielding face.

"Which means, very shortly now, an all-out attack upon me, personally, does it not?"

"I would not like to consider it an attack, as such, Mr. President," the chairman of the *G.P.* said, still gently. "Just a disagreement, such as we have had before."

"Very well," he said, standing up and speaking calmly as they followed suit. "Like you, I must continue to do as I see best. As I said at the start, I should like to have your pledge that you will help me in keeping the country calm, in attacking racism, in fighting intervention, in staying out. Apparently I am not going to have it.

I shall make no attempt to conceal the fact that I am bitterly disappointed. Neither shall I make any change in the policy that I, as President of the United States of America, deem soundest and best for the country."

"So once again," Walter Dobius said, not without a certain satisfaction, "the media and Orrin Knox are at loggerheads."

"Is that really a happy thing, Walter?" he inquired bleakly. "Is it really so good for us all?"

But for that, of course, Walter had no answer. He looked, in fact, quite taken aback and, surprisingly, for a moment even ashamed of himself. Very briefly, so did they all.

This of course changed no minds, shifted no positions, softened none of the attitudes that were hardening under the terrible pressures of the hour. They parted, as they had begun so many years ago, diametrically opposed on foreign policy. Only now he was where they had been, and they were where he had been, and strange were the ways of the awful war.

"The Congress must not tie the hands of the President with this resolution," Cullee concluded in the tense and silent Senate. "We must not take sides. And above all we must not give way to ugly racial fears, for they become us not at all and weaken us most fearfully."

In the plush offices of NAWAC, at the corner of Connecticut Avenue and L Street, Northwest, the chairman reached over and snapped off the machine with a short and ugly expletive.

To this his colleague Rufus Kleinfert, chairman of the Konference on Efforts to Encourage Patriotism (KEEP), responded with nothing more informative than a grunt.

From his colleague the chairman of DEFY came a response more emphatic.

"What the hell do you mean by that?" LeGage demanded sharply.

"I mean screw the black son of a bitch," Fred Van Ackerman said with an angry impatience. "I've had more than enough of his crap, I can tell you."

"I'm a black son of a bitch," 'Gage said with an ominous quiet.

The former Senator from Wyoming gave him an appraising look and a shrug both lazy and arrogant.

"That's right," he agreed, "but don't tell anybody, 'Gage, boy, and maybe they won't notice." He raised a casual hand as LeGage started from his chair.

"So I'm a white son of a bitch, so what?" he inquired blandly.

"Does it really matter? We've got a war to get into, 'Gage. It's no time for us to start fighting each other."

"I'm not so sure I'm going to get into any war," LeGage said dourly. "I'm not so sure DEFY is going to follow you on this racial shit. In fact, I know we're not."

"So?" Fred Van Ackerman asked, sounding perfectly confident and not at all disturbed. "What is that supposed to mean?"

"It means just what I said," 'Gage said flatly. "DEFY is pulling out."

"Well, well," Fred said softly. "So DEFY is pulling out. Did you hear that, Rufus? DEFY is pulling out."

"It iss no time for dissunity," Rufus Kleinfert observed in his heavy accent. "It iss a time to stick together."

"So it iss," Fred said, unable to resist his usual unkind mockery even with an ally. "You do as Rufus says, 'Gage. We need you, boy. In fact," he said, and his tone became suddenly cold, "any attempt by DEFY to break away at this particular time, just when we're gearing up to bring old Half-Ass Orrin around to do the job he's got to do to save this country and Western civilization, would be regarded most unkindly by a majority of your fellow members of NAWAC. Most unkindly. I think I can promise you that, LeGage."

"You never asked me about that statement of yours," LeGage said angrily. "You never consulted me before jumping on this race bandwagon about the war."

"I didn't jump on it," Fred observed, not without satisfaction. "I started it going, boy. I got in the driver's seat before this stupid country even knew where it wanted to go. I told it it had arrived before it even knew it had started. As of course," he added with a curiously impersonal thoughtfulness, "it had. . . . Hell, 'Gage! Grow up, man! If you want to stampede this country, how do you do it better than by appealing to race? It isn't *your* race, after all. They're yellow, man, *yellow*. You-all's black as de ace of spades, I do b'lieve."

"*You listen to me,*" LeGage ground out, and suddenly he had the chairman of NAWAC by the lapels, half lifted out of his chair. "I don't want any more of your eternal crap, *Senator*. You turn on one race, next thing you're going to turn on another. I don't like that, hear? *I don't like that!*" And he slammed Fred, who had possessed the sense to let himself hang limp and not fight it, back into his chair.

There was a silence broken only by their heavy breathing and Rufus Kleinfert's gently drawn and carefully unobtrusive respiration.

Then Fred looked up at him with a glazed and ominous expression in his eyes.

"I don't like that kind of business either, boy," he said softly. "I don't like it at all. I consulted Rufus. I didn't do it all by myself."

"Consulted another white man!" 'Gage exclaimed. "Of course! Of course! Why didn't you consult me, you damned coward? Because you knew I'd object, that's why! And you knew why I would, too! Because one of these days after you've accomplished this evil purpose, I've no doubt you're planning to turn on the black people in your own country for some other evil purpose, damned if I know what it is but I'm sure you've got one. That's why you didn't consult me! Well, I've said it and I mean it: we're leaving. DEFY's getting out of NAWAC and you and your fat friend here can take what's left and shove it."

"Suppose *you* listen to me," Fred said, becoming suddenly, in one of his lightning changes, perfectly calm, perfectly reasonable, "before you go flying off the handle to do something you'll regret. Whatever the reason, the United States of America *cannot* let Russia be defeated by China. We've got to save her. Our whole civilization depends upon that. Why, hell! You talk about your precious race! What's going to become of it if the Chinese win? Do you think they're going to say, 'Come on, brothers and sisters, we love you now, 'cause black is best?' *Are you kidding?* They're going to say, 'Lif' dat barge and tote dat bale, brothers and sisters! *Yellow's* best. Haven't you heard, soul folk?' . . . It's *your* skin, too, 'Gage, baby, that's why I didn't bother to consult you. I knew you'd react this way without stopping to think. I knew you'd listen to some blind stooge of Whitey like Cullee—"

"You leave Cullee out of this!" LeGage cried angrily. "Cullee makes more sense than you ever made in all your twisted, empty life!"

"Oh, so we love Cullee now, do we?" Fred inquired softly. "We love big old black Cullee, now. Well, well, well, well. *And don't hit me,*" he cried harshly as LeGage started forward, apparently intent upon doing just that, "or you won't live long, either!"

"What do you mean, 'live long, *either*'?" 'Gage shouted. "What are you going to do to Cullee?"

"We're going to give him and his damned President a lesson!" Fred shouted back, for once genuinely carried out of himself by anger. "We've got to do something to jolt that damned fool in the White House into doing what he has to do to save this country and Western civilization!"

"You leave Cullee alone," 'Gage cried, old unhappy bitternesses with his life's friend-enemy forgotten as a conviction of terrible danger to Cullee overwhelmed him, "or I'll kill you!"

"The plans are all made, boy," Fred said, suddenly coming out of his schizophrenic high to turn cold and composed again. "All made, and nothing you can do about it. Nothing at all. And if you want to take your damned DEFY out of NAWAC, God damn you, go ahead. We'll manage very well without you to save our"—and he spat out the words—"*white* civilization, thank you very much!"

"You—" 'Gage cried in a harsh, wounded voice. "You—"

"Too late," Fred said blandly, and no one would ever know whether it was fact or just another of his cruel and cruelly enjoyed threats. "Just too late, baby."

The last thing LeGage heard as he flung himself blindly out the door, knowing he must get to a telephone, go to the Hill, warn Cullee, do *something*, was the mocking laughter of the chairman of NAWAC and Rufus Kleinfert's heavy voice saying politely, "KEEP iss quite ready for whatever you propose, Fred. Unity iss *very* important if we are to save the civilization of the West."

For several moments thereafter there was silence in the room while Fred stared down at the hurrying traffic along Constitution Avenue, a strange, twisted, moody half grimace still on his lips; not really amusement, Rufus decided, but something wild, remote, uncaged, uncontrollable beyond the ordinary ken of ordinary people: the impersonal amusement of an animal, perhaps, feral, vicious and on the prowl. Rufus, who was far from being the most sensitive and perceptive of men, found himself shivering.

"That slimy little black son of a bitch," Fred said finally, his voice very soft, his eyes still riveted on his unsuspecting countrymen below but obviously not seeing them. "That slimy, worthless, no-account nigger! *Nigger, nigger, nigger!* . . .

"Why, listen!" he said, and he rounded on Rufus Kleinfert with a sudden savage motion of his entire body that made Rufus jump and instinctively half raise a hand to ward him off. "Do you think I'm going to let a stinking black tramp like *that* get in my way, when I've got this whole country moving behind me now? When all of America is listening to *me?* To Fred Van *Ackerman?* To the guy old Half-Ass Orrin thought he'd driven out of public life forever and ever, amen? When I'm leading the whole parade? When I've put my finger on all those silly stupid sheep down there, and all their silly, stupid, craven, hypocritical fears that they won't admit to themselves but can't wait to give in to? When they're loving me for it? . . .

"It won't be long now," he said, and his voice and thoughts seemed to turn inward to some vision that Rufus Kleinfert knew was far away from him and perhaps from all sane human contact. "It won't be long. Russia's falling and we've got to save her, and the man who stands in the way is going to be wiped out by the people of this country. They'll kill him or they'll impeach him or they'll do something—anyway, they'll sweep over him. And when he's gone, which won't be very many more days or maybe even hours, now, they'll turn to the man who's leading them the way they want to go, the man who understands them and knows how to appeal to what they *really* want, not all this idealistic crap we've had to feed them in recent years to get them to follow us. I won't have to feed them *anything* to get them to follow me, after this—except maybe"—his eyes looked oddly tortured for one seeing a vision apparently so attractive to him—"except maybe a few of the damned niggers and the damned kikes and the damned conservatives, and maybe even"—and for a moment a savage humor touched his face—"maybe even a few of these high and mighty *liberals* whose asses I've had to kiss for so long to get where I'm going. . . .

"And nobody," he said, his eyes returning at last to Rufus and at last appearing to focus upon him, "but nobody, Rufus, baby, is going to stop me. You stick with me and NAWAC and we'll *go* places. Because nobody"—his eyes swung again far away to some inner landscape unknown to reason, and again Rufus shivered—"*nobody* can stop me now."

But in this, of course, he was mistaken as some demagogues—sometimes—fortunately are: not all, but enough to permit the human race, when its members are very, very lucky, to just scrape by the pitfalls of a destiny that would be perfectly justified.

Even as he finished speaking there was sudden turmoil in the outer office, the scream of a secretary, a door flung open.

On the threshold stood a black man, looking, grotesquely, almost white-faced in his terrible anger.

He held a knife that glistened ferociously in the light.

The chairman of KEEP, and presently the chairman of NAWAC, screamed too.

The chairman of DEFY had come back.

RUSSIAN ROUT CONTINUES AS CONGRESS ENTERS SECOND DAY OF DEBATE ON AID RESOLUTION. BOTH GOVERNMENTS FLEE DEVASTATED CAPITALS FOR SECRET HIDEOUTS. EUROPEAN LEADERS MAY MAKE DIRECT AP-

PEAL TO KNOX AS YELLOW TIDE SWEEPS ON. U.N. RELIEF AGENCY PLEDGES A-CLOUD AID.

HAMILTON GIVES SENATE ADMINISTRATION CASE FOR NEUTRALITY BUT PARTY LEADERS IN BOTH HOUSES CONFIDENT RESOLUTION WILL PASS. MANY MEMBERS FAVOR SURGICAL STRIKE TO END THE WAR.

Surgical strike! the Vice President thought with a weary disgust as the afternoon dragged on and speech after lengthy speech repeated Arly Richardson's catch phrase. It had been a true inspiration, that slogan, sounding so neat and clean and antiseptic, one of those ideal softening substitutes, beloved of democracies, behind which men could hide in comfort from the harsh realities of what they proposed to do. Surely a *surgical* strike could not be something frightful, dreadful, awful, atomic; a *surgical* strike could only be something nice and quick, free from horror and in some magical way not involved at all with the blood, brains, guts, lives and small, desperate worlds of human beings. He had seen it happen often on the Hill in regard to less cataclysmic matters; not surprising that it should happen with the gravest matter of them all. Even more imperative now, in fact, that men hide themselves from what they contemplated.

On the House side, he knew, the same situation prevailed. Bill Abbott had walked over a while ago to sit and chat with him for a few minutes on the dais, invoking murmurs from floor and galleries and a desperate craning from the press seats above their heads as members of the media tried to guess what they were saying. But they kept their voices low and against the drone of speeches nothing could be heard. It was obvious from their expressions, however, that they were not happy. The headlines were quite accurate: the resolution was on its way to passage, either late tonight or, at the latest, at the special early session already set for 9 A.M. tomorrow.

"I can't understand it," he said moodily as he contemplated Hugh B. Root of New Mexico, whistling and roaring in his usual unintelligible fashion but somehow managing to convey with his mushy voice and wildly waving, cellophane-wrapped cigar that he was in favor of the resolution. "I just can't understand it. The country's being stampeded—just stampeded. People are *terrified* of atomic war. And yet here they go, wanting to rush into it."

"Apparently," Bill Abbott said bleakly, "they're more terrified of the Chinese. You and I don't want to believe that, but it seems to be true. They see those 'hordes,' you see—the 'hordes' are very vivid, now, yellow and savage and menacing and running amuck. And let's face it, Cullee: the hordes *are* there, there's no getting away from it. They *are* advancing. They *are* managing to absorb their losses, which must be fantastic, and still move on. To many, many minds they *are* beginning to seem almost superhuman, larger than life, doubly terrifying. They *are* beginning to seem invincible. And the Russians *are* falling back, falling back, falling back. The result has raced with an inevitable progression in the past few hours: the Russians are losing, the Chinese are winning—*people like us* are losing, *foreign people* are winning—*WE* are losing, *THEY* are winning— . . . Ah," he broke off with a sad disgust, "it's a hell of a situation."

"But it isn't inevitable," Cullee protested. "They *aren't* invincible. They must be close to exhaustion, they can't keep going much longer—"

"Long enough," Bill Abbott said sadly. "Long enough. . . . Anyway," he said, his tone more comforting, "you've done your part very nobly, I think. That was a fine speech."

"I tried to make it that way," the Vice President said. "I didn't know how much good it would do, but the President and I thought it should be said for the record."

The ex-President grunted.

"If there's even going to be a record. . . ." He made a wry, unhappy sound. "One man must be happy, though. Freddy Van Ackerman's got a new parade to lead now."

"I wonder how far it will take him?" Cullee mused.

"I'm sure he thinks the White House," William Abbott said. "And he may be right amid the ruins. This is the kind of time when jackals find their rewards."

But when, a moment later, one of the page boys rushed up to Cullee's desk with the bulletin—SHELBY STABS VAN ACKERMAN, KLEINFERT TO DEATH, SUICIDES IN CONNECTICUT AVENUE LEAP. NAWAC HEADS DIE IN APPARENT ROW OVER RACE ASPECTS OF PRO-WAR POLICY—neither the ex-President nor the Vice President could really comprehend for a few minutes the reality of the reward the jackals had finally found.

And when Cullee turned over the chair to Powell Hanson and left a Senate chamber beginning to buzz and whisper and exclaim with the news, he still could not realize it.

It was only some time later, after Sarah had called in tears and after he had sat for a long time alone in his office staring unseeing out the window at the winter-bound city, that it finally began to hit him; and it was only some time after that that he suddenly sobbed aloud, put his head in his hands and cried for LeGage Shelby, ex-roommate and ex-friend, whom once he had liked so much and would have liked to have befriended for life had not 'Gage's ambitions, jealousies and unconquerable inferiorities where he was concerned, made it impossible.

Rufus Kleinfert had an elderly widowed sister and brother living together in St. Petersburg, Florida, who cried for him. But no one at all, as far as could be discovered, ever cried for that flaming young liberal who had come out of Wyoming on the welcoming wings of the media, so long ago in thought if not in time, Fred Van Ackerman.

That night, shortly after the session ended at 10:21, the headlines heralded the coming day:

SPEAKER, MAJORITY LEADER CLAIM SUFFICIENT VOTES TO PASS AID-RUSSIA RESOLUTION IN BOTH HOUSES. RICHARDSON, SWARTHMAN PREDICT "GOOD CHANCE" FOR OVERRIDING KNOX VETO AS RUSSIANS CONTINUE TO FALL BACK IN CENTRAL PLAINS.

SHATTERED NAWAC PLEDGES CONTINUED FIGHT TO SAVE WESTERN CIVILIZATION FROM YELLOW HORDES AS NEW LEADERS PLAN MAMMOTH PARADE AND FUNERAL IN WASHINGTON FOR FALLEN VAN ACKERMAN, KLEINFERT. VAST OUTPOURING OF SUPPORT SWAMPS HEADQUARTERS.

WHITE HOUSE SILENT ON INTERVENTION GAINS.

But not for long. Half an hour after the first batch of headlines hit the streets another was added:

PRESIDENT ANNOUNCES HE WILL VETO AID-RUSSIA RESOLUTION "IN BEST INTERESTS OF AMERICA AND THE WORLD."

Half an hour after that he faced three old friends, as desperately tired and strained as he, who had come to the Oval Office on the direct and frantic orders of their superiors.

"Orrin," Lord Maudulayne said, and corrected himself hastily, "Mr. President—"

"Please," he said, "if it makes it easier. I don't mind." He assayed a small joke, though none of them really felt like humor. "The Protocol Office will never know."

"No," Claude Maudulayne said after a second, "I think better not. Because it is truly not in your capacity of old friend but in your capacity as President that we address you."

"As you like," he said. "Though," he added somewhat bleakly, "I should like to think I still had a few old friends."

"Of course you do, Mr. President," Krishna Khaleel said with a rush of emotion that brought actual tears to his enormous dark eyes. "Of course you do!"

"Thank you, K.K.," he said. "At the moment I'm not too sure. Why are you all here?"

"I am authorized to bring you the direct appeal of the President of France—" Raoul Barre said quietly, and paused for his colleagues.

"And I the direct appeal of the Prime Minister of India—" K.K. said with great solemnity.

"And I the direct appeal of the Prime Minister," Lord Maudulayne said, and added quietly, "*and* Her Majesty the Queen—"

"That you commit the resources of the United States of America," Raoul continued, "to the defense of the United States of Russia. And do so," he added firmly, "immediately, before it is too late."

He studied their intent faces for a long time, these three whom he had known and liked and argued foreign policy with over so many years in Washington and at the U.N. Then he asked with a directness to match their own:

"Why?"

"Because you cannot let Europe be exposed to the onslaught of the Mongol tide and let our common civilization be destroyed," the French Ambassador said crisply.

"The Western heritage rests with you," the British Ambassador agreed. "We need waste no time on the pretense that any of the rest of us can save it."

"Neither can you let India and all the wisdom and values of her ancient culture be conquered and destroyed by the same evil force," the Indian Ambassador asserted stoutly. "We all look to you."

The President sighed.

"Obviously you do. And how do your principals suggest that I go about this?"

"By an immediate ultimatum to China," Lord Maudulayne said.

"An atomic ultimatum, if necessary," Raoul Barre agreed.

"An ultimatum that will make them *obey*," K.K. said emphatically, "and obey *now*."

"I suppose you represent the overriding sentiment in the U.N., too, don't you," he said slowly.

"Overwhelmingly so," Claude Maudulayne said. "As Ceil must have told you, there is great sentiment for a joint meeting of the Council and the Assembly to pass a resolution appealing to you direct. But" —and he too sighed—"it has been decided that there isn't time."

"I have my own resolution to worry about," he said with the slightest trace of wry humor. "That's going to be problem enough."

"Apparently not," Raoul remarked. "You say you intend to veto it."

"So I do."

"Then you would similarly ignore anything from the U.N.," Claude suggested.

"I would."

"But, Orrin—" K.K. protested unhappily. "Mr. *President!* You *cannot* abandon us all to the Chinese! They are savages—savages! They will destroy us all!"

"And not least, in due time," Raoul said in a tone in which worry, fear, disapproval and a certain satisfaction were curiously mixed, "you—yourselves—proud America."

"My old friends," he said quietly, "I still do not believe so. I still do not believe this is the end. I still think that the Chinese are nearing exhaustion. I still think that there will be a turning point, and very soon, if the Russians can just hold out a little longer. I think they, and you, and, I am sorry to say, far too many of my own people, are being stampeded by a wave of terror that is rapidly approaching universal hysteria. It must be stopped. *It must be stopped.* China is almost exhausted—the turning point is coming—it has to come. I beg of you, let us stand firm, and believe that.

"I cannot intervene because I am not sure I could control intervention once it started. And if I did not"—his voice sank to a somber note —"the results then would indeed end the world."

"You take a fearful risk, Mr. President," Raoul Barre said.

"You gamble with us all," Lord Maudulayne said bleakly.

"You will not help us!" Krishna Khaleel cried desperately, as though he had only now begun to believe it. "You will not help us!"

"It has not reached that stage yet," he said with a stubborn quietness that they, who knew Orrin Knox, finally accepted as final. "A turning point is coming. Believe me: a turning point is coming."

But when it came it was not, as he had hoped against hope, the turning point that he and the world's few other remaining rational men might logically have expected.

2. "MEMBERS OF THE SENATE—" Arly Richardson said gravely at 9 A.M. next day, even as Jawbone Swarthman was saying with equal gravity, "Members of the House—"

"I have in my hand a message just received, addressed jointly to the President of the United States of America, to the Majority Leader of the United States Senate and to the Speaker of the House of Representatives, from the President of the United States of Russia."

There was a gasp of astonishment, a sudden tensely humming silence. In both chambers the television cameras slowly swung from face to troubled face.

"It reads," Arly said, and in the House Jawbone simultaneously began its transmittal, "as follows:

"'Distinguished and honorable friends of the West!

"'The Russian peoples and their government address you in their hour of deepest peril and greatest need. We appeal to you for help!

"'As you know, the mongrel hordes of China are at this very moment moving toward Europe across the face of Mother Russia. We have met them on the ground. We have met them in the air. We have bombed their cities and their supply lines. And still they come, in untold millions.

"'It is so even in the dead of winter.

"'It is inhuman.

"'They are no longer people, they are animals.

"'Many, many of them have died.

"'And still they come.

"'In the face of this, as you know, the peoples of Russia have made a determined and gigantic effort to turn the tide. But we are outnumbered two, four, sometimes eight or ten, to one, all along the line. We have tried to hold but we have been unable to hold. We do not apologize for our failure, because we have done our best. In the face of such millions from the alien world of China, it has not been enough.

"'At the very moment you read this, our government is in hiding. Our peoples are taking tremendous blows. We are returning tremendous blows. But they are not enough, and we are falling back.

"'We have already retreated almost a thousand miles into European Russia.'"

A groan of dismay, fear, anguish, broke almost unnoticed from many lips in both houses, and from wherever, in America and around the world, frightened men and women listened.

" 'Because of this, the government of Russia faces immense dangers, not only from the Chinese but from some evil elements within our society which seek to profit from our distress. It may not be possible to suppress much longer the outbreak of civil rebellion which could destroy the last vestige of organized control in Russia.

" 'Thus the doors will be opened completely to the onrushing hordes of alien China as they advance inexorably upon all of Europe.

" 'Next will come the Pacific and your own shores.

" 'We have already retreated a thousand miles. We are unable to hold much longer. We hope to regroup and make a further stand at some point further back to be determined by our military leaders. But unless we receive immediate help from you, the great American Republic with whom we have always had such close fraternal bonds of friendship, mutual trust and common culture, we cannot succeed. We cannot win.

" 'We will fail, and with us, you will fail.

" 'Then the yellow hordes of China will sweep over Europe as well. Then they will swarm across the Pacific and eventually to your own shores. Then you, too, will stand outnumbered two, four, eight or ten to one, and there will be no one—*no one*—to answer your cries for help.

" 'Russia is dying. Europe is dying. Western culture and civilization are dying.

" 'Help us, we beg of you! Help us! Help us!

" '(signed) SHULATOV, PRESIDENT,
UNITED STATES OF RUSSIA.' "

At approximately the same moment, Arly in the Senate and Jawbone in the House finished reading. And at approximately the same moment in the Oval Office, the President of the United States of America looked at the Secretary of State and the Secretary of Defense and said grimly, "That does it."

Yet even then he would not yield, or deviate from what he honestly believed to be best for his country and the world. He would not believe that Russia was really that weak or that the Chinese could possibly still be that strong. He knew the effect Shulatov's words would have upon the world. He understood the impact they would have upon him personally. But he would not yield.

When the decision came an hour later—

CONGRESS PASSES AID-RUSSIA RESOLUTION AFTER DIRECT APPEAL FROM PRESIDENT SHULATOV. VOTE NARROW BUT DECISIVE IN BOTH HOUSES. ENORMOUS PRESSURE BUILDING ON KNOX TO INTERVENE AS RUSSIAN

LEADER TELLS WORLD, "RUSSIA IS DYING. EUROPE IS DYING. WESTERN CULTURE AND CIVILIZATION ARE DYING. HELP US!"

—he still would not yield.

"The President," he said in a one-sentence statement issued immediately through the press secretary, "finds in the action of the Congress no reason to change his views on intervention."

An hour after that, refusing all calls from the Hill, all importunings from the press, all contact for the time being with anyone but Bob Leffingwell and Blair Hannah, he was studying the disposition of American forces and going over such fragmentary intelligence reports as were coming in from the war zones, when there came suddenly a great stir and bustle in the halls. Excited Signal Corps officers hurried in, microphones, screens, tape recorders, transmitters, were set up. Within ten minutes all was completed. Five minutes later, on a blurry signal that faded shakily in and out but remained reasonably clear for the duration of their brief conversation, he found himself face to face via satellite with the man he had last seen a week ago in New York.

Even through the flickering transmission it was apparent that he was desperately tired, strained and tense. But in him, too, there was something unyielding, even in so desperate an hour.

"Mr. President!" Shulatov said. "When will you begin to help us?"

"Mr. President," he said, "when will you realize that there must be a fundamental change in Russia if we are to do so?"

"It is too late for that," Shulatov cried with an angry anguish. "It is too late for such bargaining!"

"But it was not too late in Moscow two weeks ago, or at the U.N. a week ago," he said in a cold, cold tone. "It was not too late then to save you from what you are undergoing now. Why didn't you believe me when I warned you then?"

"You wanted to destroy our sovereignty!" Shulatov cried in the same angry, anguished voice.

"I wanted you, I wanted all of us, to modify and curtail it," he said. "I wanted to destroy it for no one, only to place upon it bounds within which the world could live. You would not do that. You were too arrogant. You had other plans. You were not afraid of war. Well," he said, and his tone was colder still, "you have war. Are you happy with it?"

"Save us!" Shulatov said, and for a moment a genuine desperation filled his voice. "*Save us, save us!*"

"I cannot plunge in as you would want," he said, more calmly. "The situation must become clearer, it must stabilize. I believe it will stabilize. I believe *you* believe it will stabilize. I believe you want to involve us irrevocably on your side instead of letting us act as I believe we should act, as mediator, peacemaker, stabilizer."

"You want to rule the world," Shulatov said bitterly. "You want us to be destroyed so you can rule the world alone."

"Goodbye, Mr. President," he said, reaching forward to turn off the transmitter. "Good luck."

"Mr. *President!*" Shulatov cried for the last time, on an angry, anguished, upward wail. "*Mr. President!*"

But the President's hand went forward and the machine went off. A shaky image of a contorted, desperate face lingered for a split second, then was gone.

He found that he was trembling all over with the terrible uncertainties of what he had just done and the things he must yet do; but he still did not honestly see that he had any choice but to do them.

PRESIDENT VETOES AID-RUSSIA RESOLUTION, SAYS HE WILL CONTINUE COURSE OF "PRUDENT NONINTERVENTION UNTIL SUCH TIME AS THE BELLIGERENTS AGAIN SEEK OUR MEDIATION." CLAIMS THIS IS "ONLY COURSE CONSISTENT WITH MY OATH, THE CONSTITUTION AND THE SAFETY AND FUTURE WELL-BEING OF AMERICA AND THE WORLD."

CONGRESSIONAL LEADERS ADMIT VOTES INSUFFICIENT TO OVERRIDE VETO. SOME TALK OF IMPEACHMENT.

BITTER OUTCRY BREAKS OVER COUNTRY AS KNOX PURSUES UNYIELDING POLICY WHILE RUSSIA RETREATS TOWARD POSSIBLE SURRENDER.

"The situation of Russia has now almost passed desperation," the *Times* declared in a front-page editorial appearing in an almost unprecedented extra that reached the streets in early afternoon. "With it has gone, or is going, what may be the last hope of preventing the pagan hordes of China from carrying their alien domination successfully across the map of Europe, and then in due time across the Pacific to our own endangered shores.

"Civilization itself is at stake—that Western civilization which over the centuries has come to carry almost all that men know of dignity, of beauty, of intelligence, of grace. At stake also is the very existence of the Western European nations, all those other nations that generally draw their traditions and culture from the West, and of the United States of America itself.

"In this crisis, the President tragically has once again justified the unhappy suspicions many of his fellow citizens have long harbored concerning his judgment. After a brief period of statesmanship lasting approximately three weeks, he has reverted to type: obstinate, reactionary, destructive of human freedoms and the desire of all true liberals to save mankind—and in the present case, very likely destructive of the life of the planet itself.

"He has vetoed the Congressional resolution calling for aid to Russia, and he is safe from political reprisal in doing so. The veto cannot be overridden, and it was, in any case, simply an advisory to him, not a mandatory requirement.

"But it *was* mandatory in the sense that it represented the overwhelming desire of the American people to stand with our gallant Russian friends in defense of all the traditions, the history and the culture of our mutual civilization. It was mandatory in the sense that it represented the firm belief of most Americans that it is absolutely vital that Russia be saved and the yellow hordes of China be driven back within their own borders.

"This newspaper now believes that the West, unless the President changes his stand within the day or possibly even the hour, is doomed, and with it, this land we love.

"We beg Orrin Knox—for that is all that is left us, to beg, since he will apparently not listen to our most urgent admonitions—to save Russia, to save the West, to *save us*.

"Do not let us go under, Mr. President! Help us! The need is terribly desperate and the hour is desperately late. . . ."

"Orrin Knox, stubborn to the end—and the end looks to be just around the corner—" the *Post* said in a similar extraordinary extra that afternoon, "is apparently adamant in his refusal to take America into the war in time to save our gallant Russian allies.

"In so doing he is condemning not only Russia but the West, including his own country, to death at the hands of the pagan hordes now swarming out of China toward the very gates of Europe.

"If Russia goes down, as now seems very likely, those gates will stand open. Through them will pour the yellow tide. Once Europe has been subjugated the tide will flow into the Pacific Basin. And then will come the turn of the United States of America, which no one, as President Shulatov so accurately said in his eloquent appeal to Congress, will be left to save.

"*No one at all. . . .*

"The President was within his rights to veto the purely advisory Congressional resolution urging aid to Russia. His veto cannot be overridden, and there is no time for the cumbersome process of impeachment some are advocating, even though we agree that in all justice it should be done.

"Apparently he will impose his will. But what a will it is!

"If he has his way—

"Russia will be lost.

"The West will be lost.

"We will be lost.

"The world will be lost.

"Aside from the brief period when he was showing true statesmanship in his journey to Moscow and Peking and in the United Nations, we have always been actively opposed to Orrin Knox. We believe we were justified, and we believe our temporary endorsement of his policies was a sad mistake, since underneath he was apparently the same old reactionary illiberal conservative we always saw in him.

"But today we beseech him, if he has an ounce of feeling left for his own country and for Western civilization—

"Save Russia from the onrushing yellow hordes of China, pagan, heathen, illiterate, barbarian!

"Save the West!

"Save the world!"

"*Save us! . . .*"

"Here on Capitol Hill," Frankly said in a special late-afternoon roundup on Congressional opinion, "it can only be said that enormous apprehension, possibly even terror, grips a majority of the Congress. Based on the phone calls and telegrams members are receiving, the same can undoubtedly be said of a majority of the American people. This country and most of its leaders are scared to death, and with complete justification. For the hordes of Genghis Khan are descending once more upon the West.

"Gallant and alone, Russia at this moment holds the frontiers of Western civilization against the advancing yellow tide from China. Even as I talk, those frontiers are crumbling all along the vast, chaotic battleline. Russia is being pushed back—and back—and back—and back. If the rout continues, it can only end very swiftly in her complete surrender. And after that, Europe lies open to the terrible tide.

"Once Europe goes, most here are convinced, the Pacific will go, and then, in due course, an isolated and completely alone America. And thus will the policies of Orrin Knox have borne their last, bitter fruit.

"Congress did what it could when it passed the resolution of aid to Russia just vetoed by the President. It does not have the votes to override his veto, it does not have the time to impeach him, as some demand. It cannot force his hand further. For whatever outcome fate has in store, Orrin Knox is in complete and unchallengeable command of the destinies of Russia, America and the world.

"It is no wonder, then, that most here are united now in one universal appeal which might be expressed in these words:

" 'Save us, Mr. President! Save Russia! Save the West! Save your own country, and save the world!' . . ."

"The fate of the world," Walter Dobius wrote rapidly in the special office maintained for him by his friends at the *Post*, "rests now with one stubborn, unyielding, unimaginative American politician who, with Russia dying, continues to act as though he could operate entirely independently of her fate.

"Orrin Knox, having risen briefly to statesmanship during his ill-fated journey to Moscow and Peking, has reverted to type. All humanity is likely to suffer. If he ever had qualities of greatness—which some in this now frantic city mistakenly thought for a few days—then they were not enough to stand the test of true crisis.

"For this, his country, the Russians and the West are likely to suffer most grievous and probably final damage in the days immediately ahead.

"At this very moment the Russian retreat is approaching full rout. President Shulatov was deadly accurate and in deadly earnest when he told us this a few short hours ago. The only bastion that now stands between Western civilization and the oncoming pagan tide of China is falling. Our history, our culture, our traditions, our very lives and freedom stand in the ultimate jeopardy before the barbarian yellow hordes that continue steadily on across the icy plains, in a wave of hatred and anger for the West that have turned them, as President Shulatov said, into an animal force that Russia apparently cannot withstand alone.

"A great beast is coming out of China to fall upon the West. And the President of the United States of America refuses to commit the only power left that can possibly force it back into its lair.

"Here in this fear-haunted capital, and indeed everywhere in America and throughout the world, all hearts, all minds, turn to the White House and the man who resides there. Will he really let Russia fall? Will he really let China conquer her and then move on into Europe, into the Pacific, eventually into America itself? Will he really let Western civilization, and soon the world, be destroyed?

"It seems impossible to believe. On every side the universal cry goes up to Orrin Knox:

"'*Save the Russians! Save the West! Save America and all humanity!*'

"Obdurate, stubborn and unimaginative though he may be, Washington cannot quite believe that the President will finally refuse that appeal, which comes from everywhere. . . ."

So said Supermedia, and so, as reports came in from all over the country, said an impressive majority of Middlemedia and Minimedia as well. Editorials, columns, broadcasts—letters, telegrams, telephone calls—riots by NAWAC and spontaneous protests by less-organized groups—sentiment respectable and sentiment suspect—all seemed to be running two to one for intervention following his veto.

There were still, he knew, great reservations among many of his countrymen, an intellectual horror of atomic war, an instinctive gut desire to stay out. Had he time to muster it, there was probably a sizable body of support for his policy. But this was all being drowned out in the great hysteria that was sweeping America and the West.

He read the papers, watched the broadcasts, received reports on the mail and the protests, began to hear in steadily swelling numbers from the frantic heads of other governments.

From everywhere came an insistent, steady, desperate drumbeat:

Help us! Protect us! Preserve us! Save us!

From the White House, silent, remote, mysterious and unknowable, its floodlit portico gleaming softly in the misty winter dark, there came, at his orders, not a word. . . .

Shortly before 10 P.M. new extras reached the streets. And now the bell seemed truly tolling, for the Russians, for the West, for him and his country, for everyone.

SECOND RUSS GOVERNMENT FALLS! NEW MILITARY JUNTA TAKES OVER! SHULATOV, CABINET SLAIN!

NEW LEADERS SAY: "WE WILL FIGHT TO THE LAST RUSSIAN."

PRESIDENT LIN RETORTS: "WHEN WE KILL THE LAST RUSSIAN THERE WILL STILL BE TEN CHINESE."

FINAL STAGES OF DEATH STRUGGLE APPEAR ABOUT TO BEGIN AS YELLOW TIDE ROLLS ON.

3. "ORRIN—" the familiar voice said, and on the screen of the Picturephone the familiar, craggy old face looked tired and exhausted, as tired and exhausted as he was, as the whole world seemed to be in this haunted hour nearing midnight. "Do you need any company down there?"

"Thanks, Bill," he said gratefully, "but I've got plenty. People are running in and out of here on shuttles with intelligence reports, news bulletins and what-have-you. I'm swamped in company. In fact, I think in a few minutes I'm going to kick them all out and just try to think for a while."

"It doesn't look good, does it?" the ex-President said gloomily, and he responded with a sigh.

"No. It does not look good. What would you do, Bill?"

"I'm beginning to think," William Abbott said slowly, "that I might —I just might—go in, Orrin. I never thought I'd come to that conclusion, but in the last couple of hours I have. I hate to see us do it, but—it may be we cannot survive in the long run if we permit the balance to be upset so terribly as it seems about to be." He too sighed. "It's a hellish thing. I'm sorry to complicate it more for you by putting myself on the other side, particularly at this moment. But this is the moment when it has to be decided, isn't it? One way or the other, it can't wait much longer."

"One way or the other," he echoed quietly, "it can't wait much longer. I agree with you, this is indeed the moment. . . . Suppose I were to intervene—and," he added quickly as his predecessor gave him a sudden sharp look, "I haven't decided yet, though I know I'm going to have to sometime before this long night is over—suppose I were, how should I go about it? Suppose you were me, as in a sense you were and still are, of course, the only other man living who genuinely understands this job from the inside—how would you do it? Where? When? On whose behalf?"

"I wouldn't want to presume to tell you—" the ex-President began, but he interrupted, "I'm asking, Bill."

William Abbott looked away for a long moment into far distances. Then he looked back.

"I keep remembering," he said finally, "a tired old patrician in Mandarin robes saying that he *would* go to Geneva."

"Yes," the President said gravely, "I keep remembering him too. But that was a long time ago, Bill, as history has moved these past few days. And how much of this—this"—he gave an ironic, unamused smile —"how much of this 'yellow tide' can he control at this moment? He's let the beast loose, to quote our friends of the *Post,* and I'm very doubtful that he and his colleagues have any real control of it any longer. It will go until it exhausts itself, and by that time *he* may not be there any longer, either. Right?"

"It will go until it exhausts itself," William Abbott said softly, "or until it meets a real stone wall."

"Yes, I agree with that."

"And if it meets a stone wall, and simultaneously the old Mandarin and his government are strengthened in their control by the most affirmative and vigorous measures of support coming from the Pacific side—"

He nodded.

"It could just possibly be done. On the other hand, if he cannot keep control in the next few days and if the tide tosses up new leaders as fanatical as itself—and Russia really does go down altogether—and Europe and the West do lie open—and we in time do become the beleaguered citadel . . ."

"The man wants certainties," Bill Abbott said with a momentary humor. The President smiled, a brief second of relaxation in the midst of so much chaos. Then his expression turned serious again.

"The man would like to have them," he conceded, "but he knows they aren't available. There is a lot to be said for siding with the Russians, Bill, difficult and hostile as they have always been, under whatever government. They *are* the West's 'bastion,' feeble though it is. They *are* occupying the space between, certainly not very effectively, but at least they're there, a buffer, a mass, something for the tide to exhaust itself against sometime soon. They are, as our frantic friends from the media now advise us, part of our general Western heritage and culture. They *are* 'like us' and the Chinese *are* 'not like us.' So maybe the liberals have a point: maybe we should make the decision in Russia's favor."

"And with a new government in charge now, apparently a fighting government—perhaps if the tide meets a stone wall with a strong Russian government on the other side of it, a fighting government that has our very strong and vigorous support—"

"And a government in Peking that would have very strong and vigorous opposition coming from the Pacific side—" Again he nodded. "It could just possibly be done. . . . Those, I take it, are the options as you see them?"

"Pretty much the only viable ones now, I think," Bill Abbott said, "because though I know you have most sincerely tried, Orrin, I don't really think nonintervention is any longer feasible. Don't you agree?"

It was his turn to look far away, while several long and obviously difficult moments passed. Then he nodded slowly, for the third time.

"Yes," he said, forced by events to concede at last. "I agree. . . ."

"And so?" the ex-President asked.

"And so," he said with a return of some of their old joshing humor, "I think you have contributed greatly to my confusion—or possibly my clarification. I don't really think you would want me to give you a preview of what I intend to do, though. Or would you, Bill?"

The ex-President smiled.

"Not if you don't know yet, Orrin," he said. The President smiled back.

"That's right," he said. "But stand by, Bill. I may want you down here at any time."

"Any time at all," William Abbott said. "The only thing I might presume to urge is that you decide fast."

"Before the night is over," he said quietly. "And that's a promise."

Before he reached that moment, however, there were other calls, most of which he refused, a few of which he accepted. He cleared his office of official intruders, gave word he was not to be disturbed until further notice. In the next half hour Bob and Dolly Munson, Warren and Mary Strickland, Lafe and Mabel Anderson, the Vice President and Sarah and Ceil and Valuela, all called with concern, sympathy and support. All the men were gravely worried. The women, he could tell, were quite genuinely terrified of what might be coming next. Yet all gave him proof of friendship that strengthened him enormously: all were selflessly concerned with *his* feelings, *his* mood, *his* confidence, *his* courage: all were brave. The last call he accepted before returning to the Mansion came from an old and often difficult friend for whom he felt, nonetheless, a strong regard and a deep affection.

The little Justice looked as tired as any, but his perky spirit remained unchanged.

"Orrin—" he began. "Mr. President—"

"Orrin will do, Tommy. How nice of you to call."

"How nice of you to accept my call," Justice Davis said. "When you have such terrible things to decide. . . ."

"Help me decide them," he offered, and for once was surprised by Tommy's response: he refused.

"No, sir," he said firmly, "I will not. Now, that doesn't mean that I don't sympathize and don't want to help, Orrin, but I just don't feel it's my proper place to give advice. And anyway," he confessed with a sudden smile that lightened the moment, "I don't know what I would advise if I *did* advise. That," he said, starting his sentence lightly but ending abruptly somber, "is how scared *I* am."

"Don't be scared, Tommy," the President said, moved by this show of desolation from one normally so bright and chipper. "At least, don't admit you are."

"Aren't you?" the little Justice asked, giving him a look at once shrewd and oddly humble.

"As hell," he acknowledged quietly. "But I'm not going to show it for one minute."

"You couldn't," Tommy Davis said fervently. "It would absolutely devastate us all."

"Don't worry, I won't," he said, and meant it. "Of course, I do want your advice, as always. Bill Abbott and I were discussing a couple of options a little while ago. Tell me what you think of them. . . ."

"Well," Tommy said slowly when he had finished, expressing no surprise that nonintervention seemed to be no longer among them, "I think those ideas pretty well cover what's available."

"Which one, or which combination of them, should I follow?"

"You know my sympathies in general have always been with Russia," Justice Davis said frankly. "Not that I liked their old system, or their new one, either, for that matter, such as it is, but just because I felt that we simply had to get along with them if the world was not to be blown apart." His eyes widened thoughtfully and he spoke in a musing tone. "I suppose it never really occurred to me that it might be blown apart by them and the Chinese. I suppose it never really occurred to any of us liberals that anything like that could actually happen. Oh, we knew it *intellectually,* but we have always been so quiveringly sensitive about the possibility that the world might be blown apart by the Russians and *us* that we pushed the other possibility into the backs of our minds. We were always so harshly critical of what our own country did because we thought it would make the Russians angry and so increase the chances for world disaster. We took China more or less for granted, off there on the side—although rationally, of course, we always knew the chance was there. . . . And now it's come."

"And now it's come. So what do I do, Tommy?"

"I don't know," the little Justice said, "I honestly do not, Orrin. But I do say this to you: as far as I am concerned—and I like to think you will find this true of most of those I think of as genuine liberals, as distinct from the 'phony' or 'professional' liberals who dominate so much of our thinking nowadays with their automatic blind reactions to things—as far as *I* am concerned, I shall support whatever you do loyally and affirmatively and with genuine acceptance, because you are my President, doing the best you can, and I think I owe you and my country that."

"Well, thank you, Tommy," he said, genuinely moved. "I warn you, I may take you up on that. That informal 'war council' I was thinking about a while back may become a very necessary reality at any moment. I may need you right here beside me."

"I shall be there," Justice Davis said. "In the meantime, if you want a statement from me supporting your decision—*whatever* it is—you will have it."

"Good," he said. "Sometime in the next twenty-four hours. You'll know when."

"Fine," the little Justice said. "Count on me. And, Orrin—Mr. President: God bless you, and do be of good heart. There is great strength in this country still. It won't let you down."

"If I didn't believe that, Tommy," he said simply, "I literally could not go on. Good night, old friend. Thanks for your call."

"Not at all," said Justice Davis with a quaintly old-fashioned dignity. "I should be a poor friend indeed if I could not give comfort when it is needed."

And comforted he was, he thought as he left the Oval Office and walked slowly, past the respectfully watching guards whose faces, worn like all faces by the strain of these days, brightened a little as he passed, to the Mansion. Comforted by old friends, comforted by a faith as basic as Tommy's in the good heart of the country, comforted by faith in himself and comforted by the Lord, though he did not spend too much time directly addressing Him. Like many pragmatic people, the President had a basic feeling that the Lord would be there when he needed Him, and usually, he had found, the Lord was.

He knew he must touch base with three more people, and then he would reach the decision which he now knew to be very close. He paused before a door some distance down the second-floor hallway from his and rapped gently a couple of times.

"Yes?" Hal called promptly. "Is that you, Dad? Come in."

"If you aren't asleep—"

"Asleep!" Hal said, opening the door. "Is anybody in the world asleep tonight?"

"I suppose not," he said, entering to be greeted with a kiss from Crystal. Both were in robes, a fire was burning brightly in the grate, a tray with milk, cake and cookies was on an ottoman. Facing their two chairs, a television set chattered urgently on. He caught a glimpse, photographed from a plane high up, of a long, dark column winding, winding, with a certain inexorable, implacable slowness, across a frozen waste. With a sudden, almost harsh movement, he stepped over and snapped it off.

"Do you mind? I want to talk."

"Sure," Hal said easily. "We've had enough for a while, ourselves. It doesn't change: they just keep coming along." He drew up a chair to face theirs. "Want something to eat? The kitchen sent up a pretty good supply."

"I will, thanks," he said, helping himself to a piece of cake and a glass of milk and settling into the chair.

They watched him with an affectionately attentive concern while he ate. He looked, they thought, very tired, but, in some almost indefinable way, less tense than when they had seen him briefly at breakfast that morning. Hal, who knew his father, voiced the conclusion he drew from this.

"You've decided, and you want to bounce it off us and see what we think."

He smiled.

"Not quite decided yet, but close." The smile faded. "God help me if I'm wrong."

"Who's to say now what's right or wrong?" Hal inquired moodily. "Only history will be able to tell us that someday—if there is any. Basically, I would guess you've decided we're going in."

"What makes you think that?" he inquired with some sharpness.

"Because I know you," his son said. "You've given nonintervention the old school try and done your best with it, but events have caught up with you and now you feel you must move one way or the other. Right?"

For a moment he contemplated bluff, then abandoned it: Hal did know him.

"Essentially," he said. Crystal leaned forward.

"Why?" she asked earnestly, not reproving, just asking. "Before the war broke out, when you were facing the Russians and Chinese in Panama and Gorotoland, you held out against the Congress, the media, a lot of the country, most of the world. You were adamant. We were kidnapped"—and her eyes darkened for a second at the memory, and so did his—"and still you were adamant. Now you've held out for a while—but you aren't going to hold out any longer. I don't question your decision, because you have many more facts than I do. I'm just curious, as many people are going to be. Why?"

"That's a fair question," he said slowly, "and no one has a better right to ask. That's why I wanted to talk to you. I feel you deserve an explanation, and I also want to clarify my own thinking about it. . . ."

He paused, thinking back to an hour ago, when, almost casually, he had conceded to Bill Abbott that the policy he had defended so vigorously up to now would have to be abandoned.

Why *had* the concession been so quick and so casual?

Because the situation had changed . . . and because he had known, subconsciously perhaps for days, that he was going to have to change with it.

It was as simple as that.

The problem remaining was to state it in terms objective enough and convincing enough so that the country and the world would understand and accept what he was now beginning to perceive as his only possible course.

He looked at the two earnest young faces before him. All right, here was the world: make them understand.

With a little affectionate smile at their solemn expressions, he began to do so, fumblingly at first, then with increasing fluency as he proceeded, selecting, rejecting, polishing, perfecting—writing the speech which now was inevitable.

When he had concluded some twenty minutes later, Hal gave him a glance as straight and uncompromising as his own.

"That clarifies *that* decision. Now what about the other one?"

"What's that?"

His son smiled.

"Don't be innocent. Who are we backing, the slippery Slav or the heathen Chinee?"

"Now, that," he replied lightly, "is my secret." But when he saw their expressions, a little amused but basically disturbed, disappointed, somewhat crestfallen at his almost flippant tone, he dropped it and spoke with complete seriousness.

"In due time . . . in due time." His tone became lighter again. "I have to hold back some secrets, otherwise you kids wouldn't listen, you'd have heard it all. Isn't that right?"

"We'll listen," Hal promised, knowing he wouldn't get farther by pressing. "You'd better get to bed and get some sleep. You've got a busy day ahead. And"—he looked much older than his twenty-seven years for a second—"so have we all."

"Yes," he said gravely, kissing Crystal good night. "Sleep well, you two, and I shall try to do likewise."

In the Lincoln Bedroom as he began methodically preparing to retire, he spoke to the last and final arbiter, whose picture smiled at him from a dozen places in the room, as young girl, fiancée, mother, political partner, encourager, comforter, adviser, friend.

You see, he told her, here is Orrin Knox being inconsistent again—or consistent, I don't quite know which. He says one thing—he means it. He changes his mind—he means it. He defies circumstance—he means it. He yields to circumstance—he means it.

I guess the old boy is pretty human, after all.

But, he said almost defensively, though he knew that he never really had to defend himself to her, in one thing he has always been consistent, and that is his desire to serve his country. It has been a curiously old-fashioned desire, maybe, in an age when the tricky win power and the sly abuse it. A curiously old-fashioned thing, that Orrin Knox should have basically no other aim than to do the best he knows how for his people and for all the other peoples whose destinies the destiny of his people might affect. . . .

Now the test had come, as it had so often, but never in such cataclysmic, imperative form: was that basic principle enough to guide him through the morass he faced? Because if it was not, then the world would quite literally end—or survive in such awful disarray that it would literally be generations, perhaps centuries, before it could ever put itself together again in any semblance of recognizable order.

Maybe good will, good faith, good heart, sincere, compassionate and idealistic purpose, were not enough. Millions had possessed them, since history began, and look where it had all brought the world at this moment: to an almost insoluble tangle of desires, ambitions, motivations—hopes, fears, loves—terrible, unyielding hatreds . . . to monstrous dealings between man and man and between nation and nation . . . to atomic war.

Millions before him had wanted to make the lot of mankind better.

Millions, also, had not.

It appeared that history might very well be about to render final judgment that the millions who wished mankind ill were the final winners, bringing all down with them in one last spasm of hate that would leave the world an empty sphere, drifting lifeless in the universe.

And against that judgment stood Orrin Knox and many other good men—still, he believed, the majority.

But he was the one to whom history, in its inescapable way, had given the final chance. He would have the support of the majority if he proved to be right. But it was not the majority who must make the decision, deliver the speech, push the button or not push it as some last inspired gleam of inspiration might advise.

It was Orrin Knox, President of the United States of America, alone at the pinnacle, alone in the vortex.

Hank, he told her simply, *I wish you were with me now.*

But she was not, and so he told her:

I will do my best.

And after three final telephone calls, went quickly to sleep, comforted in the final knowledge that she knew this, and supported him, and understood, as always.

At 1 A.M. a bleary-eyed and exhausted press secretary called together the bleary-eyed, exhausted night watch of the media, who were now on around-the-clock vigil at the White House, and gave them the morning headlines:

PRESIDENT TO MEET WITH MILITARY ADVISERS AT 8 A.M., ADDRESS NATION FROM WHITE HOUSE AT NOON. INTERVENTION DECISION EXPECTED.

4.

"MY COUNTRYMEN," he said and perhaps for the last time—who knew what would happen, who could say?—America and the world quieted down to hear a President of the United States.

"I speak to you today at perhaps the gravest moment in the history of the world.

"Atomic war is raging in Asia, pushing toward Europe. A massive Chinese onslaught, undertaken without regard to human life or the restraints of caution that normally condition nations, is striking deep into the Russian heartland. One Russian government, unable to stem the tide, has gone down. A new one fights on, but who knows for how long or with what success? The sheer massed weight of eight hundred million Chinese is being hurled against the enemy. Devastated cities, atomic blows, deaths in the millions, are apparently meaningless when there exists such an overwhelming mass of humanity to draw upon. It is awesome, and it is terrifying.

"It does indeed seem, as many in the Congress believe and as many millions of you agree, that there will be no stopping the Chinese drive—that it will sweep over Russia, and then, carried perhaps simply by its own momentum, will continue on into Europe; and then, eventually, will turn to the Pacific and so, in time, to our own shores.

"Inspired by this fear, the Congress passed a resolution urging that America intervene on the side of the Russians. As you know, I vetoed that resolution. I did so because I believed that the best course for us was to stay out, to preserve our own strength, to stand ready to mediate, to pacify and ultimately to help rebuild.

"I still think that this could have been a viable policy."

("'Could have been'!" they exulted at the *Post:* "We're going in!" "*Now* we're getting somewhere!" they jubilated at the *Times.* "Bless that foolish bastard, Orrin Knox!")

"However," he said gravely, "events have moved past that point. With the fall of the Shulatov government in Russia and the apparent rising Chinese determination to push the issue to a final conclusion as rapidly as possible, a new set of circumstances prevails.

"This is no less than the very real possibility of a complete rearrangement of the balance of power in the world. Despite the wishful thinking of recent years in our own liberal community, balance of power is the only practical way to keep the peace because it is the only method that takes into account the endless deviousness and boundless treachery of the human animal.

"Men try to be good, but far too many of them are not good. They need restraints, particularly when they organize into nations. They have to be made to behave, otherwise they do not behave. They can love you on Monday and kill you on Tuesday. And unless they know that they will be punished when they break the law, they will break it with impunity. And if they are men acting as nations, when they break the law they have the capacity to bring down the world, as witness what is going on at this very moment.

"For this reason I have concluded, reluctantly but I think realistically, that the situation has now deteriorated to the point where the United States of America, as the sole remaining uncommitted major power, has a duty to see to it that balance is restored.

"I do not say this because I am afraid of any 'Yellow Peril' from China, or because I am afraid of any 'alien culture' there. The Chinese nation is an ancient and honorable one, with aspects of great culture far antedating the great majority of the Western nations, including our own. I respect the Chinese history, the Chinese people and the Chinese culture. I do not respect the present Chinese vindictiveness toward Russia which is destroying both countries and which will lead, unless stopped, to the ultimate catastrophe for us all. The same applies, of course, to the Russian vindictiveness toward China, which they must bitterly regret, now that it is too late.

"That, too, must, for the sake of mankind, be stopped.

"It is solely on those factors that I base my decision. It is not based in any way, I hasten to add, on any great admiration or love for the Russian nation, which in recent decades has been the world's greatest troublemaker, its greatest deliberate saboteur, its most vicious, most ruthless and most unprincipled imperial power.

"Nothing it has done in recent decades gives it any right to expect anything from the United States of America. We would be entirely justified in sitting back and letting it be destroyed—were it not that if we did so, even greater troubles would probably ensue for all mankind.

"I am quite sure that satisfied abandonment would be all that we could expect from Russia were the roles reversed. But America still has, I think, sufficient conscience and sufficient responsibility so that it cannot indulge itself in that pleasure. We, at least, have some continuing concept of responsibility to the world—imperfect as it may be, and imperfectly as we may have expressed it on many occasions, as our good friends abroad always make sure to tell us.

"We possess some demon that will not let us sit by. And for that demon, the world can thank God, for it has brought the world a lot of headaches but it has also rescued the world from many troubles.

"And while I am discussing Russia and China," he said, and his tone turned a little sharper and his head came up and he looked straight into the eyes of his countrymen, "I think there are a few things to be said about America, too—since we're getting right down to cases here, and since no one knows whether intervention as my advisers and I have conceived it will work or not work, and no one knows whether we will all be here tomorrow morning or not. . . ."

(A ghostly humor flickered across the nation. In spite of the situation no one could quite believe he meant this, though of course he did, absolutely.)

"America has not been so perfect, either, in these recent years.

"We have had an intellectual community, dominated by certain influential sections of the media, which has consistently denigrated, downgraded, vilified and sabotaged every worthwhile impulse and effort of its own country. Certain influential members of the academic world have eagerly gone along with this, where they have not directly inspired it. At their hands our history has been sneered at, our principles have been attacked, our society has been condemned, the basic good heart and innocent good will of the great majority of our people have been made the mockery and the destructive target of the arch know-it-alls who presume to control our thinking.

"And they have, my friends: they have. Through the schools they have turned out two generations, now, of whom a great many think very little of their country because they have been taught to think very little of it. Through the courts they have engaged in a steady campaign to weaken, destroy and subvert the laws necessary to maintain in our own society the same balance and order that must be maintained in the world, if both the world and our society are to survive. Through a certain intellectually fashionable segment of the churches, they have steadily and implacably chipped away at all those moral acknowledge them, we have nonetheless accomplished here mirac-perfectly and humanly they may fail to measure up to them, still try to conduct society's business, for society's sake.

"And all this they have done in the name of a spiteful and shallow cleverness, a snide, in-group superiority, an intellectual arrogance, which, take it all in all, has been the greatest combination of reaction, intolerance, unfairness, hypocritical suppression of opposing viewpoints and downright ruthless *il*liberalism ever foisted on a great nation."

("Oh, come, now!" they hooted at the *Post*. "Hey, hey!" they chuckled at the *Times*. "Get *you!*")

"And, my friends," he said quietly, "it has hurt. Make no mistake about it. It has hurt this country grievously in many areas. It has *not* been just an intellectual joke. It *has* been important. It *has* mattered.

"So we come to this time of ultimate testing not the confident nation we should be, given the fantastic story of our beginning, our subsequent history and all the great and generous good that we have done in the world. For all our many faults, and I am the first to acknowledge them, we have nonetheless accomplished here miraculous things. Our thought manipulators should have accorded us the right to believe in them; they have not. They should be our pride and our strengthening; they are not. Because of the incessant attacks of some of our own people in influential position in the thought-controlling institutions of the country, we are uncertain of our heritage, crippled in our purposes, weakened in our ideals. It is a grievous burden, and a fearful responsibility rests upon those who have done it.

"But—here we are. Someday there may be a redress of balance and a return of perspective, and we hope there will be. In the meantime, we have today's situation and today's demand, and to that we must address ourselves.

"My friends," he said, and again he looked straight into the cameras, "the situation in the heartland of Russia is obviously now moving toward some kind of climax. We do not know at the moment what this climax will be, nor do we know whether, if left alone, it would work itself out in the long run in a Chinese victory or a Russian victory.

"We do know, or at least my advisers and I believe, that we cannot wait any longer to find out. We must place our weight where it will do the most good for threatened humanity.

"Starting at eight this morning I conferred with the Secretary of State, the Secretary of Defense, the Joint Chiefs of Staff and other advisers, including President Abbott and Mr. Justice Davis of the Supreme Court. We decided upon a plan of action.

"That plan of action began when I began to speak to you. It is now under way with many methods in many areas. During the next forty-eight hours, in a carefully phased, step-by-step program, it will progress to what we hope, and believe, will be a termination of the war.

"If we are right, we can begin to rebuild a sane and a better world.

"If we are wrong, it will not matter either to history, or to us.

"There are some of you, I am sure, who will greatly applaud what we are going to do. There are some of you who will violently condemn. To all of you I say:

"Suppose *you* were the President of the United States of America, faced with war between Russia and China.

"Suppose *you* had to make the decision to stay out or go in, and if your decision was to go in, who to help, and how to do it.

"Suppose *you* carried the burden on *your* shoulders, not in a relaxed time of easy decisions, but *right now.*

"Suppose you had *my* share of our joint responsibility to the world.

"What would *you* do, my friends, you who applaud and you who condemn? How would *you* handle it?

"Think about it.

"*Think about it!*

"And then move on, with tolerance, with understanding and with compassion, to join me in the job we have to do.

"As I said to you before, when I addressed the Congress:

"'It may be that we will survive to put the world together again—or we may just as likely go down with it. It is all uncertainty, all conjecture, all dark and desperate, all filled with frightful peril for us all.

" 'But we must be brave—and we must be strong—and we must look to our own defenses—and we must hold ourselves ready to help where we can—and we must pray.

" 'The Lord has preserved us through many perils, for some purpose. We must be confident that He will continue to do so. I make no pretense to you whatsoever that it will be easy. But I call on you to join me in meeting whatever the future holds, with courage, with determination, with unity and with faith in ourselves, our traditions and our purposes.'

"At noon our intervention began. Within forty-eight hours we will know whether it has succeeded, and whether peace can come.

"I bid you farewell for now, not in pessimism or foreboding, but in courage and in hope. I commend to you the same positive approach.

"We are doing the best we can, and we are doing it selflessly, generously and, we hope, helpfully for all mankind. The event rests in the hands of God, but you and I, his servants, bring to it the best that is in us. I am confident He will accept our offering, and to it give His blessing, and success.

"God bless you and God bless the United States of America.

"Until we meet again."

And the anthem thundered up, the flag rippled across the screen. Against it his tired but confident face looked out for a last impressive, calmly emphatic moment before it faded slowly away.

For several moments, everywhere, there was silence. Typical of those who finally broke it were his friends of Supermedia.

"Do you realize," somebody asked in an awed voice at the *Times*, "that he never told us *who* we were intervening for, or *how* we are going to do it?"

"That's right," somebody else agreed in an equally hushed tone at the *Post*. "He never did."

5. LATE THAT NIGHT, after the world's response had poured in, turning gradually from initial dismay and condemnation of his deliberate vagueness to a more optimistic note as the outlines of the invasion plan became clear and its progress began to pick up speed and meet some small indications of success, he walked alone down the second-floor corridor to the elevator and went up to the solarium overlooking the Washington Monument, the Potomac, Tom Jefferson and Abe Lincoln in their softly lighted temples.

He stood for a long time at the window.

No pedestrians were on the streets, very few cars passed. Winter lay cold on the city.

A tiny, cautious hope was beginning to come back into the world, but it still was a long way to spring.

A long way to spring, and a long way to the point where he, his country and the world could really begin to plan for peace—*if* they could plan for peace. The enterprise appeared to be moving well in its opening stages, the first signs were good. But an infinite amount remained to be accomplished and there was enormous room for error still.

At the moment, it was still entirely unclear whether his plan would really succeed or whether the whole world would be blown up in the wake of what could still turn out to be history's most disastrous gamble.

Yet he felt confident, perhaps because he really had no choice. Having set into motion the monstrous terrifying machine of a modern military enterprise, he must remain calm and ride Juggernaut to the end, hoping it would follow the paths to which he had directed it. There was nothing else to do now.

Reviewing the final thinking that had gone into his decision, the thinking ratified after somber conference by the Joint Chiefs of Staff, by Robert A. Leffingwell and Blair Hannah, by Bill Abbott and Tommy Davis and Bob Munson and Cullee and Ceil and Hal and the rest, he felt that he was justified in confidence. He had indeed done the best he could, and so had all he trusted and relied upon; and so they could commend the event to the hands of God and await its outcome with a fair serenity.

He had been amused by the immediate reaction to his speech. Frantic indignation had shouted from every page, spouted from every broadcast. How could he do such a thing? How could he keep them guessing? How could he take refuge in such a cop-out?

He had been tempted to tell them scathingly, "Shut your yapping mouths and wait a couple of hours, and it will all come clear." But he had restrained himself, and within a couple of hours it had come about as he could have told them. And so the chorus softened and began to change tentatively but increasingly in his favor.

He was glad that he had given them that time in which to think, and he was glad he had put it to them squarely in his speech:

Suppose you *were the President of the United States of America, faced with war between Russia and China.*

Suppose you *had to make the decision to stay out or go in, and if your decision was to go in, who to help, and how to do it.*

Suppose you *carried the burden on* your *shoulders, not in a relaxed time of easy decisions, but* right now.

Suppose you had my *share of our joint responsibility to the world.*

What would you *do, my friends, you who applaud and you who condemn? How would* you *handle it?*

Think about it.

Think about it!

He wanted them to know that it wasn't all that easy, and perhaps now they did, though he would not wager on their retaining the memory for very long.

So it was going forward as he had planned it, intervention on his terms, where and in such manner as he thought would be successful. The event was indeed in the hands of God. And supposing it would succeed, as he believed likely, what then for his frightened country and the shaken world?

He knew the answer.

Infinite pains, infinite patience, infinite struggle and strain. Infinite labor that would have to go on for years, decades, possibly generations before it could be said that a truly stable peace had finally been achieved.

And that, perhaps, was the key to it: the unceasing struggle, the fugitive joy, the recurrent pain, the endless, mostly heartbreaking endeavor.

"'Let us,'" Lafe Smith had said, quoting on a dark and dismal night, "'wear upon our sleeves the crepe of mourning for a civilization that held the promise of joy.'"

The promise of joy.

Not the easy certainty.

Not the painless assurance.

Not the comfortable guarantee.

Just—the promise.

That, perhaps, was all that the American experiment, all that any experiment in human governance that sprang from essentially decent motives, could hold out—the promise of joy. A promise always elusive, always fleeting, never quite captured, never quite achieved, here today, gone tomorrow, back again next day—if you kept working and hoping and struggling and, above all, if you never gave up. If you hung on and kept trying, all of you, unto the last generation.

If his successors—for successors he still believed there would be—were strong, were determined, never lost sight of the essential goodness of the American experiment and the essential goodness of all other sincere and well-meaning peoples wherever they might reside on troubled Earth—then just possibly, somewhere far off beyond his lifetime and maybe far off beyond many other subsequent lifetimes, the promise of joy might sometime—somehow—someday—be kept for his country and for all mankind.

But more likely that was all it was, or could ever be: a promise.

A promise forever worth the seeking—but only a promise.

All ye of faint heart and wavering will who seek the *certainty* of joy, he told them quietly in his mind, forget it.

It does not exist.

So the missiles and bombs and planes and submarines raced on through the winter night to keep their fateful appointments in the warring lands, over the oceans, over the continents, over the good, bad, decent, crafty, devious, straightforward, honest, dishonest, mean, generous, cruel, kindly, gentle, brutish races and nations of the globe, about to find out whether history still had a place for creatures so strangely composed of great ideals and unhappy compromise as they.

October 1973–June 1974.